时光你悄悄走过

Time you quietly passed

赵舒娴 著

By Zhao Shuxian

Billson International Ltd.

Published by
Billson International Ltd
27 Old Gloucester Street
London
WC1N 3AX
Tel:(852)95619525

Website:www.billson.cn
E-mail address:cs@billson.cn

First published 2024

Produced by Billson International Ltd
CDPF/01

ISBN 978-1-80377-100-7

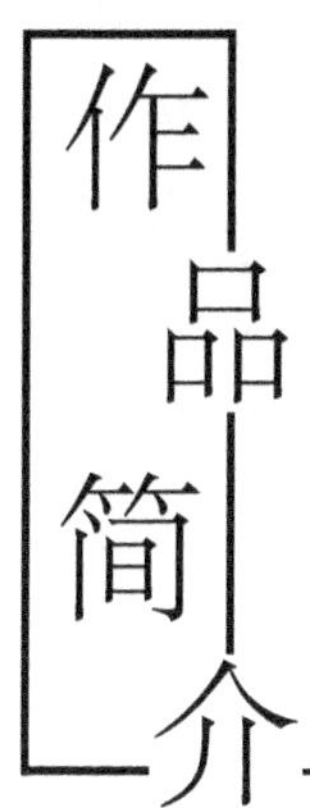

作品简介

女主人公李华遇到婚姻挫折，被爱人背叛后，历经一系列的情感纠结。正义与虚伪，善良与邪恶的矛盾情感在内心反复煎熬。

李华在追求幸福生活的过程中，一直保持善良的品性，悟懂了幸福快乐的人生哲理，找到自救的方法。李华积极创业实现自我的价值。在努力拼搏的初期，李华同时身兼三职，于多个行业投资学习。李华从事过保险行业，开过服装店，成立门窗公司，兼职做红酒销售十多年，投资房地产。为了成为更好的自己，李华不断进取，勤劳工作。

李华在努力实现人生价值的同时，孝敬父母，关爱姐妹，呵护女儿，帮助朋友，竭力为家人创造更好的生活。

生活的磨难，让李华终于活明白，女人要依靠自己的力量过上幸福生活，才是人生的赢家。人生还有比爱情更重要的事情，就是先好好爱自己，然后才有能力驾驭自己的命运，才能照顾好家人活得有价值有尊严，才能过上自己想要的美好生活。

经过 20 多年的岁月洗礼，李华最终成为自信自强的知性女性，经济独立事业如意，获得物质财富和精神财富双丰收，过上了自己喜欢的生活。

The heroine Li Hua encountered marriage setbacks, betrayed by her lover, after a series of emotional entanglements. The contradictory feelings of justice and hypocrisy, good and evil are repeatedly tortured in the heart.

In the process of pursuing a happy life, Li Hua has always maintained a kind character, understood the philosophy of happy life, and found a way to save himself.

Li Hua actively started his own business to realize his value. In the early days of hard work, Li Hua held three positions at the same time and invested in learning in a number of industries. Li Hua engaged in the insurance industry, opened a clothing store, set up a door and window company, part-time wine sales for more than 10 years, investment in real estate. In order to become a better self, Li Hua keeps forging ahead and works hard.

Li Hua strives to realize the value of life at the same time, filial piety parents, love sisters, care for daughters, help friends, and strive to create a better life for his family.

The hardships of life, let Li Hua finally live to understand that women should rely on their own strength to live a happy life, is the winner of life. There are more important things in life than love, that is, first love yourself, and then have the ability to control their own fate, to take care of their families to live a valuable and dignified life, in order to live the good life they want.

After more than 20 years of baptism, Li Hua eventually became a confident and self-reliant intellectual woman, economic independence and career success, obtain material wealth and spiritual wealth, and live their favorite life.

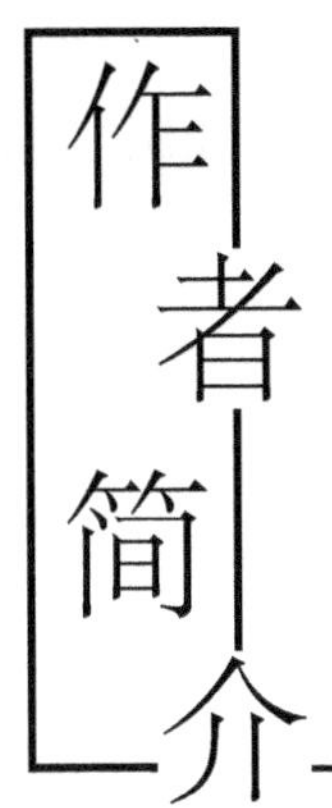

赵舒娴，笔名金豆奕铭，武汉作家协会会员，华夏精短文学学会武汉分会会长，华中分会常务会长，精短文学作家，淮南作家文化传媒副主编，毕业于湖北师范学院。热爱写作、读书、文艺，喜欢旅行体验生活。

文学作品在《新看点》《作家文苑》《海华都市报》及多个媒体平台发表，其中《漂浮姻缘》《凭着爱》《岁月轮渡》在喜马拉雅有声平台多人广播剧，收听率达 69 万多听众，每天点击率还在递增。

现已出版的纸制书籍作品有《岁月轮渡》《凭着爱》,《恰好美时遇见你》(已签约出版中),《彼岸花开》（中英文版）《时光你悄悄走过》《春风吻上我的脸》（中英文版）等多部文学作品已签约，正在筹备出版中。

Zhao Shuxian, pen name: Jin Dou Yiming, member of Wuhan Writers Association, president of Wuhan Branch of Huayia Short Literature Society, Executive chairman of Central China Branch, short literature writer, deputy editor of Huainan Writers Culture Media, graduated from Hubei Normal University. Love writing, reading, literature and art, like to travel to experience life.

Literary works in the "New perspective", "Writer Wenyuan", "Haihua City Daily" and a number of media platforms published, of which "floating marriage", "with love", "years ferry" in the Himalayan audio platform multi-person radio drama, listening rate of more than 690,000 listeners, the daily click rate is still increasing.

Now published paper book works include "Years Ferry", "With love", "Meet you at the right time" (has been signed for publication), "The other Shore

Flowers" (Chinese and English versions), "Time you quietly passed" , "Spring breeze kissed my face" (Chinese and English versions) and many other literary works have been signed and are preparing for publication.

序：让内心的光芒照亮人生的道路
Preface: Let the inner light light the way of life

我喜欢写小说，也喜欢看小说，我认为小说的一项魅力在于让读者获得体验。有些事情我们没有机会亲身经历，但通过小说阅读，我们跟随小说人物的视角见证他们的故事，能获得一些新奇有趣的体验：也许是一些没有看过的风景，也许是一些没有接触过的生活现象，也许是一些从未想过的问题——甚至作者还在作品中给了你答案。

当我们回忆往昔，我们能够记住一些画面、声音以及当时的一些想法和情绪感受。当我们回想起某一部小说，我们的头脑中也可能会浮现出当时想象的画面、声音，以及当时的想法和情绪感受。真实的经历和想象的经历对我们都有意义，也许在某些层面上这两者的运作方式是高度一致的。一段重要的人生经历可能会改变人的一生，一部小说可能会影响一个人很多年。

"逆袭"是近年来常见的网络流行语，网民大众对它的理解已经偏离原意，一般都将它理解为"扭转乾坤"，而这个词也经常以"人生的逆袭"这样的组合出现。这一部作品就是讲述一个关于人生逆袭的故事。女主角李华在中年阶段遭遇了极大的挫折，处于人生低谷中的李华内心非常痛苦，但是她没有被逆境打败，而是积极地展开自救，让自己恢复勇气和信心，活得自由而精彩。

这些年来我经常想到一个问题：我们该如何度过这一生，如果人生需要符合一些规律准则，那么这些准则是什么？我在不同渠道找到的答案都是相通的，简单总结下来就是"自强自爱"和"施益他人"。在李华的故事中，李华在熬过最艰难的阶段过后，往后的人生就像"开挂"一样。我相信这些事件不是凭空捏造的，而是有现实的原型，李华能获得这样的幸福也是应该的，因为她的所言所行不断在践行自强自爱和施益他人。

李华向理发师推荐保险业务时，先帮理发师购买了洗发月卡服务，让对方赚到钱后再跟他谈保单。李华担心忘年之交的朋友染了黄发会遭人误会，用心劝说并亲自陪同她将头发染黑。李华回家看病过程中帮好友卖掉了房子，并解开了对方的心结。李华的感悟也影响了合租室友，让她们明白到人生最终要依靠自己，要爱护自己，要利及他人。

李华从小就爱护家人，多年来一直为家庭付出。当她有能力买房时，她也先给自己的父母买房，报答父母的恩情。在创业过程中，李华也经常先考虑别人，先让顾客和合作伙伴获得利益；李华当老板的时候，宁愿自己吃苦，她也从不拖欠员工的工资。李华后来的人生之所以"开挂"，是因为她在人生的每个时期都在积累福德，于是善缘不断，时时遇到贵人，而她也成为很多人生命中的贵人。

在阅读这部作品的过程中，像是有一道光照进心中，我不时有这样的感觉：虽然不知道未来的路该怎样走，但如果我们待人接物的心态能像女主李华那样，我们的人生不会过得太差。当你对人生感到迷茫时，你可以看看李华是怎样面对：在人生的低谷中不消极埋怨自暴自弃；在工作中积极成全别人；在生活中尽量帮助朋友家人；在获得财务自由之后不困于金钱欲望，而是积极学习，扩展丰富自己的精神世界。

修行圈子里有这样的观点：生活处处是修行，红尘就是最好的修行场。在人生这场游戏中，李华已经是一个通关者，她的经历和感悟就是人生游戏的攻略指南。让我们知道如何安身立命，如何待人接物，如何达到精神和物质的双丰收。

这部《时光你悄悄走过》作品值得我们细细品味，它不仅仅讲述了一个故事，也展现了很多做人的道理。"一部小说可能会影响一个人很多年"，但愿每一位有缘人都能在这部作品中获得启发，点亮内心的明光，创造出精彩丰盛的人生。

作家老师：一鸣

I love to write novels and I love to read them, and I think one of the charms of fiction is that it gives readers an experience. Some things we have no chance to experience personally, but through reading novels, we can witness their stories from the perspective of the novel characters, and get some novel and interesting experiences: maybe some scenery we have never seen, maybe some life phenomena we have never touched, maybe some questions we have never thought of - even the author gives you answers in the works.

When we recall the past, we can remember the sights, sounds, thoughts and emotions of the time. When we recall a novel, we may also conjure up images, sounds, thoughts and emotions that we imagined at the time. Both real and imagined experiences make sense to us, and perhaps at some level the two operate in a highly consistent way. An important life experience can change a person's life, and a novel can affect a person for many years.

"Counterattack" is a common network buzzword in recent years, the understanding of the netizens has deviated from the original meaning, generally understood it as "turning the tide", and this word often appears in the combination of "counterattack of life". This work is to tell a story about the reversal of life. Heroine Li Hua in the middle age stage suffered a great setback, Li Hua in the trough of life in the heart is very painful, but she was not defeated by adversity, but actively start to save themselves, let themselves restore courage and confidence, live free and wonderful.

Over the years I've often thought of a question: How should we live our lives, and if there are rules to follow, what are those rules? The answers I found in different channels are all the same, which can be summed up simply as "self-improvement and self-love" and "benefiting others". In the story of Li Hua, after Li Hua has survived the most difficult stage, the life in the future is like "opening and hanging". I believe that these events are not fabricated, but have a real prototype, Li Hua can get such happiness is also deserved, because her words and actions continue to practice self-improvement and self-love and benefit others.

When Li Hua recommended the insurance business to the barber, he first helped the barber buy a shampoo monthly card service, so that the other side can make money and then talk to him about the policy. Li Hua was worried that her old friend would be misunderstood if she dyed yellow hair, so she tried to persuade and accompany her to dye her hair black. Li Hua went home to see a doctor in the process to help friends sell the house, and untie the other party's heart. Li Hua's perception also affected the roommates, letting them understand that life ultimately depends on their own, to love themselves, to benefit others.

Li Hua loves her family since she was a child and has been paying for her family for many years. When she was able to buy a house, she also bought a house for her parents first to repay their kindness. In the process of entrepreneurship, Li Hua also often consider others first, let customers and partners benefit first; When Li Hua was the boss, she would rather suffer by herself, and she never defaulted on her employees' wages. The reason why Li Hua's later life is "open" is because she has accumulated ford in every period of her life, so good karma continues to meet noble people from time to time, and she has become a noble person in many people's lives.

In the process of reading this work, like a light into the heart, I have such a feeling from time to time: although I do not know how to go in the future, but if we can treat people and things like the mentality of the heroine Li Hua, our life will not be too bad. When you feel confused about life, you can look at Li Hua is how to face: in the trough of life not negative complain about self-abandonment; Actively help others in your work; Try to help friends and family in life; After obtaining financial freedom, I am not trapped in the desire for money, but actively learn to expand and enrich my spiritual world.

There is such a view in the practice circle that life is all about practice, and the world is the best practice field. In the game of life, Li Hua is already a clearance, her experience and perception is the life game guide. Let us know how to settle down, how to treat people and things, how to achieve a double harvest of spirit and material.

This "Time you quietly passed" work is worth our careful taste, it not only tells a story, but also shows a lot of truth in life. "A novel may affect a person for many years", I hope that every person can be inspired in this work, light up the bright light of the heart, and create a wonderful and rich life.

Writer Teacher: Yiming

前言

Preface

    在生活的长河中，我们都是漂泊的旅人，或喜或悲，或起或落，经历着种种磨难与挫折，但重要的是我们如何应对这些困难。翻开《时光你悄悄走过》，我们能够看到一个坚韧不拔、永不言败的女性，在生活的洪流中砥砺前行：主人公李华在经历婚姻挫折后，凭借自己的勇气和智慧，大胆创业，一步步走出人生低谷实现自我价值，最终成为自信自强的知性女性。

    在赵舒娴的作品中，女性的情感、婚姻、个人成长等方面是她尤为关注的主题。她通过细腻的笔触，描绘出女性在各种情境下的心理变化和情感体验，既展现了她们的柔情似水，也揭示了她们在面对困境时的坚韧和勇敢。在这部作品中，李华是一个遭遇婚姻挫折的妻子，一个辛勤工作的母亲，一个不断学习进取的创业者。她从最初的茫然和痛苦中一步步逐渐成长为一个自信、坚强的女性。这个过程并非一蹴而就的，反而充满坎坷和荆棘，这样的情节设置使角色塑造极富层次感，也使故事更具启发性和思考性。

    此外，透过作品可以看出作者非常擅长从生活中汲取素材。故事描绘了李华在各个行业中的学习与投资经历，如保险、服装店经营、门窗公司创立以及红酒销售等。这些丰富的职业背景和行业知识为小说增添了现实生活的厚重，使故事更加真实可感。同时，赵舒娴还善于在细节中见真章，通过一些看似微不足道的小事，展现出人性的光辉与善良。例如，李华在向理发师推荐保险业务时，先在对方那里购买洗发月卡服务，这种设身处地为他人着想的品质，让我们感受到了她内心的善良与真诚。

    在赵舒娴的笔下，李华的形象栩栩如生，她善良、坚韧、乐观，充满进取精神，她用自己的实际行动诠释了"自强自爱"和"施益他人"的人生准则，让我们在感动之余，也深受启发：人生并非一帆风顺，但只要我们保持善良与坚韧，积极面对生活中的挑战与困难，就一定能够找到属于自己的幸福与成功。

这种积极向上的生活态度，不仅带来了正能量，也让我们更加珍惜自己的生活与身边的人。

正如作者所言，"人生，就是一场奋斗"，而《时光你悄悄走过》则是这场奋斗的见证和记录。

汇文书联编辑：衔青

2024 年 3 月 2 日

In the long river of life, we are all wandering travelers, or happy or sad, or up or down, experiencing various hardships and setbacks, but the important thing is how we respond to these difficulties. Open the "Time you quietly passed", we can see a tenacious, never say die women, in the torrent of life: the protagonist Li Hua after experiencing marriage setbacks, with their own courage and wisdom, bold entrepreneurship, step by step out of the trough of life to achieve self-worth, and eventually become a confident and self-reliant intellectual women.

In Zhao Shuxian's works, women's emotions, marriage, personal growth and other aspects are the themes she pays special attention to. Through delicate strokes, she depicts women's psychological changes and emotional experiences in various situations, showing not only their tenderness, but also their tenacity and bravery in the face of difficulties. In this work, Li Hua is a wife who suffers from marriage setbacks, a hard-working mother, and an entrepreneur who keeps learning and forging ahead. From the initial confusion and pain, she gradually grew into a confident and strong woman. This process is not overnight, but full of bumps and thorns, such plot Settings make the character development is very layered, but also make the story more enlightening and reflective.

In addition, through the works can be seen that the author is very good at drawing material from life. The story describes Li Hua's learning and investment experiences in various industries, such as insurance, clothing store management, the founding of a door and window company, and wine sales. These rich professional backgrounds and industry knowledge add the weight of real life to the novel, making the story more realistic. At the same time, Zhao Shuxian is also good at seeing the truth in the details, showing the brilliance and kindness of human nature through some seemingly trivial things. For example, when Li Hua recommended the insurance business to the hairdresser, she first bought the monthly card service from the other side. This quality of putting herself in the shoes of others makes us feel the kindness and sincerity of her heart.

In Zhao Shuxian's pen, Li Hua's image is liflike, she is kind, tough, optimistic, full of enterprising spirit, she uses her own practical actions to interpret the "self-improvement and self-love" and "benefit others" life rules, so that we are moved, but also deeply inspired: Life is not always easy, but as long as we remain kind and tough, and actively face the challenges and difficulties in life, we will be able to find their own happiness and success. This positive attitude towards life not only brings positive energy, but also makes us cherish our lives and the people around us more.

As the author said, "Life is a struggle," and "Time you quietly passed" is the witness and record of this struggle.

Editor of Huiwen Book: Qing

March 2, 2024

目录

C ontents

Chapter 1: A painful blow

On August 5, 1998, it was a hot, hot and irritable day, and what happened on this day was more bloody than writing a novel.

On the way back home, Li Hua's heart was cold to the extreme, the whole body felt cold, walking in the hot sun directly on the ground, the soles of the feet were hot and did not feel. A hot wind in the air blew on Li Hua's face, she still couldn't feel the heat of the summer. Li Hua only felt disheartened, bowed his head and hurried on, accelerating in the direction of his home. Her hands were clenched into fists, her eyes showed a look that could shock people, her face was angry, and she wanted to hit someone hard.

It seems that something big has happened, Li Hua has never shown such a terrible look on weekdays, even in this hot summer, see Li Hua's cold eyes, others will feel cold.

Li Hua just received a phone call from her daughter Xiaolin, and learned a shocking news: Yu Ping, who had been envied by her friends and was a good husband to Li Hua, and everyone thought that he was a good man, betrayed Li Hua and slept with a woman in Li Hua's home, Li Hua's bed!

Li Hua hate themselves how so dull, did not find a little trace.

Li Hua's mind involuntarily flashed a question: Who is this woman? How dare you! This woman must be familiar with Li Hua's family situation, otherwise how could she appear at Li Hua's home when Li Hua and her daughter had just left home?

Li Hua is most worried about her daughter Xiaolin! Daughter is only ten years old, because of homework this forgot to take school, return home is met in the home cheating Yu Ping and an unidentified woman, two people naked in Li Hua master

bedroom big bed. At that time, two people are breathing up and down to push, was home to take the exercise of the daughter small Lin ran into.

Yu Ping how also did not think, he obviously will anti-theft iron door plug in, the wooden door into the gate is also locked, daughter Xiao Lin how to come in? He even opened the master bedroom, and he and the woman who was having sex were unaware of it!

Li Hua hurried anxiously to the telephone booth where her daughter was. When she saw her daughter Xiaolin, Li Hua didn't say anything, just held Xiaolin tightly, and she could feel her daughter's body trembling. Li Hua held Xiao Lin slim thin hand, the small hand as cold as their own.

Li Hua also do not know how to go upstairs into the house, at the moment of opening the door, Li Hua saw just got a marriage certificate less than two years husband Yu Ping, a person half squatting in the corner of the balcony. A pair of frightened little eyes a little flustered, the upper body is still naked, a look will know is the revelation of the affair, have not had time to tidy up their own clothes. It is estimated that the woman who cheated, also just ran away in a panic... Li Hua despise the man who betrayed her, before this look of Yu Ping let Li Hua feel strange. Li Hua is really out of sight, how to choose such a disorderly man!

From outside the room, the bed looked unkempt. Suddenly Li Hua broke out of the power, she like crazy, suddenly rushed into the bedroom, all the bedding picked up and kneaded into a ball, severely fell to the ground, with a foot up, rubbing hard, kicking...

Li Hua's tears could not help pouring out, that kind of grievance and helplessness, the first time to feel that the days are going to fall down. How can you lose face with this! Always confident Li Hua, for a while really do not know how to face this sudden family ugly. This one. Can you stay?

Li Hua asked his heart, while cleaning up the nightstand on the ornaments, their own performance of the dance photo was placed in the dresser drawer. Li Hua suddenly remembered that every time he came back from a business trip, the photos on the bedside table were placed in the dresser drawer... It seems that Yu Pinghe cheated on this woman more than once!

Li Hua thoroughly understood that Yu Ping's husband and wife life in the past two years was not premature ejaculation impotence, nor was it impossible, but when he slept with Li Hua, there was always the shadow of that woman at Li Hua's bedside, like a ghost, watching Yu Ping's every move of guilt. Yu Ping has been out of the body, nature can not give Li Hua's love and past tenderness.

Unwitting Li Hua also consulted the hospital expert doctor all day long, with a lot of nourishing tonifying kidney nutritional supplements, has been a little bald Yu Ping also eat every day. Li Hua back from a business trip will bring some good supplements to Yu Ping to eat, two years down is not no effect, but are filled to the wild woman to go. Li Hua suddenly realized at this moment, think of Yu Ping with her husband and wife life changes, Li Hua hair all over the body, the more want to be more terrible, the more want to be more hateful, the more want to more wish to remove the house.

Why is this man so ungrateful? ! How sorry was she, Li Hua? Although the two were married for the second time, it was also Yu Ping pursuing Li Hua. At that time, Yu Ping used a lot of friends to catch up with Li Hua. This marriage only how long, Li Hua did not think, she and Yu Ping's marriage was so vulnerable. What woman wants her man? Who is it?!

Li Hua suddenly calmed down, stopped all the rough action, and slowly began to shake out of bed supplies. When she was lost in mind, she suddenly found a very small phone book booklet, Li Hua found the clue, she carefully looked page by page, and finally saw a woman she knew name and phone number, with a pencil line below.

The woman named Wang Qinlan, in Li Hua impression is a long face freckles yellow face woman. The receptionist who let Li Hua despise, the woman who is not outstanding in the pile of women, is the bitch who cheated with Yu Ping? This makes Li Hua suspect Yu Ping's taste, Yu Ping will be interested in such a woman?

Can not imagine her Li Hua lost to such a woman, to beauty is not beautiful, to

look no looks, the only bright spot is a waist long hair fluttering. Yes, Yu Ping love women long hair, when the pursuit of Li Hua, Li Hua is a screw coil long hair, like a female singer in Taiwan, very gentle and elegant fashion soft. At that time, Yu Ping did not see Li Hua a day, just like lost soul, with his personal driver, everywhere to ask Li Hua's BFF Jane where.

Li Hua is not willing, her eyes look terrible. She walked out of the room, scanned the man hiding in the corner of the balcony with her peripheral vision, and looked at him with disdain. Li Hua did not want to say anything to the man, holding her daughter Xiaolin hand and walking out.

Yu Ping immediately got up from the balcony and went to the gate to hold out his hand to stop Li Hua: "Sorry! I'm so sorry!"

Li Hua also did not know how to treat Yu Ping in front of her to relieve her hatred, she grabbed Yu Ping's hand and put it into her mouth, biting it down with hatred...

Yu Ping shouted. Li Hua knows that kind of pain is just flesh pain, and Li Hua is painful in the heart. Li Hua feel very hate, with a kind of contempt contempt eyes look at Yu Ping, this look even Li Hua himself are shocked! At this time the eyes must be murderous, Li Hua saw Yu Ping a sudden shock, block Li Hua's hand also hurriedly collected back.

Li Hua pulled up her daughter Xiaolin to turn around and go, the door fell hard, giving vent to his anger. Li Hua was also shocked at his decisiveness at this moment. She has not yet figured out how to deal with Yu Ping, do not know when, but certainly not now.

Li Hua stood outside the door and looked at the door for a few times. "Can we live here? That wild woman has been back and forth several times." Li Hua thought of here, felt by Yu Ping touched the hand is very dirty.

Li Hua understand that the responsibility is to protect her daughter Xiaolin young mind, worried about leaving a shadow in Xiaolin heart. Li Hua suddenly remembered that her daughter had to rush to school. On the way to school, Li Hua said to Lin: "Don't tell anyone about the ugly things you saw today, go back to

Grandma directly after school, I want to think about how to deal with this thing tonight!"

Xiao Lin nodded very sensibly. Li Hua was relieved to see Xiao Lin walk into the school. In any case, the daughter is the first time to catch the adultery in bed witness, when the mother only hope that her daughter can safely leave the scene.

Chapter 2: I can't tell you

Li Hua returned to work at the unit, told himself to be calm, can not let colleagues see that he has just experienced such ugly things. If colleagues, classmates, friends know this matter, Li Hua really do not know how to face them. Li Hua to protect themselves, try to calm their emotions, so that they do not think about this unfortunate thing.

It is not as good as God, Li Hua wanted to spend the future years with Yu Ping, live together sincerely, after all, two people really love each other. I really can't believe that Yu Ping would like a woman who is worse than Li Hua in every way, and even a married woman!

In the early days of their acquaintance, Li Hua has been focusing on work and deliberately avoiding Yu Ping's sight. Because of the frustration of marriage once, Li Hua is more cautious about marriage.

At that time, Yu Ping would chat on the phone until midnight when Li Hua was on a business trip, and chat for more than four hours on winter nights. Yu Ping had been in the pursuit of Li Hua in the days of tender infatuated said, with his roommate friend Lu always envy him and Li Hua's love. At that time I don't know how there are so many things to say in the heart, in the days of Li Hua's business trip, Yu Ping constantly told how he missed Li Hua.

In the era when real estate changed from the planned economy to the market economy, units implemented the index of buying and distributing houses, and property rights were privately owned. Li Hua inadvertently chat with boudoir Zhen Zhen buy out the house of the moment difficult. Yu Ping with Zhenzhen is also a friend, from Zhenzhen that Li Hua's difficulties, Yu Ping specially in the bank to take out 50,000 yuan, wrapped in an oil envelope. He handed the money in the envelope of oil paper to Li Hua, and then whispered, "Go pay for the house!"

To tell the truth, Li Hua was determined to marry Yu Ping from that time. Li Hua is not a person who craved material comforts, but was moved by Yu Ping's kindness. Now think of these, Li Hua nose sour - are ready to give up people, but suddenly think of Yu Ping so many benefits!

At this moment Li Hua's mood is very complicated, how she can not understand why it has become this situation.

Li Hua suddenly remembered that the third sister had called Li Hua several times unintentionally and asked, "Are you and Yu Ping OK?" I wanted to come and see you. Is your brother-in-law home?"

At that time, Li Hua did not understand what the third sister wanted to say, but she did not say anything, she told the third sister: "Yu Ping is not at home, on a business trip for two days..."

The third sister only asked one sentence: "Do you know where he went on a business trip and who he went with?"

Li Hua really did not ask Yu Ping where to go the habit, and never nervous worried that Yu Ping will have a change of heart one day. Yu Ping has been doing a good job, the kind of good that makes anyone envious.

Li Hua suddenly reminded of bestie Zhenzhen to Li Hua also had a reminder, remember two bestie call to tell Li Hua, she is working in the unit of Yu Ping, met Wang Qinlan in the office sofa rest in Yu Ping, very casually come out.

"If you're not busy, come over for lunch and see what's going on?" Zhenzhen really said to Li Hua on the phone.

Li Hua called back and just said, "I have a customer here, and I want to invite the customer to dinner at noon." Busy ah, can not come, there is nothing, I hang up!"

Zhenzhen still could not help but ask Yu Ping, Yu Ping understated explained: "She came to take a bath."

Zhenzhen all asked about this, see Li Hua did not respond, it did not mention.

But that period of time Zhenzhen work and foreign companies have contact, later in the lunch break, and saw Wang Qinlan from the rest room to take a bath!

At that time, Zhenzhen remembered very clearly, it was a winter, when it was very cold in winter!

Be awakened fragment like lightning memories, Li Hua to himself, as if to find Yu Ping betrayal of their own time. Half of the responsibility for Yu Ping's betrayal lies in Li Hua's carelessness and never thought of Yu Ping's abnormality. Men who used to come home from work on time suddenly often stay out playing mahjong. Yu Ping did not ask where to go, Yu Ping told Li Hua on the phone, Li Hua believed what! Thought it was a normal work-related social connection.

At this time Li Hua distressed to the bones, stuffy even breathing are very uncomfortable, the chest came a colic, do not know who is sad?

The day was so long, the office building was all gone, but Li Hua didn't know to go back there. Daughter has returned to Li Hua mother's home, Li Hua just make a phone call with Xiao Lin said: "Be good, finish your homework, go to bed." Don't wait for mom, listen to grandma, don't think about what you found today, listen!"

Li Hua wanted to be alone quietly, think about how to face the future life, she was distraught out of the office building.

The hot August is really the autumn tiger that people often say, and it is more sultry than ever. Li Hua looked so helpless and irritable that night. Li Hua looked in a trance, and a car passed by the side of the road. Li Hua walked to the intersection and looked at the brightly lit downtown. Once so noisy night, Li Hua now only see the dark long road.

A car horn startled Li Hua's thinking. "Are you deaf or blind? You'll die!"

Li Hua dull was scolded by the driver, but could not say anything. Think of yourself in a trance, feel really poor and helpless, not even have a place to talk.

Li Hua unconsciously habitually walked on the way home from work, unconsciously walked to Yahui food stall, which is a night market street close to Li Hua's home, where people are still coming and going, people come in groups to eat late night snacks. Seeing this familiar night market street, Li Hua felt particularly uncomfortable in the heart, thinking of Yu Ping and her daughter Xiaolin, in summer, they will have a night snack together in this most lively night market.

Just in front of Li Hua this familiar place can not be familiar again, in front of this table, Li Hua's footsteps involuntarily stopped. Maybe she was hungry -- Li Hua didn't eat any food all day after she found out about her husband Yu Ping's affair at 9 am.

In front of so much, Li Hua thought: good health first, I have to eat, a good meal. Can't go down without getting back at those two.

Li Hua asked the waiter to order a full table, the previous favorite barbecue, green bean soup, kelp soup, roasted chicken feet, smelly dried meat, lamb kebabs. The waiter asked kindly, "Is your Mr. Yu and your beautiful daughter coming?" Or do you eat it and take it home?"

Hearing the waiter's familiar voice, Li Hua realized that the waiter has been very familiar with his family, and Li Hua also realized that some things are not the same after all, and can no longer hide it. Li Hua only said to the waiter: "You serve the food first, I am hungry!"

Waiter: "Oh! At once, what would you like to drink first?"

Li Hua said to the waiter: "A case of cold beer."

Li Hua suddenly stuffy nose, sour, feel sad up. Originally a good home, originally a warm and sweet family sitting in front of the table, but now only Li Hua a person, and she also here strong pretend nothing happened, pretend not to be knocked down strong, dead support, repressed.

While the waiter was busy preparing, Li Hua's mobile phone rang. It was her good classmate Huizhu who called, "Where are you?"

Li Hua paused for a moment, and finally said truthfully: "A person in Yahui night snack, if you are free, come here to drink beer together!"

The female classmate who grew up with Huizhu lived very close to the night market, Li Hua often asked her to dance together. Huizhu said directly without pushing, "OK, I'll come in ten minutes!"

Huizhu is very punctual, ten minutes on time, far saw Li Hua sitting alone at that table. Huizhu approached Li Hua and patted her shoulder and said, "Why do you have this pleasure to eat so much today, and who did not come?" I really have food!"

Li Hua silently shook his head, his eyes did not dare to look at Huizhu, only said: "Eat it, no one please, please yourself, can't you?"

After the words were said, Li Hua's tears came out, she pinched her stuffy nose with a tissue, forcefully cleared out the snot, and quietly wiped off the tears on her face. This scene was careful Huizhu looked in the eyes, she immediately realized that something was wrong.

Huizhu is really understanding, did not ask anything, did not say anything, directly open the beer bottle, put in front of Li Hua. Huizhu himself also took a bottle and touched Li Hua: "Come, let's drink!"

Huizhu know Li Hua must be met with sad things, it must not be small. Huizhu is Li Hua grew up with bare feet, play together, grew up with the old classmate. From small to large, Huizhu has never seen Li Hua cry. In Huizhu's impression, Li Hua is the most sunny, the most filial parents, the most will manage the family woman, is also the best strong woman.

Huizhu did not persuade Li Hua, just keep helping to clip food, mouth has been to Li Hua said: "eat more quickly, don't drink with an empty stomach?"

This wine is Li Hua's life, drink the most sour, the most sober, the most daring of a wine. Looking at a table full of dishes usually like to eat, Li Hua has no appetite, but still desperately to the mouth with dishes, filled with the mouth, is unable to swallow...

At this time is already in the early morning, Huizhu reminded Li Hua: "The phone in your bag has been ringing, answer the phone!"

Li Hua took a look and turned off the call, and the mobile phone continued to ring. Hui Zhu said: "Take it, have something to say."

The phone was answered, and Yu Ping's anxious voice came from the other end of the phone: "Huahua, where are you?" I'll come get you."

Li Hua really do not know is alcohol to give courage, or really drunk, she raised the octave voice, back to the past: "I will not die, rest assured!" You get the hell out of my house! You better not let me see you two motherfuckers. I hate you! Fuck you! Stop pretending to me, you heartless thing. What more do you want? "

It was the first time that Li Hua cursed like a shrew, the first time that he shouted from his heart like crazy!

Chapter 3： Difficult Days

That night Li Hua was so uncomfortable, she still said to Huizhu in a sober state: "You can go home, I'm okay, I know how to deal with this pair of dogs and men!"

Huizhu looked at Li Hua like this, suddenly distressed Li Hua, she has never seen Li Hua so sad. Love marriage these words really harm ah, Huizhu also doubt this world really have a trusted love. Yu Ping and Li Hua love period that happy match scene, Huizhu had seen with her own eyes, but from this night Li Hua sad degree, she is by how much grievance, hold how much can not tell?

Yu Ping according to the call Yahui night market street noise, judge Li Hua in the night market stalls. He and Zhang driver two people really found Li Hua here. Seeing Li Hua this look, Yu Ping only quietly approached Li Hua and sat down quietly beside him, speaking in a very small voice: "Come, let's pack it and take it home to eat."

Li Hua suddenly picked up a bottle of beer and poured the whole bottle of beer on Yu Ping's head, wetting Yu Ping's entire hair. At this time Li Hua very resented and said: "What do you care about me, you go to find that bitch ah, you go to find it!" I will not embarrass you, you go away, as far away as possible!"

Li Hua suddenly pushed Yu Ping, at this time Zhang driver immediately protect Yu Ping, in the middle of Li Hua, humbly said: "Sister Li, have something to say, don't make everyone embarrassed."

Li Hua determined to let Huizhu home, also forced to let the driver take Yu Ping. Chapter driver see at this time of Li Hua unyielding posture, had to persuade Yu Ping to leave here first.

Li Hua sat alone for a while. May really drink too much, and she did not eat anything at all, the stomach turned, Li Hua vomited a bitter water. But this time Li Hua is still very sober, she asked the waiter for a bottle of water to gargle, the rest of the water all washed the face, the face all washed again, tears, wine, spit of bitter water, all erased.

After spitting out, Li Hua felt better, she went on the familiar road, staggered back to his small home, that has let Li Hua sad home. Li Hua knew that she could not go back to her mother's house in the middle of the night, and her daughter was there. Li Hua has been very sad, can not let his family know, so the family will be more sad; I can't go to my sister's house. It'll alarm them. Li Hua doesn't want his family to worry about him, so Li Hua must go back to the home that used to be warm, but now it is dirty by that wild woman...

Li Hua thought while walking: I can't have something, do not pack up these two cheating dogs and men, I will not give up... What's going to happen this night? Is the man who betrayed her still in the house, or is he up to something, and this dog's not gonna strike first, is he?

At that time, Li Hua was still very alert, but he did not know that he was afraid, and he was really calm and did not say his pain to the outside world. She thought that when she recovered from her condition, she would find an opportunity to get back at the bitch...

At the moment of opening the door, Li Hua didn't think that Yu Ping was sitting on the sofa. Yu Ping immediately got up and said to Li Hua, "I'll give you a good pot of chicken soup, give you a bowl."

Yu Ping timidly said, went into the kitchen to make soup, he from time to time out of the corner of his eye to Li Hua back. Li Hua walked directly into the room where her daughter lived, locked the door behind her, and put her back behind the door. Li Hua thought: Do I dare to drink the chicken soup made by Yu Ping? People are changed, love also out of the soul, wish I die early, in the way of him and that woman's good, this soup may now be poisoned; Maybe I did, but would I believe it? Can I trust him?

Li Hua simply won't believe Yu Ping, from the moment he knew he had an

affair with that woman, even if it was true love before, now there won't be a little bit of trust.

Li Hua needs a cooling-off time and needs to figure out how to deal with the two of them. Now the two bad things are exposed, Li Hua endured the pain and became sensible and indifferent, which is forced out. Li Hua was lying on the bed, his face had lost the color, his eyes were empty and blank, staring at the ceiling thinking about all this sudden happening during the day...

Outside the door sounded Yu Ping gently knock on the voice: "soup on the living room table, come out to drink some, I have been heated several times."

Li Hua listened to the man's voice outside the door and really wanted to throw up at the moment. This sound once let Li Hua happy drunk, but at this time she is eager to plug the ears, even want to rush out, and then hard bite down.

Emotional, Li Hua suddenly just had a late night snack and food, together with beer all spit out. Li Hua uncomfortable ah, she cried, but did not make a sound, did not open the door to rush out. Just hand bedside paper towel wiped the corners of the mouth, and picked up the nightstand water cup, drink a big mouth, but all spit out. Shielding the light, Li Hua continued to lie in bed thinking: What should I do? Giving up marriage is a sure thing, it's just a matter of time. But just let the dog and the girl go? It's not that cheap!

Li Hua was not in the mood to sleep that night, and leaned against his daughter's desk, flipping through the usual subscription to the Zhiyin marriage magazine.

Li Hua suddenly thought that she could write a letter to the editorial department, asking the editor to advise when a woman encountered this kind of marriage affair how to face, how to deal with, how to retaliate. She did not want to do something stupid because of impulse, she wanted to find the best revenge plan, not to ruin her life for revenge.

Li Hua wrote full of three pieces of paper, in one go, will see the process of the whole affair adultery between men and women, and the feelings after the occurrence of all written out. It's like talking to a person who can keep a secret the most, and all the grievances in the belly are vented. She knew it was the safest way to vent, and she wanted to limit the damage to what she could control, because she had to protect her daughter, Lin. The daughter is just 10 years old, she and her daughter Xiaolin will have to rely on each other in the future, and currently have to live in this city. If only Li Hua lived alone, perhaps she would not have such good patience, perhaps under the impulse of anger to cut this pair of dogs and men, and then left to leap to the Yangtze River, whether she is dead or alive!

Li Hua thought back to the table, see the finished paper. At that time it was more than five o 'clock in the morning, Li Hua felt much better after writing the letter, no longer the clueless state yesterday. Li Hua seemed to know how to deal with this matter, with ideas and firmness in her eyes. Li Hua stuffed the written letter into the hanging bag on his back to work, ready to send the letter on the way to work. At this time, Li Hua seemed to have accomplished a big thing in his heart.

In the time since the letter was sent, Li Hua did nothing to the couple. After a month, there is no like Lu Xun's Xianglin sister-in-law to see people to tell. The scandal was scarcely mentioned in the presence of anyone. It's not how smart Li Hua is, but the less people know about it, the better she can get revenge!

Yes, that was the idea, and the main motive was not to let the woman know that she was going to take revenge. Besides, it's not a glorious thing. She Li Hua is also a woman of face, she clearly knows what she can do and what she can't do. She didn't want her family to find out and worry about her and grieve for her.

For Li Hua, the appearance of calm is really an ordeal. Every time when he woke up, Li Hua remembered that he dreamed of the dog man and woman again last night, and every time he couldn't help looking at the handbag. There is a fruit knife in the bag, this knife is mainly used for self-defense, if the two people happened to have an affair, use this knife to kill the dog man and woman.

These days, Yu Ping and that woman called Wang Qinlan also have a hard time, after all, such ugly things can not see the light. One is a husband with a wife, a talent, in the unit or the executive general manager of foreign companies; One is a married wife, is the front desk subordinate of Yu Ping, a half-old Xu Niang

freckle-faced temporary worker woman. Two people are still in the same unit, the relationship between superiors and subordinates, in the eyes of the factory, I do not know whether it can be seen as the relationship between men and women. Who would have thought that this couple would be having an affair in the office break room before they were caught? Wang Qinlan lived on the third floor of the factory dormitory, only 100 meters away from the factory office. It was a convenient place for cheating!

Li Hua calm more and more let Wang Qinlan out of mind, and Yu Ping is helpless, although every day can see Li Hua home as usual, but still ignore him. In the face of no expression of Li Hua, Yu Ping some panic, he felt Li Hua more and more strange.

Li Hua kept waiting for the editor's reply, wondering whether what he wanted to do was appropriate. She must punish the man and the woman, but no mistake must be made. This evil breath could not come out, Li Hua felt uncomfortable. The strong idea of revenge tormented Li Hua day and night, she has been patiently waiting for the editor's reply. Li Hua wanted to know how the editor would reply, and then make a specific revenge plan.

Chapter 4: Tracking

That month Li Hua suddenly lost eight catties, no appetite, eat anything is not sweet. In fact, Li Hua has forced himself to eat more than usual, but there is a concern, which can grow well? That month almost suddenly thin, from a very standard weight 103 pounds thin to 95 pounds, Li Hua do not know how thin into this. Sometimes looking at herself in the mirror, Li Hua could not support some, looking forward to the end of this day soon, she was about to bear it.

Li Hua had all these crazy ideas in his head. A month of oppression, Li Hua heart resentment can not be eliminated, she can not control their own idea of revenge. Can reason let Li Hua awake a lot, those two people are not worth their own hands, they are not worthy. Li Hua is so silently remind themselves, must endure for a while, in order to get rid of the heart of hate!

The editor's reply and Li Hua's idea, there are some rational suggestions coincide, but Li Hua's idea of planning revenge, but day by day clear up. The more understanding Wang Qinlan this woman, Li Hua more want to revenge this woman as soon as possible, otherwise really can not rest at ease, may not sleep a day.

Reason and hatred entangled in the contradiction, this day is like a year, who can not understand the mood of Li Hua, sometimes rational and sometimes crazy, really wish to end all this as soon as possible.

One weekend Li Hua's chance for revenge came. That day, Yu Pinglin went out and said to Li Hua, "The workers are working overtime today. I want to go to the factory to have a look."

Weekday Yu Ping Saturday does not work, today Yu Ping again can not bear to be lonely, or began to secretly with Wang Qinlan? Li Hua thought of this, and an idea quickly formed in his mind.

"I really hope that this time we catch a man in the act and catch him with stolen goods..." Li Hua thought so, she hopes to block this pair of dog men and women, it is best to catch the current, but also use the camera to take down as evidence.

Yu Ping saw that Li Hua did not pay attention to him, so he directly grabbed his bag and walked out of the door gently. Yu Ping out, Li Hua immediately took out the address book, find Wang Qinlan home phone number, also quickly go out. Of course, she is not tracking Yu Ping, Li Hua must put Ping free, let him relax will have the opportunity to know his whereabouts. Li Hua ran quickly towards the public telephone box, which was far from home.

Li Hua stood in the telephone booth and paused for a moment, cleared his throat, picked up the telephone receiver, and dialed the past according to the number. The bell rang, Li Hua's heart also beat faster, she hopes that the voice of the phone is a woman, if it is a woman, it means that the woman did not work overtime; If it's a man's voice, it's that bitch's husband, Wang Mu.

"Hey! Hey! Please speak! Can you hear me? Why don't you speak?" Wang Mu followed the phone, there was no sound on the other side for half a day, he shouted at the phone.

Li Hua suddenly heard a man's voice coming out of the phone, which disturbed Li Hua's thoughts, she wanted to tell Wang Mu directly, "Your woman has cuckolded you, you don't want to know who it is?" The words suddenly stopped on the lips.

Li Hua thought, if so straight, not cheap that bitch? If the two of them have a quarrel and split up, it will definitely push the woman directly into peace. In any case, Wang Qinlan's current husband conditions are not as good as her boss Yu Ping. If she was with Yu Ping, she got a great deal!

There is another outcome, Wang Mu severely beat the bitch, and then divorce. But before forcing the woman to divorce, Wang Mu is likely to take the opportunity to blackmail Yu Ping, after all, Yu Ping to Wang Mu "cuckold".

These rational thoughts ran through Li Hua's mind at the phone booth. "Bear with me!" Li Hua consoled himself, and finally held back the rash of vomiting for a while! The original preparation to stir Wang Qinlan's home, let this bitch try home to scatter the taste, but this is not the thing to do at the moment. Li Hua suddenly changed his mind and hung up the phone.

After calm, Li Hua remembered a question: where will Yu Ping and Wang Qinlan have an affair at ordinary times? They're not likely to see each other at home too often, and they're not likely to mess around at work too often - after all, they've been found to be very effective. Li Hua suddenly remembered Zhang driver this person, Zhang driver must know the inside story, he acted as a pimp role to please the master, will seamlessly arrange two people's appointments. The society of that time had these bad habits.

The driver could not tell Li Hua directly how long the woman had been with Yu Ping, where she lived, and what dirty things she had done. Li Hua had to investigate by herself.

Half an hour later, Li Hua came to Zhang driver's car repair shop outside. Li Hua didn't go in at once. She looked around at several roads leading to the car repair shop, which was at the T-junction. The left side of the garage door leads to the direction of Li Hua's home, the right side leads to the brewery where the woman works, the front of the door is leading to the city's commercial center, the garage has a side door, and behind the door is a small backyard.

The original car repair shop is located here, no wonder they go to Li Hua's house so convenient. Li Hua alone along the outside of the garage house walked a circle, and then turned around and slowly walked in from the gate. The shop can only accommodate two car repair space, the backyard can park three cars, it looks very shabby. Li Hua was watching, a repairman came up warmly and asked: "Who is the beauty looking for?" Or fix the car?"

Li Hua subconsciously replied: "Looking for your boss Zhang driver."

The repairman shouted at the backyard: "Brother Zhang, a beautiful woman is looking for you!"

After a while, Li Hua saw Zhang, a driver wearing a yellow T-shirt and jeans, leaning against the door from the back yard and looking into the store. Li Hua and

Zhang driver's eyes meet at the same time, see Zhang driver immediately take the backyard door, to Li Hua walked up.

Li Hua see Zhang driver eyes skip panic, Li Hua suddenly understand he found the right place. Her analysis was right. This is where the dog and the dog hang out. Maybe that bitch waits in this garage when she needs a date. Driver Zhang was Mr. Yu's full-time driver when he worked at the brewery; Rest time, Zhang driver will receive private work in the repair shop, equivalent to telephone command; If you're out of town doing market research, take this woman with you. Yu Ping want to use the rest time to go to the field for a few days, chapter driver will accompany the whole way. Zhang driver is almost Yu Ping's personal butler, Li Hua has learned many times, before Yu Ping often let Zhang driver pick Li Hua in the city to do something.

Li Hua did not use Zhang driver's car much, but Li Hua often sent some tea and cigarettes to Zhang driver. In Li Hua's eyes, she sympathizes with Zhang driver, she knows Zhang driver's wife with two children is still in the countryside, the family is very difficult, the couple separated. Li Hua has seen Zhang driver's wife, a beautiful and thin woman, who is very honest and simple. Just to pity the mood of the driver's wife, Li Hua never let the driver do things empty-handed, will find a reason to give some fruit or eat food to the driver to add to the family.

Li Hua quickly thought of here, but in the mind, Zhang driver has forgotten the benefits of Li Hua. In the face of interests, there are many people like Zhang drivers who do something against their will. After all, Driver Zhang serves his boss Yu Ping, not Li Hua.

Driver Zhang was surprised and asked, "Sister Li, why do you have time to come here today? Mr. Yu is not here."

Li Hua replied very calmly: "To do something here, I came to see your car repair shop by the way, I have not been to it." Well chosen, easy to find. I am not looking for Yu Ping, will Yu Ping come after work today?"

Driver Zhang said: "I don't know whether Mr. Yu is in the factory or in the company today, I will call later to ask where to pick him up." Why don't I give you a ride home, or do you want to stay and have dinner with me? I'm going to cook the crawfish."

Li Hua looked around while coping: "Will Yu Ping also come to eat today?"

Zhang driver did not react, and did not continue to answer Li Hua's question. He barely smiled twice, and then ran to the backyard: "Sister Li, you sit down first, I'll go and arrange it, see a few pounds of lobster, and then call Mr. Yu!"

Looking at the back of the driver, Li Hua thought: See what kind of tricks you still play!

Chapter 5: Wake Up

Not long after, the driver Zhang looked from the backyard, approached Li Hua and said, "Sister Li, Mr. Yu is still in the company, and asked me to pick him up later, should I take you home first?" Or is it Mister with me?"

Li Hua naturally understand Zhang driver wants to ask her to go. Li Hua said: "No trouble, see you are very busy, I go shopping myself, you are busy." Tell Yu Ping to come back early. I have something to tell him."

Zhang driver immediately agreed: "OK, then you go slowly." Sure you don't need a ride?"

Li Hua waved his hand and went to the gate. She thought that when she went out, the woman would come out. She wanted to stay in the shadows and see the woman emerge.

Li Hua also really did not think that this woman is so shameless, she is too brazen. After seeing the bad thing exposed, there was no movement on Li Hua's side, and the woman thought that the tuyere had passed. "This bitch takes herself too seriously, we'll see!"

Li Hua head also did not go back to the direction of the intersection, she also knew that the driver was still looking at her back. The driver looked at the backyard with obvious panic, Li Hua thought that the yard must be hiding people,

Li Hua thought, Zhang driver is guilty, saw Li Hua and Wang Qinlan at the same time before and after appear in the garage. Driver Zhang was glad that the two women did not collide directly, otherwise he did not know what would have happened. So he could only politely send Li Hua away first and tell Mr. Yu in detail by phone.

Li Hua waited for a long time without seeing anyone come out, and she couldn't help but wonder if she was too sensitive. She waited patiently for another hour, her legs numb, but still no one came out, she finally decided to give up.

Li Hua along the side of the road, walking listlessly, she looked back at the row of broken small doors next to one another. Li Hua feeling in the heart, the environment is so run-down, Zhang driver still have the mood to engage in extramarital affairs, but also to help his boss mess with men and women. Perhaps the chapter driver in order to live, keep the job of serving the boss, so they flatter flatter flatter, let themselves live humbly.

Li Hua silently walked to the teahouse, ordered a pot of Tieguanyin tea to the waiter, and chose a dark table to sit down. Picking up a cup of tea, slowly looking at the slightly warm yellow electric lamp cover, a sad heart. Li Hua mused, drank down the Tie Guanyin tea is really bitter...

After sitting down, Li Hua could not help but think of Yu Ping again, think of that cheap woman, think of the endless pain he endured during this period of time, and his heart was a pain.

Had it not been for the two bad things that made such a mess today, Li Hua really would not have followed these ridiculous things and made himself crazy. I really did not think that the original scene of tracking the mistress in the movie was also staged here in Li Hua today. Li Hua felt sorry for herself when she thought about it.

This is not Li Hua really want to live, without self, day by day depressed, around a man, the pain is overwhelmed by themselves. Seeing himself become like this, I really do not know whether it is revenge on the pair of dogs and men, or revenge on Li Hua himself. At this time, Li Hua remembered the editor's reply: "If you go to get revenge, is it worth destroying yourself for these two people?"

The editor's earnest words made Li Hua wake up suddenly. Li Hua can't let these two bad things ruin his life! Li Hua wants to live well, this is the best redemption for himself, but also the best revenge for men. Let yourself live better and happier, and then let go, let the man regret, than conquer by force more retaliatory power!

Li Hua said to himself, "Thinking of what the editor teacher said in his reply, we can't be like them, we were right." If a dog bites you and you bite back, doesn't that make you a dog? We are human beings. We can't treat dogs like humans!"

Li Hua felt that the knot in her heart had loosened. Such days are coming to an end, Li Hua hopes to put down resentment.

Exiting from the teahouse, Li Hua walked along the river in autumn and summer. Still hot and stuffy, some suffocated, Li Hua slowly exhaled a long breath, and walked vacantly to the direction of home. Summer night, it is still the scene of red and green, noisy situation, the size of the stall are placed on the roadside. Li Hua walked aimlessly, feeling the hot air flapping towards him. At this time Li Hua really want to jump into the Yangtze River waves, wash away the woman to the home on the bad luck.

We got home at 11:40 p.m. Unexpectedly Li Hua just walked to the door, did not take out the key, the door was opened. Yu Ping immediately greeted her and said, "Why are you back so late? Have you eaten yet?"

Li Hua looked into Yu Ping's eyes a little angrily, walked over and went straight into the room to rest, not listening to what Yu Ping said.

That night, Li Hua was in her daughter's room next door and had a good sleep. It seems that in more than a month, I have never slept so comfortably as this day.

Chapter 6: Nasty People and things

Three days later, Zhang driver gave Li Hua a phone call and said: "Li sister, I tell you, you don't call people to play, Wang Qinlan's brother in the underworld also has people, if you find someone to retaliate against her, her brother will find you." I hope you don't mess with her any more. It's not good for anyone to make things worse."

Hearing the tone of Zhang driver's voice like this, Li Hua didn't even think about it and shouted to Zhang driver: "You call her to come, have the courage to come!" Also evil, he has a husband and son, but also to steal people, steal in my bed, now caught adultery. Did she tell you anything she wasn't ashamed of? Why did you hit her? She stole someone into the house! As long as she's cheating, tell her to be careful. I'm not gonna hit a bitch. Get my hands dirty. As long as she has adultery with another man, ask her cuckold husband Wang Mu to fight. If she still does not know the face, you go and tell her husband Wang Mu, that she stole a man to sleep in someone else's bed. This time has left a bitchy woman a little affection, and then steal, let her husband Wang wood tidy up! It will not be a matter of slapping, it will be a matter of breaking up the bitch's house like mine."

The driver on the other end of the phone was silent when he heard this. He certainly didn't know about the scandal that the woman was caught in Li Hua's bed. Guilty of doing something wrong, certainly dare not tell her husband Wang Mu.

At this time, the driver himself realized the seriousness of the problem, but also worried that things will be implicated in him. He's been involved in all this thieving. If it were not for his daily help to make this man and woman convenient, the woman would not dare to be so wild. So that the woman went to Li Hua's house to have an affair, so is it a habit to come in and out of Li Hua's house? Is there anything the driver doesn't know?

Li Hua with Yu Ping after marriage, inexplicably failed to live husband and wife life, in essence is Yu Ping spirit and body are derailed. Sometimes Yu Ping very want to give Li Hua warm, but the memory is Wang Qinlan crazy moans, where he still have the mind to see Li Hua innocent implicit expression? The disharmonious sex between these couples suddenly cold hurt, Yu Ping felt very deep. He's not sick. He's mentally guilty. In the words of psychologists, there are sexual disorders in the heart, physiological functional disorders, and the wife has become an innocent display. Yu Ping is caught in the exciting cycle of cheating, because the stolen seems to excite him. The man and woman who were doing harm to two families, undetected, grew emboldened. This is also Yu Ping was confused, self-righteous found a new love, he did not know that destroyed the second half of his life demon, has gradually begun.

Zhang driver's wife in the countryside called Suqin, a very simple woman. He had a son and a daughter with him, and they were married for twelve years, but they did not know that he also had a lover outside, and it was his own cousin Luo Qiong. If one day be honest Suqin found, do not know what is going to happen, then Suqin must be more painful than Li Hua. After all, Suqin is a rural woman, there is no economic source, and on weekdays, some temporary workers in clothing factories subsidize the family, and others rely on the income of the driver to maintain the life of the family. Suqin life also only a man chapter driver, this is the parents designated marriage. In fact, suqin son long compared to chapter driver cousin Luo Chun five official look good, beautiful and beautiful. Luo Qiong is only a little younger, no married children, but has been secretly eating forbidden fruit with Zhang driver for more than two years.

I remember one weekend, Suqin suddenly found Li Hua's mother's house on Saturday morning and asked Li Hua, "Do you know where my child's father Zhang, the driver, went with Mr. Yu?" I've been in town for three days and I haven't seen him. It's the weekend. The factory shouldn't be working." Suqin said her husband was with Mr. Yu, had not gone home for three days, his sons and daughters were waiting for his tuition, and the school was about to sign up for school.

Li Hua looked at the edge of the road, standing in the dust Suqin, the thin body, it looks like the wind will blow down. Li Hua heart really for Suqin uncomfortable, so weak and kind woman, Li Hua how to tell her worse things?

Li Hua know the pain of being betrayed by his man, do you want to let Suqin taste the pain of being betrayed by her husband again? Thinking of this, Li Hua felt a pang of sadness in his heart: such a good woman, a son and a daughter are around, holding her hand from left to right, asking Li Hua to tell her, where the husband chapter driver went.

Li Hua, of course, knew that it was the information that her bestie's husband inadvertently revealed. At that time, he asked Li Hua: "Why didn't you go to Zhejiang to inspect the market with Mr. Yu and Wang Qinlan, Zhang Siji and his cousin Luo Qiong?"

Li Hua froze: "I don't have so many days off, they said to take a week."

Li Hua at that time just guess Zhang driver with cousin Luo Qiong a little abnormal relationship, but she never thought of his man will have a problem with Wang Qinlan. Li Hua is too confident and careless. These four people went to Zhejiang Putuo Mountain, in fact, by business research sales market. At that time, Li Hua and Suqin, is also in the dark, the four people are like two couples go together, stay in the hotel to open two suites, travel in pairs.

Li Hua answered Suqin, "I really don't know where they went, I only know that several of them are on a business trip together and can't see each other for a week." They were doing their job, so I didn't contact them."

Suqin heard Li Hua say these words, showing very helpless eyes. Li Hua always remembered such a look in her eyes, how poor a woman she was.

Li Hua and Suqin are equally simple, and never thought that Yu Ping would have a leg with the freckle-faced woman beside him. Now think of that time four people together day and night, in the hotel do not know how unrestrained indulgence.

If not for the bestie's husband and Yu Ping is the same unit of management, Li Hua is in the dark. He heard that several people in the factory on a business trip gossip, really can not listen to couldn't help but tell Li Hua. Li Hua just knew that their line is to Putuo Mountain, nominally to investigate the promotion of beer sales market, in fact, is a vacation tour together.

Putuo Mountain is in Zhejiang province, where Yu Ping is from. Yu Ping has a cousin who lives there. She is a very simple person who runs a clothing tailor shop in Jinhua, Zhejiang Province. This time to see Yu Ping did not bring Li Hua along, cousin Yu Ping asked some information by the way, Yu Ping perfunctory cousin said: "This is a business trip, so did not bring Li Hua."

Two years ago, Yu Ping's mother took Li Hua to his cousin's home, as a full member of the family, the future daughter-in-law to meet relatives. This time Yu Ping with Wang Qinlan this woman, cousin see two people play ambiguous, so not very warmly entertain them four people, no less to Yu Ping face.

Yu Ping is very embarrassed, so with a line of four people in the nearby town hotel opened two suites. Something happened to them that night that shouldn't have happened, and that's when their affair began, in plain sight. Match up as a couple away from home, take a vacation like a real couple.

Later Zhang driver with Li Hua bestie Zhen Zhen talk accidentally said slip mouth. Zhenzhen at that time in order to help open up the sales of beer market, asked about the work of things, talking about Zhejiang Jinhua Yiwu to see some details of the market. When talking about the food problem, Zhenzhen said that Li Hua likes to eat seafood, like to eat big crabs, Zhang driver said that they also ate a lot of seafood. Yu Ping eyebrows up at that time, do not let the driver Zhang said. Zhenzhen suddenly understand, but Zhenzhen worry that this will affect Li Hua husband and wife feelings, not with Li Hua said.

A few years later, Zhang driver said back to the situation at that time. Zhang driver said: "Wang Qinlan that a few days to help Mr. Yu wash underwear, the woman in the hotel that night, the opportunity to Yu Ping throw." "Female subordinates sleep with their superiors in an undisturbed space, so it's natural for them to sleep together."

From then on, Yu Pinghe, the woman, had her own needs.

Zhenzhen is surprised by the change of Yu Ping, for Wang Qinlan such a soil woman derailed? She could never figure out that Yu Ping would like this woman. Zhenzhen thought, this in Ping is too no taste, is a sow meeting?

In the face of selfish interests, a little passion is burning, that kind of fresh feeling of heartless instead of plain husband and wife life. What else are lonely men and women doing at night? With the intentional arrangement of the driver, it is naturally more smooth. Zhang driver also need to stay with his cousin Luo Qiong, Zhang driver in the convenience of the same time, in fact, in order to better facilitate themselves.

Li Hui really does not understand, a temporary driver in the economic conditions are not good, why still have extramarital affairs, but also take it for granted...

At that time, the reform and opening up had just begun, and some weak-willed people, like callous people, lived day by day. They have no sense of shame, no moral conscience, and the social atmosphere is corrupted by these people. In the eyes of the driver, he did a lot of good things for the master, satisfied with the desire of flat and Wang Qinlan. He thinks it is perfection, but in fact it is evil. Let sexual pleasure trump morality, and there will be retribution for those who fall into it.

Li Hua still can not forget the innocent and cloudy eyes, the car to the dust of the roadside Suqin, she held her son's hand, while holding her daughter's hand. Li Hua thinks that the hate of extramarital affairs is to make a good home, home like a temporary hotel, the people in the home God has scattered, leaving an empty home.

Chapter 7: Hair Cuts Ruin Your Image

At dusk in early September, the room is still a little stuffy, and there is occasionally a cool breeze outside. Li Hua felt a little cool at this time, perhaps because the hair was cut short, she was not used to it - Li Hua just cut off his long hair for many years in the barber shop.

In the barber shop, Li Hua looked in the mirror, the woman in the mirror is just like a tomboy, but Li Hua smiled with understanding: I like even I do not know the image, is to this capable and strong image.

Barber Xiao Ying said: "It's a pity you don't have this long hair!" Li Hua smiled at Xiao Ying without a word, said thank you, and then readily pay to leave.

When walking, Li Hua still used to grab long hair to the back of his head, and felt empty there before realizing that he really cut off his long hair. Li Hua of course understand that cut long hair will "destroy the image", she also knows that pretend to be indifferent, is forced to smile relaxed. Li Hua does not know the cost of self-destruction image, for many years, the kind of elegant and fresh woman charm has become Li Hua's "standard", in the eyes of friends, Li Hua should be a woman of this temperament.

Although Li Hua himself ordinary features, but it is the kind of durable type of woman - familiar with Li Hua's friends have so evaluated, they think Li Hua's long hair back is very attractive. On the appearance of clothing, Li Hua is also very good at dressing, wearing a good look and personality.

On the way home, Li Hua remembered the editor's reply mentioned in this way: be sure to calm down, and make a decision when you are most calm. Even if you decide to break up after enough calm reflection, it's not too late to make the decision.

After more than a month of calm thinking, Li Hua had some insight and decided to maintain the status quo and do nothing. Li Hua wouldn't give up her job and career for a man. Li Hua loves work, every day with work to fill the time, like a machine numb work, and did not affect the work because of frustrated marriage.

Li Hua is not used to her strange image at this time, but she does not regret it. People are always changing, Li Hua hopes to have a new start from now on, to be the best and most confident self again, even if there is no husband, no marriage, no love, she also has affection and friendship. She could have a wonderful life, a warm friendship.

Li Hua suddenly felt that this day is not in vain busy, she did a thing to make themselves happy, resentment in the heart seems to be reduced some, the pace also slowed down.

When I got home, it was dark, and Yu Ping was already at home, sitting in the hall. When Li Hua opened the door, Yu Ping said, "I've come back."

When Li Hua and Yu Ping face to face, Yu Ping looked stunned: "When did this happen?" Why did you cut off your long hair?"

Li Hua said, "I just cut it. If you like women with long hair, the streets are full of them, choose for yourself."

Li Hua thought to himself, just change what you don't like!

Yu Ping shook his head and said, "You really, this is not even ugly yourself." Do your colleagues think it looks good?"

Li Hua said dismissively: "This ugly is nothing, it is better than some people steal people?" Now everything Li Hua says to Yu Ping has to be barbed.

Li Hua took advantage of the situation to continue to say: "Love to see, you look at it yourself, and no one is blocking you." Go to whoever you like, as long as you don't bring it home. If you do it again, I'll beat you up with it!"

Li Hua repented and walked into the kitchen, lifting the kitchen knife in his hand and cutting the pears on the counter. Li Hua did not eat, recently was forced to anger and heavy, think or to health, pay attention to health first, so with pear and rock sugar steamer cooked instead of dinner. This period of time wasted eight

pounds, Li Hua saw his appearance is very distressed. Tonight play a mouth lawsuit, see Yu Ping very angry look, Li Hua really enjoy, the heart is very cool, restored the momentum of the former queen, and finally have an appetite.

The next day, when Li Hua went to the office for work, his colleagues looked surprised. My colleague Xiao Wang asked, "Why do you cut your hair so short?" I didn't hear about your haircut yesterday. How did you get yourself into this? Why, I almost didn't recognize you!"

Li Hua said: "Just want to change the mood, try another style."

Xiao Wang said, "I think you are strange these days. I really don't want to cut such a good long hair so short, like a tomboy, it will take at least two or three years to grow."

Li Hua made up some excuses to stave off his colleagues' curiosity. Organs and units are like this, everywhere careful, with a tail between his legs, Li Hua really don't want to be colleagues see what flaws. Although Li Hua is not a scheming woman, she still knows the importance of understanding. In the organ has been more than ten years, what people have not seen, people are awesome, Li Hua does not want to become some people laugh at the object. Colleagues do not know what happened to Li Hua during this period, Li Hua can not mention to anyone. Li Hua wanted to change the subject and added: "Easy to take care of, simple!"

Li Hua does not say a word of nonsense, afraid to say a little more will expose emotions, let colleagues see the clue. Li Hua is afraid that one day suddenly can not help but expose all these things, how to deal with the eyes of their friends and colleagues, how will they see?

Li Hua did not think about how to break up with Yu Ping first, but from that day on, Li Hua heart has no relationship with him. In the emotional part has long gone their separate ways, but the divorce paper, the legal certificate, has not yet gone to handle.

This period of time Li Hua is basically eating in the unit canteen, that family no longer want to cook on the stove. And she didn't want to go back to that house for a while and just sleep there. It was the home of Li Hua's relatives. Li Hua wanted Yu Ping to leave, not her.

In that era of reform and opening up to attract investment, there were many foreign companies in the city of Li Hua, with Hong Kong businessmen investing and Taiwan businessmen investing. Yu Ping's business is a Taiwan-funded enterprise, the boss adopts a private family-style management, due to poor management, the business went bankrupt. The factory has stopped and the workers are being discharged. The factory retains more than a dozen people to keep the factory, others are all dismissed, including the cheap woman Wang Qinlan, including Yu Ping, old eye ah, pack up this pair of dark men and women!

This is the internal news, bestie Zhen Zhen told Li Hua the news. This is the best chance for Li Hua to break up with Yu Ping, and it is needless to say to break up, very in line with Li Hua's mind. Breaking up is easier, less embarrassing, without living together. Maybe it was providence. As long as this man is not there, Li Hua does not have to pretend to be happy in the eyes of so many people.

Li Hua said to Zhenzhen, "How nice! That way the guy can get out of here, and I can save my face. What if someone asks Mr. Yu? I can answer, no, I have gone to other places to develop!"

Zhenzhen very agree with Li Hua put in a horse, let Yu Ping decent to leave. The man's career is suddenly gone, his relationship is in shambles. Li Hua thought that there was no need to do so, but also think of the man used to be good to themselves. Let go of Ping, let Yu Ping regret. This is better than Li Hua to take revenge on him in person, and he will be more painful.

Zhen Zhen said, "Mr. Yu must have felt your kindness, and this is perhaps what Mr. Yu regrets most." Unfortunately, there is no regret medicine in the world to buy, Mr. Yu also knew that if he had not derailed, even if the factory closed, he would not be bad. I'm definitely going to help him with his career, and your contacts will help him with that, and he'll be able to carve out another niche."

Zhenzhen is right, losing Li Hua's trust is Yu Ping's biggest loss, losing not only marriage, but losing a chance for career development.

Li Hua said: "I think there is no need to spend time with him, after he left the city, we will slowly fade." Even if Yu Ping doesn't ask for a divorce, I can still find a way to divorce my marriage."

Zhen Zhen said, "You didn't file for divorce before Ping left? This can affect the rest of your life, and you're too young to pay for someone who hurt you. In case someone likes you in the future, you can have a new love, there is no need to give up beautiful pursuits for peace."

Zhenzhen kindness Li Hua is very moved, but also understand the future of a long way Li Hua have to learn a person to go on, she also understand Zhenzhen said passive.

Li Hua said: "You don't worry, equal to a walk I will face everyone." As time goes on, I will deal with the relationship rationally. Give yourself two years to sort it all out. Whether Yu Ping and that woman want to go on or not has nothing to do with me."

Zhenzhen found Li Hua's new hairstyle at this time, shaking her head and saying: "I really convinced you, you can ruin your image into this."

Li Hua said: "It's the determination to bounce back and start again. When my hair is long, I'm sure everything will be better. I don't believe in love and marriage anymore. I just want to work and make money. Now only money makes me trust."

Li Hua at this time suddenly remembered the old colleague Honghong said a sentence: "Anyone can betray you, lover, friend, but money will not betray you."

Li Hua lowered his head to think aftertaste, and really understood the motto of Honghong life. This is indeed the words of the heart, Li Hua with a living example of frustration, to remind himself. She also summed up the motto: "A woman should be loyal to herself!" Must be financially independent, independent personality, independent thinking, to be a wealth free woman."

Chapter 8: Getting to the ground

Autumn in the river city is coming, in the evening wind blowing by the river, Li Hua walk alone.

After a bad breath, Li Hua is still often preoccupied, working normally in the unit during the day, staying in her daughter's bedroom at night.

Li Hua came home from a walk by the river. Yu Ping at home said to her, "Li Hua, I want to talk to you about something today. Can you sit down and talk about it?"

Li Hua knew in his heart that it was not practical to always avoid him like this: "OK, you say it as soon as possible!"

The brewery where Yu Ping is to be dissolved, Yu Ping was ordered by the chairman of the Taiwan-funded enterprise boss instructions, after processing the release of the factory staff buyout severance pay, he himself would be fired by the chairman, and the executive position of the general manager would be revoked. Yu Ping could not save himself at this time.

Li Hua understood that at this time, Yu Ping did not have the capital to take the woman to start a business. Yu Ping also knows that only to find a new job, first have to support themselves. As for the woman Wang Qinlan who cheated for a while, Yu Ping how to deal with it, the heart naturally knows. Wang Qinlan this woman also had to go back to her husband Wang Mu side, the current affair is not exposed, Wang Mu still in the dark. Wang Qinlan and Wang Mu have a son, life is still to live.

Yu Ping will not go to break this relationship, to find himself an extra burden. Once Wang Mu know his wife Wang Qinlan with Yu Ping cheating, will be on Yu

Ping. Wang Mu home was already poor Jingle, now facing the wife laid off, will not let go of the opportunity to blackmail.

Thinking of these, Yu Ping felt afraid. He wants to preserve the marriage with Li Hua, no matter how to say how to compare, Li Hua than Wang Qinlan this woman is worth staying in the marriage. He will not break up with Li Hua because of extramarital affairs, he needs to get Li Hua's understanding and give him a chance to come back. In private, he wants to get the help of Li Hua's contacts and continue to seek good career development; Yu Gong, Li Hua is stronger than that woman Wang Qinlan in every respect.

Yu Ping also regretted that his casual and modest personality hurt himself, was seduced by the woman's warmth, did not reject the door, leading to a chaotic situation in life, so that he was passive embarrassed. He knows that the upper body has wisdom, but the lower body is the male hormone of the animal, and can not restrain the animal sex impulse that should not happen...

So far, Li Hua did not fight back against him, break and say out, and still maintain his image outside, which more and more let him feel panic. The worries of recent months, coupled with the shock of unemployment, Yu Ping's appearance is still swagger, but it is obvious that much older, only fifty-one years old middle-aged man, completely lost his former style, hair began to thin hair loss, which is the beginning of baldness signs.

Yu Pingqing cleared his throat and said slowly, "Our Taiwan-funded factory is going to be dissolved, you may have heard." I may take a job as deputy director of a garment factory of a Taiwan-funded enterprise in Guangzhou next month. I have already received the application notice. It is also possible to work for another Taiwanese clothing company in Shanghai. I'm going to work for a while, and when I'm stable, you can come and see me. Or I will come back to see you after the Spring Festival holiday. My daughter Xiaolin has arranged a private school in the city, and I will pay the tuition fee to you."

Li Hua listened to the man in front of a very organized arrangement, the heart mixed feelings to surge. She and Yu Ping are the second marriage, can make her daughter so kind arrangement, in today's society is not many men's mind. This may be the reason why Li Hua did not move a finger to Yu Ping. She still had the happy situation that Yu Ping loved her in her heart. She had to admit that she really loved the man in front of her, and a strange pain pierced her heart! They say the more you love, the more you hate!

On the surface, Li Hua was calm as usual: "Of course, work is the main thing, you can find a job so soon, you must cherish the present moment, don't waste your energy on useless people, you understand!"

Yu Ping quickly continued: "I will contact you by phone in the future." I was wrong this time, please forgive me, and we will continue to live a good life in the future, okay?"

Li Hua was silent for a few minutes, did not answer, then slowly looked up with a little thought, looked at the man and said: "You can go to work at ease, if my friends ask me why I did not see you, I will say that you are developing in other cities." I won't talk about anything else, is that all right?"

Yu Ping was very moved, "Thank you, I will come back and spend the New Year with you." Maybe try to go back to my hometown for the New Year and have a reunion with my mother."

Li Hua paused for a moment: "See then say, maybe I will go before you, my unit immediately want me to work at the grassroots station."

Yu Ping spoke with his head down, his voice so low that it buzzed like a mosquito. He knew that Li Hua did not want to face himself and wanted to avoid him, so he chose to stay away from and not divorce this way of getting along. He understood that Li Hua did not say tough words, to prove that he is still in his heart, reluctant to give up him.

Yu Ping guessed half of Li Hua's mind, Li Hua really dont have the heart to make any decision when in pain, so just think of this move, with time to dilute these unpleasant things. It is precisely at the time of the call of the leaders of the units that some comrades have been working in the grass-roots front line for three years, and

at this time these comrades should be replaced, and at the same time another group of comrades are needed to work at the grass-roots level.

This night Li Hua slept very soundly, the two sides talked, basically each has a plan and plan, the heart can be opened. Li Hua actually wanted to heal himself and go to the farthest place to work.

The next morning, Li Hua decided to go to the women's and children's hospital before going to the grassroots, and took out the contraceptive ring. Although it was a small operation, Li Hua took the doctor's advice to take three days off sick leave, directly tore it up and threw it into the trash can on the roadside.

Li Hua had heard Sun, director of the Trade union Women's Federation, say to her: "If a woman does not want children, she can bring an IUD; If you are not married, you can get rid of the IUD."

Li Hua is the latter, although he has been married to Yu Ping for more than two years, he has already lost those things between husband and wife. Always thought that his man kidney deficiency, bought two years of Chinese medicine kidney health care products to the man to eat, the result to the wild woman.

There was no color on her face. It was white. She only eats vegetarian food, the only thing is to love to eat some fish and shrimp, plus the recent occurrence of these unspeakable things, has been depressed in the heart, people are thinner than before. Li Hua, who was originally very cheerful and optimistic, almost changed a character and was taciturn.

Li Hua slowly walked to the unit, can not help but shake his head and smile bitterly. Li Hua thought well, decided not to rest, try to set out the day after tomorrow. Today I'm here to pack up my office supplies. The office was organized, and it was evening after the handover. Li Hua is afraid of the coming of the night, others are talking and laughing day by day, she is a number of days a day.

Three days later, Li Hua simply packed enough clothes for a month, with the unit inspectors down to the grassroots station, research sales. Li Hua only statistics inventory, every week to the municipal bureau to make a sales, inventory, funds to complete the report. The heavy work of moving boxes in the station did not let Li Hua do, and there were only four people working in the following station, stationmaster, salesman, warehouse keeper, and a financial accountant named Li Lianhua.

Li Lianhua is the only female colleague in the station, and this job has been for three years. Working at the grass-roots station can be said to be a touch of miscellaneous, what work is not so clear, and sometimes when a person takes a turn to rest, you must have to do all the work. Li Hua came, Li Lianhua is very happy, finally have a female colleague company. In the evening, Li Hua was arranged in Li Lianhua's dormitory, a room with two beds of 1.2 meters.

The first day of dinner in the station, the stationmaster said, let the custodian do a few dishes, specially for Li Hua made a big pot of boiled fish, a plate of ginseng fish, a big bowl of their own vegetables, really delicious. Li Hua was not picky, after eating it realized that she had not eaten hot food in recent months, feeling that the rice in the countryside was delicious.

Stationmaster said at the table: "Our basic station life is bitter, there is no amateur cultural life, but our rice raises people." The vegetables you tasted today were all planted by the keeper. The fish is bought live from the villagers who raise fish; Rice is also bought in the hands of farmers in the season of new rice, do not eat vegetables can eat two bowls. Director Li Hua, you are sent down by the Municipal Bureau to inspect and guide our station's work, and to eat, live and work with us.

Li Hua heard the stationmaster simple words, from the heart feel very warm. In all honesty, she had never in recent months been so relaxed as she was today, nor had she had such a good appetite as she was tonight, eating so much food, and concentrating on these earthcooker dishes. Coupled with everyone's kindness and concern for her, Li Hua did not know what words to express her gratitude, raised her glass to all the colleagues present and said: "Today I am the person who eats the most delicious food, and I have not drunk so much as today for a long time." In the future work, I will fully cooperate with everyone's work, thank you for your concern and help. Thank you very much."

Li Lianhua took over and said, "Li Hua, director, don't be polite. What we eat, you eat what, you have such an easygoing director Li Hua, and I also live in the same room, I am so happy. You have no AIRS at all, and you are much more down-to-earth than the previous staff. I used to have meetings, eat dinner, walk around and go back to the city, never standing still."

Li Hua said: "Now the bureau leadership attaches importance to the construction of grass-roots stations, the municipal bureau organs to supplement the work of grass-roots stations, hit the goal of sales winter, breaking through the same season sales indicators in previous years."

Everyone sat around the table, you talk to each other, the atmosphere is happy. Everyone is not sleepy, from work to talk to life, Li Hua saw these lovely colleagues from the grassroots, suddenly felt very happy with them, very contented, temporarily forgot the pain in his heart.

Sleeping in bed at night, Li Hua looked at the light on the wall with his eyes open. "Lotus, are you afraid to sleep alone every day?" Li Hua chatted with Lotus affectionately.

Lotus said: "Not afraid, it is very safe here, there are duty officers in the station, and there are colleagues living in the next room." We don't soundproof here, you can hear anything, you can rest easy."

Li Hua said, "I may snore after I fall asleep. Don't bother you."

The Lotus said, "It doesn't matter, when I fall asleep, I can't hear anything. My husband said, I am like a pig, I also belong to the pig, haha."

Hearing Lotus's words, Li Hua couldn't help laughing.

Chapter 9: Farewell to the past

Sleepiness hit Li Hua, and she fell asleep unconsciously. Li Hua in the dream climbing a mountain, climbing, climbing, was about to grasp the root of a tree on the top of the mountain, suddenly slipped, unable to grasp the rope in the hand, fell down the mountain. Li Hua shouted loudly, but could not make a sound, she struggled to wave and grasp, and finally caught another tree vine.

Li Hua was suddenly awakened by a dream and sat up on the bed with his hands. Li Hua look lotus is still sleeping, dare not wake her, and quietly on the bathroom, back to bed to sleep a cage sleep. Can no longer sleep, Li Hua remembered a few days ago a person lying on the operating table in the hospital, heard the doctor said: "Your uterine mouth is very good." A 40-year-old woman should be at the age of 30 like a tiger and 40 like a Wolf, which should be a period when husband and wife's life is flourishing, why do you have to take off the contraceptive ring, and you are not afraid of being pregnant?"

Li Hua dared to blurt out to the doctor who was not familiar with her: "We have not been together for two years, how can we have that kind of life? Imagine how impossible it will be."

The doctor in turn advised her: "That can not, you are cold, if you need any medicine to tell me, I suggest you drink some Chinese medicine, Chinese medicine has no side effects, adjust for a period of time will be better."

Li Hua said: "Thank you doctor, no need, I just want to take the ring, will not think about husband and wife life this thing."

The doctor wondered. And Li Hua at that time was thinking like this, and very calmly insisted on his own opinion, and took the ring until later did not reveal half a word to the peace, there was no need!

Yu Ping lived with his former wife for five years and had no children. Yu Ping and Li Hua were already on their second marriage. After finding that Yu Ping derailed, Li Hua did not have a little want to share the same room with Yu Ping. Li Hua is tired of this estranged marriage, she has to learn to let it go. This initiative to work at the grassroots level is her first step, she wants to stay away from Ping's sight, her heart to Ping's remaining love will be a little less light, light to her heart can really put down, her heart will not hate nor pain.

This is one of the reasons for Li Hua to escape, otherwise with Li Hua soft-hearted character, if you hear Yu Ping with a magnetic voice, say lingering love words, she was afraid that she could not help but be cheated. If Yu Ping leads her around by the nose, she will hurt more. She is no longer the age of a teenager, and she needs a mature and rational mind, not romantic and childish feelings.

Li Hua thought of this, could not help but knock heart to ask: "I can still believe in love and marriage?" Now Li Hua quickly mature a lot, she does not have the past unreasonable temper, become gentle and quiet. She seems to realize that if marriage life only brings her cheating betrayal, she would rather not choose marriage and not live in the eyes of others. She needs a safe haven for herself, not a broken marriage like this.

In a small society where people are afraid of words, cold words are killing people, so she must listen to what the editor teacher said: "To deal with the problem calmly, the better way is to let time and years dilute everything, can not be impulsive, must reduce the damage to the minimum time, and then follow the heart." If the marriage stays or goes, then you will definitely come out of the shadow, live your life, and live a better life."

Thinking of these words of encouragement and relief, Li Hua thought: What else can I not put down? No love, no marriage afraid of what? I still have a good job, good relatives, good colleagues, good friends, the most important thing is that I am no longer a naive woman, I should mature, is to say goodbye to the past days!

Li Hua a month after the grass-roots station work, back home in the city is already the weekend. It was raining that day, and the beginning of November was the beginning of winter. The key had just been inserted into the lock, but Yu Ping opened the door from inside the house and said softly, "I'm going to work in Guangzhou the day after tomorrow, and I'm still thinking about going to the grassroots station to see you, I didn't expect you to come back tonight, how nice!"

Li Hua put down his small box, Yu Ping handed the slippers in time. Li Huahuan looked at the living room of the house, there are two large boxes on the side of the coffee table sofa, a look will know that it is Yu Ping's suitcase, the kind of large. She knew that in two days, she would really go her separate ways. This is God's will, know Li Hua can not make up his mind, and do not know how to treat in peace, the two people finally separated on the grounds of work needs, get along not so awkward. This is the way Li Hua wants to deal with it. Usually always for the sake of each other, kind Li Hua can finally use this way to dilute the rational treatment of a chicken feathers mess, let the years to erase the scars of the heart, light gone!

Either way, let's cut it some slack. Li Hua asked, "I've packed my bags. Shall I go to Guangzhou by train or by plane?" Is anyone delivering?"

Yu Ping said, "By train, driver Zhang will take me to the railway station."

After saying that, it seems that there is no plan Li Hua sent him the meaning.

The station was close to the brewery and the woman's home, and Li Hua suddenly had an idea: I'm going to see this man off. Li Hua thought, that woman will also send this man! According to Li Hua's understanding of Zhang driver, Zhang driver will definitely provide convenience for the woman and go to the station to see her off. If they do, they will lie and say that the unit sent someone to see Mr. Yu off; If you don't meet, maybe buy a train ticket to go with you.

This idea is Li Hua sixth sense, Li Hua thinks her sixth sense is very spirit, on the one hand, she hopes that she guessed right, on the other hand, she is very angry, if everything is true, what should she do? To make a scene? Or just play dumb again?

Li Hua was not too concerned about this man and woman screwing shit, but the thought of these, Li Hua head big again.

Li Hua thought: Whatever, as long as I am not caught, steal once and steal ten times what relationship, he is not derailed? What's the difference?

So Li Hua said quietly, "Let me see you off."

Yu Ping stunned: "If you are busy, you can not send me, my driver will help me to arrange everything."

Li Hua asked, "Why, is it inconvenient?"

"No, I'm afraid you don't have time. I'll be back from vacation."

"I'll take you to the station. What time is the train the day after tomorrow?"

"1:20 at noon, may not have time to eat lunch, we have to leave."

Li Hua remember the time, no more questions, and then said: "Rest early today, after you leave, I will quit this relative's house, no longer live." Anyway, you don't work in the city anymore, I moved back to the unit of the house to live alone, work is convenient."

"Do you need help moving? If your colleague asks you why you didn't see me, what will you say?"

Li Hua first bowed his head and was silent for a while, then raised his head and stroked his head with his hands. Li Hua forgot his short hair and looked at Yu Ping thoughtfully: "Don't worry about this, I will tell all the friends who care about you that you have gone to other cities to develop." It's true, it's honorable, and I won't say a word about anything that's not on the table. In the future, you will master a degree in how you speak to outsiders and be careful."

Yu Ping heard Li Hua so reply, finally put down the words hanging in the throat. He also did not want everyone to look down on him, after all, it was he who had damaged his good impression in the eyes of everyone.

Li Hua pays more attention to the frightening reality than Yu Ping. Yu Ping patted his butt and walked away, and Li Hua also continued to live and work in this land, and his family and relatives were in it, which could be handled as simply as Yu Ping. Li Hua had to pretend that nothing had happened and bear it in silence. Rather than let go of Yu Ping this man, it is better to let go of herself.

Yu Ping needs to work more to earn money to support her family and raise her daughter, and she is a dutiful daughter, but also to earn money to honor her parents and take care of her younger sisters. Li Hua can not afford to lose this ugly, but also do not want outsiders to see her and Yu Ping joke. She also knew that everything would get better slowly, and that it would take a long time to heal the most painful wounds in her heart.

She can be so rational and calm to say these words, Yu Ping feel a little uneasy, he did not know Li Hua's real idea. According to the routine, Li Hua will certainly make trouble, will be strong to repair him; But Li Hua's performance in recent months has left him a little confused. He was thinking that as long as Li Hua did not make a fuss and did not expose him, he had to be a man with his tail between his legs and take good care of the home, otherwise he was really embarrassed to return to this city and this home.

Yu Ping said to Li Hua, "After I settle down my job, I will save more money and try to go back to my hometown for the Spring Festival together."

Li Hua had no words, nor was she moved, because she had heard too many promises from this man. The day after tomorrow the man will leave, Li Hua must face the reality, for the sake of her daughter, she also have to work and live well, can not go to fantasy rely on who.

Chapter 10: Farewell

Yu Ping left that day, he woke up early, early to go downstairs early stall to buy weekdays Li Hua favorite beef rice noodles plus a fried stick, and Jiangcheng people love to drink tofu brain, glutinous rice chicken each two. Yu Ping knew that it was too late to eat lunch, so he ate more breakfast and should not feel hungry until noon.

Li Hua heard the sound of closing the door and got up, saw the breakfast on the table, she also understood that Yu Ping was showing her good will. After washing, Li Hua sat down unceremoniously. Yu Ping picked up two pairs of chopsticks in the kitchen, handed a pair to Li Hua and said: "Eat this beef powder while it is hot, this is your favorite Master Peng beef powder, there are many people today on Sunday."

Yu Ping himself could not wait to eat. Li Hua buried down to eat breakfast, Yu Ping see Li Hua did not speak, also eat quietly. The restaurant occasionally made the sound of sucking rice noodles and drinking beef soup. Finally, both men tore the churros into small pieces, dipped them in the spicy beef broth, and put them in their mouths. They both ate contentedly, as if they had met the most delicious food under the sun.

Yu Ping said, "I won't be able to eat this authentic taste in Guangzhou in the future! I ate so clean today.

Li Hua did not accept Yu Ping's words, just stood up and said to him, "Your taste will change, there is more food in Guangzhou metropolis, you don't have to worry about anything."

Two people organize and check the things to take until the time to leave. Yu Ping left two hours ahead of schedule, only one hour to drive to the train station, leave one hour for the station, and have a short rest in the waiting hall. Chapter driver must be listening to Yu Ping told, waiting downstairs on time. Driver Zhang did not talk as much as usual, just focused on driving. Sometimes he glanced at Yu Ping and Li Hua sitting in the back row through the reflector. Li Hua noticed. Yu Ping is also looking at the driver's eyes, seems to have something to say...

In less than an hour, the train arrived at the station. The driver parked the car and took out the two large boxes, and Yu Ping himself carried a small box with him and walked with the driver one after the other. Li Hua deliberately fell behind Yu Ping, observing the crowd around her, she was looking for a familiar figure. Zhang driver bought a ticket to send Yu Ping into the station, until the sound of "this train will leave in 15 minutes" broadcast, Li Hua did not see the familiar figure under the platform.

Li Hua with the crowd into the station, Zhang driver urged Yu Ping quickly on the train. Li Hua's curiosity came out immediately, anyway, there was still time, she followed Yu Ping to the carriage. Yu Ping wanted to stop, worried to persuade Li Hua said: "You don't have to send, more than one person crowded can not get off the train, that can be troublesome."

This said as if to be anxious for Li Hua, but Li Hua sounds like the man who feels panicked in front of her is afraid of what she sees. Li Hua made an effort to push Yu Ping into the carriage: "Go, you sit down, I will go right away."

Driver Zhang also shouted strangely: "Excuse me, excuse me, Mr. Yu and Sister Li hurry up, just two rows in front." Screaming Zhang driver in front of the road, Yu Ping and Li Hua closely followed. When the driver Zhang put the two big boxes away, he immediately made a look at Yu Ping and said to Li Hua, "Hurry up and get off the train."

Li Hua stood for a while, quickly swept the car has come in the people, also looked at the next compartment, and did not see the people she wanted to see. Yu Ping anxiously remind Li Hua to get off with the driver, then Li Hua had to walk quickly to the outside of the car. When he was about to get off the bus, Li Hua instinctively looked back at the row where Yu Ping was sitting, and a woman's back sat down towards Yu Ping's row. At this time, the train was about to start, Li Hua had to get off and run to the carriage on the platform. Li Hua wanted to prove her judgment, she jumped up to look at the carriage, jumped a few times, did not see the front. The train was already moving at this time. Li Hua panted out of the waiting hall. The driver had already been waiting for her in the parking lot.

After getting on the car, Li Hua did not say the doubts in his heart, just sitting in the back of the car, constantly thinking about the scene just now. Is it really that bitch? Why else would it be so familiar?

The driver's question interrupted Li Hua's thinking: "Sister Li are you going to the unit, or go home?"

Li Hua said, "Take me home! In addition, I forgot to tell you that some time ago your lover Suqin and the children came to me and asked if I had seen you. The days when you were on a business trip with Mr. Yu and your cousin and that Wang Qinlan. I see the eyes of Sukhin and the two children, how I look forward to seeing you. I only said to Sukhin that you and Mr. Yu were on a business trip, and I didn't see you. I did not say how many people went, I will not lie, did not dare to stay. They'll be gone in a few minutes. I hope you're nice to Sukhin. She was so nice, she really believed me. When he turned around with the child, he turned his head and waved at me, telling me to hurry in, because it was windy outside. You know what? How much I hated you and Mr. Yu at that time, did you deserve your wife and children?"

The driver did not reply to Li Hua's words, and the car continued to drive forward. Li Hua also did not look at the driver, she thought in her heart, this is to tell the driver, you do those shady ugly things, I do not know, don't put Suqin and I are fools. It's just that we were kind enough to give you a chance to correct your mistakes. If you are still stubborn, there is no impervious wall, I do not say, there are always people who say, or more points of virtue, good for yourself.

The car slowly to Li Hua's downstairs, out of the door when the driver said: "Thank you did not say anything to Suqin." Now I have been laid off, today is the last day to work, from tomorrow I only have that car repair shop to work for myself. Fortunately, I listened to Mr. Yu and asked me to open a car repair shop, otherwise where could I find a job in a while? If you need my help in the future, you come to me at the store!"

Li Hua stood in place and listened, then turned to the driver of a little repentant attitude and said: "A good home, you have to be good to suqin." Sukhin is really kind and simple. Where can you find a woman as simple as Sukhin? Do you have the heart to hurt her? It's not too late to live well, you have children."

Zhang driver said: "I know, after I was laid off by Luo Qiong hung aside, no contact, sister Li, you don't blame Mr. Yu, he still loves you, you ignored him first, can you forgive him?"

"We'll see, just go with the flow. You see, I didn't do anything to him, so it's a good thing he left for work, God damn it! Let's just get on with it!"

The next day after Yu Ping left, Li Hua, while there is still a day off, hurriedly asked the moving company, all the furniture to the father of a relative in the countryside, the only piano gave to the second sister who once took care of her daughter, and then put himself and her daughter's daily necessities into the unit house. Li Hua also asked a cleaner to clean the empty house, and suggested that her relatives hang the house in an agency to sell it - because the bitch had slept bad luck, she did not want to damage her relatives' home. After doing this, Li Hua seemed to have a lot of clean heart, she wanted to completely forget this thing. Not here, not here. She needs a fresh start.

After working in the grass-roots station for a month, she realized a truth: Only by having the strength of economic independence can she remove the shadow in her heart. She needs to heal on her own, she has to put her energy into her work, so that she can stop her thoughts...

Chapter 11: A Decisive Retreat

A few years passed, Yu Ping in the second year of development in the field transferred to Guangzhou garment factory as deputy director. The relationship between Li Hua and Yu Ping is hanging, anyway, people are not around, we will slowly get used to Li Hua shape single shadow in and out of the unit community.

One day in June 2002, the Municipal bureau convened a meeting of mid-level cadres and above, and the leaders first listened to the report of comrades from the grass-roots stations, and then the bureau leaders announced two major reform measures, one of which aimed at the excessive number of personnel in the administrative departments of the Municipal Bureau, and the positions of sinecures could be cut and merged. One is to encourage the mid-level cadres of the municipal bureau to actively respond to the call for reform, the age of 45 can apply for internal retirement policy, suspended enjoy 80% of the salary; One is to work as a heavy worker in rural basic stations.

For a time, some middle-level cadres of the municipal Bureau were panicked and some were excited, and they discussed one after another, Li Hua was the most calm one. Li Hua is trying to escape the emotional hurt that this city has brought to her. The man who hurt her is gone, but those things, and the people who knew about them, she has to deal with. She was afraid that one day she would not be able to carry on and do something stupid, she could not be stuffy in her heart for a lifetime, pay for those painful memories. She wanted to go out, she even felt a pity that this opportunity had come two years earlier!

Li Hua thought that a regular eight-hour work day could not bring her more wealth. Now that her home is in name only, if she still stays where she is, living like a robot, the next twenty years will be the same scenario. The life that can see the head, the unchanging life is not the state that Li Hua wants, she wants to fight. At present, the unit policy is very good, and 80% of the salary is taken. At the very least, even if the business is not successful, Li Hua does not have a sense of crisis. Since you can't die of hunger, why not have a try?

Li Hua already had an idea in mind. She couldn't miss the chance. In accordance with the call of the bureau leaders, she actively responded to the application for retirement. She feels that she did not choose wrong, she needs to change an environment, to a place that does not know her to find business opportunities, and then start a business, so as to achieve a house and car life in the metropolis early.

Among the middle-level young female cadres in the unit, Li Hua was the first to apply to the organization for internal retirement. At that time, many people did not understand her, and the leaders who wanted to train her advised her to think twice; Those who do not have the real skills, take the opportunity to stir up the fire to let Li Hua leave the unit as soon as possible: "If you apply, go out to make it better than now."

These people want to occupy her mid-level cadre post, hoping that she will go quickly, so that she can vacate the position to climb, mix for a few years, when an official post. There are also individual selfish leaders have other plans, if Li Hua really go, leave the vacancy can also get benefits, such as promoting a person who wants to be the director, by the way to sell personal feelings.

Li Hua saw clearly what these people were thinking. She thought well, did not want to put the future of work and life, to deal with interpersonal relationships. I mean, she can't pull off that kiss-and-tell thing. In the face of such a situation, Li Hua only go all out, decided to retreat, nothing great. "Isn't he just a center director? In the future, if you do well, you may be the president of a company!" Li Hua is very confident in himself and must seize this opportunity.

Li Hua's application for retirement was unanimously approved. The application for internal withdrawal has been submitted, and there is still half a month to wait for the official notice. We need to engage in handover work. A colleague asked Li

Hua, this time is not to go to Guangzhou to take refuge in Yu Ping, Li Hua vaguely brought this topic. All to Yu Ping probe Li Hua fidgeting, waiting for notice days Li Hua day like a year, she does not know whether he can always pretend to be a light wind clouds. She is looking forward to the early approval of the application, so as to save long dreams.

In recent years, Li Hua has handled the affair of Yu Ping very well, few people know. Li Hua also does not want everyone to know that her reorganized family has been riddled with holes, and she has not figured out how to deal with this mess. Li Hua want to leave Yu Ping marriage bondage, but do not want everyone to know because Yu Ping did ugly things that lead to family breakdown. She must let everyone think that she and Yu Ping are still a happy couple.

Yu Ping has been away for a few years and has returned several times during the Spring Festival. Everyone's temptation and concern let Li Hua very uncomfortable. These concerns and greetings are like merciless mockery in Li Hua's heart. Once Li Hua thought that with Yu Ping away, she would feel better; Did not expect Yu Ping people left, his side of the network is staring at Li Hua all the time. It was as if she were being peeped at without clothes, and she felt ridiculed by everyone. She wanted to leave the city and let the past fade away.

After deciding to retire, Li Hua also had her own plan, she wanted to go to the southern city of Shenzhen to study insurance. She knew what kind of job she was suited to, and only as an insurance agent could she work and live in any city in China, and only in this way could she escape the people she knew around her.

A week later, Li Hua received a formal notice from the personnel section, and the financial aspect passed the normal pre-handover audit. On the third day after receiving the notice of approval, Li Hua went to the residential school alone and told his daughter about his next life plan. She is going to Shenzhen to study insurance, and try to stay in Shenzhen to work, she has found the next goal and challenge. Li Hua asked her daughter to study hard and gave her confidence that she would make her daughter's life better. She told her daughter that she would go back to her grandmother or second aunt during the school holidays.

After all the arrangements were made, Li Hua was relieved to get on the train to Shenzhen. That day is the night of the train, leaning on the window to look out at the Mercedes train, the scenery along the way let Li Hua can not sleep. Loneliness and longing are intertwined, Li Hua thinks about a lot of challenges she will face in the future: to a strange city to start over, no one knows her, everything from scratch. But she was very relaxed, and slowly felt that the stone in her heart had been removed from her, that no one would know her past in the future, that she would no longer be wronged, and that she would begin to live for herself.

The train arrived in Shenzhen at half past seven in the morning. Before Li Hua walked out of the hall, he went to the bathroom to wash his face and put on a light makeup. She changed from the box into a dress suitable for Shenzhen climate, and then with the long straight hair that has grown up, it appears young and energetic, only like a small woman in her 30s, you know that Li Hua was 45 years old at that time.

According to the detailed address recorded in the book, Li Hua came directly to the vicinity of the Imperial building. Seeing that it was not time to go to work, Li Hua first walked into an early dumpling restaurant, bought a bowl of vegetarian dumplings and ate them slowly. Then find the agency that has been contacted and get through the phone. Ten minutes later, a girl really came to pick her up in front of the dumpling house and went to the private apartment booked to settle her luggage. Li Hua picked up the hanging bag that he carried with him, and went out with the beauty, the two of them asked and answered to understand the surrounding life situation.

It's a great setting, so close to the Imperial Building, only six minutes' walk. The dumpling house is also very close, if in order to save money, there are snack stalls and noodle shops here. She was surprised to find a Hunan restaurant that she particularly liked to eat. She wanted to have a good meal in the evening, so she went to Hunan restaurant to eat. She must not be wronged herself any more.

Li Hua has learned on the phone that the agent training of Smith Barney Insurance Company must be studied for two months. Li Hua passed the insurance

agent qualification certificate and finally became a new person in the insurance career.

Li Hua, through an intermediary, rented an apartment with a bathroom in a private building next to the Imperial Building. Mainly for convenience, you can walk to the class place and save time to learn the insurance agent qualification training course. In order not to be late, Li Hua began to walk around the rented house on the first day in Shenzhen, familiar with the breakfast shop, Limin supermarket, wet market and bus station, as well as beauty salon.

Li Hua got up early on the first day of class and bought a bowl of medium pork dumplings with Chinese leeks at a nearby Shanghai dumpling house. After eating there is still plenty of time, Li Hua unhurried into the next hair salon trim hair.

Li Hua looked at the hairdresser to blow her finishing, looking at himself in the mirror: the hair has been long from the length of the inch to the hair of the ear show, has recovered the appearance of gentle beauty. After the barber repair type care, now Li Hua looks very professional, capable temperament appeared.

Chapter 12: Insurance training in different places

It was almost time to cut the hair, Li Hua picked up the bag and walked quickly to the imperial building, and arrived at the sixth floor insurance agent training classroom 10 minutes before attending the class. I really didn't expect there were so many people there, not a familiar face, everyone from all over the country.

Shenzhen is a special zone city, in the era of reform and opening up, people who come here are people who have dreams of entering the world. Many bold investors, as well as college students, migrant workers, officials who have abandoned politics for business, and employees like Li Hua, have flooded into this young city.

Li Hua also inadvertently caught up with the tide of The Times, Li Hua did not think to join the party, but caught up with the fashion. Had it not been for the avoidance of gossip, Li Hua would not have had the courage to retire early from a secure job and squeeze into the unfamiliar insurance industry. Don't even know the depth, she came, the newborn calf is not afraid of tigers, everything starts from scratch. Li Hua think do not know how to study, the back road are broken, hard to learn early through the training, as soon as possible to get the insurance agent exhibition certificate. The goal is clear, the place to live has been decided, everything is ready, and the rest only needs to focus on learning.

Li Hua swept the whole classroom at a glance, see some empty bags, some chairs with clothes, Li Hua cushion to the countdown to the middle of the row, there are a few empty places. Li Hua sat down on an empty chair. The host was already at the podium, taking the microphone and addressing everyone: "Quiet, everyone. First of all, I would like to thank so many students for being here today. On behalf of American International Assurance Company Shenzhen, I would like to welcome

you. You are welcome to pass the insurance agent training, pass our exam, and become a real member of our insurance industry. Thank you, the insurance company team has a new strength. You are welcome to show your qualifications and become our future diamond business elite. Like me, you are welcome to come to this stage and share your learning and experience in the insurance agency industry. I hope that more insurance elites can gather here and walk on the peak of our life value. I wish the students work hard to complete the training, I wish you can successfully pass the training exam!"

The whole venue applause, this passionate scene, Li Hua has not felt for a long time. Li Hua clapped and looked around. These people were as excited as Li Hua and looked forward to it. That look is Li Hua in the previous unit has not seen the scene, make people energetic.

Then Li Hua picked up a notebook and pen, wrote down the class notes, these contents include the concept of insurance agents, insurance clauses, insurance claims, insurance exhibition in the random appointment, insurance foreign insurance clauses, insurance life, the relationship between the insurer and the policyholder and the beneficiary, and so on. Learning insurance knowledge is really much, Li Hua thought, if not to learn, how can not catch up with the development of The Times.

Li Hua's learning attitude of taking notes carefully attracted the attention of a beautiful woman next to him: "Hey! Your handwriting is neat and beautiful. I'll copy it after class. There are two passages in between that I didn't write down."

Hearing the northeast accent, Li Hua immediately laughed: "OK, you are from the Northeast?"

The Northeast girl said, "Yeah, you recognize my local accent?" My name is Niu Niu, what's your name?"

"You call me Li Hua is good, because I also have friends in the northeast, so familiar with this kind of voice, feel very cordial."

The two people quickly met, Niu Niu's character is frank, often say a few words between classes can cause the surrounding students to laugh. Then Niu Niu made a face and spat out her tongue, and several handsome boys in the front and left seats were laughed by Niu Niu!

After class, many boys touch Niuniu intentionally or unintentionally, pleasing her with fruit and snacks. I really don't see Niu Niu has such a move, and anyone can hit hot. Li Hua looked at Niuniu carefully, in fact, Niuniu looks general, there are acne on the face, and the dress is also general, but she is very good at talking. This cheerful personality must be very suitable for being an insurance agent, I believe she will do well in the insurance business in the future.

A week of learning time quickly passed, Niu Niu and Li Hua familiar with up. Niu Niu saw Li Hua dressed in a workplace style. She looked like a lecturer rather than a student. Li Hua a black short-sleeved professional dress, that dress is still very famous clothing brand. Wear simple and generous grade, can be said to be never obsolete. Niu Niu saw Li Hua is very workplace style, but also a woman's charm. As long as the class Niu Niu followed Li Hua into the same bathroom, the two people changed to see the bag occupy the position; Every day, whoever arrived first would take care of each other and occupy the usual place of class. For a long time, the students around are very conscious, sit in each position. They also ate together on weekends -- splitting the bill, of course, which was quite fashionable in those days.

On the third weekend, Niu Niu and her classmates went to Hunan Restaurant again for dinner. Li Hua likes to eat spicy, often eat there, did not think that the students also find this shop, economical, and the taste is really authentic. Li Hua had refused the invitation several times before. This time, when I heard that my classmates were going to have dinner in Hunan Restaurant, Li Hua immediately joined in. Niu Niu shouted happily, "Who dares to drink today?" There was an immediate response, "I want a beer!" "Me too!"

Li Hua also asked for a cup of stout, Shenzhen in July is really hot, eat spicy with a cup of cold beer, should be very comfortable. When the owner of the Hunan restaurant saw Li Hua coming, he received him warmly. The boss always thought that Li Hua brought everyone to eat here and took care of his business, so he was particularly enthusiastic about Li Hua.

Li Hua usually a person to eat in this shop many times, every time to change a dish to eat, almost every dish in the store tasted. Therefore, Li Hua is responsible for ordering food. She knows which dishes are heavy in taste and which dishes are delicious. That meal we eat very happy, checkout boss also see in Li Hua face a discount. Eight people spread out and paid less than 50 yuan! The students clamored to come back next week, and of course the boss was happy. That is, the boss knew that Li Hua and they were from the insurance company.

After the show, Niu Niu asked Li Hua, "Li Hua, where do you live? Why don't you come stay with me at my place today? I hail a cab alone and I live alone. I have two rooms. You can really stay at my place. I want to discuss something with you tonight!" Li Hua thought that Niuniu needed to help with the exam review, so he politely invited her to live with him.

Li Hua said, "Don't worry, I have printed two copies of the review questions for next week's exam, I will give you one, you don't have to worry." If you review according to the above, there will be no problem in the exam.

Niu Niu was talkative in class and didn't listen much. Li Hua sorted out the key contents and wrote out the answers to some questions.

Niu Niu said: "Thanks, I need these review questions, but I still want you to stay for one night!"

Li Hua saw Niuniu sincerely invited, thought Niuniu was afraid, and went back with her.

Shenzhen night, red and green, tall buildings, in Li Hua's eyes fly over, the taxi in the spacious highway. If not accompanied Niu Niu to her home, Li Hua did not know that the night in Shenzhen is so beautiful, with bright lights along the way. Li Hua on weekdays after class, in addition to eating, washing hair and walking outside, never go out at night, let alone go to the night market.

About 20 minutes to Niu Niu rented the community, where the environment is really beautiful, several electronic card swipe door seems very safe, there are security guards. Niu Niu lives in Room 9 on the 6th floor, with two bedrooms, one living room, one bathroom and one kitchen. Niuniu and Li Hua took a bath and sat down to chat. Niuniu did not feel sleepy and said directly to Li Hua, "I want to go to the talent market center together after the exam, because we have a base salary of 600 plus commission, and do insurance while working, you see?"

Li Hua said, "That's a good idea. Do you know anyone?"

Niu Niu said: "Yes, you are like a manager, the boss will definitely hire you." Anyway, go to the report every day, there is a basic salary of 600 yuan a month, the living expenses are earned, we do insurance will not affect."

Li Hua: "OK, you really have an idea, you think I can do it."

Niu Niu said, "And tell you, this house is actually rented by my boyfriend in Hong Kong, 3,000 yuan a month." You come here to live in my room, only pay me 500 a month, here is certainly better than your private apartment, yours is 600 yuan. What do you think?"

Li Hua stopped thinking for a second and replied, "OK, I will reply you before the expiration of this month." When the exam is over next week, when you pass it, you can decide where to live then."

Niu Niu said: "Well, I think it is you who is at ease, if others I will not share the apartment." But my boyfriend only comes here for two days every two weeks. When he comes, you don't say we are roommates, you say we are students in the same class."

Li Hua said: "OK, you have all the bedding?"

Niu Niu said: "There is a bed Simmons, no bed, other covers have blankets."

Li Hua saw that Niuniu's brain turned so fast, she was very impressed, young than Li Hua's institution for more than 20 years of people also appear smart and capable.

In this way, Li Hua and Niuniu have passed the insurance agent training exam. After the exam, they first discussed moving. Three days ahead of the end of this month, Li Hua simply cleaned up, with only daily necessities, did a renunciation of the apartment, moved into Niuniu's house. The days outside are very simple, a person has enough to eat, a place to sleep, it is very good.

Li Hua felt fortunate to see Niu Niu's quick arrangement for help. When the

insurance exhibition industry was about to start in Shenzhen, with the help of student Niu Niu, I not only settled down to a good place to live, but also found a decent job that did not conflict with insurance work hours. Can earn more is a little bit, 600 yuan can also be a house rent has landed, live together the house environment is better, and there is a companion.

Chapter 13: Challenge Yourself

So Li Hua in Shenzhen in August began the insurance agent exhibition industry. At that time, the new insurance agent must buy a one-year accident insurance policy by himself, and he needs to complete 5 single tasks in a month, so that he can get the new diamond reward, and the monthly income will have a commission of more than 5,000 yuan. Li Hua carefully learned the knowledge of the insurance exhibition industry, and started with the five important people around him.

Before sharing an apartment with Niuniu, Li Hua wanted to sell insurance randomly and naturally by starting with familiar faces near her home.

Li Hua first went to the talent market center to report, after a busy morning every day, soon to noon to go to the familiar target area, to look for insurance exhibition opportunities.

On the first day, Li Hua wanted to dress herself up. The first stop she thought of was the hairdresser she often went to. The No. 6 barber, who often serves Li Hua, greeted her warmly as soon as she entered the door: "Hello, are you washing or cutting your hair today?"

Li Hua said: "I'm looking for you today to do a shampoo monthly card, there are activities discount?"

No. 6 barber said happily: "Thank you for taking care of me, I must wash you comfortably, today is not in a hurry?"

Li Hua said: "Not in a hurry, just chat with you to wash hair."

The barber helped hang the bag and asked, "Why is the bag so heavy today?"

Li Hua mysterious smile: "Ha ha ha, that is a package of money ah, don't lose crushed!"

The barber heard Li Hua's words, and took the bag down nervously: "You still hold it, this can not be careless."

Li Hua said: "You can also have so much money, wash your hair and tell you about it!"

The barber asked curiously, "What can I do to earn so much money?"

Li Hua said: "It is a life insurance policy, the insured amount is 100,000, only 120 yuan a month, the younger the insurance premium is less, how old are you?"

The barber said, "I'm 22 years old, how much can I insure for 500,000?"

Li Hua said, "I suggest you don't insure 500,000 yuan, you try to insure 100,000 yuan first." Only 120 yuan a month, so you have no financial pressure. Only insure for one year, when you have the money and stability, and you believe in the benefits of insurance, then do the whole life insurance plan. It only costs 120 yuan a month, and there is a security guarantee, you see?"

Hairdresser wash hair side and Li Hua happy chat, hairdresser is very assured. After washing the head, Li Hua first at the counter to wash the monthly card, by the way, directly take out the insurance form, ask the barber the basic personal information, and then ask: "Show me your ID card, register the number."

The barber did not hesitate to take out his ID card from his work box and show it to Li Hua, who took a picture with his mobile phone: "It needs to be used as a copy." Just sign here. Do you want to pay every month, every six months, or every year?"

The barber said, "I'd better pay every six months."

Li Hua said, "No problem, it only costs 720 yuan for half a year. Pay now and I'll apply for insurance for you tomorrow. Then I'll send you a receipt and other insurance policies. You see, you have the same coverage as me, and my premium is much higher because I'm older!"

The barber looked and nodded: "Really, young insurance pay less premium." I trust you, you always take care of my business, anyway, only 120 yuan a month, I can afford it."

Li Hua said: "That's right, to plan for their own financial management, meet accidents do not panic!"

In this way, the first day of the exhibition industry success! After Li Hua went out of the store, he encouraged himself happily and silently said: "I am the material for insurance!"

To tell the truth, this insurance policy randomly recommended success, so that Li Hua found confidence.

The next day Li Hua went to the Imperial building company, paid the insurance premium, issued a good receipt, and got a few insurance applications. About noon, Li Hua came to the Hunan restaurant she often goes to, chose the old place (leaning against the most table) and sat down, this time was personally received by the boss. Li Hua intended to come early, the guests are relatively few, she knows that after 1 o 'clock is the peak of the restaurant, now not busy.

Li Hua said to his boss, "Boss, can you talk with me for 15 minutes now?"

Boss: "Sure, what do you want to eat?"

Li Hua calmly took out the insurance application form from the bag: "Boss, I sent you the security and money, do you want it?"

"What could be so good? Do you want me to buy insurance?" The boss sat down, because he saw the insurance application form on the desk. The boss knew that Li Hua was in insurance, but Li Hua had never recommended him to buy insurance before.

Li Hua said directly: "If you only need to pay a monthly premium of about 200 yuan, pay a year of insurance coverage of 150,000 yuan, are you willing to buy?"

"Is there a good insurance product?"

Li Hua took out a pen on the paper, calculate to show the boss. A few strokes draw a picture from low to high, and the boss can understand it at a glance. Li Hua explained the advantages of insurance to share the risk of accidents. Li Hua also added: "There are five cooks and handymen in your shop, plus the investment in the renovation costs of the shop, I have planned for you the most affordable insurance

protection, to fight small, the burden is still very small, the staff is also guaranteed, you are willing to insure!" To share, each employee only pays a few dozen yuan per month, your boss has no pressure at all, and improve employee safety awareness! Why not?"

The boss looked at several people drawn on the sketch, the average insurance tens of dollars, the top of the arrow above the protection of 150,000 to 300,000 two kinds of plan insurance policies.

The boss smiled, he knew that Li Hua had spoken out his worries. In this analysis, it also solves the problem of employee turnover that the boss is worried about, and the employees have the guarantee that they will not resign casually and go away; The boss can also take out part of the bonus to buy insurance for employees as a guarantee reward, and both sides are happy!

Undoubtedly, the insurance policy of the owner of the Hunan restaurant has been negotiated. Of course, this is also because Li Hua has been an old customer of this store, and the boss has become friends, trust each other, so it is easy to close a deal. After two successes, Li Hua got the hang of it.

Li Hua thought of the old classmate of the securities company who came to Shenzhen to struggle for business. The old classmate is Li Hua's classmate. He has always been the top student in the class, and he writes well. He is the proud student of the homeroom teacher and a good example for boys. In those days, old students rarely moved around, let alone male and female students. Li Hua alone to Shenzhen this matter, had inadvertently said to the class teacher lover, did not expect the class teacher after listening to the pillow wind know, immediately called to tell his proud student Chen Xiong. Chen Xiong contacted Li Hua several times during Li Hua's study, and asked her to have dinner, but Li Hua refused. Li Hua thought this time it was time to ask the old classmate to have a meal, and by the way directly explained that he was officially involved in the insurance industry, so that the old classmates would support him.

Li Hua had known Chen Xiong also lived in the imperial building not far from the securities company dormitory building. When she first came to Shenzhen,

Li Hua didn't want to cause trouble for her old classmates because she hadn't decided what job to do, so she didn't tell Chen Xiong that she also lived near there. Now is different, Li Hua think their own life things have been solved, now is entrepreneurship, is to talk about work, you can ask the old students to support. Thinking of this, Li Hua knowingly smiled, picked up the mobile phone to Chen Xiong number called the past: "Hello! Hello!"

There came the voice of Chen Xiong, Li Hua smiled and said: "It is me, today about you for lunch tomorrow, how about my treat?"

Chen Xiong said: "Ha ha ha, the sun is coming out of the west, how can you have time to invite me to dinner?" I've asked you several times, and you don't give me the honor to say it. I've been in Shenzhen for almost two months, but I haven't been seen. If the head teacher had not told me, you would not have met! Why, something's wrong?"

Li Hua said: "Invite you to dinner, must have something?" Are you free for lunch or dinner?"

Chen Xiong said, "OK, I'm busy in the morning. I'll have a little meeting in the afternoon. In the evening, let's meet at a Shanghai dumpling house near the Emperor Building.

Li Hua thought what a coincidence, Chen Xiong also know that dumpling house. The world is so small, but how come two people never bump into each other?

Li Hua said, "OK, that's up to you. Let's meet at Shanghai Dumpling House at six!"

Li Hua knew that this old classmate must be dressed up. Chen Xiong's residence is very close to his work place, Li Hua also wants to leave more time for Chen Xiong, so that the old classmates can get together and talk slowly. Two people are old classmates relationship, Li Hua can directly let Chen Xiong buy an insurance, this time Li Hua does not have to turn to talk.

Chen Xiong and Li Hua arrived at the store within two minutes of each other. They both arrived five minutes early. The two of them were particularly happy to meet, Chen Xiong did not put Li Hua as an outsider, and did not put her as a

female classmate. Li Hua originally wanted to ask Chen Xiong to eat better, eat the boiling fish of Hunan restaurant, Chen Xiong said: "Do you also like to eat this dumpling?"

Li Hua said: "Yes, but please eat dumplings, is not too wronged you?"

"Oh, this dumpling house is delicious, don't run around." We can talk more. It's near where I live."

"Well, since you don't think it's cheap, don't say I don't treat you well."

"The dumplings in this shop are better than anything else!"

The two people said a smile into the dumpling house, choose a table by the window to sit down. The waiter approached and asked, "Are you still eating the same way?" Both men nodded at the same time: "Yes! Same old!"

Both of them laughed at the same time and pointed to each other and said, "So you often come to eat ah, how did you not meet?"

After laughing, Li Hua directly said to complete the task of insurance policy, she only needed Chen Xiong to buy a small insurance policy, a year of accident insurance.

Chen Xiong said: "Buy to buy life insurance!"

"I do not recommend that you buy life insurance now, because you have just come to Shenzhen, the career is not stable, and the economy is not rich." When you get rich and you buy a house, you can think about buying a big policy, okay? Just a little insurance now!"

Chen Xiong said: "OK, just listen to you, buy the kind of insurance of 100,000 yuan a year?"

"Well, fill out the form for yourself and give it to me."

In waiting for dumplings on the table, the two people very tacit agreement reached a consensus. No sooner had the form been filled out than the dumplings were served. Li Hua took the opportunity to go to the bathroom, by the way to buy the single, and added two cold dishes. Back slowly eating dumplings and chatting, Li Hua thought this old classmate really interesting, did not do any ideological work on insurance.

Li Hua knows this is a friendship insurance policy!

Four small insurance policies have been completed, if the pace of progress, Li Hua can not only get the new diamond award, but also may be on the Red honor list this month! But Li Hua knows that she still needs to complete a big single, life insurance policy!

Li Hua thought of what her little sister had said to her: "Sister, if you have difficulties in Shenzhen and need help, you can go to my friend, General Rong!" I told him that a sister came to Shenzhen to develop. He insisted on inviting you to dinner, and I refused for you."

Li Hua counting the date, approaching the end of the month, had to get through the Rong total phone, a simple appointment to meet the place to hang up the phone. Li Hua handled the call carefully, because she was a student friend of her sister, she did not know how to talk about insurance. This is really difficult for Li Hua, she has been encouraging themselves, this is to talk about work, thick skin is not ugly, the insurance industry is very exercise.

This lecturer said is true, a month of insurance exhibition time countdown, so that Li Hua is very nervous, which also affected self-confidence. Li Hua gave himself a pep talk, decided to see the situation again, the atmosphere is not suitable for talking about insurance, she will not say, can not let the sister's friends feel embarrassed.

Saturday night finally arrived at the appointed time, the dinner place is the little sister Xueyou Rongzong booked the restaurant. Li Hua just entered the restaurant, the waiter led Li Hua into a box, General Manager Rong was already sitting waiting for Li Hua to arrive: "Hello, sister, is it easy to go on the road, is there a traffic jam?"

Li Hua said: "OK, smooth, give you trouble."

General Rong said, "I have wanted to invite you to dinner for a long time, and it has been difficult to disturb you." According to your little sister, you are doing a good job in insurance, do you need my help?"

Hear Rong total straight to the subject, Li Hua worry is superfluous, she really

did not think of little sister's friends so straightforward asked her. She had thought of many opening lines, but nothing straightforward! Now Li Hua is not worried, she told the truth according to the topic, Rong general listened and smiled and said: "To my son do a child's life guaranteed insurance!" Premiums within 5000 per year can be insured. Plan to pay twenty years, is a life insurance, to your professional can recommend me to choose a kind of insurance on the line, big sister say!"

Li Hua excited speechless, this is another little sister a big favor! Li Hua carefully analyzed the situation of Rong's son and calculated the most suitable life insurance. As a result, General Rong looked at the insurance and said happily: "This child's life happiness guarantee is good, thank you big sister thoughtful!"

The dinner was getting warmer and warmer, and it was also the richest meal Li Hua had ever had in Shenzhen. Li Hua has never been so pleased as today, she looked at the Rong general generation with appreciation, really worthy of being a young generation with achievements. Li Huachen is proud of her little sister, and also admire her understanding. These days, the young generation is amazing.

At the commendation conference at the end of the month, Li Hua stood in the center of the stage and raised the diamond trophy of this month, and took a group photo with all the senior leaders of the company in the cheers. Photos record this glorious moment, Li Hua's insurance exhibition industry opened a good sign!

Chapter 14: Visiting Friends

In these days when he just came to Shenzhen, in addition to work and study, Li Hua often read the information of new real estate through the newspaper. She likes to spend her weekends alone by looking at houses to pass the time. Li Hua insisted on the good habit of looking at houses before, never make friends of the opposite sex, she no matter whether she has money or not, will go to see the new real estate, will also look at the model house under the recommendation of the sales department miss, calculate how much money down payment, pay how much can be a transaction plan, looks like really want to buy a house hostess. The waiter can be attentive, Li Hua like this feeling, she secretly to their own refueling: must be a rich woman!

One weekend after he arrived in Shenzhen, Li Hua went to visit his girlfriend Wan Mi. At that time, they saw three new developments in Futian District, of which one was a small, 16.67 square meters one-bathroom one-bedroom apartment type. Li Hua joked to Wan Mi and said: "I can afford this house, if only the down payment, I want to buy it." I don't want to rent all the time, what do you think?"

Wan Mi replied, "Forget it, it's only been a few days, take a look." Don't buy a house on impulse. There are plenty of good houses. Take your time. To buy a house, you have to wait for the job to be stable, you are sure you want to stay in Shenzhen, I will accompany you to other places to see. Really don't be too impulsive."

Friend Wan Mi is single, because her husband cheated with the nanny and gave birth to a child. Wan Mi in anger to the bank unit resigned to Shenzhen struggle, now take refuge in Shenzhen brother, has hit a day. Wan Mi has her own house, she put her house as an investment, rent to earn rent, and live in her brother's house.

After her early divorce, Wan Mi never wanted to get married again. Every year

when Wan Mi returned home, Li Hua and bestie Zhenzhen received her together, bowling, singing, eating, going to the beauty salon, foot spa wash feet... In short, several women have a lot of happy time together, and this is also the friendship of misery.

Li Hua said, "OK, I will listen to you and will not buy a house randomly. But I really like the feeling of looking at the model homes and enjoying the feeling of being served like a rich person. It's really fun!"

"Yes, I also like buying and selling houses, because it seems that only houses can give women security." I've already found out, you and me and Jen, that all three of us women love houses, which means we're still insecure and lacking good men. Well, I'd better rely on myself. After I make money, I can buy whatever house I want. I can only rely on myself."

Li Hua said, "You are so right, relying on men is not reliable. Now you know about me. No man can be trusted! Now I want to start over in a new environment, so I must start to learn to earn more money and live the life I want! I'll say goodbye to that man when I'm on my feet and strong. Right now, I'm not sure how to deal with the situation. I am not reconciled at all, that woman is so ugly, how dare to cheat on my home, that man is blind! It makes me feel bad to think about it, but it's true. I certainly won't want this man, but I don't know how to get rid of him, I am so difficult!"

Wan Mi said: "Anyway, you are now separated, rest assured to do your thing, find a suitable work to earn more money, and take a step by step in the future." Li Hua nodded in agreement.

At noon, the two men said: "Let's eat fish, brain!" Ha ha ha, all think of the same!"

It's called understanding. It was a lovely meal. Keep looking at the house after dinner. Think of it as a walk to help digestion. In this way, through looking at the house, Li Hua understands the actual demand information of many real estate in Shenzhen. This weekend passed like this, lived a full and happy.

The following weekend, Li Hua arranged to visit her sister's students. My sister's student is also in Shenzhen, named Huang Wen, is a Macheng rural boy, he is doing auto parts and car modification business, he also opened a car wash shop.

My sister introduced that Huang Wen went to Shenzhen to work first, and the result was that in less than two years, the rural family got to Shenzhen to start a business and work. Now a few shops, all the family to their own work, really not simple. Such a talented man, Li Hua has wanted to meet him long ago.

The day has finally arrived. Li Hua made a phone call to Huang Wen: "Hello Huang Wen, I am Miss Li's sister!"

The other end of the phone immediately heard the response: "It's sister Li, you send me the location, I will drive to pick you up."

Li Hua did as he was told, after the location was issued, he waited in the parking lot near the imperial building. In less than half an hour, Huang Wen arrived by car. Li Hua saw the Toyota car down a head is not high, fat, smiling a young man. The guy is very strong, short-sleeved shoulders, people to Li Hua in front of the voice also reached Li Hua's ear: "Li Jie hello, get on the car, let's get on the car to talk!"

"Well, thank you for coming to pick me up, for the trouble!"

"You're welcome, as long as you don't mind, you can live in our staff dormitory." This time I will take you to see my three shops first, and then at noon my family, who are also my workers, plus my wife and son, will meet together to take care of the dust for you. I booked the hotel before I came to pick you up!"

Li Hua said: "Don't be too much trouble, I want to learn from you, how you are in less than two years, the family received Shenzhen business, but also bought three houses." Listen to my sister, you are too clever!"

Huang Wen has no shelf, looks very simple, silly look, Huang Wen smiled and said: "That is Teacher Li looked up to me." I got into the auto parts car wash business by accident!"

Originally, Huang Wen came to Shenzhen's first job is also to do insurance sales, unfamiliar with life at that time, starting from the shop every day. Huang Wen believes that if you want to sell insurance, you must choose rich people and people

with insurance consciousness. So he started from the car decoration shop, car wash shop and auto parts shop, began to search one by one, visit one by one contact, leaving business cards. Of course, in the exhibition industry has also eaten a lot of doors and cold faces, encounter does not understand is also rejected.

One day just at noon, no single success for several days in a row, when Huang Wen was in a dilemma, his stomach was hungry and thirsty, and his money was not much. He couldn't bear to get a ride back to the rental, so he walked back along the road. Encountered an auto parts shop, really can not walk, stopped, advised himself to visit a customer, try luck.

Huang Wen slowly walked in and said hello to the middle-aged man who bowed his head in front of the counter. The middle-aged man did not look up and continued to write something. So Huang Wen himself introduced the benefits of insurance, but the man in front of him looked up and replied: "Tell me all the insurance products again."

At this time, a woman came out of the car wash shop next door, holding a mop, a rag, carrying a bucket into the store from the back door, and said to the counter man: "Oh, boss, the car has been washed, but the customer seems to go out to do business." Please move your car to the side of the road so we can continue washing the cars behind you."

The conversation between the woman and the man made Huang Wen shout happily: "Oh, we are fellow townsmen!" It's so tearful to meet my fellow countrymen here. I've met someone today. We're from the same town. I am from Macheng, you must be from Macheng."

Counter man early heard Huang Wen like home, so let Huang Wen say the content of insurance again, in fact, is to confirm where Macheng people. The man smiled and said to Huang Wen, "If it weren't for the fellow villagers, who would listen to you say insurance ah." My name is Luo Fat, I opened these three shops, the whole family to help me work together, in fact, in order to support themselves. We've only been here three years. Business is good. In recent years, I have been busy with business and have not taken care of buying insurance. After listening to you, I still plan to buy an insurance for peace of mind and protection. You've been in Shenzhen for a few years. How long have you been doing insurance? Could you please give each member of our family a medical insurance today?"

Huang Wen was so surprised that his mouth opened wide and said excitedly: "Boss Luo, thank you for taking care of my fellow countryman!" I will definitely recommend the most suitable insurance products to you, and make a family insurance plan! And it will please you!"

In this way, Huang Wen's insurance career really began from this day. With Boss Luo's insurance policy for a big family member, a single for ten people! Boss Luo a family of three, plus his sister and sister two families, a total of ten people, all invested in life insurance and medical insurance.

From then on, Huang Wen came to Boss Luo's shop whenever he had time and walked around like his relatives. Sometimes the shop is busy with customers, and even the boss of Luo has to personally dismantle and repair cars. Huang Wen is very diligent, help in the field to see things to do things, mop the floor to do health, move and unload goods, did not put himself as an outsider. Boss Luo's family and employees all like this hard-working little countryman Huang Wen.

Chapter 15: Investigate Shenzhen real estate market

Another sunny weekend, Shenzhen summer heat up, do not work are sweating. As soon as Huang Wen entered the store of Luo boss, he saw Luo boss lying on his back under the car, his face was dusty, and his hand kept twisting accessories. Luo boss called Huang Wen put the first frame of goods, Huang Wen cleverly quickly found, and handed Luo boss one by one. I do not know how long it took, the car was finally installed, the debugging was successful, and the sound performance of the engine was normal.

At this time Luo boss face dirty, like a big face. Huang Wen could not help laughing when he saw it: "You really look like a woman singing, go and wash yourself!" I'll help you sort it out and put it away."

Luo boss is not welcome to the staff dormitory shower shampoo hair, put on a clean clothes. When he entered the store again, Huang Wen had arranged the spare parts on the floor and shelves neatly. To tell the truth, Luo boss himself also loves orderly and regular placement, but did not think that Huang Wen did better than him. Huang Wen is seriously writing the accessory model, specification origin, price list, did not find Luo boss into the store.

Boss Luo stood behind Huang Wen, looking at his beautiful and neat pen writing, couldn't help but pat Huang Wen on the shoulder and said: "College students are different! I think you, why don't you quit your insurance job, come to me, and let's do it together. I'm planning to open another auto parts store, and I've already picked out an address, but I need people. How about you, like me, bring your rural family members to Shenzhen, I'll train them, and we'll open a chain store? I'll give you three days to think about it, and in three days I'll have to hire someone, and if you agree to do it, we'll cooperate and promise to bring you in and make money."

Huang Wen did not wait for three days, he just thought about one night, he helped Luo boss obligation to do things after these periods, has understood the operation mode of this industry, this is the best opportunity for him to stay in Shenzhen, so the next day promised Luo boss. The same day directly into the Ping An insurance company headquarters to apply for resignation, decided to go back to Macheng hometown with Luo boss. Luo boss also went home together, do Huang Wen family to Shenzhen business mobilization work. In this way, the boss of Luo smoothly opened the chain store as planned, and also changed the living conditions of the three families of Huang Wen, from rural unemployed people to Shenzhen builders, entrepreneurs. The family business shared the profits equally, and now they have bought three houses and three cars!

That is, from that day on, Huang Wen changed Luo boss to Luo Big brother. Huang Wen said: "I am really grateful to my fellow countryman Luo Brother today!" Huang Wen introduced the situation of the shop, while telling Li Hua that he changed from the insurance industry to the process of opening an auto parts shop. Li Hua listened with admiration and awe.

Huang Wen also said that when Luo boss told him to bring his family out of the reason for struggle: Shenzhen mobility, entrepreneurial opportunities, to survive in Shenzhen must hold warm. Starting a business with a small group of family members will contain each other, and we must have the idea of sharing joys and sorrows in order to survive cohesiveness. If the day workers were hired, the church a car repair technician would leave one employee; But family is different. If Luo boss only asked Huang Wen a person, the chain would not have opened so smoothly. Luo boss said these words, Huang Wen has been impressed.

At lunch, Huang Wen's entrepreneurial story was almost finished. Li Hua still feel very shocked after listening, a long aftertaste. Huang Wen suddenly thought of looking at the house, afternoon will take Li Hua to see Luohu and Longgang district four real estate houses.

Huang Wen said: "This weekend, I will be the driver of Sister Li all the way to see the model house." Can't finish today, continue to watch tomorrow!"

Li Hua was very excited to thank Huang Wen: "This time is really not in vain, listen to your entrepreneurial history can let me write a book for you, this is definitely the value of life dry goods!"

Those two days Huang Wen took Li Hua to look around the house, Huang Wen on the real estate situation and the future development trend of the analysis, Li Hua has a reference basis. Li Hua was very excited, and at the same time strengthened the confidence to invest in real estate in the future. Huang Wen said that sentence, Li Hua remembered the most clearly, "Li sister, tell you ha, in recent years, as long as you have money, invest in big cities to buy a house, house prices will definitely rise." Buy a house is to earn money, Li sister buy a house is the time!" The young city of Shenzhen gives Li Hua a lot of hope and business opportunities.

On the following weekend, Li Hua took the initiative to make an appointment with Chen Xiong, an old classmate who wrote well. Li Hua explained his idea, let Chen Xiong go to see the sea view room near Xiaomeisha, meet company, and watch the seaside real estate, as if it was a different weekend.

Chen Xiong received a phone call and agreed: "Well, I have come to Shenzhen for several years, often work overtime on weekends to study the market research reports of securities companies, and have never rewarded myself." Just in time to open houses with you this week, enjoy the beach life. Please bring your swimsuit and go swimming at the beach. Let's meet on Saturday at the dumpling House."

Li Hua said: "OK, but tomorrow will not eat dumplings, we meet and change a place, to eat beef rice noodles!" I know which one is good!" Chen Xiong said: "OK, see you tomorrow!"

In this way, the next morning more than six o 'clock, Li Hua and Chen Xiong before and after not less than three minutes to the dumpling house. After the meeting, Li Hua directly took Chen Xiong to the snack street and skillfully walked into the beef powder shop. The owner's wife greeted Li Hua very warmly: "Would you like two today?"

Li Hua said to the owner's wife in a friendly way: "Yes, add two churros."

"Yes, I'll be right there. Sit down and have your tea." The owner's wife is from Chongqing, and she is cheerful and enthusiastic. The food is authentic.

Li Hua introduced to Chen Xiong said: "The more spicy the rice noodles, the more delicious, the last remaining soup do not waste, you dip in the soup with dough sticks, soak for two seconds and then eat, that taste you absolutely like!"

Chen Xiong said, "In this respect, I have to learn from you to combine work and rest, and enjoy myself while working." Are you still thinking about investing, are you going to buy a house to live in, or do you want to try your best here in Shenzhen?"

Li Hua said, "First of all, I really like to look at houses, that feeling makes me so comfortable. Second, to the right opportunity, if there is a suitable investment opportunity, I will certainly not let go. Just in Shenzhen, there are no other people who know everything, we are old classmates to talk together, trust each other. Even our middle school teacher, Mr. Yuan, supports us to contact more and move around! Your phone number was given to me by Miss Yuan, who really likes you very much."

Chen Xiong said: "That is, Teacher Yuan likes me most, I know." Miss Yuan also likes you girls, otherwise Miss Yuan would not have asked me to take care of you and bring you a little. I think this is the teacher too much, in fact, you are taking me to play, feel that you are more familiar with Shenzhen than I am!"

Chen Xiong's feeling is right, Li Hua does not have a day idle. She used the rest time on the weekend to investigate all the real estate information in the surrounding and central suburbs. Speaking of real estate analysis, Li Hua is more thorough and clear than Chen Xiong! Chen Xiong said with admiration, "If I didn't have a wife, I would definitely pursue you!"

Li Hua smiled and almost choked: "Stop, don't make fun of me." Who doesn't know you? You were the girl in school, the one who could dance. There is

a good writing Yajun also secretly love you, you are also very good to others, but you chase the school flower! What were you thinking? What an amorous genius, I dare not think. No one else is here today, so why don't you tell me about your love history? Ha ha ha!"

Chen Xiong said: "That is the past, are not sensible, don't laugh at me." Tell me about you, how you gave up that respectable office job, you are really brave, follow the fashion to go to sea?"

Li Hua suddenly quiet down, low voice self-deprecating said: "Forced ah, forced helpless...... Now, don't talk about me, but about you!"

Li Hua does not want to let her hometown acquaintances know her second husband Yu Ping derailment scandal, classmates and colleagues will not say. Li Hua can bear it, the more people know, the more trouble there will be. Old classmates together, there is a lot to talk about. Get along easy and kind, but there is no evil between men and women, but nothing to talk about. As long as you don't talk about your marital status, you can talk about anything.

After breakfast, the two quickly boarded the bus to Xiaomeisha Beach. Along the way, the two people are chatting, with company is good, about an hour to arrive. At that time, Chen Xiong had not bought a car, and the bus was comfortable and air-conditioned. After this car, I saw a beautiful woman in the sales department holding a house advertising sign, and introduced to the people who got off the car: "Go with us to see the sea view room, there are free tea dessert fruits, and provide buffet."

"You are well informed, admire! Let's go with this beautiful woman and see the model house!" Chen Xiong see beauty happy to catch up with words.

Li Hua and Chen Xiong on more than 20 people sit to see the RV, along the way can see the sea view. Miss in the car began to use the radio microphone to introduce the housing, surrounding environment, traffic and other conditions, a variety of exciting benefits, the price per square as long as 4300 yuan. At that time, Luohu 6000 yuan per square meter, Futian District price is 6600 yuan per square meter, Longgang house price is about 4000, the difference in prices in each district is clear.

This trip came, Li Hua put Shenzhen in 2003 real estate market statistics, know. According to Li Hua's plan, if she has money and finds a job suitable for her, she will choose her favorite city life and struggle in the big cities of the country. Huang Wen those words she listened to, she now very believe that they see the momentum of real estate, as long as there is money, we must find a way to buy a house.

Chapter 16: "Cough" causes illness from overwork

Li Hua has been in Shenzhen for some time. On an autumn night in Shenzhen, Li Hua was lying on a small bed alone, staring at the roof and thinking about how to further carry out insurance work. At this time Li Hua felt very lonely, every night is such a person to stay in a small apartment. There were only a few simple items in the room to make do with life, which was not the environment she wanted.

Before she goes to sleep, she thinks of the home she's looking forward to. For her, home is where people are and where the house is. She didn't like the idea of renting. This time to Shenzhen is to start from scratch. Li Hua chose a new city and a new environment. While Shenzhen is a special zone city, there are more opportunities for development prospects. But it is not easy to survive in Shenzhen, and it is not easy to buy a house in Shenzhen. But Li Hua has confidence, she is so diligent, keen to pay attention to real estate information, this idea persistence, one day there will be Li Hua a place to live, she has a feeling that she will be in the immediate development, there must be their own place to live in a small world.

After several months of intensive training and study, as well as the hard work of rushing about and eating some spicy food, Li Hua's throat has been sore recently. It is also because of the recommendation of insurance, to say a lot more than before, and also pay attention to the topic, can not directly say insurance, have to say as if it has nothing to do with insurance content. Bring up the topic of insurance by making small talk. After this, my throat is tired.

At this time, Li Hua's sore throat can not stand, can not drag any longer, have to take medicine and give an injection to suppress. I'm under the impression there's a small private clinic near this apartment building. On the way to the imperial building during the day, Li Hua saw a small clinic with a white and Red Cross curtain hanging in front of the door. Although Li Hua was very uncomfortable, he still had to get up from bed to see a doctor. She casually put on a loose coat and picked up the bag that she carried wherever she went, which was Li Hua's most valuable thing, containing her ID card and bank card.

At nine o 'clock in the evening, there are still some patients sitting in the small clinic getting injections. Li Hua saw that there were two empty beds inside.

Li Hua said to the doctor: "Doctor please take a look, I have a cough, can you play a few bottles of anti-inflammatory needles?" My throat is so dry and sore!"

The doctor took out a small wooden sign and called Li Hua to open his mouth, and pressed down his tongue with a small wooden sign to check: "Yes, your throat is bleeding, it has been red and swollen, you have to give three days of acupuncture to reduce inflammation, play it?"

Li Hua said: "Play, play now, can you lie on the bed to get an injection?" I think it would be better to sleep?"

The doctor said, "Yes, it will cost you 10 yuan for the bed."

Li Hua at the moment just want to go to the doctor and get an injection, get better early and suffer less. She nodded violently to the doctor, took her bank card out of her bag and swiped three days' worth of injections, plus some anti-inflammatory medicine and cough syrup.

The small clinic has two people on duty, a doctor and a female nurse, the service attitude is very good. In less than ten minutes, the nurse finished the medicine, went to the inner bed, and called Li Hua's name. Check to confirm that it is Li Hua, began to do skin test. After 15 minutes, the nurse looked at the skin test and said to Li Hua: "Fortunately, you are not allergic, you can play the bottle!"

Needle water into Li Hua vein, Li Hua almost did not feel, the nurse is light, no pain injection. Looking at the potion drop by drop into the body, Li Hua seemed to be mentally comfortable, perhaps it is the role of thought.

At this time, Li Hua's cell phone rang in his pocket. Li Hua asked the nurse

to take out her mobile phone, put it through and handed it to her. Her familiar voice came from the phone: "Huahua, how are you? What are you doing?"

She did what she was afraid of, and the sound disturbed her. She hid so far away, or was found by Yu Ping. From the derailment of Yu Ping, Li Hua felt that he was not worthy of the customary call "Mr. Yu", so the heart has been called full name.

"Yu Ping, please stop calling me by my nickname Hua Hua, and now please call me by my full name Li Hua!" How did you know I was in Shenzhen?"

Yu Ping telephone voice into Li Hua's ear: "It's not important, it's easy to find you." Most importantly, I should tell you that my garment factory in Guangzhou is very close to Shenzhen, only about 40 minutes by train. I can come and see you! You sound hoarse. Are you sick? Tomorrow is the weekend, give me the full address, I will come to see you?"

Li Hua on this end of the phone listened quietly, thinking that she must not let Yu Ping know where she lives now. The environment here is too bad, if let Yu Ping see, it is not let him see the joke?

"You don't have to come to see me, I'm getting an injection, the medicine will be fine, nothing, I hang up!"

After a while the phone rang again, the nurse did not go far, very clever and put the phone on Li Hua's hand, indicating Li Hua or answer the phone, otherwise the bell will be noisy other patients with injections. No way, Li Hua had to lower his voice and said: "You tell me, what else?"

Yu Ping's gentle magnetic voice sounded again: "Then when you get well, come to my Guangzhou garment factory." I will pick you up at the train station. I am living in a one-room dormitory in the factory and eating in the staff canteen. Come to my place next week when your voice is better. My factory has a batch of women's and children's clothing export surplus orders back to the warehouse clothes, with the disposal price can buy genuine quality clothes. You come to play, by the way you can choose some of your favorite styles, you can also help your family to bring some suitable clothes! I've picked out some for you. Think you'd better do it yourself. You can buy more."

Yu Ping knows Li Hua too well, listen to Yu Ping's tone of speech is sincere, because before Yu Ping also like to buy some very fashionable clothes for Li Hua.

What to do? Li Hua did not want to let Yu Ping come to Shenzhen to see her temporary residence, do not want to let Yu Ping see her weak and sick look, had to perfunctory promise: "Wait for the illness to recover, I will go to Guangzhou to see." Now I want to get some sleep, I must go!"

The phone was finally quiet. In fact, Yu Ping is a person of temperament, he is good to everyone, soft ears, if not for his good character, Li Hua would not risk second marriage to marry him. But Yu Ping touched the most taboo bottom line in marriage, single-minded loyalty did not do. So even if Yu Ping is good, he has fallen in Li Hua's mind. Only once had love and lingering, often tormented Li Hua.

Li Hua secretly will also compare Yu Ping with some men who show her kindness, which proves that Li Hua still has not completely put down. In Li Hua's heart, she is still very much in love and care about Ping, so far have not let go, not really put down.

Close your eyes lying on the hospital bed injection time, Li Hua's head like in a dream, a past in the brain quickly flashed. She did not notice when the injection was finished, or the nurse's voice interrupted her thoughts. The nurse pulled out the needle and let Li Hua hold down the wound patch of the needle eye on the back of her hand.

Li Hua walked out of the clinic at 11 o 'clock in the evening. The clinic is open 24 hours, and it's not easy for the private doctor to watch the clinic's patients so late! Li Hua walked to his rented apartment, went home to sleep on the bed, this sleep until dawn.

Timely medical treatment, three consecutive days of injections, Li Hua physique is still very good, quickly recovered.

It was almost the weekend, and she was thinking about going to Guangzhou to see Yu Ping's garment factory and find out how he was doing. This is also an

opportunity, no matter how she must face the flat, whether it is divided or combined must deal with, can not always avoid and drag. Look at Yu Ping's specific situation, then make a plan. But also to see the real estate in Guangzhou, this is the real reason Li Hua went to Guangzhou.

Strange to say, every time Li Hua thinks of something, something will appear. At this time, the mobile phone shows that someone is calling, and a look at the mobile phone number will know that it is called by Yu Ping.

"Well, that's better. Why don't you come to Guangzhou on Saturday this weekend? Can you buy your train ticket today? I'm waiting for your information, tell me the train fare, I'll pick you up!"

Li Hua's heart has actually convinced himself, but somehow, for the invitation of flat, she is still very tangled very contradictory. In other words, love and hate.

Li Hua thought for a minute and said, "OK, I'll go to the train station now to buy tickets for Saturday." Besides, can you accompany me to Guangzhou Baiyun Mountain on Sunday? I want to see a new building that has opened for sale."

Yu Pingsec replied: "Yes, you come on Saturday, choose your clothes, and take you to eat Guangzhou dishes in the evening." You should drink more Cantonese soup to supplement your nutrition. On Sunday, I will accompany you to look at the house, take you to the railway station after dinner, and we will buy the return train ticket when we get to the platform. There is no hurry to return, and it is very convenient to leave at what time."

Yu Ping said carefully, Li Hua heard Yu Ping tone almost coax her. She thought to herself, if I had known today why should I have started!

There are many trains, tickets are easy to buy, and express trains are less than 100 yuan. Li Hua took a picture of the train ticket and sent a text message to Yu Ping. Everything was ready, and on Saturday Li Hua simply took a small bag and a mobile phone and went out, just like visiting the door, wearing the taste of a very intellectual woman. After the illness recovered Li Hua is still some weak, but looks more gentle and charming, more feminine charm.

Li Hua specially selected a very soft dress, the upper body white vest, the lower body light yellow flower skirt. It was 1999. Li Hua, Yu Ping and their daughter Xiaolin bought the suit when they were visiting Shanghai. It still fits them perfectly. Li Hua is in good shape. She is of average weight and looks slim. Li Hua wears a pair of ink glasses and a big white sun hat, and hangs a small hanging bag on his shoulder, which can only hold a wallet and a mobile phone. Li Hua like the quality of the skirt fabric, too suitable for the southern city to wear, the appearance of light pack than Shenzhen people also like city people, to Guangzhou this outfit is like Guangzhou woman. Li Hua thought, although thin a circle, but also become beautiful, thanks to Yu Ping ah! No need to lose weight to preserve the charm of the year!

Li Hua fell asleep as soon as he got on the train. It was as if he had squinted for a while before the train arrived in Guangzhou. In recent years, with the rapid development of railway, people who are far away can meet each other in the same day. This technology is developing too fast. With the rapid change of the motherland, urban roads are in the expansion, and immediately there is an intercity high-speed rail into the major cities, the development of the special zone Shenzhen is more favorable, Shenzhen is the leader in the accelerated development of the city.

Chapter 17: Never see you again

At the moment of leaving the railway station, Yu Ping saw Li Hua standing in a bright place at a glance, and came forward to hold Li Hua's hand and said: "I recognized this familiar skirt at a glance." You're slimmer and prettier. You had a good trip. You see how convenient, in the future, you can rest, you can often come to hang out."

Li Hua did not answer, just looked at Yu Ping, thinking: let me slim down is not you? I guess it was a blessing in disguise!

Li Hua left the station behind Yu Ping and directly got into a royal blue car in the parking lot. This is the car of the clothing factory sales department, to the factory, Yu Ping directly took Li Hua to the warehouse room, select the export to domestic sales of clothes. From children's clothing to women's clothing and elderly clothing, Li Hua has selected clothes that suit her family. She chose selflessly, even forgetting that her body had only recently recovered and was still a little weak.

Li Hua finally chose more than thirty pieces, never so cool, should let the man spend money! In the past, Li Hua saved money and was reluctant to buy many clothes for himself. Every time he was on a business trip, he always bought souvenirs for Yu Ping. Ties, clothes, and wallets were not bought less. Now, if you still save money for Yu Ping, who knows what bitch he will use it for? Li Hua thought of it this way, and suddenly felt at ease. Anyway, Li Hua is still Yu Ping's legal wife.

When Li Hua thought of this, he cursed in his heart: "This man is really cheap, and he does not cherish when he is good; Instead of treating him as a family, he sticks to him like a lapdog!"

Assistant Yu Ping said to Li Hua, "Sister Li, don't worry. The factory director has already paid for all the clothes you want to buy. I'll wrap it up for you and put it on the desk in the director's office."

Women like to buy clothes, have things to do time is fast, a flash to the afternoon work time. Yu Ping paid for the clothes and carried them to the dormitory apartment to put them away. He took a shower in the shower room, put on a new suit of clothes, and looked much more energetic than he had looked when he took orders at the factory. The clothes make the man and the saddle. That's true.

Yu Ping and Li Hua went to a Chinese restaurant for dinner. There was a band playing and the atmosphere was romantic. The soup was light and delicious. Li Hua didn't eat much after he finished it. After losing weight, it seems that the stomach has also become smaller, Li Hua's eating amount is like eating cat food.

The next day, Yu Ping took Li Hua to Guangzhou Baiyun Mountain real estate to see the house, where the house looks very high-end, the most expensive house price with the east third ring road in Beijing, about 6700 yuan a square. The design of the model house is reasonable, square, and there is no waste of space. Li Hua likes this house, but does not like Guangzhou very much, just through the addiction of looking at houses, by the way to understand the prices of houses in different cities, the final decision to develop in that city, where to choose a house to do a comparison, you can quickly come up with a decision, because the opportunity is always left to those who are prepared, while saving money to find a way out, while working hard is the most effective way for Li Hua. Is action, do a good job of each stage should do what can be done, time is very fair to everyone, Li Hua will not waste a little time, is a short weekend rest, but also with the idea of a dream to approach the goal to work hard.

During this period of time, Li Hua's biggest gain is to compare the housing prices in Shenzhen and Guangzhou, where is suitable for life, Li Hua knows. She also realized that it was impossible to renew the relationship with Yu Ping, although they are not divorced, but have been separated for nearly two years. This time to visit Guangzhou, in front of the factory workers, they are a family; But on the night of the dinner, Yu Ping was like a thief who had done something wrong - a thief who stole women.

Li Hua has also seen Yu Ping living in the dormitory, can not be more simple and ordinary living environment. Yu Ping showed confidence and superiority in front of the factory workers. Li Hua found that Yu Ping is no longer the man she once loved, and now Yu Ping is not worthy of himself. Li Hua lived in the factory dormitory that night, Yu Ping made the bed for Li Hua, in the vague moonlight, Li Hua silently looked at Yu Ping's back, she saw that Yu Ping's hair is scarce, and some places have been bald. She suddenly thought of Yu Ping with Wang Qinlan together, suddenly lost appetite, want to vomit. She ran into the bathroom, spit a few dry spit, wash the mouth, wash the face and brush her teeth, and then came out of the bathroom for a long time. At that time, Yu Ping, who was lying in bed, was already asleep.

Li Hua covered the sheet and slowly lay on the outside edge, not knowing when he fell asleep. When he woke up, Yu Ping got up early. Li Hua knew that she was like Yu Ping, there was no solution to the knot, and the life of the two people was always just atonement and careful politeness. Both men bear the emotional burden of the scene.

This trip to Guangzhou, is the beginning and the end, is Li Hua and Yu Ping's last reunion. Li Hua has foreseen their future, if the two people live together, there is no love in their hearts, only sad and heartless guilt. Is such a marriage necessary?

Through this trip to Guangzhou, Li Hua found out the real estate market in Guangzhou, and also knew how to face it in the future. She will go back to her home city and quietly handle the legal process to dissolve their marriage. Li Hua felt it was time to leave this man, and felt no love or hate for him, only pity. She also understands the reason why Yu Ping only likes to stay in the factory, in that environment he has the confidence of a man, can pretend. Now he is not the Yu Ping of the past. Li Hua even do not want to break up with Yu Ping said, or afraid of hurting him, want to leave a man's dignity to Yu Ping. Or don't say it, quietly put down, let go of the flat, also let go of their own.

It was seven o 'clock at night when we left Guangzhou Railway Station. Yu Ping helped Li Hua with her big bag of clothes and sent her to the seat of the carriage. Told Li Hua a few words and immediately went out, standing on the platform, waiting for the train to start before leaving. Li Hua watched his distant shadow shrink and become blurred. The train sprinted forward in the night, the train galloped faster and faster on the track, like saying to Li Hua: Everything is not natural, will end, you will break through the shackles to the new goal!

Back to Shenzhen is already the night, the autumn wind and leaves blow through the streets on both sides, vaguely in twos and threes, there are many couples walking, snuggling together. This is the only way to go back to the dormitory, there are many people eating and talking at the night food stall, and there are boxes of empty wine bottles placed under the table, it seems that business is very good.

Instantaneously Li Hua remembered the scene of having supper with Yu Ping in his hometown, when the love of the two people was no less than these young people now. At that time, their love was also enviable. Yu Ping was tall and handsome and spoke pure Mandarin, which always made women like him. Even the elders also like Yu Ping that style, gentle temperament makes him unconsciously have a good impression on him.

Now Li Hua can really get rid of the knot in her heart, she and Yu Ping as if to make an end this evening. Li Hua told himself that this time must be completely out, after all, for the flat that hate and love, has been replaced with a poor feeling. There is no need to tangle with Yu Ping, in fact, has proved that between each other, no matter how hard tolerance and efforts, will touch the scene, bring just forgotten and re-ignite the heart that hidden in the heart of the sting, really better not see, let the years fade away naturally disappear that has been lost love, go, go far away in the heart will be cleaner!

Thinking of it, Li Hua decisively moved into Niuniu's community room the next weekend. Li Hua pays the 500 yuan rent to Niuniu every month, which is 100 yuan less than before. You can save 100 in the beginning. Starting a business is not easy, but fortunately the environment is good, and the two people can be company.

Since Li Hua moved into Niuniu's house, the room often heard the laughter of the two of them. This used to be a cold house has also become popular, they go in with the same, the kitchen also often see two people busy figure. Niu Niu will make a northeast chaos stew, Li Hua will Hubei's special dishes for each meal. Niu Niu do northeast chaos stew for a while, two people drink some beer, eat while talking, poor happy day is also very simple.

This little life of complementary heating is very comfortable. Niu Niu said to Li Hua, "A woman can live a handsome life without a man, can't she?"

In fact, Li Hua moved to Niuniu's residence, but also to put an end to their own soft heart. She was afraid that if she ever found a reason to visit her in the future, she would politely refuse on the grounds that it was inconvenient to rent a house with her female companion. Because it's true. It's easy to say. Li Hua is not good at telling lies, but also hate lying people, even for a man who has betrayed himself, she still insists on treating with true temperament.

Chapter 18: Confessing Secrets

Niu Niu and Li Hua went to the talent market during the day to do reception registration work. Because it is the employment registration recommended by a friend, the company will hit the guarantee fund on the card every month on time. RMB is very good, has received two months of guaranteed wages, eat box lunch money also has a guarantee. Other expenses, planning to buy a house must save money, will be made into an insurance policy, there will be performance salary incentives. Those days in addition to the normal necessary living expenses guarantee, other than the cost of all reduced, Li Hua will all change collected and saved, saved to can be used to pay the first house down payment, one day, will find suitable for their own and have the ability to buy housing opportunities, Li Hua is not dreaming, she began to move forward toward the goal of the plan, never flinched, and even more to see the dawn!

For newcomers, the first three months are the observation period of the exhibition industry. Is not suitable for joining the insurance industry, in the initial sprint stage can be seen, can stick to the new in the sprint stage, generally do the insurance industry is no problem.

One night, Niu Niu was talking to Li Hua when she suddenly mentioned her family. Niu Niu took a very old photo album, sat down on the sofa in the living room, opened the album and took out a picture of a five-year-old girl: "Look at my brother's child is beautiful, I often go to see my brother's child in my hometown, I miss her very much now."

Niu Niu talked about her family affairs, talking about her niece, she could not help but bend her head to touch the girl in the photo, and then sorted out her emotions and talked about her boyfriend in Hong Kong. She said: "I will probably

leave this place in the next half of the month because the boyfriend has not been here for over a month, which is not normal. He used to come for two days every weekend. You've seen my boyfriend. He looks like the boss. He's very handsome. Does he look like he's unmarried to you? He had only paid half a year's rent, but it was about to expire, and he had to renew the rent before he could live in it, and he had to pay half a year's rent in one go.

Li Hua said, "I feel like he has a family. If he doesn't come in the near future and the house is due, there is no need for you to renew the lease. The rent of 3000 yuan a month is not cheap, and there is no need for you to live in such a big house. I suggest you leave a few days before next month, don't you?"

Niu Niu said: "There are many cases of Hong Kong men taking second wives in Shenzhen, I dare not think about it. But maybe, I accidentally become his second wife, and I don't want to live like this. The insurance learned, but I haven't made many orders yet. My boyfriend took care of me once, and others bought two, and I did not complete the performance. It seems that I am not fit to stay in Shenzhen. If this Hong Kong boy will not be my boyfriend and help me, I will have to go back and see my brother's children."

As he spoke, Li Hua seemed to hear that Niu Niu had deep feelings for her niece, both missing and sad, as if she were missing her own child. Li Hua guess that is Niuniu's child, two people look very similar.

Niuniu inadvertently let it slip and asked Li Hua: "The child looks like me, don't you think?"

Li Hua slowly looked up at Niuniu and said, "Compared with your face shape and thick lips, little girls are like you." And it feels like you're talking about this kid like you have something to say. If you have something on your mind, you can talk to me. First of all, I don't know anyone around you, and it won't do you any harm to talk to me about it. Second, you'll feel better if you talk about it. Third, there are no outsiders here who are not afraid of leaks. I have a bad cough recently, so I may return to my hometown earlier than you."

At that time, in 2003, Shenzhen and Guangzhou were already severely affected by SARS. Li Hua said: "Under the SARS epidemic, my cough is very delayed insurance work. As long as there is a cough, people are far away, it is really not suitable to talk about insurance. If you decide to change to a smaller apartment, I can help you move before I leave."

Niu Niu said: "In the future, you can still have the unit to reimburse, I can only go back to my hometown, and I don't know what to do." It's so cold in the northeast that I don't want to work when I go back. I think I'll go see my daughter first. To tell you the truth, I still want to come to Shenzhen to find a job. You guessed it, that girl is really my child. She is five years old. I'm divorced, I can't take care of the kids by myself, and I can't bear to leave her. My ex-husband is aggressive, irresponsible, and always beats people. Do you know anything about domestic violence? It was horrible. I was with him, and he used to hit me and pull my hair. So I sent my daughter to my brother, and I came out to work to make money to send to my brother, to pay the monthly child support. I can assure you, and please don't blame me for cheating you before."

Niu Niu opened her clothes and let Li Hua see the scars on her body. In addition to the face is good, the whole body is covered with scars, especially the teeth around the breast. Li Hua felt sad and said to Niuniu, "It doesn't matter, you are not cheating me, this is a good way to protect yourself." Li Hua understood Niuniu and placated her with understanding: "Don't be too sad, go home and have a look at the child, and it is not too late to develop later." This month is also about to expire. Recently, I have completed the leaving procedures with the landlord agency in advance. I can try to help you move out and return the house before I leave, so that you will not default on the rent of the house. And if he doesn't show up, you don't have to pay any more. If you don't rent a house, that's the end of your relationship. Tell him by the way, QQ message or phone number tell him, do not expect to hurt each other, after all, have been good for a while, maybe the man can not give you points, only quietly leave you in this way, confession?"

Niu Niu said, "I rarely call him, and I don't want to. I know this is not a

normal relationship. Come on, men can't be trusted... What are you going to do when you get back home?"

Li Hua said: "I am going back to my hometown, first hospitalized to cure the disease, and then take advantage of this time to sell my home." Also sell the parents' old house, and then buy a bigger house, the name of Mom and dad, let the two old people rest assured. So I can settle them down and start my own business. Maybe go back to Shenzhen like you, maybe never come back. I feel that I can only take care of myself when I come to Shenzhen, and I don't care about my parents and daughter. I want to go to the city where my daughter will go to college and start a business there to see if I can do some small business, open a small clothing store or a small tea house. I like that kind of petty bourgeois life very much, do not need to earn a lot of money, but to be very clean, very warm, very decent literary work. I like writing, but I always want to wait until my job is stable and my mind and temperament are mature before I start to do it. Dream must have, I can first feed myself as the foundation. I can also save some money to open a small shop, read books to learn the kind of "book bar", I like the small tea house, can heal my own heart. I like to challenge myself and try out various kinds of work that I like. If I don't try, I won't be willing!"

"Whoaa! Talking about the idea of the future, you say what you want to do, as if it is very close to your life, really cool! I admire you for your ambition!" Niu Niu replied Li Hua with a smile.

After the two chatted and giggled, Li Hua said, "We are all having a nice day dream. But if I didn't dream my dreams, I wouldn't have the courage to live."

When Li Hua saw Niuniu telling her her privacy, she couldn't help but say a few words to Niuniu and told her about her husband's affair. Li Hua didn't know how to deal with it. Persuade Niu Niu has a set of principles, but they are still a little at a loss, but also explore how to live a good life without marriage. Li Hua has no confidence in love and marriage, and she doesn't want to depend on a man. She wants to go back to her hometown first, take good care of her parents, take good care of her daughter, and start a business while accompanying her study. The provincial capital is not far from his hometown, Li Hua plans to develop the next stage in the nearest provincial town.

Looking out of the window, you can see the bustling Shenzhen at night, which is the city where Li Hua and Niu Niu once struggled. The tall buildings and low apartment buildings, as well as the small, cluttered houses, were witnesses to their entrepreneurship.

Two people on the balcony looking at the shining lights of the scenery, Shenzhen night scene let how many people yearn, Li Hua is the same, looking at the stars in the sky said: "You see, we are like so many stars, a flash." People like us, we have to be like stars wherever we go, bringing our own light. We must live better than before to be worthy of ourselves." Li Hua's persistent and resolute eyes affected Niu Niu, and gave her hope: a divorced single woman can also rely on her own to create all the beautiful belonging. Niu Niu seems to have a direction and a head in her heart.

Chapter 19: Leaving Shenzhen

A few days ago Li Hua in the talent market and know a fellow countryman, is a beautiful woman in Xinzhou, Hubei, named Jing Wen. Li Hua see fellow especially feel kind, so the jing Wen recommended to the northeast Niu Niu. In the future, three people often eat together, although it is called a box lunch, each person points a dish, and everyone changes to eat, so that you can eat three kinds of flavors. They all know how to live economically on the outside.

Jing Wen, like her name, is a very quiet girl, small in stature, and speaks in a very special voice. Jing Wen is very elegant, at a glance, three-dimensional big eyes and high nose, almost half of the face. Niu Niu think Jing Wen is particularly gentle, very envy her young and beautiful.

Jing Wen before the dress looks a little coquettish, a head of dyed yellow hair. Li Hua also reminded Jing Wen for this: "Can you dye your hair back?" You were a very good girl, if I don't know you, I think you are a bad girl, now people are more judge by appearance. Besides, in this line of work, the best first impression you make on a stranger is to dress nicely. I'm old enough to be your sister, so let me get this straight: Do you mind if I accompany you to get your hair dyed naturally black?"

Jing Wen said: "I also know that you are for my good, dyeing back to black hair is of course no problem." In the past, working in the factory required uniform work clothes, all the girls did not look prominent, some girls use the way to dye their hair to attract others' attention, I am one of them, you don't laugh at me!"

Now Jing Wen just realized that she has changed the working environment, she has been sitting in the office to work, in this environment should be generous and mature.

Jing Wen said: "I listen to you, thank you for not treating me as an outsider." I appreciate your direct reminder to get rid of the bad habit of putting things off. I'll get it done after work tonight."

Jing Wen has been in Shenzhen for two years. She worked in a Taiwan-funded factory in Longhua and only recently rented a one-bedroom, one-bath apartment near Shenzhen's job market. Jing Wen said to Li Hua: "Before my factory's Taiwan boss wanted to chase me, just know two months, but feel like the boss is a family." Do not want to have an ambiguous relationship with the boss, so from the Longhua side to move here. I want to find a job here, can not work in the previous factory, refuse the pursuit of the boss of the Taiwan company. This is just based in the center of Shenzhen, I know that I have to rely on myself to be reliable, and this is my goal in Shenzhen."

Jing Wen's work in the factory is too closed, the factory's working sisters are foreign sisters. Working 12 hours a day, a lot of mechanical manual work, or feel the city life easier. Jing Wen came here is also providence, here the recruitment threshold is low, although it is only to do some small things without technical content: according to the list of hired employees, agreed by the boss by Jing Wen to take people to the unit to report. Li Hua and Niu Niu are also doing the same job, connecting the hired employees with the unit. Send employees to the unit, as to help the new candidate to complete the work handover process.

Jing Wen moved that day Li Hua also came to help, Jing Wen said: "I have done well here, you can live with me." I live here alone, and sometimes my brother comes over on weekends, eats one meal and then goes away." Jing Wen is really stay Li Hua live in her small apartment, here is also convenient Li Hua work.

Jing Wen very glad to know here fellow Li Hua, although the age is bigger than her a whole circle, but see Li Hua heart is very friendly, really like Li Hua. Li Hua is also very assured and simple Jing Wen friends, so naturally help Jing Wen do some practical move. Li Hua did not think of any idea of glory, purely to the townsmen to give a hand.

Li Hua said to Jing Wen: "Do not move to your side for the time being,

because I just moved to Niuniu there, living well." Can we wait a little longer? I have to talk to Niu, so I don't get the wrong idea. Moreover, I feel that the climate in Shenzhen is not suitable for me. I always cough in Shenzhen for several months. I also love to eat spicy, just after the injection voice just right, the result because eat spicy old trouble again. Now my throat has become chronic bronchitis, and I often feel like coughing. You know what? When I was doing insurance, I was having a conversation with someone, and after saying a few words, suddenly my throat itched, and I had to cough and endure. Halfway quickly ran to the bathroom, or did not have time to avoid, in front of the guests cough out, really embarrassing! SARS is so serious recently that everyone is very cautious and careful to avoid it. I know I'm not SARS, but others don't know it, especially when I cough, others subconsciously want to stay away and have no mood to talk to me. At this rate, there is no energy to negotiate insurance, so recently it has been very difficult. The insurance customers I haven't followed up at all this month have been struggling to return to their hometown to cure their cough and then come to Shenzhen to work." Jing Wen understand Li Hua, no longer insist on Li Hua moved into her apartment.

At that time, Li Hua suffered from a cough. Sometimes Li Hua can only sleep for half a day, and even coughed up urine. She was afraid to wear a skirt and carried a pair of underwear and sanitary napkins in her carry-on bag. If you have a bad cough, you can solve it immediately.

This Shenzhen autumn, the climate is very hot, wear not many clothes. One time, it was really ugly. I peed on the outside of my pants. Li Hua quickly in the mall to buy a set of casual clothes, in the bathroom to change, so as to solve the temporary embarrassment, in order to insist on the afternoon to visit the exhibition industry to see customers.

Li Hua's injection seems to have failed, and his family has been worried about Li Hua. Take the train back home also need to check to take the temperature, if found to have a fever, must be locked in the quarantine area, can not be cured in time to cough. At that time, there were many people with fever caused by SARS, and the symptom of SARS was also cough. Li Hua knows in his heart that he is not

SARS virus, but others do not know. People don't know what causes her cough, and they're right to stay away from her.

Li Hua weighed a lot, or ready to return home for treatment, one of the one is that there is medical insurance in the home. I can't work until I'm cured. This time I may really have to leave Shenzhen. After Li Hua made up his mind, he chose a few days before the end of the month to discuss it with Niuniu and Jing Wen.

Li Hua said: "These days fortunately have you, there is a friendship between us." I go back to cure cough first, I don't know if I will go back to Shenzhen. If I do not go back to Shenzhen, I think I will not choose to develop in my hometown, I will choose the provincial capital near my hometown, this is just my preliminary plan. In fact, I like Shenzhen very much, it is a young city, there are many opportunities for employment and entrepreneurship, but I really can not adapt to the environment here. I have been here for several months, and I cough almost every other month. I can't stand it. Health is very important, you see I came to Shenzhen has been thin, and now continue to thin, like this is not normal. I can't eat well or sleep well."

The weather in Shenzhen was fine the day Li Hua moved out. Li Hua put all their daily necessities are left to Jing Wen use, Niu Niu ready to leave the house, also together with their luggage, all available can not take things, are given to Jing Wen. Before and after coming to Shenzhen for more than half a year, Niu Niu left, Li Hua also left, leaving Jingwen, and people who are suitable for fighting there. In that land there are still people who continue to struggle in the confused search.

Li Hua said in his heart, "Shenzhen, I like you very much, but I have to leave you." However, I do not regret that I have come, struggled, and found the right turn in my life!"

Niu Niu said to Li Hua: "I really thank you, let me make up my mind to find the purpose of life. You've changed my perspective. I used to expect that finding a man who loves me would lead to a good life, but the fact has made me realize that a divorced woman can only be happy on her own."

Jing Wen said: "You are all gone, I am really sad, but also very glad, very

happy and you become good sisters." If you come to Shenzhen again, whether it is to start a business or to travel in the future, you will come to me. Don't despise my little family. You are welcome to live here. This is your home."

On the last day of the end of the month, Li Hua came to the railway station in Shenzhen. Back to the train station, looking up at the sky, looking at the distant traffic, people coming and going. She realized that she would soon leave here. Li Hua already had a deep attachment to Shenzhen.

Chapter 20: Back Home

The whistle of the train brought Li Hua's thoughts back to her hometown in Hubei Province.

On the day of getting off the bus, the station was inspected very seriously, and everyone had to take their temperature. Fortunately, Li Hua prepared a packet of syrup tablets in her bag before getting on the car. The tablets were put in her mouth. When she wanted to cough, she drank some water to moisten her throat. Li Hua always had a glass of water in his hand, so as to ensure that no cough symptoms occurred all the way.

After getting off the train, Li Hua did not alert her family and friends to pick her up, but directly came to the familiar bus stop to take the bus. There is just a bus to Li Hua's community, the community has a platform in front of the door.

"My hometown is back!"

Li Hua really feel at home a thousand days good, go out of the truth of this sentence. When Li Hua came home, his parents were so happy that they felt that Li Hua had lost a lot of weight.

Mother distressed to ask: "outside to eat a lot of suffering?"

Li Hua smiled and said, "When I come home and see you all well, I don't feel bitter." Don't worry, it's all in the past. Now I want to go directly to the hospital to get rid of the cough, so that mom and dad don't worry."

Li Hua's father said: "You know back, so a good job to quit quit, also do not want to think about this age." Also not small, more than 40 years old, daughter is studying, this family without you not scattered? Forget about you. Just come back. Hurry up and take care of the illness, this cough has made people thin like this, and you really don't care about yourself."

Li Hua's father is a hothead, but the most painful eldest daughter Li Hua, she was raised as a boy. In Li Hua's childhood, every time his father went fishing on weekends, he took Li Hua with him. Li Hua went fishing with his father and caught eels to improve his life. In the 1980s, the father worked hard to manage the family, and the life of the family was arranged by the mother, and the two worked together to improve the basic life of the children as much as possible.

Li Hua put down the suitcase, a simple pack up, the mother must Li Hua to drink a bowl of pork ribs lotus root soup and then go out. Li Hua saw a bowl full of his favorite soup, and did not refuse to drink it in one breath, and his mouth was full of oil. She's really hungry after all this.

Mother said, "Don't worry, take it easy, don't burn it." There's soup, and I can give you another bowl."

"Mom's pork rib pot lotus root soup is really good, full, never eat so full." Mom, Dad, I'm going to the hospital for a thorough examination, don't worry!"

Li Hua ready to see her daughter's things will be arranged after discharge, Li Hua dont want to affect her daughter Xiaolin study. The second sister took good care of her daughter and did a lot of things in life for Li Hua when she was a mother. Li Hua rest assured that Xiaolin will be taken care of by her sisters, she trusts this big family, and her relatives take care of her daughter more thoughtfully than themselves.

Out of the compound, came to the bus stop, two stops directly to the Women's and Children's Hospital. After examining Li Hua's throat, the doctor said to her: "You have chronic pharyngitis and bronchitis, your throat inflammation is very heavy, and you are coughing up blood." It's been a long time, what, months?"

Li Hua replied, "Yes, I started coughing three months ago. After more than ten days of injection, he got better, and then accidentally ate spicy food and coughed up. When the climate is dry, I have a cough over and over again, which has not been cured, and I get injections every two or three days."

The doctor shook his head and said directly: "You need to be hospitalized, go through the hospitalization procedures as soon as possible." The unit is near here, opposite so close, why not come to see a doctor?"

What the doctor said is not wrong, Li Hua's work unit is diagonally opposite the hospital. The doctor does not know that Li Hua is no longer working in the unit, but far away to Shenzhen to struggle. Li Hua is also not good to explain, just smiled and said: "Yes, now the cough can not stand, just to see a doctor, want to be completely cured!"

The doctor said, "You must stop eating spicy food." Give up spicy food and don't eat it any more. Otherwise it will be repeated, will get chronic bronchitis disease, that is more trouble, later treatment is difficult, must cherish yourself ah!"

Li Hua smiled again and again and said: "OK, I don't want to, I really don't dare to eat pepper!"

Take out diagnostic medical records, exit the doctor's clinic to go to the hall for admission procedures, the medical fee unit can report 80%, Li Hua only paid the admission fee.

Li Hua realized how good it is to be a unit worker at this time, and these benefits are given by the state. She is grateful from the heart to be born in China, and to enjoy such a good welfare, to comfort her when she is sick, not to worry about looking down on the disease, but to treat it with peace of mind.

During the period of hospitalization, the chairman of the unit trade union also came to the hospital to visit Li Hua on behalf of the unit leadership and brought a cordial greeting. Comfort Li Hua: "Be sure to treat well, internal and retired people are our employees, we are consistent colleagues." You are also responding to the call of the organizational policy of that year, so you are all colleagues." This made Li Hua put down the mental pressure, from the heart grateful to have a country to have a home, a home to have a good socialist environment of personal development, this feeling is out of the leadership organization to realize how good it is!

Li Hua remembered her good friend Xie Hua is also a single woman, when the city leaders met at the spring gala. The leader also joked: "You two names with

China, fortunately not in the same unit, don't make a mistake in the future, to often interact with each other yo!"

Xie Hua's husband died of cancer, only two years older than Li Hua. Xie Hua, who had big eyes and a long braid, was a remarkable woman at the time. Li Hua and Xie Hua live close to each other. After they met, they often met around the garden lawn of the municipal government and walked along the lake to chat. Sometimes we play badminton together in the morning, sometimes we play table tennis together in the afternoon of Li Hua unit on weekends, and sometimes we go shopping together and then go home.

Li Hua thought of here, immediately picked up the mobile phone to Xie Hua sent a message. After a phone call to learn that Li Hua was ill in hospital, Xie Hua asked Li Hua directly in the hospital several rooms: "Wait for me for half an hour, I bring some food to you, do not eat hospital meals, I do some bring over, wait for me!" We can finally see each other, but I didn't expect to see you at the hospital. Really, no wonder you didn't play with me, ran so far, and came to see you."

Xie Hua's friendship with Li Hua is really nothing to say. Xie Hua is a very cheerful person, and now her daughter has grown up and gone to college, she is alone at home, playing with some flowers in the terrace all day, she likes to grow flowers. Li Hua has been to Xie Hua's house and sometimes has dinner at Xie Hua's house. Xie Hua's cooking is very good and he's definitely improved now. Xie Hua said that nothing is often thinking about how to do a good job of eating dishes, and now I don't want to fall in love with a person, anyway, I have to take good care of my body.

Xie Hua walked into the ward and smiled at Li Hua: "You are finally honest, you are only good when you are sick." When did you go to Shenzhen? You didn't tell me. If I knew you were in Shenzhen, I should have promised my classmate, the boy who has always been good to me, he has always advised me to go to Shenzhen to develop and let me work in his company. I just retired. Is it appropriate to go to Shenzhen at this age? I didn't expect you to come back from Shenzhen, did you feel good in Shenzhen?"

Xie Hua is the kind of woman who speaks in a loud voice, the person does not arrive at the house, the voice arrives at the house first. A series of questions, Li Hua laughed: "I know you will say me." Listen to the truth, Shenzhen climate is very good, if there are acquaintances there, you can go to work directly, it is really worth starting your new life. Besides, your male classmates are also single, so good to you, they must be serious to you, you should think about it. You've been single for a few years and haven't had a boyfriend to take care of you since your husband died. If someone is really good for you, I suggest you go!"

Xie Hua said: "I still can't make up my mind, and I have been thinking about my house. And some things at the back of my unit, how to deal with it?"

Li Hua said: "This is easy to say, you have a good contact with Shenzhen, decide to go, you will sell the house here." Now the housing reform has become 100 percent of their property rights."

Li Hua persuaded way, also put their ideas to Xie Hua all out. Li Hua took the book with him out of the bag, called Xie Hua remember the phone number, is the contact of the real estate agency. Li Hua wants to do the same thing. She wants to sell her house and her parents' old house. At that time, Li Hua listened to the suggestion of the third sister, has chosen a very good green residential house, ready to buy a big house. To finish these ideas, Li Hua is eager to operate immediately, the execution of super super like Li Hua's father, the same A blood type of personality, with organizational leadership, there are two kinds of personality, adaptability is also strong, but also very calm, but also like romantic feelings.

Li Hua face to face to teach Xie Hua, in front of Xie Hua through the real estate agent's phone: "Hello! My beautiful little Qin, is it convenient for you now?"

Xiao Qin replied: "Convenient, beautiful sister, please say, what do you want me to do?" Which house are you selling?"

Li Hua said, "Haha, how did you know I was selling my house? Are you Sun Wukong drilled into my stomach?"

Intermediary Xiao Qin said: "I know, as long as I see your phone, I know you have good things, must be rich again." Selling the house and buying the house?

You tell me the neighborhood, the floor, the square footage, and the price you want to sell the house. I will help you hang on the Internet, positively recommend!"

Li Hua said, "OK, I will send you a text message with my mobile phone and send you all the information." In addition, I have a friend who also wants to sell the house, I will tell her your mobile phone number, this beautiful sister's name is Xie Hua, let you contact directly. You must get a good price for her, too. She is a very good friend of mine."

Li Hua, who hung up the phone, immediately smiled at Xie Hua and said: "Copy the phone, just look for this small Qin, she is very good, I have several houses are her help to contact the buyer to sell my house, don't you worry." Keep your phone, call her directly, go to her office and tell her the details of your house, she will help you."

Xie Hua smiled happily and said: "You can sell the house with three or two, really convinced you." I paid you a visit this time. It seems that you will be in the hospital for a few days, and I will have to come every day to stay with you. I didn't think you could fix my heart, after all these years I couldn't make up my mind, you made me make up my mind. I'll do what you say. Sell the house. You know what? Every time I go back to that house, I think about my daughter's dad. So you really need a change of scenery, a change of hill, and a fresh start."

Li Hua said: "Don't be polite to me, don't thank me, in fact, women are very difficult, first of all, love yourself." It takes about a month to sell the house. Do it early, do not drag, our time is money!"

Chapter 21: First home with Parents' names on it

Hospital seven days quickly passed, in these seven days, Xie Hua really do every day to accompany Li Hua, two people have endless topics. Xie Hua's house was only hung for five days, which is not surprising, the section of the house is really good: Xie Hua walked from her home to the hospital as long as five minutes, if you add two minutes downstairs, seven minutes to arrive. Xie Hua told Li Hua the good news that the house has buyers, and sincerely thank Li Hua for helping himself to solve the big problem.

Li Hua's house was also inquired about on the Internet, and Li Hua's mother's small house of more than 80 square meters was taken a fancy to. Li Hua according to the market price of 45,000, the result of the other buyer counteroffer. The buyer was a young boy, ready to get married and use as a new house. The buyer is very sincere, just want to buy over, the second year decoration wedding. This is a rural boy, after graduating from college to work in this third-tier city. I talked to a girlfriend in college and planned to get a license with my girlfriend some day. If there is no marriage house, the girl's parents do not trust the girl to marry him. He did not want to let his parents in the countryside worry, so the young couple rushed to buy a house and do a good job.

The intermediary Xiao Qin told Li Hua about the actual negotiation situation: "Sister Li, I also want to sell you a good price, but this young man is really sincere to buy a house." He's been here twice, and I'm embarrassed to tell you. I mean, your price wasn't high, but he's haggling, and I don't even know how to negotiate. Now to tell you the facts, I want to hear what you think."

Li Hua's sister introduced a new house to Li Hua, pay a deposit of twenty

thousand can be settled, and later you can operate and sign the purchase contract. Because of the special relationship, you can turn key decoration first. Thinking of this, Li Hua immediately called back and said: "Xiao Qin, you talk to him, if I reduce the price by 5,000, then 40,000 yuan is a deal, but he has to pay a deposit of 20,000 yuan, and must ensure that I extend my check-out for five months after moving." The contract must note the check-out time, and make up the remaining payment of 20,000 yuan on the day of check-out. If he agrees to sign, that's my bottom line. I can't give in any more."

Xiao Qin said happily: "OK, I will talk according to Sister Li's meaning, there should be no problem." And I told him, the owner of the house is very nice. The young man has met a gentleman, and I'll do my best to follow your advice when you help him. Thank you for understanding, Sister Li, it is difficult for you not to be rich!"

After Li Hua put down the phone, he was nervous about buying a big house, which would be his parents' home in the future. People often say that parents in the home is the best feng shui treasure, Li Hua must operate well, so that parents live comfortably!

After Li Hua discharged from the hospital to do this thing, choose an auspicious day, according to the mother's meaning to bring an apple, figure a safe. Li Hua in the business, or some nervous, because there is no male master at home to make decisions for her, she must be careful, all by their own judgment, signed the contract there is no chance to look back, if hesitant will miss the opportunity.

Three sister with Li Hua came to the sales department, the house has been optimistic, Li Hua directly with a deposit of 20,000 to sign the contract. The contract says to pay the total amount in five months, and then take the key to open the door to inspect the existing house.

Li Hua took into account that time point, her own current housing must have sold, so that the house money will be landed, today's payment of 20,000 deposit is the deposit for the sale of parents' housing. It all fits together beautifully, and there's no need to sell your parents' house and then scramble to find a place to live.

Li Hua thought well, get the key can ask the decoration team to enter. She talked to the decoration contractor, two months to finish the decoration, put three months to breathe and smell, just five months time, should not be much of a problem.

Thinking of the later arrangement, Li Hua felt that he had business to do again, and his heart was very full. This is to do practical things, to do the greatest good for parents, but also when the daughter should pay the most filial piety. Li Hua knew that this matter must be done successfully, and give his parents a good home in their old age after a lifetime of hard work. Parents have been thinking for their children all their life, never thought of enjoying life, always scrimp and save to subsidize Li Hua's life. If the children are not home, parents eat two vegetarian dishes at each meal; But when the children come back, there are always good fish, good meat and good dishes to entertain them, so that the children can eat well. Food arrangement on the two old simple make do with their own, Li Hua found several times, the heart is very uncomfortable. In this life, we can't let our parents suffer! The living conditions of parents must be improved. To improve their living standards, start by improving their homes.

After coming out of the sales department, Li Hua breathed a long sigh of relief. The house has been sold, the parents can continue to live in the old house until 5 months to move to the new house. This is Li Hua's trip back home to do the first big thing.

Li Hua ready to tell the intermediary Xiao Qin, the house to seize the time to find customers as soon as possible to sell, because there is not too much time, she can not delay. Li Hua wants her parents' names on her new house. If she wants to do that, she can't get a loan. Therefore, it is necessary to sell the house before handing over the house and pay off the full amount of the house.

Li Hua did this so that his parents could live at ease. As the eldest daughter in the family, Li Hua led a good head and set a good example for her sisters to honor their parents. To do these things, Li Hua did not discuss with his sisters, but talked with his parents about the idea of replacing the house for a long time, and then boldly and securely operated the procedure.

Li Hua said to his parents, "You can rest assured that I will do it well." The house was sold with a deposit, which I used to buy a new house. The contract is signed. Your names are on the deed. You can live in the old house, the new house is decorated and open to breathe for three months, and then Mom can choose a good day to move."

Li Hua's mother asked with concern, "Have your father and I really sold this house?" When someone buys a house, they're gonna wait that long for us? You're not going to chase us off, are you?"

Upon hearing this, the father was anxious to ask again: "So soon sold, others still let us live for several months?" What a good buyer!"

Li Hua said, "He is not an idiot, he agreed to let us stay for a few months, because he reduced us by 5,000 yuan in the total price of the house." It's like we're giving him the benefit of the bargain. That's equivalent to rent, and for the next five months from the date I signed the contract, it's his house. It would save the buyer $5,000 and benefit him. Of course he agreed, but let us rent it for five months! Do not operate in this way, we have to go out to temporarily find a house to rent, temporary and move home more trouble, furniture are moved scattered frame!"

Mom asked again: "The down payment of the new house has not been paid off, only give the deposit of 20,000, they can give you the key to the new house?"

Li Hua was eager to explain: "This is the face of the three sisters, he greeted the boss and told him my idea and feasible plan to buy a house." The boss knew I could pay the full amount, so he vouched for me with the developer. Execute according to the remarks in the contract. If the buyer breaks faith and defaults, I will double the compensation. Of course that will not happen, and I will actively cooperate with the agent to sell the house. Don't worry about it, I know how to do it, and I'll take the time to do it."

The two old people really have nothing to say, Li Hua's father just sighed: "Lived here for more than 30 years, your sisters are married from here." From small to big on this two rooms and a half, a living room, a bathroom, a kitchen and a balcony of the house, our family of six people live quite well, and do not feel that the house is small. Now we're just two old guys, and we get to live in a new house, a big house. I never thought I'd see the day, old lady."

Li Hua's mother replied, "This is not the filial piety of our daughter! Madam, you should stop thinking that you are inferior if you do not have a son, and put an end to these feudal ideas. Of those families with sons, how many can help their parents buy a house? How many sons and daughters in our unit buy houses for their parents? In the future, do not say to your daughter what 'married daughter, poured out of the water, the daughter is a loss of money', really can not say so! Our children are good, are very filial to us two old, there is nothing to say!"

Li Hua's father said: "My daughters are good children, I am content, contented and happy!" After moving to a big house, those old colleagues, old friends, will be happy to envy us. I'm only going to talk to Mr. Dong and Mr. Lu about this."

Li Hua's mother said, "Yes, you are two good colleagues and good friends, have known each other for 40 years, are worthy of deep friendship." When you move to a new house, invite them over and have a nice drink. I'll cook and treat them well. Lao Dong and Lao Lu, these two friends are really good, and they are also your introducers for joining the party. It was only with their approval that you were promoted to be president of the service company union. These two friends are your noble people, and we should remember their kindness and be grateful."

Chapter 22: Repay Your Parents

Li Hua saw his parents ask and answer the chat, the heart gushed out a lot of emotion. When I was a child, although I lived in poverty, I was very happy and warm, and my parents did not ignore the education of their children because of poverty. In Li Hua's impression, parents treat each daughter's basic education, are very open-minded, and actively encourage their daughters to study hard. As long as their daughters want to study, their parents will send them to the best schools.

When Li Hua was in middle school, the school often engaged in learning industrial and agricultural activities, and almost half of the time in a semester was working in agriculture. The school would be linked to farms and factories, and students would be regularly arranged to study working class work-study programs and learn how farmers cultivated fields and cut grain. In the course of half a semester, only a part of the Chinese, mathematics, physics, chemistry, politics, geography, sports, these seven courses, there was no English course.

In the eyes of Li Hua's parents always feel that their child has not learned real cultural knowledge, so when Li Hua was in the second grade, Li Hua's father had asked someone to pick her up from the farm, and the next day sent her to the best county No. 1 middle school of that year to study high school. Not long after Li Hua transferred to this key middle school, several students from the same junior high school were transferred to this key middle school. They studied with Li Hua in primary and junior high school. They all got good grades, they just weren't in the same class. Here high school penniless classes, science classes, key classes, ordinary classes. Li Hua first studied in the ordinary class, and later, because of her good composition, she was assigned to the liberal arts class and served as a labor committee member.

Li Hua's father transferred her from the factory children's school to the best high school in the county, which was not understood by many people. At that time, the bourgeoisie was criticized, and the intellectuals were criticized as stinkers. Li Hua's father did not take his children's study lightly. In his eyes, it was a major event in life. Parents attach great importance to their daughters' study, and have been sending their daughters to good schools to study, so that children can cultivate a good thirst for knowledge. When Li Hua thought of this, he could not help admiring the wisdom of his parents.

Later, Li Hua's mother encouraged her second daughter: "Second, you that year, the college entrance examination, has been admitted to Hubei Art School, painting major, because there is no tuition, the family economy is not rich, did not let you go to college, in order to improve the economy, you like big sister too sensible, because of this family ah, you became a temporary worker, and now the factory children have two places to apply, as long as the test can be enrolled in a technical school, Your dad and I are rooting for you to go to school. Don't be a temp. Your hands look like meat buns, red, swollen, and split. Children ah, good, obedient, test out to study for two years, to become a teacher, than this job is more suitable for you!"

Two younger sister listened to the words of parents, carefully reviewed, from the practice of work to pass the technical secondary school. The second sister is smart and studious, and was admitted to the exam until the completion of school graduation, and was honored to stay in school as a junior college teacher, and the later work was named senior lecturer every year.

After a year, Li Hua's mother also encouraged her third daughter to become a kindergarten teacher. The third daughter can sing and dance, especially suitable for kindergarten teachers. People in that era think that there is no diploma, there is no strength, when the kindergarten teacher must have a job certificate. The third daughter silently used her spare time to review the contents of the kindergarten teacher professional culture class exam, and finally got the kindergarten teacher

qualification certificate in the second year of participating in the work, and became a kindergarten teacher class teacher.

Later, Li Hua's parents trained their youngest daughter to be equally excellent, and the youngest daughter won the second place in the national mathematics competition in high school, and was directly recommended to study in the University of Science and Technology of China, and the state paid all the learning expenses. After graduation, the youngest daughter was assigned to the northern Province City bank to work for eight years. The younger daughter worked while learning, and finally through self-study, and was admitted to the University of Cambridge in the UK, studied in the UK for two years, and obtained an actuary degree.

Li Hua thought, their sisters are now in work and life are very good, this with the love and careful cultivation of parents can not be separated. Li Hua is deeply aware that it is parents who give their children their selfless love. Now the girls are grown up, and everyone has a family and a career and a good life of their own. Every little family has its own property and home!

Although Li Hua suffered the blow of two bad marriages, her family never discriminated against her, but comforted and helped her spiritually. Try your best to help Li Hua so that she can concentrate on her work. Li Hua felt guilty to her parents, who were always worrying about themselves, and she could never repay the gratitude of such selfless upbringing.

Li Hua rushed according to the procedure, dealing with selling houses, and dealing with buying houses, but also dealing with the decoration of the house. Finally, in the third month, the final payment of the two houses and the full payment are processed in place, and the new house can be checked out at any time. At present, the full payment time is less than five months, and the promise is fulfilled ahead of schedule.

This is a memorable good day, Li Hua's mother according to the book of changes, combined with the birth of the husband and wife of eight characters selected a auspicious day, set the 16th move. It was a good day, a happy day, a happy day! Finally settled down, Li Hua finally made his parents have a big house with their names.

This is indeed a large house, duplex, 160 square meters per floor - because it is the top floor, enjoy two-for-one benefits, the actual area of 320 square meters. There are 6 rooms, 3 bathrooms, 3 living rooms, 1 kitchen and 1 balcony. The house was big enough for the whole family, and each family could stay while the four daughters returned to their parents' home. Parents really enjoy the four generations of warm and happy life, at those times, Li Hua will feel that she is not lonely, this is her happy family!

Although this house is Li Hua personal money to buy for his parents, but the sisters each in the identity of family members sponsored twenty thousand decoration money, but also to their parents have bought new furniture. In addition to the antique five-ladder cabinet, the clothes mirror, and the pendent clock left by the ancestor, the rest of the furniture and electrical appliances are sponsored by the younger sister: the second sister provides the refrigerator, the third sister buys the TV, the younger sister buys the washing machine and the marble round automatic dining table. The small knick-knacks and practical life items in the room are all bought by the daughters. When it comes to holidays and parents' birthdays, we should also find reasons to buy some practical clothes and household items for our parents while celebrating.

Under the influence of Li Hua, when the second sister in Kunshan also bought a small apartment type of existing house, to the two brother-in-law used as a commercial and residential apartment investment. Because the second brother-in-law works for a senior executive in a foreign company, this operation will subsidize the rental fee of the unit, plus only invest a little money to repay the bank loan. The property rights of the house also belong to the two younger sisters, which is equivalent to supporting the two sisters to work at ease and creating an investment environment for self-living. Kunshan real estate that year to buy, investment only need a down payment of 40,000 yuan, other bank mortgage loans, live for five years, later due to two brother-in-law work to move the Shenzhen headquarters, this house as a rental for four years, to rent back loans, the tenth year after the loan paid off, after selling Kunshan house profit 290,000 yuan.

Three younger sister also in the second year to encourage Li Hua next together and bought two small facade, a face to sign a ten-year lease contract hairdresser, on the one hand for stability, on the other hand also for the benefit of friends to rent affordable introduction. In order to repay his friend, Li Hua promised not to increase the rent every year. This front room is also to rent to repay the loan, two sets of front rooms, are to rent loans, easy to make money.

In the following year, my younger sister bought a villa in Beijing and invited the whole family to accompany her parents to Beijing. My sister and brother-in-law were invited to their new home in Beijing, where they spent a meaningful March day in spring. After that, the family often went to Beijing in warm March to reunite with her, all at her expense.

The younger sister said, "Since Mom and dad moved into the house that big sister bought, it must be a good place for feng shui." My mom and dad were much happier and my career was going well, so I didn't expect my job to improve so much in my second year in Beijing. This time I invite my family to share my four-story villa, I want my family to accompany my parents to enjoy their happiness. Let my relatives add to my popularity, I heard a Buddhist master here say that the house is to be lively, to plant more green plants, especially to raise more water bamboo."

The little sister pointed to a pot of bamboo with a height of one person and said to her family: "This is the bamboo sent by Wayan, it has been growing for a year, so high, very strong!" I love it, big sister help decorate for a month, really help a lot! "

As the saying goes, filial piety is the first thing, only to honor the parents of the family, the family will cause like a fish in water, all the best! Li Hua and his sisters all feel that since their parents moved to move, Li Hua's whole family has shown good luck, everyone's career smoother.

The girls also realized how much work their parents had put into their development. When they see their parents' wrinkled faces and white hair, they can still feel their kindness. The hands of the parents are covered with age spots, and the wrinkled skin shows the signs of age.

At this time, the parents see the family and Meimei, from the bottom of my heart, pleased that the children have grown up, pleased that the daughters have become, have lived a good life. The kids' lives are so much better now than they ever were.

The mother is a vulnerable side, and the youngest daughter is the first to see her mother wipe the tears from her face with her hands. The younger daughter said, "Mom, don't cry, you and dad should be happy, as long as you live a long and healthy life, better days are still to come!"

Li Hua took the words: "Mom is happy to cry, and must think of the sad things that we suffered in the past!"

The father said: "Your mother is happy, finally can not worry about you!"

The second daughter smiled and advised her mother: "You see, our mother's new hairstyle is like a big professor?"

The third daughter followed: "My father said, my mother looks like the central female leader Wu Yi!"

At this time, the mother was laughed by her husband and daughters, and the tears of excitement could not stop pouring out. The mother choked up as she spoke: "The children are good and the work is smooth, which is the happiest thing for me as a mother." Children, with your filial piety, to see your sisters united and helping each other, this is the family I would like to see the most, and the family should be so close."

The father added, "Your mother has always said that each of our daughters is better than the sons, even better! Last month, our old colleagues, your Uncle Dong and Uncle Lu, said that your daughter is a hundred times stronger than their son, that their son is eating the old, but your daughters are supporting you, how happy you are!" The father's words completely pulled the mother back from the sad mood, the father will advise the mother, the daughters have a good life, but also their two old people's blessing, should be happy.

Let alone buy a house for parents, is to give everything to parents, Li Hua are willing to take it for granted. Li Hua did these things without seeking fame or profit, just wanted to let her parents live a better life than before, to let their parents enjoy life, this is her daughter should do the obligation.

Sometimes Li Hua almost in the tone of command to parents said: "you should enjoy the happiness, don't worry about it, now each of our children's small home is living in a new house, and you still live in the old house of the 80's, let us do the younger generation of what?" Must be trying to improve your old couple's living conditions. If we only care about living well for ourselves, regardless of you, won't we be scolded by others?"

Li Hua is want to give parents a big enough house, let everyone stay together during the holidays, but also spacious and comfortable, let parents enjoy the happiness of family reunion there is a home atmosphere, parents in the home is a happy home, the daughters do not want to leave regret, or want to do filial piety to their parents as early as possible. This family style is that parents teach their children well, the daughters are nurtured into talent, so that Li Hua parents and peers of friends envy! Li Hua's parents are very pleased!

Chapter 23: I bought a school district house for my daughter

In order to repay his parents, Li Hua finally sold his house, bought a duplex building for his parents in his hometown, wrote his parents' names, and fulfilled his wish as the eldest daughter to be filial to his parents.

House decoration into the final link, the installation of doors and Windows project Wu boss and Li Hua settlement of doors and Windows installation and renovation money. Boss Wu in order to show that his company's business is big, has done the provincial city big developer's project, inadvertently talk to the next day to go to the provincial city and developer's project money also want to settle. It is the largest developer in my hometown, and the commercial real estate project invested in the provincial capital is being pre-sold, with small existing houses.

Li Hua heard the news very excited, she could not wait to go to the provincial capital with boss Wu, so he asked him: "Boss Wu you go to the provincial capital tomorrow, can you take me to see the provincial capital development of the house?"

Wu boss did not want to think about it said: "Of course, it is convenient for me to drive a person is also to go, take a person only, drive at seven o 'clock in the morning, and try to arrive at nine o 'clock sales department opening time." I will go to the finance department to settle the bill, you are in the sales department to see the house selection, it is best to let the staff take you to see the model of the existing house!"

Boss Wu performance is frank, one is to prove his strength of cooperation with big developers, the second is to tell Li Hua his company doors and Windows aluminum quality is good, in order to cooperate with provincial developers, but

also want Li Hua to introduce some home improvement company customers to him. When you go to check out, take Li Hua to look at the house, see Li Hua is well-connected, filial to parents, good heart, but also willing to climb the business relationship. Boss Wu is very happy to say that in the past few years with developers in the provincial capital investment cooperation of several large projects, the address is in different areas, but are good places, convenient transportation! Wu boss and Li Hua all the way to chat with the company is currently the main project, and talk about some big developers are in several other areas of the provincial capital is, next year and next year to sell the information, Li Hua silently listening, did not interrupt the boss Wu's speech, but the heart has a lot of ideas into the provincial capital development!

Li Hua this day has a lot of ideas suddenly come out, she recently just took all the scattered funds on the hand of the bank card are on the body, as if there is a hunch is to go to this matter. She must seize the moment and buy the right type of house. This matter is imperative, in order to take good care of their parents, but also take good care of their daughter, Li Hua chose to start a business in the provincial capital close to his hometown. In Li Hua's opinion, if you want to start a business, you must first live and work. She believes in the goal of having a home as the theme, and buying a house is a stepping stone to starting a business in the provincial capital.

At this time, Li Hua also considered her daughter's studies, her daughter will be admitted to the provincial city in the next two years to study university, then you must provide her daughter with the provincial city school district house. In this way, you can also start a business, you can take care of your parents, and you can provide convenience and care for your daughter during college, you can also facilitate her to find a job after graduation, and provide provincial hukou, so that there is a good foundation for employment distribution.

Woke up early the next morning. It is August, the tail of summer, the beginning of autumn, the autumn air is crisp, the morning air is very crisp. The small hometown of the breeze blowing past the ear, let Li Hua feel very comfortable. If it were not for the derailment in marriage, Li Hua loved his hometown very much, how did not think it would be for this reason, leave home, go to the provincial capital development. Perhaps the goal was set, and she felt relaxed, as if today were the first stop on a short tour of the actual house.

Li Hua wants to buy a house in the provincial capital to make her daughter and family rest assured. Since the early retreat to start a business, this state of mind out of the venture, there is no way back must actively do a cause. In order to give his family a better life, Li Hua is in urgent need of a place to live in the provincial capital, but also to improve living conditions, maybe even Li Hua has to prepare for thinking, looking for a second career, a third career. She considered that as long as the investment is not beyond her ability, will think of small and big. Strong execution, quick action, this is the characteristics of Li Hua's success, and consider mature, must be a short time to act. In the early days of Shenzhen, Guangzhou, Beijing, Shanghai, Suzhou several cities of investigation, Li Hua has mastered the real estate prices in the actual situation of the country. This trip to the provincial capital to buy a house, Li Hua has been fully prepared to investigate the data.

Wu boss at the gate of the community on time waiting for Li Hua to appear, he said, if the concept of time is not strong, did not see Li Hua, he will drive away. Li Hua remembered this sentence and came earlier than Boss Wu.

Boss Wu's black Toyota car, slowly drove into the community, the guard stopped, pressed the electric window to Li Hua said: "Please come up, you are quite on time, a strong woman doing business." At first glance, you are a woman with strong opinions, reliable in doing things, and everything is easy. It seems that there is nothing you cannot do, and don't forget to take care of me when you are developed in the future!"

Li Hua said: "Boss Wu praises this I like to hear, at least I also want to seriously do this thing." Also thank the boss today by the way to take me, let me less detours, go directly to the sales department to take a look, maybe today will set a minimum unit."

Boss Wu said, "Let me tell you, this project is really good, developed by the biggest developer in our small city." I've been working with them for years. There

are two other development projects that I can show you today if I have time, and you can compare them. I personally think this project is more suitable for you, there are small units you want, and the investment is not large, the total price of a little more than 100,000 can get a house, the average per square area of 2030 yuan. Having a house in a provincial town is good for children' s future study and college, and there are more options for starting a business in the provincial town in the future."

Li Hua said, "Yes, the unit price of this house in the provincial capital is indeed lower than that of Beijing, Shanghai and Guangzhou, and the price is the same as that of Suzhou and Yunnan." Compare, there is just need and investment space, worth investing. I think prices will continue to rise in the future, and in the last two years they have definitely gone up."

Li Hua and boss Wu chatted while driving to the provincial capital, talking very happily along the way, the two sides exchanged information about all aspects of real estate, and talked about the future trend of real estate. Li Hua on this trip, more in mind, thought this time must seize the opportunity to march to the provincial capital, this is the first step to go steady. Li Hua always feel in the dead, this is because of her kindness filial piety for parents to do good met the opportunity of the provincial capital, if not for parents to buy a house renovation balcony doors and Windows, how will meet Wu boss talk about these timely need to understand the information? It is true that the speaker is not interested, the listener is interested, Li Hua attributed these timely information resources to God to take care of her, help her point out the direction!

More than an hour to the destination, the sales department of the center door has not opened. Boss Wu said: "Let' s have breakfast nearby, this provincial city' s breakfast is very rich, cheap, wide variety." What do you like to eat, today I treat you!"

Wu boss parked the car, two people walked into the opposite alley. I don' t know. I was shocked to see it. Look at the humble place, but there are so many stalls and roadside food shops. Provincial capital said to eat breakfast as "too early" , the pattern is so much, Li Hua can not see. She likes to eat the taste, such as beef powder, soup dumplings, fried dough sticks, noodles, rice wine dumplings, onion rolls, millet porridge, red date porridge, pork ribs lotus root soup...... I'm really confused. I don't know which one to eat. In the end, Li Hua still came to a bowl of beef rice noodles and a churro. This is her favorite heavy, spicy beef powder.

At this time, Li Hua more determined to buy a house here, she felt that the life here is too convenient, living in this neighborhood feel very comfortable. Li Hua was glad to catch a ride this time, so he was very grateful to quietly buy the breakfast order first. She felt she had to pay to get a little more variety, otherwise she would be embarrassed to order something else. Li Hua ordered a plate of small glutinous rice dumplings, ordered a noodle nest and chives, everything tastes a little, can not finish the package. Li Hua couldn't help laughing because she felt greedy for food.

Wu boss ready to pay after eating, did not think that Li Hua will single has bought. Boss Wu said: "I just agreed to treat, why have you already paid?" Well, thank you. Isn't this the right place?"

Li Hua said, "It's delicious. I didn't expect it to be so convenient. It's time for the doors to open and we should go to the sales department."

Boss Wu said, "Yes, it's only a few minutes' walk. You must be the first guest, I know all the staff of the sales department of the developer, they will patiently introduce the suitable room type to you, I ask them to give you a discount."

Li Hua said: "Thank you for giving me a discount, thank you, thank you!" What Li Hua needs most at this time is to save a little investment cost, even if it is less than one point, it is the most affordable help.

Wu boss feel Li Hua very grateful, in the recent contact, give Wu boss impression in mind, Li Hua is a good faith speech arithmetic woman, worth helping and communicating. Boss Wu thought of here very warmly into the sales hall, to the staff XiaoQin said: "I brought you a new guest, is our hometown, please give her the biggest discount price." She's a client and a friend, and she would definitely buy one of your developments. She loves this area. Please look after her." Boss Wu said good words to the person in charge of the sales department, and turned to say hello to Li Hua, and went straight to the financial department.

Li Hua in Xiao Qin patient and enthusiastic recommendation, went to the scene to see the existing house! Immediately back to the sales department signed the purchase contract, the house is set down, the down payment of twenty thirty thousand yuan, the rest do commercial loans, such as bank loans approved, you can hand in the room decoration use! Li Hua has something to do again, and every link of this connection is compact, without dragging, and even can be said to be a quick decision.

When Boss Wu came out from the finance department, he saw that Li Hua had signed the contract, and gave a thumbs-up in front of the staff and said: "Admire, too admire, the first time to see the room, less than three hours decided to sign the contract." With your style of doing things, you will be able to get up in the future, today can celebrate, this is the first step into the provincial capital business, if there is a need to choose a house to see the house in the future, keep in touch."

Li Hua can not help feeling: finally have their own small nest, this is a new turning point in life. Perhaps in the future, I will have my own development field in this city, manage my own life well, and bring my parents to the provincial capital to live with myself, so that my parents can enjoy this kind of family life.

Li Hua thought it was his responsibility, a burden. She must move forward, first to survive, then to find a dream, one small goal after another to achieve it. Invisible power and spiritual ideas to promote Li Hua difficult forward, encountered great difficulties, she never complained, not to tell relatives. Only report good news to their loved ones, and infect the single girlfriends around them with an optimistic attitude towards life. At that time, Li Hua's friends were almost all single divorced career-oriented women. Li Hua encouraged themselves to take them as an example, with the wise, with the diligent, with the successful teacher! I believe that one day after hard work, I will be on the road to success, become a member of the role model, and be admired and proud of the successful woman!

Chapter 24: Exchange pre-marital property for daughter

Li Hua bought a small school district house, the surrounding environment is very good. The opening prices were much lower than those in Shenzhen, Guangzhou and Beijing in the same year. At that time, Li Hua's capital on hand was only 30,000 yuan, and the house with the down payment for investment could only choose a small unit of 38 square meters of school district housing. First, it is also affordable, and in the future, my daughter will go to college and it will be convenient to go home every week. Li Hua bought the house without any pressure. The transportation here is very convenient, from the university campus to the residential area only need to take five or six stops on the bus.

In order to save money Li Hua only hired a decorator, only spent 7000 yuan simple decoration configuration. This is the first house that Li Hua invested for her daughter in the provincial capital, Wuchang District of Wuhan City.

On the day when the decoration was finished, Li Hua was full of joy to take her loved ones to visit the house she designed. It is a very warm residence with an open kitchen in the main hall at the entrance, a small bathroom and shower area on the left, a master bedroom on the right, a washing machine on the balcony, a sun terrace with an air conditioning unit, and a sliding salsa door and glass door between the balcony and the hall. The bedroom makes full use of the corner space, the top is filled with wardrobes, and the entire storage cabinet is considered. There is a big bed in the bedroom, which is enough for Li Hua and her daughter to sleep together as a place for rest.

Since then, Li Hua felt full of strength in those years, for her family, she must spell out, work hard to earn money, so that her family can live a happy life. Li Hua

just want to earn breath, divorce is not terrible, husband betrayal is not terrible, she does not need marriage can also live a good life they want.

Li Hua is a restless woman, during the renovation of her parents' house, as long as the information about the provincial capital house, she is very concerned. Can smoothly buy this provincial city house, which is also the accumulated results of the early stage. Before Li Hua went to every big city to investigate the local real estate market. Just do not have the goal of the day, Li Hua went to Beijing to help my little sister decorate the house, get Beijing's house price information. In Kunshan to help two younger sister decorate the house, we understand Suzhou and Kunshan house prices. During several months of insurance in Shenzhen, Li Hua learned about the housing price information in Shenzhen and Guangzhou. Because of his own eyes, fully grasp the real information, Li Hua can quickly compare and judge, make decisions can be fast and ruthless.

In those years, house prices rose rapidly, almost as long as the investment in the city center of the house, there is no price, as long as the sale can make money. It can be said that buying a house can double the money. Of course, for Li Hua, who just came to the provincial capital to start a business, it is really an opportunity. On the one hand, life is just needed, on the other hand, after three years of buying a house, you can also adjust and improve the housing needs according to the actual situation of your own and your daughter's placement planning. Later, Li Hua saw that there was a hukou policy for house purchase, and it was a preferential welfare policy formulated by the government for the majority of intellectuals.

The days passed so fast, Li Hua's daughter also spent three years in the provincial capital. In the fourth year of the university, I immediately need to find a unit internship, and it takes half a semester to complete the subject study. In order to let her daughter get a good opportunity to work as an intern, but also in order to make her daughter become a provincial hukou, Li Hua wants to buy a larger area of the house in her daughter's name. Must do the time, only in this way, in order to enjoy the conditions of the purchase into the provincial city account: the house money reached more than 500,000 yuan, the area of 100 square meters, to be eligible for settlement conditions.

This matter must be settled in 2006, the daughter will graduate from college, the internship unit is the provincial city telecommunications industry company. Li Hua didn't want to miss the chance to buy a house. Li Hua thought the safest investment in wealth was a house. She gave a house to her parents. If you want to give her daughter the most affordable much-needed love, Li Hua still thinks that the house is the best gift. To buy a house for her daughter is to give her a sense of security, a warm harbor. That is to give her daughter a high platform starting point, raise children, guide children to grow up healthily, do not want to bring low self-esteem to her daughter because of single parent families, to set up a good example in her daughter's mind to be a good example of economic independence, this is Li Hua want to give her daughter the most practical and largest motherly love.

Li Hua took a fancy to Wuchang school district house, the surrounding traffic developed, can be regarded as the Wuhan cultural center, a few minutes through the Wuhan Bridge until Hanyang, direct Hankou commercial street. There are more than a dozen buses at the bus stop in front of the community, which can directly reach Zhongnan Commercial Building, Donghu Han Street, and Hanzheng Street by boat. These are the commercial and cultural centers of Wuhan City. There are supporting hospitals, schools, kindergartens, wet markets, and Shouyi Square at the foot of the Yellow Crane Tower. How convenient it would be for my daughter's future to live here. If my daughter settles down here in the future and becomes a member of the residents of the provincial capital, there will be no problem in employment.

Think of these, Li Hua full of energy, a little tireless, hard work to do a variety of tedious and must be solved things. Li Hua's whole mind is for her daughter's consideration, did not think about themselves.

In order to buy a new house, Li Hua needs to raise a down payment. My first thought was to sell the house I had lived in for three years. It's the best way to get the money. The house has doubled in price. Looking at the house that is about to be sold, which has lived in the house for three years, everything around has witnessed

Li Hua's decisive wisdom three years ago. In this respect, no one taught Li Hua, parents did not expect, the eldest daughter Li Hua in a short period of three years, quietly doing these things to invest in the house, all by their own understanding of the unexpected surprise and wealth brought by real estate investment.

These years of experience has cultivated Li Hua's intuition of investing in real estate. As long as he sees a house in a good location, what Li Hua has to do is to actively collect the down payment funds for the purchase of a house, and then immediately go to the sales department to sign the purchase contract. The next step is to apply for commercial loans according to their good bank credit points. Because the loan is timely, credit is good, Li Hua is divorced and single, their own things, do what things are very smooth, this is Li Hua most willing to do, is in the house contract to sign the name of the moment the most enjoyable, the mood is great.

Li Hua also has the advantage of being low-key. Doing something as big as buying a house is just a matter of talking to her family supporters and confiding in them about her ideas and every step she can take. Before it was done, Li Hua kept a low profile. Family, friends, colleagues and classmates only know that Li Hua is very busy. Sometimes phone wechat to find people, Li Hua is not in the building materials market, is in which city travel to see the house, sometimes in the move, sometimes in the decoration. In fact, to implement these things, we really need to do a lot of practical things. Moving in those years was the norm for Li Hua, and this time he began to face the daily affairs he had done before moving. Li Hua is sometimes the image of a tough woman, a camouflage pants, sneakers, T-shirts and tops, to create their own image of a contractor, how to look will not think of her is the landlord. The house is not well, Li Hua will not let her family see her dress up.

Although Li Hua likes the life of a laid-back bourgeois, she is also a woman with a romantic taste. But at some time, she is like a tireless work maniac, a selfless dedication of the mother, but also a reasonable elder sister, in the eyes of the elders, is a big filial piety of the eldest daughter, from a young age to develop a strong and assertive personality, no affectance, no redundant nonsense, decisive practical work. Li Hua always gives people a feeling of calm, full of vitality, as if never tired, towards her goal, perseverance, never affected by other people's words.

Li Huabian on the network to contact the housing agency, will own this small school district housing entrusted to the intermediary company quickly sold. When the small unit was bought, the total price of the house was 108,000 yuan, and it rose to 180,000 yuan after living for three years. Li Hua heart is really reluctant to give up, but this is the first step of small broad operation, in order to sell smoothly, finally make a profit of 20,000 yuan, sold at a total price of 160,000 yuan, in order to give her daughter Xiaolin household name to buy a house, with the provincial capital settled down payment for a house, this is the first step to successful operation.

Li Hua near a primary school, found his hometown to develop a new property in the provincial capital, selected a set of can enjoy the transfer account policy conditions of the area of the house, the total price of more than 500,000, the area is 102 square meters. Li Hua bought in the name of her daughter, signed a house purchase contract, two months later can be handed over to decorate the use. The plan is a set of links, the deal closing time is important.

Chapter 25: Li Hua's entrepreneurial history

Time is money, at this time really true, Li Hua knew that only the small house sale of funds to hand, after the purchase procedures can be logical. Otherwise missed business opportunities and capital supplement, the new house side is only under the deposit, has not paid the down payment. Although I found an acquaintance to coordinate the time of the down payment to be paid one month later, once the overtime delivery, the deposit will not be returned, and the room number will not be retained. It was a risky move, but Li Hua had no other way. She never wanted to borrow money from her friends to invest, nor did she want to make trouble for her relatives. She would rather compromise on the total price of the small unit to close the deal as soon as possible. After the goal is clear, Li Hua looks very calm.

Soon after the sale of housing information hung on the Internet, the intermediary Xiaochen informed Li Hua to take customers to see the room. Li Hua is actively preparing to facilitate the house sale. The city is a city of stoves, and the hot summer winds make people feel stuffy and irritable. Li Hua wanted to buy a house to leave a good first impression, she deliberately chose a bunch of flowers, arranged in the living room the most prominent place. Li Hua is reluctant to turn on the air conditioner on weekdays, but on this day she adjusted the air conditioner to the right temperature. The room was thoroughly cleaned, and the whole room gave a warm and romantic atmosphere. The room was quiet and comfortable with soft music playing. It seems that people have the illusion that it is not summer here, but the spring garden!

When everything was ready, there was a knock on the door, "Sister Li, here we come." Xiao Chen affectionately called Li Hua outside the door. Li Hua slowly opened the door, stood side by side, showed the spacious and bright living room, and handed over the guests' disposable shoe covers one by one. Li Hua is good at service, just like meeting the customers who look at the model house.

Intermediary little Chen Yu quickly said: "Sister Li's house is really beautiful, like a new house." If you buy it, there is no need to invest in renovations."

Li Hua said, "Although the house is small, it has a complete set."

The buyers were a young couple who came in full of joy. Electrical appliances, furniture, decoration, all show the owner's cultural taste, buyers see the eyes shine. The female buyer asked, "Is this all arranged by Sister Li?"

Li Hua said: "Yes, I like to design house decoration, every item is carefully selected by me. Even though I sold them, I loved them. Perhaps this house is more suitable for you and your young couple."

Li Hua arranged the environment of her home very well, answering all the questions of the buyers, and chatting with them was very pleasant. Looking at it, the young couple said very anxiously: "Let's go to the agency today to sign a contract, we have no time to look at other houses." With Sister Li, let's deal with the information hanging on the Internet. We are a commercial loan. The bank approves it quickly. Sister Li, we can't afford that much at once, but we can pay you 100,000 yuan in advance and take out a loan of another 60,000 yuan."

Xiao Chen said: "It's easy to say, let's go to the intermediary to sit down and talk." If you can buy a house without renovations, you're buying the right one. Check in with a suitcase! All home appliances delivered!"

Li Hua could not keep down his joy, stabilized his mood, very polite said, "This is fate, I also hope to buy a house friends like it as I do, this happy romantic happiness of the cottage!"

A couple of young people said: "We like it here, we want to stay." Leave this music CD for us too!"

Li Huashu took a breath and fondled the disc and said, "I also like this music very much, which is found in the music house shop." Well, I'll give it to you!"

Xiaochen with the two people looking at the house talking and laughing to the

intermediary, the same day the deal. It was the fastest sale of another house in Li Huayou's life.

The next day, Li Hua took the 100,000 yuan deposit for the sale of a small house, plus the 20,000 yuan deposit for the purchase of a new house in advance, which was just a total of 120,000 yuan for the down payment. The total house payment of her daughter's new house is 406,000 yuan, which is Li Hua's most satisfied house sale transaction and the most successful connection! Although deducting the brokerage fee reward Xiaochen cashing, Li Hua made less profit on this side, but timely replenishment of investment housing funds, which is more important. Li Hua seized the opportunity to solve the problem of the implementation of her daughter's hukou, and also laid a good foundation for her daughter to work in the provincial capital. Li Hua gave her daughter a home, a veritable first house before marriage, a safe harbor. This incident also opened the door to the wisdom of Li Hua's daughter's investment and financial management, which is equivalent to getting the golden key to open the treasure wealth box, so that she knew that the sense of security given by economic independence was more reliable than anyone else.

Since then, Li Hua's daughter's studies, career, marriage and children have all benefited from this house. This house not only brought Li Hua and her daughter a bucket of money in business and investment, but also brought a lot of good opportunities for business cooperation and entrepreneurship. After buying this house, Li Hua started her own business. For several years, she took several jobs and worked hard to make money all year round. Li Hua did a line of work, and soon saw results in just three years of investment, breaking through the starting point of one million yuan, and paying off all the loans of her daughter's house. He also invested all the after-sale profits and principal into a second and third downtown property. It has changed from a small house to a large one, and from a set to three sets of investment houses. Under the good influence of Li Hua's example, Li Hua's daughter also showed investment wisdom among her peers.

Over the years, in the dead of night, Li Hua often thought of his first business scene. After buying a small school district house, she thought about doing something to make money and solve the pressure of the mortgage. Li Hua's initial idea was to open a tea house, a small tea house of about 100 square meters with a little bourgeois art style. Every March, Li Hua accompanied his parents to Beijing for a reunion with his sister. Li visited Beijing teahouse, teahouse, teahouse, book bar, coffee shop market model.

In March, Beijing is brimming with spring scenery, with lush leaves on the roadside and prosperous buildings along the way, you can feel the rapid change and development of the motherland. Li Hua accompanied his parents on a sightseeing tour arranged by his sister. Several major scenic spots and some major city landmarks in Beijing were visited. In the evening, Li Hua went out to visit and learn about some small music bars, small book bars, cafes and other cultural petty bourgeois style tea houses in Beijing, and also investigated some simple style tea art culture small tea houses. Li Hua visited dozens of small teahouses in Beijing during that time.

Later, Li Hua also told his family about the motivation of the investigation and asked them to give some advice. We talked about capital investment, budget, actual decoration costs, staff hiring, and the implementation plan of the management operation mode after the store. The family put the problem in front of Li Hua: the investment of money and energy is too large, and the late store plan is immature. These problems forced Li Hua to abandon his plan to open a teahouse.

My little sister said to Li Hua: "Sister you think, you are to start a business to earn money to pay the mortgage. If your business does not achieve this purpose, it will not only lose meaning, delay your time, but also add a greater financial burden to you!"

Li Hua listened to the silence for a while and asked, "Do you have any good advice, what do you think I am suitable for?"

The second sister should voice: "Sister, you don't like our hometown Huanggangsha Street that woman brand discount store clothing?" Buy a bunch at a time and see if your girlfriend and classmates like it too. Every time you buy a dozen

pieces, and you are familiar with the store owner, you might as well open a clothing brand discount store. I think it will work, you know the industry, the clothing is cheap, the investment cost is low, you can try this project."

Li Hua's heart lit up, when she was in her hometown, she often patronized the women's clothing brand discount store. I heard that a friend of the female owner of a clothing store specializes in shipping in Beijing, she has opened three brand discount stores, although the stores are in the county and urban areas, but the business is very hot, almost women into the store did not come out empty-handed. Li Hua and his girlfriends love to buy them. They buy seven or eight pieces each time.

The third sister also said: "Yes, the eldest sister loves to buy, and the surrounding friends also like it." Every time I go shopping, I always return with a full load, no empty handed back, there must be your consumer market. If you join this clothing store, you will have no shortage of goods to sell. It's easier than opening teahouses and cafes!"

The little sister then spoke again: "Yes, do what you are familiar with and can invest in." The most important thing is to talk about how to survive first and then dream."

Li Huajing sisters point, head of the emergence of clothing store boss Hong in the store busy appearance, every time to the store to see a lot of customers, customers look at every piece of clothing like looking at the baby, those clothes as long as the retail price of two discount, customers buy a little distressed hand soft. Li Hua himself has experienced the excitement of buying these clothes, indicating that the suggestion of opening a clothing store is the best investment project at present, and there should be no problem if you follow it.

Thinking of this, Li Hua immediately said: "I have a solution, I first call the brand discount store owner Xiaohong." I have heard that she lives in Beijing delivery, you can talk to her about franchising stores, what conditions are needed, I call to consult, if she is now good in Beijing!"

Chapter 26: First Survive, Then Dream

Li Hua is impatient, decisive, after the idea is determined to implement immediately. Li Hua confidently called the owner's wife Xiaohong's contact number and learned that Xiaohong was just in Beijing.

Xiaohong just in the company ready to purchase, a heard that Li Hua came to Beijing, immediately to meet a face to face to talk. Xiao Hong said directly: "I came to pick you up, you personally inspect the company for a few days, and live with me on the company side." I have an apartment that I use to deliver goods, and I basically live here now. This time you come at a good time, I am in Beijing, and I just bought a red sports car. Which ring road are you on in Beijing? I'll come get you."

This little Hong boss is also a person who can do something, heard Li Hua said in Beijing's East second Ring Road Wangfujing water show Street, let Li Hua in the silk Street Starbucks coffee shop waiting for her.

On the phone, Xiao Hong boss also said: "Tomorrow I am going to the company to pick up goods, you will accompany me to know how to purchase." Let me introduce the process of the company to you by the way, if you join my company, I will not charge you franchise fee, but I can add two points to your clothing wholesale cost? The advantage is that you do not need to stay in Beijing for a long time to buy goods, I will help you choose the spot. You just tell me the styles that sell well, the styles and styles that customers demand, and I will deliver the goods to you according to the market situation. I'll take two points off the cost of each dress, and anything else is your profit. I don't need you to join the fee, you go home to find a suitable store address, you can simply decorate the opening, so cooperation?"

Xiao Hong continued: "I won't let you suffer. We have known each other for many years. You have brought many customers to our shop. I will treat such good customers as friends. Our franchise is really profitable, I believe you can do it in Hubei province. In order to ensure your interests, I will not charge you the franchise fee. Tens of thousands of yuan saved for operating decoration costs, but also used as purchase funds. We'll discuss it when you get here."

The good news came too suddenly, Li Hua was moved by Xiao Hong's words, and suddenly hooked Li Hua's thoughts. She lost her marriage, she must not lose her career, Li Hua is eager to try the clothing industry to bring benefits. The little sister's words reminded her that she must first earn more money, first seek survival and then seek dreams, which is the king's way.

With Xiao Hong's specific guidance and help, Li Hua took many detours less, which is really an opportunity. After personal investigation and family analysis, Li Hua also believes that the capital cost of opening a tea house is too large, and it is impossible to achieve. Especially in the early stage of entrepreneurship, Li Hua can only invest in small cost projects to achieve the goal of fast mortgage payments.

The idea of joining the clothing store is more mature, the investment is small, tens of thousands of dollars can immediately open a store to earn income. Li Hua thought that he would try to make money first, and then realize his dream of making a small tea house. Li Hua knows that you must have rice before you can cook. With a financial foundation, you can be what you want to be. After listening to the clothing store owner Xiaohong's words, Li Hua, who has a pleasant personality, promised Xiaohong without saying a word: "Good, today in this Beijing second ring Starbucks cafe waiting for you." Give me a call as soon as you get there. I'll be ready to come out."

About an hour later, Xiao Hong called: "You can come out, I am at the intersection of Starbucks." The red car with the flashing lights on the side of the road is mine. Be safe and watch the road. Come here quickly. I'll wait for you in the car.

Li Hua told his sisters to go back to Beijing and visit the clothing company for two days. Li Hua soon find little Hong car, after getting on the car with little Hong and Li Hua two people especially excited, they all talk about home dialect, talk very freely. I really did not expect that the hometown customer and the boss can meet in the metropolis of Beijing, and still talk about business, become Allies.

Li Hua seems to be serious this time and has come prepared. Xiao Hong smiled while driving and said: "Action is strength, say dry, really admire your aggressive, it seems that the tea house did not open, to open a clothing store."

Li Hua also said happily: "That's for sure, I think following you to open a clothing store, certainly can do it." Because I know you, and I love the way your family dresses. I can accept the price, I also have these consumer groups, friends of the guests with customers, when the friends support, the price is moderate, a cheap love, this clothing discount store can be done. Besides, I am as good as you, easygoing, and I can do it. I will not toss open what tea house, there is no fixed guests, there is no stable consumer flow market. Peace of mind to learn from you, but also have to earn money first, and when you earn a lot of money, then go to open a teahouse."

Xiao Hong replied, "I will also go to your place to have a rest and drink a cup of tea." This afternoon I will take you to the company to see, I show you to choose the goods, see how much to achieve. If you join a clothing company, the company will take a commission of intermediate management, which is too much pressure on you, because you do not know the skills to adapt to the sales link of the market. So I suggest you become my distributor open a small shop, franchise fees do not need. How much do you sell directly? I'll give you two points in between. In this way, your financial pressure is not big, I will deliver to you, you can sell goods at ease. If it is operated in this way, it is like the three branches of Huanggang in my hometown. That's how all three stores operate. They don't buy stuff, I ship it, they sell it. As you can see, business is good, and there are no fewer than three or four people coming in, often seven or eight. You've experienced it. It's a pleasure to buy."

Li Hua was moved by Xiao Hong's words, and immediately said happily:

"Today, I may want to fly back and get up early." If it is what you say, I will open more such clothing stores in the provincial capital and have business."

The two chatted all the way, Li Hua excitedly looked out of the window of Beijing, traffic, people come and go. The car passed the tall buildings and gradually drove towards the Middle Road of the Fifth Ring Road in Beijing. Xiao Hong drove very fast and it wasn't long before he got near the company. The original clothing company in Beijing five ring nine peaks, Li Hua this just know Beijing nine peaks wholesale clothing market was originally here.

Li Hua asked: "Clothing wholesale market how to choose in such a partial place?"

Xiao Hong replied, "Is this still wrong? The houses in Beijing's Sixth Ring Road are selling very expensive! If you want to develop here is not impossible, but here is not more comfortable than Hubei. Small cities are much more moist, and you can make money without pressure. It's hard work in Beijing. You need money for everything."

Li Hua said: "So all need to start a business to earn a living. I had to put aside my dreams of writing, of book bars, of tea houses, of cafes, and do real things for a few more years. After earning money, I will work hard to realize my dream. Do you think I'm going to earn my first startup fund?"

Xiao Hong immediately replied: "You must be able to, against your decisive and wise spirit." I am confident that you will succeed, so I am willing to help you. When you get to the company, you can see the scene of the purchase of clothing styles, and when you see the price and quality, you will definitely decide to return to the provincial capital to open this brand discount store."

Chapter 27: Open a specialty clothing brand discount store

Li Hua with small Hong choose clothing delivery, as expected by the company's atmosphere and clothing prices shocked. Li Hua was moved and determined to open this clothing store. Think of the future and her daughter's life, think of the future to buy a house for her daughter, Li Hua must start a business to make money, otherwise a lifetime also don't want to buy a house. Thinking about this, opening a clothing store is the most urgent thing to do.

Li Hua looked at all kinds of clothing piled up, are classified packing stacked, by the buyer to choose. Some are squatting, some are standing, some are looking like eyes, not knowing where to start. Most people are constantly immersed in choosing clothes that they like and that their customers want.

Li Hua excitedly said to Xiao Hong boss: "Thank you for bringing me to the head office, I trust you, from now on, I do not hesitate." Today, I will buy with you, I decided to learn to do with you, join directly in your store, give you two points of sales commission."

Boss Hong said happily: "OK, we will help you choose goods from today." I know you will agree to do this line of work, you need to make money to do what you want to do. As long as I bring home the people, not one is not tempted to open a shop. I hope you open up the situation in Hubei province, I fully cooperate with you to choose goods delivery, you go back to your hometown just choose the store location, simple decoration, shop sales."

Li Hua smiled cheerfully and nodded continuously, and saw all the clothes all over the ground in his eyes, and the importers were busy. It's also like the future of her clothing store, with customers coming in and out of the scene.

Li Hua has returned to his hometown of Hubei Province in advance according to the plan, and ordered a house for his daughter at the same time, and also looked up the address of the brand clothing discount store. The site is located on the side street of the new community, where the flow of people is very large. This street leads directly to the wet market, and there are always crowds passing by in the morning and during the working hours. On the right is a row of breakfast stalls, barber shops, and small restaurants. Walk to the T-intersection is the famous key experimental primary school, and the famous art school. The famous People's Hospital in the provincial capital is further ahead. There are many bus stops here.

All in all, choose this address as a clothing store, is really very suitable, quiet, there is a stable flow of residents of the community, there are teachers and students of the art college, and people who visit patients on the way to go shopping. The most important is that the side street stores all opened different brand style clothing stores, jewelry stores, shoe stores, children's fashion stores, there are three beauty salons, nail shops, foot massage shops around. This is a complete supporting facilities, mature quality living community. Here to open a brand clothing discount store suitable for young and middle-aged people, there must be suitable women to buy.

Li Hua think this shop opened in this area, business will be able to do, the most important is the clothing price style suitable for different groups of women. Think of here, Li Hua full of energy, find two just want to transfer the boss to talk. There is an empty shop without decoration, but the landlord must pay half a year's rent in advance, the rent is calculated at 3000 per month, half a year 18000, without any hesitation, because the geographical location here is too good. The transfer of the jewelry shop next door, due to the luxury decoration of the transfer fee is too high, more than Li Hua's budget investment cost. There is no way, Li Hua only give up ready-to-decorate the storefront.

Li Hua said dry, soon with the empty shop landlord signed a contract, and to the landlord to give half a month decoration time, other terms are in accordance with the landlord's provisions to do. Landlord boss Liu saw Li Hua is sincere to rent a shop, and personality bold and unrestrained, he likes to deal with such tenants. He thought that the vacant time not only can not collect rent, but also be a favor. So Liu boss promised to rent to Li Hua, and give half a month to Li Hua decoration.

The location of this shop is close to Li Hua's new home, since the decision to open a shop, we must move early, without delay. Li Hua saw this facade, satisfied with his heart, decisively signed the rent contract, and immediately began the design and layout of the house in an orderly manner. In order to save investment costs, only a woodworker was invited to saw the discarded wood piles into pieces, and nailed up the three characters "Lotus Lake edge" in his handwriting toward the middle of the upper part of the door. Not only saved the advertising cost of 5000 yuan, but also the effect is special, and the name of the front shop in the whole woman street looks unique.

Li Hua visited a teahouse in Beijing to take some photos of the door decoration style, clothing store facade design reference to such a style: eye-catching, artistic, natural, nostalgic, simple, fashion. Suddenly attracted the attention of the passing female crowd, the decoration characteristics are just in line with the preferences of art college teachers and college students, but also suitable for housewives who come out to buy food and hang out on weekdays.

This was a successful site selection, and the decoration design benefited from the homework done in Beijing. There is no white road in the world, people's thoughts and efforts to act, always bring unexpected harvest!

The decoration clothing store is being carried out in a nervous and orderly way, while Li Hua also pay close attention to the Beijing delivery of small Hong boss communication, full power to let Hong boss as soon as possible in half a month to organize a good clothing store to open supply guarantee. In the store decoration above, Li Hua also in the color, music, lighting, mirror design layout, so that the whole only up and down 60 square area of the pavement, looks not only unique, but also very practical, there are enough hidden space to place things.

Li Hua set the whole downstairs into a clothing store, half of the whole wall has a mirror, above the design of a purple gauze cover guests try on the space. A small bar in the left corner serves as a cash register with a computer playing music. On the right is a clothing display cabinet from the bottom to the top, the background is also purple, with the three words "lotus lake edge", echoing the sign outside the store. There is a small but functional bathroom in the furthest corner of the aisle, with an electric water heater above.

Store decoration details Li Hua thought, in the end is engaged in the decoration of people, but also fortunately Li Hua like their own decoration, design. When Li Hua is doing the work of these men, he does not feel how tired he is, doing things he likes, covering all the grievances and difficulties.

"Lotus lake edge" clothing store opened as scheduled, Li Hua is both the boss and the waiter, a touch with ten miscellaneous, what do. She slowly learned to be a clothing store owner, but also to observe the taste of guests to see goods. After two months of guarding the store, I gradually accumulated some resident customers. Gradually, there were art school teachers and college students. Because the price is reasonable and affordable, it is easy to get customers to buy. Li Hua's clothing business so into the right track, business day by day better, more customers back up.

Li Hua later found that the row of side street shop owners are all single women, really such a coincidence, Li Hua how also did not think, he suddenly became a clothing store owner, in order to improve the living conditions of the environment, better for the family, they must first be rich, have rice to cook, have the strength to help the family! This is real life!

One day, when it was closing time at night, a middle-aged woman walked into the store in Li Hua, looking not like buying clothes, looking very tired. She's got a lot of stuff on her hands, looking around. Li Hua was still eager to ask the woman to put things down and slowly see if there were any clothes she liked. The woman listened to this. She put her things on the ground in the corner and said to Li Hua, "May I go to the bathroom?"

The woman looked a little anxious, Li Hua quickly pointed to the position of the bathroom: "Yes, go inside to the left is!" The woman nodded gratefully and walked straight inside. Li Hua helped the guests take care of the things on the ground, and glanced at them, feeling that they had just bought shoes and clothes.

It may be that the woman has been shopping all day, and now she just walked in casually by Li Hua's clothing store. There may also be no way to urinate, go in and try to solve the problem of going to the toilet. Well, it's definitely not about clothes.

The woman walked out of the bathroom easily and stood opposite Li Hua pointing to the clothes on the hanger and said, "Can you take it down and feel the fabric feel?"

Li Hua took it and said: "OK, you slowly see if there is anything you like, I will take it down for you." I have many people here during the day, because it is the price of the brand discount store, compared with the new model of the last season, this old model is much cheaper, and the next year will be new. There are fewer guests at night, so you can take your time!"

The woman's eyes suddenly lit up, slowly look slowly touch, turn around, and turned to Li Hua said: "Boss, do you have water to drink?"

Li Hua quickly filled the disposable cup with water and handed it to the woman's hand and said, "Please sit on this sofa and drink slowly. Sit down and rest. Just sit and watch."

The woman really sat down and talked with Li Hua while drinking. On the coffee table in front of the sofa, Li Hua moved the fruit plate that usually put sunflower seeds and candy to the woman, "You haven't eaten dinner, first cushion your stomach." This apple and orange fruit is very sweet, eat some!"

The woman took the fruit and laughed and said, "I have not bought clothes, yet you give water to drink and fruit to eat." You are such a good boss, so friendly, why do I feel that you do not like the boss? Are you really the boss?"

Li Hua laughed loudly: "Beautiful sister ah, I am a person bored, have you to talk with me, but also take care of my business, this is the guest I can not beg." People said that the customer is God, a look at you is a fan of the Lord! It doesn't matter whether we buy it or not, we are destined to come and sit down anytime later!"

The woman said with satisfaction, "I saw that the sign of your shop has some characteristics, and I was curious to come and have a look." I didn't expect you

to be patient, affordable clothes, and most of all, the style I like. But I have bought so many things today, but I still want to buy a few more clothes in your store, I am afraid it is an impulse!"

Li Hua said: "It doesn't matter, I will keep the clothes you like tonight, and you can return them at any time within a week!"

The woman did not hesitate to buy seven pieces, and even selected three accessories, and the winter coat that was hanging was also bought by this woman! The woman was really happy to leave the store.

Li Hua closed the shop late. It usually closes at nine o 'clock, but today it is ten o 'clock. Li Hua looked at the time of the electronic clock on the wall, and shook her head happily while smiling silently, with a look of hard work on her face. The original business should also be kind to every guest, who is not sure who is a big buyer, a good guest who likes you. Li Hua's business is prosperous is reasonable, she in the street, and finally became the female bosses dinner point, chat and chat small tea house, because the female bosses of the woman street, almost like visiting next door, come to visit Li Hua's shop, drink tea and talk about some interesting things, often make customers laugh, and even have neighborhood neighbors. Li Hua has also become a frequent visitor and friend in the store!

Chapter 28: Hospitality

It is often said that peers are competitors, but Li Hua broke this saying, Li Hua made friends with peers.

"Lotus lake edge" clothing store next door is a first jewelry store, the boss named Xiao Lin, she opened a genuine jade shop, hair crystal, crystal, amethyst and so on. In contrast, Xiao Lin shop business is slow, almost no people patronize. Later, Xiao Lin and Li Hua got familiar with each other, and often went to Li Hua shop to sit and chat.

One day two people are eating melon seeds while talking, next to sports leisure clothing store female boss Xin son also smiled and walked in: "Your business is very good, always see your guests more, I want to see to take experience."

Li Hua got up and said, "Come sit down and eat some claws." The main thing is my clothes are cheap. They're ten bucks cheaper. I see a lot of students in your store to buy!"

Xin 'er said: "I am for fun, doing to pass the time." My shop assistant Xiaojun said to me, you go to the edge of the Lotus Lake, the business of that store must be good, always see in and out of the guests, so I came to see. Anyway, we are not making a style brand, there is no conflict ha!"

Xiao Lin also chimed in: "I also want to buy some clothes with Lianhu edge, so I also come to sit down."

The three female owners of a street began to talk intimately in this way, and the business of the store did as it was.

A guest came in and pointed to a floral dress hanging on the wall and said, "Is this dress what your computer says it is?"

Li Hua said: "Yes, only this one!"

Xiao Lin boss then said: "If I wear the size, I will buy it!"

Xin son boss said: "Your shop clothes how so affordable, where is the purchase?"

Li Hua knew that it was the two bosses who helped the guests make the decision to buy, and they wanted to help Li Hua make a deal one by one.

The fashionably dressed young guest, who appeared to be an art college student, asked the trio, "Which one of you is the owner of this shop?"

Li Hua came out and said, "I am." Xiao Lin and Xin 'er simultaneously pointed at Li Hua and said in unison: "She is!" Ha ha ha laughter began at the same time, and the guest and the three owners all laughed.

Li Hua grabbed a handful of melon seeds on the coffee table and handed them to the young female guest and said, "Eat and watch." You really have a good eye. This dress is my shop's favorite sample. The big red flowers, the big, stylish beauty can wear that charm. You're so stylish, you're gonna kill me. If you don't believe me, I'll take it off and you can try it on for us!"

The words made the young guest try on, and the guest standing in front of the mirror was completely different from before. "Like a star, sexy and sexy!" Hin son praised. Xiao Lin also echoed and said: "Really can't see, wear on the body effect is very good." Coupled with a necklace, hanging in the chest of the chicken heart collar, it is more attractive ah! Can you get me another one of these dresses?"

Li Hua said: "The headquarters is out of goods, this is a broken code processing to have this price."

The young guest drew the curtain and said to Li Hua, "Boss, I'll take it! I'll take it off and wrap it for me!"

Xiao Lin and Xin son admire to Li Hua smile, friendly said: "The boss is really, no wonder business is good!"

During this period and into three young girls, Xiao Lin and Xin son at the same time to help Li Hua greet the reception of the guests, Li Hua assured to receive the money, the deal just negotiated. Li Hua has been used to peer boss Xiao Lin and

Xin son to take care of the store guests, Li Hua also did not think, peer on the street bosses became friends!

When it was time for dinner, Li Hua made a phone call to order food, called to send food to "Lianhu edge" clothing store. The restaurant owner immediately said: "I know, a chili poached fish fillet, a green fried red cabbage moss, a hot and sour potato shreds, three bowls of rice!" 20 minutes later, it was sent to Li Hua's shop, Li Hua pointed to the order on the coffee table and said: "Xiao Lin, Xin son eat together, this restaurant is doing Xiang food taste, taste delicious!"

Xin 'er and Xiao Lin said at the same time: "Wow! We also care about dinner, and I will come to your shop to eat!"

Li Hua said: "Eat while it's hot, there are fewer guests now. Thank you both for helping me make some deals today!"

Xiao Lin said: "Lift a hand!"

Xin 'er said: "Don't be polite, business is people support, and your shop clothing is really cost-effective, guests can afford!"

Li Hua smiled and said: "We use water instead of wine, drink and eat, another day we go to karaoke together!"

Although it was summer at this time, the three female bosses still ate Hunan food, and kept saying: "Hot, hot really fun, too authentic."

Xiao Lin looked at Li Hua's face has been red up, looking at Xin son sweating on the forehead, choking with a smile, and did not forget to grab and say: "It seems that in the future, we will bring the business of this street to life, cheers for the prosperity of business!"

Li Hua's "Lotus Lake Edge" clothing discount store in that single woman street business surprisingly good, the overall store decoration style with other store design is different, so it is easy to find. Even delivery personnel also know "lotus lake edge" clothing store, next door jewelry store opened for many years, delivery is not clear. Xiao Lin said in a hurry: "My shop is in the lotus lake edge next door!" The delivery brother immediately replied: "Oh, I know, then you take fast food at the edge of Lotus Lake?" Just lotus lake edge boss also ordered food!"

Xiao Lin said to Li Hua, "Alas! The waiter at the restaurant will only deliver my lunch to your shop. I will not eat until I come to you!"

Li Hua said: "You are not afraid of trouble, we eat together!" I also ordered a grilled fish, I think you like it!"

Sure enough, lunch together have been sent to the "lotus Lake edge", Xiao Lin and Li Hua have lunch together like this is the norm. Later this street casual wear shop owner Xin son order also sent to lotus Lake edge. Lianhu edge of the guests also increased up, in the nearby beauty salon little beauties will also patronize Li Hua's business. Li Hua is the beauty salon quality customers, know is the beauty salon boss to let the little beauties to take care of Li Hua's business. Business partners help each other at this time reflected, Li Hua is also very moved, the friendship established is gradually deepening, each other has a lot of trust.

One day in May 2008, Li Hua woke up after 7 o 'clock as usual and began to get up to sort out the winter clothing inventory placed on the second floor of the store. This is the Beijing delivery of small Hong boss suggested a batch of distribution of old red coats. Hong said that only large quantities of goods can be eligible for the minimum discount. Li Hua listened to the suggestion of Xiaohong and advanced 40 pieces, which is also to help Xiaohong distribute a batch of tasks. The retail price can be determined according to their own market demand.

Li Hua compromised some customer information needs, she did not want to backlog winter clothes a few seasons to sell, so to QQ friends sent information, but also to some love to dress up female students called. Directly tell those old colleagues who like to wear beautiful clothes, new and old friends to come to the store and choose some clothes that suit them. See according to the purchase price plus freight, do not earn money only break-even sales, as soon as possible to reduce the backlog of cost funds, by the way to help Beijing Xiaohong more distribution point inventory. Li Hua only took out a small number of winter clothes hanging in the store as promotion.

As soon as the message was sent, the first person to return the phone call was Li Li, an old colleague who now works at Industrial and Commercial Bank of

China. In the original small city inside, Lili lives in Li Hua parents home next to the community, now also handled the internal withdrawal procedures, is idle to do nothing, heard that Li Hua opened a clothing store in the provincial capital, curiosity also want to see Li Hua.

Lily and Li Hua worked in the same factory when they were 18 years old. At that time, Lili's father was a cadre in Huanggang District, and Lili also had a brother and a sister. Lili is the most beloved and prettiest daughter.

Li Hua was a strong athlete in the factory at that time. Lily often watched Li Hua playing badminton by the court. At first just looked at Li Hua sports figure, then could not help but next practice, one to two people are familiar with. Li Hua is very self-disciplined, almost can see Li Hua playing and training in the court after work. It is often said that people who have perseverance will become great things.

Lili was attracted by Li Hua's energy, and the two became good friends who talked about everything. Later, Lili introduced her boyfriend to Li Hua. Li Hua often laughed that the boy Lili introduced to him was his first love in name only.

Li Hua from receiving Lili's phone call, intentionally or unintentionally thought of these youth interesting. How time flies! After all these years, Li Hua is looking forward to Lili coming to the store early.

Thinking of this, Li Hua said directly to the phone: "Lili you come, live in my shop, I will accompany you for two days, let you listen to my better and better experience in the past few years, you are sure to be happy!"

Lili on the other end of the phone smiled as sweet as a flower: "Even the residents have arranged for me!" After all, it is the provincial capital, see you happy, I will definitely go! By the way, my classmates got together the day before yesterday, and I gave your mobile phone number to your first love Guo Qizhi. I'll send you his cell phone number, too, so be sure to keep in touch. I forgot to tell you that he is also single now, and is also the deputy director of a tax bureau in our city, and he is also making progress. I'll tell you in person! Ha ha, you two should be able to renew the relationship?"

Li Hua smiled and said: "You really like to be a matchmaker, but also mention

these jokes about me, when you come to talk about these stories!" Now I just want to think about how to earn money to support my family, not your life is good, that is, the life of an official wife, you will know how busy I am!"

Chapter 29: Friends Show up

Girlfriend Lili is a free and easy woman, really the next day came to the "lotus lake edge" store. It was the peak hour of Li Hua's business when he entered the store. Li Hua had just received a guest and was collecting money at the cashier. Li Hua looked up and saw the smiling Lili, and also took out a coat that was being promoted: "I want this dress, so cheap you will not be a loss on clearance?"

Li Hua quickly walked out of the bar: "Is that the size you wear? Let me see what you wear!"

Lili said: "I tried it on, it fits well, and I support you. Don't tell me when the shop opens, or I'll give you a red envelope!"

Li Hua leaned close to Lili's ear and whispered: "Give you a good package, give you, you don't pull with me, let the customer see bad!"

Lili wanted to speak and stopped, only to signal Li Hua to wrap clothes for himself, and then came to the sofa and sat down, slowly looking around the store, like appreciating the treasure looked at Li Hua to do business. Li Li how also did not think Li Hua will become a businessman, is the nature of The Times ah, Li Hua from the institution to exit into the business sea workplace, from the insurance industry and transformation of investment in their own shop when self-employed, these years must have eaten a lot of pain, but also must have seen a lot of the world. Lili's eyes were full of envy and admiration.

After receiving the last guest, Li Hua picked up a brochure of Hunan Restaurant and said: "See what you want to eat, order what food, we will have dinner here today." After closing, I'll show you around Shouyi Square. Have a late night snack at the night market, the food street here is great!"

Lili said: "I wish you a prosperous business! Here you are, Guo Qizhi' s phone number, set it up! Do your business first, and contact him when you' re not busy!"

Li Hua said: "Let' s see, you have seen, where am I free?" Making money is still important! I' ll ask my daughter to watch my shop all day tomorrow, and I' ll go to see a new building with you. Tonight you will sleep with me above the shop, wronged you for one night, here is not as good as your mansion, haha!"

After saying that, Lili followed Li Hua upstairs to visit. Upstairs, there is a 1.2-meter bed on the left, a wooden bed on the right, a fashion design display cabinet directly above the stairway, and a storage space upstairs, full of incoming clothing. The room is not big, but clean and orderly, there are Windows upstairs, the Windows of the front of the shop have made anti-theft iron nets, the rear window is against the courtyard of the community, there is no anti-theft nets. There was a rope tied to the foot of the bed. Lily asked, "What does this mean?"

Li Hua smiled from ear to ear: "I' m usually afraid when I sleep alone!" Afraid of robbers and fire, in case there is any disaster, the front is not easy to escape, I can tie the rope to the back window to escape. I wish I had thought about it enough to take precautions."

When Lili heard Li Hua say this, she felt that Li Hua was really not easy, so she asked with concern: "Why don' t you fall in love and get married again?" It' s nice to have someone who loves you and takes care of you, and your pension should cover your basic expenses, but you have to keep yourself so busy?"

Li Hua said, "You will come with me tomorrow to see the opening of the new building and you will know why I want to do business." I had my eye on a house and had to open a shop to earn money to get working capital. I want to buy that house. It' s bound to go up in price. You also buy a set, the price rises and then sell, you can also make money! If you want to live for yourself, it' s a great location for both living and investment!"

Lili said, "Have you looked after the house? Let' s go and have a look tomorrow! I like houses, too. Women are afraid of not having a nest!" Li Hua got Lili approval, happily nodded and said: "This I am at ease, but also worry about where you go to play tomorrow, it is better to do a good survey of the real estate industry trend, we seize investment opportunities to gain benefits, than open a shop to make money!" If there is a need for funds and I don't have enough money to buy a house, even if I sell the clothing store, I will buy that house, you know what I mean?"

Lili kept nodding to agree with Li Hua's idea, that this decision should be more suitable for Li Hua's character than the store management - the store wasted Li Hua's talent!

The next day was Saturday, Li Hua accompanied Lili all the way to see three real estate in Wuhan, talked about a lot of past events, and also planned the idea of investing in real estate in the future. Li Hua would like to give his heart to Lili, let her believe that this is a rare opportunity to make a fortune. Li Hua talked about the few big cities he has been to in recent years, and he really has development prospects in real estate.

Li Hua was very excited about this topic, but Li Li said: "I think Wuchang is also very good, my aunt used to have several houses here, and later after the movement to overthrow capitalism, they were confiscated all the houses." I'm not at all interested in buying a house right now. I already have a 180-square-meter house, the one you saw when you went to my house. I am content to have such a house, but I am not so hard as you, the house is more difficult to take care of!"

Li Hua did not say anything more, two people said this topic is not a channel. Li Hua joked: "OK, let's eat and drink well today."

After Lili and Li Hua looked at the house, Li Hua invited Lili to have dinner, and Lili looked at her watch very contentedly and said, "I have to catch the last bus, it is very close to the bus station, I will go back to the city tonight." We walk to the bus stop, you go back to the store busy!"

Li Hua said, "Won't you stay two more days? Have you got any more coats?"

Lili said: "Always in the backpack, thank you, I am not welcome." You

remember to call Guo Qizhi, people call you, remember to answer, talk about always can have a friend!"

Li Hua nodded and smiled and said: "You also see how busy I am, multiple jobs, and when the clothing store owner, and help Taiwan Bianjie sell red wine, there are doors and Windows to do the project, wish to become the sun monkey who will be split." When is there time for love? But if he calls me, I'll answer, because I have a full life, too. Still have the courage to make money!"

Lili walked to the bus station while talking to Li Hua. The two of them said goodbye at the station. Lili sat on the car and waved to Li Hua and said, "Go back to the store quickly. Give me a call if there is any situation."

Li Hua said: "That's for sure, otherwise you will make people can't sleep!" I'll let you know how it goes! Bye!"

On weekdays, Li Huashou shop business is better than other shops, basically there are always people into the shop to see. Some of the guests have changed from passers-by to friends of Li Hua, and even some of them have the residence of Li Hua small district. Today fortunately Li Hua daughter help to look at the shop, otherwise Li Hua really can not take off to accompany Lili.

Li Hua's daughter is very sensible, knowing that her mother just opened a small shop, in order to save staff costs, did not ask staff to look at the shop. Li Hua's daughter works all day from Monday to Friday on weekdays, and only on weekends and Saturdays can she help her mother guard the store, often taking her classmates and colleagues to take care of her mother's business.

Li Hua's daughter brought eight beautiful customers this time, each of them bought more than three dresses, they all bought a red coat, all said it was too cheap. These beauties said they were going to wear red coats together to look stylish.

Li Hua knew that every time her daughter guarded the store on Saturday, she would generate income, and the business in the store was supported by her daughter's friends. Li Hua thought, this kind of business by the nature of care is a number of times, but also rely on her daughter and Li Hua's popularity, acquaintances are eager to help, it is impossible to always let people spend money on underwriting.

Every Saturday when my daughter went to the store, she would put on the most overstocked clothes in the store. The red coat looked good on her daughter in any way, and the passing guests took one look and stopped their feet. A residential sister-in-law asked: "Beautiful woman, the coat you wear, have I wear the size?"

Li Hua's daughter enthusiastically agreed: "Yes, look at the row of shelves on your side, large, medium and small sizes are complete." This is the company discount the most affordable price, value for money, great deal! You see the original price is 399 yuan, now the discounted price is only 109 yuan. If you buy two pieces, the price is only 89 yuan. You can choose to try on, buy winter in summer, it is the most money saving. A young teacher bought two pieces, said to give his daughter-in-law as a New Year's gift, the meaning of the boom is good!"

Customer A said: "Really, the price on the label is still 399 yuan, this gift friends can also take it!"

Guest B said, "Does the beautiful boss have a packing bag? I'd like to buy two, one size M and one size S. One for me, one for my bestie, and this year's New Year's red dress is done. Will you wrap it for me separately for a special price?"

Li Hua's daughter said: "No problem, give you the activity price, you are satisfied!"

Daughter business is not worse than Li Hua, but also very creative. The customer is convinced, the price is real, the meaning is good, the Chinese people themselves like to wear red clothes during the New Year festival, appear happy.

In the evening, Li Hua returned to the store and settled the income of the day with her daughter, which was 1060 denominations more than usual, and the highest turnover was 3080 yuan that day.

Chapter 30: Best Friends

A week after Lili's visit, Li Hua was in the store taking stock of the coats on sale. She was relieved that only a few coats were left. At this time, several women's voices were heard outside the door of the store, "It is here, you see the three words on the edge of the lotus Lake." Li Hua said on the phone, is to use wood bark nail on the door plate. It must be here, at last!"

Another female voice said: "It's good to find, it's this one, Li Hua also said there is a jade jewelry shop next door." Then he heard another sentence: "You two really, don't you go into the store and have a look?"

Li Hua vaguely heard who was the voice inside the glass door, quickly opened the door, "Ha ha, it is you three!" Easy to find. Come on in! Old classmates so give face to support, I am so happy ah! I didn't expect the three of you to be together!"

Three students are welcome to enter the store and sit on the sofa. Li Hua took out the prepared fruit plate and tea, made hot tea, and entertained the students. But they grew up with Li Hua's classmates, from kindergarten to junior high school are members of the basketball team, art team. One of them will do business students called Min Li, the lotus lake edge of the name of the store, is to use the name of the tea house that Min Li once opened. Li Hua heard Min Li said, junior high school teacher Yuan helped her tea house named "Lotus lake edge". Did not think that Li Hua is also used as the name of the clothing discount store, a multi-purpose - of course, not in the same place, the teahouse opened in the third-level city, but also a few years ago. Now Li Hua opened a clothing store, the same name used in different industries will not cause conflict, fortunately, the name can be reused.

Min Li smiled and said: "Our teacher Yuan must charge copyright fees, we both want to give!"

Classmate Huizhu said, "Come and visit the clothing store, let's go upstairs first." Li Hua said to let us sleep in the shop tonight. I want to see where we sleep!"

Classmate bestie Sunny said: "What's the rush? I'm not leaving today, so you can see enough." Bestie Sunny said here, or follow Huizhu upstairs, and asked: "This shop is really spacious, we sleep in this wooden bed, or sleep in that small bed?" Sunny pointed to the two sleeping places upstairs and shouted to Li Hua downstairs. Li Hua replied, "You can choose where you want to sleep. Be free with me, and listen to you!"

Min Li said: "I don't sleep here anymore, you know, I also bought a house in Wuhan Optics Valley Jindi. I'm not going to bother you, just them!"

Li Hua said: "It doesn't matter, you can sleep, how tired you rush to the past?"

Min Li said: "Very convenient, just a few minutes walk outside the store is Pengliu Yang Road platform." It's easy to get from your place to mine. It's not tiring. I often take the bus to Wuguang, Zhongnan, Hanyang Zhongjia village shopping. Don't worry about me. I'm familiar with it. Have you forgotten that the two of us and Nana were looking at houses in Wuhan together?"

Li Hua said: "Did not forget, tell you, I recently went to see the new real estate, really want to buy, than we bought two years ago more than 2000." At that time, we closed our eyes to buy a house to make money, only about 4000. Now the price has increased by more than 6,000, and there is still room for price increases, because there are so many people in big cities!"

Huizhu and Sunny from upstairs said: "You two people talk about the house again, Min Li clothes fancy?"

Min Li said: "I have chosen a red coat, my favorite two beautiful women, you two quickly choose!"

Sunny also said: "I also take a red coat, just wear the New Year, red

happiness." So cheap, the quality is good. This is the same style of clothing as the Huanggang store we often go to before, you can pick some more!"

Hui Zhu said: "I think it also looks like the type of clothing in that store!"

Li Hua said: "You two really accurate vision, there is no mistake, I just joined the small Hong boss's clothing store." She shipped directly to me in Beijing, I don't worry about buying!"

Sunny said: "So, we used to go to Xiao Hong's home shop to buy clothes, a buy seven or eight pieces, each time Li Hua bought the most!" Now that you have your own shop, you can't run out of clothes!"

Li Hua laughed and said, "You all love to buy clothes, which one bought less?"

Everyone say one word at a time, like when we were young. Sometimes they argue, sometimes they break up in a bad way, but after a few days, they get better again like nothing. Classmates are classmates, something is not in the heart, said the end is over, heartless time also had a happy spent.

Li Hua looked at Sunny, suddenly remembered a few days ago Lily mentioned the "first love" Guo Qizhi. Sunny was part of a relationship that ended before it even began. Li Hua wanted to talk to sunny about it, but Huizhu and Min Li present, Li Hua is not convenient to talk about these involved in personal privacy of the past.

Just think of that past, Li Hua felt funny again, can not help but smile on his face, the wind changed: "Pick quickly, choose quickly, today at noon in the store for dinner." Close the shop in the afternoon, and eat boiling fish and barbecue at Shouyi Snack Street in the evening. Go to the dance hall tonight. We haven't danced together in years, have we? You do not come, I have no time to play, even living so close, I did not go to play!"

Hui-ju and Sunny said, "Is there a dance hall here?"

Li Hua said, "Yes, I know you two like it. Min Li don't go back tonight, let's have a look!"

The three students all chose their favorite clothes in the Li Hua store. After the guests dispersed, they all said with one voice: "The boss has to pay the bill!"

Then put the prepared money directly on the register. "No, take it! Stop it!" All three students said so to Li Hua.

Li Hua said: "You don't have to do that, one is one, two is two. I'm already so happy you're here. Really, I want you to come and play often, and do what you want to do, okay?"

Li Hua put the change that should be changed into everyone's hands, and his heart was fine. Sunny said, "Well, I'm not afraid to be so serious!"

This day lunch in the store to order takeout, mapo tofu, fish eggplant, glutinous rice cake fish, these dishes are very rice dishes. They ate together and talked about lunch, and everyone said it was delicious. When the meal was almost finished, the guests came. Li Hua looked at the sale of a lot of clothes, they closed the shop early, to have dinner around the place shopping!

For dinner, I chose a famous restaurant with boiling fish. Fish balls, fish slices into the pot, the spicy taste into the mouth, everyone said: "fun! It tastes so authentic!"

Everyone said that they were full and wanted to go out for a walk, and when they came out, it was already the time when the ballroom was about to open, opening at eight o 'clock in the evening and ending at ten o 'clock. With a band, it's a dancing atmosphere. The light shines in the crowd, flickering, the warm light of the atmosphere is ambiguous in the dancing crowd swept through the shuttle. Li Hua watched the students dancing very relaxed, and she was also dancing wildly. Jump fast three waltz, or used to choose to jump with sunny, Sunny as a male companion, Li Hua jump female companion pace, or the original familiar dance music. Although the physical strength is not as good as that year, but the two of them thought of the naughty scene of dancing when they were young, and simultaneously laughed all at once.

Li Hua said: "So long no dance, still very cool ah!"

Sunny said: "Yes, you are heavier than before, I can hardly carry you, ha ha!"

Li Hua said: "Haha, you are getting fat and fat, you should continue to exercise yo!"

Sunny said, "Yes, when I go back to the city, I will ask my friend Ah Xiang to do square dancing."

Min Li was dragged into the ballroom together. Huizhu was asked to run by a handsome man, the ballroom flying. When the slow song, Min Li was also asked by a man to jump a slow four steps. Everyone had a great time that night, and they all sweated. Li Hua said: "This is the best exercise for beauty, sweating is the whole body detoxification!"

Until 10:00 the dance floor, all of them are not satisfied, walk back to the shop. After showering, the four of them huddled directly on the wooden bed on the floor, chatting in their pajamas and laughing at each other from time to time. We talked until the second half of the night, and then slowly fell asleep. Four people were lying across the plank of the floor, and the 1.2-meter bed in the room was empty. The students really wish never to grow up, heartless in the age of pure students to stop, this friendship can not be false, a reunion is so happy.

This is the close relationship between the little bestie, do not know whether there is such an iron relationship in the future, what can be said, what can also not care about, you can not decorate to cover up their emotions, such friendship is really expensive, just like the song sung by a Taiwanese singer in that era, love is priceless!

Chapter 31: Advice from Friends

The next morning, the three old classmates woke up early, and Li Hua ate breakfast together, according to the agreed plan, Sunny and Huizhu directly walk to the river by ferry, to the opposite Hanzheng Street, a famous wholesale market in Wuhan; Min Li gets on the bus at the nearby bus stop and goes back to her home. Li Hua waved goodbye to his classmates and then walked back to the shop alone to open for business. Li Hua was trying to read the memo on the calendar when suddenly the phone rang: "Hello! Li Hua, tomorrow I will come to Wuhan in the morning to hold a meeting on epidemic prevention of the WHO. In the afternoon, I may come to your shop with the driver and help me choose some clothes suitable for me to wear! See you tomorrow afternoon, and I'll invite you to dinner tonight!"

Wei Yue happily said on the phone, Li Hua was very happy to say: "Nothing, with your time to come, I am waiting for you in the store." I'll text you the address of the store on your phone, and your driver will know how to get here!"

Li Hua thought, today is really a good day, just sent off a wave of old classmates, and received a high school female students to the store Wei-Yueiyue phone. On weekdays, Wyatt didn't say much. She was the most simple of Li Hua's friends, but she always gave warm support to Li Hua. Wei Yuet-Yue's lover Xianghe is also Li Hua's classmate, but also in the last semester of high school when the graduating class cadre, as the league branch secretary. Did not expect this classmate auspicious into the society became Wei Yueyue lover. One works in medicine, the other in business. What's more, because of Wei Yue's kind and good character, Li Hua and the couple of classmates also became the best friends. Later, Li Hua knew from the mouth of Wei Yue that Xiang and his classmates were

hospitalized for a period of time because of illness, during which he met Wei Yue and began to pursue.

Li Hua and Wei Yue's classmates friendship has been very stable, from Li Hua married, gave birth to a child, birthday, Li Hua remarried please witness the students, also only please Wei Yue and peace two people. Later, Li Hua also became a matchmaker with Wei Yue, and promoted a marriage for another single female student!

Li Hua thought that he could see Ms. Wei tomorrow afternoon, and his heart was filled with joy. Li Hua likes Wei Yue's low-key, steady and easy-going personality. Li Hua has a lot of confidant will tell Wei Yue talk, she knows Wei Yue never pass words nor laugh at her, always in need of help in Li Hua's side, silently listening to Li Hua pour out the distress! This kind of friendship let Li Hua rest assured at ease, looking forward to the arrival of Wei Yue in the afternoon of the next day, she wanted to talk!

Sure enough, in the afternoon of the second day, "Lotus Lake edge" to meet the arrival of Yue Wei. The driver entered the store and said, "Director Wei, you and your classmates talk first, I'll park the car and come back!"

"Xiao Li," said Wyatt, "you first take the fruit in the car to the shop, and then you go and park the car, and then come and sit down!"

Ms. Wei calmly treated her colleague Xiao Li, the driver, with a very modest attitude and no shelf. Wei Yueyue is relying on the hard level of professional technology, growing day by day in the professional cadres stand out, and finally become a well-deserved chief physician!

Wei Yue took over Li Hua handed over a few clothes, into the curtain behind the try, not only fit, but also stylish and decent! Coming out of the curtain, Ms. Wei said, "You picked really well, and then help me choose a few more clothes to see if there are any peaceful clothes to wear?" There are also the clothes that Xiao Li, the driver, is wearing, you help him choose some of them!"

Li Hua knows that this is Wei Yue to take care of her shop business, it is not easy to come. Li Hua also know that the medical work is very busy, after the meeting all thought of looking at her, this friendship is very rare.

Li Hua said, "If you really need all of it, take it away; Don't buy anything you don't need, don't take care of my business, understand?"

Wei Yue's driver Xiao Li quickly came forward to Li Hua and said: "You don't know, Director Wei told me on the road, today to the classmate shop to pick more good clothes, absolutely affordable." A look in, it is really real, but also the brand discount, sure we all need to buy!"

Wyatt said, "Why should I be polite to you? I really do! It's really cheap. Two XL for men, and two tops for my son. Otherwise they'll say I'm selfish and unfair. You can't go back empty-handed on a trip, count it together, divide it into two bags. After that, we'll go to dinner together, and we'll take care of you and close the shop early today!"

Li Hua did not speak much, she thought in her heart, this is the intention to take care of her business. False words Li Hua also said not to export, she to Wei Yueyue this high school classmates is really plain to see the truth. They are busy on weekdays, and once something happens in their work and life, the two people will think of each other and try to help.

At the hotel dinner table in the evening, the dishes ordered by Xiao Li, the driver, are all Hunan dishes that Li Hua likes to eat, which is really careful to take care of Li Hua's heavy taste. These are all Wei Yue told the driver Xiao Li order don't forget the main menu, still remember Li Hua love to eat, and even more some staple food, let the waiter pack, let Li Hua take the store to eat tomorrow.

Wyatt said: "My sister used to open an auto parts store, long-term store, eating is not convenient, I often send food to." So I understand it's not easy being on your own. When you eat, you can turn the microwave oven and eat it, and cooking in the store is not convenient, and it is not easy to make good taste, do you think?"

Wei Yue always thinks for Li Hua in the details of life, this move makes Li Hua especially moved. After Li Hua divorced so many years of single life, only Li Hua put himself as a man to make money to take care of his family and daughter, no

one can accompany to take care of themselves in small things in life. Wei Yue these natural and intentional care and consideration, so that Li Hua in the heart is very warm, Li Hua some appreciate Wei Yue sincere simple and approachable kindness. Li Hua appreciate Wei Yueyue tepid quiet character, good impression is also the main reason for friendship together.

Li Hua said: "I want to buy a house after some time, I think I have to sell the house next, so that I can have funds to invest in real estate." I think it's better to invest in a house, and it's not so hard. I work 12 hours a day, all by myself, the salesperson, the boss, everything, I've been trained, everything. To start a business is to be prepared to worry!"

Li Hua talked a little more that day, but he was telling the truth. That night ate a lot and talked a lot, through the exchange, Wyatt also said good advice: "You are suitable for doing anything, in fact, we all see real estate opportunities to make money than the current clothing store."

Li Hua then said: "Yes, to do this clothing store is to invest less, the money back quickly." But the time spent in the shop limits me, and I can't get away to do other things. So this time to inspect a few big real estate to find a breakthrough. These several real estate is really good, like Wuchang jade bridge Jindi, as well as the landmark green property, and Han Street real estate project. These big buildings, if you have money to buy it, you earn it. Do you have any plans to buy a house for your children in the provincial capital in the future?"

"I only have one son, and we let the child follow us, so that when I retire, I can take care of my son and help him," she said. But you are different, since you are already in the provincial capital, you must buy a house as soon as possible, and live in peace and contentment. If you invest in a house, you can free up time and make more money. Then seize the opportunity, time is money!"

Li Hua's mind was Wei Yue understand, and very support Li Hua. Li Hua knew something in mind: "I may make a decision in the near future to let the clothing store transfer out during the period of business earning money." Recoup the investment costs and profits, and invest all the down payment of two housing projects. That's how you get a home loan. If you decisively make a clothing store, you can connect to seize this good real estate project investment. I'm done with it, let's do it!"

Wei Yue said to Li Hua with a gentle smile: "In fact, you have your own mind, but you must get the affirmation of others." In the future, you can ignore the advice of others and follow your own feelings. I'm a medical student, but I also think sometimes a woman's sixth sense is very accurate, trust yourself!"

The dinner was more than just a meal. The more important meaning for Li Hua was to gain recognition and carry out his plan firmly. Li Hua considered a whole package of transfer plans and made three very attractive terms. Sure enough, within a week, it quickly turned out and returned the rent in the first half of the year in the landlord's hands. According to the contract, half a month's rent will be directly awarded to the owner of the transfer shop. In this way, it seems that Li Hua lost half a month's rent, but in order to transfer smoothly, appease the landlord not to make trouble to stop, in the case that various conditions do not affect the interests of the landlord, the landlord has to compromise and cooperate with Li Hua to transfer smoothly.

Due to the timely integration of funds, Li Hua put all the recovered costs and profits, all invested in the already optimistic two real estate: one is Wuchang Jidi Garden, one is Hankou Vanke real estate. All as Li Hua hoped, Li Hua's investment property operation was successful again, for her daughter to invest in the real estate under her name before marriage, but also for themselves in the provincial capital to invest in a small apartment in the downtown area.

On the last day of the clothing store, an unexpected visitor appeared outside Li Hua's store. Who was he?

Chapter 32: Meeting Your First Love

After the transfer of Li Hua's clothing store, the first time to set the house things, deal with all the most urgent things. According to the terms and conditions of the contract, Li Hua's stored things should be cleared out within a week. Just two days before the check-out, Li Hua still had an electric water heater to tow away. These days have put Li Hua busy enough, a moment is not idle, the daughter also use the rest of the time to help. At this time, Li Hua's phone rang: "Hello! Is it Li Hua?"

Li Hua listened to the call and asked in surprise, "Who are you, are you not wrong?" Just say what you want, I'm busy right now!"

The other party did not hang up: "It's me! Lily didn't tell you? I am Guo Qizhi, now outside the clothing store, why does it look empty?"

Li Hua said: "You stand there don't move, I clean things upstairs, immediately downstairs!"

Although Guo Qizhi and Li Hua have not met for more than ten years, but the voice between each other can still be heard. At that moment of meeting, everyone seemed to be familiar, not strange at all. Guo Qizhi said hello to Li Hua, "I didn't think of it, I came to see you." Bad timing. Why'd you get transferred out? If I hadn't come today, I wouldn't have found you! This is God help me, just in time! Is there anything I can help you with? I can follow your command today, I have nothing else to do!"

Li Hua is anxious to find someone to help, Guo Qizhi uninvited, the Li Hua's "first love object" appeared too timely. If in the past, maybe Li Hua will pretend to refuse euphemistically, the woman's reserve to show. Now Li Hua more calm, Guo Qizhi also count their own acquaintances, greatly accept each other's help. Looking at Guo Zhiqi not seen for many years, Li Hua did not consciously think of that period of the past.

At that time, it was the 1980s, Li Hua and Lili met because of playing ball, and the two became good friends. Once Lili was ill in hospital, Li Hua went to the hospital to visit Lili. Just into the ward, Li Hua saw Lili sitting on the bed turning over the magazines and books, as if ready to go out for a walk.

Lili asked Li Hua, "Oh! Why are you here?"

Li Hua said, "Why didn't you tell me you were sick?"

Lili said, "Nothing is wrong! I came to the good body weak, can not go to the late night shift, came to the hospital after examination, said I was weak, need to recuperate the body. Stay here during the day, and I'm going home at night! Fortunately, you came early, or I would have gone back!"

Li Hua said: "No serious illness is good, so I quickly came to see you!" Let's sit down and go back together."

Lili said, "I just want to tell you two things, do you know Wenbin, the elder son of the finance section?" Every day when we play badminton together, the person who plays the guitar to the side of the court, you should remember?"

Li Hua nodded and remembered that there was such a person. Lili said, "It seems that people like you and ask if you have a boyfriend." When I said no, he asked me to ask you if you would like to be his girlfriend."

Li Hua was shocked: "Make no mistake! You must not tell me, I will not fall in love in the factory, I do not want to find a factory boyfriend!"

Lili said, "No, I don't want to make friends with people who work in the factory." You're on the same page as me. Why don't I set you up with a boyfriend? My classmate just returned from the army, his father is the director of the office of the administration, his mother used to work in our factory, and then found a connection to transfer. One day I will help you contact, let you know, you can be friends to understand. He certainly looks younger than the treasurer's son. He is coming to visit me in the hospital tomorrow, and you should come to see me in the hospital tomorrow at this time, as if by chance. This is an opportunity, my

father's comrades to introduce me to the boyfriend also lives in the administration compound, my boyfriend's father is the commissioner of the administration, they two families I know, are cadres family, you rest assured. Don't tell anyone I have a boyfriend!"

Hearing so many secrets at once, Li Hua's heart beat nervously. She did not think about the problem of boyfriend, she felt that she had a colorful life: she went to work when she was working, played ball games after work, or practiced dancing and singing, and went to the open-air swimming pool to learn swimming at weekends. These days are also very happy. I didn't expect to face the problem of falling in love soon, maybe fate came to it.

Li Hua is the oldest daughter in the family, as the saying goes, "A family of adopted daughters want a hundred." In order to eliminate the idea of the factory's finance section chief son, Li Hua also want to quickly open the news of a boyfriend, so that the son of the finance section chief can not take the initiative to refuse and offend him, Li Hua is also afraid of offending his father, the finance section chief - after all, Li Hua is still working and living in this temporarily, Li Hua does not want to "do not eat mutton but get embarrassed." This aspect must be dealt with a good sense of proportion, so Li Hua promised Lili's arrangement, when the chance encounter with Lili's classmates to meet on one side.

Li Hua arrived the next day. This time Li Hua's footsteps are deliberately light, she does not want to disturb others, she wants to see what Lili introduced the retired soldiers look like, and also want to hear what they talk about. Li Hua stood gently at the door for a while and heard Lili say, "I introduced you to your girlfriend, but she has never been in love before." Some of the leaders' sons fancy her, but she just doesn't look up to them. She has a really nice personality and she's very capable. After you meet, you leave your contact information, ask other girls more, you won't let me teach you to fall in love?"

The retired soldier was none other than Guo Qizhi. Guo Qizhi said: "Thank you Lili for the introduction, I am also serious. My mother said that as long as she became a member of our family, she would help transfer Li Hua out of the factory and go to a better work unit in the future. Depending on fate, my family relationship is simple, there are four people in my family, my parents and a sister."

Li Hua looked at the back of the lily to speak to Guo Qizhi, listening to what he just said, feel this Guo Qizhi really calm!

At this time, Lili had already seen Li Hua standing at the door, took a look at Li Hua, and continued to ask Guo Qizhi: "When are you going to take Li Hua to meet your parents?"

Guo Qizhi said: "Depending on Li Hua, I can choose any weekend to go to my home for dinner. I'm all set for the greeting, a yellow women's army bag, a women's watch, and a women's army uniform. These are all from the former female soldiers when I was in the army, both stylish and memorable, and now it is very popular for girls to wear military uniforms. I have gifts that money can't buy."

Guo Qishi said the truth, in the early 1980s, can wear the army women's pants, yellow hanging bag on the back, and put on a pair of high-heeled shoes, just like the dress of the high-level children of literature and art soldiers. In this dress, the girl looks dignified and has an unusual temperament.

Li Hua is also a mortal, hearing here in the heart and Lili like a little happy and proud, can not help but laugh out loud. Guo Qizhi turned and looked towards the door. The woman standing in front of him was Li Hua. He saw Li Hua petite curve slim, just match his height, a round baby face, looking simple and sweet, is the type of girlfriend he likes.

Guo Qizhi said: "You are Li Hua, we are talking about you!"

Li Hua looked at some dark skin color Guo Qizhi: big eyes very bright, wearing a white shirt, with the army army pants, a pair of black leather shoes, looks very elegant and stable, with the military habit of standing straight posture is standing in the ward, there is a military style. Li Hua had a good feeling, but after all, it is the first time to meet such an occasion, Li Hua is still embarrassed to look at Guo Qizhi a glance, directly to Lili walked with a smile.

Lili came forward to take Li Hua's hand to Guo Qizhi and said: "My task

is completed, you will agree on your own appointment time, I can not care." Remember, you are a man should take the initiative!"

Guo Qizhi smiled and said: "Thank you old classmates for helping, I will!"

Li Hua's brain quickly thought of these, and suddenly felt that time passed really fast, and it was middle-aged in a flash. The former young man has now become Uncle Guo, Guo Qizhi is slightly overweight, and now Li Hua himself wants to laugh, she can also calmly talk with Guo Qizhi like a friend, and there is no other meaning. Like the feelings of an old acquaintance and old friend, generous and casual but measured distance, just to cover up the initial germination of a little "hypothesis and then continue the leading edge" idea.

Through the baptism of time, love and friendship see the light at the same time, and soon distinguish. A man who has become Uncle Guo knows that he is doomed! Because Li Hua, standing beside him, no matter in the face in the body in the cause, did not leave traces of years, but felt in reverse growth, but more of a mature woman's charm, still have the charm of the young age, really no less than the first time to see the same appearance.

Chapter 33: Once Upon a Time

Young people in the '80s were shy when they first fell in love. Every time Li Hua and Guo Qizhi date will call sunny together, three people side by side, walk along the edge of the road, Li Hua in the middle, right is sunny, left is first love Guo Qizhi.

On the first date, Li Hua dare not stare at Guo Qizhi casually, call bestie Sunny more secretly observe. In this way, the weekly date has become a date of three people, each time will start to walk from Li Hua's unit, send Sunny to the unit dormitory, the two people return to Li Hua's unit dormitory building. On the way, we will pass a big stadium of a technical secondary school, and the two people will walk two circles along the big playground and chat all over the country.

In that era, lovers in love will even hold hands and their hearts will speed up. Once they encountered a ditch, Li Hua followed Guo Qizhi to jump over, and was pulled by Guo Qizhi's hands tightly at that moment, both of them were embarrassed and embarrassed to loosen. It was a summer evening, only scattered people walking, no one cared about them. The night breeze blew over the leaves nearby, and the chirping of cicadas in the trees made a ditch of frogs sing -- even the small animals laughed at the two men. At that time is Li Hua in love with the beginning of the season, Li Hua this embarrassed look, let Guo Qizhi see fascinated. He wanted to take things to the next level. Guo Qizhi couldn't wait to say, "My whole family would like to meet you. Can we come to my home this weekend?"

Li Hua smiled and said nothing, this is like the wind blowing past the ear, listening to the ear, the heart feels warm. Girl love open, just began to germinate may be such a feeling? By this time the two people have been walking while talking, back to Li Hua's unit dormitory gate. The time to get along is really short, the love road is shallow, just started to go. This time, Li Hua was shy and did not reply Guo Qizhi's invitation in time.

Another weekend, Li Hua was practicing badminton with Lili on the court. Sunny had been invited to stand next to the court, and after some time Guo Qizhi also came.

Guo Qizhi looked at Li Hua on the court swinging a badminton racket figure, Li Hua every youth jump vigorous vitality have tightly attracted his eyes. When Li Hua came off the court, Guo Qizhi handed water to Li Hua and said to Li Hua, "I really can't see you playing badminton so well."

Lili then said: "Old classmate you don't know, Li Hua has been our two consecutive women's competition runner-up, you come to date today?" Lili made a face and smiled and said: "I am not a light bulb, I go home, you go around!"

Sunny smiled and said, "I watched you play from beginning to end, and it got better and better!" Where shall we go later? I'm working a late night shift today, so I can stay with you for two hours as long as it doesn't interfere with the 10:00 p.m. shift."

It was summer, and though it was already past seven o 'clock in the evening, it was still light and dark. Li Hua looked at Guo Qizhi and asked, "Where are you going to take us today?"

Guo Qizhi affectionately looked at Li Hua in front of him, wanted to say something and did not say it, shaking his head while looking at the foot and whispering: "My mother asked me to invite you to my home this Saturday to have dinner and meet my family, today I am here to tell you about this matter." You didn't answer me last time, and my family is still waiting to hear from me. Let's just walk around the neighborhood, don't you think?"

Li Hua thought for a moment and said: "Then let's take Sunny back to her unit to catch up with the night shift, we walk back slowly, we can talk on the way, OK?"

Li Hua and Guo Qizhi dating always have girlfriends Sunny accompany, in that era is also very normal, as if if there is not a witness, it will be uncomfortable. Li

Hua is such a psychological, with a BFF beside their courage is also big, dare to play some jokes, active atmosphere, showing the naughty nature.

From the Li Hua unit through a technical secondary school stadium, walk to a street, and then walk forward for 10 minutes, you can see Sunny's bed sheet factory gate. Li Hua and Guo Qizhi every time will send sunny to the other side of the road bed factory gate, see sunny walk in, the two talents turned back to Li Hua's unit.

On the way back, Guo Qizhi asked curiously, "Have you always been this good with Sunny?"

Li Hua said, "Yes, we have been going to school and playing ball together since we were young. I went to her home to learn to make dumplings, she likes to eat our mother made salted fish salted vegetables. Since childhood, we have been so good that we are not divided into you and me, and I want to give her a share of what is delicious. She has a good personality and always comes to my home to have classes with me every day. I am the eldest in the family, there are a lot of housework I have to do, she helps me take out the garbage bag. Later, they worked together, but they didn't share the same factory."

Guo Qizhi listened to Li Hua say some interesting things with Sunny children, and forgot to ask Li Hua about the answer to see the family next Saturday. Soon returned to the gate of Li Hua unit. Guo Qizhi only said, "Good night, maybe I will come to the factory some time on Friday afternoon to see you and see the workshop where you work?" Can we just meet and talk about this this time?"

Li Hua responded quickly: "This is not good, the workshop is a place of work, what is good to see?" Who dates at work?"

Guo Qizhi wanted to speak and stopped, and finally did not ask export. Looking at Li Hua turned into the dormitory building, only to quickly turn around and leave, the pace is like a soldier's appearance, decisive, resolute, as if to make a decision to themselves, "Friday afternoon I must promise Li Hua!"

Soon it was Friday, Li Hua was working in the workshop, the machine was buzzing. In front of the workshop came a stranger, pick up the plumber master Yan

asked, to the young man into the workshop: "Young man who are you looking for? This is where the workshop works!"

The bearer is not others, it is Guo Qizhi, he is really line, really found Li Hua's work workshop. This will cause a bad impact, Li Hua was Yan master called out, in a hurry to ask Guo Qizhi: "How you come here, so the impact is not good!" What's the hurry?"

Guo Qizhi looked around, seemed not anxious at all, just slowly said: "My mother, father and sister, the whole family set this Sunday, must I bring you to my home for dinner, you promise me!" I'll leave at once."

"Alas! Is that what this is about? Why don't you find me when you're working in the workshop?"

Li Hua worried that the workshop leader saw the criticism can not be good, which apprentice fell in love was chased to the work place? Li Hua urged: "You go quickly, my mother said, a girl in love must be the man's parents first on the woman's home, the woman can then go to the man's home, this is a social custom." Your family is a cadre family, don't you know how to respect these customs?"

Guo Qizhi was puzzled and continued: "What kind of problem is this, it is already a new society, and it is still so feudal and superstitious?" What's wrong with just having dinner and getting to know each other? You must go, our family have prepared for you to meet the gift, a watch, a set of green military uniform and yellow military hanging bag, which is the most popular now. Come to my house first this time, and prepare to go to your house next time, OK?"

Li Hua's mind was running fast, like a row of spinning machines. A few seconds later Li Hua seemed determined, lowering his voice but very serious to Guo Qizhi said: "You go first, I think well, I can't go to your house." If my mother knew that a girl's family went to the man's family first, she would be very sad, and even accuse me of being ignorant. My mother said, a girl must be reserved, in order to get the real respect of the man's family! If you want to go, you should go to my home first, my family agrees, and then you can go to your home!"

Guo Qizhi did not speak, he went to the workshop a little angry, and finally slowly turned back to Li Hua said: "Then we scattered it, if you insist not to go, I only with the family account!"

Li Hua also angrily pushed back: "Is it important? Go or break up? When they break up, they break up! That's what you said! Okay, I agree it's over, and you can tell your family whatever you want. No, I have to get back to work!"

The two parted on bad terms. Is this the end of the first love? Even Li Hua feels confused. It's over before it starts. Think about it all feel so wrong! To be a good girl is to give up the chance to love? Li Hua is a little irritable, listen to mother's words should not be wrong, what about him? If you don't respect a girl's advice, then it's gonna be harder to listen to who?

Li Hua didn't say much, just buried himself in his work. This is the third time she refused the opportunity to fall in love, in order to listen to her mother's words, be a good daughter, be a sensible daughter. Li Hua felt that he had done nothing wrong, but Guo Qizhi also seemed to have done nothing wrong, so what went wrong? At that time, the ideology was created, and the selection criteria were chosen according to the traditional rules, which would not be wrong.

Anyway, this thing is yellow, there is no game, fortunately, Li Hua is a person who loves life, hobbies are extensive, playing basketball, volleyball, badminton, swimming, cycling, dancing, singing, knitting hand-work, all take up all of Li Hua's rest time. This life is also very fulfilling, Li Hua is just back to the happy single life. Lili didn't say anything about Li Hua after knowing that, just said: "You are very picky about finding a boyfriend, if you marry Guo Qizhi, you will certainly be able to transfer out of this factory and arrange a more comfortable job." Li Hua also answered and said, "Yes, Guo Qizhi said that his mother is from my unit, my workshop to work in administrative institutions." It would matter if he had the skill, but not the patience."

Three months passed quietly. One Friday afternoon, Li Hua was getting ready to go to work when Guo Qizhi stopped him by the side of the road.

Guo Qizhi said: "I want to ask you for help, I want to talk to your bestie Sunny friends, do you mind?"

Li Hua did not react at the moment, she really did not expect Guo Qizhi to find himself because of such a purpose. At that time Li Hua felt ridiculous, almost self-amorous thought Guo Qizhi regret, to recover themselves. I really did not expect that the first love in life would change so dramatically.

Li Hua pretended to be relaxed and dismissive and said, "Well, I wish you all the best. I don't mind, I don't mind, really!"

Li Hua finished walking directly to the crowd of work, who knows Guo Qizhi chased up and said: "Can you accompany me to say it in person today?" Sunny wants you to say you don't mind kissing!"

Chapter 34: Perfect Atmosphere

Li Hua stopped, looking at Guo Qizhi in front of him, thinking: Anyway, why not be a good person and help them. Although some unhappy in the heart, actually and such a man talked about love when friends, Li Hua felt funny, but very fortunate, and Guo Qizhi nothing happened.

Of these two people, one is a good friend, and the other is a boyfriend who has just started his first love and has not yet had passion. Li Hua did not love Guo Qizhi to the depths of the feeling, has not experienced the kind of dead and alive love. They seem to have just held hands, not even hugged and kissed. The date between the two is a movie. This is not a bad emotion to put down, at least Li Hua has not suffered, lost; Neither let Guo Qizhi look down on, no big mistake in principle, no hatred, and did not say words that hurt each other.

Thinking of this, Li Hua shouted the name of a workmate in the crowd: "Chen Xiang, please tell Ben Sufen for me to go to work, I have something urgent, let her cover my class!" I'll take her shift tomorrow!"

He turned to Guo Qizhi and said, "Let's go, this favor will help you, and don't look for me in the future."

Li Hua's decisiveness surprised Guo Qizhi and immediately said, "OK, let's go now!" She should be off duty!"

Li Hua felt good atmosphere, if other women listen to this, must be angry. But Li Hua is unusually calm, two people walk one after the other. The road at this time is exactly the road they have walked countless times, the place has not changed, but the heart has changed.

Really unexpected, Li Hua admire themselves can be so calm, treat Guo Qizhi and Sunny this thing is like a contradiction between friends. Li Hua also understand,

with Guo Qizhi know, almost every date with sunny three people together, this relationship in the participants are three people. If there are feelings between them, it is also normal, after all, love is a matter of two people, you love I want to go together.

The only date was Li Hua watching a movie with Guo Qizhi. The film is Shaolin Temple, Li Hua also learned the film's theme song "Shepherd song". For a long time, as long as went to the K singing hall, Li Hua will intentionally or unintentionally sing this song "Shepherd song". This is the spiritual brand left by that era, Li Hua also used it to commemorate that short-lived feelings. Li Hua thought of himself as the first love, in fact, with the modern sense of the world, it is not called love, not first love, it is just in life after getting on the car, passing a station must pass the road, did not arrive at the destination, got off at the halfway station.

Ten minutes of journey is not long, but Li Hua thought all the way, think about it or feel shallow fate with Guo Qizhi.

Soon came to Sunny's dormitory door, Li Hua often come here, is very familiar with it. Li Hua and Guo Qizhi stood side by side knocking on the door, in the dormitory Sunny promised: "Who is it?" Come in!"

Li Hua push the door at that moment, sunny see Li Hua side of Guo Qizhi, everything understood. Without waiting for Li Hua to say it, he was anxious to say: "Don't listen to him, I haven't promised it!"

Li Hua was very calm and peaceful to Sunny said: "I am specifically asking for leave to come and tell you that I really don't need to consider my reasons, you talk about friends, I really have no opinion, because nothing happened between me and him." As long as you don't mind us talking about friends, you have my blessing and I have to go!"

Li Hua finished speaking and turned to walk away. Guo Qizhi was also driven out by Sunny: "You go, I'm going to work the night shift soon!" Don't come to me again! What a mess!"

After doing this, Li Hua was relieved, as if he had completed a task and completely put it down. Who says women are in pain when they lose love. Li Hua did not feel pain, but rationally felt sorry. Sometimes Li Hua will feel that this regret may be a kind of psychological camouflage, pretending to be relaxed for missing a love. Li Hua was so calm and poised at that time, just slipping away a little bit of unhappiness in his heart, and this thing passed quickly. It seems that it is not the first love, just let Li Hua experience the feeling of love.

Since then, I saw Guo Qizhi again, it was in the Li Hua unit building. After more than ten years, Li Hua did not think about the fate of meeting Guo Qizhi, which is like a movie. At that time, Li Hua was already a divorced single woman, focused on work, was the director of the center in the municipal Bureau office, mainly responsible for the administrative affairs of the unit, the management of the canteen, including the purchase of ingredients, the management of chefs and waiters, and the reception of business guests in the province and the city, but also to catch the food and beverage work of the canteen of staff cadres.

One day, a tall man walked into the office on the third floor. He knocked on the door and asked, "Excuse me, is Director Li Hua there?"

Li Hua just in the office to review the purchase bill invoice, looked up at the middle-aged man, very handsome, but do not know, and asked: "Excuse me, what do you find her?"

The man said in a Huangzhou dialect, "I'm not looking for her, but our director Guo is looking for her."

Li Hua heard the accent and asked puzzled: "Which director Guo? Are you from Huanggang?"

The man immediately replied, "Yes, it is Director Guo Qizhi." He's waiting in the hall downstairs to see Director Li Hua!"

Li Hua thought: Is it him? How did he find his way here? I haven't seen each other in years! Li Hua thought for a while, came forward to the man said: "She is not available today, to have a meeting, you go back!"

The man asked unwillingly: "Then when free, let me go down so that I can reply!"

Li Hua thought about it and said: "Then on January 16, if you Guo director leadership still remember this day."

The man seems to be whitening. The woman in front of her should be Director Li Hua. Her dress is also a little strange. The man exited the office and walked slowly toward the elevator with his head down. Li Hua was relieved at this time, fortunately, she came early in the office, and the people in other departments did not meet.

Li Hua's heart accelerated, thinking: What is the wind to blow him to come, I can no longer be afraid of you, you think when the director of the great? Hey hey, I'm not bad, there's nothing to be afraid of!

Li Hua thought and took out the mirror of the drawer and looked at himself. Take off the sunglasses and slowly look at the nose, which was enlarged only two weeks ago, and the swelling is slowly going down. "If you want to see me, I have not met for more than ten years, we must let him see the best side." Even if there is no purpose, also have to maintain a good image, not to mention such a first love, even fall in love are changing, fortunately did not talk, just did a good job, the feeling of rejection is really cool!"

Thinking of these, Li Hua looked forward to the arrival of that day with peace of mind. She didn't understand why she was doing it, to prove her charm.

God knows what Li Hua was thinking. It doesn't matter. Li Hua said the day is his birthday. Li Hua, give each other a chance to meet, as an old friend together once.

On her birthday, Li Hua went to work as usual, only wearing a bright silk scarf on the basis of professional clothing. At 11 o 'clock Guo Qizhi's phone called Li Hua on time: "I am in front of the office building, the car parked in front of the road, or parked in the backyard of the unit?"

Li Hua said: "You park in the roadside parking space in front of the building, you go directly to the second floor of the rear auxiliary building, I will wait for you here!" I'll treat you to lunch!"

Guo Qizhi said: "You know what, I brought wine, go out to eat!"

Li Hua said: "It doesn't matter, to me here to see me, I invite you to eat a potluck just, don't be polite with me!"

The other end of the line paused for a moment: "Well, respect is better than obey!"

Guo Qizhi said awkwardly, Li Hua stood on the second floor walkway, looking at the first love that has not been seen for more than ten years, the heart suddenly felt funny. She herself does not know why to this man so warm hospitality, it should be a little hate, after all, he had chased Li Hua's best girlfriend girlfriends, this matter for a woman how is a kind of harm. How could Guo Qizhi forget this? Why did he have the courage to find himself? What a strange man!

They met and looked at each other again and again, "You haven't changed a bit!" "You have become beautiful and well maintained!"

The two complimented each other, sat down in the small box for guests, Guo Qizhi looked around the clean and bright restaurant, took the red wine he brought on the table, "Drink this bottle today, good wine!"

Li Hua thought, micro plastic surgery is still necessary, she is not beautiful for others, but to please yourself happy! Young is good, to let the face can not see the traces of years, she is glad to invest in themselves.

At that time, micro plastic surgery was one of the most luxurious investments, and not many people were willing to. Li Hua is willing to spend money for study, sports, but also buy beautiful clothes, do beauty; No gambling, no smoking, no bad habits, self-control, and can withstand temptation!

This is the first feeling that Guo Qizhi met Li Hua this time, mature and intellectual beauty, more connotation than Li Hua when she was a girl. He knew that Li Hua in front of him had experienced the temper of life, and was no longer the simple girl of that year, but he could still feel her kindness and humility in her bones. Li Hua is still charming, from the professional clothes can see that the figure is full and playful, the high heels in the corridor knocking the sound is very appealing.

Now Li Hua's shadow is churning in Guo Qizhi's mind, appearing in front of him scene by scene. I thought before I came here, and I'm too embarrassed to say

it. He thought that he was single, and when the director of the tax bureau, he should still be qualified to chase Li Hua. Don't know how, after seeing Li Hua, he was afraid of losing the opportunity to contact, dare not mention emotional problems, only like visiting old friends calmly talk about old times.

The two talked about the movie they watched together before, and Guo Qizhi's own time as a child, only to know that he was also insecure. Guo Qizhi's father was sent to work during the movement, when he was young, but also to take care of his sister to eat, and his mother often worked overtime, rarely to take care of him and his sister.

Li Hua received the working dinner has been on the table, and ordered two dishes, Li Hua remembered that it was Guo Qizhi's favorite braised crucian carp, spiced steamed pork. Guo Qizhi was very moved, he did not know why Lili wanted to tell him Li Hua's recent situation and mobile phone number. He only knows that Li Hua is single, so is he. Maybe Lily wants to push them to renew their relationship. The two of them are purely historical fate, so that there are less strangers between them, and more trust in tolerance!

Lili always felt that it was a pity that they were separated, and did not make any big mistakes, and even thought that they were young at that time and missed a good marriage that should have been there - otherwise why did God let two people be single again? Lili is the witness of their beautiful times, she hopes Li Hua has a companion, she always wants to promote Li Hua and Guo Qizhi fate again, but Lili forgets that people are changing, let alone Li Hua who has ideas and opinions.

Chapter 35: Special Birthday

After the two of them finished eating, Guo Qizhi asked Li Hua, "Can you take a half day off today and we can drive around?"

Li Hua on weekdays to work, rarely rest, promised Guo Qizhi, leave for half a day. Fortunately, the company is not busy today, and there is no leading guests to visit, Li Hua birthday proposed a half-day off, the leader immediately agreed, as long as Li Hua arrange the work on the line.

Guo Qizhi asked happily, "Where do you want to go?"

Li Hua answered without thinking: "Want to go to the Eastern Mountain, worship Buddha temple, draw a sign!" Is that OK?"

Guo Qizhi promised, said to go! They went downstairs together and walked to Guo Qizhi's white car. Guo Qizhi opened the door for Li Hua, very kind and considerate to let Li Hua sit on the co-pilot first, then sit in the driver's seat, fasten the seat belt. Li Hua did so and asked by the way: "Is this your private car or your unit special car?"

"I told the driver to take a rest. It's convenient to drive my own car," Guo said.

Li Hua said nothing, this is the first time to take the car of first love. When I was young, I did not have such conditions, and all dates were walks, and all walks were on foot, which was also quite fun. There is no comparison, no one has ever hated poverty. But now love to talk about the room and car, now people have become very material, but Li Hua has no concept of the car, and do not know what car is good, what car is a luxury car. Li Hua is never vain, she only likes the house, it is after the divorce, she feels that she has her own house, a house is the feeling of home, there is a sense of security.

Guo Qizhi asked, "Can you drive? Have a car?"

Li Hua said, "I can drive and I have a driver's license, but to be honest, I don't like driving. I am very good at driving in empty places, but once on the right road, I am afraid of driving, my heart beats, my hands and feet are not good. Aych! I didn't want to drive after that."

Guo Qizhi asked again: "Do you have any plans in these years?" For example, personal issues, don't you want to start a family again?"

Li Hua looked up to Guo Qizhi and said, "You'd better drive at ease, we'll go to the Oriental Mountain Temple and draw a sign, and we'll know my fate." Let it be, even if I have a plan in my heart, it still depends on the will of God!" Li Hua really meant what she said. She was worried about what to do next.

She likes working, but she doesn't like her present job. Li Hua wants to change careers or transfer work, go to a non-small unit circle work. Li Hua does not like the ambitiousness of the working environment, she does not have so many colorful eyes, rely on hard work. However, some leaders still like to form cliques and puff each other up, play dirty tricks, engage in petty actions, operate false interpersonal relationships, and promote promotion! Li Hua was ostracized, a little uncomfortable, but I do not know who to tell, only pray for Buddha margin Avalokitesvara Bodhisattva to give guidance, in order to find comfort!

Li Hua these occasional pessimistic and helpless emotional reaction, is also understandable. In real life, a single divorced woman, need to do not be bullied by a few villains, must pay more efforts than ordinary people, but also have a toughness of steel temperament, brave, righteous! Only with strength can everyone be convinced!

The car a chat, time passed quickly, 40 minutes the car drove to the Dongfang Mountain parking lot. Because it is not a festival, there are not many people on the mountain, temple fair pavilions before and after incense stove, a wisp of incense smoke floating into the sky with the wind. Li Hua knelt down religiously one by one. Guo Qizhi also stood nearby, clasping his hands together to worship Buddha. After the procedure was finished, Li Hua went to the hall to find the monk who drew lots and shook out a sign.

The monk replied, "Ah! If you sign it, good luck!" The content of the signing is: if you travel out of the customs, half a life silver two do not worry, let you go to the southeast, northwest, the four seas are still for you honor.

It's really easy to sign, on the sign, but Li Hua can't believe it, how is this possible? Li Hua thought: I want to leave this working environment, do not work can also be rich? I can not do without a job, divorced women must have a better job, if the transfer to the province of the job landed, it is also the work of the "silver two" ah?

Li Hua is very happy to sign on this, but not sure what the content of the signing is really their own guidance, there is a little doubt in the heart, the signing over and over again to see several times.

At this time, Guo Qizhi took out 200 yuan from his wallet and gave it to the monk, who humbly and politely rang the bell three times, indicating that the money should be placed in the Gong De box, and signed the name of the donor. Guo Qizhi picked up a pen and wrote Li Hua's name on the donation list. At that moment, Li Hua wanted to refuse can not, this is to do good deeds! Li Hua accepted with delight.

It seems that Guo Qizhi is really concerned about Li Hua, he understands Li Hua think, if this time to send material things, Li Hua will certainly refuse, after all, no work is not paid!

In this line, this birthday is really meaningful, and I really did not think that Li Hua's 39th birthday would spend a meaningful day with his first love. Li Hua has a habit, when encountering big things, no opinion, she will read some Buddhist books and famous philosophical stories, slowly fade the heart of anxiety. Over time, you will go up the mountain alone, worship the Buddha temple, listen to the bell, will make the heart quiet down!

After that day, Li Hua and Guo Qizhi did not have too close contact. Li Hua met Yu Ping and became his wife. Guo Qizhi also knew this, and his marriage with Li Hua also failed to develop. This flash is many years past, when we met again is

Li Hua's clothing store out of the day, Guo Qizhi appeared in time to help move the store.

Li Hua suddenly thought of Guo Qizhi and her fate is not shallow, this time and the last eastern mountain, after seven years, the two met again in Wuhan. No fate to be lovers, but between each other became familiar friends.

Guo Qizhi naturally helped Li Hua clean the heavy objects in the store and put the water heater in the trunk of the car. According to the address said by Li Hua, transported to Wenzhou Mall in Huanggang City, where there is a three-story shop that Li Hua invested many years ago.

This time Guo Qizhi was surprised that Li Hua also bought a front room in his city! An hour's drive, finally arrived in Li Hua investment of the facade, Guo Qizhi familiar with the situation of the mall, quickly moved the water heater to the third floor. He looked at the renovated shop, which looked vacant for many years and had not been rented, only a small increase of tens of thousands of yuan.

Li Hua laughed at himself: "This is the first time I have no experience in investing in real estate. It's not much money, but it hasn't been bullish for almost a decade. I was the Wenzhou real estate group pit, a love real estate girlfriend clever mouth persuaded me to play a good person to give the benefit of this facade to me to take over. A fall into the pit has taught me a lesson. Since then, I have invested in houses accurately every time, and almost everywhere I put my money, it went up! If you sell it, you can more than double the profit."

Li Hua talked to Guo Qizhi naturally and generously as he talked about other people's affairs. Guo Qizhi said in a joking tone: "Since you have come to Huanggang to invest, what house are you going to buy?" I have a new apartment available. Are you interested? If I go to Wuhan to develop, I will not buy a house, I will live in your place, how about that?"

Then he laughed and saw that Li Hua did not seem to be deterred, Guo Qizhi went on to say: "I know that our small city house is not worth much, or you have a good vision, invest in provincial real estate, and buy it is to make money." I suggest this shop be sold as soon as possible!"

Li Hua is also considering this, before coming to an appointment to see a housing agent, ready to hang online transfer out. Li Hua is quick and resolute in doing things. The intermediary manager Li came and quoted the market price of the house to Li Hua. Li Hua knows that the sale of this property only needs to earn back the principal and interest. The remaining profit will be awarded 10,000 yuan directly to Manager Li, the only condition is to sell it as soon as possible. If you find a buyer who pays the full amount in one time within a week, Li Hua rewards the intermediary 15,000. Manager Li immediately signed the sale contract, immediately said within a week to listen to the phone notice, keep in touch.

Li Hua also added: "The house you have seen, is not doing business when housing is also cost-effective." The decorations are done. Even the water heater was installed today. The furniture of the whole house will not be removed, all are given away. The only condition is full payment in one lump sum!"

Guo Qizhi smiled admiringly to Li Hua and said, "Things have been done, it's time to go to dinner." I invite you to eat special dishes, roast chicken, marinated glutinous rice cake fish, braised crucian carp, are you love to eat, by the way, there are rice porridge. In this life, I have not married you as a wife, I am blind, I still have a chance?"

Li Hua smiled brightly, whether she married or not is not important, but at present the relationship between the two people makes her feel very comfortable. Life has no permanent enemies, no permanent friends, let alone choose a lover? Li Hua never regretted her experience, at least she got sublimation and respect in Guo Qizhi's mind. So many years have not been wasted, should be that sentence: kind people, smart struggle will win! Looks like all roads lead to Rome!

The dinner was delicious and the wine was well drunk. Li Hua also insisted on inviting the housing agent manager Li to dinner, laughter from the small restaurant outside the house, the night is tantalizing. Three people in a happy atmosphere in the toast to the smooth sale of the property.

After the meal, Guo Qizhi also promised to help Li Hua deal with the reimbursement of her father's hospital expenses. But a few days later, Guo Qizhi found his ex-wife working in the relevant department. Guo Qizhi worry ex-wife if know Li Hua and Guo Qizhi delicate first love relationship, and the ex-wife's character is harsh, if know Guo Qizhi is to help Li Hua handle this thing, will certainly misunderstanding deeper, with the ex-wife's temper, make some trouble how to do? Guo Qizhi thought of these, and a little afraid, he did not want to go to provoke his ex-wife, from the fire.

In order to avoid causing unnecessary trouble to Li Hua and himself, Guo Qizhi helplessly called Li Hua to inform the inside information. Li Hua understanding let Guo Qizhi dont have to put in mind, it is not a big problem, she can handle it on her own.

Guo Qizhi that helpless was hung up, think about his own only this courage, clearly can take this opportunity to please Li Hua this is still single first love. I missed her more than 20 years ago, and I missed her again seven years ago, and this time it may not be possible. Only feel that Li Hua is stronger than when he was young, as if anything is not a matter in Li Hua's eyes, always find a solution to the problem. In a word, the method is always more than difficult problems, as long as the problem is calm, there is no problem that can not be broken.

Guo Qizhi hated his inability to pursue his favorite people, he felt very sorry, such a good opportunity once again slipped away. Lili once joked with him: "Your whole life is for the official hat." You didn't do what you should and shouldn't do. You don't know what you're afraid of? Your mother was bullied by your ex-wife, and you are also responsible for not honoring her. I lost my wife and became an enemy. It is not easy for Li Hua to tolerate you, regardless of the past, you did not seize the opportunity. When you were young angry after Li Hua bestie talked about a love, this thing must hurt Li Hua, but Li Hua did not hate you, where can you go to find such a good woman? And you have also wasted the opportunity, if Li Hua is not in favor of you, what woman is willing to invite you to dinner?"

Lili is also a bystander clear, Guo Qizhi think Lili analysis is too in place. But there is no way, he Guo Qizhi is such a character, all to the cause of heavy, in order to secure the position of deputy director of the tax Bureau, but also wronged their own heart! While there is no clear confession to Li Hua, withdraw from the difficulty and leave some man dignity for himself. Life for face alive! It' s okay to be careful.

No one can feel the helplessness of Guo Qizhi at this moment, he also blame himself. He understood that Li Hua would soon put him aside, Li Hua was young when he treated him like this, he knew Li Hua is not for love and marriage put down the career of the woman.

Li Hua did, and she learned her lesson in her second marriage. After being hurt by Yu Ping, Li Hua dared not try to fall in love any more. Li Hua' s calm is the perseverance forced out by the years, Li Hua survived these years is really not easy. A person left the familiar city to struggle in different places, free from the shadow of revenge.

Time is really a cure, after so many years, she has gradually learned to silence, let go of the past. For those who hurt her parties, there is no hate, and Yu Ping has long forgotten about her persistent love.

After meeting Yu Ping in Guangzhou, Li Hua put Yu Ping down. Soon after returning to her hometown, Li Hua quietly unilaterally sued the divorce procedure, and she needed to make another decision for herself. After that, Li Hua was not in a hurry to fall in love and get married, and she was a little afraid of marriage from then on. But what I did not expect is that when Li Hua has several jobs and a successful career, there are many people who show her love, and Guo Qizhi is just one of them.

So Li Hua to Guo Qizhi' s ingratiating handling of the cloud light, as if it is met a dozen years ago an old friend, courtesy exchange only. There is no right or wrong, there should not be, fate in the past is over, meet and see, and even calm to not mention it with good bestie Sunny. Said but not good, Li Hua is so think, there are words buried in the earth forever, than the wind to rely on. She still cherish the pure friendship between children and bestie Sunny, but also left Guo Qizhi to her that pure good feeling. Kindness makes everything easy. Li Hua' s life has stepped into what she wants to be, wealth freedom, spiritual freedom. The state of having both in life is a rare balance in life.

Chapter 36: The single female bosses on that street

After dealing with the facade of the small county town, Li Hua returned to the provincial capital to deal with the cleaning up after the store. The female owners of the shops next door to the clothing store invited Li Hua to their own shop to chat, they want to know Li Hua's shop said transfer immediately transferred out of the experience.

They want to get out of the business, too. It is too difficult to operate the store, it takes a long time, and the business needs have not reached the work of asking employees, so basically the owners are their own store management. Running a small shop, the boss has to do everything himself. This also has advantages, first, the purchase price bosses themselves know that in the encounter of love bargaining customers, you can have a minimum price profit, do flexible, earn less earn more their own say.

Li Hua came to these familiar circle of friends, suddenly lively up. Li Hua first went to the next door jewelry shop Xiaolin that sat for a while, to help out some ideas, but also to help deal with some goods inventory. Xiao Lin, the owner of the jewelry shop, said: "I really admire you, and said that the change shop was decisively transferred out, how did you do it?"

Li Hua patiently said: "As you can see, I put all goods and clothing at the purchase price plus freight, all first promotion out." There are also some clothes half sold to friends, classmates, colleagues, let them come to the store to take away at a discount price. There are also some customers who pass by to pick up bargains, we must meet their psychological advantage, and tell them that there is only this one activity, after the village there is no shop, so everyone is willing to spend money to buy affordable things."

"Of course you're selling luxury goods here, you can't sell them at such low prices. You have to find out the reasons for buying from different customer groups. You can suggest that customers buy what they earn, use it as a relationship-building gift, and keep it for friends, siblings, parents, etc. It can also be suggested that young people buy to give lovers objects, as a commemorative jewelry. In this way, the customer base of your sales will be more. You can also engage in buy one, get one free activities, all the ornaments as empty as possible. In this way, the cost of transferring the store is low, and the new tenant only takes over the empty store and only pays the rent, so it is easy to find a tenant. You don't have to be passive, and you also have to prepare for two things while you wait. Once it's due, you don't have a backlog of goods, so it's easy to deal with. For expensive items such as air conditioners, sell them early and at a discount.

Xiao Lin said, "After you say that, I understand how to act." I go for it, discount, buy one get one free, this way!"

The two people are saying, leisure clothing boss Xin son also walked into the Xiaolin jewelry shop, "Li Hua, after you change the shop, my shop is also out." Today I came to check out, I have a group of cabinets have no place to put, if you have a place to put, I will give you. I don't want to give the new tenant, she bargain too hard, don't want to cheap her!"

Li Hua looked at Xiao Lin and asked, "Do you need it? Keep the store in the future!"

Xiao Lin said, "Oh, I will keep it for you, if you have a garage, put it first." Whoever needs it will use it!"

Xin 'er also said: "Yes, put it in Li Hua's garage first, how you use it is up to you." I'll give it to you anyway! Come, come and see with me!"

Xiao Lin said: "You go quickly, we have lunch together!"

Li Hua followed Xin son to the store a look, good guy! Such a beautiful set of

display counters, square black painted wood cabinets, double glazed Windows, look heavy and strong, good cabinet! It's a shame to lose it. It takes a lot of space.

Li Hua called the company that helped her move the day before yesterday, talked about the address of the store and talked about the price, the moving company immediately sent three strongmen to come, and spent two hours to relocate all the cabinets in the store to Li Hua's garage. Seeing all this, Xin 'er said happily: "You really do! I was so worried about this set of cabinets that I didn't sleep well at night! Tonight I invite you to sing, let's have a good time!"

After dealing with the son of the thing, go out just meet the garden cloth boss Hu Qing. Hu Qing was born in the same year with Li Hua, opened a clothing store for many years, she is the only female boss on the street to stick to it, and Li Hua has become a peer friend without talking. Li Hua sometimes think about it also feel strange, isn't it said that peers are enemies? Li Hua has become friends with all the single female bosses in this street!

Hu Qing saw Li Hua came back, quickly closed the store, came to say hello to Li Hua: "You do the clothing business is better than I manage, why turn?" Besides, the style of clothing you sell complements the style in my store, so it's a shame you're not in business. How can I play with you from now on? You are welcome to come back and play with me often, anyway I will always drive here, come and sit down!"

Li Hua took Hu Qing's shoulder and said: "Rest assured, I will come to your shop to pick my favorite clothes, because I have always liked your style of clothing, there is a national flavor, and a woman's charm!"

Hu Qing smiled and said: "Your evening activities count me in, I just have a few cases of beer, we drink all tonight, a drunk!"

Xin 'er said happily: "I am ready to ask you to sing together!" Close early today, see you at Shouyi Road song Hall at 7 o 'clock!"

That evening, almost all the female proprietors of the costume street were there. Xin son has been helping her to look at the shop with a single girlfriend Chen Jun, Xiaolin with the pursuit of her boyfriend Sue, Hu Qing with her single female classmates, Li Hua with two customer girlfriend - from the customer to become a personal friend of Li Hua, and the same street beauty salon owner and store manager of two beauties. What is most unexpected is that there was an uninvited male guest that day - General manager Chen of the property management company on the street, a handsome man who speaks fluent Mandarin and can sing love songs! This is a lot of fun.

That night, everyone really had a crazy time, drank too much, and everyone played a few songs. I've never had so much fun! Li Hua is really reluctant to give up the good sisters on this street.

Li Hua looked at the girlfriend who was singing, the warm light gave off an ambiguous and mysterious atmosphere, and the music was filled with talking words, and everyone looked so charming and sexy and rich in emotional appeal. Li Hua also wore his own style of dress that day, really worthy of being the bosses of the clothing industry, everyone looks like they do not lose the charm of a woman, each has its own merits. Su and Chen saw them all thumbs up and praise, Chen said: "Really did not find that there are so many beautiful bosses hidden in the street, we these single dogs can not find their own flowers in the flowers, this is our men's sorrow!"

Chen sang on stage, "to the beauty of an old song" I don't want to say ", I hope the beauty like."

Xin 'er said: "Chen's Mandarin is good, I did not think of singing more affectionate and good!"

Xiao Lin snickered: "It's a pity, he's too short, I like tall people!"

Hu Qing whispered, "Su always speaks with a northeast accent, but she is as tall as Dunzi, haha!"

Xin son and Chen Jun laughed at the same time, the water was sprayed out, and did not forget to hurry to say: "Be careful, we are not to choose the prince to find an object, everyone together!"

Li Hua pointed to the singing Chen on the stage and said: "You listen to the

songs and choose the songs, go and sing a few love songs with Chen." How about a little orgasm? Every beautiful woman has to go! Not one less, not one missing!"

Xiao Lin said: "Yes, singing fun!"

Li Hua took Xin son handed to the microphone, "I take the lead, the beauties follow." Li Hua came to the stage and stood side by side with Mr. Chen and began to sing. Perhaps the two people are very invested in the role of the song, the two people's soulful eyes, so that the atmosphere reached a climax, the expression of the two people singing like it is true, the performance is perfect!

Xiao Lin waited for Li Hua to sit down, attached his ear to her and said, "I can see that Mr. Chen likes you. When you sing, you look like a couple! Don't you like his Mandarin voice? I see a chance!"

Li Hua quickly bowed his head and whispered, "Don't say that, I can't find a young man who is 17 years younger than me." Think of it as a child! Don't talk nonsense, it's impossible!"

Kobayashi said: "I can see that, before he always said 'bring a few staff to sit in your shop'. At first I thought it was the job, but then I realized that if you suggested something, his employees would do it in a timely manner."

Hu Qing said: "This evening can be understood, otherwise how could this general manager Chen come to our party uninvited?" I'm sure I want to hang out with Li Hua. Box singing is Sue always pay, Chen always shouted that will go out to ask everyone to eat dinner. Keep drinking beer then, I have more in the car!"

Xin 'er said: "Originally I wanted to return Li Hua a favor. Li Hua always invited me to dinner before, and tonight I can't turn, then the next time to sing together!"

Li Hua said: "Don't mention it, you send me so many things, that can also be your treat!"

That night, the crowd dispersed from the karaoke hall and rushed to the night market food stall. It was a really fun evening. There were so many people. This night market in Wuhan is full of lights and a bustling scene, this group of single female bosses have such a colorful night life, where there is time to be sad for the past? Li

Hua thought: We these wise single women are not worse than anyone. Look at each one is beautiful and capable, EQ IQ is no less than a man's master! There's nothing wrong with being single. It's easy!

The single female owners of this street, although the store was transferred, but since then have lived a very good quality, each is a connoisseurs of wealth freedom. It is said that Xiao Lin went to Singapore to make a fortune in the health care product business, and sent his daughter to Singapore to study at university. Xin son became a music piano teacher of the art college, accompanied her mother to live together, and some spare time also took students to do pre-performance training classes, and had a stable income. She was as sweet as ever, and the years had not aged her at all. Hu Qing is still doing a stable clothing store business on that street, wearing beautiful and fashionable clothes every day, more and more like a rich woman. Chen Jun also found a good man eight years younger than her and got married, and the days were very sweet.

Li Hua at that time, in the investment of real estate, almost every buy a set can earn money. After so many years of accumulation, and encountered a good investment era, as long as hard-working wisdom, business vision, in this prosperous era is not rich. Li Hua has everything except no marriage.

Li Hua, like all the other women on the street, is happily single. One is that their vision is higher, and the average man can't handle it. The main reason is that women have a sense of security after having money, if they meet a man who loves them, and worry that the other side only loves their money, it is more and more difficult to choose a partner.

Several friends have been in touch, to discuss if the old has not met the object of love, then choose a good place, together to buy a house to live together for the aged! Li Hua has been holding a sincere two kinds of preparation of the idea, yearning for a true love of marriage and love life, but not deliberately to find. She knows that love is not wishful thinking, but the collision of two people's hearts, can not be met. So she made her own rules and went with the flow. You do what you

have to do. You don't wait for something to happen. She never fantasizes about unrealistic things and prefers to keep things down to earth.

Li Hua dry dry now has a sea view room, the city has a school district room. Under the positive recommendation of bestie Zhen Zhen in the suburbs of the city, two single women have been neighbors together, investing in a small villa for the aged, a 3-story house is enough to live in. Two people on weekdays are busy with their careers, met holidays in the villa community agreed to meet time. Take a look at the renovations of your neighbors in the same area while relaxing, in case you need to prepare for the renovation before moving in. Some time ago, the two women have carried out the simple decoration of the basic water and electricity layout according to their own preferences, the frame diagram effect has come out, and the two people have their own ideas! Li Hua does not need to marry a good man as a sense of security, she has already relied on their own to find a sense of security.

Chapter 37: Invest in two hardcover rooms downtown

After the transfer of the clothing store, Li Hua took the time to do two real estate investment houses, and finally signed the purchase contract before the price rise.

That was in early March 2009, a slight increase of 100 yuan per square meter compared with the price at the end of 2008. Li Hua took a fancy to Wuchang river view room fine decoration of a small apartment; There is also a Vanke fine decoration of small house, located in the three towns of Wuhan, the most prosperous Hankou railway station near.

At that time, considering the type of these two houses, one is to solve the problem of Li Hua's daughter working nearby, and invest in pre-marital real estate in her daughter's name. After the clothing store was transferred out, Wuchang investment community housing has doubled in price, relying exclusively on the transfer of funds out of the store, not enough to invest in the cost of two houses. For this reason, Li Hua wants to sell a house, this house because of the convenient transportation, not far from the school and the hospital. As soon as it was posted online, it was ordered by a young doctor at a nearby hospital.

The sale of this housing, in order to save the cost of investment clothing store rent, Li Hua will rent this house to a good condition of the art school female students. Think of students have graduated due, then is the best time to recover the sale, Li Hua decisively contact the housing agent sold the prosperous house.

Think about it or some reluctant, but Li Hua thought as long as the sale of a set of investment housing, you can solve two sets of investment housing, or a very successful operation. This is also the first time that Li Hua has made a very

successful investment transformation in a multiplier way. It is convenient for my daughter to work in the provincial city, and also convenient for my single life in the provincial city.

Doing the right thing at the right time, Li Hua felt a sense of accomplishment, so he actively recommended his family and friends to see the investment house. After Li Hua did several successful things silently, the family naturally looked at Li Hua and trusted him very much. At the end of 2008, global housing prices fell madly, Li Hua has been mobilizing his family to persuade his parents to move to the provincial capital early, so that everyone can take care of each other and take care of their elderly parents together. So Li Hua can rest assured!

Li Hua little sister listened to the suggestion, the Spring Festival in early 2009, little sister for their parents to invest in this set of provincial capital housing, is because Li Hua actively recommended. At that time, Li Hua said firmly: "If you do not buy in time, the price will rise later, you will certainly regret it!"

Look at this house, the total price of 1 million, 136 square area, good location, old street alley market are nearby. There are three major banks, the front of the community is the avenue and the bus station, the opposite of the house is the Yangtze River, it can be said that there are very future development prospects. To really buy is to earn a fortune. Li Hua suggested that the little sister to parents to buy a house in the community, the late expansion of the subway station line at the gate of this community, the instant real estate and due to the favorable factors of convenient transportation and increase in value.

First, the original intention of investment is based on filial piety, the second is to judge the information, the third is the right time, this time Li Hua recommended little sister successful house purchase is a sense of accomplishment. Li Hua saw his family profit and reduced the cost of buying a house, and he was more happy than he benefited.

On that day, Li Hua was looking down to help his parents sign the house key, and a woman's voice next to it attracted Li Hua's attention: "Is there still a big house?"

Property staff replied: "early sold out."

Li Hua looked up and saw the woman with her back to her side, and patted the woman on the shoulder with surprise: "It's really you, Li Lin! What a coincidence, you also bought a house in this neighborhood! Do you live on your own, or do you invest?"

Li Lin said happily, "It's you, Li Hua! We haven't seen each other in years. How can we meet here? What a destiny!" Li Lin happily pulled a man standing beside him to Li Hua and said, "This is my husband, Lao Li! This is my old colleague! We weren't even 20 at the time!"

Li Hua said, "Yes, after a few decades, I have to be neighbors." You have good taste to buy here."

Li Lin said: "I have bought, I want my brother to buy a set, in a community to take good care of each other!" Alas, just asked, a suite is not available, only wait for the second phase of the room to be launched, then take a look. How about you? How many houses have you bought?"

Li Hua and Li Lin talk about investing in the house this common hobby topic, the two people talk endlessly.

Li Lin said: "Did you find the back decoration?"

Li Hua said, "I just made an appointment today with Zhao, the decoration company who helped me decorate before, to talk about it. We'll bring the blueprints. You see my house first. If you think Mr. Zhao's renovation plan is real, you let him go to your home to see the house, and also make a quotation of the renovation plan, you talk directly! More comparisons are good."

Li Lin and Lao Li nodded: "Yes, you can take a look at the rough house your sister bought for her parents, and take us to talk together!" Would you like to visit the small hardcover apartment you live in?"

Li Hua is a warm-hearted character, met a young colleague, happy to decorate the company boss Zhao recommended to Li Lin, and explain Zhao to Li Lin the most favorable most economical most real price. Li Lin felt that Li Hua had not changed at all, and was as sunny and friendly as when he was young! Li Lin is also

a quick and decisive woman, the same day with Zhao signed the decoration contract, the scene let Zhao general decoration.

Lao Li said, "Can I be a supervision consultant?"

Zhao said: "No problem, we like the owners to keep in close contact with us!" We can discuss the construction details in advance!"

Li Hua added: "No problem, go to my small apartment to sit and have a cup of tea, while resting and talking." Talk about the decoration plan first, so that the decoration will avoid doing a good demolition, waste costs!"

This time, Li Lin learned that Li Hua's family has invested in a large and small two sets of housing in this community, and the starting point is to facilitate the care of their parents, without affecting their living habits. Li Lin also happily told Li Hua that her brother had also invested in a house across the road in the Jiangjing real estate. How fortunate it is to meet the same interests and three views of the confidant! Two people from meet to separate, has not stopped to chat. That intimate friendship, let the next people are envious, let alone family.

On that day, everyone was very happy, and Zhao, who was responsible for the decoration, said happily: "Please rest assured, two sisters, I must put your house as a residential model room decoration!" And inexpensive, package two sisters satisfied, must be worthy of the trust of the sisters!"

In this way, two colleagues many years ago began to start neighbors, and it is the same unit. Li Lin lives in No. 2003 and Li Hua lives in No. 2907.

Since then, the two often look at houses and inspect investment houses together. Later, Li Hua invested in Hankou Vanke fine decoration house in the name of his daughter, and on the day when the developer handed over the house to the owner for acceptance, Li Lin also accompanied him. I really did not expect to enter the age of retirement, the two met the bosom friend! This is also the fate of the wish!

That year, Li Hua successfully accomplished these two major events of investment housing, which is of great significance to Li Hua. In the provincial capital for their own home and career laid the foundation, convenient for her daughter to work back and forth to save time, but also more convenient to take care of their parents. In their own investment at the same time, but also affect the family to get better day by day.

This is why Li Hua has the motivation to run hard, in order to live better for her family, as the oldest daughter, she must work hard. Li Hua has a responsibility in her heart, and her wish is that her relatives can live a better life! You have to do in front, when the guide is very worried!

Chapter 38: Travel in England

The house is a big deal in Li Hua's eyes, don't laugh at her, she really cares about the house after the divorce. During the first marriage, in order to subplan the house into commercial housing, Li Hua needs to take money from her ex-husband to buy it, the husband of the money, only threw Li Hua three words "no!" I really don't care.

From then on, Li Hua realized the importance of money, she can feel without the right to speak, if she does not even have a house one day, then she really has no home.

From that time on, Li Hua tried her best to ask friends to help, and finally got the money through bank loans, and successfully turned the planned house into a commercial housing property right, when it really belongs to her and her ex-husband. Later quarrel with her husband cold War, Li Hua from the bone no longer rely on her husband. As a result of the divorce, Li Huaning was willing to pay her husband half of the property and asked the court to judge the divorce request.

Before the divorce, Li Hua is not material at all, the monthly salary is handed over to her husband, Li Hua's husband is in charge of life. Oil, rice, tea and salt all need money, and the daily expenses of the family are all in the management of the husband. Li Hua often works on business trips, so she is not in charge, and she is afraid of trouble. But when you need to buy something big for the family, you want to take money from your husband, you will never have it. The contradiction intensifies, the three views are different, and the life will be troublesome. Three days a small quarrel, the husband coax Li Hua the next day.

Li Hua has never taken the initiative to admit defeat, her character is forced out by her husband. Each time let Li Hua angry, and then coax Li Hua to continue to pay money, but has not solved the substantive problem. So Li Hua tired, she did not want such a life, so there is the idea of divorce, what can come again. Within two years of the divorce, the couple had separate families, but both later divorced again.

Li Hua and Yu Ping' s marriage is based on love, this time Li Hua did not want Yu Ping to buy a wedding house. Their marriage ended because of Ping' s betrayal. This love, come fast and go fast, almost hurt Li Hua' s bones. Li Hua heart is very painful, confused for a long time, listless, often sullen during the day to work, go to the blind massage parlor massage.

In the heart of disappointment and bitter, Li Hua do not know who can say, she felt she could not afford to lose this face. When she was pursued by Yu Ping, Li Hua was confident and proud of her own charm. Also thought that after the two married, Yu Ping will spoil her like a princess. The life of the second marriage, she lived is very heart, romantic for a period of time. Li Hua has been busy with her work, she thinks that work is better than love and marriage, and she is glad that she did not give up her work because of marriage, but she ignored marriage management because of work. Her overconfidence and overconfidence led to another failure of her second marriage.

Li Hua heart pain, early she anesthesia their way of relief, is to go to work less talk, quietly enjoy the massage after work! Because the masseuse is blind and can' t see the face of Li Hua, Li Hua enjoys the feeling of not being disturbed and not being snooped on. The blind technician seemed very clever. Every time Li Hua came in and said "one hour" , he knew who it was. He also never spoke much, as if he knew the pain of Li Hua' s frustration. There were even two blind technicians who did not accept Li Hua' s money. It turned out that there were classmates who often went to massage, and the big boss who knew Li Hua helped Li Hua pay the bill. It turns out that not only Li Hua has something on his mind, but the guests here may all have some unspeakable anguish. The advantage of massage is that when the body and mind are tired and hopeless, you can still let the body relax, let the blind hand smooth the pain in Li Hua' s heart, and get a little inner peace.

After many years Li Hua in the bottom of my heart to thank once those chaos, if not for the pain of the past, how today so capable Li Hua. Li Hua heart really thank hurt her people, years to polish her into a stronger mature warrior, at this time Li Hua very sense of accomplishment. If it were not for those unfaithful and cheap little three, she Li Hua would not have today, for the family to do these seemingly very ordinary things for themselves, and never thought, pick up a pen in the real estate contract to sign his name, the purchase of the event of his own say this kind of pride.

Those painful experiences in Li Hua heart is not a matter, now began to wake up, what can not let go? Men and marriage did not, but let Li Hua career wealth thriving, and every investment is successful, wish to achieve.

When the two sets of hardcover room acceptance is completed, the short-term plan has been realized, Li Hua relaxed a little, she decided to thoroughly fly once, reward themselves for a trip, enjoy a good life, may encounter what good luck. This time on the advice of his girlfriend, Li Hua decided to travel to England.

In mid-April 2009, Li Hua's application for a UK visa was approved. The friend who went with him to sign and submit the application in person did not approve because he did not have real estate as a financial guarantee, and Li Hua successfully got the travel visa to the UK in half a month.

The staff smiled and said, "Congratulations, British visa passed!"

Li Hua took his time and asked, "Are there any special conditions for visa approval?"

The staff said: "You must pass, you have two sets of purchase contracts, but also a copy of the facade property certificate, the economy is really strong." You will not stay in Britain as an illegal immigrant."

Li Hua said, "That's for sure, China is so good. I'm just going to see things, take a trip. How long can I stay, please?"

The officer said: "1 month to 6 months of visa!"

Li Hua looked at the visa and thought: So long? I don't need it! I'm just going on a trip to relax.

Li Hua quickly listened to his girlfriend sister Xu's words and bought a plane ticket to London, England. I'm really flying out of the world on my own this time.

On this long trip, Sister Xu asked Li Hua to bring a set of skin care products for her daughter. Sister Xu's daughter has acne on her face. This is the cream for the treatment. Sister Xu is the benefactor who introduced the job to Li Hua's daughter. Elder sister Xu Li Hua 5 years old, do a public institution financial director, good enthusiasm, help others. She helped Li Hua's daughter arrange work and did it without giving gifts. Li Hua felt very sorry in the heart, this time Li Hua went to Britain to bring something to sister Xu's daughter naturally is willing. Li Hua and Sister Xu's friendship has been more than ten years of friendship, two people are very grateful.

From Wuhan, China to Beijing to London, England, it only took 11 hours. It was dusk and the sun was setting when the plane landed at London Airport. Sister Xu to the handsome friend of the United Kingdom, a just retired second-line emperor police Allen explained Li Hua holiday, Allen took the initiative to meet Li Hua at the airport.

When leaving the airport, waiting for a long time Allen recognized Li Hua at a glance, holding a sign with Chinese Li Hua two words. Li Hua laughed, just like the scene in the movie theater. The British friend met Li Hua in this old-fashioned way. Li Hua in the face of Allen, with a mobile phone to take a group photo sent to sister Xu, tell each other has arrived safely.

After traveling to London for a month, Li Hua set out for another city to see Sister Xu and her daughter. It takes more than six hours to drive from London to the city where Xu's daughter studies. Li Hua joked to herself, "If Alan had not helped me on this journey, I would have struggled with my English." I really want to thank Ellen, a British friend, for driving Li Hua to the university of Cambridge, where Sister Xu's daughter is studying for a master's degree.

Found in the campus where waiting for a long time Wang Wei - Xu sister's daughter. Li Hua will bring things one by one to Wang Wei hands. Completed this task, Li Hua this just breathed a sigh of relief, also Allen sent a large jar of candy, all to Wang Wei, Allen read Wang Wei as a child. Later it was known that Allen and his wife had no children after marriage, happened to be Allen's wife derailed, the

two divorced, Allen from then on there is no woman. Alan lives in a community of retired police officers. The town is quiet and peaceful. Li Hua was invited by Alan to visit, it is a one-family two-story villa, the actual area is only 160 square meters.

Wang Wei really sensible, is catching up is the point of dinner, she took everyone to the restaurant to eat. Allen Wang Wei as a child, but people Wang Wei can be clever, while ordering the menu, Wang Wei will settle the account. When Li Hua went to pay the bill after dinner, the salesperson smiled and said: "The single has already bought, three people on your table are going to pay the bill, really funny!" So Alan came to buy the order! Friends of the same kind are so comfortable. Don't play games!

Li Hua for sister Xu after the heart, the heart relaxed a lot, but in turn let Wang Wei the single buy! This little girl is too much like Sister Xu's style of doing things, even grab the bill to learn. That night Li Hua will tell the information to sister Xu, not to praise Wang Wei sensible, let Li Hua do aunt are lost, no wonder why Sister Xu so assured, the daughter Wang Wei sent abroad for further study. According to the words of Sister Xu, "girls are to go out and see the world more, and in the future life, they will not be cheated because they do not know anything, nor will they lose confidence because of ignorance."

Chapter 39: Preparing for Entrepreneurship while Traveling

After dinner that day, Li Hua and Alan did not return to the city where Alan lived in time, and stayed in the nearest hotel for a rest for one night, of course, staying in different single rooms.

At breakfast the next morning, Alan said to Li Hua, "On our way back, we can go to the little town of Ingnan, where you can see women in plaid dresses." There are still some places of interest to visit. Would you like to go there?"

Li Hua immediately said, "If you are not tired, let's go." As long as we don't take detours and can visit more places, it's certainly good." Li Hua used the translator to communicate with Alan, and soon entered a state of natural communication. Li Hua is not polite, directly agreed to agree!

Li Hua has been used to saying that go on the trip, but also can do very free and easy. In this point, Li Hua and Alan are still a little different. Now Li Hua and Alan are already very good friends, familiar with each other, get along very natural and comfortable, without any pressure. Allen is very quality, enthusiasm just right sense of proportion, let Li Hua relax and release a naughty lively cheerful character, sometimes happy smile, let Allen shy shy.

Thinking of the first time to see Alan, Li Hua also felt that the 1.86 meters tall man a little pressure, straight waist, a look can feel that the other side is a well-trained man. But when Alan laughed, Li Hua found that his two teeth were a little angry, and was embarrassed to say it.

Li Hua thought on second thought, he is not a blind date, the other party is just a friend who picks up the airport, why should you pick each other's shortcomings? Li Hua felt that he was a little too much at that time, and made the shortcomings

of judging people by their appearance. His girlfriend once gave Li Hua a nickname called "Appearance association"! Because Li Hua on the appearance, like handsome handsome men!

After the divorce, Li Hua did not lower his criteria for choosing a mate because of his divorce! With economic strength, Li Hua will not be wronged to let himself marry down. If fate comes, meet a good quality man, Li Hua can consider getting married; If fate does not come, it will always be a happy and free single woman, more free, want to buy a house a person sign arithmetic, want to travel, buy a plane ticket.

Li Hua thought of the impression of the first day to London Airport, here is not so bustling as imagined, the old public facilities, let Li Hua put down the worship and excitement before. Just looking around, talking to Alan and walking out of the airport. It took two turns and passed a bus stop outside the airport, which could only hold about eight people. Alan was walking ahead with a big box. Li Hua followed Alan and asked, "Where are we going?" Alan said, "Now go get my car. My car is in the parking lot of the hotel near the airport."

Ellen is a British friend introduced by Sister Xu, Li Hua trust Sister Xu, also trust her friends introduced, very assured to follow him, there is no match in simple English conversation. Before coming, Li Hua specially went to Xinhua Bookstore to buy three English pamphlets, carry with him bad English short sentences, very practical use. Friends also praised Li Hua: "I really admire you, take a few English book pamphlets dare to go to the United Kingdom, very brave!"

Li Hua really has courage. She made a great determination to travel abroad this time. The first is to reward themselves for the successful transfer of clothing stores, the second is to sell the shops invested many years ago, and the third is to book two sets of provincial housing has been accepted. These big things have been done in a short time, Li Hua also has a sense of accomplishment. Li Hua has a good habit of never being stingy to himself, so he must give himself a holiday to enjoy life.

After the divorce Li Hua figured out, life to live a transparent point, in addition to work to earn money, or to invest in the old line of real estate as their favorite investment. She believes that this kind of investment can achieve time freedom and economic freedom. You can invest two more sets of money, you can contribute less money, and you have to invest one set of bank loans. As long as it is a good landmark house, or a house in the city center, no money should be considered! Years of real estate investment has brought economic benefits to Li Hua, she was willing to pay out of her own pocket, travel abroad at her own expense, cash their own rewards. In public institutions, you have to be a deputy director in order to enjoy the number of government-funded study Tours. Li Hua felt that it was much better to go abroad than to rely on the welfare of the unit.

Li Hua chose London for her first trip abroad. The first stop was a trip to London's Chinatown for a leek and meat dumpling. The dumplings here are very expensive, 30 a plate, 30 pounds, the exchange rate at that time is 1 to 11, the price of a plate of dumplings is 330 yuan, two or three people in the country can eat a big meal. Once converted into RMB prices, Li Hua felt a little distressed, but it has been pointed, can not be returned.

After Li Hua every time to buy things, eat food to convert RMB, calculate in the heart, spend the row is not cost-effective. The rest of the day doesn't count. Try to save it.

After staying in the UK for two months, Li Hua has been very used to Taobao in the UK, and will go to the second-hand currency market to buy their favorite clothes. At first, she did not know that it was a second-hand store, and occasionally passed a store to see a lot of people buying things, she also went in to watch. She saw a rosy red dress, looking like a cheongsam, the belt is particularly beautiful, and suddenly attracted Li Hua, looking at a classical woman charm.

Li Hua used the translation tool to ask the boss about the clothes, and then looked at the label, almost did not call out: my mother yo, so cheap, only 6 pounds! It's only 66 yuan. It's worth it. Buy it now.

I ended up buying a lot of clothes, bags, and shoes that day, only to find out that it was a second-hand grocery store that sold all kinds of goods. What Li Hua didn't

think of is that most of the people who buy things in British second-hand shops are British. There are Asian faces from Japan, Korea, China, Vietnam.

Li Hua often regards Japanese women as Chinese women, and several times he came forward to ask questions in Chinese, and the result was explained with a humble smile: "I am Japanese!" After admitting mistakes several times, Li Hua was no longer embarrassed to ask casually. The passing Asians are tourists, students and visa workers from all over the world. The world is so big, Li Hua's trip to England has opened his eyes!

With Alan's help, Li Hua signed up for a local tour group and toured the major attractions and royal castles in Britain. Li Hua carries a multi-language translator, each tourist has a card on his chest, holds a tour guide booklet, and follows the tour guide holding a small colorful flag along the way. The hotel is also arranged with the team, which is convenient. It is said that the tour group of Li Hua Newspaper is the best local travel agency, the service reputation is the first, the cost is higher than other travel agencies, but it is safe, where there are buses!

This long vacation trip, let Li Hua again lit up Li Hua entrepreneurial enthusiasm. She saw that the doors and Windows of the British people's homes were still made of the white plastic aluminum sheet materials that the Chinese people had long been outdated, and the window design was still very old-fashioned. Before going abroad, there was a friend in Northeast China who wanted to cooperate with Li Hua to open a door and window engineering Co., LTD. Prepare Li Hua to take the job, sign the project contract; Northeast Friends is responsible for technical production, aluminum purchase, engineering construction team cooperation and other work. This business plan only talked about the beginning, Li Hua is considering whether to join the industry that does not understand. Friends in the northeast are very optimistic about Li Hua, and talked with her several times. Li Hua acted cautiously, and then replied to friends in the Northeast with a comprehensive plan.

Although this trip abroad is a trip, Li Hua can not help but pay attention to the doors and Windows of various houses, and also take photos of various furniture matches and save them in her mobile phone. Although she gave herself a long vacation, she never forgot to go back and do a big job. This trip has also become a pre-business market investigation, the play process from time to time to collect materials, in addition to Li Hua himself and the city scenery, most of the photos are about a variety of styles of houses, doors and Windows as the background of the photos. Also the photos in the UK local all washed out, Li Hua afraid of mobile phone storage is not enough, so save rest assured!

Li Hua thought well, after returning to China to talk to friends in the northeast about investing in the door and window company. She already has an idea, and she is mainly responsible for sales negotiation business engineering. In terms of technology, public relations, and engineering construction, we will hand over to our friends in the Northeast who understand technology and our future partners.

Once he had the thought of starting a business, Li Hua's trip to the UK would not be idle. In the later one-month trip, Li Hua would record the housing construction of the place almost wherever he went, taking photos of landmark houses and various doors and Windows. Even the bathroom of tourist attractions, the bathroom door of the hotel lobby, as long as the shape is special, she will choose an Angle to take pictures, and the photos are all washed out in the photo studio.

These moves made the British friend Alan curious, he asked Li Hua: "You are going to do doors and Windows related business?"

Li Hua replied with a smile: "I want to save these beautiful pictures and take them back as a modeling reference, suitable for use as a combination of Eastern and Western cultures." Some of our private houses have also been built in the style of villa areas, for those who require Western charm of the house, we can provide these Western characteristics of the door and window products, there will be market demand!"

Other people's travel is sightseeing, eating, drinking and fun, and Li Hua that line of long vacation has laid the foreshadowing of entrepreneurship in his mind. Li Hua realized that no matter where he lived, he needed an economic foundation and he needed to be a human being. She realized that in order to prove

that her post-divorce life was going well, she had to make a profit financially. And entrepreneurship can achieve the goal more quickly, as long as it can grasp the market demand of the era.

Now is the market economy, those years and real estate related industries, will be driven by the social construction industry market, for example, real estate, decoration industry, door and window engineering, housing agents to rent and sell houses, these industries can earn money. With the general direction of investment, Li Hua has her own opinion, she pays attention to the news and pays attention to the price comparison information of real estate in any city. Opportunities are left to those who are prepared. The trip to Britain opened Li Hua's mind and broadened his horizon.

Alan admired Li Hua's intently looking at the picture and asked, "Can you stay in England?" I can help you stay!" Li Hua looked up at Alan. He had a serious expression on his face. Li Hua was a little surprised but very embarrassed to say, "My English is not good, I have my career and family in China, my eating habits are not adapted to the UK, I prefer the life in China." I'm just relaxing on holiday, not planning to stay long. Thank you for your invitation. If you have a chance to travel to China for sightseeing, I will be your China guide!"

Li Hua said all the words in his heart in one breath, and did not hide his true thoughts. That's probably why Alan admired her, pure honesty. When there is no scheming Li Hua appeared in Alan's vision, has left the charm of Chinese Oriental women. Alan also do not know when to start, has been quietly from like to fall in love with Li Hua so a kind of emotion, in Alan's heart, silently covered up for a long time, today Alan also do not know why he dared to express it.

Aware of Alan's subtle emotional changes, Li Hua had to end the trip to England early. She has so many things to do that it is impossible for her to have the time and mind for love right now. She is afraid of love, although men like her first, but the final marriage ended in divorce. Although love regardless of national boundaries, regardless of age, but she really can not afford to love, she does not want to be hurt by emotions. She was now feeling good about being a happy single woman, free to make her own decisions. Now Li Hua already feels that his life is like a fish in a duck's water. At present, the most important thing is not love and marriage, but work, to have an independent economic foundation, have their own career!

On the day we left London Airport, it was cloudy and drizzling. Alan was a gentleman to help Li Hua move a big suitcase, and bought some fruit to eat on the road, but also quietly put 200 pounds in Li Hua's bag. After entering the security check Li Hua only found, looked up to see Alan reluctant to part with the eyes, Li Hua only bowed to escape from Alan looking forward to the eyes, she understood that she could not give love, the love came at a bad time. She could only play dumb, pretend to be relaxed, wave her hand in Alan's direction, and turn away at once. Li Hua did not dare to look at Alan who was still standing there. Thinking it would be good to say goodbye, she wished Ellen happiness when she met him: "Good-bye, Ellen! You are a good man, but I can't give you love!"

Chapter 40: Starting a Windows and Doors Company

Li Hua came back from the dust, and partners of northeast friends Xiao always hit it off, immediately began emergency planning to open doors and Windows engineering company, quickly prepared for two months, the site opened.

Li Hua's first single gift to the company was an office building project in a third-level city that she helped negotiate. After the customer is introduced to Xiao, the technical solutions are handed over to Xiao to follow up and exchange. After the pre-approval, the construction team will be arranged by General Manager Xiao. The installation period is written in the contract, a total of four months, the project payment is settled according to the progress, the down payment is 30%, the interim is subject to the installation of materials, the final payment is paid in full after the completion of the project, and 5% maintenance deposit is reserved! The contract is simple and clear, because it is dealing with the government, everything is simple, and efficiency and quality are trusted to ensure the smooth completion of the first project.

Xiao is always very happy, he did not want to Li Hua from the UK travel back immediately into work, this said to do the courage to do, really not all women can do. Li Hua has forgotten that he is still a woman, in addition to following up the construction with Party A to recover the project money, but also go to the site with Xiao every day. Sometimes with workers to eat a box lunch work meal, that a camouflage pants with a white shirt, also very heroic! As described by bestie, standing on what hill to sing what song, Li Hua's appearance is too suitable for the workplace, not losing to men. Able, steady, decisive, organized and strong affinity.

The workers were convinced of her, and Xiao said admiringly: "How can we men listen to women?" A northeast accent Xiao finished speaking, the workers laughed. Some make faces, some beep, and some shout directly: "As long as Li Zong comes, he will give us more food, more food, Xiao Zong will know to yell at us to work!"

Xiao continued: "You do this job well, I invite you to eat sour cabbage stew ribs, and dumplings, the whole two bottles of Erguotou!" How about that?"

The workers said in unison: "Well, then have a good drink, now let's go to work!"

To tell the truth, this construction team, really have no words, all are the skilled technicians who used to work with Xiao. One of the foreman managers is Xiao's brother-in-law, that is, Xiao's lover's brother. Xiao always in a kindergarten door and window project to know the kindergarten teacher Xu, one to two people know. We got married two years after we started dating, and we had a kid the next year. Since Xiao General Manager and Xiao Xu married, never delayed the wages of the workers. Sometimes Party A does not settle as scheduled, when the capital turnover is not good, what material money can be temporarily released in a turnaround period, but the workers' wages are not a lot.

This is also an important reason why this team is willing to follow Li Hua and Xiao. The key is to work with the workers in one mind, do the project quality well, and complete the installation of doors and Windows as scheduled. This is a construction team that can be assured, the company has a clear division of labor, responsibility to the post, and good coordination and cooperation. When the manpower is not enough, Xiao always eats and sleeps with the workers. On weekends or major festivals, Xiao would invite workers to the company to eat dumplings, a pot of sauteed ribs with cabbage, a northeast delicacy.

Li Hua must be one of the people invited, Li Hua was originally single, usually devoted to work, rarely cook, this is Xiao always interested in taking care of Li Hua. Li Hua, who does not eat coriander, has learned coriander dipping sauce, scallion dipping sauce, and scallion dipping sauce, according to Xiao's Northeast words, "Li

has been used to eating our Northeast food, which is like taking the leader of this rural migrant worker team!"

Indeed, Li Hua has no shelf, easy-going work style, care about migrant workers in life, let workers feel kind. They know that the company's business engineering work is Li Hua, she is also responsible for all Party A contracts and interpersonal relationship follow-up. Li Hua is not easy, a bowl of water is a delicate balance, the average person can not do, let alone Li Hua is a woman. Li Hua in public relations to give full play to Xiao total Northeast people's bold character advantages, with a northeast accent to tell jokes, like the TV skit actor Xiao Shenyang at that time, the party leader coax happy, said to laugh to death you. It cost less PR and got the contract renewed. After that, Li Hua took all the contacts of the party to let Xiao know, to the military background, Xiao Xiao, 16 years younger than Li Hua, all follow up, the two people have a happy tacit understanding.

When a project was completed, Li Hua encouraged Xiao to say: "You will march to ten million assets in the future, I only need to reach half of it!"

Xiao always suddenly remembered one thing, "Listen to the big leader of the party said, there is a place in Huanggang, there is a bearded master fortuneteller is very accurate." Before we go to settle the bill for the project today, we'll explore the road and do some math. What do you think?"

Li Hua concurred and stared at Xiao and said: "Today is still early to go to the engineering department to find Sheng director, to apply for the project payment report." By the way, ask Director Sheng what requirements and difficulties, and the director Li who is in charge of our quality, must modestly ask her about the settlement situation. Who to talk to first, which leader to talk to, you have to be smart and improvise. I went to the accountant's office to find out about the allocation of some specific project billing plans. It is said that seven construction teams need Party A to settle the project payment, and the time is tight. If these plans are not reported and signed by the eight leading directors, we still cannot get the project funds, which is an urgent need. When this is done, I will surely take you to a fortune-teller and ask about your future."

Shaw always said, "Okay, this is a big deal. Next month, the festival will also pay the workers' saving fee, and the aluminum material payment. The factory also has to settle with our company, and the next batch of aluminum can be sent to us!"

Li Hua took a deep breath, "How did I listen to your words, set up an industry I don't understand, and really opened a company." I'm tired of thinking about so many relationships to deal with. I've only been doing this for almost a year, and I've aged five years. You're a man, you know what you're doing, you fuck more, I only cooperate with your work. Need me to come forward and people, I help you about, you do public relations is good, nothing you can't do!"

Xiao always joked: "Make fun of me again, open a company with you, I am your full-time driver, executive general manager, errand runner, or public relations manager." You really know how to use people. You're killing me. Let's do it! Who wants me to be a man?! If you don't make money, you certainly won't take me out!"

Xiao always said to say, do anything really dont let Li Hua worry, meet things to discuss to do, details than a woman is also careful and thoughtful. Party A director Li is very appreciative of Xiao, like the horse of the northeast young man. The project payment of that phase was approved as scheduled, which really solved a big problem!

Li Hua fulfilled his promise, deliberately chose a sunny weekend, let Xiao always drive the second-hand black Audi car bought during the company's entrepreneurship, to the direction of Huanggang County West Mountain!

The scenery is beautiful on the way, the leaves are lush, and the fragrance of a branch permeates both sides of the path. Drive down the hill to the parking lot, then walk up the hill. The mountain road is like a winding circle, slowly walking up to the top of the mountain. Up a road, down a road, go halfway up the mountain, want to retreat are difficult.

Li Hua walked in front and looked back at Xiao, who fell dozens of meters away, and said, "You can't climb anymore?" We have to go up while we have some strength. We can't stop. To the mountain have Dongpo cake to eat, limited

queue to buy. That is the specialty of this mountain, after eating with a bit of Xianqi, fortune-telling more spirit. Draw one and you'll be happy to come. We will eat our fast today and make sure you are satisfied."

Xiao always said with a mischievous smile, "You sent me like this today and asked me to eat vegetarian food." I know that I like meat, no meat is not happy, this whole person is not good to eat, I have no strength to drive back to the company!"

Li Hua tilted his head to look at the sky, "Go, maybe it's going to rain, run!"

Xiao hurried to follow. Looking at the sky, the sun hid in the clouds, and the woods felt cool. In the mountains, the climate is changeable, the air is unusually good, and the fragrance of flowers and trees is also refreshing. Small running mountaineering, stop and go, talking and laughing, less than 1 hour, we arrived at the gate of the West Mountain Pavilion. Li Hua bought two tickets and took Xiao directly to the place where the monk was chanting.

Quietly follow the crowd waiting in line, those young men and girls how to ask for Buddha, Xiao always how to do. Li Hua also religiously according to do, kneel in front of the Buddha, silently read the heart of the three wishes, wish the Buddha bless everything smoothly, wish the business is booming, financial resources widely enter, wish all the wish!

After kneeling in silence, General Xiao kowtowed three heads in succession, and then quietly told Li Hua: "I drew a sign, asking me to go to the merit box to donate money, how much should you give?"

Li Hua looked at the Buddha worship, whispered: "Your own heart, there is good faith!"

Xiao put his hand in his pocket, took out the 600 yuan prepared in advance and put it into the merit box, "Picture a good idea!" Let our company make more money, so that I can buy a house this year and become a multimillionaire!" After saying that, Xiao laughed all the time. He also knows that this is money to buy a spiritual sustenance, a wish, come there is sincerity, Xiao always stuck in the heart than painted "Buddha bless me smoothly."

Xiao always took it to the monk master to unsign it. Sign said "know the wind and risk, but sincere has set, ride the wind and waves, will win the universe!"

"Good sign, good sign! The monk smiled and looked at the big round red face of Xiao General, rang the bell three times, Xiao General quickly knelt down and kowtowed three sounds. This is a 180-degree bow and kowtow. Li Hua, with the same sincerity, took the signature in his hand and hurriedly hid it in his bag. She understood the meaning of the signing, the heart is very happy, this trip was not in vain. Sign said "Mingjun heart, performance all over the world, no matter the ends of the earth, there is a seat, mountains and mountains, must be right and wrong of the idle!"

It is this good sign to give Li Hua faith, no matter where, Li Hua all draw on the sign hidden in her world!

Chapter 41: Three Years of Hardship

After signing on, Li Hua's attitude is more positive, she does not consider anything, hard work, and partners Xiao total together to do a few good projects. In the three towns of the province, several important landmark buildings have her company's doors and Windows project! Several big developers have joined hands with Li Hua Company. Due to the good quality and timely delivery of the construction period, the reputation has been well-known in the same industry, and the qualification has no words.

Xiao always found a large private enterprise in northeast Liaoning to rely on as an aluminum base, due to good reputation and timely payment of goods, but the factory gave Li Hua Company greater preferential conditions for cooperation, to achieve a three-way win-win situation. This is exactly the development concept that Li Hua is willing to see, we all get rich together, develop together, and seek the greatest cooperation benefits together. Three years of cooperation, Xiao and Li Hua cooperation has been very happy, never in the profit dividend distribution of disagreements and contradictions. Xiao always satisfied, he wanted the company to have a bigger and better development.

Soon to the third anniversary of the establishment of the company, at the celebration wine party, Xiao always with a northeast dialect, passionately said: "I actually do not speak seriously, everyone usually said to me 'where you do, we will follow you', I was really touched by it." I really appreciate everyone being so hard on me. I have nothing to say, I am just a rough man from the military background, and in the past three years, everyone has given me great support and help, so that I can overcome the most difficult times."

"This has been smooth along the way, but also thanks to our company chairman

Li Hua Li's support and strong help." In the most difficult year to start the company, I had no score at all, it was Li Dong who gave us the first project contract; In the later stage, when our company was facing the critical moment of capital loss, it was Li Dong who sincerely asked Party A to timely allocate the project payment of our company. That's really timely, the money back is used for workers' wages, raw material settlement, freight, plant rent, water and electricity and all expenses. I remember at that time, Xiao and Li Dong's remaining funds were just enough to pay for the reunion dinner that year."

"But these, Li Dong never let me complain. Li Dong said, "The difficulty is temporary, the eight people will go to work at the beginning of the year, do a good job has signed the contract project, they will get the down payment." We do good quality, let the leaders rest assured, you don't have to worry about money. 'You know what? I Xiao general from that moment on, determined to follow Li Dong. Today to say this, but also to celebrate the wine, to Li Dong a cup, thank you! I'll leave it at that! Now please ask Li Dong to speak to us all, everyone welcome!"

At that time, the company and the construction team of more than 30 people, the number of people is not much. The venue is located in the small venue of the Westin Hotel on the edge of the river view, once only to sign a contract with the party to go to this high-end hotel, but today the workers and teachers who work together to fight together are invited here. This is a very meaningful measure, Xiao always said is to let the workers know that this is called sharing the good and bad, encourage everyone to share the joys and sorrows with the company. The company is good, the workers have hope, now the company is not Li Hua and Xiao total two people's company.

There was warm applause in the venue, Li Hua, as a legal person of the company, is ready to say a few words on this occasion - the summary of the official field must have the meeting agenda. But did not expect is that Xiao can really talk, the situation is talked about the actual, which let Li Hua moved, temporarily forgot the prepared speech, the mind is blank. In the cheers to the venue on the platform of Li Hua, a hard to think, I say which sentence when the beginning?

Li Hua thought and slowly picked up the adjusting upright microphone and looked up at the crowd. At that moment, she could not see who was who, only that people were waiting for her to speak. "My God, why so nervous!" Li Hua thought on second thought, as usual and workers chat on a piece of it. 'Yes, from here! Li Hua slowly relaxed the mood, the microphone expanded a touching show of true feelings.

"Hello, everyone, I wanted to give you a summary, the results of Xiao's words are too touching, I also because of moved confused thinking, forget the original plan to talk about the content." Now I'll say what I think, and don't take it personally if I'm wrong."

"First of all, I have to thank Xiao General, convinced me to join the company to work together, and insisted on cultivating me as a layman to become a member of this professional door and window team." Thanks to our efforts, we have seen hope and development prospects in the past three years of project cooperation. At the same time, what I am most grateful for is that everyone is kind, hard-working and resolute in their work, and everyone has a spirit of indomitable defeat. Seeing the workers and teachers on the construction site without complaining and silently paying to complete all the installation tasks during the construction period, I have sufficient confidence and confidence to negotiate with Party A and submit the application form of project payment return report. It is everyone that let me have the face and courage to fight with Party A, get the company's project payment in time, and save the company's fund disconnect problem in time."

"I can be a good logistics work, with Xiao general technical construction tasks, are trivial things." Compared with the hard work of the workers and teachers, it is much easier. Thank you all for your love and understanding. Because of everyone's concerted efforts, the development of our company today is a good situation. I cannot express my gratitude in one sentence or two words. I can only take this wine to express my best wishes to all my colleagues present here. I wish you all health and happiness, all the best! Cheers!"

Li Hua discussed with Xiao before, and decided to make a high-profile summary in a five-star hotel with luxury specifications on the occasion of the third anniversary of the company's establishment, in order to boost everyone's morale. And this time the celebration party did achieve the desired effect. Li Hua saw that the company has slowly entered the right track, the project increases every year, but also expanded to the door and window projects in other provinces. In the past three years, Li Hua's responsibility is getting bigger and bigger, there is no day's rest time, when it comes to the festival, the workers can have a holiday, but Li Hua can not relax down, but also have to consider the company's further development.

On the New Year's Eve of the Spring Festival, Li Hua sat in front of the TV to watch the Spring Festival Gala. It seems to be the first time after the establishment of the company so comfortable, indulge in the living room sofa lounging, a pair of elegant small feet on the coffee table. It's rare to relax so much and enjoy that warm feeling in your own home without any scruples.

When I bought this suite, Xiao, who was doing the door and window project, insisted on persuading Li Hua to install the floor heating facilities. Li Hua in order to save natural gas, has been reluctant to open geothermal heating. I really did not expect that the Spring Festival of that year, the furnace city of Wuhan in Hubei Province came a heavy snow, and the weather was surprisingly cold. Li Hua had to turn on the geothermal heating and felt really comfortable.

Old people often say that no matter how much you want to visit relatives, do not choose to go out on New Year's Eve. The local custom is that you must guard your home for the New Year and guard the God of wealth. Since doing business, Li Hua has listened to all these customs, in order to figure out a good luck and pleasure. Coupled with the cold weather, Li Hua is more at ease to stay at home, do whatever you want, look at the Spring Festival Gala program, relax your mood, is really a rare time!

On this day, only Li Hua was at home alone, and her daughter went to her father's place for the New Year. This is the first time the daughter has been invited by her father since she started working. Before going to see her grandparents, her daughter said to Li Hua: "My father called me and told me that my grandparents wanted me to go to their home for the New Year dinner, Mom, do you want to go?" I listen to you!"

Li Hua thought for a few seconds and asked her daughter, "What do you think? After all these years, you want to see? You tell me the truth."

The daughter carefully looked at Li Hua and said, "Listen to my father's tone is very good, that is to say, I did a lot of Chinese New Year dishes that I loved to eat when I was a child, and want me to go to the reunion dinner with you." Also said grandpa grandma always mention you how good, dad said grandma pointed to the wall hanging you hold me that picture said, look at the granddaughter has grown up, still don't come to see us. She said you were a good daughter-in-law and her son was not blessed. So, I want to see my grandparents! Their families only recognize you as their daughter-in-law."

Li Hua thought about what her daughter said is also reasonable, after she divorced her daughter's father, she handled the relationship with her ex-husband's family very well, and did not break face. Li Hua said to her daughter, "You go to have a look, and bring my unit's oil and two bottles of good wine to my grandparents." In addition to the two cashmere sweaters for business relations, you give them to your father to wear, but do not say that these are from me, understand? Just don't mention my name."

The daughter said happily, "Well, you agree, then I will go to my grandparents' home for the 30th New Year's Eve dinner." So are you gonna be home alone for the New Year? Why don't we go together?"

Li Hua went on to say, "You just go, what do I do?" You can tell me that you have graduated from college, found a good job with a stable salary, and can honor your grandparents. You bought all this, okay? Cut the rest of the crap."

The daughter knows Li Hua is very stubborn, the family will not go back to the past. Before, her father was too unkind to Li Hua, now Li Hua put down personal grudges, let her daughter bring so many gifts, rebuild the family, this is Li Hua's kind atmosphere. After all, Li Hua and the father of the child have no contact for more than ten years, and the feelings are weak; But a daughter's blood bond can never be broken. Li Hua himself can not walk around, can not affect the daughter's thoughts! Li Hua is Mingli's mother, and her daughter is in charge of this. Her daughter had more family affection, more love from the big family, and she was pleased. After all, it was once a family, and it was Li Hua who insisted on divorce, and how many of her daughters had some guilt.

On the afternoon of New Year's Eve, her daughter went out early and Li Hua stayed at home alone. The TV was playing all the time, but Li Hua didn't know when to fall asleep. It was a sound sleep, undisturbed. Li Hua thought, maybe only she will worry about work during the New Year, people all over the country are celebrating the New Year, this time who will bother themselves because of work? So Li Hua turned his mobile phone on silent and enjoyed the peace and quiet of the festival.

Li Hua, who slept to wake up naturally on the first day of the New Year, was hit by the knock on the door loud and lazy: "Who is it?"

Li Hua opened the door and saw that it was Xiao with his wife and the project manager's brother-in-law and his family who came to pay New Year's greetings to Li Hua. Xiao always can not forget the New Year to partner Li Hua New Year. In private, Xiao always directly called Li Hua, 16 years older than him, Li sister, in some occasions called big sister. "Sister Li, it is our family to give you a happy New Year, may you come into a good fortune, a happy New Year, all the best, smooth sailing!"

Xiao has not entered the door, the northeast voice has been in Li Hua's ears. Li Hua sounds very kind and warm in his heart. At this time, the friendship of friends, partners and colleagues is better than the concern of relatives, which is really rare. Li Hua sorted out the clothes, drank a sip of water, quickly put the blanket on the sofa into the bedroom, and then went straight to the gate and ran.

The moment I opened the door, I saw Xiao's family, all wearing red coats, red scarves, children wearing red hats, a jubilant holiday dress.

Li Hua hurriedly greeted them into the house: "The family is prosperous to celebrate the holiday! Come in. It's cold outside and warm inside. '

Mr. Xiao's wife said, "Sister Li, happy New Year. This is my local specialties, glutinous rice dumplings, and apples, in peace, you accept it, as the New Year to open a meat, eat some vegetables, taste some fresh."

Brother in law walked to the living room, said: "Sister Li, the floor heating effect is very good, this year is cold, really use it." Were we right to advise you to install it that year?"

Xiao then said, "Your big sister is reluctant to enjoy, this is the first time it has been opened under heavy snow this year?"

Mr. Xiao and his family are sitting in the living room eating tea and chatting 突 but Li Hua's daughter also came back, when she entered the house, she shouted: "Ah! It's so busy, I thought I'd be the first one home to call my mom. Xiao is good, everyone! Thanks for seeing my mom!"

Then he said to Li Hua: "Mom, this is the spicy dish that dad made for you, I know you like this taste." Grandma put it in a bottle and let me bring it to you. And this is the stove grandpa gave you, and this is the glove aunt gave you, saying that we have time to get together!"

The daughter said a bunch of words in one breath, are the care and blessing of her husband's family. Li Hua heart moved, eyes are also wet, she did not obviously show, said to her daughter: "You have a good time, go to wash your hands, eat reunion dumplings together." This is the whole vegetarian dumplings made by Mr. Xiao himself, you can eat at ease!" Li Hua's family are vegetarians, Xiao always knows it with his friends.

Li Hua this year really unforgettable also very happy, the daughter tied up the family again, the previous resentment knot opened. That year was the third year of the company's creation, and everything was developing in a good direction, including family and friendship. Li Hua suddenly felt that the grievances of these ten years had been relieved. She thinks it pays to be a good person. No matter how hard it is, Li Hua has adhered to the bottom line of being a good person, and only by being a valuable person can he get real respect. He is confident from the inside out and exudes a strong personality charm. Li Hua has been refined out of a pair of things do not panic attitude, when things are not anxious, mature and stable.

Chapter 42: Transfer of Company

These years Li Hua work life is very full, but also know different industries of high-end people, learned a lot of knowledge can not be learned in school. In this mixed society of dragons and snakes, grow up step by step, recognize people long lessons, and eat countless small losses. Have encountered no quality of enterprise leaders; I also met good leading cadres who did not touch alcohol and were not greedy for money. What kind of people, depends on how to deal with.

When Li Hua met male leaders more social, basically rely on Xiao general accompany. She knew Shaw had a knack for telling jokes, and he could handle it. Li Hua see Xiao total ability has exceeded their own, Li Hua began to plan to withdraw from behind the scenes, by Xiao always take the lead over the work. She wants to sign the project contract by Mr. Xiao as the company' s New Year' s gift. Also want to take advantage of this handover, find Xiao to have a good talk, will be 50% of the company legal person, all transferred to Xiao a legal person. Li Hua intends to completely delegate power, and he will specially follow up the expansion of business engineering negotiations, take the sale of aluminum as the leading, and cooperate with Xiao General operation of the entire company.

These three years of overwork and worry, Li Hua has been physically and mentally exhausted. In the dead of night, Li Hua after taking a bath, sometimes in order to improve sleep, before going to sleep will drink a glass of Taiwan boss sister Bian sent red wine. Looking at myself in the mirror wearing a robe, it seems that I have aged five years in the past three years. Looking at the thin face in the mirror, Li Hua suddenly thought that when the completion of the project, after the dividend profit must be good to themselves. When the transfer company let Xiao general officially took over, Li Hua quit the second line, at ease to arrange micro plastic surgery hospital, for their all-round beauty micro whole design.

This decision seems more important than continuing to work hard at the company, after all, Li Hua is the most beautiful. She can not write the unbearable years on her face, she wants to live out her favorite appearance. The current life is not the state she wants, money earned but premature old. She needs a sunny and confident self more, and now she can do this, she has such economic strength. In those days, the most fashionable way to show off your wealth was your own beautiful face. The face can break itself, the face is beautiful than a thousand words. This change of thinking made Li Hua generous to herself and willing to invest money in her talent and beauty.

Thinking of this, Li Hua made up his mind that he could not make money without face and good health. I have not had a good rest in these three years, and I have stayed up late and spent many sleepless nights. When a woman gets old, she's afraid to look at herself. Think of what if one day, those who have hurt their exes, or want to see her jokes to see their old faces, how humiliating! These vanity is also reasonable, Li Hua is not an immortal woman, but also ordinary women have the love of beauty.

People alive is a struggle for breath, if others only see the vicissitudes of life on Li Hua's face, a bruised bitter melon phase, there is no amount of money and house difficult to always hang in the mouth to say? If you see a person with poor spirits and an old face, who will believe that you are living a good life? If Li Hua really met those who hurt themselves, she would go to them to explain, to show off? Li Hua Kenning can't do what these children do. The only thing that can be changed is your state of life, give yourself a physical and mental vacation, and completely release yourself.

It is not difficult to save yourself, that is, to learn to let go. Li Hua thought that these years has been from poverty, step by step to achieve a house and a career. At present, her daughter is academically successful, and she can also take into account filial piety to her parents. Her economic level is increasing year by year, and she can

meet her basic expenses. Everything is good enough, there is nothing to take hard, and there is nothing that cannot be put down.

On the eighth day of the Spring Festival, Li Hua Company and Party A entered the construction site normally. After arranging the workers and handing over the task to Xiao's brother-in-law, the company immediately divided into two ways, leading the relevant management personnel of the party, small to the cashier accounting, large to the director cadres, invited to a local famous foot massage city, entertainment and relaxation. One is to thank them for their support and cooperation last year, and the other is to do a good job in the next year's business connection for Xiao, and recommend the key leaders of Party A to him. Li Hua wanted to bring all the business relations of the company to Xiao without reservation.

Invited leaders have arrived, at that time, the company only a second-hand Audi car, Xiao is a person. Li Hua contacted a business taxi with long-term cooperation and said to the driver, "You are responsible for sending these leaders you picked up, and remember that everyone should send a pre-prepared gift package to them." Now wait for these leaders to enjoy playing mahjong, you accompany the good service."

Li Hua finished the driver, and went to tell Xiao: "You go to sing with the leaders who love to sing, I will accompany Li director and cashier husband and wife to pedicure." Let's division of labor in this way, if there is a leader to go ahead, must send a text message to tell me, take care of each other, do not fall the leader. Don't talk about work! Remember, just relax!"

The eighth day of the day, the snow is flying, is never cold in previous years. This activity even the ordinary family members of the cashier were invited together, not only to invite the powerful leaders, so the leaders of the director can rest assured to participate in this party. Because it is a group event, everyone who participates feels sincere and respected. Everyone was happy and relaxed. These projects are much more real than just eating and drinking outside, and for people with different hobbies, they basically meet their own entertainment.

Moreover, the eighth day is the day of group worship, not the real working state, in fact, it is the buffer period of the holiday. After a long holiday, I have not really put my mind back to work, which is the norm in the office of public institutions. Li Hua too understand the work of public institutions, so not anxious not impatient to Xiao said: "Today only with good leadership, you unified checkout, open the voice to sing the first song." Say a little thank you before you sing."

That night the sky was full of white goose feather snow, haze and snow hanging on the roadside branches. The snow bent the branches, the leaves are seen as a white flower, the snow on the roof is already a thick layer of white cotton quilt. But there were buses on the road, moving very, very slowly. The city is really not simple, such a big snow or a succession of firecrackers, east and west not far from the sky rising colorful fireworks.

Li Hua chose to sit on the recliner beside Director Li and soak his feet. The hot water temperature was just right. Director Li is also filled with a large wooden bucket of hot water, Director Li said to Li Hua: "Mr. Li you are too polite, this work have any ideas, need my help in the place you feel free to say, I will support your work."

Li Hua said, "I am very grateful for Director Li's words. Today is to let everyone relax and thank you for your support of our work. In the future, on my company's side, Xiao will consult Director Li, please take care!"

The indoor heating is really enough, and everyone has a red face, enjoying the sleep brought by foot therapy. Li Hua quit the pedicure room first and finished her pedicure massage in advance. She quietly said to the technician: "Don't disturb them, if you finish, please let the leaders lie down and rest, don't wake them." Bring a snack halfway and leave on the coffee table."

After telling the waiter, Li Hua, Xiao and the taxi driver are waiting at the entrance to the living room. The leaders came out one by one, as arranged in advance, Xiao always sent him to the leader please into his car. The taxi driver brought his leader into the commercial car. Li Hua said hello to each leader, shook hands to say goodbye, and sent to the car.

Until the car started to leave far away, Li Hua did not enter the pedicure city to

look around and sit on the single sofa in the hall to look at the schedule. There are still 15 minutes to 9:30 PM, and the last bus can go directly to Li Hua's residential area. It takes about 40 minutes to get to the nearest bus stop.

Thinking of this, she immediately got through to Xiao General phone: "Xiao general, it is me, you don't have to say, I say you listen." It's late today, and the roads are slippery, so be safe. You sent the leader home, you don't have to rush back to pick me up, I can take the bus home by myself. When you're done, go straight home."

After the phone hung up, Li Hua quickly went outside the door, a deep and shallow step on the ground footprints, to the bus station across the road, accidentally fell a big fall. Hurry to get up and see that no passers-by have seen her funny appearance, the wind is biting, blowing in her face, and the snow is falling on the down hat curtain above her head. After a few minutes, Li Hua looked at himself like a puppet snowman, very cute. It's okay when we get to the platform. The train hasn't come yet. Wait outside here.

This day is finally busy, whether there is no result, but the company's sincerity and will, these leaders should feel. They feel that Li Hua and Xiao are real people to do things, go out to get on the car when the leaders shake hands with Li Hua, I can see that they sincerely thank Li Hua.

The bus arrived 10 minutes late and arrived at the station at 9:40. When Li Hua got on the bus, he had become a snowman. After stomping and kicking on the platform to ward off the cold, I got on the train and sat directly in the last row by the window and chose a corner to lean against. With the bump of the car, staggered to sleep. I do not know whether it is nervous or dare not sleep at all, Li Hua is always half awake and half asleep, afraid of sitting over the station, it is not convenient to return to the road. Li Hua is so close to the window, with his hand to wipe off the fog on the window to look out, outside has become a white snow city!

Do not know how long after, the bus automatically announced the name of the station: "Pengliu Yang Road station, to get off passengers, please get off from the back door in order." Li Hua woke up, got off the bus and looked at the highest building on the roadside, "Finally arrived, tonight is another sleepless night!" I'm too tired today, and when I enter the company tomorrow, I must talk to Mr. Xiao about the handover."

Li Hua remember that a lifetime of snow, taking the bus home lonely and tired scene, may also meet so big snow in this life.

By the next day, the snow was still falling, and basically the employees of the company were still in the holiday spirit. Li Hua sat in his office early and waited for Xiao to talk. Xiao always knew Li Hua's character, she decided things must be considered very mature, will say to him. Both sides openly exchanged hearts, Xiao always very reluctant to say: "I understand your intention to quit the company, so that everything can start again." But can you be my adviser forever, have a good network to continue to help introduce. What do you say we reward individuals for the projects we receive according to company regulations, subject to signing a contract with Party A?"

Li Hua smiled and said, "I knew you were afraid I would take off the burden and leave you alone." No, I will, as always, help you negotiate a good project, introduce you to Party A, and you will contact directly. The specific matters and work arrangements are up to you to decide, I will not interfere in any business of the company, do not interfere in all your personnel work arrangements in the later stage, I will only cooperate with you to sign business contracts successfully, so that you can grow rapidly. As for the individual bonuses, we will follow the rules we set before. In fact, you are already on your own, don't be afraid, you think about the autograph we drew at the Xishan Temple fair. The intention is clear, you are a future multimillionaire, I am only half of your ambition, a few million is enough. When you really become a multimillionaire, say that we will go together to pay the wish!"

This year, Li Hua completely realized the philosophy of life, when the wealth reaches the level of their expectations, there are more meaningful things than trying to make money. At this stage, Li Hua just wants to start slowing down and thinking calmly about some problems. She is not a woman who makes money just for the sake of making money, but to make life more meaningful. Life can not lack of

money, but money is not the source of happiness. Wealth can make people free, have more time to accumulate precipitation, and realize their dreams of life by investing in themselves, which is a virtuous circle and a perfect realm. Spiritual wealth and material wealth combined with the life, can enjoy the real happiness and happiness, the two kinds of wealth can not be short of one. With double happiness, is the real winner in life.

The next week, the sun finally shone on the city, and the snow gradually turned into water droplets, running into the ground from leaves, tree trunks, and cracks in the rocks. Such a good spring season, taking advantage of the good weather, Li Hua and Xiao successfully handled the handover procedures, the company legal person column of the form filled in Xiao's name. Xiao always smiled shyly to accept the formal transfer of the text, Li Hua said easily and happily: "No official a light ah, really can sign up to learn some interests and hobbies."

Li Hua already has the next learning goal in her mind, and she has not put down the literary dream in her life. Li Hua has written the mail into the nearby post office box, it is a written letter to register for learning, Li Hua will attend the Beijing humanities writing correspondence class. This will be a new level. Li Hua does not stop the learning requirements of self-improvement, in each stage of growth, will give themselves a goal, will also be surprised in that field. The achievement of a writer who wants to do the writing dream, is imsubtly from Li Hua's inner germination of a kind of power. It is time to build up the basic knowledge and practice writing, and it should not be too late to start.

Chapter 43: Developing a market for wine Sales

In the 1990s, the city mainly focused on attracting investment policies, and bestie Jane units were just responsible for receiving and negotiating to follow up the implementation of foreign companies. Jane is very responsible and organizational ability, in order to let foreign companies in the mainland business as soon as possible, usually in addition to normal working hours to receive these foreign companies and relevant responsible person, weekends or holidays with them to organize some networking activities. Jane always says there are no working days and days off in this job.

Taiwan enterprises Bian total husband and wife is one of the main service objects of bestie Jane. Jane did everything she could for them and was always there for them when they had fun. In the weekend entertainment activities, Jane often took Li Hua to participate in those high-level small gatherings, attended the party has the public institution section level, bureau level cadres, and sometimes the mayor who is in charge of this investment promotion work also invited.

At the event, it is said that there is no talk about work, but when there is a big leader present, Bian will sometimes inadvertently ask some preferential conditions for policy. These leaders have done the work of foreign companies at the grassroots level, implemented it, and sometimes it has become an on-site office. Always a wise female boss, Bian made important decisions when she and her husband's private company came to invest in the mainland. Bian was always a forceful woman.

Bian was almost sixty that year, and Jane and Li Hua were only in their thirties at that time, the prime age for their careers. They were the kind of women Bian always liked. Mr. Bian once said in front of the mayor: "Thanks to the leadership to

take care of our Taiwan enterprises, and arrange such capable beauties to cooperate with our work, I am very assured that the enterprise will be introduced to the city and enter the next step of investment in the wine market."

That's when Li Hua met Bian as a friend. Later, during the opening of Li Hua's clothing discount store in the provincial capital, Bian always heard about it, and personally went to the "Lianhu edge" clothing store to invite Li Hua out of the mountain, and again invited Li Hua in many cities inside and outside the province to open the wine sales market, expand business, and sell to provinces and cities throughout the country.

At that time, Li Hua had multiple jobs and did not agree to Bian's request, just said: "I will help Bian recommend wine on occasions when I need to use wine, free service." After I have been busy for a while, I will help Manager Bian to arrange a few orders before the festival. Would you like to see Manager Bian?"

Bian always saw that Li Hua was really busy, and the words were all said to this, and there was no reluctance. She knew Li Hua was well connected and had a flexible business mind. Li Hua has promised to help with the recommendation, and Bian is also a good harvest. She is very grateful to Li Hua for her help. After that, Mr. Bian made an appointment with Li Hua from time to time to maintain the relationship. Of course, Li Hua was also paying attention to the wine business of Mr. Bian everywhere, so every time they got together, they would always make an appointment with friends of different professional identities and introduce them to Mr. Bian. Late wine market several major customer girlfriend, are Li Hua often go to the beauty salon boss Qin Qin, and similar to other industry circles girlfriend.

When Li Hua transferred the door and window engineering company to partner Xiao, Li Hua actually arranged the future career direction. She did not forget the sincere invitation of the husband and wife, she did not forget that she had done insurance, had done wholesale station director, those business model and customer dealing skills are Li Hua's strengths. Bestie Jane often said: "can be a man, do not worry about no career."

Bestie Jane said in front of Bian: "I introduce Li Hua to you, I promise you will regard her as a treasure in the future." Li Hua is a talented person, a real sales champion, with a quick brain. The most important thing is that she always thinks of the other side, and will not lose money on profits when cooperating with her. People like to do business with real people. She can close a business, whether it is an individual or an organization, or a private wedding, she can do it all! Mr. Bian, now you have set up your home and company in Wuhan, and Li Hua is also in Wuhan. This is really the right time, the right place and the right people. Together, you can definitely push the wine to more cities, and the sales will only be bigger than in previous years!"

Bian said excitedly, "Thank you for introducing me to my good sister Li Hua. I only trusted Li Hua in Wuhan. Whether Li Hua comes to the company or not, I will take Li Hua as a long-term partner of my company, she can work at home and abroad by phone. For Li Hua, I do not require Li Hua to work eight to five in the morning."

Bian experienced a successful random sales of Li Hua, that is, a phone chat, the leader of the wife about to the beauty salon, asked her to do facial and body maintenance, the wine business became! Bian always knew that Li Hua was not deliberately to recommend the sale of red wine, her marketing model is the first consideration to make friends comfortable, this is the first person! Friends recognized Li Hua's character, think about what win-win project to talk about later, will not be moved?

After Li Hua's parents moved to the provincial capital, Li Hua found time to go back to his hometown and sell the spare house he had bought for his parents. In order to promote Bian's red wine, Li Hua can give the wine as a favor for free tasting, or as a gift to partners.

This time, she suddenly thought of a friend, the bank branch high president, he knew that some customers have the need to buy a house, but also have the economic strength to buy a house. After getting through to President Gao's phone, President Gao asked a few polite words with concern: "What good project did Mr. Li have back home this time?" Don't forget to let me know!"

Li Hua said seriously: "There is really one thing, you can help me."

President Gao also said seriously: "Anything, as long as I can do it, I will help."

Li Hua went on to say, "OK, please ask President Gao to get together at the teahouse on Phoenix Road after work and have a good talk." If you have friends around you who are trustworthy, have economic strength, and need to buy a house, you can also bring them to the teahouse and chat while drinking tea. Of course, today you can bring sincere friends to buy a house better!"

President Gao thought about it and immediately replied: "There really is a business friend who wants to buy a house because he wants his children to go to school in the city." I can ask him to talk to you directly at the teahouse. I won't send a message. You two do it in person. He's got the money in my bank, so there shouldn't be any problem. Then I will contact you and meet you directly at the teahouse after work!"

President Gao is Li Hua's fellow townspeople, people are very simple and enthusiastic, do this position today, all rely on a good person, have a good service attitude, and business fine, in the line savings task completion is always the first. His job scope has gone beyond the requirements of the savings task, and he treats his clients as friends and helps them out. So clients are willing to help support his work. Li Hua is in the business contact, understand President Gao's person, know that he is willing to help, trustworthy, so this time the first thought of letting President Gao to introduce the need to buy a house and rich big customers.

Back in her hometown, Li Hua likes to go to a beauty salon near the teahouse for a two-hour relaxation program, facial moisturizing and neck treatment, and then have a good sleep there. Because of the annual card, usually come back halfway, and do not want to trouble friends to entertain, she went to the beauty salon to spend time. This is a good place for Li Hua to meet her girlfriends.

Three hours soon passed, the spirit of Li Hua who had done beauty was very good, and a pair of small hands of the beautician stroked the finger on the face skin was really comfortable. Li Hua when tired, always like to listen to the gentle hypnotic music here, enjoy the kind of gentle massage in place. Being single for many years, Li Hua has developed a good habit of loving herself. In order to work in the spirit of some, Li Hua often use this way to quickly recover their physical strength, eliminate the journey fatigue. So in the eyes of friends, Li Hua always looks refreshed, feeling Li Hua in reverse growth, more and more the kind of mature intellectual beauty charm of women.

Bestie Jane also came to the beauty salon, did an hour of the project, and then Li Hua said the purpose of the trip. Bestie Jane did not say a word, Li Hua invited himself to buy a seven-seat new car. Jane said happily, "This car will be the special car to pick you up, as long as you go back home, I will pick you up." In addition, if you buy this owner to help Benson always do some wine sales, convenient to send some goods. I still work and can't be in the wine business full time like you."

Li Hua said, "That's a good idea, I was wondering how you could buy such a big car because you are so slim." Now I understand that you really wasted your talents by not doing business."

Jane said: "Our unit does not have a good policy for your unit, I have to work until the age of 55 to retire!" I'm just bringing some of Mr. Benson's wine to my restaurant friend, not like you, which is 40 cases of wine in a cart. You're selling your house today. How many more cases of wine are you selling?"

Jane's joke really reminded Li Hua that she had a good idea!

Chapter 44: The All–Win Scenario

At six o 'clock in the evening, Li Hua and Jane sat in the seats near the window of the designated teahouse. Just ordered a pot of fruit tea and snack fruit platter, high president came, along with a smiling middle-aged man. Before sitting down, President Gao introduced to Li Hua: "This is my friend boss Liu, today to talk to you about buying a house, tea and chat!"

Li Hua to President high and boss Liu introduced the boudoy Jane, this is like a serious business, Li Hua could not help but laugh to himself. Liu boss said: "Can you show me the real estate certificate?"

Li Hua took it out of the bag, handed it directly to Boss Liu and said, "I like Boss Liu's style of doing things, straight!"

President Gao also added: "General Liu is this character, if the agreement is settled today, tomorrow can follow the procedure." Can I see the existing apartment later?"

Li Hua took out the key and said, "OK, here it is, let's have a look today!"

"Where does Mr. Liu work and what kind of company does he run?" Jane asked Liu about the general situation from the side and wanted to know what company he was the boss of.

Liu general while looking at the real estate certificate, answered: "I will do some steel, building materials business!" Then he said to Li Hua, "Is this house on the top floor? The area is OK, but will it be very hot in summer? Listen to President Gao introduced the situation of your community, I feel good, I do need to buy a house. If there is no problem after seeing the existing house, I will buy this house. As for the price, I offer 520,000, what do you think?"

Li Hua quoted a price of 540,000 yuan before, hearing that Liu cut 20,000 yuan, Li Hua was silent for a while and smiled to President Gao and said: "President Gao, didn't you tell Liu the total price?"

President Gao said, "I have told Mr. Liu about your offer. As for the transaction price, you two talk directly, I will not intervene."

General Liu then said: "My side of the idea is very simple, you Li general take care of it, we save the intermediary fee, Li general here does not lose." If you agree, I am also a pleasant person, and immediately give you a deposit of 20,000 yuan, how about? I know Mr. Li is also busy, and it would be good for Mr. Li to close the deal as soon as possible. The most important thing is that I am really busy, if it were not for the invitation of the high president, so save you and I common roundabout links, Li Zong you set!"

All said to this, bestie Jane took a look at Li Hua, and then shouted the waiter: "order food!"

The waiter asked enthusiastically: "What kind of soup do the leaders want?" This is a picture of the latest recommended dishes in our teahouse."

President Gao took out a concession card and handed it to the waiter, "Use this card to pay!" You can order whatever you want!"

Mr. Liu smiled and ordered a soup rice with chicken. Mr. Gao said, "I want a steak and a fruit salad." Jane ordered a fish fragrant eggplant pot, Li Hua ordered a braised fish soup.

It's really hard to say, like this four people four meals, or to the teahouse is more appropriate. Li Hua thought that her best friend Jane had given her a few minutes to think. Jane's eyes told Li Hua, accept the deposit first, such a price is reasonable, the current local second-hand house prices are this market, can be closed.

Li Hua realized that the difference between these intermediary fees is equal to directly transferring profits to the buyer Liu, and this time it is President Gao to come forward, the funds are guaranteed, and do not worry about receiving the housing money after selling the house. Because there is no real estate agent to guarantee, we can only trust President Gao, and there should be no problem with him being the President.

After a few minutes of mental evaluation, Li Hua joked: "Oh, Liu will really bargain, the agency fees are directly reduced." You are President Gao's friend, the first time to meet, talk business is also easy. Listen to the general meaning of Liu, the loss of only this good house. Now that we're all friends, I have to take more care of my wine business! That's it! You can have it! This house is a feng shui treasure! You see, our family has been promoted to a provincial capital."

General Liu Lingguang, immediately picked up a glass of beer to Li Hua said: "Cheers to the deal!" And took out two envelopes of bank paper bag banknotes to Li Hua, "the twenty thousand yuan deposit first take!" Gao President also picked up the cup, and bestie Jane also raised her head, together with the head to drink the wine in the cup!

President Gao put down the cup and said: "This is the easiest business connection I have ever dealt with, and the two ceos are really refreshing!" I can say a few more words today. Although Mr. Li is a lady, she is no worse than a man. I admire her. Let's have a drink! As for the red wine recommendation, it is really possible to ask General Liu to help sell! This favor, you General Liu should help, others General Li suddenly let you 20,000 yuan, atmospheric people, do not make money is difficult!"

President Gao used the method of encouragement, and General Liu had to say: "I am willing to try, just before the Spring Festival can get a batch, get a few boxes to send related households to drink first, see how the effect is."

Li Hua thought about it and said, "President Gao is like this, I said before, who helps me sell the house, the agency fee of 20,000 yuan will be given to who." Did not think that the intermediary fee was given to General Liu - well, the fat water does not flow outside the field, now we are friends. Now President Gao brokered the business of buying and selling houses between the two sides, and I did not get any benefits. And now you're setting me up with Mr. Liu to sell wine. That's too much. I want to deal with it like this, after the house is completed the transfer procedures, the house is in place, and the house is handed over on the same day. Before the Spring Festival, I will first send 40 cases of red wine to President Gao and General

Manager Liu. The wine tasting is my gift, and if there is a sale, I will reward President Gao for doing something good and helping me. I'm giving away all 40 cases of wine! How about, no pressure to help me!"

Li Hua send wine to open up the market bold approach, let boudoir Jane long experience. No wonder Li Hua often heard, reluctant to give up sheep, can not set the Wolf's hunger promotion law, Li Hua gave her a lesson with examples today.

Later things are also very smooth, Li Hua's house not only in time for the Spring Festival before the transaction, received 50% of the house payment. Li Hua thanked President Gao for his timely help with wine. Li Hua thought, this is more beneficial than giving a red envelope of twenty thousand yuan. First, the market profit part of the wholesale price and retail price of 20,000 yuan red wine gave President Gao a gift; Second, gave President Gao to continue to help recommend the red wine market, first to supply shops to pave the way for goods, so that President Gao no pressure to accept the wine; Third, on the occasion of the Spring Festival, many human exchanges need to send wine as the best time to help Bian expand a multi-level sales platform.

When bestie Jane with Benson always said Li Hua cushion 40 boxes of wine to friends, Benson always more appreciated Li Hua. Manager Bian said to Jane, "Li Hua also paid 10,000 yuan in advance for wine last time, and brought his friend's son to learn the wine business. The profits from that batch of wine went to the son of the best friend. Later, the young man continued to purchase several batches of red wine, and really earned the first bucket of gold in life. Li Hua's good friend, the young man's mother, later became the godmother of Li Hua's daughter. I really admire Li Hua as a person, she has great wisdom, she has developed some good friends with sales potential into wine recommendation winners, not only earn money, but also win friendship."

On New Year's Day that year, Bian and his wife gathered together all the friends who had developed the wine business in Li Hua, not only organized everyone to dine and sing, but also presented high-grade new wine products. Bian head office to Li Hua returned a big favor, but also pushed the red wine to a variety of sales channels virtuous circle.

Li Hua that year is the private needs of the scattered business to do a living, such as beauty salon owner activities, Li Hua suggested to do a member of the customer to send wine; For private wedding venues, they are also sold to the host at a wholesale price, so that they can get a profit margin of red wine. Li Hua to do these means of distribution is simply for the sake of each other, put the profits on the table to say, the interests to the recommended party. Sometimes it is their own money first, after the transaction to make money, in the receipt of profit sharing at the same time, the cost of recovery.

One day Bian received a phone call from Qin Qin, the boss of Ruan's beauty salon: "Sister Bian, Li Hua asked me to come to you directly. I want to order 30 cases of Winery wine for the Spring Festival this year. Can you give us the same price as Li Hua?"

Manager Bian replied, "Li Hua is in charge, and I will give you the price." Only to count the sales of Li Hua, in order to enjoy this three-level wholesale price!"

Qin Qin said happily, "Thank you Sister Bian, no wonder Li Hua helped you and me so much." You two are so nice! Come to our beauty salon then, send you to do the project! Next month, we will open a beauty salon in Zhongnan Road 2, with higher specifications. Now I will verbally invite you, Mr. Bian, and you will certainly come to enjoy the premium service treatment of members. It will please you!"

Li Hua has long been a lifetime senior member of five stores of Qinqin Beauty Salon. Li Hua was tired of struggling outside, or came back late from the province to send wine, will do several sets of projects in the beauty salon of Qin Qin. Facial cleansing, neck care, ovarian maintenance, hip lift, breast enhancement and other beauty physical techniques, doing doing Li Hua will unconsciously fall asleep. Sometimes it is noon to the store, to seven o 'clock in the evening to come out, Li Hua slept for a few hours, full of energy. This is also a way for Li Hua to coordinate and relax, Li Hua is also a woman, and is a woman who is willing to love beauty. My daughter godmother said to Li Hua: "I just appreciate Li Hua this, generous to friends, also willing to themselves." Unlike some women, when misers, women who do not invest in themselves, will be willing to be good to others!"

Classmates Huiping and Sunny have personally seen Li Hua a beauty salon membership card value of 170,000 yuan, almost did not scare off the jaws of two people, this is seen with their own eyes yo, see Li Hua in the cause of their own hard, in the life of beauty maintenance of the cost of large, also have the strength of really hard really willing ah! Envy Li Hua has the strength also want to open. Should Li Hua said: "to be the master of money!"

Li Hua did red wine sales in those years, red wine sales to beauty salons, restaurants, three wholesale stations, back to the overall company wine market to expand outside the province, everywhere. Li Hua also brought out a lot of female friends to do wine sales, these elite women detachment from different industries, have obtained the nickname of "beautiful girl rich sister" ! Li Hua was called "beautiful sister" by them.

Chapter 45: Permanent Employment

Bian always in Hubei Province in the past few years of wine sales, took a fancy to Li Hua's loyalty, practical style of work. Every business is sold naturally, and there is no forced sale. But from the details, for the other side to save costs, so naturally do things. Li Hua directly did the promotion of red wine by example, and turned all the opportunities he needed to return the favor into sending red wine as a thank you gift. This has contributed to many natural sales success. She also helped several unemployed young people learn to go out into the world and to market themselves. After earning the first bucket of gold, I gained confidence in doing business and learned to find a suitable business world for myself. They also understand that it is not easy to work and earn money, and they also see the hard work of their parents.

Li Hua cares about the growth of the younger generation, her love for them is not to give red envelopes, but to teach them to do business. Let them be familiar with the various processes of purchasing, delivery, warehousing, and checkout, and learn to distribute profits. It also teaches them to tap new demand groups and carry out circular purchase and resale. The first support principal, into the principal plus profit, and then buy again to make money, like the successful business model said in the book, snowball the profit increase.

As long as the friends who have done wine business with Li Hua have seen the hope of making money from sales. Li Hua not only earned money, but also learned to think for his partners, and realize that the more interests of others, the more benefit himself. Human nature is so, you are really good to others, everyone wins, everyone wants to cooperate with you, and they will think of you when they make money. Everyone trusts a person who can lead them to earn money. Li Hua is such a person.

Bian saw that every single red wine sold by Li Hua had a touching story. With the simple help of Li Hua, Bian's overall wine market development slowly benefited from the vast number of consumers. Also teach the younger generation in the classroom can not learn social knowledge, wisdom, patience, kindness, sincerity, toughness, flexibility, all aspects of the words and deeds!

Bian never wanted to lose such a good friend as Li Hua, who was both a sales expert and the company's most effective partner. Bian discussed with her husband and decided to hire Li Hua as a salesperson for the company on a long-term basis. It was up to Li Hua to decide whether to work part-time or full-time.

Li Hua also knows how many pounds she has, she understands what she needs most, and what work is suitable for her current life status. Over the years, Li Hua has also experienced a number of industries, in each industry she is not reluctant to fight, can quickly turn around gorgeously. When the clothing store business is booming, she can decisively transfer the shop; When the business of the door and window company is booming, she is also willing to transfer the company. She knew that she could not blindly pursue money and wealth, while ignoring her spiritual needs.

She needed life to feed her dreams, and she needed time to slow down. She needs more time to do something more meaningful. While doing wine sales part-time, while doing her favorite real estate investment, this is the most suitable job for her. Through a year of amateur wine marketing, she also learned the truth of business.

The measure of selling the house also sent 40 cases of red wine, Bian was very moved after knowing that Li Hua really helped her to expand the wine market and open the sales within her power. On the eighth day of the Spring Festival of that year, President Gao called Li Hua as soon as he went to work and said, "Happy New Year, today I have asked Mr. Liu to come to the bank and remind him to pay the balance of your house, and all of it will be in place for you today." In addition, years ago to send out to taste the red wine, some as a gift, which recommends two secondary red wine wholesalers interested in talking to you about business. You see how it works, I will be the introduction to help you recommend!"

Li Hua was very happy to say: "Thank you for taking care of President Gao, the red wine sent out is counted as a gift I should thank you for." For the rest, please negotiate with the two secondary wholesalers directly, and directly send the retail invoice and the receipt of the purchase wholesale price to the distributor. You can share the profit with the distributor directly. This is to thank you and of course encourage you to recommend more wine to me in the future, and I can also get sales incentives from the head office."

President Gao said, "Give so much? How dare you!"

Li Hua said, "It doesn't matter, you will help me recommend more and sell more, and we will make money together." Small profits and quick sales, expand the market! Cake is everyone together to eat a long stream, thank you is my duty!"

Bian always knew that Li Hua's house payment was in place, and his heart was at ease. On the fifteenth day of the New Year, the weather was particularly good. Bian asked Li Hua to come to Jiangjing Tea City for dinner. Li Hua just have the development of new customers to book wine plans, also have to face to face with Bian total husband and wife talk about the plan, ready for delivery.

The tea town was Li Hua's favorite place to talk business, and Bian always respected Li Hua's preferences. Bian was very punctual. He went to the tea city in advance to choose a private room that was more suitable for talking. Li Hua arrived on time according to the address and room number that Bian said. They invariably give each other the gifts they bring. Bian took out a beautiful Hangzhou silk scarf and said, "It's too cold this year. I gave it to you to keep you warm. It also looks good with your clothes.

Li Hua smiled and said: "The two of us think of together again, but I only consider warm, two big red velvet scarf!" A little something for President Bian and Meng Dong."

Meng Dong said, "You have helped us innovate sales in the past year, and the company is ready to equip you with a full-time delivery driver." Price on the basis of the past, reach 100 boxes reward 10% profit! Only for you!"

Li Hua gratefully said, "Thank you, this is what I should do." I also benefited a lot by helping the company develop the wine market. Thank you Bian and Meng Dong for giving me multi-directional support and cooperation, so that I have a platform to display! Honestly, I accept to be a part-time recommended salesman for the company forever!"

Bian said, "That's just what we two old guys wanted to say, a formal invitation to you to be my company's off-staff sales director forever!" This seat is always for you!"

Meng Dong said, "Today we drink the best red wine of our company, and we have prepared two bottles of our new product for you to take home to your loved ones."

Bian said, "There is nothing else to do today. After dinner, we will sing together. Meng Dong wants to sing a Taiwanese song with you," Love to Fight Will Win!"

Just like the lyrics of the song, it takes hard work to win, and both Bian and Meng Dong are still struggling in their late 30s. With them as examples, Li Hua was naturally encouraged and continued to work hard. It is often said that "birds of a feather flock together" and people like to be with their own kind. People with positive energy attract Li Hua, Li Hua has a group of such strong people around. It is Bian's outstanding ability and decisive character that attracted Li Hua, and the two of them became friends of age and confidants in career and life. Li Hua wanted to be as successful as Bian, not to say that he must do much work, but to not let himself be idle, to do practical things like Bian, to be a useful person to society.

Manager Bian once said to Li Hua earnestly, "It's not just for money that Meng Dong and I are still doing this at our age. Our kids don't do what we do, they don't do what we do, and we both get sick. Since doing this industry, I feel very relaxed, as a friend to do business. Also, when you find a job for yourself, do your best to do it, spread the benefits out, and do not think that the cause is getting better and better, especially after the introduction of this wine from Spain. China is a big market, a large population, and the state has a good policy toward foreign enterprises. When we meet good friends like you to help and support us, we are more and more relaxed. The two of us have always advocated the concept of earning money, happy cooperation, common prosperity, doing healthy business, and making happy friends!"

Meng Dong also said contentedly: "Come to Hubei through the red wine friends, through your introduction, we all know the good friends around you, they have become our partners, we are really happy." Like Qinqin, the boss of the beauty salon, Zhou, Zhenzhen, Sunny, your daughter's godmother, your girlfriend's son, your sister's daughter, and the telecommunications sister Xu, and Unicom's Yan... They are all experts in sales. You have opened up another big wine market, which is something that neither of us can do, and neither of us thought of. It seems you don't want us two seniors to retire!"

Bian kept nodding and holding Li Hua's hand and said, "You know what? When Jen retires and joins us as a full-time wine salesman, she asks if you have any other ideas."

Li Hua smiled and said, "Don't praise me like this, where do I have any tricks?" Sister Bian, I sell to every customer, every package, you know how to make it happen. I have your company to support and cooperate with, and treat each other honestly. For partners, all profits on the table to talk about, reasonable distribution, 50/50 division, mutual help and win-win. In this way, every business profit is settled in time, profits are in place in time, and they are never hidden. Profit transparency, integrity, losses to themselves, benefits for each other to think. This way to treat people, cooperate to work together, but also afraid of partners do not find a trustworthy person to cooperate? I don't have much experience, but I'm practical."

Bian kept nodding his head and saying, "Yes, yes, it's called a blessing for the honest." Everyone likes to do business with someone like you, talk about projects, keep working with them. I don't care, you are me and Meng Dong forever partner, forever friend!"

Li Hua smiled excitedly and said: "We patronize to talk, I have this opportunity to sing an old song" Love is priceless "for the two bosses, to my business partner sister Bian Meng Dong. I wish you health and happiness, money rolling in! Wish us a happy cooperation and smooth sailing!"

The strobe light shone on the stage of Li Hua in the box, singing with a focused expression, singing with the true feeling and soft voice, and singing the theme of the song: Love is priceless.

Chapter 46: Investing in landmark homes

Li Hua has a good habit, after the promotion of wine business, will ask partners to do beauty nail art, in order to express gratitude. In addition, the girlfriend who is interested in red wine will be pulled up to drink tea together, so that the partners who have benefited from the order can share the joy of success with new friends casually and naturally. Li Hua is only responsible for paying the bill and introducing new friends to get together. Such a natural way of recommendation is a virtuous circle, so that Li Hua less say a lot of polite and hypocritical words, Li Hua sincerely treat people, extend the deep influence of more friends, voluntarily interested in cooperation with Li Hua.

Li Hua's sales success is based on this, never "Wang Po selling melons, boasting", but with the joy of sharing after the success of friends, speaking with facts, so that new friends are interested in red wine sales. Then teach by example, the scene by a friend to teach each step of the simple procedure. Friends demonstrate successful examples, new people see the hope of a deal and want to try in person, experienced friends are also willing to teach. This is also one of the reasons why Li Hua's sales network is getting wider and wider. Li Hua has another advantage, like to thank as soon as possible, even if it is a verbal commitment on weekdays, will be in the heart, at the right time to friends one by one to honor friendship, honor interests, honor gratitude.

Li Hua and Bian general cooperation, Li Hua vacated more free time, free Li Hua will search for valuable real estate investment information. On this day, Li Hua found a good investment project, and asked a friend to sit in a nearby teahouse, and he inadvertently talked about business opportunities.

In Wuhan in June, the weather is getting hot. Partner beauty salon Qin Qin has just promoted a single red wine business, Li Hua invited her to the highest specification of Jiangjing teahouse tea. Li Hua has a girlfriend QiQi who lives in a riverview room. She is also a beauty, beautiful and powerful woman. This time Li Hua made an appointment with Qiqi.

Li Hua thinks it's time for Qinqin and Qiqi to get to know each other. Although the age difference of the two is eight years, but the situation of the two people is very close, both are powerful single sex women, successful economic independence, are willing to spend money on their own health, we can interact in the same circle of friends. When people get together, they can speak freely, exchange and inspire a variety of intelligent ideas, and think to change people's fate.

The cry of Qin Qin interrupted Li Hua's thoughts: "Li Hua, you are so early, I arrived five minutes early." Has your good friend come yet?"

Li Hua got up and said, "Sit here and wait for her." Cookie's family lives in an upscale neighborhood around here. She has a little bourgeois charm and is doing well in her career, building and designing houses. She is a delicate little woman with good taste!"

Qin Qin confidently said, "I understand that all of your friends are strong people, including me."

Qin Qin mischievously praised Li Hua's friends, also praised himself, sweet mouth like wipe honey. Li Hua saw in Qin Qin clever inner show, also very good at talking, really want to learn from Qin Qin who is eight years younger than himself.

Qiqi walked through the glass door into the teahouse, wearing her floral dress, covered with gauze, which was enchanting and graceful like a fairy, as the breeze blew. "You're all here so early, I'm not late, am I?"

People and voices come into Qin Qin and Li Hua's sight at the same time. Qin Qin's jaw drops: "Li Hua, you said that your friend Qi Qi is the same age as you. You are both beautiful women! How old are you? I'm so jealous! Nice to meet the last two fairy sisters. Be sure to go to my beauty salon to do body care, I send you two project maintenance cards, let you enjoy!"

After saying this, Qin Qin not only introduced herself, but also praised the two

sisters smiling from ear to ear. Li Hua directly said to Qi Qi, "This is the young, capable and generous beauty salon owner Qin Qin, who has the strength of 5 beauty salons!"

Cookie reached out her little white hands and took Gin's slender hands. Qin Qin praised: "Wow, so will maintain, hands are so beautiful, a look is to know how to invest in themselves, will maintain the beauty!" Seriously, there are no ugly women, only lazy women! After tea, go to my place to do the body easy open back! Free!"

Li Hua looked at Qin Qin actively recommend their own beauty salon, just the right natural introduction, appreciate her business ability. Li Hua smiled and took out an envelope from her bag and handed it to Qin Qin: "This is the money for the wine that was paid yesterday. Mrs. Yu you recommend is really generous, Bian the driver will deliver the goods, she directly signed the invoice payment. Here's your 50 percent. Take it!"

Qin Qin replied, "So soon? So easy to make money?"

Li Hua looked at the tea and ordered drinks, replied Qin Qin: "You can do, relationship iron, Yu total goods received, also said thank you." She gave her employees bonus wine on the Dragon Boat Festival, she was a private enterprise, she said!"

Qin Qin and Li Hua came to a matching conversation, Qi Qi understood and said to Li Hua, "You two can make wine so easily, why don't you bring me?"

Li Hua patted Qi Qi's hand and said, "You know I always make wine, and I also introduced you to Manager Bian." You've been focusing on your engineering instead of this little business. We just do it for fun, we also like to drink some every day, good sleep! If you are interested, ask Qin Qin to teach you how to get started."

"I think Cookie can do a better job than me because she has more connections and needs more people," Gen said. We can only move the mouth to make a single, other delivery, collection, all by Li Hua to cooperate with your service, really very simple!"

Qin Qin said and looked at the money on the envelope, "So, tonight I want to sing, just I invite two beautiful sisters, give me face ah!"

Li Hua poured the new best bottle of red wine for Qiqi and Qinqin and said with a smile, "OK, today I will go to your place to enjoy the beauty." If you think it is suitable and effective, I will apply for an annual skin-care card."

Qin Qin said: "First go to the beauty salon to enjoy the experience, if suitable, then need to do the frozen age skin care to enhance the firming of a New Year card, the most important is to sing beautifully tonight."

Qi Qi has almost choked with laughter, slowly said: "Listen to the beautiful ladies arrangement, Li Hua said to do a card, I also need to do an annual card." Anyway, the beauty project must be done, it is better to take care of Qin Qin to do it elsewhere, and today you can get a gift project. No wonder your beauty salon has opened five stores. It's not easy. That's a deal, you will teach me how to specifically do wine business, earn all the money invested in a beauty card, to become beautiful."

Three women a play, talking about the beauty and wine to talk about happy. By accident, Li Hua looked at the real estate advertisement outside the window and asked Qi Qi, "I heard that it is a landmark building, Qi Qi, you are an engineering designer, can you confirm whether it is true or not? When will it open for foreign sales, and whether the house price will be high, these information also help to ask. Let's go and see if there are any model houses open to the public sometime."

Cookie loves houses just as much as Li Hua. It's the right person to ask. Qi Qi quickly said, "I know, this is the river view room built by Greenland Group." To build the third tallest landmark building in the world and the first tallest in Wuhan. Create real estate high-end residential areas, office buildings, business circles for the integration of good planning projects. The first phase of pre-sale will be more than 12,000 per square area, and the model house seems to be open to the public on July 1 next month. You really asked me right. A few days ago, my sister asked me if Wuchang has a room with a river view, so I got to know all about the surrounding situation. There is also a point to add, I heard that the subway line 5 will be opened here, just at the entrance of the sales department in the community. This building is a great value. I'm going to look at it and plan to buy it. You're not buying a house again, are you? This is the most expensive property in Wuhan."

Li Hua looked down at the cup in her hand, quietly thinking about what she would do if the house looked like Cookie said it would. She is keen to invest in a landmark house, even if it is improved. In fact, Li Hua currently lives in the community environment is very good, all aspects of the supporting facilities are very complete, she just does not want to let go of this investment project.

Qi Qi said to Li Hua in a creamy voice, "Beautiful woman, what did you think of again?"

Li Hua smiled and said: "You are really a roundworm in my stomach, I think what you can see!"

The three women laughed at the same time, and Qin Qin made a face and spit out his tongue, "Others look at our table and think they have picked up a big ingot!"

Cookie patted Li Hua on the arm and said, "I bet you want to buy that house in the middle of the green space again, right?"

Li Hua smiled and nodded without a word, but he worried and asked Qi Qi and Qin Qin, "You two help me make an idea. If I sell my current small apartment and use the money to book a house in the Green space center, how will it work?"

Cookie said, "In terms of investment development, the housing prices in your neighborhood have doubled. If we can sell it quickly and invest in landmark buildings in the center of greenbelt, there will be room for appreciation.

Qin Qin also added: "If you invest in the green center, I also want to find a community facade over there, and open the beauty salon there." Call me when you open the house, and I'll take a look. Where do you get it? Where's my beauty salon?! Ha ha!"

Li Hua smiled and put his index finger to his mouth: "Hush, well, it's settled!"

Li Hua took out his mobile phone and called the housing agent who often kept in touch with him: "Xiao Huang, how many square meters can the house prices of the residential area of our subway station bank be sold now?" Can I find a serious buyer for my small apartment soon? Please help to find out the situation, try to tell me the truth as early as possible, I will send you the details of the house later. The agency fee is still according to your store's rules, if the transaction is completed within one month, I am willing to pay you more than the agency fee as an extra bonus."

The intermediary yellow phone said happily: "No problem, immediately help you push to the website, the first time to reply to you!"

Li Hua's expression is decisive and serious, it seems that the matter is really settled. Qi Qi stared at Li Hua to say his doubts: "Or you are bold and careful, so decided, began to operate?"

Li Hua said: "If you want to invest, you must be prepared for the capital. I don't have any other sources of funds, and I don't want to borrow money from friends and family. If you can solve it yourself, you will never tease your family about financial difficulties. Besides, I have been used to buying and selling, which is the best way to solve the money problem. So I have maintained a good business reputation with the real estate agent! Rest assured, smooth is my fortune, not also can not affect my existing life! As long as you do your best, there is hope. It's now or never!"

Chapter 47: My Daughter's Money Teacher

Efforts pay off, Li Hua seize the time to operate the investment landmark housing plan, on the one hand with the housing agency active contact, on the one hand to seize the integration of scattered funds. Under the active promotion of the intermediary, there were two buyers soon, one was a white-collar young man who came back from Shanghai to Wuhan for development, and the other was the owner of the community, who wanted to buy in the same community for his family and have a look after each other. The intermediary Huang asked Li Hua: "Sister Li, which one do you want to sell to?"

After understanding the customer situation, Li Hua said: "Try to give priority to buyers who pay a one-time payment, in the case of the same price, choose customers who can pay a one-time payment." If it is the way of mortgage loans, choose the buyer is a single buyer, the parties can directly handle the transfer procedures."

Huang said: "That or choose from Shanghai back to Wuhan business white-collar young people!" He can afford it all, and he's sincere about buying it. But on the total price, the buyer asks for a reduction of 2000 yuan. What do you think? If you agree to cut off this part, I can inform the buyer to come tomorrow morning with a deposit of 60,000 yuan for processing. Also please bring the real estate certificate and all the invoices of the purchase contract to the intermediary store to sign the entrusted sale contract, see you tomorrow!"

Huang has always had the courage to do things, this is Li Hua optimistic about the reason for Huang manager. Of course, Li Hua gives Huang more intermediary fees than others every time. Li Hua wanted to sell the house early, grab the next investment opportunity, and connect the source of funds, which is more cost-effective than going to the bank loan interest. Good location of the house is relatively difficult to find, and this green center project real estate, only three stops away from where you live now by bus, convenient transportation, there are brand-name kindergarten, bank, wet market. Mainly, there are landmark buildings, which have more room for appreciation than the houses we live in now.

Although it is a bit of a toss to deal with, after selling the old house, you have to check out and move furniture. But the thought of living three years later, but also earn a net profit of twice the price of the house, is also worth the toss. It's just that the process is a little hard, cleaning, hauling, cleaning, packing, etc. In order to invest and make money, Li Hua currently does not have the strength to enjoy life, she still needs to struggle, but also need to move residence, as long as there is a profit margin to make money, Li Hua will decisively sell. Look for a good place for your retirement later.

Li Hua immediately promised Xiao Huang manager, agreed to sign the contract time. Then immediately call her daughter: "Darling, come back early from work today, we will drink chicken soup together downstairs across the chicken soup house, something to tell you!"

The daughter said, "You tell me now, I won't be home until 7 o 'clock!"

Li Hua said: "Or wait for you to chicken soup house face to face, that's all!"

My daughter is so obedient that she met Li Hua directly at the chicken soup house after work. "What is it you want to talk about so mysteriously?"

Li Hua has ordered two chicken soup cans, two cold dishes, and a roast chicken paw, which is a simple dinner that Li Hua and her daughter love to eat. The daughter has been used to the mother's style of doing things, entering the store and sitting down, smiling to say hello to Li Hua. Li Hua this mother also smiled and said: "Tonight you get ready, put your favorite daily necessities and clothes in order; Organize the things you don't need or want. I think we have to move our things to my third aunt's empty house for a while. We can stay in Grandma's guest room. I'm going to sell the house I'm living in tomorrow, and I'm going to get the money,

and I'm going to buy that greenfield house I showed you. It opens next month, and I want to convince your second aunt to buy one, too."

The daughter smiled and said, "I guessed, but I didn't expect you to sell the house so soon." Which agency did you talk to? Don't be deceived."

Li Hua proudly said to her daughter: "It is the house agent you know Xiao Huang shop manager!"

The daughter said: "It was her again, Huang manager really, a week to help you find a buyer?" But our small apartment is selling well, and there are plenty of people who can afford it. I heard that the house has room to rise, but I'm used to it, anyway, it's your house, as long as you can make money, you want to sell it, I have no problem. Anyway, I didn't open a big bag of shoes from my last move, and I didn't open a few clothes! Hey, I knew my new home wouldn't last long."

Daughter naughty and very understand Li Hua's mind, Li Hua is a little embarrassed, "mother temporarily vacated a few times the house to make money, will give you a big house, a good house." You believed Mom could do it! It is hard now so that we can live in a better house later, believe me."

The proud daughter joked, "You know what? My classmates and colleagues all said that my mother looked like my sister and that my mother must be rich. Students who have come to my house say that there are my houses here and there. I said live a few years those houses are sold, they still do not believe, insist that my mother looks like a rich sister, said I am a rich second generation! Hey, I have no name!"

Li Hua said to her daughter very cool, "What do you think? We lived in a good house every time, and it got better and better with effort, didn't it? After a few more years of struggle to make money, we will live the life we want, and live in a good house that is more suitable for both of us. For now, choose a suitable investment project and make money make money. The best way for me to make money is to invest in a house. I don't understand the stock way, and investing in physical stores is too much trouble, and you have to keep the store management.

Running a company is also tired, too many things to deal with. Therefore, it is more comfortable to invest in a house."

The daughter kept smiling and nodding: "Of course I understand you, my classmates and colleagues also said that in the future, their families buy houses, please go to see and take them to make some money." They really envy me and praise you to the sky, as if I was born to enjoy the blessing of mother! They don't think about how hard it is for me to move so often!"

Li Hua quietly listened to her daughter's words, and then said: "Your classmates and colleagues are not wrong, you are really lucky to have me this mother." You have taken a lot less detours, your starting point is higher than others, and the experience of having two sets of housing investment before marriage will definitely help you grow your investment horizon in the future. Besides, you've been with me since I was a kid, so I never let you live in a rental, did I? Looking back, we both moved everywhere, did we move from a small city to a big city, from a small apartment to a big house, from a school district to a downtown house? The more we change, the better. The harder we work, the happier we are."

Li Hua and her daughter are like friends with business and quantity teasing, no wonder her daughter's classmates and colleagues envy this mother-daughter relationship. My daughter is also influenced by Li Hua's imperceptible influence, and has her own unique views on financial management and investment in housing.

Li Hua here is ready, the next day went straight to the theme, went to the intermediary store to sign the sale contract, the same day received a deposit of 60,000. Transfer procedures within a week, the day of the transaction to receive the full payment of the house!

Everything as Li Hua hoped, the house money came in time, just to catch up with the first phase of the greenbelt center to sell houses opened only a few houses. Li Hua also persuaded his second sister to buy a set of real estate in the greenbelt center by selling houses, and also solved the problem of entering Wuhan Hukou, killing two birds with one stone. Since then, two younger sister buy a house to listen to Li Hua's advice, invest in a value-added a place, get money money happiness.

Second sister's job is an ordinary teacher, but also through this way of investment to achieve a well-off standard of living, do not have to worry about relatives. Li Hua likes to do these things that can help her family and friends get rich together and improve the quality of life.

Lili, who did not listen to Li Hua's suggestion to buy a house, often regretted that she had missed a good time to buy a house to make money. There was not only one regretting friend, but also a classmate from Hubei Normal University, Zhaodi. Cookie hesitating to buy an ocean view. Qin Qin, who had promised to buy a shop with Li Hua, did not miss the opportunity, not only really opened a beauty salon in a landmark building there, but also invested in several sets of downtown housing for himself. Qin Qin is also one of Li Hua's many single girlfriends. She loves her house and enjoys the security it brings. Since then, Qin Qin seems to be more willing to follow Li Hua's vision, where you will see where to invest! Qin Qin in the real estate investment, is already familiar with the point, start!

Li Hua ear often think of the usual chat mother said, "In fact, I like the most is the kind of home with a small yard, have their own piece of heaven and land, no one else lives in our home head, there is independent space, feel very comfortable."

The speaker is not interested, the listener is interested, Li Hua silently began a new life plan in the heart. There is filial piety in the heart, where to think of Niang, Niang is the real home. Li Hua's heart is surging out of a new financial goal, have the motivation to explore and try to execute. Li Hua thought he must let his mother realize this wish. Li Hua secretly smiled, thought to continue to work so hard, should not be a problem!

Chapter 48: Bringing Parents to the provincial capital

People often say that you can live and work happily, Li Hua has achieved this goal in the provincial capital, with a good environment of living units, business is also doing smoothly. Li Hua's younger sister helped her parents buy a new house in the provincial capital. She also listened to Li Hua's suggestion and bought the same residential area so that Li Hua could take care of the elderly. The house is of a very good size, with an area of 137 square meters, which was renovated under Li Hua's supervision and ventilated for several months.

About to leave the small hometown city where he has lived for decades, the old man is still reluctant to part with his heart, after all, it is where his four daughters were born and grew up. They had spent most of their lives there, their jobs, their youth, their old colleagues, their old neighbors.

Li Hua's mother often encouraged her daughters to "be good in all directions, people go high, water flows low." So Li Hua's mother also convinced her husband to try to experience the new living environment, life will have more fun. It's a gesture from the girls. Just accept it. And living close to her daughter, the children can rest assured of struggle.

Li Hua family where there are big and small things need to choose a day, everyone listens to Li Hua's mother's advice, let the old man choose a good day. This time, Li Hua's mother, after calculation, chose to move from her hometown town to the downtown house of the provincial capital on September 16, 2009, so that her daughters could fulfill their wish to honor their parents.

The day I moved to the provincial capital was indeed a good day. On the day of the move, when all the furniture had been loaded into the car, it began to drizzle. On the way to the provincial capital, Li Hua sat in the passenger seat of the big van, and worried that it would rain and wet the furniture. Mom always picked the right day, why did it rain when she moved this time?

Parents sitting on the third sister's private car, the third sister asked her mother: "Just the sun is shining, why did it rain this moment?" Mom, didn't it rain on your moving day? How can we move things if it keeps raining?"

Li Hua mother unhurriedly said: "Third daughter, you don't worry, to the provincial capital rain will stop, this is called good weather!" Just drive!"

Li Hua mother really said, nearly to the provincial capital half of the road the rain stopped, the sun in the sky, the weather is clear, there is no trace of rain.

The third sister said happily: "My mother really can count the days!" There is really no rain here in the provincial capital, this is really a good day, too God!"

Li Hua's mother did not speak, closed her eyes in the back seat of the car, listening to her daughters ask about the family. From Li Hua's mother's look, all this is expected things, there is no fuss.

At the gate of the provincial town, Li Hua's truck started first and arrived first. Li Hua did a good job in advance of the property community pass note, stopped in reverse under the command of the doorman staff, and then began to move to their own unit floor. Looking at everything according to the department to do, Li Hua just in the big truck also worried about rain, now has to rest assured.

After a while, Li Hua's third sister also arrived at the community with her parents. After opening the door, Li Hua listened to her mother's words and went into the house. She carried the stove and held a plate of apples and oranges in her hand. Then the third sister entered the room, she wanted to carry half a bucket of water, and rice and broom. This is according to the custom of moving to do, the first entry items are exquisite. All in all, follow Li Hua's mother's instructions. This move should make the parents comfortable and like, after all, this is the parents' new home. The parents feel at ease that this time they and their eldest daughter Li Hua live in the same community and can take care of each other.

There is a regular moving company responsible, the move is very smooth. After all the things were installed and placed in place, Li Hua measured the size of the old furniture that his parents liked in advance and kept it and moved into the new home. Which room to put it in is all arranged by Li Hua. It's a mix of old and new, but it has a Chinese style. Li Hua's mother's study, made a whole wall of bookcases, from bottom to top all filled with books. Moving master said: "This box a box of books is really heavy, why so many books?" Li Hua's mother looked at the bookcase and said to the master: "The masters have worked hard, but this book is a golden house!" Carefully placed, thank you masters!"

Parents looked at the new home is very satisfied, Li Hua is also very happy, directly approached the parents around the finger room, "This is mom's master bedroom, this next door is dad's second bedroom." Dad went out diagonally opposite is the bathroom, but also for the convenience of dad, specially made decoration design. Now I'm going to take you around the neighborhood and make room for the teachers to move things."

Li Hua led his parents and family to take the elevator downstairs and walk through the green belt environment outside the community, where there are water fountains and five green flowers. Walk along the tree-lined path, see the chair let the parents sit for a while, smell the fragrance of leaves. Li Hua excitedly introduced: "Come out here in the morning to walk, exercise, enjoy the fresh air." Go to the east gate, there is a barber shop, foot massage shop, dry cleaning shop; Go to the back door and you will find the wet market and the Middle hundred supermarket and the school. Go to the main entrance and you will find the bank, the subway, the bus station, the morning stand, the Chinese restaurant and the beauty salon. Across the road is the river, the river scenery at night can be beautiful and spectacular. There are dancing on the dam, walking, walking dogs, love, very lively. This is the river city you see in real life and the famous river city Wuhan."

Li Hua walked while introducing, choose nearby the largest green tile brick courtyard farmhouse happy restaurant to eat. After the family sat down, Li Hua's father said: "It's really convenient here, everything." My dear friend, are you satisfied?"

Li Hua's mother replied: "Certainly satisfied, I also said that 'good son aims at the four sides, people go up, water down'!" The children have worked hard, and we are both satisfied!"

The third sister added, "Order now, everyone is hungry. There are many local dishes that Mom and Dad love to eat! It's delicious, I'm sure you'll come back again!"

This is the first reunion dinner of housewarming, and the family gets together happily. Li Hua second sister has been busy looking at things, younger sister has come back from Beijing by plane. The happiest time for parents is the reunion with their children and the happy atmosphere of family when everyone is present. At this moment, the mother said to everyone: "Children, sit down, eat more, busy from morning to evening, and finally figure out a smooth." Rest assured, the crowd here is very prosperous, we for four generations together, a glass of wine, my wife is happy today!"

The second day of the move, little sister brought good wine good tobacco and fruit specialties to honor the two old. The parents were able to move to a new home in the provincial capital and settle down, relying on the financial support of the little sister to buy the house. She also took two days off from her busy schedule to come back and reunite with her family. After seeing the new house, Li Hua took the family to the foot massage parlor near the community to do foot massage. The little sister said to her father, "Mom and dad can come to the pedicure shop once a week and swipe the card, I just got you an annual card." Foot massages are good for your body and improve your circulation!"

My little sister is very considerate and proud of her parents at home. Sisters are proud of little sister, good reading, good character, clever, kind, opinionated, self-control. My younger sister was one of the best in her studies since childhood. She was first recommended to HKUST and then went to the UK to study. After completing her studies, she returned to China and settled in Beijing. My younger sister has been working in the financial industry and provides the most financial support for her parents every year. The three sisters admire the little sister, the appearance seems to be weak and petite, but it is very connotation, is a mature and stable intellectual management type. Little sister's style is peaceful, never seen her say a harsh word, nor speak loudly, but if you chat with others, every word will say to each other's heart. Parents like to talk with their little sister most, and they love their little sister most.

After the parents finish the pedicure, love the little girl spent too much money, said to the little girl: "Don't worry about it, there are several of your sisters to take care of, everything is very good." Your big sister got your dad a membership card for a shave and a shampoo, and the salon is right around here. Your second sister also led me to the stall where the grain was sold. Everything we need in life has been satisfied, you can rest assured, you can fly back to Beijing tonight and rest assured. Don't spend any more money on us, there's enough!"

The third sister replied and added: "I have hired a part-time worker for my mother and do the whole house cleaning every week." We've arranged everything. Don't worry."

Li Hua nodded to her little sister and said, "If you don't worry about it, you can fly back often when you are free, and we can get together more."

Li Hua said the whole family laughed, the atmosphere is good, the family and beautiful. Li Hua's daughter Xiaolin envy this older generation of family affection, let her feel the warmth of the big family, all solid mutual support! This warm and thick scene has set a good example for the younger generation of Li Hua's daughter to respect the old and love the young.

Li Hua's parents lived in this new house for a few years, like other ordinary people, living an ordinary and simple life day after day. Li Hua sometimes goes back to his own small house to live, and sometimes stays in his parents' guest room, which is reserved for relatives who come to take care of their parents. Whoever comes to visit their parents can rest in this room!

It's a great idea to buy in the same neighborhood to take care of each other without disturbing each other. In large families, there is no generation gap. When it comes to holidays, Li Hua's parents often have four generations under the same roof

and get together. A table in a restaurant; Coffee table next to a few children dinner; Living room, balcony, study can sit down and talk and laugh with loved ones, such a scene is envied. Li Hua's parents' colleagues and old friends of the older generation often come to the provincial capital from small cities to visit them. When a guest came, Li Hua's parents were more happy than the holiday, and warmly entertained their old colleagues and relatives and friends in their hometown. That is the spiritual pillar of parents, Li Hua's father loves to say to an old friend: "Free often to sit down!"

Chapter 49: That year my father was found to have advanced lung cancer

Li Hua took his parents to the provincial capital to live together, the old man lived a comfortable life, such a day passed for several years.

During the physical examination in the first half of 2016, Li Hua's father was diagnosed with lung cancer. After hospital treatment, discharged directly back to his hometown convalescence. In order to facilitate the life of her father after surgery, the third daughter deliberately bought a four-room, two-bathroom and two-hall house for her father on the first floor, and asked a caregiver to take care of her for 24 hours. Li Hua's mother has been accompanying her, looking at her parents who are getting old day by day. Li Hua is in a race against time. She hopes to do her job well and earn more money, so that she can give her father more nutrition expenses and pay for the long-term care worker. But my father died on the night of December 8, 2016.

On the day his father left, Li Hua made two trips to the provincial capital and his hometown. Li Hua more want her father to live well, she can go to work in peace, she is not afraid of hard work is not afraid of tired, afraid of losing relatives Yin and Yang. The reality did not change because of Li Hua's fear and unwillingness, everything developed according to the law of nature, Li Hua's father was still sick and took away his life.

On the day of his father's death, Li Hua still thought about finishing the last thing tomorrow, and must accompany his father to bask in the sun, take a walk, relax and talk... But all this is Li Hua's wishful thinking, father still did not leave Li Hua this time, father this sudden leave, to Li Hua left a lifetime of heartache!

Li Hua's father put some of his favorite items in a drawer before his death, and these things became the old man's relics. The drawer was full of gifts that his

daughters had given him in various periods: gold rings, watches, Buddhist beads chains, clothes, hats, ties, gloves, scarves, and so on. These things were neatly arranged in drawers, some unused, and my father could not bear to put them on.

Seeing these items left by the father, it seems to tell the daughters that these are foreign things, which can not be taken away. The father is gone, but the things he loved most during his life are left to his daughters - returned to their original owner. This is the father has told Li Hua before his death, will return each daughter's gift to the giver himself.

Father is very handsome, young by the factory's largest leader introduced to the mother, the mother also took a fancy to red and professional father. My father was born in a poor rural family, and the whole village cultivated a rural boy with a junior high school education level. My father was the first worker from the village to enter the factory. His father was diligent and studious, carried out technical transformation of projects on the factory production line, and also made a lot of contributions to machine reform and innovation. He gradually became the backbone of the factory, was selected to the Beijing Auditorium, participated in the May Day commendation conference, was awarded high honors: five good pacesetters, excellent Communist Party members, advanced workers and so on. The honor roll often has a picture of his father wearing a big red flower.

At that time, Li Hua's mother was very young and a descendant of the revolution. Secretary wife personally matchmaking for the two people, become a lifelong partner. When they got married, Li Hua's mother was just 19 years old and his father was 23 years old. Li Hua's mother once said to her daughters with a smile, "At that time, your father was very poor, and in order to get married, he wore black rain shoes as leather shoes to marry me." The living conditions were simple and simple. We lived in a one-story room in the factory. There was only a table, a wooden bed, and a kerosene stove. The marriage of the old man when he was young, without any material basis, but also in the ups and downs of decades of love, has been spent the golden wedding years!

Li Hua looked at the wall of his father 23 years old photos, then the father really good handsome, quiet and handsome, lips purring smile upward arc, a pair of small single-eyelid eyes deep, like looking at Li Hua. Next to it hung a black-and-white photo of my father himself taken at a photo studio, showing that he was still sixty-six years old. On the wall is a family photo of the two old men and the four sisters of Li Hua. It was the last family photo taken before his father died at the age of 75. In March 2013, my younger sister held a golden wedding celebration for her parents in Beijing, and the two of them took a photo together. This precious photo hangs next to the family portrait.

I remember the father once said to his daughters, "Your mother and I have moved seven times in my life." The first two moves you are very small, then called the factory workers dormitory bungalow. The third time they moved to the first suite, three floors up, where the eldest had graduated from high school and the younger daughters from elementary and middle school. For the fourth time, I moved to Room 501 on the left side of the 5th floor, which is an 87 square area house with two and a half rooms, one living room, one bathroom and one kitchen. Your three eldest daughters are all working, that is, the youngest daughter is studying at HKUST. The last three moves are, is the boss in the city to me and your mother's name bought a big house, upper and lower duplex 320 square area. I did not think that my younger daughter would later buy the house where our old couple lived in the provincial capital. Six years later, my third daughter bought a big house of 200 square meters on the first floor for our old couple in our hometown. Life has always had a second child to improve our food, a variety of ways to make a bunch of delicious, wrapped vegetarian dumplings in the refrigerator standby, with your good daughters to honor us, this life is worth it!"

When my father said these words, he had been discharged from the hospital after major surgery and returned to his hometown. When he saw the spacious and bright new house, he said these words from his heart.

My father's bedroom in his later years always lived in the second bedroom, and my father always left the best master bedroom for my mother in order to let her rest well. Like many marriages of the older generation in China, the father's only

wife, the mother of his daughters, was protected all his life, and the two people went through a lifetime of bumps and bruises. My father never said "I love you" to my mother, and never heard any gossip about my father. Although they often say a few words, for the livelihood of the grumble - the father's temper is not very good, but when the big things will be mutual tolerance. In this way, he went through the golden wedding years for several decades, and his father spent his life.

Li Hua picked up the gold ring she had given her father for his 70th birthday and recalled some details of that year. At that time, in order to increase the weight of gold grams, Li Hua quietly told his mother, "I want to take all my gold jewelry, necklaces, earrings, earrings, studs and rings to the gold processing shop, replaced with a big ring, for my father's 70th birthday gift." I often hear my father say that his ring is small, and playing mahjong with old colleagues always looks stingy. Dad always said that the official Uncle Ho was wearing a big ring from his son. I know dad is saving face, anyway I don't love these old style accessories, give dad a big ring, to save my dad always feel that raising a daughter is not worth raising a son!"

The mother said: "Your father is this knot, raised several daughters, always want to have a son how good." You're the eldest child, so you can make our family feel good and your father feel good. But you changed all the jewelry. You don't need it?"

Li Hua said, "It doesn't matter, the old doesn't go, the new doesn't come." Well, since you're okay with it, I'll exchange it at the gold jewelry store, which is doing an event at the mall. Don't tell dad about this, you just know, this time I want Dad to wear a big ring to play mahjong with his old friends, show off!"

At that time, Li Hua was still in the early stage of entrepreneurship, and there was not much cash flow on hand, so some funds would be saved and used to invest in real estate. When the benefits were not achieved, Li Hua was afraid that his family would worry about him, always hiding from his father, silently getting up early and coming back late to do what he saw, and never mentioned the problem of difficulty and lack of funds.

Once, when investing in the downtown landmark house, Li Hua saw the business opportunity, but the hand was short of tens of thousands of yuan deposit. After the mother knew, quietly saved for many years to Li Hua: "Boss, this 100,000 yuan to take urgent use, don't worry about it!"

Mother's move let Li Hua nose a sour, tears are about to come out. She could not say a word for a long time, but her eyes were red. Li Hua hurried into the bathroom and washed away the tears and snot on his face. Li Hua did not dare to go out for a long time, because he looked in the mirror and his eyes were still red, swollen like a lantern.

Li Hua secretly vowed that she must let her parents live a decent and good life and let her father be proud of her! What's wrong with raising a daughter? Raising a daughter must be better than other people's sons!

Thinking of this, Li Hua was calm and firmly said to himself: I will let my father wear the most prominent ring, must let my father live in the big house of the listing center, must not let my father disappoint and regret, must let my father be proud of our good daughters!

Li Hua and his sisters have done it, are very successful, in 2008, the little sister in the provincial capital for their parents to buy a new house at the entrance of the subway, from home to live in the provincial capital for six years, life is getting better and better. After the father took the gold ring sent by Li Hua, every time he went home to play cards, he would also talk to his mother about some outside things: "Old man, do you know what those poker friends say?" Ha ha, praise us two old lucky, better than the official name He. These days, the surname He did not come to play mahjong, poker players said that his son had committed economic problems. You see, if you don't have integrity in office, things go wrong. What's so good about that? It is still safe to be common people!"

My mother likes to read and write diaries on weekdays, and has developed a good habit of loving learning since she was young. In the family position, all important matters are decided by the mother. The mother's voice was not big but very dignified, the mother said in a solemn tone: "Old man, you play your little card, don't laugh at others." The idea of raising children for old age and adopting

children without happiness is the product of feudal superstitious society. It's different now, The Times have advanced, it's time to change your mind! Less cards, less smoking, nothing to do sports! How good it is to learn Tai Chi!"

The father said: "Yes, now three lack one, also can not play!" Starting tomorrow, I will go to the community to learn taichi."

My father took my mother's advice and really began to quit smoking. From two packs a day to a pack of cigarettes, and then a few cigarettes from a pack. When my father was admitted to the hospital, the doctor solemnly said, "You must not smoke a single cigarette." My father finally quit smoking for more than 30 years.

Speaking of smoking, Li Hua felt very guilty. After working, Li Hua insisted on sending cigarettes to honor his father, 4 articles a month has never been interrupted, and every New Year's festival is more to send good cigarettes to his father to prepare for the needs of guests. Li Hua sent cigarettes as many years as his father had smoked. Later Li Hua felt that she had caused her father to get lung cancer. Li Hua thought, father is smoking too much?

Chapter 50: The Comfort of Parents

Li Hua's father was found to have advanced lung cancer during a physical examination in the first half of 2016. After leaving the hospital, he did not return to his residence in the provincial capital. Considering the father's recuperation during the frequent travel to breathe the sun, often up and down the stairs will be very inconvenient. Mother and three sister considerate, persuaded the father to return home to live in a new house. When his father was discharged from hospital, Li Hua had moved all his parents' furniture to a new house in his hometown.

Father on the way back to feel the spirit is particularly excited, Li Hua and his family have been hiding the real cause of his father, did not tell his father is lung cancer. They knew their father wouldn't take it well if he knew the truth. Li Hua also often heard many people say that cancer is not terrible, terrible is that people lose the spiritual support, the fear of the heart is very harmful to the body. So some white lies are both virtue and helplessness, Li Hua and his family all hope that his father can maintain a peaceful and cheerful attitude without knowing it, so that there is no bad emotional pressure, and cooperate with rehabilitation treatment, maybe his father will live longer.

In the doctor's office, Li Hua was the first to know about her father's condition, she clearly heard the doctor say: "Even if your father has an operation, maybe only three months." After that, whatever he wanted to eat and wherever he wanted to travel, he tried to satisfy him. If he is well nursed, perhaps he will live longer, perhaps six months."

Li Hua asked the doctor, "Can't you control it?"

The doctor said, "It's too late, the lung cancer cells have already spread around." More metastasis was found during this lung incision..."

The second sister and the third sister are in the hospital corridor with their mother, waiting for Li Hua to come out. Li Hua's mind went blank, came out to see his mother and sisters, only to truthfully answer every word the doctor said. They had a brief family meeting in the hallway and decided to keep it a secret from their father. Otherwise, with his father's character, if he knew the truth, his spirit would inevitably break down. We agreed not to mention the illness and to pretend it was nothing. As usual, talk as you like, without letting father see it, and without making him suspicious.

My mother, supported by her sisters, walked into the hospital room and looked at my father, who had just woken up from surgery. His father was lying on the hospital bed, trying to move his body with effort, but he could not move, possibly because of the effect of anesthetics, and his father was weak. The doctor said to the father, "The operation was a success. If you want something to eat, tell your daughters." Look how nice your daughters are, they have come to see you! '

The old man in the next bed began to cry, complaining about his fate and crying very sad. The father later heard from the nurse that the old man was only two years older than his father and had three sons and a daughter, but none of the sons came to see him and it was the daughter who sent him to the hospital. But the daughter is very difficult, is a sanitation worker, in the economy can not help him, only after work, do some food sent to have to rush home, because there are two children at home need her to take care of.

My father, in this room, suddenly discovered his sense of superiority. The father was content to comfort the patient and said, "Old man, don't think too much, eat a little more nutritious fish soup, my daughter has done a lot for me." We get better early, is to reduce the burden on our children!"

Father comfort others to say easy, to their own head still have concerns. Not a few days later, I heard that my father's patient friend was transferred to the intensive care unit two days after the operation and died. The head nurse asked Li Hua not to tell his father the news because a new patient had been added to the ward. You can't talk about the patient's affairs in the ward, which will have a psychological shadow on the patient. Since the change of patients, the father's language is less, often noisy to go home to recuperate.

The doctor agreed, wait for the wound to heal and remove the wire for another week, if there is no problem, discharged. At that time, my father's face was haggard out of shape, pale and thin, and it looked a little scary. Li Hua saw his father like this, the heart is very uncomfortable, a sad mood from the heart. Li Huaqiang tried not to let the tears fall, and quickly stood at a different Angle, not to be seen by his father. She turned her back to her father, took the bowl on her head to the bathroom to clean it, and did not dare to enter the ward again until she was calm. Li Hua let his father rest assured to sleep, she will look at the medicine bottle needle finished, call the nurse in time to change the dressing.

It was only when he was asleep that father felt more comfortable. Drugs and painkillers to kill cancer cells should not be used too much, and father should not be allowed to think too much in his waking hours. When the wound healed and the stitches were removed, the doctor discharged my father to recuperate at home. The doctor knew that no medicine could save my father, but he said that he could only prolong his life by his own constitution.

Without knowing it, the father thought that his body had recovered, so he arranged to be discharged. After leaving the hospital, his father's mental condition improved and he felt good, but Li Hua and his family were particularly uncomfortable. I thought it would be great if I could extend my father's life with a drug. The daughters are all good, in their respective positions to do a good job, can let the father feel pleased, but the father has to leave them in a short time. The more Li Hua think, the more uncomfortable, the time is very hard, the heart clearly know that his father's life has entered the countdown, but can not show in his face to let him see.

On the day of discharge, the weather was fine. When I got on the car, my father looked up at the sky for a long time and felt the comfort of the breeze blowing on his face under the sun. The father took a deep breath of fresh air and said, "I haven't

seen the sun in the hospital for a long time. I feel really comfortable today. I'd better go home."

Li Hua said, "Yes, Dad! The doctor just told you to get more sun when you get home. We also bought you an automatic control wheelchair at home, and the caregiver you like at home often pushes you outside to bask in the sun. Eat healthy food with plenty of soup and calcium, and you will recover quickly.

The third sister also quickly helped his father to get on the car and said: "The family is arranged, Chen Zhi (three brother-in-law) is waiting for you at home, do the cuttlefish soup you like to eat." And the house is finished, he told his brother that he can catch live fish for you to eat every day. The new village contracted fish pond, local chicken stew, you will like it. This time, Chen Zhi deliberately chose the first floor to buy a house, and there is no need to go up and down the stairs, which is convenient for you to travel. Don't worry about it. Just eat. Chen Zhi's colleagues heard that he gave the house to his mother-in-law to live in, all praised him for his filial piety and good character, and said that he was too happy to be Chen Zhi's parents, and the story of filial piety to his mother-in-law was passed from one to another. Chen Zhi is very happy that all the people in the company praised him for his filial piety to the elderly, and the more he praised the more vigorous he did!"

Li Hua said, "To be honest, Chen Zhi has done a great thing this time. There's nothing wrong with treating your in-laws like they're your own parents. This son-in-law is just a son, and my father liked him very much, so he told Chen Zhi directly about everything."

The father listened to the conversation between the eldest daughter and the third daughter, and understood in his heart that this was directly returning to the new home prepared by the third son-in-law. The father looked at his wife sitting next to him and said with a smile: "My wife or you are right, raising a daughter is good!" Our daughters are good children, we than the son of the old Dong Lao Lu Qiang. During the hospital, my eldest brother ran up and down every day to take care of me. Several daughters arranged their work and took turns to take care of me.

The youngest daughter lived far away, but she paid the most for treatment. I really figured it out this time, it's better to have a daughter!"

The mother replied, "Yes, the old Dong and his wife, who have a son, save money together to buy a house for their son and marry a wife." Your good friend Lao Lu and his wife have saved a lifetime of money to buy a house for their two sons, but also because the size and area are not the same. Now they are living apart and raising grandchildren for their two sons and have no old age of their own."

Father nodded his head with satisfaction: "They are still working for their sons when they are old, which is like our early happiness, I smoked the good cigarettes sent by the boss for decades, the daughters often send good wine and good fruit filial piety, good clothes are not finished, I am satisfied!"

My mother quickly went on to say, "My wife, this time you will take good care of your body when you go home, and don't delay the work of the children." Let the eldest brother hurry to sell the house in the center of the provincial capital, the market is good now, and the money can be returned to the younger daughter, who now needs money for her two children studying abroad."

Li Hua immediately answered and said, "You two don't worry about it anymore, I have already hung up in the housing agency." Rest assured, Dad take good care of the body, mother accompanied to eat better, let us all worry. I'll let you know when everything's done. You live in peace, as the saying goes, there is always our treasure at home!"

The third sister said, "Just listen to the elder sister, and don't worry about it." Better food, better drink, less worry than anything. Only if you two are healthy and happy, our career will be more and more smooth, and we can make more money!"

Li Hua and his sisters took their father from the hospital to their new home, arranged everything, and invited a male nurse who accompanied him 24 hours a day. This is Li Hua from the hospital intermediary contact with the male nurse, a monthly package to pay 4,000 yuan nurse fees. The money is shared between the four sisters, in a joint account kept by their mother, and paid in time every month.

After his father was discharged from the hospital for several months, Li Hua

and his sisters hurried to seize the time, they were busy with their own small family life and work, and the day still had to continue. Li Hua realized the importance of money after his father was hospitalized. If there was no working capital in hand at that time, it could not help his father pay 100,000 yuan in hospital expenses in time, and later my little sister also took out 100,000 yuan. Although the father has been discharged from the hospital, but later nutrition costs and nursing fees, also need to spend money.

Li Hua thought of what the doctor had said, "Your father only has a few months to live!" She also realized that the phrase had another meaning: to be prepared for the future.

This idea filled Li Hua with fear, Li Hua panicked to escape the reality of his father, and the only reason to escape reality is to keep working to create more opportunities to earn money. Li Hua will his father used to live in the house all cleaned up clean, the father used things, all arranged to transport the car back to the storage room of the new home, including photos are also all packed up, transported to the hometown.

Li Hua did not ask people to do these health work, she herself took time to tidy up. When the house was vacated and cleaned, it was immediately recommended by the intermediary buyer, and only looked at three waves of people to finalize the time of pre-sale check-out. Li Hua signed the sale contract as a full agent! Deposits and down payments were also collected. This is the most reluctant to sell a house in Li Hua, the most emotional house, here records Li Hua and parents together happy time.

Chapter 51: Emergencies

My little sister lives in Beijing, and this house has carte Blanche for Li Hua to handle all the transfer procedures. The time is set on December 9, 2016, and it will soon be the time to make an appointment to transfer the account.

On the afternoon of December 8, Li Hua and the manager of the decoration company Zhao were busy in the building materials market until more than 3 o 'clock in the afternoon. Two people casually ate a bowl of hot dry noodles, went straight to Hanxi building materials market, ready to buy some basic decoration materials.

On the way, the mobile phone in Li Hua's bag kept ringing. Zhao, who was driving, took a look at Li Hua, who was sitting in the co-driver's seat, and indicated that Li Hua had a phone call. Li Hua was tired and dozed off. After being woken up, he took out his mobile phone and pressed the answer key. On the phone came the second sister and the third sister's anxious voice: "Sister, you hurry back today." Dad hasn't eaten anything since yesterday, just some porridge. Mom asked us to call you and tell you to come home and see Dad if you're not busy. My uncle has come from home. Come back today, too!"

Li Hua's eyes widened immediately: "What is the situation, tell me to go back now?" I'm busy, can't it take a few days?"

Li Hua is a little anxious and impatient, muttering to his mobile phone, "I am not finished yet, and I am preparing to arrange this urgent matter at hand." The house will be transferred tomorrow, and I have to go through the formalities myself. I'm ready to finish this big thing, and then go back to spend some time with dad, just wait one day?"

Li Hua finished hanging up the phone, the whole person unhappy. Zhao, who was driving, heard what was said on the phone and asked with concern, "Sister Li,

something is going on at home, you'd better go home and see it." You can rest assured about the decoration here, I will choose the good materials of the decoration standard according to your account."

Hearing General Zhao's words, Li Hua was a little relieved from the worry, just at this time, the mobile phone rang again. Li Hua quickly answered the phone, it turned out that the little sister called: "Big sister ah, today you don't busy with other things." Gotta get back to see dad. Isn't the transfer tomorrow? You should take the high-speed train back today and tell me in time if there is anything wrong with Dad!"

This side of the news are notified in Beijing's little sister, little sister also urged Li Hua hurry back. Receiving such a desperate phone call, Li Hua was very helpless and wished to deal with these two important things at the same time. The visit to my father was important, as was the transfer of the house sale the next day. The buyer signed the purchase contract as early as two months ago, and Li Hua has received the deposit. Agents had lined up a month ago to make an appointment for the transfer on December 9. The three parties agreed to handle the transfer at the municipal hall tomorrow. If the contract is violated, Li Hua will pay double compensation for the deposit and the down payment of 1 million yuan.

These two things are very important, are at an important juncture, no matter what goes wrong, Li Hua will cause a painful blow, so Li Hua is so helpless anxiety. On the surface, Li Hua looked very impatient and angry, but he did not know who he was angry with. She still quickly picked up her mobile phone to search for a high-speed train ticket to buy back home, and looked at several trains that showed that there were no tickets today.

Li Hua some collapse, the heart of a colic, helpless to the extreme. General Zhao looked at the anxious Li Hua and said, "Sister Li, let me drive you home." The selection of materials for decoration can be put aside today. I'll take you right back. You'll feel better. If there's nothing wrong with your father, we'll drive back in time. It'll make you feel better."

Li Hua gratefully said to General Zhao: "Really thank you, then you have worked hard, I will give you the cost!"

General Manager Zhao has cooperated with Li Hua for more than ten years, and the decoration of all the houses of Li Hua's relatives and friends is entrusted to General Manager Zhao. Zhao total good character, price management, the two people have been very happy cooperation, they have cooperated in the decoration of 13 houses. Zhao always work to make people dependable, Zhao is trustworthy, so Li Hua is willing to give all the work to him to do. After years of cooperation, Li Hua has treated General Zhao as a brother sincerely, never hiding his joys and sorrows, and General Zhao also knows some family situations of Li Hua.

Zhao began to turn around, open the car GPS navigation, while operating said: "Don't separate so clearly, sister Li take care of my company for so many years, I go to see your father should also." I haven't seen your father once since he was taken ill in hospital and moved back home. It happened to me today, so don't mention it!"

All the way Zhao drove silently, occasionally to Li Hua to determine the direction is right. Li Hua thought thousands of thoughts, thought of many, many scenes to see his father, one scene at a time, there is a bad hunch...

Zhao always sent Li Hua to his hometown at the fastest speed, the whole journey of more than 100 kilometers, 1 hour and 20 minutes back to the new home prepared by the three younger sisters for their parents. Li Hua just entered the house was surrounded by mother two younger sister three younger sister, said a hello together into the father's bedroom. Li Hua entered the door and saw his father lying on his side facing the wall, with his uncle and a nurse guarding the bed.

Seeing Li Hua come in, his uncle immediately shouted to Li Hua's father, "Brother, the eldest Huazi has come back to see you!" Uncle called Li Hua nickname, the father woke up. Li Hua motioned his uncle not to wake up his father so loudly, let him sleep, and wait for him to wake up naturally.

"Your father is not asleep," said the uncle. "He is waiting for you to come and see him, and he knows it!"

Sure enough, the father slowly moved his hands and feet, and seemed to stand up from the bed to see Li Hua. He did not turn over for a while, and with great effort, he reached out a dry, old, bony hand to hold his eldest daughter's hand. Li Hua saw his father, who had not seen him for several months, was already thin and out of shape. The former tall body was now skin and bone, the body bowed and thin into a weak mass. It's like you can't even see someone under the covers.

Li Hua wanted to touch his father's hands, but he was afraid to take it back - it was not his father's hands in memory. Li Hua's eyes have gushed full of tears, throat blocked, throat can not make a sound, nose sour. Li Hua only shouted out two words dad, the rest of the words were choked. Li Hua gently patted his father's shoulder with his hand, paused for a minute, stabilized the mood, stuck in his father's ear to hold back sobs and said softly: "Dad I'm back, you sleep at ease."

At this time, Li Hua has been unable to hide his sadness, do not want his father and uncle to see her fragile sad appearance, quickly ran out of his father's room, to the bathroom closed the door silently shed tears. The tears wiped and wiped, but couldn't stop. Li Hua approached the mirror heavily, opened the faucet, and quickly poured cold water on his face. Let the cold water wash away the tears on his face.

Li Hua wanted to calm herself down as soon as possible so that she could face her family outside waiting for her to speak. Li Hua is the eldest, is the eldest daughter of the family and the breadwinner, her parents raised her as a boy. In the eyes of parents, she is the strongest child, but also the most daring, is the backbone of the sisters. Li Hua walked out of the bathroom and saw his mother and two sisters sitting in the hall. His uncle and General Manager Zhao were also sitting beside him.

Li Hua said with difficulty: "Look at dad like this, as long as he eats something, should be able to get better?" Why don't we take him to the hospital?"

The uncle shook his head and said, "There is no use sending him to the hospital, the doctor has already said that it is only three months." You've done a great job. It's been extended to six months, three months longer. There is not much time. If you eat porridge, you can last a week; If we don't get anything to eat, it's only for a few days, and we have to be ready." The uncle was telling the truth, and then he made some important preparations. Li Hua and his sisters explained some things to be done, one by one to implement everyone.

In addition to the little sister in Beijing has not come back, basically the father's closest people have met, I believe he will not have regrets. Li Hua looked at General Zhao sitting beside him, suddenly remembered another important thing, and hurriedly said to his family: "Mom, uncle, and two younger sisters, three younger sisters, you are all here, today I will return to the provincial capital with General Zhao." I really need to go through the house transfer procedures tomorrow, the agreed time is 10 am, and only after signing the transfer can I receive the final payment of 2.3 million yuan. If I default, I'll pay double the deposit and down payment. If the change is notified to others, it will be very troublesome. I'll be back as soon as I'm done with this."

The family understood Li Hua's difficulty, the mother had to say: "You go, finish the job and hurry back." Your father understands children. Let me take you to say hello to your father."

Li Hua came to his father's bed with his mother and shouted: "Dad, you want to eat, I will come back to accompany you for a period of time when I finish tomorrow."

The mother then said, "Wife, you can rest easy, we are all here." The boss is so busy and has come back to see you, and now she has to go back to work on tomorrow, and when she is finished, she will come back to accompany you. Don't hold the children back, the children are hard too!"

The father seemed to understand the mother's words, gently waved his hand, and then fell asleep on one side. Li Hua pulled up the corners of his father's quilt to cover his father a little more tightly. After a few moments of silence, nothing could be said. There is nothing to say in this situation, what is more important than father at this moment? But today must go, tomorrow is also very important.

Li Hua said to his father in his heart, "Dad, please give me one day tomorrow. I will come back to accompany you, go out in the sun with you, catch up with your

old friends, have a daughter filial piety. I can also listen to your nagging, I promise not to argue with you, all listen to your young things..."

In order to hurry, Li Hua said hello to his family and went back. General Zhao also said goodbye to Li Hua's family and said: "Rest assured, I will send Sister Li safely home!"

Li Hua did not turn back and hurried to the door of the car. Three younger sister caught up with the car, handed a bag of oranges and two apples, a few bottles of water, told: "Zhao sum big sister on the road to eat, drive slowly, safety first!"

The second sister said: "Something we will call you, you can do your business tomorrow, we are here!"

Zhao General for Li Hua and his family nodded goodbye, at this time Li Hua did not dare to look at his family, low head whispered to Zhao General said: "Drive away!"

The car started, Li Hua's tears and not to vent out like Yongquan, completely can not stop. Li Hua don't know why cry, why so sad, why life is so difficult! She is a good daughter of her parents, a good mother of her daughter, a good elder sister of her sisters, a strong woman admired by her colleagues and friends, but how can all this be done? It would be a dream to keep my father alive for a few more days. Li Hua's success was enough to make his father proud, but his father did not live a long life because of Li Hua's efforts and success.

Chapter 52: The Last Company

Zhao always sent Li Hua to the roadside downstairs in the community, the car stopped: "Sister Li, already home!"

Li Hua opened his eyes from the confusion: "I don't know when I fell asleep, Zhao always came to my home for dinner and then went away, this point for dinner has passed!"

Zhao said: "Sister Li is welcome, you go home early and rest." You have that big thing tomorrow!"

Li Hua thought about it and said to General Zhao, "OK, thank you so much for today, I will ask you to do pedicure health care some other day." The decoration of the small villa is up to you to choose a good day to start."

General Zhao replied: "Don't worry, you do your job, everything will be done for you!" I'm leaving!"

Looking at the direction Zhao drove away, Li Hua did not walk quickly to his daughter's house until he could not see the car. Tomorrow there are a lot of things to be ready, the transfer of property information, power of attorney, their own identity card, the sale contract all need to be sorted together, tonight is also very busy. Think of this, the elevator has reached the 27th floor, pressed the doorbell, daughter Xiaolin opened the door and said: "Have not eaten dinner?" There's chicken soup in the pan. Have some! How is Grandpa today?"

Li Hua said: "It seems that time is running out, it should not last a few days." I'm really worried about your grandfather. I wish he could live longer! I'm going to transfer your aunt's house tomorrow, and I'll finish the paperwork tonight."

Xiao Lin put a bowl of chicken soup on the table: "Mom, drink a bowl of chicken soup before finishing it, drink it while it's hot!"

Man is iron, rice is steel, Li Hua has not eaten dinner all day. See daughter sensible and considerate appearance, Li Hua heart warm, buried down to eat up. After eating the soup, I went directly into the study to sort out the materials.

When it was nearly nine o 'clock, Li Hua's mobile phone suddenly rang. Li Hua froze for a long time, afraid to answer the phone. Her daughter picked up the mobile phone that was charging on the bedside table and handed it to Li Hua. The phone is Li Hua's mother called, "Boss, your father just left half an hour ago, tell you, come back!"

Li Hua's father really left, and he couldn't hold on for a day. Li Hua is afraid of this phone call, the result is still unable to hide. Li Hua said to himself: "This father is really, must fight with me for time, must go at this time, fight with me to rob!" Xiao Lin interrupted Li Hua: "Mom, you don't say that, hurry back." I'll call Aunt Bear to take Xiao Bao, and I'll drive you back to your hometown!"

Li Hua was a little emotional at this time, like a child arguing with his father before he died, and continued to say: "This father is unreasonable, stubborn and old love to fight with me before he died, and I have to fight for time." I'm really angry. This is excruciating! A good day, but must rush to heaven!"

Xiao Lin silently arranged everything, waiting for aunt bear to come and set out. Li Hua, like a wooden man, stared at the clock on the wall, and the second hand continued to move forward with a swing. Time waits for no one, it is the same for everyone, it will not stop because you want to stay in the world a little longer. Li Hua can not and do not want to accept the fact that his father has passed away, do not believe that also have to face the reality.

Li Hua said, "What about my things tomorrow? If I go back tonight, I must come back early tomorrow to do my business!"

Her daughter said, "If you don't go back tonight, you won't sleep well all night." Why don't I drive you home with me and listen to the arrangements, take care of things at home, and hurry back in the morning." Li Hua sighed gently and also approved her daughter's plan.

Aunt Bear is the aunt that Xiaolin has been asking to do cleaning at home, and has been getting along with her daughter for 5 years, and the two have exceeded the employment relationship and become relatives. Such a big thing happened at home, Aunt bear did not say a word, catch the bus before nine o 'clock immediately to Xiao Lin's home. As soon as he entered the door, he said: "You hurry up to go, I will take care of Xiao Bao here these days, you can go at ease!"

Xiao Lin said, "Thank you, Aunt Bear. We may have to stay in our hometown for three days."

Li Hua said, "I may take the high-speed train back to the provincial capital tomorrow morning, and then take the high-speed train back home to take care of my father's funeral." Home our little treasure please you! Thank you Sister Bear!"

Xiao Lin drove the car, looking at Li Hua in the rear seat from time to time through the rearview mirror. Xiao Lin comforted and said, "Mom, grandpa left is relieved." Cancer pain is very painful, my classmate's mother is also lung cancer, when the pain is unbearable, can not eat, can not drink. In fact, Grandpa left is also a blessing, did not suffer so much pain, otherwise how painful ah."

Li Hua did not answer the question and was sitting back in tears. It was as if for the first time she felt guilty for her father, knowing his days were numbered, but not being there for him; When his father left, he blamed his father for having trouble with himself. In any case, in my heart, I just can't accept that my father went to heaven at this time. A few hours ago the father was still there, but in order to do business or cruel abandon the father to return home. I didn't think it would be so soon. My father didn't even leave Li Hua a day. This is Li Hua's father, go also let Li Hua uncomfortable! Don't let Li Hua worry.

Xiao Lin parked the car at the back door of the home, the front door of the car are parked full. At the moment of entering the gate, Li Hua saw his father already lying on a piece of wood in the center of the living room, and the portrait and funeral hall were located in the living room. As he entered the door, his uncle called out, "Brother, Huazi has come back to see you again. Please close your eyes, the children are on their way back to see you off!" Say with Li Hua and small Lin to the shrine on three heads.

Strange to say, Li Hua saw his father like asleep, his face is also smiling with lips, like a dead look, the feeling of sleeping peacefully. Li Hua was depressed and asked his mother: "After I left, is my father very angry? I must blame me!"

The mother immediately came over and said, "I don't blame you, your father is not an unreasonable man." Boss, you are the eldest daughter, and you will be here tonight waiting for your father's funeral and writing the words for the memorial service."

Li Hua asked, "Is it appropriate for me to write?"

The three sisters came up and said, "You're the perfect person to write." Here's a pen and paper. Write it tonight. On the day of the funeral, you will read it and burn it, completing the memorial service for Dad."

Li Hua did not say anything, quietly and carefully sitting at the table beside the funeral hall, looking at his father's portrait, thinking of the little life with his father. Starting from the age of seven, he wrote four turning points in his father's life. Father for the family to pay, all vividly, like a movie, scenes emerge in Li Hua's mind. Li Hua looked down silently and quickly began to write it out, a piece of paper in order, unconsciously wrote eleven pieces of letter paper, three hours in one go!

Writing the process, Li Hua has been buried head, sometimes the tears blur the eyes, wipe and continue to write. Li Hua wrote that he missed his father deeply and felt the softest and delicate warmth. She writes about a father's interest in the development of his daughters. In the poor early sixties, the sisters and their parents prepared for the Lunar New Year each year. At that time, it was the father who washed, cut, pickled and fried the fruit and gave it to his daughters as a snack. No matter how difficult it is, parents will buy new clothes for their daughters to put on the bed. Li Hua thought of her father's work trip, and could not forget to buy an orange sweater for Li Hua, which warmed her the whole winter, and also made Li Hua, a young girl, spend several beautiful autumn and winter -- it was the most beautiful clothes Li Hua wore.

That era has gone, but can not dilute the daughter's dear memory of parents. Parents to their daughters simple selfless dedication, daughters are in the process of growing up to absorb the good character of their parents. In the old age of parents, great love has been revealed and returned to the parents. But Li Hua felt that it was not enough, she always felt that when her parents grew old and needed her care and companionship, she was still unable to wait for her parents for various reasons, which made Li Hua deeply ashamed of her father!

Li Hua's parents never worry about not having new clothes to wear, the daughters provide the best living environment for their parents, so that they can eat the most delicious food. The second daughter, who is careful and hardworking, serves as the chef for the annual reunion dinner, making hearty meals for her parents and family. These delicious dishes, once made by their parents, have become the pure and simple taste that their daughters love. These delicacies are passed down by the daughters, which is also a return of affection and great love. This kind of family virtue of respecting the old and loving the young, imperceptibly affects the growth of the daughters, to the good, forward, towards a better future, showing gratitude and feedback day by day, and continuing the warm family affection.

Li Hua also recalled his father's efforts in education, in order to help his daughters get better learning opportunities, his father repeatedly asked for help and transferred the children to key schools. At work, the father also supports his daughter's decisions and choices. Li Hua remembered that once upon a time, he was greatly wronged at work and hesitated for a decision. His father gave Li Hua the strongest support at a critical juncture. Father said to Li Hua, "I believe in you, there is no obstacle that can not be overcome, and boldly go in the direction that you think is right." I will stand by you no matter what lies ahead." These simple and unpretentious words are enough to let Li Hua stress relief. Think about the decades, the daughters grew up through every step of the father accompanied, father love mountains, each child has left the father's encouragement and silent traces of pay.

Li Hua got up and walked to his father's funeral hall, bowing deeply and handing over the memorial speech he had written to his mother. Did not think of Li Hua's mother after reading the direct tears collapse, kept nodding, looking at the written first draft of the memorial to his father's body said: "My wife, you will feel

relieved under the nine springs, the eldest wrote well ah." The eldest daughter has taken your responsibility for your family and your love for them in your heart. You see how sensible the children are, they all remember your kindness, you can go at ease!"

Li Hua supported his mother beside him and said, "Is it OK to write like this? I did not write according to the format of the memorial words, I am according to the heart to think of little bits and pieces of my father's love for us to write, where I want to write, is that OK?"

The mother put the letter paper on the father's funeral table, said to Li Hua: "The eldest brother is very good, there are true feelings, a word does not have to change."

The mother turned around and approached the father's funeral hall and said, "Old man, you did not raise our good daughter in vain." My little girl is also on her way back to see you today, you can rest assured."

The memorial speech wrote about the sincere feelings between father and daughter, and the article was recognized by her mother, and Li Hua was relieved. She did not expect to suddenly think of her father so many bright points. This eulogy content is very smooth, Li Hua will write the ordinary story of his father's vivid and touching, but also wrote the father's feelings for his daughters to guard a lifetime, the heart of his father's love is vividly expressed. Li Hua regrets not telling his father before his death how much his daughters love him, Li Hua regrets that she did not personally say to his father, "Dad, I love you!"

Hope the father of heaven can hear Li Hua's voice: "Dad you rest in peace, we love you!"

Chapter 53: The Meaning of Life

Considering that she had to deal with the problem of housing transfer in the morning, Li Hua had to go out and return to the provincial capital in the morning to catch the earliest high-speed train. Li Hua whispered with the mother account, and with the second sister said: "I must go back to the provincial capital early, here during the day home guest arrangements, you and the third sister to discuss." The transfer of the house is also very important. It's time for me to do it. I think Dad will understand."

The second sister nodded and waved to Li Hua: "Big sister you go quickly, I understand, dad also understand you." You are doing things for your little sister, you are concerned about this for the better life of your family, you know that you have responsibility!"

Get the understanding of relatives, Li Hua does not want to trouble his family, recruit a network about the driver immediately to the high-speed rail station Mercedes.

Li Hua, sitting in the high-speed train, breathed a long sigh of relief at this time, looked at the scenery outside the window and fell asleep unconsciously. Li Hua is too tired, from yesterday to today is like a war with time, has not had a rest, she really want to have Sun Wukong as a split. Li Hua realized that she could not fail at this moment and had to do it well. It's not just a question of money, it's a question of credibility. The integrity of business has become the basic principle of Li Hua over the years, and because of this personality charm, Li Hua has made great gains in any industry. For decades, Li Hua has tried various industries, from small white to achievements in each field, all come from Li Hua being serious and thinking of others. In the business operation, not only to measure the interests, but also to see the

character, there is an inspiring positive energy to gather strength, in order to become bigger and stronger.

Li Hua arrived at the provincial municipal Hall in advance, and the three parties successfully completed all legal procedures according to the agreement procedure. When Li Hua saw that the mobile phone showed that the transaction was completed and the whole house payment of 2.3 million was received, the stone in his heart finally fell to the ground. She took a deep breath of air, picked up her mobile phone and sent wechat to her little sister in Beijing, "The housing transaction was successfully completed, and the balance payment was immediately transferred to your designated bank account, please check the reply information in time." I'm now ready to take the buyer and the agent to the house to hand over the keys and the utilities. After all the handover of this house is completed today, immediately take the high-speed train back home. Little sister rest assured, keep the information flowing."

At this time, the younger sister had flown from Beijing to her hometown in Hubei Province, and when she saw Li Huafa's message beside her mother, she replied to Li Hua: "Elder sister, I have received the house payment and arrived at home, you can rest assured." Take your time, be safe, and eat before you go out. Just come back before dinner tonight, and we'll all be waiting for you at home!"

Everything is done, Li Hua really admire themselves, they are so capable, two things that seem to need to be done, Li Hua has successfully handled. Li Hua walked out of the residential building, looking at the community that had once allowed her to accompany her parents, she felt both kind and reluctant to part. She looked at the green leaves everywhere in the community, and looked at the blue sky, that day the sun was shining gently overhead her. A soft breeze with a little drizzle, began to fall on Li Hua's body. Li Hua feel this is the father to her timely rain, a warm hug, she understand must be father in the sky looking at her, Li Hua think so, otherwise how to explain the rain in the sky suddenly stopped?

Li Hua finally relaxed down, she thanked her relatives for their understanding, but also felt a warm feeling, must be the father pleased to say to her: "Go back, you work I rest assured, my good daughter is capable!"

Li Hua thought, if her father was still alive, he would praise her again in front of his old friends and show off. Thinking of this, Li Hua hurriedly took the subway to the high-speed rail station, went straight to his hometown, and then told his family about the process. She knows that her family must care about the process and relevant details of this matter, and she will give her family a satisfactory answer.

The third day is the father out of the hall ceremony to return to his hometown memorial service, held in his father's hometown rice field. That day my father really met heaven, the blue sky. In the breeze came Li Hua for his father, personally read his own written words of condolence, rice field floating over the memory of the emotion, this condolence words so warm and touching, so that all present mourning mourning relatives and friends are in tears. Li Hua's sincere feelings for his father must have touched his father's soul, I believe he can feel the sadness of his relatives, and will be proud of the performance of his daughters.

That was my father's most glorious day. Li Hua always thought that his father was the most face-saving, and sometimes he always thought that his father lived too tired and lived for vanity. His father always regarded his daughters' gifts of filial piety as his greatest treasure. His father was already in heaven, but the gifts of his daughters' filial piety were quietly placed in the drawer.

Li Hua suddenly cried, she instantly regretted that she understood too late, father like to show off in front of people, not because father vanity is strong, it is the father in showing off his daughters filial piety, show off as a father to enjoy the happiness. He recognized his daughter's filial piety, and also hoped that others would recognize the good quality of his daughters, which was also a declaration of love for his daughter. Li Hua recalled the scenes of his father triumphantly talking and laughing, and realized his father's good intentions. Father love is greater than the mountain, Li Hua a little self-blame, the original has been misunderstood father.

On that day, relatives and friends who were present to attend the memorial were infected by Li Hua's heartfelt and tearful eulogy. We think back to everything that

Dad did for his work, his family and his daughters, every effort. His deep love for his daughters will remain in the hearts of his relatives forever. They also understand that the father's show off is the daughter most want to see happiness. That's because a father's love is always with her as she grows up.

The death of his father made Li Hua have a new understanding of life, especially in the material wealth and spiritual wealth has a great spiritual impact. Li Hua saw in the life and death juncture, material wealth seems so pale. There are so many precious gold ornaments that my father carries with him before his death, and when people leave the world, these things can not be taken away, leaving only the memories of the living relatives. With the passage of time, I am afraid that even memories will fade with the years.

Is there any point in saving money when you can earn more money in life but can't spend it? Li Hua began to wonder if he still needed to work so hard. There is more to life than just working and making money. There are many things you can do and ways of living that are more meaningful than money.

Li Hua began to readjust her work, life, study, entertainment and rest time. She began to slow down the pace. I remember a philosopher who said, "You have to have balance in your life, otherwise you'll get out of control, you'll get burned up, and your life will be a mess."

The death of his father made Li Hua realize a truth, people alive also have a sense of value, should create spiritual wealth. Because spiritual wealth is the experience that people themselves can share, feel, and blend with the soul. No one can replace that feeling. Giving a poor man a sum of money can improve his life in the short term. If a positive life belief is implanted in his heart, it may change the fate of his life. Over the years, Li Hua has been influencing people around her with a positive attitude, which is the spiritual wealth she has created herself. However, a person's contact with a limited number of people, influence is also limited, can there be a better way to share their spiritual wealth to more people? Soon, Li Hua found the answer: to achieve this goal through writing. That's what I'm going to do for the rest of my life, that impulsive desire to create literature from the bottom of my heart is coming back, if not now, when will I do it? Li Hua thought this was her father telling her that it was not too late to do it now, live in the moment.

Chapter 54: Reward Investment to Improve Yourself

Li Hua will reward investing in himself every time he benefits from investing in real estate. This virtuous cycle of good habits has been maintained, can encourage Li Hua to continue to work hard to find new investment opportunities projects.

In the past, Li Hua's reward for himself was mainly focused on the material aspect, or the investment in body maintenance. Since experiencing three years of hard business doors and Windows, and experienced the death of his father, Li Hua is not as important to material wealth as in the past. At this stage, she can slow down the pursuit of material wealth and turn more energy to the pursuit of spiritual wealth.

Li Hua loved writing when he was young, and later was busy with life, busy with livelihood, busy with entrepreneurship, and could only keep the writing dream in mind. Now Li Hua no longer needs to work hard for money, and has achieved basic financial freedom and time freedom. In recent years, Li Hua's investment in himself is mainly to improve his mind and spiritual outlook.

Just after the Spring Festival in 2017, Li Hua signed up for the city's university for the elderly and reported two classes, one is a singing class and one is a runway model class. She also increased her investment in writing, signing up for a book writing bootcamp class and signing up for short book writing. Later, I also successively applied for teacher Qi's prose biography writing class, Teacher Ning's novel learning class, and Teacher Wang's documentary writing class. He also participated in the 2019 Zhiyin Story Contest and won the winning prize. Being recognized in the study of writing has aroused Li Hua's strong interest in writing and learning.

In the following years, Li Hua continued to study the writing of stories and novels. First, I attended Mr. Chen's short story writing class, and later, I attended Mr. Yiming's long story writing class. While studying to improve herself, Li Hua has written two novels, the first drafts of which have been published in newspapers. Li Hua sorted out these newspapers, arranged them all over the ground, took pictures and sent them to his mother's wechat. Her mother has always supported Li Hua's writing and is also happy to share her daughter's achievements in writing.

During the years of writing, Li Hua kept writing and got a series of achievements: Li Hua joined Wuhan Writers Association; Won the 2019 "Bosom Friend" story contest and won the winning prize, including tax bonus of 1000 yuan; His works have been published in Huainan writers' cultural media, You book, simple book, beautiful piece, 17k novel network media, daily reading story media, short novels, marriage stories, city stories and other publications and network platforms, including two novels and dozens of fine short stories. He also published a series of articles in provincial newspapers.

Li Hua imagined her mother looking at her work seriously and felt very happy. As expected, the mother was very proud of Li Hua's writing, and kept saying, "How meaningful it is, leaving a house for the children is more important than leaving a book." When the money runs out, there's nothing left, and you can't take the house with you when you leave. And left behind works, future generations can read, spiritual wealth can be passed on forever, how meaningful writing ah!"

Sometimes the mother after reading Li Hua's works will also publish some reading impressions, "Boss, I am reading the article you wrote" I bought the first house in the name of my parents ", the story made me cry, the child ah! It's very well written..."

Li Hua's mother said these words, is sent to Li Hua's wechat voice segment by segment. Hearing her mother's choking voice, Li Hua felt her mother's comfort and pride. Parents have the wish of the son, the mother in emotional life and spirit are very dependent on Li Hua. Li Hua was born in the 1960s, at that time there was still a phenomenon of son preference, and the feudal idea that the adopted daughter was not as serious as the man. Mother always hopes that Li Hua will be better than

the boys. She cultivated Li Hua from a young age must study hard, be a good man, Li Hua's requirements are much stricter. But over the years, Li Hua never let her mother down.

My sister told Li Hua on wechat: "Mom likes your article, sometimes she will draw a wavy line under some paragraphs with a steel pen, mark these wonderful parts and read them repeatedly."

Sometimes my sister also pretended to be jealous and said to Li Hua: "You have always been mom's pride, we are good to her, but mom still likes you the most!"

Mother often talked to her sister about Li Hua when she was a child, Li Hua would make a fire stove to cook at the age of seven, and use small hands to make coal balls in winter, wash greasy work clothes on weekends, and take care of her sisters. When talking about emotion, the mother also shed a lot of tears: "At that time, your elder sister suffered a lot." Primary school teacher Chen often praise your elder sister sensible, learning and serious, after school to go home to help adults do housework. Your big sister always gives you all the good food. When I first received a salary of 22 yuan, I paid 10 yuan to my family, left 6 yuan for living expenses, and ate vegetarian dishes in the cafeteria for a month. Then she came home every week to bring you back fried sesame strips and other snacks, sweet and salty half, ten ten to buy. She also brought small salted bream, which she never returned home empty-handed. These things are given to you to eat, your sister herself reluctant to eat, the eighties is still a very difficult period ah!"

Mother's love never said, she always encouraged and influenced Li Hua must learn more knowledge, to make progress, must be excellent, so as not to be bullied. Later, Li Hua sisters did not lose to the children around the same age, which is inseparable from the mother's teaching and influence.

Mother's eyes let Li Hua still forget, her spirit has been affecting Li Hua. Li Hua suddenly understood, why these years have been able to insist on writing, is for the mother's expectations of the eyes. Li Hua enjoyed her mother's gratified look, which was the original expectation that had been met.

Becoming a writer is Li Hua's dream, but also the mother's expectation, the mother hopes that the family can produce an intellectual female writer, and this wish was realized by Li Hua. Thanks to the introduction of her writing predecessors, Li Hua has joined Wuhan Writers Association. Li Hua is expected to join the Hubei Writers Association if he can publish his novel in paper. This is not only Li Hua's own goal, but also the community's recognition of Li Hua's writing achievements. Li Hua now has a greater literary goal in mind, so that he can write more and better quality works, and strive to become a member of the Chinese Writers Association!

After that, Li Hua had a stronger motivation to write, and kept writing at least 8,000 words a week. Li Hua was excited and happy when he saw his works published in newspapers and magazines. In order to publish the novel into a book, Li Hua lived to learn and strive for perfection, greatly revised the whole novel, from the outline of the story, story structure, plot scenes, character dialogue, character portrayal, and written sentences, and upgraded the work to a higher level. Make the reader's reading experience better, but also easier to feel the theme expressed by the work. Li Hua's works have been appreciated by the editor, has signed a paper book publishing contract, and soon can be sold on the shelf.

In the long-term writing process, Li Hua thought while learning, and Li Hua's three views were also sublimated in writing. Li Hua is not for writing and writing, nor for the book and the word count, but with the soul to express the inner feeling, and strive to let the reader gain, and get the resonance of the reader's emotions. Li Hua's goal is to write good works and leave a spiritual wealth for future generations, not just a house, a car, and a bill. She also hopes that the spiritual wealth she left behind can be enjoyed by generations. She firmly believes that no matter how The Times develop, the way to do things, the right beliefs, and the quality of kindness are what everyone needs to have.

No matter how much money he made over the years, or how many houses he successfully bought, Li Hua found it less fun than publishing his work in the form of a book. It was a genuine joy and pride. Li Hua secretly decided, in order for the mother to continue to share their happiness, but also let the mother proud of

 themselves, Li Hua at home and Wen Youyi teacher, all expressed, must write the old! Live the rest of your life for writing!

Chapter 55: Duplex apartment with sea view writing

Li Hua continued to focus on investing in real estate while investing to improve herself. No matter which city has good housing information, Li Hua will rush to the field to see the house. Li Hua once took five female classmates to Yangjiang, Guangdong Province to see the sea view house; To take his girlfriend to Guangdong Zhuhai and Zhongshan house inspection; Take my hometown girlfriends to see villas in suburban areas; Take your family downtown to see school district housing...

Li Hua actively search for investment real estate information and practical implementation, in order to save costs, in the house decoration has been hands-on. It also develops the process of decoration into a personal preference. Everyone knows that decoration is hard work, but to Li Hua here, but can not see the hard work. She's shaping the house like a work of art. Being able to turn the blank house into what you want is the process of achieving your dream. Li Hua enjoyed the satisfaction of having her creativity at her disposal from beginning to end. The decoration process is very tired, but it makes Li Hua feel very full.

Li Hua's pace of life is sometimes tight and sometimes slow. One day Li Hua received a phone call from his girlfriend Yang Yang, inviting him to get together. Li Hua is decorating the construction site, without thinking about it politely refused: "Beauty, I have been too busy recently to have time to party, and I will find a video to show you."

Li Hua then hung up the phone, immediately gave the phone to the project manager, took a short video within 1 minute, and sent it to Yang Yang's wechat. Yang Yang saw in the video Li Hua wearing a white T-shirt shirt, wearing a white sun hat, the lower body wearing a green camouflage pants and a pair of black high-

top shoes, the whole person looks mentally competent. From the dirt on the shoes, we know that Li Hua is still doing civil construction site. There was also a lot of cement, sand and floor tiles piled up at the site. The video also saw workers at work, coming from a variety of noisy sounds of work.

Yang Yang said, "I see, it seems that you really can't come." Where are you decorating?"

Li Hua modestly whispered, "It's in a small town in the countryside. I'll ask you to come out again when I'm done."

Li Hua can only explain politely, and attach now shooting video to Yang Yang. Yang Yang had invited Li Hua several times before, and every time it was an inappropriate time, Yang Yang called Li Hua several times, and she was working, either buying decoration materials in the building materials market, or adjusting the design plan with the designer, or doing some emergency things on the scene like today: connecting electricians, plenders, painters and woodworkers. Because it is half a package project, so what things have to do themselves, control the entry and exit of workers handover.

The project manager and the general manager Zhao who do the decoration are on site to arrange the staff and decide the relevant decoration process. Zhao always understand Li Hua, let Li Hua rest assured to leave to attend the party, here he presided over the overall situation. Li Hua waved his hand and said, "How can you think of singing now? Mr. Zhao, if you don't get the overall layout and site construction drawings out one day, I can't rest assured."

Zhao said, "You just give me a year to pack the bag for you." It's not like you're in any hurry to move in. There are so many nice houses downtown anyway."

Li Hua said: "This is two different things, the first period of decoration must be arranged reasonably, can not think of where to do!" It's a waste of time and a waste of money. Must be well planned and arranged, in order to get things done. Don't rip it apart and then redo it. You'll lose money and time."

Zhao always understood Li Hua's meaning and stopped trying to persuade him. He knows Li Hua's personality very well, after all, Zhao always worked with Li Hua to decorate 13 houses, each time with a tacit understanding, but also save money and trouble. Li Hua every time to decorate the details of the house thoughtful, and remind Zhao.

Refused friends entertainment, Li Hua is also worried about being misunderstood by friends. So shoot a video to clarify, let her know that she is really busy, can not rush back downtown. On the one hand, it saves the time of explanation, and on the other hand, it saves the misunderstanding caused by roundabout. When a friend asked whose house it was, Li Hua could not just say that it was his own house, he said that he supervised the management with the boss of the decoration company and learned to see how their workers dealt with some on-site construction problems.

Li Hua is used to keeping a low profile and doesn't like to show off her wealth. Some people guess how many houses Li Hua has, how much money he earns, want to ask about Li Hua's strength, turn a corner to explore Li Hua's strength. Li Hua smiled at these temptations and kept his mouth shut about it. Li Hua does not buy a car, does not wear big brands, with his girlfriends shopping is also to buy brand seasonal discount clothes, bags, shoes. But the girlfriends all know that Li Hua likes to enter the beauty salon to do maintenance and micro-rectification. Li Hua has the concept of fashion, she cares about the strong heart, but also care about the appearance. What woman does not love beauty, unless false. Li Hua has always believed that the best way to show off wealth is a woman's face and a healthy body that leaves no signs of age.

Returning to single life these years, Li Hua not only does not look old, but looks younger and younger. Less mental pressure, temperament is good, according to Li Hua's own words, it is to grasp both spirit and material, both are not wrong. Not only the qualitative change, but also let those who have hurt her see that she will only get better and better, let those people see her thriving, see her more and more confident, see her more and more noble. Li Hua has been in the heart to admire themselves, encourage themselves, comfort themselves, to do rather than angry.

These few years have inadvertently come along like this, and along the way went smoothly.

Li Hua sometimes finds time to visit cities such as Zhuhai and Zhongshan in Guangdong Province to check the authenticity of real estate information on the spot. To personally experience the road transportation, urban traffic, the pace of life, life supporting various aspects of the situation. This time Li Hua will go to Zhongshan to handle some invested real estate projects, two sets of house procedures, one set of value-added sale, one set of reserve.

Take the intercity high-speed train from Wuhan to Guangzhou, then turn to Zhuhai and Zhongshan. Li Hua has been used to traveling alone, going out on the train for a few hours alone, often let Li Hua can calm down some problems, but also learn a lot of independent skills. Driving from Guangzhou to Zhongshan North Railway Station, Li Hua had a wonderful hunch that he would often go to Zhuhai and Zhongshan in the future. It is likely that in the process of viewing the existing house, she will pay the purchase deposit.

Coming out of Zhongshan North Station, Li Hua has seen Chen driver who picked her up. Chen driver is a local town people, very familiar with the purchase of units related to the route, which is also the sales department of small non-yun recommended Chen driver one of the reasons. From Zhongshan North Station to the sales department has more than 20 minutes by car, Xiaoyun has been waiting for Li Hua in the hall. Chen driver said to Li Hua: "You look at the house by the sales department accompanied by beauty, there are batteries to see the RV." Call me when you're done, and I'll take you to your hotel. At night, you can go to the seafood street to eat shrimp, fish and crabs."

Li Hua replied to driver Chen: "OK, thank you. I'll call you when I'm done. The scenery is beautiful and the temperature is like spring. Is there too few buses, there are no buses? It would be very inconvenient if it weren't for Chen."

Sales department Xiaoyun immediately said: "It will be very convenient to develop in the future, there will be a battery car to the bus station in the community, and the people in the community will go to the station." There is also a hot spring hotel here, the purchase of guests will be discounted, 168 yuan standard room."

Li Hua nodded and smiled to Xiaoyun who had been in close contact on wechat and said: "Go, take me to see the house first."

Li Hua has a soft spot for the house, as long as it is to see the house and choose the house, all the troubles are gone. The day is sunny, the weather is beautiful, the sales department hall is decorated in the atmosphere and luxury, which has made Li Hua like it. All afternoon Li Hua followed Xiao Yun to see six sets of existing houses, in addition to see the sea view room apartment model room three types of rooms. Li Hua has his eye on two houses. She wasn't impulsive, she was prepared. She chose a boxy 138 square house with four bedrooms, three bathrooms and two living rooms; And I pre-selected a duplex on the beach.

When he saw the real scene of the existing house, Li Hua's mood became better. Standing on the balcony of the existing house looking at the sea, you can see the mountains far away, and the sea waves are beating to the shore, constantly blowing the water with the wind. Then open towards the balcony of the community, the small bridge water in the community, the green plants along the courtyard of the path with small flowers colorful, and the pond lotus, garden flowers, Li Hua only feel good, but can not call out the name of the flower, Li Hua looked at thinking into the fan.

At this time, Li Hua has the strength to come to romance, the poet Haizi's famous sentence flashed in his mind, Li Hua quietly said to himself: "I already have a sea view room facing the sea with spring flowers."

This day Li Hua can realize it and own it. The distance between the sea is so close, looking at the blue sky, smelling the fresh air, hearing the sound of waves beating, from far and near the wide, can not see the edge, this environment has made Li Hua's mind surging. Li Hua made up his mind without hesitation: Buy! Must have it!

Xiao Yun said to Li Hua: "Sister Li Hua, here is beautiful?"

Li Hua said, "Yes, it's beautiful! The most important thing is that this apartment is square, like the home I live in Hubei now, the same layout, at a glance, it feels familiar. Let's go. Let's go sign the contract. These are the two. Your advertising says well, hot springs coast!"

Xiao Yun happy face smiled and opened flowers, very happy to Li Hua said: "You are the most cheerful good customer I have seen this week!" Last month, a boss from Macau also looked at the house in the morning and signed two houses in the afternoon. She said that the house is close to Macau, and it is suitable for living or investing on weekends. She also said the house was worth it and would definitely go up."

Listen to what Xiaoyun said, a message to Li Hua wake up, you can also take like to buy a girlfriend to invest in seascape apartment, let them also benefit. I'm sure Cookie and Jen would love this house, too. Li Hua often does these things to share good information with a group of girlfriends who like to invest in real estate.

Xiao Yun happily said to Li Hua: "Go, we go to sign the purchase contract." Just pay the deposit today, pay the full amount in seven days, and I'll give you a free month's property fee. "

In addition, Xiao Yun told Li Hua, pick up her Chen driver is actually the boss of the decoration company. Chen also takes into account to help the owner do the property rights certificate, because he is familiar with the address, plus Chen's wechat is a lot of convenience.

This day Li Hua was in a particularly good mood, and suddenly found that the hard work was worth it when signing. Perhaps one day to visit again, Li Hua from this investment will benefit far more than today's pay. She believes that every effort will be rewarded, and she believes that people who are prepared at any time are more likely to succeed.

I did not expect the time to pass so quickly, and then several years have passed. Li Hua is himself again, and can be free as he pleases. Li Hua enjoys the happiness brought by this growth, and enjoys this pleasant state of life. Li Hua took a circle in life, and found that the life that he is in charge of is a meaningful life.

Li Hua affectionately turned her eyes to the direction of the sea. It was so beautiful here. Here she could be alone, here she could daydream, here she could do her favorite writing. Here to create stories and novels, the text will be published into a book, here to realize the winding Li Hua's literary writer dream for many years!

Xiao Yun smiled at Li Hua, eyes can see the obvious emotions: admire, envy, worship. Xiao Yun said: "Sister Li, you are too ox! I can do what you're doing now in my life, and I'll wake up laughing when I sleep."

Li Hua said: "You work so hard, you can also!" As long as women are financially independent, security comes. Remember, no one is better than you, especially us single women! "

Chapter 56: Fade in Time

Li Hua's life is busy and full spent, she herself did not realize that the single life has passed for more than ten years.

The previous marriage life is like the jade bracelet she wears on her hand, if it is broken, broken, can not be restored, can only throw away, and then choose a new bracelet that suits her. Li Hua understands the truth that "if the old does not go, the new will not come". This is the real life, if there is no love and marriage, the original can also live smart confident beautiful.

Li Hua has long left the resentment far behind, the clock does not stop rotating, as the years run forward, resentment has been in the years faded away. Li Hua's life is getting better and better, the quality of life is constantly improving, the original sense of loss is gone forever! Thinking of some people and things in the past, Li Hua has been relieved, she learned to understand human nature, treat themselves kindly and let go of others' mistakes. After the loss of marriage, family and friendship have always brought Li Hua support and warmth.

It has been more than 20 years since the first divorce, once Li Hua just returned to her daughter's home from the Suzhou pen friend book launch, Li Hua habitually greeted her daughter Xiaolin: "I am back, where are you?"

Xiao Lin ran from the master bedroom to the living room and said with a smile, "It is good to come back, these days are too busy, I asked my father to help me cook a few meals." His wife aunt is also helping to clean the kitchen, and we will have dinner together later!"

Li Hua did not react, hesitantly asked her daughter: "What happened? Well, I'm gonna go before they see me in the kitchen, and you guys can eat. This is awkward!

I want to know they're here, and I'm not coming back. Why didn't you tell me? I raised you for nothing!"

Li Hua said while handing over the luggage box to Xiaolin, with eyes signal quickly put the box into the bedroom, that is the daughter specially reserved for Li Hua bedroom.

Li Hua then lowered his voice and said: "I went to the beauty salon to do care, just rest for a few hours, you eat it." They left to tell me on wechat, I'm gone, don't say I'm coming!"

When the door was open to go out, the ex-husband took out the dishes from the kitchen and put them on the table, and saw the ex-wife Li Hua and her daughter standing at the door. The ex-husband froze for a moment, immediately like nothing, walked forward to say hello: "Yo, back, just have you like to eat braised fish, as well as shredded mustard stir-fried chili, to eat!"

Her ex-husband is much older, and from the appearance, he does not seem to be of the same age as Li Hua. Her ex-husband is still the same loud voice, speaking with a real Chinese accent, and his character has not changed at all; And Li Hua from the appearance of dress, but appears young, energetic, generous, fashion, intellectual beauty. It is the nature of The Times, ah, Li Hua suddenly saw her ex-husband like this, thinking of the marriage between them. My husband always thought that he was from a big city and was proud, and looked down on Li Hua from a small city. But now it feels like they've switched places.

These memories flashed in Li Hua's mind for a few seconds, fresh memories, suddenly there is a point of the wrong door of the illusion. Li Hua very politely declined and said: "I really have something, you eat."

At this time, her ex-husband's wife also came out of the kitchen, Li Hua's mind quickly flashed what her daughter Xiaolin said: "Dad's current wife is three years old, and aunt conditions are also very good." Is the aunt chasing dad, dad is still pretty popular with women, I am also very good..."

The ex-husband's current wife, looks simple and skilled to help her daughter

do housework, really did not put himself as an outsider, but also polite and polite to Li Hua said: "have done it, sit down to eat together!"

At this time, it appears that Li Hua is not like his family, standing is not, sitting is not, busy back outside the gate, waving and saying: "You eat it while it's hot, I really have something!" Li Hua is actually happy in her heart, and she has put it down over the years. Daughter more loved ones love, this is not Li Hua want?

Li Hua said blushing, head also dare not go back to the elevator door, press the elevator key to feel more relaxed. The daughter chased him out: "Mom, do you go to dinner?" Really, they're all so easygoing. As you can see, you're so young, they can't compete with you! People don't care about it in their hearts, but you still hide?"

Li Hua directly refused to say: "Fuck you, let them come and don't talk to me, make me really embarrassed!"

Xiao Lin couldn't help but laugh and added, "Mom, you can have new material to write stories, ha ha ha!"

Li Hua stared at Xiao Lin, "Oh, worry about it! You go to eat, I go to the community beauty salon to do care, hungry me. You're an asshole. I raised you no better than your dad can cook, okay? The dog ate the heart! Oh, I understand, my own father is still my own father!"

Xiao Lin quickly replied, "Oh, it's all over." You all have your own lives. You're all family. As you can see, Dad remembers your favorite dishes and is good to you. Dad still has a picture of you holding me at home! I don't hate you at all, but you didn't want your father!"

The elevator door opened, Li Hua rushed in, pressed the door key, and made a face to her daughter standing in the aisle, "You hurry into the house to eat, they are waiting for you!"

Elevator from the highest level to the first floor, Li Hua breathed a sigh of relief, to the community next to the shady tree path to the back door of the community, the beauty salon is nearby. Beauty maintenance is Li Hua's favorite kind of leisure consumption. Li Hua thought that if she finished her beauty care and her ex-husband had not gone, she still had a place to go. Li Hua did a pedicure club membership card near the community, then do a pedicure care again. If they have not gone, Li Hua went to the hairdresser to do a set of head care, anyway, also did the card. In life, Li Hua is very reasonable arrangement and enjoyment, but also pay attention to health maintenance. Over the years, thanks to Li Hua, she knows how to manage her own life. Whenever I am tired from work and want to be alone quietly, I will rest in the above ways to relieve physical and mental exhaustion.

Years passed in a flash, those past people and things, now is in the eyes of Li Hua, also can not arouse resentment. Time is a great healer. Li Hua all wonder how he willingly put everything down, sometimes Li Hua think of these things can not help but laugh, can not help shaking his head. Li Hua thought, these things are not a big deal, everything is over, and now only Li Hua himself, not also very good? Other people aren't as bad as she used to think. Not many people care about who and who's past. Besides, who doesn't have a past?

Li Hua thought and fell asleep on the comfortable beauty bed. Beauticians a pair of small hands, massage techniques in place, let Li Hua feel very comfortable; The soft hypnotic music in the store also makes Li Hua extremely relaxed.

A few days before the Spring Festival of this year, my daughter said to Li Hua: "Mom, aunt LAN LAN and dad said, let us go to grandma's New Year's Day, thirty eve dinner, what do you think?"

Li Hua followed her daughter's meaning and said, "You can go, I'll let it go, otherwise how would your father think?"

Xiao Lin said, "Grandma said that she didn't invite dad's current wife that day, just to let you go back to the New Year dinner." Dad said aunt is very understanding, specially said his mother's family also want to eat New Year's dinner, deliberately not present!"

Li Hua was silent for a moment and said, "That aunt is so good to your father, I don't need to go." You want your dad to be nice and live a good life. This time you go to my unit to take the material, the fruit for grandparents, the cashmere sweater is for your father, the gloves for your stepmother, the silk scarf for your

aunt. These things don't say I gave them, say you work rich to honor them. Just hope they're nice to you and don't hate me. When you went to see them on my behalf, you told them that Mom was going to keep her new house for New Year's Eve. Just say that and don't talk about anything else!"

Li Hua really just wants to have a quiet year in his new house. It feels as if you are the queen, lying on your back, with your legs up on the coffee table, so you can comfortably watch the party than anywhere else. You can also quietly look at a copy of a letter from her daughter Xiaolin, which is an email that Xiaolin has hidden for many years.

Li Hua has not been in contact with that person, but also almost forget that betrayed her hurt her man Yu Ping. That letter is written by Yu Ping, this time Xiao Lin took it out to Li Hua to see, must have a special purpose.

Years have passed, small Lin realized that mom has been no longer in love no longer married, the heart has been to Yu Ping love and hate, and did not put him down. Xiao Lin didn't want her mother to live in pain and hatred, she wanted her mother to completely let go and walk out of the shadow, so it was time to take out the letter to her mother.

The letter was forwarded by Yu Ping to his daughter's email address after Li Hua's divorce from Yu Ping took effect through court proceedings. At that time, Li Hua could not operate a computer, and her daughter set up a shared email account. Li Hua would have forgotten the existence of this email address had he not seen the letter. Xiaolin often use the computer, what information she will see first, this letter is in Li Hua did not know, was daughter Xiaolin saw after collection.

Li Hua didn't want to open it, but he remembered what Lin said before she left: "Mom, if you feel bored, you can read this letter." But when you're done you can burn it, dispose of it, don't keep it!"

Li Hua at this time, curiosity germination, what content is written inside, read to burn?

Chapter 57: Yu Ping's confession

Li Hua quickly picked up the envelope, leaned on the most comfortable position on the sofa, put her legs on the coffee table, and casually looked at the letter. Looking at it, the expression solidified, the brow locked deeply, unconsciously the eyes filled with tears. Li Hua silently wiped away the tears that blurred his eyes and continued to read the letter.

The letter read:

Dear Hua Hua, I have already received your complaint. Luckily, I got it and saw it. Mom didn't see the letter. Mom died before she knew you were divorcing me. Of course, I didn't get a chance to say that to mom.

When she was 83, she was admitted to the hospital with Alzheimer's disease and died that year. Uncle Cheng, who has been accompanying her, sent her to the funeral home. Cheng Bobo so infatuation love mother, guard the latter half of life, two old people have not been together, is now heaven two separation. I suddenly feel, I really not human ah! The person I am most sorry for in this life is you, my Huahua.

As I write this, it was me who spent my 60th birthday alone in the hospital. I have seen the notice of summons, and I know that it is my fault that you were disappointed in your marriage and filed for divorce in this undignified manner. I know that once you've made your decision, there's no point in saying anything. It's too late.

And I'm grateful that you didn't mention my marital affair on the docket, saving a man's face and my pride. It dawned on me that you were the one who was really good to me. But I don't have the face to ask you to come back to me. Although I have broken off contact with that woman, I also know that you will not be able to get back

together with me. I know you are stubborn and will never forgive me. I know this, I don't blame you, only blame myself, please don't hate me, I only have a penitent heart. I have no mind to fall in love with another woman in this life, I messed up our love and marriage, lost, I love dearly! Now there is no woman around, but my mind is full of your shadow, I think of the happy time we used to be together every day.

As I write this letter to you, I am being treated alone in a hospital in Shanghai. I have been hemiplegic in the bed for two months. The doctor said I might have inherited my father's condition, a cerebral thrombus. I don't know which day will suddenly have a heart obstruction, and then suddenly die. Divorce court, if I don't show up, you can get a court order, divorce, single. I'm a dying man, and that's all I can do for you.

Perhaps by the time you read this letter, I will no longer be on this earth. I know you don't spend a lot of time at your computer checking your E-mail.

Finally say a few words of truth, I'm sorry to you, please forgive me for the stupid thing I did wrong! Please don't punish yourself for me, Hua Hua, be good to yourself, I am alive or gone, I want to say goodbye in this way, because I have no face to see you again. The thing I regret most in this life is that I did not cherish the days with you. My confusion stabbed your kindness, let me completely become a ghost!

Forgive me, or I will die.

The person who still loves you: Yu Ping!

November 5, 2012 (Do you remember? Today is my birthday.

Yu Ping is a heart of Li Hua, life can not also a debt of love. Yu Ping may not even know that Li Hua will not see this letter until many years later. Yu Ping knew that the kind-hearted Li Hua would forgive him for his mistakes; But Yu Ping did not know that Li Hua was once loved by his infatuation, hurt very deeply, so that from then on, Li Hua no longer believe in love.

The text in the letter like sentimental seed, miserable Xi Xi text scene let Li Hua sad sad. She did not know whether to feel sad for herself or feel sorry for Yu Ping. At this time, Li Hua understand Xiaolin's mind, understand the daughter's good intentions, hope Li Hua cheer up. The past is gone, the people who loved and hated are gone. Stop punishing your life for people and things that don't deserve it, and look yourself in the face and come out of the shadow of your heart. In addition to life and death, what other frustrations can not be overcome? Let go of all grudges and live well is the most powerful farewell to the past hurt. Facts proved that Li Hua also came this way, without love and marriage, not also very good?

As in the past, Zhenzhen agreed with Li Hua on the phone to meet on the fifteenth day of the year, or meet in the old place - about the villa they bought together in the community. On the fifteenth day of the first month, Zhenzhen and Li Hua before and after 5 minutes were respectively to the villa area property company to meet.

The green belt in the district makes people relaxed and happy, the fresh air in the outskirts of the provincial capital, and the festive red lanterns hanging on both sides of the gate of the district bring a jubilant traditional cultural atmosphere to the festival. People who can live in this community are not simple, and have a pair of discernment, especially those who bought here in the first phase. Choosing to buy a house here, whether it is an investment or a home, is worthwhile and wise.

The housing prices of these communities are cheap and good, and the environment of the community after several years of development is becoming more and more beautiful. Li Hua and Zhen Zhen both like this place very much. It is a masterpiece of their investment real estate projects. It seems that they want to go or decide to stay as a good place for their future retirement! Here the green grass, to the provincial capital traffic is very convenient, is a noisy take quiet leisure good place. Zhenzhen love photography, Li Hua love writing, weekdays have their own work and hobbies to study to be busy, the two people do not disturb each other; But when we get together, we can talk all night, and we can be together. Life has such a confidant, life is enough!

Li Hua and Zhenzhen walk along the path of the community while talking, Zhenzhen said to Li Hua: "I have a notarial letter of Yu Ping express to you, which is handed over to me by Yu Ping's lawyer." I wonder how long it's been there?

It was on my tenth day of work that I found a pile of letters on my desk, and among them was this big mail delivery box. When I opened the carton, I saw a notarial certificate that I had handed over to you, as well as a suite key and a private letter that Yu Ping wanted to give you. I'll give it to you right away. My job is done! Open it and take a look."

Li Hua took a look at Zhenzhen, opened the letter face to face, the letter line by line, the handwriting Li Hua is too familiar. The letter reads as follows:

Hua Hua, by the time you receive this letter, I may not be alive anymore, so please read it patiently, OK?

I did some bad things to you when I was alive, and now I want to do two right things to make up for my guilt toward you when I'm about to die. First, after my death, I will donate all my useful organs to help patients in need. Second, I have notarized the property in Shanghai that I only kept for you. After doing these two things, I have nothing to worry about.

I felt better after I had done it. I know it never occurred to you that I would buy the Shanghai property privately. Now the property is worth tens of millions. This is the real estate we bought after marriage, the real estate information is also highly recommended by you at that time, but later I did not have the chance to tell you, I bought this house in time. It was Mom's money, and I don't know how to tell you this. I dreamed that one day you would forgive me and we would go on living in this house that you love... These unexpected increases in wealth remind me of your investing wisdom. Because I benefit from your vision, which should belong to you and me.

Over the years I have experienced a lot of women around me, most of them are greedy for my money and play, when I found that I was ill hemiplegia, the women around have disappeared. During my stay in the hospital, it was my loneliest and most enlightened day, I quietly looked at the ceiling on the ward, the cold walls on all sides, and suddenly felt the sadness of my life.

I think of everything about you, when we were together, your goodness, your kindness, your carelessness. You were stupid enough to believe my lies until you found out about the affair. I see your pain and your despair. The tooth mark you bit on my arm, still on my wrist, is a stain on my life. I didn't fight you back. I put up with it so you could get over it. After the accident, during the Cold War, I knew that you kept the letter of repentance that I wrote the next day. I remember the content of those two sentences, it is my life difficult to say regret.

Of course, Li Hua will always remember the content of the note left by Yu Ping: "I'm sorry for you, I left to develop in another city, I left..."

See here, Li Hua eyes red, nose began to stuffy: "really uncomfortable!"

Li Hua pretended to be very relaxed, back Zhenzhen directly concerned about the eyes. Zhenzhen very understand Li Hua's state of mind at the moment, eyes only look at the road ahead, continue to walk while saying: "Look light, to the good side to see." Yu Ping can repent in this way, showing that he really regrets doing those things that hurt you. No one's perfect. We have to remember what he did to you. Thinking of the last days of his life, his heart is full of your goodness, he will always remember your kindness. Yu Ping heart in action, for you to repay this debt. After all these years, aren't you here by yourself? In fact, you have let go, but the two of us never mentioned the past days, never mentioned Yu Ping this person, deliberately avoid this matter, this person. But I know that you have always had him in your heart, so you have not accepted other people's feelings. As a friend, I want to tell you that you can now accept these facts in peace. Time is the best healer, I will always understand you!"

Li Hua continued to carefully open the express bag with a face covered, which showed the notarial certificate and the key. It was that year that Li Hua and Yu Ping went to Shanghai to see the house in the community - Shanghai Wenmin District, only ten minutes away from McDonald's. It was one of the suites 2001 that saw the final end of the market. What I did not expect was that Yu Ping went to settle down the next day. And I didn't mention the house to Li Hua.

After so many years, the real price of the house has risen to more than 10 million yuan. This also proves that at that time, Li Hua's eye to see how powerful. That year, Li Hua and his daughter came to Shanghai to travel with Yu Ping, Li Hua

accidentally saw the housing publicity information on the newspaper, and insisted on seeing the end of the existing house. After reading, Li Hua insisted that if you have money to buy this house, the price will rise with your eyes closed. At that time, Yu Ping agreed to buy, but later said some reasons did not buy, in fact, after two days to order the house, thinking that the future will always give Li Hua a surprise. As a result, the unpleasant thing happened soon after, and Yu Ping never told Li Hua about it.

See the content of the notarial certificate, the property right of this house was given to Li Hua, and passed to Li Hua in the form of legal documents. Li Hua's mind is myriad, she is thinking, now everyone is gone, but what is the use of leaving the house?

Li Hua looked at Zhenzhen with a very calm eye and said, "I have decided that I will sell the real estate of Yu Ping in Shanghai, and all the money sold will be donated to the children in the poor and far mountain villages." It is best to build a Project Hope school for children in remote mountain villages, so that children can go to school! Zhenzhen, you are now the vice mayor, the relationship channels are wider than me, this matter is still by your friend to help me operate, find a lawyer to enter the auction, I will be there to handle the formalities!"

Zhenzhen is not surprised that Li Hua will do so, she knows that Li Hua's existing wealth has already exceeded the value of the house given by Yu Ping.

Zhenzhen know Li Hua love the house, for many years a person struggle, the house is no longer Li Hua sense of security on the dependence. Spiritually confident Li Hua has already achieved wealth freedom and grown into an economically independent woman. No marriage, no love, she can still rely on their own money to buy the ideal house, no longer the old Li Hua!

Chapter 58: I like the way I look

After dealing with the house given by Yu Ping, Li Hua was relaxed. Zhenzhen play heart admire Li Hua so calm and calm, do not hesitate to calm attitude. Think of if there is such a friend in old age, two people still live in the same community, still worry about loneliness?

Zhenzhen also thank Li Hua trust her, Zhenzhen just proposed to buy a house together, the two met to see a house, Li Hua signed a house purchase contract in the second month. It is good to have economic strength, one-time full house payment, this is the goddess of the model! In the eyes of Zhenzhen, every investment project, Li Hua as long as the field investigation, will think of all the details, the best and worst interests of thorough analysis, and decisive attack.

Li Hua execution is very strong, as long as there is a reasonable plan, anyway try to do it, do it on the road, encountered difficulties one by one to deal with the solution. If you think about all the difficulties and then implement the perfect plan in order to avoid all the risks, it is likely that nothing will be done, and you will have scared yourself before you do it.

Li Hua often met Zhenzhen in the villa area on weekends, and sometimes discussed some things by the way. For now, the two still live in different cities.

Li Hua looked around the lush environment of the community and said to Zhenzhen: "This time you gave Yu Ping this set of house notarial certificate to me, it is a hot potato." Fortunately, I never expected the pie to fall on this day, to deal with it so plain, but also for Yu Ping to do the last good thing. The past is the past, and I have moved on. I hope he can see good results in heaven, and children in remote areas can grow up healthily and study well. Doing something good for the country is more meaningful than putting my house in my name."

Li Hua never thought about her marriage after she separated from Yu Ping, nor did she plan to pursue perfect love for the rest of her life. Li Hua in addition to work is to invest wealth investment to improve themselves, fill their time, let themselves run like a machine, do not feel lonely.

It is often said that the more you want something, the harder it is to get it. Instead, the good things that you don't want will suddenly come around and make people surprised. Li Hua recently met a good thing that made her perplexed.

After Li Hua and Yu Ping separated, over the years, there were actually many men to Li Hua friendly, such as the clothing street property management company Chen general manager, and Li Hua's "first love" Guo Qizhi. At that time, Li Hua was more than forty years old, busy with career struggles, and had no mind to respond. Many years passed, Li Hua did not think that she could have any love at the age of sixty. But now I have really met and am remembered by two wonderful men. Is there any truth in this world?

Li Hua began to alert to remind herself, they love her this person? Li Hua thought that he would indeed maintain ten years younger than his peers, but even if he had beauty and charm, he could not afford the traces left by the years, after all, he was over half a century. Li Hua is worried that they are just aiming at their own good conditions of wealth. Just curious attention to get some good feelings.

After thinking about it, Li Hua sometimes felt that he wanted to think too much, the two people's "thinking" may be just their own illusion. Because both men have good careers. Li Hua does not believe that he can meet a dim love. No matter how good and excellent men, also can not enter Li Hua's sight and heart. She has been used to being lonely for decades, and she does not think in the direction of love and marriage. Can continue to be free after half a life, already do not know how many people envy themselves, Li Hua contented.

Over the years, Li Hua has also met a lot of men who can say sweet words, and has become a little numb to men's ingratiation. She can calmly cope with the temptation of men, will give no true feelings of men consciously quit the step, will also deal with those who only to maintain a career cooperation relationship.

Li Hua has a very good ability to read people, can grasp the distance and sense of proportion.

Li Hua does not resist the truth, but does not deliberately pursue it. If there really is a suitable candidate at this time, Li Hua will not be as happy as when he was young. She will observe silently for a period of time, if the other side has true feelings will inevitably have perseverance. If the two people are indeed destined, the other party will not retreat because of a period of "observation" - if Guo Qizhi can persist in pursuing Li Hua for a year or two, he may not have no chance of success.

Not long after, Li Hua's novel was published. The publisher held a small book launch specially for Li Hua. At the scene of the conference, there was a man who always paid attention to Li Hua's every move and showed infinite appreciation. This is a plump, stocky, broad-shouldered middle-aged man. Li Hua recognized him, in a developer held a real estate project first sales meeting, introduced by three brother-in-law, Li Hua met the real estate company chairman Yin.

Yin Dong is a genuine northern man, prudent and generous, patient and delicate, usually do things silently never speak much. Yin Dong is 1.8 meters tall, his eyes are very small, and he squints into a slit when he smiles. With his slightly fat body type, he seems to have a simple and honest temperament. Li Hua has a good impression on him, always feel this kind of people simple and safe. It is said that Yin Dong's wife died several years ago, after which Yin Dong devoted himself to his career and remained single.

I do not know what reason, although Li Hua did not have a deep friendship with Yin Dong, but each other left a good impression. Li Huai concerned about developer housing new real estate information, naturally also often pay attention to the project direction of Yin Dong company, but also invested in three sets of housing in these projects. One by one, Li Hua several times to see the real estate company chairman Yin.

One day the three brother-in-law said to Li Hua at the cocktail party, "Elder sister, we Yin Dong people are really good, single for several years." A lot of single female friends around like to be close, but Yin Dong did not put in mind. Last time I heard me talk about your book launch, Yin Dong asked me which day to hold it, and asked me to get admission tickets. I feel a little sudden, is our Yin Dong attracted to you? Can you get me some invitations for the book launch?"

Li Hua smiled and said, "Of course you are welcome to come to the show, but you must come with friends who are sincere about buying new books." For the friends you bring, there is no limit to the number of books you buy."

The next day Li Hua will give the invitation to the third sister, let her forward to the three brother-in-law. As for the three brother-in-law to whom, Li Hua did not care to guess, she only knew that the more people to the better. The more people there are, the more lively the atmosphere of the conference. Li Hua's literary dream, which he had been looking forward to for many years, finally came true. She wants her book signing to be a success!

Soon it was the day of the book launch. Standing on the stage to speak Li Hua, the first to the audience swept a glance at the guests, she saw relatives, see friends, see girlfriends, see old classmates, also saw the front row right aisle sitting Yin chairman, a pair of eyes have smiled into a seam of men. It is strange to say, Li Hua saw him want to laugh, the simple and honest look of the tiger, even let people feel a little funny and cute. This is the Yin Dong in Li Hua's impression. In my mind is already an easygoing old friend, seems very familiar, there are many good feelings.

For Yin Dong came, Li Hua did not feel surprised, but a little secretly happy. Three brother-in-law before mentioned Yin Dong to his intention, Li Hua is listening to it, but did not reveal too much. Decades of single day shadow lonely, Li Hua just deep, can only be on the cause of the heart, to the opposite sex friends indifferent become some numb. In the career and workplace, Li Hua put himself as a man to get along with the opposite sex only talk about cooperation, do not talk about romance. In the past, there were also some friends of the opposite sex who cared for Li Hua, but they were skillfully avoided by Li Hua. Why is it different this time? What's really going on? Li Hua thought of the "ghost".

Yin Dong did not deliberately show kindness to Li Hua when facing, but they can get along with each other as easily as acquaintances and friends, and there are several unexpected encounters - Li Hua think this is also a sign that the two people are destined. Sometimes the two people will naturally care about each other's news, wechat circle of friends also like each other. Sometimes Li Hua felt that Yin Dong was really like a good big brother, helping her secretly, intentionally or unintentionally, for example, providing the best information on the opening of new houses for sale. As long as Li Hua fancy to buy, Yin Dong will say hello to the sales department, the company's most preferential internal staff prices sold to Li Hua and his family! Of course, the third sister also helped a lot. Sometimes directly encourage remind Li Hua to invest in Yin Dong company's real estate projects, indirectly to Yin Dong company. And these are good projects, Li Hua every time they invest in their property can get a good return. Therefore, a good cycle has been formed, and Li Hua and Yin Dong have cooperated indirectly for several times.

Today, Yin Dong came to support the show, and as expected, he signed and sold 500 new books in one breath. When the host read the book purchase unit, name, quantity, this let Li Hua was surprised. Does Dong Yin eat his new book as a meal? Buy so much to underwrite?

Li Hua certainly does not doubt Yin Dong's economic strength, but the book is used to read, bought so much if only to support, let these books in the dark corner of the dust, Li Hua felt too meaningless. Yin Dong seemed to see Li Hua's heart, the eyes seemed to say to Li Hua: "Rest assured! I will help these books find the right audience for them!"

A moment of eye contact, Li Hua embarrassed to quickly put the eyes back. According to the previous arrangement, it is Li Hua's turn to speak next. When Li Hua was ready to speak, she suddenly found that the eye contact had disturbed her thoughts, and she suddenly forgot her words! Fortunately, Li Hua has seen the scene experience, silence for a few seconds immediately adjusted back, slowly issued a gentle, not slow voice: "First of all, thank you for coming to participate in the signing of new book activities of the leadership, friends and relatives. Thank you for your encouragement and support! As the author, I would like to express my sincere thanks to all of you. Thank you all for accompanying me on the writing road; Thank

you for your encouragement to make me write a good work; Thank you all for your love and affection. Finally, because of everyone's encouragement, I have the motivation to keep writing. I will write better literary novels in the future. Finally, I wish the book launch a complete success! Thank you all!"

It was not the first time for Li Hua to make a speech in a meeting room with hundreds of people. Yin Dong was very nervous mood, was Li Hua after the applause diluted. Yin Dong quietly rose from his seat and spoke a few words to Miss Manners. Then Miss Manners conjured three bouquets of pink flowers from the bottom of the tray. Wearing a fitted red cheongsam, Miss Manners led three beautiful women to the center of the stage in the sound of music, and presented three bunches of flowers to Li Hua who had just delivered a speech.

Li Hua saw that it was her favorite pink lily, and could not help but be overjoyed. She understood that Yin Dong sent her these meaningful lily flowers. She could not help but also unabashedly, accept the flowers in the crowd cheers, also accept Yin Dong's deep friendship. At this time, Yin Dong did not dare to say what sweet words, but Li Hua has felt the sweet heart full of joy.

Yin Dong always take action instead of speaking, Li Hua is fancy Yin Dong this excellent simple side. This kind of strength, responsibility, and responsibility, good man quality. At the age of Li Hua, to have such a deep relationship with Yin Dong, it is indeed impossible to meet. At this time, Li Hua's frozen heart for many years once again palpated, and the long-lost girl's feelings filled Li Hua's heart. Did you meet true love in the sunset of sunset? Li Hua really did not expect to be able to feel such a heartbeat at this age.

After the release of the new book, bestie Zhen Zhen said excitedly: "Li Hua, you can now use part of the money earned by entrepreneurship to improve the writing environment." Pick up a previous dream, open a book bar or tea house, cafe - drink a cup of coffee can also refresh your mind, suitable for you to write. Now you can plan your dream."

Li Hua was said to be tempted, seriously think about this matter, now is indeed the best time to implement the operation. Jiajia, a good friend, reminded Li Hua beside: "Oh, you can transform your small villa of one to three floors, and the first floor is all decorated according to the teahouse club." Ready-made house, community environment is good. You can live and write there every day; Invite some like-minded friends, painting friends, photography friends, and friends who can sing and dance together at the weekend, how comfortable!"

Li Hua should voice: "I think so, Zhenzhen, Jiajia you two listen to my design arrangement." The first floor hall set up a wall as a display cabinet, from the bottom to the top of the wall can be placed on my published books, as well as all the literature books, as well as the paintings made by my family. I framed them and hung them where I wanted to display them. The corner of the living room pillar is decorated with a big tree, and the top of the living room is all arranged into a banyan tree, and the green leaves are lush at a glance, like spring. We feel like we are drinking tea under the big tree, chatting, and enjoying the good time. I have a drawing plan for this decoration design for a long time! I'm telling you, that tree is full of cabinets, and when it's closed, it looks like a real tree. I specially in the hometown of the Red Army Hongan county, found a very famous folk craftsmen Ruan teacher made simulation tree. When the renovation project is complete. You two could be regulars. Ha ha, you two are busy!" The three men laughed.

At this time, Yin Dong smiled and came over, looked at the design drawings that Li Hua put on the table, pointed to the central design kitchen of the restaurant on the first floor, and said: "If you need to ask the chef, I am happy to cook for the beautiful women, lulu cooking." I do Lihua like to eat boiling hot pot fish banquet, package you all like to eat! I wonder if you can hire me."

Yin Dong said to Li Hua seriously, but also in a polite way, also want to let Li Hua's friends know that he has taken Li Hua as the future to spend the rest of his life together. Yin Dong knew that Li Hua was the partner he wanted to choose. With the strength of Li Hua everything has, in Yin Dong's mind, Li Hua is wealth freedom, do not want his money, because Yin Dong has been worth more than 100 million.

Yin Dong is more willing to help Li Hua from practical matters, he understands the value of life that Li Hua wants most, he is willing to pay for it. Fine points to see

the truth, once signed Li Hua published 500 new books; In the decoration, secretly provide the best and most affordable construction materials to reduce the decoration cost for Li Hua. Yin Dong is real, has let Li Hua moved the heart of the hidden Xu, but she never revealed - after all is about to enter the old age of the woman, Li Hua dare not to hope for love. But in front of the girlfriends are happy for Li Hua, in his old age can meet such a virtuous confidant, can entrust the rest of his partner. They all shouted out with one voice: "Li Hua quickly promise, we agree!"

Friends all hope that Li Hua hire Yin Dong to be her senior chef for a lifetime! Li Hua and Yin Dong smiled shyly, Li Hua like a young girl in love, cheeks quickly flushed up, a heart pounding. This feeling of first love is hidden in Li Hua's heart, and she silently enjoys this long-lost happiness.

Today's Li Hua has been praised by friends, envy she has lived to their own want of life realm: food, clothing, housing and transportation carefree, writing six hours in the morning, half a day to raise flowers, do some of their favorite things, reading and learning, insist on doing fitness exercises. On weekends, we can enjoy tea and dance with our friends, talk about the future, and sometimes travel to faraway places together.

Li Hua did what she once dreamed of, and now everything is ready, just ride the wind and waves again, go with the tide, and live the moment.

Chapter 59: The Years are so enchanting

Like many people, Li Hua also cherishes every day of life and enjoys the years. As a literature lover, she needs to keep learning and thinking about the source of her creation. Now that Li Hua is financially independent, she wants to visit the beautiful mountains and rivers of her country more. In order to create the sense of reality in his works, Li Hua went abroad by way of travel, and has been to the United Kingdom, Australia and the United States, to personally experience the local lifestyle and cultural customs, and interviewed a large number of characters, some of which have become the role models in the novel.

Through such visits and investigations, Li Hua has created two novels in more than two years, totaling more than 600,000 words. These works were serialized in the newspaper media and later successfully published as paper books. While creating novels, Li Hua also wrote a large number of short novels and essays in the fields of women's emotions, marriage, opinions, emotions, etc., which were published in various provincial journals and online platforms.

At the beginning of writing, there are many people do not understand Li Hua, put a comfortable day, but also in the middle of the night to write toss, is really blessed not to enjoy ah. Others believe that Li Hua is just a whim, can not last a few days. Others say that if the article can be published in the journal, or even published into a book, it is called a writer - these Li Hua have done it with strength, and do it very well.

At the beginning of hearing these sarcastic remarks, Li Hua seemed to have expected it, not angry, still go her own way, do what you should do. Never because of the cynicism of others to argue, as usual enrolled in the writing class. After two years of continuous learning of writing knowledge, combined with the writing task

given by the teacher, continue to write and submit, reject and revise, revise and submit again. In this way, Li Hua every once in a while, there are essays, short stories, novels have been published in major media platforms.

Li Hua achieved these writing achievements, not pie in the sky, that is ordinary people can not do the pay. Li Hua has a highly responsible attitude towards writing, taking writing words and sentences seriously, reflecting the good and evil, beauty and ugliness in the works as objectively as possible, guiding people to advocate justice and goodness, and warning women to be economically independent, independent thinking and independent action.

At the end of the novel, Li Hua felt both excited and anxious. On the one hand, he wanted to finish the work that took two years as soon as possible, and on the other hand, he was worried that the end would be too hasty. Li Hua is often half asleep at night, although his eyes are closed, but his mind has been thinking about how to layout the story line of the work.

Li Hua has not dreamed of becoming a writer for a long time. When in the trough of life, Li Hua when their own reserves of spiritual wealth, the material in life and even suffering, processing into a good way to encourage people to Chongshan self-improvement. She cherished every person who gave her help in life, every teacher and every like-minded friend. She is glad to have such a good family understanding, encouragement, support, let her become a member of the literary creation, a future, just want to silently write a good work of the author.

Li Hua wanted to say to his relatives that for the rest of his life, I would write more beautiful and moving novel stories in the seascaped room facing the sea, or in the suburban villa in the spring. Over the years, Li Hua has been inspired to write wherever she travels. Li Hua has always had a sensitive insight, just as he got a lot of inspiration about door and window products when he was traveling in the UK.

Li Hua wrote a book as an indispensable part of her life. She wants to pass on all the good feelings and wisdom gained in her life in writing. She believes that the meaning of life is to contribute their own value to the world, material or spiritual can be shared. And she wants to let future generations get their own spiritual wealth, it is a positive, hard working spirit, not discouraged, do not bow, like sunflowers under the sun, always facing the light!

"You must be kind at all times and places." This is Li Hua's mother often whispered in her ear.

In the past, when Li Hua encountered grievances and anger at work, the mother often said to Li Hua: "Children, you have to learn to look light, give way to the villain, you turn the corner in the past, the villain rampage will always encounter the roadblocks that trip him, you do not need to hand." In addition, letting go of those who hurt you is also letting go of yourself. The world still likes kind people more, and some things will make you because of your kindness. The world follows the law of cause and effect, and good is rewarded with good and evil with evil, not without time. Because you are kind, a lot of things will be confused and broken; And because of your kindness, good things will return to your future life. You should know that the ancients were right, and remember to be a kind person."

Li Hua with decades of life experience, repeatedly verified that the mother's words are right, the world is such a law.

Li Hua grew up under the influence of his parents, in the process of growing up to learn patience, humility, empathy. Of course, a bottom line is also added to identify people: you can let the opponent three moves, give three opportunities to reform. That is Li Hua life added a law to protect themselves, but three!

Li Hua's life is like "open hanging", to the positive energy of things, with a positive attitude to pursue; Subtract negative people and distractions. Be strict with yourself, lenient with others, not happy with things, not sad with yourself!

Li Hua sometimes think of the divorce with her daughter's father, glad that he was kind and inclusive of her ex-husband's selfish fault, when her ex-husband was sick, Li Hua secretly extended a helping hand, sold jewelry to raise money, so that trusted relatives handed it to him. At that time, Li Hua did not go to the hospital to visit, because his relatives understood Li Hua's difficulties. At that time, the ex-husband was already on his second marriage and was being snubbed by his then-wife. The man regretted his rash impulse and got married in anger. After that serious

illness, the ex-husband also gave up the second marriage and went back to single life.

After the daughter Xiaolin coordination drive, the ex-husband has moved with Li Hua's family like relatives.

Li Hua in the remote writing period, one day Xiaolin home crowd sent a video. In the video, there appeared a person who Li Hua was familiar with - her ex-husband who had lived with her for ten years. Li Hua looked at the man in the video carefully with wide eyes, now also a man of sixty years old, wearing a thick gold necklace on his neck, a big gold ring on his hand, and his hair was still hot and curly. He was dancing loudly and telling stories about taking care of his mother. In order to please Li Hua's mother, the ex-husband did not treat himself as an outsider.

The ex-husband in the video speaks eloquently about how he cooks food for his elderly parents and nurses his mother, who has Alzheimer's disease. During that difficult period, because of his meticulous care of his parents, he won the reputation of a filial son in the neighborhood. Then he is attracted to his current wife and pursues marriage. Now her ex-husband also has a happy family and found a happy marriage that loves him and suits him, Li Hua silently gives blessings in her heart.

The ex-husband will these years of experience, with a real Chinese accent to Li Hua's family and sisters to listen to, made everyone nod, laugh from time to time. Li Hua felt the peaceful atmosphere of the big family from this scene, she did not expect to be so harmonious. At this moment, Li Hua felt very pleased, she understood her daughter's pains, understand the reason why her daughter let her ex-husband approach the big family: in order to complete her father's wish, can not become Li Hua's husband, but also when relatives!

Li Hua's mother is eighty years old and likes to live quietly all the year round. Life is too simple, and do not like to cook, resulting in insufficient nutrition. Li Hua's ex-husband learned this information from his daughter and wanted to do something for Li Hua's mother, so the scene in the video appeared. Her ex-husband also persuaded Li Hua's mother to pay attention to her body and diet by talking about his experience of taking care of the elderly. After that, he will come to Li

Hua's mother from time to time to do some delicious food, so that Li Hua's mother can accept his kindness.

The ex-husband's live broadcast of the truth and sincerity, let the family accept him again, trust that he is sincere, but Li Hua's mother still politely refused. Li Hua's mother said: "Your mind I take, can come to see me, I am very happy. However, I still prefer quiet, just two days on the weekend, I do some cooking by myself. I'm not that pretentious. Don't bother you with both. I am glad to see that you are all well now."

Seeing here, Li Hua was glad to listen to his mother's words and be a kind person. Li Hua's ex-husband acted very unkindly, but Li Hua forgave him later. When he divorced his ex-husband, he moved out all the furniture and appliances, leaving only an empty house for Li Hua and their daughter. Even before preparing for the second marriage, under the direction of the second marriage woman, Li Hua unit office forced Li Hua to write down a promise to give up the court judgment that the ex-husband should give her daughter's maintenance, so that he would no longer entangle Li Hua's future life.

Thinking of these past events, Li Hua also really admire his atmospheric tolerance, these good intentions are now in different ways to return to Li Hua side. At this time, Li Hua's heart has no hatred, only infinite happiness. Did not think that although her marriage is not, but the family still enjoy the affection brought by kindness, and this is the ex-husband willing to repay.

Li Hua admired her mother's wisdom, and her mother had taught her many times: "There are difficult and confused things, don't rush to vent your emotions, be understanding, think for each other, slow down and calm down, and let it go." To be a kind person, you must have a broad mind. Only this kind of person has the personality charm of not being surprised, and can overcome anything!"

Hearing these words from her mother before, Li Hua would feel bored. Now she understands her mother's kindness and wisdom, which have been passed down through generations of Li Hua's family. The older generation of colleagues and friends around the mother envy her, kua mother to cultivate the children all filial piety, but also envy her the older the more children and grandchildren, every New Year's festival is a family reunion, four generations under the same house.

The scene in the video is warm and real, Li Hua even looked at the illusion that the man inside is still her husband, nothing happened between them, a flash of decades, he has been a member of the big family. Li Hua looked at her ex-husband wearing a scarf in the kitchen, making a delicious meal for Li Hua's family, and sometimes going to the living room to say a few words. It was like being in your own kitchen, going in and out, real and natural. Li Hua heart feeling, because of their kind people, once cut the family again after decades. Although Li Hua did not have direct contact with her ex-husband, this affection returned to the big family.

When Li Hua saw the video, she was living and writing in a sea view room between Zhuhai and Zhongshan, enjoying the leisure life facing the sea with spring flowers. Li Hua bought this ocean view room a few years ago, in order to realize the good wish of writing in the sea breeze and the sound of waves in the future. After the completion of the renovation, Li Hua has been busy with her career, and also rushed about family affairs, and has no time to enjoy this leisure vacation life, and has not lived here.

When Li Hua's novel was published, she began to find the balance between writing and life, and also found her own way of writing. After some time alone in a quiet environment, Li Hua's inspiration and writing state is better. She realized that the ocean view house was the perfect place to write for a long time. In this seasonally springlike beach, she can really enjoy the open and pleasant feeling of facing the sea. Under the sun, the waves are lapping on the silvery soft sand, the sea breeze is blowing in the air, and the air is filled with the fragrance of green plants. Looking at the sea view in the floor-to-ceiling window, I am bathed in the sunshine while writing. As long as he is in such a beautiful environment, Li Hua's heart will gush the impulse to write.

Li Hua believes that encounter is fate, as long as the good efforts, years will be a good return. Look, the years are so enchanting! What better blueprint could there be?

Li Hua immersed in the time quietly passed by, pleased to enjoy the infinite scenery of nature, the release of the heart of the piece of fragrant years, time such as edge, hard, good, those who have been the pain have gone with the wind, she is confident that the future life, will be better and better, the temper of life makes her gradually become gentle and elegant.

In front of the windowsill of Li Huayi's house, looking at the rising sun in the east, the afterglow of the sun shines on the sea, waves of waves rise, the blue sea and the comfort of the blue sky echo each other, white clouds in the vast sky, freely dance and fly, really beautiful.

All this seems like yesterday, the long river of years as if time quietly passed...

postscript

"Time you quietly passed", lasted more than two years, and finally put into print. Outside the window, the autumn sun spread, the sky is particularly clear, the blue sky swim clouds, make me happy.

The planning, start-up, writing process, completion and revision of the first draft of the book "Time you quietly passed" have received strong support and enthusiastic help from family, friends, teachers, chief editors, publishing houses and other parties in spirit, heart and writing aspects. It makes me deeply feel that there is great love in the world and great goodness in the world. I am deeply moved by all these, and I would like to express my gratitude here. Therefore, I will also write as a part of life, seriously into writing, write good works, write more works, repay all those who have been grateful to me. Writing is endless, I will continue to create literature, continue to write new articles, live in the moment!

Zhao Shuxian

February 28, 2024

第一章　沉痛的打击

1998 年的 8 月 5 日这一天，正是骄阳似火闷热烦躁的一天，这天发生的事情，比写小说还狗血。

在急赶回家的路上，李华的心冷到极点，全身感觉到寒意，走在炎热阳光直射的地面上，脚底发烫都没有知觉。空气中一股火热风吹在李华的脸上，她还是感觉不到一点酷暑的温度。李华只感觉到心灰意冷，低头快速赶路，向着自己家的方向加速。她的一双手情不自禁地握成了拳头，一双眼睛流露出可以电击伤人的眼神，一脸怒火的样子，恨不得要狠狠地揍谁一顿。

看样子是发生大事情了，平日里李华从没有表现过这副可怕的样子，即使在这炎热的夏天，看到李华那双冷眼，旁人都会感觉到冰凉。

李华刚刚接到女儿小琳打来的电话，得知一个令人震惊的消息：曾被朋友们都羡慕嫉妒对李华好的丈夫于平，所有人都认为的好男人，却背叛了李华，带着女人睡在了李华的家，李华的床上！

李华恨自己怎么就这么愚钝，没有发现一点点蛛丝马迹。

李华脑中不由自主地闪出疑问：这女人是谁？胆子真大！这女人对李华的家庭情况，一定很熟悉，不然怎么会在李华和女儿刚刚离开家的时间里，出现在李华的家中。

李华最担心的是女儿小琳！女儿才十岁，因作业本忘带学校，返回家中正碰上正在家里偷情的于平和一个不明身份的女人，两人赤裸裸一丝不挂在李华的主卧大床上。当时两人正喘息上下推动着，被回家取作业本的女儿小琳撞见。

于平怎么也没有想到，他明明将防盗铁门插上了，进大门木门也锁好了，女儿小琳怎么就进来了？甚至打开了主卧室，他和正在偷欢的女人都没有觉察呢！

李华焦虑着急地赶到女儿所在的电话亭旁边。见到女儿小琳的时候，李华什么话也没有说，只是紧紧地抱着小琳，她能感觉到女儿的身体紧张得直抖动。李华握住小琳纤细瘦小的手，那小手跟自己一样冰凉。

李华也不知道自己是怎么样上楼走进家门，在打开门的那一瞬间，李华一眼就看到刚刚领结婚证不到两年的丈夫于平，一个人半蹲在阳台的角落里。一双惊恐的小眼睛有些慌乱，上身还赤裸着，一看便知道是偷情败露后，还来不及整理好自己的行头。估计那偷情的女人，也是刚刚在慌张中跑掉了……李华鄙视这个背叛她的男人，眼前这副模样的于平让李华感到陌生。李华真的是看走了眼，怎么就选择了这么一个乱性的男人！

从房间外面望去，床上凌乱不堪入目。突然间李华身上爆发出力量，她像发了疯一样，猛地冲进卧室，将所有床上用品抓起来揉成一团，狠狠地摔在地上，用脚踏上去，使劲地搓着，踢着……

李华的眼泪再也忍不住涌了出来，那种委屈和无助，第一次感觉到天都要塌了下来。怎么丢得起这个脸呀！一向自信的李华，一时真的不知道如何面对这突如其来的家丑。这家，还能待吗？

李华边在问自己的心，边收拾床头柜上的摆件，自己的那张表演舞蹈的照片被放在梳妆台抽屉里。李华突然想起来，自己每次出差回来，床头柜上的相片都放在化妆柜子抽屉里……看来于平和这个女人偷情不止一次！

李华彻底明白了，原来于平这两年来的夫妻生活不是早泄阳痿，也不是不行，而是在与李华同房的时候，总有那个女人的影子在李华床边，像幽灵一样，注视着于平心虚的一举一动。于平已经灵魂出窍了，自然给不了李华的爱和往日的温存。

不知情的李华还一天到晚向医院专家医生咨询，配了一大堆滋阴补肾的营养补品，已经有点秃顶的于平也天天在吃。李华出差回来都会带些好的补品给于平吃，两年下来不是没有效果，而是都补到这个野女人身上去了。李华此刻恍然大悟，联想到于平跟她夫妻生活中的变化，李华全身发毛，越想越可怕，越想越可恨，越想越恨不得把这房子都掀掉。

这男人怎么就不知好歹呢？！她李华那点对不起于平啊？虽然两人是二婚，那也是于平追求李华。当年于平可是动用了很多朋友的关系，才追到了李华。这结婚才多久，李华想都没有想到，她和于平的婚姻竟这么不堪一击。是哪个女人非要抢她的男人，是谁！

李华突然冷静下来，停止一切粗暴的动作，不紧不慢地开始抖起床上用品。正在六神无主的时候，突然发现了一个很小很小的电话簿小册子，李华找到了头绪，她一页一页地仔细查看，终于看到了一个她认识的女人名字及电话号码，下面用铅笔线勾了一下。

这个女人名叫汪芹兰，在李华印象中就是一个长着满脸雀斑黄脸婆。这个让李华不屑一顾的前台打杂人员，在女人堆里也不出众的女人，就是跟于平偷情的贱人？这让李华怀疑起于平的品位，于平会对这样的女人感兴趣？

无法想象她李华输给了这么一个女人，要姿色没姿色，要长相没有长相，唯一的亮点就是一头齐腰长发飘飘。对，于平很爱女人留长发，当年追求李华的时候，李华就是一头螺丝卷的长发，像台湾一位女歌手，很温雅时尚柔美。那个时候于平一日不见李华，就像丢了魂似的，带着自己贴身司机，到处托李华的闺蜜珍打听李华在哪。

李华不甘心啊，她的眼神看起来很可怕。她走出房间，用余光扫了躲在阳台角落的男人，很鄙视地冷眼瞧了一下。李华什么也不想跟这个男人说，牵着女儿小琳拉着手向外走去。

于平马上从阳台起身走到大门口伸手拦住李华："对不起！真的对不起！"

李华也不知道怎么样对待眼前的于平才能解恨，她抓起于平的手放进嘴里，恨恨地咬了下去……

于平大叫一声。李华知道那种疼只是皮肉之痛，而李华是疼在心里。李华感觉很不解恨，用一种轻视鄙视的眼神直视于平，这眼神连李华自己都震住了！此时的眼神想必杀气腾腾，李华看见于平蓦地一震，挡住李华的手也赶紧收了回去。

李华拉起女儿小琳调头就走，将大门使劲地摔上，狠狠发泄着自己的愤怒。李华也震惊于自己此时此刻的果断。她还没有想好怎么收拾于平，不知道哪一天，但肯定不是现在。

李华站在房门外，看了几眼家门口。"这里还能住吗？那个野女人都来来回回几多次了。"李华想到这里，感觉到被于平碰过的手很肮脏。

李华明白此时责任是保护女儿小琳幼小的心灵，担心在小琳心中留下阴影。李华突然想起女儿还要赶到学校上课，在送小琳去学校的路上，李华跟小

琳说："不要把今天看到的丑事对任何人说，放学后直接回姥姥那里住，我今晚要想想怎么处理这件事情！"

小琳很懂事地点点头。看到小琳走进学校后，李华才松了一口气。不管怎样，女儿是第一时间捉奸在床的人证，当妈妈的只希望女儿能安全离开现场。

第二章　有苦说不出

　　李华回到单位工作岗位上，叮嘱自己一定沉住气，不能让同事看出自己刚刚经历了那样的丑事。如果被同事、同学、朋友知道了这件事，李华真不知道要怎么去面对他们。李华要好好保护自己，极力平复自己的情绪，让自己不去想这件倒霉的事情。

　　真是人算不如天算，李华本想好好地跟于平度过未来的岁月，一起真心实意地过日子，毕竟两人确实真心相爱。真的不敢相信，于平会看上比李华各方面都不如的女人，而且还是有夫之妇！

　　在他们相识初期，李华一直以工作为重，有意避开于平的视线。因为有过一次婚姻的失意，李华对待婚姻比较谨慎。

　　那个时候的于平会在李华出差的时候，电话聊天到半夜，在冬天的夜晚聊上四个多小时。于平曾在追求李华的日子里温存痴情地说过，跟他同房朋友吕总都羡慕他和李华的爱情。那个时候不知道怎么就有那么多要说的心里话，在李华出差的日子里，于平不断诉说他是如何想念李华。

　　在房地产从计划经济转向市场经济的年代里，单位实行买断分房的指标，产权私人所有。李华无意中跟闺蜜珍珍聊起买断房子的一时难处。于平跟珍珍也是朋友，从珍珍那里得知李华的困难后，于平特意在银行取出 5 万元，用油皮信封包好。他将那包油皮纸信封里的钱交给李华手上，随后低声说一句："快去付房款吧！"

　　说实话，李华就是从那个时候铁了心愿意嫁给于平。李华不是贪图物质享受的人，但被于平雪中送炭的情意感动。现在想起这些，李华鼻子酸酸的——都准备要放弃了的人，却突然想起于平那么多好处！

　　此时此刻李华的心情非常复杂，她怎么也想不明白，为什么会变成如今这种境地。

李华突然想起来了，三妹曾经几次无意打电话问过李华："大姐你和于平还好吗？我想过来看看你，姐夫在家吗？"

那个时候的李华不理解三妹想说什么，可又什么都没有说，她告诉三妹："于平不在家，出差两天了……"

三妹只问了一句话："他在哪里出差，跟哪些人一起去，你知道吗？"

李华还真没有追问于平去哪里的习惯，也从来没有紧张担心过于平会有变心的一天。于平一直做得很好，让任何人都羡慕嫉妒的那种好。

李华猛然又想起了闺蜜珍珍对李华也有过提醒，记得有两次闺蜜打电话告诉李华，她正在于平的单位办事，碰见了汪芹兰在于平的办公室沙发上休息，很随意地走出来。

"如果你不忙，中午过来一起吃过饭，你来看看怎么回事？"珍珍在电话里真切地对李华说着。

李华回电话只是说："我这里来了客户，中午要请客户吃饭。忙啊，来不了，没有什么事，我就挂了！"

珍珍还是忍不住问了于平，于平轻描淡写解释说："她来洗澡的。"

珍珍都问到这份上了，看李华没有反应，也就没有提了。可是那段时间珍珍工作与外企有联系，后来在午休时间，又看到了汪芹兰从于平的休息间洗澡出来！

那个时间，珍珍记得很清楚，是一个冬天，是在冬天很冷的时候！

被唤醒的片段闪电般回忆着，李华自言自语，好像找到了于平背叛自己的时间。于平的背叛有一半责任在李华太粗心了，从来没有想过于平的不正常。以前总是按时下班回家的男人，突然常常以打麻将留宿在外。于平在哪里去也没有问过，于平电话告诉李华说什么，李华就信什么！以为是正常工作上应酬关系户。

这时候的李华心疼到骨头里，闷得连喘息都很难受，胸口传来一阵绞痛，不知道是为谁难过？

这一天是那么漫长，办公大楼的人都走光了，可李华不知道该回到那里去。女儿已经回到李华妈妈家，李华只是打一个电话跟小琳说："乖点，做完作业，就睡觉。不要等妈妈，听姥姥话，也不要想今天发现的事情，听话！"

李华想自己一个人静静，想想怎么面对今后的生活，她神不守舍地走出了办公大楼。

炎热的八月真是人们常说的秋老虎，比以往还要闷热。这个夜晚李华显得那么无助烦躁。李华神情恍惚，路边一辆辆车从身边驶过。李华走到十字路口，看着这灯火辉煌的闹市中心。曾经那么喧闹的夜晚，李华此刻只看到黑灯瞎火的长路。

一声汽车的喇叭叫声惊吓了李华的思索。"你耳朵聋了，还是眼睛瞎了，不要命啦！"

李华木讷地被司机骂着，却说不出话来。想想自己恍恍惚惚的状态，感到自己真的可怜无助，连一个说话的地方都没有。

李华在无意识中习惯性走在下班回家的路上，不知不觉走到了雅惠大排档，这是离李华住的家很近的夜市一条街，这里依旧是人来人往，人们成群结队来吃夜宵。看到这条熟悉的夜市街，李华心里特别难受，想起和于平还有女儿小琳，一到夏天就会一起在这最热闹的夜市吃夜宵。

就在李华眼前这个熟悉得不能再熟悉的地方，这张桌子前，李华脚步不由自主地停了下来。也许是肚子饿了——从上午九点钟知道丈夫于平偷情的事情后，李华一整天没有吃任何食物。

眼前顾不了那么多了，李华心想：身体健康第一，我得吃，好好吃一餐。不能还没有报复那俩人，自己先倒下了。

李华叫服务员点上满满一桌，以前最爱吃的烧烤、绿豆汤、海带汤、烤凤爪子、臭干子、羊肉串。服务员好意询问："你家于先生和漂亮的女儿要来吗？还是你吃后，打包带回家？"

听到服务员熟悉的声音，李华才意识到这位服务员已经对自家人很熟悉了，而李华也意识到有些事情终究已经不一样了，也无法再掩饰下去。李华只对服务员说了一句："你先上菜吧，我饿了！"

服务员："哦！马上，你先喝点什么？"

李华对着服务员说："冰啤酒一箱。"

李华突然鼻子不通气，酸酸的，感觉到伤心了起来。本来好好的家，本来这个桌子前坐下温馨甜蜜的一家人，却如今只剩下李华一个人，而她还要在这里强装着什么也没有发生，装着不被打倒的坚强，死撑着，压抑着。

　　在服务员忙去准备的同时，李华的手机响了，是好同学惠珠的来电："你在哪里呢？"

　　李华稍停顿了一下，最后还如实说了："一个人在雅惠夜宵，你若有空，来这里一起喝啤酒吧！"

　　这位从小一起长大的女同学惠珠住处离这家夜市很近，李华常常约她一起跳舞。惠珠二话没有推，直接说："好吧，我十分钟后过来！"

　　惠珠很守时，十分钟准时到，远远看见了李华一个人坐在那张桌子。惠珠走近李华跟前，拍着肩膀说："怎么今天有这个雅兴出来吃这么多，还请了谁没有来吗？我还真有口福！"

　　李华默默地摇头，眼睛都不敢看惠珠一眼，只说："吃吧，谁也没有请，就请自己，不行吗？"

　　话一说完，李华眼泪一下涌了出来，她着用纸巾捏着已经不通气鼻子，用力清出鼻涕，悄悄擦掉满脸的泪水。这情景被细心的惠珠看在眼里，她马上意识到不对劲。

　　惠珠真是善解人意，什么也没有问，什么也没有说，直接叼开啤酒瓶，放在李华面前。惠珠自己也拿一瓶，向李华碰了一下："来，我们喝酒！"

　　惠珠知道李华一定是遇到伤心的事，这事一定不小。惠珠是李华从小一起光着脚丫子，一起玩，一起长大的老同学。从小到大，惠珠没有见过李华哭。在惠珠的印象中，李华是最阳光，最孝敬父母，最会持家的女人，也是最好强的女人。

　　惠珠没有劝李华，只是不停地帮夹菜，嘴里一直对李华说："快多吃点菜，别空着肚子喝酒？"

　　这餐酒是李华有生以来，喝得最酸涩，最清醒，最壮胆子的一次酒。看着满满当当一桌子平时喜欢吃的菜，李华一点食欲都没有，可还是拼命向嘴里夹菜，塞满了嘴巴里，就是咽不口下去……

　　此时已是凌晨，惠珠提醒李华："你包里手机一直响着铃声，快接电话吧！"

　　李华看了一眼，就把来电关掉，手机铃声继续响着。惠珠说："接吧，有话好好说。"

　　电话接通了，电话那头传出于平焦急的声音："华华，你在那里呀？我来接你。"

　　李华真的不知道是酒精给了胆子，还是真的醉了，她提高八度的嗓子，回了过去："我不会去死的，放心吧！你给我滚出我的家！你最好别让我看见你们这一对狗男女，我恨你！去你的！少在我面前装了，你这没良心的东西，你还想怎么样？！"

　　那是李华第一次像泼妇一样骂街，第一次像疯了一样从心里喊出声音！

第三章　难熬日子

那一夜李华好难受，她还是在清醒状态下对惠珠说："你可以回家了，我没事，我知道怎么处理这对狗男女！"

惠珠望着李华这般模样，突然心疼李华，她从没有见过李华这般伤心。爱情婚姻这几个字真害人啊，惠珠也怀疑这世界上真有可信任的爱情吗。于平与李华恋爱期那愉悦般配的情景，惠珠曾亲眼所见，但从这晚李华伤心程度上看，她是受了多大委屈，憋着多少不能诉说的苦衷？

于平根据通话时雅惠夜市街道喧闹声，判断李华在夜市大排档。他和章司机两人果真到这里找到了李华。看见李华这副模样，于平只悄悄走近李华身旁静静坐下，说话声音很小："走，咱们打包带回家吃吧。"

李华突然拿起一瓶啤酒，朝于平的头上将整瓶啤酒倒下去，淋湿了于平整个头发。此时李华很解恨地说道："你管我干吗，你去找那个贱女人啊，你去找呀！我决不为难你，你给我滚，滚得越远越好！"

李华猛地推开于平，这时候章司机马上护着于平，挡在李华中间，低声下气地说："李姐，有话回去说，别这样搞得大家难堪。"

李华执意让惠珠回家，也强行让章司机带走于平。章司机见此时的李华毫不退让的姿态，只好劝于平先离开此地。

李华独自坐了一会儿。可能真是喝多了，而她也根本没吃什么东西，肠胃翻动着，李华吐了一地的苦水。可这个时候李华还是很清醒，她向服务员要了一瓶水漱漱口，剩下水全用洗了脸，将脸上全部洗了一遍，泪水、酒水、吐的苦水，全部抹去。

吐出来后，李华好受了些，她走上熟悉的路，摇摇晃晃地回到自己的小家，那个已经让李华伤心的家。李华清楚，这半夜时分不能回到妈妈家，女儿在那里。李华已经很伤心了，不能再让自己的家人知道，那样家人会更伤心；妹妹的家也不能去，也会惊动她们。李华不要家人替自己担心，所以李华必须回到那个曾经温暖，但现在却被那个野女人弄脏的家……

李华边走边想：我不能有事，不收拾这两个偷情的狗男女，我不会罢休的……这晚会发生什么？那个背叛她的男人还会在家里吗，还是在准备干什么呢，这狗东西不会先下手为强吧？

那个时候的李华还很警惕，但就是不知道害怕，还真沉得住气，没有将自己的痛对外说。她寻思着等自己的状态恢复过来，就找机会报复那个贱女人……

开门的那一瞬间，李华没有想到于平正坐在沙发上。于平立即起身对李华说："我给你煲好土鸡汤，给你添一碗吧。"

于平胆怯地说着，走进厨房里盛汤去了，他不时用眼角余光瞟向李华背影。李华直接走进女儿住的房间，将房门反锁，背靠门后，李华心想：我还敢喝于平做的土鸡汤吗？人都变心了，情也出魂了，恨不得我早死，碍着他和那个女人的好事，这汤现在没准下毒了；没准是真的悔改，可我会信吗？我还能信他？

李华根本就不会再相信于平，从知道他跟那女人偷情那一刻起，即使以前是真爱，现在也不会有一丁点的信任了。

李华需要冷静的时间，需要想好对付俩人的办法。现在俩人坏事败露，李华忍着痛苦变得理智冷漠，这是给逼出来的。李华躺在床上，脸上失去血色，眼神空洞茫然，死盯着天花板想着白天突然发生这一切……

房门外响起于平轻轻敲门的声音："汤放在客厅餐桌上了，出来喝点吧，我都热了几遍了。"

李华听着门外那个男人的声音，此刻真的想吐。这声音曾经让李华欢喜沉醉，可此时她却恨不得将耳朵堵住，甚至想冲出去，再狠狠地咬下去。

情绪激动下，李华突然将刚刚吃过夜宵和食物，连同啤酒全部吐了出来。李华难受啊，她哭了，但是没有发声，没有开门冲出去。只是顺手将床头纸巾擦了嘴角，又拿起床头柜的水杯，猛喝一大口，但全又吐出来。拉黑灯，李华继续躺在床上想着：我该怎么办？放弃婚姻是肯定的，只是时间问题。但就这么放过这对狗男女吗？没有那么便宜！

李华这一夜没有心情睡觉，和衣靠在女儿的桌子边，随手翻看着平常订阅的知音婚姻杂志。

李华突然想到她可以给编辑部写一封信，请编辑指教当一个女人遇到这类婚姻外遇该怎样面对，怎样处理，怎样报复。她可不想因为冲动做出傻事，她寻思着要找到最好的报复方案，不能为了报复的事毁了自己的生活。

李华写了满满的三张信纸，一气呵成，将这对男女整个外遇通奸看到的过程，及发生后的感受都一一写了出来。就像对一个最能保守秘密的人倾诉，将一肚子的委屈，全都宣泄出来。她知道这是最安全的发泄方式，她要把伤害缩小在自己能控制的范围，因为她还要保护好自己的女儿小琳。女儿才刚刚十岁，她和女儿小琳今后还要相依为命，目前还不得不在这个城市生活。如果只是李华自己一个人生活，也许她就没有这么好的耐心，可能在气愤冲动下斩了这对狗男女，再剩往长江一跃，管她是死是活！

李华思绪回到桌面上，看到写完的纸上。那时已经是凌晨五点多钟了，写完信后李华心里好受多了，再不是昨天那毫无头绪的状态。李华似乎知道怎么去应对这件事情，眼神里有了主意和坚定。李华将写好的信塞进上班背的挂包里，准备在上班的路上就把这封信发出去。此时李华心里好像完成了一件大事情。

信发出后的这段时间，李华对那对男女什么也没做。一个月下来，也没有像鲁迅笔下的祥林嫂那样见人就诉说。在任何人面前，几乎没有提起这桩丑事。不是李华有多么聪明，只是感觉这事越少人知道，她越好实施报复！

对，就是这个念头，最主要的动机，是不想让于平和那女人知道她将要报复的心思。再说，这也不是光彩的事情。她李华也是有脸面的女人，她清晰地知道，她能做什么，不能做什么。她不想让家人知道后为她担心，为她伤心。

对李华来说，表面上风平浪静真是一种煎熬。每次醒来的时候，李华都记得自己昨夜又梦见那对狗男女，每一次都情不自禁地看看那个随身的手提包。包里有一把水果刀，这把刀主要是用来自卫，如果刚好碰见那两人偷情，就用这刀了结这对狗男女的命。

这些天来，于平和那个叫汪芹兰的女人也不好过，毕竟这样的丑事不能见光。一个是有妻之夫，一表人才，在单位还是外企执行总经理；一个是有夫之妻，是于平的前台下属，一个半老徐娘满脸雀斑的临时工女人。两人还是在同一个单位，上下级的关系，在工厂众人眼里，不知能否被看出是偷鸡摸狗的男女关系。没有坐实捉奸之前，谁会想到这对男女会在办公室的临休息间里偷情？汪芹兰就住在离厂办公室只有 100 米的厂宿舍三楼，那是多么方便的偷情地方！

李华的平静越发让汪芹兰魂不守舍，而于平也是束手无策，虽然每天都能看到李华照常回家，但依旧不理他。面对没有什么表情的李华，于平有些慌，他觉得李华越来越陌生。

李华一直等待编辑的回复，思索着自己想干的事是否妥当。她一定要惩罚这对男女，但不容有闪失。这口恶气不出，李华憋得难受。强烈的报复念头日夜折磨着李华，她一直耐心地等待编辑的回信。李华很想知道编辑怎么回复，然后再制定具体的报复计划。

第四章　跟踪

那一个月李华一下子瘦了八斤，没有胃口，吃什么都不香。其实李华已经强迫自己比平时吃得更多，但有心事，哪能长得好呢？那一个月几乎暴瘦，从很标准的体重103斤瘦到95斤，李华都不知道怎么会瘦成这个样子。有时候对着镜子中的自己，李华有些支撑不住了，心里期盼着这个日子快点结束吧，她快要受不住了。

李华脑子里尽是这些疯狂的念头。一个月的憋屈，李华心里的怨恨消除不了，她控制不住自己要报复的想法。可理性让李华清醒很多，那两个人不值得自己亲自动手，他们不配。李华就是这么默默提醒自己，一定要忍一时之快，方能除掉心头之恨！

编辑的回信与李华的想法，有一些理性的建议不谋而合，但是李华策划报复的念头，却一天天清晰了起来。越是了解汪芹兰这个女人，李华越是想尽早报复这个女人，不然真的无法安心，可能一天觉也睡不着。

理性和仇恨在矛盾中纠缠不清，这日子度日如年，谁也体会不了李华的心情，时而理性时而疯狂，真恨不得早点了结这一切。

在某一个周末李华的报复机会来了。那一天于平临出门对李华说："今天工人加班，我要去厂里看看。"

平日里于平星期六并不工作，今天于平又耐不住寂寞了，还是又开始跟汪芹兰暗中来往呢？李华想到这里，一个想法迅速在脑子里形成。

"真希望这次抓个正着，来个人赃俱获……"李华这样想着，她希望能堵住这对狗男女，最好能抓现行，还能用相机拍下来当证据。

于平看到李华没有搭理他，就直接夹着包，轻手轻脚地走出了门。于平一出门，李华立马拿出通讯录，找出汪芹兰家里的电话号码，也迅速出门。当然，她不是跟踪于平，李华得放于平自由，让他放松才会有机会知道他行踪。李华朝着离家很远的地方向公用电话亭快步跑去。

李华站在电话亭内停顿片刻，清清嗓子，拿起电话筒，按照号码拨打了过去。铃声嘟嘟嘟地响着，李华的心脏也跳动加快，她希望接电话的声音是女人，如果是女人，那说明那女人没有加班；如果是男人的声音，那就是那个贱女人的丈夫王木。

"喂！喂！请讲话！听得见吗？怎么不说话？"王木接着电话，另一边半天没有声音，他冲着电话里喊着。

李华猛然听到电话那头传出男人的声音，这声音扰乱了李华的思绪，她本想直接告诉王木"你的女人给你戴绿帽子了，你不想知道是谁吗？"结果话到嘴边突然停住了。

李华心想，如果那样直说，不是便宜了那贱女人吗？他们两夫妻要是闹矛盾分开了，那肯定会直接把那女人推向于平。无论怎么说，汪芹兰现在的丈夫各项条件都不如她的上司于平。她要是跟于平在一起，那还捡了大便宜！

还有另外一种结果，王木狠狠地揍一顿贱女人，然后离婚。但王木在逼女人离婚之前，很可能会趁机敲诈于平，毕竟于平给王木"戴绿帽"。

李华在电话亭子前，脑子里闪过这些理性的想法。"先忍吧！"李华劝慰着自己，终于忍住了吐一时之快的冒失！原准备搅得汪芹兰的家鸡犬不宁，让这贱女人尝试家要散的滋味，但这不是此刻要做的事情。李华突然改变了主意，挂下电话。

冷静过后，李华想起了一个问题：于平跟汪芹兰平时会在哪里偷情？他们不可能经常在家里见面，也不会经常在工作单位乱来——毕竟被发现了效果很严重。李华突然想起章司机这个人，章司机一定知道内情，他充当拉皮条的角色讨主子欢心，会天衣无缝地安排好两人的约会。那个年代的社会就有这些坏风气。

章司机不可能直接告诉李华，那个女人跟于平来往多久，住在哪里，还干了哪些见不得人的丑事。李华只能自己去调查。

半小时过后，李华来到了章司机的汽车修理厂外面。李华没有立刻走进去，她看了看四周通往的几条公路，这汽车修理店正处在丁字路口。修理厂门口左边通往李华家方向，右边通向那女人工作的啤酒厂，门口正前方正通向市商业中心，修理厂还有一扇侧门，门后是一个不太大的后院。

原来这个汽车修理厂设在这里，难怪他们到李华家偷情那么方便。李华独自一人沿着汽车修理厂房屋外围走了一圈，然后再调头从大门慢慢走进去。店里只能容纳两台车的修理空间，后院可以停放三台小车，看似很破旧。李华正看着，一个修理工模样的人热情走上来问："美女找谁？还是修车？"

李华下意识地回复："找你们的老板章司机。"

修理工冲着后院喊："章哥，有美女找你！"

不一会工夫，李华就看见身穿黄色 T 恤衫下穿牛仔裤工装的章司机，从后院倚在门口站着向店内探头看了看。李华与章司机的眼神同时相遇，只见章司机立刻带上后院的门，向李华走了上来。

李华看到章司机眼神跳过慌乱，李华顿时明白自己找对了地方。她的分析是对的，这是那俩狗男女常来的地方。也许那贱女人要约会时，就在这修理厂等。章司机在啤酒厂工作时是于先生的专职司机；休息的时间，章司机会在修理厂接私活，等于平电话指挥；若是去外地市场调研，就带上这个女人。于平想利用休息时间去外地偷情几天，章司机会全程陪护。章司机几乎是于平的私人管家，李华已领教过多次，以前于平经常让章司机接李华在市内办些事情。

李华没少用过章司机的车，只不过李华经常送点茶叶、烟给到章司机。在李华眼里，她很同情章司机，她知道章司机的老婆带两个孩子还在农村，家里很困难，小夫妻分居。李华见过章司机的老婆，长得漂亮很瘦弱的女人，人很老实朴素。就冲着怜惜章司机老婆的心境，李华从没有空手让章司机办事，会找着理由给些水果或者吃的食物给到章司机补添家用。

李华快速想到这里，心里却在想，章司机早已忘记了李华给过的好处。在利益面前，像章司机这样做一些违心事情的，大有人在。说到底，章司机是为他的老板于平服务，而不是李华。

章司机惊讶地问："李姐你怎么今天有空来这里，找我有事吗？于先生不在这里。"

李华很冷静地回复："在这边办点事，就顺便走过来看看你的汽车修理厂，我还没有来过呢。这地方选得好，也好找。我不是来找于平，难道今天于平下班后会来吗？"

章司机说："不知道今天于先生是在厂里还是在公司那边，我等会打电话问问在哪接他。要不我先送你回家，还是就在我这里顺便一起吃饭？我准备煮小龙虾。"

李华边应付边四周扫了一眼："今天于平也会来吃吗？"

章司机没反应过来，也没有接着回答李华的问题。他勉强笑了两声，边说边向后院小跑步走去："李姐，你先坐一下，我去安排一下，看有几斤龙虾，再打电话问问于先生！"

看着章司机的背影，李华心想：看你还玩什么花样！

第五章　幡然醒悟

没过多久，章司机从后院张望一下，走近李华说："李姐，于先生还在公司，要我晚点接他，要不先送你回家？还是和我一起等于先生？"

李华自然明白章司机想请她走。李华顺水推舟地说："不麻烦了，看你很忙，我自己逛逛街回去，你忙吧。告诉于平让他早点回来，我有事要对他说。"

章司机马上答应："好的，那你慢走。真的不需要我送你一程？"

李华挥挥手向大门外走去。她想着自己走出去后，那个女人总该出来。她想躲在暗处，亲眼看见那个女人出现。

李华也真没有想到，这个女人这么不要脸，她也太肆无忌惮了。看到坏事败露后，李华这边没有任何动静，这女人就以为风口过去了。"这贱女人也太把自己当回事了吧，咱们走着瞧！"

李华头也不回向路口方向走去，她也知道章司机还在看着她离开的背影。刚刚章司机望向后院的眼神明显带着惊慌，李华心想院子里肯定躲着人，

李华心想，章司机是心虚了，看见了李华与汪芹兰同时前后都出现在汽车修理厂。章司机庆幸两个女人没有正面相碰，不然他也不知道会发生什么。所以他只能客气地把李华先支走，赶紧电话详细告诉于先生。

李华等了好长时间都没有看到有人出来，她也不禁怀疑自己是不是太敏感了。她又耐着性子等了一个小时，把腿都站麻了，还是没有看到有人出来，她终于决定放弃了。

李华沿着路边的小路，无精打采地走着，她回头看了看那一排破小的门面一间一间挨着。李华心中感慨，环境如此破败，章司机还有心情搞婚外恋，还帮自己的顶头上司乱搞男女关系。也许章司机为了生活，守住这份伺候老板的差事，于是专拍马屁讨好于平，让自己卑微地活着。

李华沉默地走到茶楼，向服务员点了一壶铁观音茶，选择一个偏暗的桌前

坐下。拿起一杯茶，慢慢地望着微暖泛着黄色电灯罩子，心中一片忧愁。李华沉思着，喝下去的铁观音茶水真苦……

坐下来之后，李华再次情不自禁地想起于平，想起那个贱女人，想起这段日子自己承受的无尽苦楚，心里又是一阵阵地发痛。

要不是今天那两个坏东西弄出这样的破事，李华真不会去做跟踪这些可笑的事情来，把自己搞得神经病一样。真没有想到电影中原配跟踪小三的场景，今天在李华这里也上演了。李华想想都觉得自己可怜。

这真不是李华想要的生活，没有了自我，一天天消沉，围绕一个男人，痛苦不堪地淹没了自己。看到自己变成这样，真不知道是在报复那对狗男女，还是报复李华自己。这时李华又想起了编辑的回信："若是你去报复，为这两个人毁了自己值吗？"

编辑语重心长的话让李华顿时惊醒。李华不能被这两个坏东西毁了自己的人生！李华想好好活着，这才是对自己最好的救赎，也是对男人最好的报复。让自己活得更好更幸福，然后淡然放手，让这个男人后悔，比用武力征服更有报复的力量！

李华自言自语道："想起了编辑老师回信中说过的话，我们不能跟他们一样，我们本来有理。如果是一条狗咬了你，你也咬回去，那不就是也成了狗吗？我们是人，不能把狗当人对待！"

李华感觉到内心中的结已经松开了。这样的日子快要结束了吧，李华心里希望能够放下怨恨。

从茶楼退出来，李华沿着还是秋老虎夏季的江边行走。依然炎热闷躁，有些憋气，李华长长地慢慢地吐出一口气，茫然地向家的方向走去。夏天的夜晚，依然是灯红酒绿的景色，嘈杂的局面，大小排档都摆放在路边。李华没有目的地走着，感受着迎面的热风往身上扑腾。此时李华真想跳下长江的水浪中，洗掉那个女人给家沾上的晦气。

到家已经是晚上11：40。没想到李华刚走到门口，还没有拿出钥匙，门就被打开了。于平立刻迎了上来说："怎么这么晚回，吃了没有？"

李华有点愤怒地盯着于平眼睛，走过去了，直进房间休息，没有听于平说什么。

那一晚，李华在隔壁女儿的房间，安安稳稳地睡了一个好觉。好像这一个多月以来，从来没有像这一天睡得这么舒坦。

第六章　那些龌龊的人和事

三天过后章司机给李华打个电话说："李姐，我跟你说，你别再叫人打了，汪芹兰的兄弟在黑社会也有人，你如果再找人报复她，她兄弟也会找你的。希望你不要再惹她了，把事情闹大了对谁都不好。"

听到章司机这样说话的语调，李华想都没有想就对着章司机喊："你叫她来呀，有种就来！还邪了，自己有老公有儿子，还去偷人，偷在我家的床上，现捉奸。她不要脸的事情对你说了吗？为什么打她，偷人到家里了！只要她还偷人，就叫她小心点。我才不会打贱人呢，脏了我的手。只要她再跟别的男人通奸，叫她戴绿帽子的老公王木去打。她如果还不知道要脸，你去告诉她老公王木，说她偷汉子睡在别人家床上了。这次已经给贱女人留了点情面，再偷人，让她老公王木收拾！到时候不是打两耳光的问题，那就是要贱女人的家也跟我的一样散。"

电话那头的章司机听了这一番话没吭声了。他肯定不知道那女人在李华的床上被逮住的丑事。心虚做了错事的人，肯定不敢跟她老公王木讲。

此时章司机自己意识到问题的严重性，也担心事情闹大了会牵连到他。这些偷鸡摸狗的事，桩桩都与他有关联。若不是他平日里帮这对男女制造方便，那女人哪敢这么猖狂。以致后来那女人到李华家里偷情，以是习惯常出入李华家里来吗？他章司机还有不知道的理？

李华跟于平结婚后，莫明其妙地没能再过夫妻生活，实质上是于平精神肉体都出轨了。有时候于平很想给李华温存，可是记忆里是汪芹兰疯狂作怪的呻吟，他哪里还有心思去看李华无辜含蓄的表情呢？这些夫妻之间不和谐的性突然冷淡的伤害，于平感受很深。他并没有生病，是他精神上有负罪感。用心理医生的话来说，就是心里有了性障碍，生理功能性障碍，妻子成了无辜的摆设。于平陷入偷情的刺激怪圈，因为偷来的好像令他兴奋。这对男女做着伤害两个家庭的事情，没有被发现，胆子就越来越大了。这也是于平被困惑，自以为是找到了新爱，他哪知道摧毁了他的后半生恶魔，已渐渐开始。

章司机农村的妻子叫素琴，很纯朴的女子。跟他生一儿一女，做了十二年夫妻，却不知情他在外面也有相好的，而且是他亲表妹罗琼。要是有一天被老实巴交的素琴发现，还不知道要发生什么事情，到时候素琴肯定比李华过得更痛苦。毕竟素琴是农村女人，没有经济来源，平日里做一些服装厂临时工补贴家用，其它的要靠章司机的收入来维持一家人的生活。素琴一生也只有章司机一个男人，这是父母指定的婚姻。其实素琴子长相比章司机表妹罗春五官长得好看，清秀漂亮。罗琼只是稍年轻，没有结婚生子，但是已经跟章司机偷吃禁果有二年多了。

记得有一天周末，素琴在星期六的早上突然找到李华的娘家，问李华："你知道我孩子他爸章司机跟于先生去了哪里吗？我来城里三天了都没见到他，这是周末，厂里应该没有上班呀？"素琴说老公跟于先生在一起，已有三天没有回家，儿子女儿都等着他的学费，学校快要报名上学了。

李华看着马路边上，站在灰尘中的素琴，那瘦小的身子，看上去风一吹就会倒下去。李华心里真的替素琴难受，这么弱小善良的女人，李华怎能告诉她雪上加霜的事情呢？

李华知道被自己男人背叛的痛苦，难道还要让素琴尝一遍被丈夫背叛的痛苦吗？想到这里，李华心里感到一阵悲凉：这么好的一个女人，一儿一女都在身边，一左一右牵着她的手，求李华告诉她，老公章司机哪里去了。

李华当然知道，那是闺蜜的老公无意中透露的信息，当时他问李华："你怎么没有跟于先生还有汪芹兰、章司机、表妹罗琼一起去浙江考察市场啊？"

李华一愣："我没有那么多天假，他们说要一周时间。"

李华那个时候只是猜到章司机跟表妹罗琼有点不正常关系，可她怎么也没想到自己的男人会和汪芹兰有问题。李华太自信又太粗心了。这四个人结伴而行去浙江普陀山，其实是借出差调研销售市场为由。当时李华跟素琴一样，也是蒙在鼓里，那四个人就像是两对夫妻结伴而行，住酒店开两套房，成双成对地旅行。

李华回答素琴："我真的不知道他们到哪去了，只知道他们几个人一起出差，有一周时间见不着。他们是为了工作，不便打搅，我也就没有联系他们。"

素琴听到李华说出这番话，流露出很无助的眼神。李华一直记得这样的眼神，那是一个多么可怜的女人。

李华和素琴同样单纯，从来没有想到过于平会跟身边这个长着满脸雀斑的女人有一腿。现在想起那一次四个人在一起的日日夜夜，在酒店里不知道有多放肆放纵。

要不是闺蜜的老公跟于平是同一个单位的管理人员，李华更是蒙在鼓里。他在厂里听到那几个人出差的闲言闲语，实在听不下去了才忍不住告诉李华。李华才知道他们那一行是去普陀山，名义上是去考察推广啤酒的销售市场，实际上是在一起度假旅游。

普陀山在于平的老家浙江。于平有一个表姐在那生活，她是一个很淳朴的人，在浙江金华开了一家服装裁缝店。这次看于平没带李华同行，于平表姐就顺便问了一些情况，于平敷衍表姐说："这次是公差，所以没带李华。"

在两年前于平的妈妈就带李华去过他表姐家，作为家庭正式成员，未来的媳妇去认亲戚。这一次于平带着汪芹兰这个女人，表姐看出俩人玩暧昧，所以没有很热情招待他们四人，没有少给于平脸色看。

于平很尴尬，于是带着一行四人在附近的小镇宾馆开了两套房。当晚他们就发生了不该发生的事情，他们的婚外情就从那个时候，明目张胆地开始。在外地以情侣关系配对，像真的夫妻那样度假。

后来章司机跟李华的闺蜜珍珍说话时不小心说漏嘴。珍珍当时为了帮于平开拓销售啤酒市场，问到工作方面的事情，谈到浙江金华义乌看市场的一些细节。谈到饮食问题时，珍珍说起李华喜欢吃海鲜，喜欢吃大螃蟹，章司机说他们那次也吃了很多海鲜。于平当时眉毛向上一挑，不让章司机说下去。珍珍一下子就明白了，只不过珍珍担心这事会影响李华夫妻感情，没有跟李华说。

几年后，章司机才说回当时的内情。章司机说："汪芹兰那次一连几天帮于先生洗内衣内裤，这个女人在住酒店当晚，趁机会向于平投怀送抱。下属女性跟上司同处无人打扰的空间，很自然就睡在一起了。"

从那以后，于平和这个女人各有所需，一发不可收。

珍珍对于平的变化感到惊讶，为了汪芹兰这样的土女人出轨？她怎么也想不通于平会喜欢这个女人。珍珍心想，这于平也太没有品位了吧，难道是个母猪都会上？

　　在私欲利益关系面前，一点激情就燃烧，那种新鲜感觉无情替代了平淡的夫妻生活。孤男寡女的夜晚还能干什么呢？加之章司机有意安排，自然就更顺利了。章司机也需要跟表妹罗琼待在一起，章司机在方便于平的同时，其实是为了更好地方便自己。

　　李会真的想不明白，一个临时的司机在经济条件并不好的情况下，为何还要搞婚外情，而且还觉得理所当然……

　　那个年代改革开放刚刚开始，有些意志薄弱的人，像是麻木不仁了，过一天算一天。他们不知廉耻，没有道德良心，社会风气就是被这些人搞坏了。在章司机眼里，他为主子做了很多好事，满足于平和汪芹兰的欲望。他认为这是成全，事实上这是在造恶。让性欲之欢压过伦理道德，陷在其中的人都会有报应。

　　李华至今还忘不了那无辜而浑浊的眼神，那车来人往灰尘扬土的路边站着的素琴，她一边牵着儿子的手，一边牵着女儿的手。李华认为婚外情的可恨之处在于把一个好端端的家搞得表里不一，家像临时酒店，家中的人神已散，留下一个空空荡荡的家。

第七章　剪发"毁形象"

九月初的黄昏，室内还是有点闷热，外面偶有凉风。李华感觉到此时有点凉意，或许是头发剪短的缘故，她还有点不习惯——李华刚刚在理发店将自己留了多年的长发剪掉了。

在理发店里，李华看着镜子，镜中的女人简直就像一个假小子，但是李华会心地笑了：我喜欢连我自己都不认识的形象，就是要这干练强势的形象。

理发师小英说："可惜你这头长发没有了！"李华冲着小英笑而不语，说了声谢谢，然后爽快付钱离开。

走路时李华还是习惯性往后脑抓长发，感觉那里空空的才意识到自己确实把长发剪掉了。李华当然明白剪了长发会"毁掉形象"，她也知道装出无所谓的样子，是强颜欢笑式的轻松。李华何尝不知道自毁形象的代价，多少年来那种雅致清新的女人韵味已成为李华的"标配"，在朋友眼中，李华就应该是这种气质的女人。

李华本人虽然五官平凡，但却是那种耐看型的女人——熟悉李华的朋友都这样评价过，他们认为李华的长发背影很有吸引力。外表衣着上，李华也很会穿衣搭配，穿得好看还彰显个性。

回家途中李华想起编辑老师的回信中这样提到过：一定要冷静，在你最冷静的时候再做决定。当你经过足够多冷静的思考，哪怕还是决定分手，那时执行这项决定也不迟。

经过这一个多月的冷静思考，李华有所领悟，决定维持现状，什么都不做。李华不会为一个男人放下工作和事业。李华热爱工作，每一天都用工作把时间填满，像机器一样麻木工作，并没有因为失意挫败的婚姻而影响工作。

对于此时自己陌生的形象，李华确实不习惯，但她并不后悔。人总是在变，李华希望从今以后有一个新的开始，重新做回最好最自信的自己，哪怕没有丈夫，没有婚姻，没有爱情，她也还有亲情和友情。她也可以拥有精彩的生活，温暖的情谊。

李华忽然觉得这一天没有白忙，她又做了一件让自己快活的事情，心里怨恨似乎又减淡了一些，脚步也慢了下来。

回到家时天色已暗，于平已经在家里，正坐在大厅中。李华开门的瞬间，人还没进去，于平就说："回来啦。"

当李华跟于平正面相对的时候，于平的神情愣住了："啥时候搞成这样子？为什么把长发剪了？"

李华说："刚剪了。你要是喜欢长发飘飘的女人，满大街都是，你自己去挑选吧。"

李华心里想，就变你不喜欢的样子！

于平摇摇头说："你真是，这还不是丑化你自己。你单位的同事说好看吗？"

李华不屑一顾地说："这丑算不了什么，这总比有的人偷人好吧？"现在李华跟于平说的每一句话都要带刺。

李华趁势继续说："爱看不看，你自己看着办，也没有人挡着你。你爱看谁就去找谁，只要不再往家里带。如果再敢做一次，我会连你一起揍！"

李华解恨地走进厨房，手里顺便提起菜刀，切着台面上的梨子。李华没有吃饭，最近被逼得火气又重，想到还是要养生，注意身体健康第一，于是用梨和冰糖蒸锅煮熟后代替晚餐。这段时间消瘦八斤，李华看见自己的样子很是心疼。今晚打个嘴巴官司，看到于平很生气的样子，李华真过瘾，心里爽极了，恢复了往日女皇的气势，终于又有了胃口。

第二天，李华到办公室上班的时候，同事都露出很惊讶的眼神。同事小王问："你怎么把头发剪这么短？昨天还没听说你要剪发。怎么把自己搞成这样？哎呀，差点认不出你来了！"

李华说："就想换换心情，尝试一下别的风格。"

小王说："我觉得你这段时间怪怪的。真不至于把这么好的长发剪得这么短，像个假小子，最起码要两三年才能长起来。"

李华随口编了一些理由搪塞了同事们好奇心。机关单位就是这样，处处小心，夹着尾巴做人，李华可真不想被同事们看出什么破绽。虽然李华不是有心计的女人，但还知道轻重的明白人。在机关也待了十几年了，什么人没有见过，人言可畏，李华可不想成为某些人取笑的对象。同事们都不知道李华这段时间发生了什么事，李华也不能对任何人提起。李华想改变话题，又补充说："好打理，简单！"

李华不多说一句废话话，怕多说一点就会暴露情绪，让同事看出端倪。李华真怕突然有一天忍不住将这一切事情曝光，到时候该怎么应对自己朋友和同事的眼光，他们会怎么看？

李华还没想好怎样跟于平分手就先拖着，但是从那天起，李华心里跟他已经没有关系了。在情感的份上早已分道扬镳，只是那张离婚纸，那张法律的证书，还没有去办理。

这段时间李华基本上是在单位食堂吃饭，那个家已经不想生炉做饭了。而且她也不想回到那个家多待一会，在家里只是睡觉。那是李华亲戚的家，李华希望于平走，而不是她离开。

在那个改革开放招商引资的年代，李华那个城市有很多外企，有港商投资，有台商投资。于平所在的企业是台资企业，老板采用私人家族式的管理方式，由于经营管理不善，企业倒闭。工厂停了，那些工人正在遣散。厂里保留十几个人守厂，其他人全部辞退，也包括那个贱女人汪芹兰，包括于平，老天长眼啊，收拾这对阴暗的男女！

这是内部的消息，闺蜜珍珍把消息告诉了李华。这是李华跟于平分手的最好机会，而且是不用说出来的分手，很合李华的心意。不在一起生活，分手就容易了，不令人难堪。也许这就是天意。这个男人只要不在，李华就不用在这么多人的眼皮底下，还假装恩爱幸福。

李华跟珍珍说："真好！这样那个家伙可以滚了，我也免去装面子。如果有人问于先生呢？我好回答，不在呀，去外地发展去了！"

珍珍很赞同李华放于平一马，让于平体面离开。这男人事业突然没有了，感情婚姻生活又一团糟。李华心想做人也没必要做得那么绝，也想起这男人以前对自己的好。放过于平，让于平后悔。这比李华亲自去报复他更高明，而他也会更痛苦。

珍珍又说："于先生肯定感觉到你的善良，这也许是于先生最后悔的事情。可惜世上没有后悔药买，于先生也知道，如果他没有出轨，哪怕工厂倒闭，他也不会过得差。我肯定会在事业上全力帮助他，你的人脉也能帮到他，他还能开拓另一片天地。"

珍珍说的没错，失去李华的信任是于平最大的损失，失去的不仅仅是婚姻，而是丢掉了一次事业发展的机会。

李华说："我觉得跟他没必要耗着，等他离开这个城市以后，我们就慢慢淡了。就算于平不提出离婚，我也有办法去把婚离了。"

珍珍说："你不在于平走之前提出离婚？这可会影响你今后的生活，你还年轻，不可以为伤害你的人买单。万一将来有人喜欢你，你还可以有新的爱情，没有必要为于平放弃美好追求。"

珍珍的好意李华很感动，可也明白今后的一段长路李华得学会一个人走下去，她也理解珍珍所说的被动。

李华说："你放心，等于平一走我会面对所有人。随着时间推移，我会理智处理跟于平的关系。无非给自己两年时间去把这一切解决。于平跟那个女人要不要走下去，都与我没有任何关系了。"

珍珍这个时候才发现李华的新发型，哭笑不得摇头说："我真服了你，你能把自己的形象毁成这个样子。"

李华说："这是重新振作，重新开始的决心。等头发长长的那个时候，我肯定一切都会更好的。我今生不会再相信爱情婚姻了，我只想要工作挣钱，现在只有金钱让我信任。"

李华在这个时候突然想起旧同事红红说过的一句话："任何人都有可能背叛你，爱人，朋友，但是金钱不会背叛你。"

李华低头思索回味，真的理解了红红那句人生格言。这确实是肺腑之言，李华用活生生的挫折例子，给自己提了醒。她也总结出一句格言："女人最应该忠诚于自己！一定要经济独立，人格独立，思想独立，做一个财富自由女人。"

第八章　到基层工作

　　江城的秋天就要来临了，在晚风吹送的江边，李华独自漫步流连。

　　出了一口恶气后，李华还是常常心事重重，白天正常在单位上班，晚上待在女儿的卧室。

　　李华从江边散步回到家，在家的于平对她说："李华，今天我想跟你说一个事情，能坐下来我们好好谈谈吗？"

　　李华心里明白，总是这样回避他也不实际："好吧，你尽快说！"

　　于平所在的啤酒厂要解散，于平受令于台资企业老板董事长指示，处理发放完厂里人员买断遣散费后，他自己也要被董事长解雇，撤销总经理的执行职位。于平这个时候自身难保。

　　李华明白，此时于平没有资本带走那女人去创业。于平也深知道只能去找新的工作，先得养活自己。至于偷情一时之欢的女人汪芹兰，于平怎样对待处理，心里自然有数。汪芹兰这女人也只得回到她老公王木身边去，目前出轨之事没有暴露，王木还蒙在鼓里。汪芹兰和王木还有一个儿子，生活依旧要过。

　　于平不会去捅破这个关系，给他自己多找一个包袱。一旦王木知道他的老婆汪芹兰跟于平偷情，一定会讹上于平。王木家本来就穷得叮当响，现在面临老婆下岗，更不会放过勒索于平的机会。

　　想到这些，于平感到后怕。他更想保全与李华的婚姻，无论怎么说怎么比，李华比汪芹兰这个女人都值得留在婚姻里。他不会因为婚外情去跟李华分手离婚，他需要得到李华的谅解，给他重新再来的机会。于私，他想得到李华的人脉帮助，继续谋求好的事业发展；于公，李华哪方面都比汪芹兰那个女人强。

　　于平也后悔自己随便谦和的个性害了自己，被那个女人的温情勾引，没有拒之门外，导致生活混乱的局面，令他被动难堪。他深知上半身有智慧，可下半身是动物的雄性激素作怪，抑制不住不该发生的兽性冲动……

　　至今为止，李华也没有对他反击吵闹，捅破说出去，还在维护他在外的形象，这越发让他感觉到恐慌。最近几个月的担忧，加上失业的打击，于平外表上还是神气十足，可明显老了许多，只有五十一岁的中年男人，完全失去了往日的风采，头发开始稀少掉发，这是秃头开始的迹象。

于平清清嗓子慢慢开口说："我们台资企业厂要解散了，你也可能听说了。我下个月可能会在广州一家台资企业服装厂做副厂长工作，已经收到应聘通知了。另外也有可能去上海的另一家台资服装企业工作。我先去工作一段时间，稳定后，你也可以来我那去看看；或者等春节放长假我再回来看望你。女儿小琳已安排好本市里一所私立学校，学费我会交给你。"

李华听着眼前男人很有条理的安排，心里五味杂陈地翻涌。她和于平都是二婚，能将她的女儿这样善待安排，在当今社会里也是不多的男人胸怀。这也许就是李华对于平一个手指头都没动的原因，她心里还存有于平爱她的幸福情景。她不得不承认自己真的爱过眼前这个男人，一种奇怪的疼痛刺进她心里！人们常说，爱得越深，恨就会越痛！

表面上李华跟往常一样平静："当然以工作为主呀，你这么快就能找到工作了，就一定要好好珍惜眼前当下，别再把精力浪费在无用的人身上，你明白就好！"

于平赶紧接着说："以后我会以打电话的方式联系你。这次是我不对，请你原谅，以后咱们继续好好过日子好吗？"

李华沉默了几分钟，没有回答，随后略有所思地慢慢抬头，看着男人说："你就安心去工作吧，朋友们若问我怎么没有看见你，我会说你在其他城市发展。其它我什么都不谈，这样可以吧！"

于平很感动，"谢谢你，我会回来和你一起过年。也许争取回我老家过年，和老妈过一个团圆年。"

李华停顿一会儿："看看再说吧，也许我会比你先走，我单位马上要我下基层站工作。"

于平低着头说话，声音小得像蚊子一样嗡嗡响。他知道李华不想面对自己，想躲开他，才选择远离又不离婚的这种相处的方式。他明白李华没说出狠话，证明还是心里有他，舍不得他。

于平猜对了李华的一半心思，李华真的不忍心在痛苦的时候做出任何一个决定，于是才想了这一招，用时间去淡化这些不愉快的事情。正是趁单位领导号召之际，有些工作在基层一线的同志已经干了三年，这个时候应该把这些同志换上来，同时需要另一批同志下基层工作。

这一晚李华睡得很安稳，双方谈开了，基本上各自都有了计划和打算，心里疙瘩可以打开。李华其实就想自愈疗伤，到最远的地方去工作。

第二天早上，李华决定下基层去之前先去趟妇幼医院，将节育环取了出来。虽然是一个小手术，但是李华拿着医生开的建议休息三天的病假单，直接慢慢撕了个粉碎，丢进路边的垃圾桶。

李华早听工会妇联孙主任对她说过："女人若是不要孩子，可以带上节育环；若是没有夫妻生活，也可以取掉节育环。"

李华是后者，虽然和于平结婚两年多了，可早已没有了夫妻之间的那些事情。一直还以为自己的男人肾亏，买了两年的中医补肾保健品给这个男人吃，结果补到野女人身上去了。

她的脸色没有一点颜色，白白的。她本来就只吃素食，唯一就是爱吃点鱼和虾，加上近期发生的这些难以启齿的事情，一直闷在心里，人就更比以前瘦了很多。本来很开朗乐观性格的李华，几乎换了一个性格，沉默寡言。

李华慢慢向单位走去，情不自禁地摇头苦笑着。李华想好了，决定不休息，争取在后天就出发。今天是来将自己的办公用品整理打包。办公室整理好，做完交接工作已是晚上了。李华很怕夜晚的来临，别人是在一天天的有说有笑中过日子，她可是一天天数着数字熬日子。

三天后，李华简单收拾了够一个月换洗的衣服，随着单位检查人员下基层站，调研销售情况。李华只是统计库存，每星期按时向市局作一个销售、库存、资金回笼完成报表。站里搬箱子的重活没让李华干，在下面站工作只有四个人，站长、销售员、仓库保管员、一位名叫李莲花的财务会计。

李莲花是站里唯一的女同事，这一干就是三个年头。在基层站工作可以说是一抹带十杂，什么活都没分得那么清楚，有时候换上一个人轮流休息的时候，必须都要什么工作都得顶上。李华来了，李莲花很开心，终于有一位女同事做伴了。晚上就把李华安排在李莲花的宿舍，一房正好有两张 1.2 米的床。

站里的第一天晚餐，站长发话了，让保管员多做几道菜，特意为李华做了一大锅水煮鱼，一盘参子鱼，一大碗自己种的青菜，真的是味道鲜美。李华本来不挑剔，吃完后才意识到她最近几个月都没吃过热烫烫的饭菜，感觉农村的米饭都好吃。

站长在餐桌上说："我们基层站日子是苦点，没有什么业余文化生活，但是我们的米饭养人。你今天尝的这青菜，都是保管员小张种的；鱼是在养鱼村民那买的活鱼；大米也是在农民手上买的当季新米，不吃菜都可以吃两碗。李华主任你是市局派下来检查指导我们站工作，和我们同吃同住同劳动，委屈你了。"

李华听到站长朴实的一番话，从心里感觉到无比温暖。说句心里话，最近几个月她从来没有像今天这样放松，也没有像今晚这样好的胃口，吃了这么多食物，而且专心吃着这些土灶烧出来的大锅菜。加上大家对她的亲切和关心，李华不知道用什么话表达感谢之情，举起酒杯向全体在座的同事说："今天我是吃得最多美食的人，很久没有像今天这样开怀畅饮。在今后的工作中，我会全力配合大家的工作，谢谢大家对我的关心和帮助。在此，感谢的话尽在不言中。"

李莲花接过话说："李华主任千万别客气。我们吃什么，你就吃什么，有你这样随和的李华主任，而且还跟我同住一室，我好高兴。你一点架子也没有端，比起以前来的工作人员朴实多了。以前都是开会，吃完饭，转转就回市里去了，从没在站住下来。"

李华说："现在是局领导重视基层站建设，把市局机关人员补充到基层站工作，打好销售冬季这一目标，突破往年同季销售指标。"

大家围坐在桌前，你言我语地聊起来，气氛愉快。大家都没有睡意，从工作聊到生活，李华看到这些来自基层可爱的同事们，忽然感觉跟他们一起很容易开心，很知足，一时忘记了自己心里的痛。

晚上睡在床上的李华，睁着眼向墙面上灯看去。"莲花，你每天一个人睡觉有怕过吗？"李华亲切地与莲花聊着。

莲花说："不怕，这里很安全，站里有值班员，站里隔壁左右房间都有同事住。我们这里不隔音，有什么动静，都会听到，你安心休息啊。"

李华说："我睡沉后可能会打呼噜，别吵着你了。"

莲花说："没有关系，我睡着后，什么都听不到。我老公说过，我像头猪，我也属猪的，哈哈。"

听到莲花的话，李华也忍不住地笑出来。

第九章　告别过去

　　睡意向李华袭来，她在不知不觉中睡着了。梦中的李华在攀登一座山，爬呀爬呀，正要抓住山顶上的一棵树的根部时，突然手滑，抓不住手中的绳子，向山下掉了下去。李华大声地喊着，可是发不出声音，她挣扎挥手乱抓，终于抓住了另一棵树的树藤。

　　李华突然被梦惊醒，双手撑在床上坐了起来。李华看看莲花还在睡觉，不敢吵醒她，自己又悄悄上个洗手间后，回到床上去睡一个回笼觉。可再也睡不着了，李华想起几天前一个人躺在医院的手术台上，听到医生说："你的子宫口很好。四十岁的女人，应正是三十如虎，四十如狼的年龄，应该是夫妻生活正旺的时期，你为何要取掉节育环，就不怕怀上了？"

　　李华敢脱口对不熟悉她的医生说："我们有两年没有在一起，哪有那种生活？想想以后会更不可能了。"

　　医生反过来劝她："那可不行，你这是性冷淡，你若需要什么调理的药就告诉我，我建议你喝点中药，中药没有副作用，调一段时间就会好起来。"

　　李华说："谢谢医生，不需要了，我只是想取环，再不会去想夫妻生活这个事了。"

　　医生感到纳闷。而李华那个时候就是这样想的，而且很淡定地坚持主见，取环这事直到后来也没有对于平吐露半句，都没有必要了！

　　于平跟前妻生活五年也没有孩子，于平跟李华都已是二婚。发现于平出轨后，李华更没有一丁点想跟于平同房的心思。李华已厌倦这种貌合神离的婚姻生活了，她得学会放下。这次主动下基层工作，是她的第一步，她想这样远离于平的视线后，她心里对于平仅存的爱会少一点淡一点，淡到她内心可以真的放下，她的心就不恨也不痛了。

　　这是李华逃避的原因之一，不然以李华心软的性格，如果再听到于平用带有磁性的声音，说出缠绵的情话鬼话，她害怕自己又被情不自禁地受骗。若被于平牵着她的鼻子转，她会伤得更深。她不再是少女的年龄了，她需要成熟理智的头脑，而不是浪漫幼稚的情怀。

李华想到这里，不由得叩心自问："我还能相信爱情婚姻吗？"如今的李华迅速地成熟了很多，她没有往日得理不饶人的脾气，变得温和宁静。她似乎悟出来了，如果婚姻生活只带给她是出轨背叛，她宁愿选择不要婚姻，不活在他人怜悯的目光里。她需要给自己一个安全港湾，而不是这样支离破碎的婚姻。

在人言可畏的小社会，冷言冷语是会杀人的，所以她必须听从编辑老师说的那样："要冷静地处理问题，比较好的办法是让时间岁月去淡化一切，不能冲动，一定要把伤害减少到最低的时候，再来跟着内心走。这段婚姻是留是走，那个时候的你一定会走出阴影，活出自我，活得更精彩。"

想到这些鼓励和宽慰的话，李华想：我还有什么放不下的呢？没有爱人，没有了婚姻怕什么？我还有好的工作，好的亲人，好的同事，好的朋友们，最重要的是我已经不再是以前幼稚的女人了，我该成熟了，是该向过去的日子说拜拜了！

李华一个月下基层站工作结束后，回到市里的家已是周末了。那天还下着雨，11月初是进入冬天的日子。钥匙刚刚插进锁眼，没想到于平从房子里面打开了门，轻声说："我准备后天就去广州工作了，还正在想准备去基层站看你，没有想到你今晚回来了，真好！"

李华放下自己的小箱子，于平及时递上拖鞋。李华环顾房子客厅，茶几沙发边也有两个大箱子，一看就知道是于平的旅行箱，超大的那种。她明白眼前于平，过两天就真的各奔东西了。这是天意，知道李华下不了决心，又不知该如何对待于平，俩人终于以工作需要为由分居两地，相处起来没有那么尴尬。这是李华最希望的处理方式。平常总替对方着想，善良的李华终于可以用这种方式去淡化理性处理一地鸡毛的乱事，让岁月去抹去心里伤痕，淡淡逝去！

无论怎样，给于平一点情面吧。李华问："包都打好了，坐火车还是飞机去广州？有人送吗？"

于平说："坐火车，由章司机送我去火车站。"

话说完，就好像是没有计划李华送他的意思。

火车站离啤酒厂和那个女人家很近，李华突然冒出一个念头：我要去送送这个男人。李华想，那个女人一定也会去送这个男人！依李华对章司机的了解，章司机一定会为那女人提供方便，也去车站送行。如果万一碰到了，他们会编谎话说是单位派人送送于先生；如果没有碰上，也许买好了火车票同去。

这个想法是李华第六感，李华认为自己的第六感很灵，她一方面很希望自己猜对了，一方面又很恼火，如果一切都是真的呢，她该怎么办？当场闹开揭丑吗？还是再装一次傻子？

李华本不是太在意这对男女乱搞的屁事，但一想到这些，李华又头大了。

李华心想：管他的，只要不被我本人捉住，偷一次跟偷了十次有什么关系，他还不是出轨了吗？有什么两样？

于是李华不动声色地说："我去送送你吧。"

于平一愣："你要是忙，可以不用送我了，我的司机会帮我安排好一切。"

李华问："怎么，不方便吗？"

"没有，怕你没时间。我休假会回来的。"

"我会送你去火车站，后天几点火车？"

"中午1：20，可能来不及吃午饭，就要出发。"

李华记住时间，就不再多问了，随后说："今天早点休息吧，等你走后，我会退出这所亲戚家的房子，不再住了。反正你也不在本市工作了，我一个人搬回单位分的那套房子住，上班也方便。"

"搬家需要人手帮忙吗？如果你同事问你，怎么没有看见我，你怎么回答？"

李华先低头沉默了一会，随后扬起头，用手抚顺头顶。李华忘了自己剪短的头发，若有所思地直视于平："这你就别担心了，我会对所有关心你的朋友们说，你去别的城市发展了。这是实情，也很体面，那些拿不出桌面上的事，我会一字不提。你以后为人处世，掌握一个度，你该怎么对外人说话，自己小心点。"

于平听到李华这样回复，总算把吊在嗓子的话压了下去。他也不想让众人瞧不起他，毕竟是他损坏了自己在众人心目中的好印象。

李华比于平更注重人言可畏的现实。于平拍拍屁股一走了之，而李华还要在这块土地继续生活工作，家人亲戚都在，哪能像于平这样简单处理。李华必须装出什么事也没有发生一样，得默默地扛着顶着。与其是说放过于平这个男人，还不如说是放过她自己。

　　于平更需要工作挣钱养家和培养女儿，而且她还是一位孝女，还要挣钱孝敬父母，照顾好她的妹妹们。李华更丢不起这个丑，更不想让外人看到她和于平的笑话。她也知道一切会慢慢好起来，需要漫长的岁月去抚平内心最痛的伤口。

　　她能这么理性冷静说出这番话，于平都感觉有点忐忑不安，他不知道李华真实的想法。按常规来说，李华一定会闹，会强势地修理他；但是李华近几个月的表现让他有点着摸不透。他在想，只要李华不闹不揭穿他，他只得夹着尾巴做人，把这个家照顾好，不然以后真的不好意思再回到这座城市和这个家。

　　于平对李华说："我安顿好工作后，会多攒点钱，过年争取一起回我老家过春节。"

　　李华没有言语，也没有感动，因为她听过太多这男人的承诺了。后天这个男人就要离开了，李华必须面对现实，为了女儿她也得好好地工作生活，不能再去幻想着靠谁了。

第十章　送别

　　于平离开的这天，他醒来很早，早早地去楼下早点摊上买了平日李华最爱吃的牛肉米粉加一根油条，还有江城人最爱喝的豆腐脑，糯米鸡各两份。于平知道午饭来不及吃，就多吃点早餐，到中午应该不会感觉到饿肚子。

　　李华听到关门响声就起来了，看到摆放在桌上的早餐，她也明白于平在向她示好。洗漱完毕后，李华毫不客气地坐下来。于平在厨房里拿起两双筷子，递给李华一双说："趁热吃这家牛肉粉，这是你最爱的彭师傅牛肉粉，今天星期天人很多呢。"

　　于平自己也迫不及待地吃了起来。李华埋头吃着早餐，于平见李华没有说话，也安静地吃着。餐厅里偶尔发出吸米粉的声音和喝牛肉汤的声音。最后两人都把油条扯成一小段，在辣辣的牛肉汤中沾一下，再放进嘴巴里。两人吃相都很满足，像是遇到了天底下最好吃的美食。

　　于平说："以后在广州肯定吃不到这种地道口味了！今天我吃得这么干净。

　　李华没有接于平的话，只是站起来对他说："你的口味会变的，广州大都市有更多的美食，你不用担心什么。"

　　两个人整理检查该带的东西，一直等到出发的时间点。于平提前两小时出发，开车到火车站只需一个小时，留一个小时进站，在候车厅小息一会。章司机肯定是听于平叮嘱了，准点在楼下等候。章司机没有往日那么多话，只是专注地开车。有时候会从反光镜向坐在后排的于平和李华扫一眼，李华注意到了；于平也在看章司机的眼神，似乎有话要说……

　　不到一个小时，车子就到了火车站。章司机停好车，将两个大箱子拿出来，于平自己提着一个随身小箱子，跟着章司机一前一后地走着。李华有意落在于平身后，观察着四周人群，她在寻找熟悉的身影。章司机买了站台票进站送于平，直到响起"此班火车还有 15 分钟就要开"的广播，李华在站台下也没有看见熟悉的人影。

　　李华随人群进站，章司机催促于平快上火车。李华的好奇心马上涌出来，反正还有时间，她跟着于平一起上到车厢去。于平想拦住，担心地劝李华说："你不用送了，万一人多拥挤下不了火车，那可麻烦了。"

　　这话说出来好像是替李华着急，可李华听起来就感觉眼前慌张的男人害怕她看见什么。李华使了一股劲，将于平推着向车厢里进去："快走呀，你坐下我就马上走。"

　　章司机也奇怪地高声喊起来："让一下，让一下，于先生李姐快点，就在前面二排。"扯着嗓子喊的章司机在前面开路，于平和李华紧紧跟着。当章司机把两个大箱子放好后，马上对于平使了一个眼神，对李华说："快点下车，火车快要开了！"

　　李华站立了一会，迅速扫了这节车厢上已进来的人，也看了一下隔壁车厢，并没有看到她想见到的人。于平焦急地提醒李华赶紧跟章司机下车，这时李华才不得已快步向车厢外走去。在快下车的时候，李华本能地回头向于平坐的那排望去，一个女人的背影向着于平的那排贴身坐了下去。这时火车已经要开动了，李华只有下车，在站台上往那节车厢跑去。李华想证明自己的判断，她向上跳起来向那节车厢看去，跳了几下，都没有看到正面。火车这时已经动起来了，李华气喘吁吁地向候车厅外走去，章司机早已在停车场等着她。

　　上车后李华没有把心中的怀疑说出来，只是坐在车的后排，不断想着刚刚的那一幕。难道真的是那个贱女人？要不然怎么这么熟悉呢？

　　章司机的问话打断了李华的思索："李姐你是去单位，还是回家里？"

　　李华说："送我回家吧！另外，我忘了告诉你，前段时间你爱人素琴和孩子找过我，问我有没有看见你。就是你和于先生还有你表妹，还有那汪芹兰一起出差的那几天。我看到素琴还有两个孩子的眼神，多么期待要见到你。我只对素琴说，你和于先生出差去了，我也没有见到你。我没有说去了几个人，我不会说谎，没敢多待。他们过几分钟就走了。希望你对素琴好一点。她那么好，真的信了我的话。带着孩子转身的时候，还扭头向我挥挥手，让我快点进去，外面风大。你知道吗？我那个时候有多恨你和于先生，你们对得起自己的老婆和孩子们吗？"

　　章司机没有回李华的话，车子继续向前开着。李华也不瞅章司机一眼，她在心里想，此番话说出来就是要告诉章司机，你们做的那些见不得人的丑事，我不是不知道，别把素琴和我都当傻子。只是我们心地善良，想给你们一个改错的机会。如果还一意孤行，没有不透风的墙，我不说，总有人说，还是多积点德，好自为之吧。

车子缓缓地到了李华家楼下，出车门的时候章司机说了一句："谢谢你没有对素琴说什么。我现在已经下岗了，今天是最后一天上班，从明天我就只有那家修车店为自己打工了。幸好听了于先生的话，要我开一个修理汽车店，不然我一时半会哪里能找到工作？以后有什么需要我帮忙的，你到店里找我！"

李华站在原地听完，随后转身对着有点悔改态度的章司机说："好好的一个家，你要好好地待素琴。素琴真的很善良朴实，你在哪能找到像素琴这么单纯的女人？你忍心伤害她吗？现在好好过还来得及，你们还有孩子呢。"

章司机说："知道了，我下岗后也被罗琼晾在一边了，没有来往了，李姐你也别怪于先生了，他还是很爱你的，是你先忽略了他，你可以原谅他吗？"

"再说吧，随缘就好。你看到了，我没把他怎么样，这样他因工作而离开也不错，天意！我们都好自为之吧！"

于平离开的第二天，李华趁还有一天假，赶紧请了搬家公司，将所有的家具全部给了父亲乡下的一个亲戚，把唯一的一台钢琴送给了曾经照顾女儿的二妹，再把自己和女儿的生活用品搬进单位的房子里。李华还请了清洁工把空房子打扫得干干净净，并建议亲戚家将此房挂在中介卖掉——因为那贱女人睡过晦气，她不愿意亲戚家受损。做完这些之后，李华似乎心里干净了许多，她想彻彻底底地忘记这件事情。不住这里，就不会触景生情，她需要重新开始。

通过下基层站工作一个月，她悟懂一个道理，必须要有经济独立的实力，才可以清除心里的阴影。她需要靠自己疗伤，必须将精力投入工作，这样才能阻止自己胡思乱想……

第十一章　果断内退

一晃几年过去，于平在外地发展的第二个年头转到了广州制衣厂当副厂长。李华与于平的关系就这样吊着，反正人不在身边，大家也就慢慢习惯了李华形单影进出单位小区。

2002 年 6 月某天，市局召集中层干部以上的会议，领导首先听从了从各基层站调研同志报告，随后局领导宣布了两大改革措施，其中一项针对市局行政部门人员超多，闲职的岗位可以减掉合并。有两种处理意见，一种是鼓励市局中层干部积极响应改革号召，年龄到了 45 岁可以申请内退政策，停职享受 80% 工资待遇；一种是到农村基层站担任重职工作。

一时间市局中层干部有人恐慌有人兴奋，议论纷纷，李华是最冷静的一个。李华正想逃避眼前这个城市给她带来的情感伤害。那个伤害她的人走了，但是那些事，还有那些知情的人，她得面对。她害怕哪一天扛不住会做出傻事，她不可能闷在心里一辈子，为那些痛苦回忆买单。她想走出去，她甚至感到可惜，这个机会要早两年来临就好！

李华心想，按部就班的八小时工作，不能给她带来更多的财富。现在她的家已名存实亡，她如果还在原地不动，像机器人一样生活，未来二十年也还是这样的情景。能看到头的生活，一成不变的生活不是李华想要的状态，她想拼一把。目前单位政策很好，退职位还有 80% 的工资拿。退一万步来说，就算创业不成功，李华也没有温饱危机感。既然饿不死，为何不去试试呢？

李华心里已经有了主意，她不能错失良机。她按照局领导的号召，积极响应报名申请内退。她感觉自己没有选错，她需要换一个环境，到一个不认识她的地方去寻找商机，再创业，这样才能早点实现在大都市有房有车的生活。

在单位的中层年轻女干部中，李华是第一个向组织提出申请内退人员。当时有很多人不理解她，想培养她的领导劝她三思而行；那些没有真本事的人，

趁机煽风点火好让李华早日离开单位："你要是申请了，出去闯闯肯定比现在混得更好。"

这些人想占她中层干部的岗位，巴不得她快点走，好腾出位置向上爬，混个几年，当上一官半职。也有个别私心很重的领导另有打算，若是李华真的走了，留下空位还可以再得到好处，比如提拔一个想当主任的人，顺便卖个人情。

这些人心里的小算盘，李华看得很清楚。她想好了，不想把未来的工作和生活，去应付人际关系上。拍马屁说假话那套，她还真做不到。面对这样的处境，李华只有豁出去，就决定内退，没有什么了不起的。"不就是一个中心主任吗？将来自己干好了，说不准就是一个公司的老总！"李华对自己很有信心，必须抓住好这次的机会。

李华当年的内退申请一致通过。内退申请递交上去了，等待正式通知还有半个月，需要搞交接工作。有同事问李华，这次内退是不是去广州投靠于平，李华模糊带过这个话题。众人对于平的打探令李华坐立不安，等待通知的日子里李华度日如年，她不知道自己是否可以一直装出风淡轻云的样子。她期待着申请早点批准，省得夜长梦多。

这几年来李华对于平出轨的事处理得很好，没有几个人知道。李华也不希望众人知道她的重组家庭已是千疮百孔，而且她还没有想好怎么去应对这个乱摊子。李华想离开于平的婚姻束缚，但不希望众人知道因为于平做了丑事导致家庭破裂。她必须让所有人都以为她和于平仍是幸福的一对。

于平已离开几年，这期间逢过年也回来过几次。众人的试探和关心让李华很难受。这些关心和问候，在李华心里就像是无情的嘲讽。曾经李华以为随着于平的远离，她会好过一些；没想到于平人离开了，他身边的关系网却无时无刻不在盯着李华。她就像是没有穿衣服被别人偷看着一样，她感觉到被众人嘲笑讽刺。她想离开这座城市，让过往的一切慢慢地淡忘。

决定内退之后，李华也有自己的打算，她想一个人去南方城市深圳考察学习保险。她了解自己适合什么工作，只有做保险代理人，才可以在中国的任何一座城市工作生活，只有这样才能逃离身边熟悉的众人。

一星期后，李华就接到人事科的正式通知，财务方面也通过了正常交接前的审核。接到批准内退通知的第三天，李华只身一人到住读学校跟女儿说了自已接下来的生活打算。她要去深圳学习保险，并尽量能留在深圳工作，她找到了下一个奋斗目标和挑战。李华让女儿好好学习，也给女儿信心，相信她一定会让女儿的生活过得更好。她告诉女儿，学校放假就回姥姥或二姨家住。

一切安排妥当后，李华如释重负地踏上去深圳的火车。那天是夜晚的火车，靠在车窗向外看着奔驰的列车，沿途风景让李华无法入睡。孤独和向往交织在一起，李华思索着很多未来将面临的挑战：到一个陌生的城市重新开始，谁也不认识她，一切从零开始。但是她很轻松，慢慢地感觉压在心里的石头被她移开了，今后再也没有人知道她的过去，她再也不会受委屈了，开始要为自己而活。

这趟火车在早上七点半到达深圳，李华在走出大厅前去了卫生间洗一把脸，化了一个淡妆。她从箱子里换上一身适合深圳气候的连衣裙，再配上已长起来的长直发，显得年轻有朝气，只像30多岁小女子，要知道那个时候李华已是45岁。

按照本子记录的详细地址，李华直接来到帝王大厦附近。看到还没有到上班时间，李华就先走进一家早点水饺馆子，买了一碗中份素菜馅的水饺，慢慢地吃了起来。随后找到那家已联系好的中介公司，打通了电话。10分钟后真的有一个女孩来到饺子馆门前接她，去预定好的私人公寓安顿好行李。李华背起随身携带的挂包，跟着美女一起出门，俩人边问边答了解了大至周边生活情况。

这里环境真好，离帝王大厦真近，走路只需六分钟。那家饺子馆也很近，如果为了省钱生活，这里的小吃排档面馆都有。她惊喜地发现了一家她特别喜欢吃的湘菜馆，她想着晚上好好地吃一餐饭，就上湘菜馆来吃，一定不能再委屈自己了。

李华在电话中已经了解过，参加美邦保险公司代理人培训学习的情况，必须经过学习两个月。李华考取了保险代理人资格证书，终于成为一名保险职场上的新人。

李华通过中介在帝王大厦旁边的私人楼房租了一间带卫生间的公寓。主要是为了方便，步行就可以到上课的地方，节省时间来学习保险代理资格培训课。为了不迟到，李华到深圳的第一天就开始在租住房的周边散步，熟悉早餐店、利民超市、菜市场及公交车站，还有美容美发店。

　　上课第一天李华早早起来，在附近一家上海饺子馆买了一碗中份的韭菜肉馅饺子。吃完后还有充足的时间，李华不慌不忙地走进旁边的美发店修剪头发。

　　李华看着理发师给她吹型整理，看着镜子里的自己：头发已从寸长短发长到齐耳秀子发，已经恢复温柔秀气的模样。再经理发师修型打理，现在的李华看起来非常职业，干练的气质显现出来。

第十二章　异地学习保险培训

剪完头发时间差不多了，李华拿起包快步走向帝王大厦，赶在听课前10分钟到了六楼保险代理培训教室。真没有想到已经坐了很多人，没有一张熟悉的面孔，大家来自五湖四海。

深圳是特区城市，在改革开放的年代，来这里的人们都是有梦想闯世界的人。有很多胆大的投资者，也有很多大学生、农民工、弃政从商的官员，还有像李华这样离职下海的职员，涌进这座年轻的城市。

李华也无意中赶上了时代浪潮，李华没有想到凑热闹，但却赶上了时尚。要不是为了逃避闲言闲语，李华不会有勇气把稳稳当当的工作提前内退，挤进这不熟悉保险行业。连深浅都不知道，她来就了，初生牛犊不怕虎，一切从零开始。李华认为不懂就学，把后路都断了，努力学习早点通过培训，早日拿到保险代理展业证书。目标清楚了，住的地方已经定下来，一切就绪，剩下的只需要安心学习。

李华扫了整个教室一眼，见有的空位上放着包，有的椅子上面搭着衣服，李华垫着脚尖向倒数几排中间地方走去，那里还有几个空位。李华在一张空椅子上坐下来。主持人已经在讲台上开始拿起麦克风向台下所有人讲话："大家安静。首先很感谢今天能有这么多同学到场，在这里我代表美国友邦保险公司深圳分公司，向在座的学员们表示欢迎。欢迎你们即将通过保险代理培训学习，通过我们的考试，成为我们保险行业真正的一员。在此感谢大家，保险公司队伍又拥有新生力量。欢迎你们以合格资格去展业，成为我们未来钻石业务精英。欢迎你们也像我一样，走上这个讲台，分享你的学习和保险代理展业经验。我希望能有更多的保险精英在这里汇聚一堂，走上我们人生价值的巅峰。祝学员们努力学习完成培训，祝大家能够顺利通过培训考试！"

整个会场掌声响起，这种激情澎湃的场景，李华好久没有感受到了。李华

边鼓掌边环顾四周，这些人和李华一样激动兴奋，一脸期待。那神情是李华在以前单位没有见过的场面，让人精神抖擞。

接下来李华拿起笔记本和笔，记下了上课笔记，这些内容包括保险代理概念，保险条款，保险理赔，保险展业中的随机预约，保险异外险条款，保险人寿生前金，保险人与投保人及受益人的关系，等等。学习的保险知识还真多，李华心想，要是不学习，怎么也赶不上时代发展。

李华认真做笔记的学习态度引起了旁边一位美女注意："哎！你的字写得整齐漂亮，等会下课后借我抄抄。中间有两段我没记下来。"

听到东北口音，李华立刻笑了起来："好呀，你是东北人呀？"

东北女孩说："是啊，你听得出来我的乡音？我叫妞妞，你叫什么名字？"

"你叫我李华就好，因为我也有东北朋友，所以熟悉的这种语音，感觉很亲切。"

俩人迅速认识，妞妞性格豪爽，上课间常常说几句话就能引起周边同学的大笑。接着妞妞又扮鬼脸，吐出舌头，前后左右座位上的几个帅气男生都被妞妞逗得笑岔气了！

下课后，很多男生有意无意接触妞妞，讨好她递上水果和零食。真看不出妞妞有这么一招，和谁都能打得火热。李华仔细看着妞妞，其实妞妞长相一般，脸上还有青春痘，穿着上也显一般，但是她很会说话。这开朗的性格一定很适合做保险代理人，相信她将来的保险业务一定会做得好。

一周学习时间一晃就过去了，妞妞与李华熟悉了起来。妞妞看李华的穿着很显职场风格，看上去不像是学员倒像是讲师。李华一套黑色短袖职业套装裙，那套裙子还是当年很有名气服装品牌。穿起来简洁大方上档次，可以说是永远不会淘汰落伍。妞妞看到李华很有职场风范，也有女人的韵味。只要下课妞妞就跟着李华同进同出洗手间，两人换着看包占位置；每天谁先到都会照顾对方，顺便占听课的老地方。时间长了，周围的学生都很自觉，各坐各位。周末还一起吃饭——当然是 AA 制了，这在那个年代还是挺时髦的。

到了第三个周末，妞妞及周围的同学又一起到湘菜馆共进晚餐。李华喜欢吃辣，常在那吃饭，没有想到同学们也找到这家店，经济实惠，而且味道真的很正宗。之前几次邀请李华都推了，这次听说同学要去湘菜馆吃饭，李华马上加入。妞妞高兴地叫起来："今天谁敢喝酒？"马上有回应，"我要一杯啤酒！""我也要！"

李华也要了杯黑啤，深圳的七月真的很热，吃辣的配上一杯冰啤，应该很舒服。湘菜馆老板看见李华到来，很热情地接待着。老板一直以为是李华带大家来这里吃，照顾自己的生意，于是对李华特别热情。

李华平时一个人来这家店吃过很多次，每次换一道菜吃，几乎店里的每道菜都品尝遍了。因此点菜交由李华负责，她知道哪道菜的口味重，哪道菜鲜美。那一餐大家吃得很尽兴开心，结账时老板还看在李华面上打了折。八个人摊起来只付了 50 元钱不到！同学们吵着下周再来，老板当然开心。也就是这一来二去，老板知道了李华他们是保险公司的人。

散场后，妞妞问李华："李华你住哪里？要不今天跟我一起去我那里住好吗？反正我叫出租车是一个人，住也是一个人。我有两间房，你真的可以住在我那里。今晚我想跟你商量一件事！"李华以为妞妞需要自己帮忙考试复习的事情，才客气邀请她一起住。

李华说："妞妞你放心，我已经把下周考试的复习题印写了两份，我会给你一份，你不用担心。按照上面的内容复习，考试没有问题。"

妞妞上课爱说话，没有怎么听课，李华把重点内容都整理出来，并将一些问题的答案写了出来。

妞妞说："谢谢，我需要这些复习题，不过我还是希望你来住一晚上！"

李华看到妞妞诚心诚意地邀请，以为妞妞害怕，就随她一起回去。

深圳的夜晚，灯红酒绿，高楼大厦，在李华的眼前飞过，出租车在宽敞的公路上行驶。要不是陪同妞妞去她家住，李华还不知道深圳的夜晚这么美，沿途灯光通明。李华平日下课后，除了吃饭、洗头在外面走走，从来不在夜晚出去，更不会去逛夜市。

20 分钟左右就到了妞妞租住的小区，那里的确环境优美，几道电子刷卡门看来很安全，也有保安值岗。妞妞住在 6 楼 9 号房，两室一厅一卫一厨。妞妞和李华洗完澡后坐下来闲聊，妞妞没有睡意，直接对李华说："我想考完试后，咱们一起先去人才市场中心工作，因为有底薪 600 加提成，一边工作一边做保险，你看呢？"

李华说："很好的主意，你有熟人是吗？"

　　妞妞说："对，你很像管理人，那个老板肯定会录用你。管他呢，反正每天去报到，每月还有底薪 600 元，生活费挣到了是吧，我们再去做保险也不影响。"

　　李华："行啊，你真有点子，你认为我可以就行。"

　　妞妞说："还有告诉你，这所房子其实是我香港的男朋友给我租的，一个月 3000 人民币。你来我这里住一间，每月只给我 500 就行，在这里肯定比你那私人公寓好，你那还要 600 元。你认为呢？"

　　李华停止了一秒的思索，反应过来回复："好的，我这个月到期之前答复你。等下周考试完了，等通过就好了，到时候在哪里住都好商量。"

　　妞妞说："好吧，我看是你才放心，要是别人我才不会合租呢。但是，我的男朋友每半个月才来住两天。他来后，你别说是合租，你就说我们是一个班学习的学员。"

　　李华说："好的，你床上用品都有吧？"

　　妞妞说："有床席梦思，没有床，其他盖毯子都有。"

　　李华看到妞妞脑子转得真快，她很佩服，小小年纪比李华所在事业单位干了二十多年的人还显得精明能干。

　　就这样，李华跟妞妞都通过了保险代理培训考试。考试过后，她们在第一时间商量搬家。本月底提前三天，李华简单收拾一下，只带了生活用品，办了退租公寓，搬进了妞妞的房子。在外的日子很简单，一个人吃饱了，有张睡的地方，就很好了。

　　李华看到妞妞麻利地安排帮助，感到很庆幸。在深圳即将开始保险展业的时候，在学员妞妞的帮助下，不仅安顿好了住处，还多找到了一份与保险工作时间不冲突体面工作。能多挣一点是一点，600 元也可以当是房租金有着落了，住在一起房子环境也好些，而且还有一个伴。

第十三章　挑战自己

　　就这样李华在深圳的 8 月份就开始保险代理展业了。当时新人保险代理人必须自己买一份一年意外保险单，一个月需要完成 5 单任务，这样能拿到新人钻石奖励，当月收入会有佣金 5000 多元。李华仔细学完保险展业知识，把随机展业人物目标从身边重要的 5 个人做起。

　　在跟妞妞合租之前，李华想从住所附近熟悉的面孔入手，随机自然地推销谈保险。

　　李华先到人才市场中心报到，每天忙一上午后，快到中午时分就去熟悉的目标地段，去寻找保险展业的机会。

　　第一天，李华想把自己打扮得精神点，她想到的第一站是她常去的美发店。经常服务李华的 6 号理发师一看到她进门就热情地问好："你好，今天是洗头还是剪头发？"

　　李华说："我今天找你办洗头月卡，还有活动优惠吗？"

　　6 号理发师高兴地说："谢谢你照顾我，我一定把你洗得舒舒服服，今天不赶时间吧？"

　　李华说："不赶时间，就跟你聊天洗头。"

　　理发师帮忙挂包，顺便问了句："今天包怎么这么重呀？"

　　李华神秘一笑："哈哈哈，那是一包钱啊，别搞丢了压坏了！"

　　理发师听到李华这话，很紧张地又把包取了下来："你还是抱着吧，这可不能大意。"

　　李华说："你也可以有这么多钱，等会洗头跟你说说！"

　　理发师好奇地说："做什么能挣这么多钱？"

　　李华说："是人寿保险单，保额 10 万，一月只缴 120 元，越年轻投保保费越少，你多大？"

　　理发师说："我 22 岁，投保多少钱能有保额 50 万？"

李华说："我建议你先别投保 50 万，你先试试投保 10 万保额。一月只交 120 元，这样你没有经济压力。只投保一年，等你有钱稳定了，你相信保险好处后，再做人寿终身保险计划。反正每月只花 120 元，还有一个安全保障，你看呢？"

理发师边洗头边和李华开心聊着，理发师很放心。洗完头，李华先在柜台办洗头月卡，顺便直接把保险单表拿出来，边问理发师的个人基本信息，随后问一句："你的身份证给我看看，登记一下号码。"

理发师没有犹豫，从自己工作箱子里拿出来身份证给李华看，李华用手机拍了一张："需要用作复印件。你在这签名就可以了，你是每月一缴，半年一缴，还是一年一缴？"

理发师说："我还是半年一缴吧。"

李华说："没问题，半年只需要 720 元。现在付款，明天我就给你申请保险，随后送收据等保险单。你看，你跟我一样保额，我的保费要多很多，因为我的年龄大些！"

理发师看了点点头："真的呀，年轻投保交保费少些。我相信你，你总是照顾我生意，反正 1 个月只用 120 元，我负担得起。"

李华说："这就对了，要给自己规划理财，遇到意外不慌！"

就这样，第一天展业成功！李华出店后，高兴地鼓励自己，暗自默默地说："我就是做保险的料！"

说实话，这张保险单随机推荐成功，让李华找到了自信。

第二天李华去帝王大厦公司，将保险费上缴，开好收据，又领了几份保险申请表。快到中午时分，李华来到她常去的湘菜馆，选择好老地方（靠在最里台桌前）坐了下来，这次是老板亲自接待。李华有意来早点，客人还比较少，她知道 1 点后才是餐厅高峰期，现在不忙。

李华对老板说："老板你现在可以和我聊 15 分钟吗？"

老板："可以，你想吃什么？"

李华不紧不慢地从包里取出保险单申请表："老板，我给你送保障和钱来了，你想要吗？"

"哪有那么好的事情？不会是要我买保险吧？"老板边坐下边说着，因为看到桌前已摆放好的保险申请表。老板知道李华是做保险的，但之前李华从没有推荐他买保险。

李华直接说："如果只需要你每月缴 200 元左右的保费，缴一年保险额有 15 万元保障，你愿意买吗？"

"有这好的保险产品？"

李华拿出笔在纸上划着，算给老板看。几笔线条画出由低到高的图画，老板一看就懂了。李华说明了投保的好处，分担意外的风险。李华还补充说："你店里厨师杂工连你一共 5 个人，加上店里装修费用投资，我给你计划了一种最实惠的保险保障，以小搏大，负担还很小，员工也有保障，你保证愿意投保！分担起来，员工每人每月只交几十元，你老板根本没有压力，而且提高员工安全意识！何乐不为呢？"

老板看着草图上画的几个人，平均投保几十元钱，高处箭头上方保障保额 15 万至 30 万两种计划保险单。

老板笑了，他知道李华说出了他曾经的烦恼担心。这样分析下来，还解决了老板担心的员工流失问题，员工有了保障是不会随便辞职走掉的；而老板给员工的奖金，也可以拿出一部分给员工买保险作为保障奖励，双方都高兴！

无疑，湘菜馆老板的保单谈成了。当然这也是因为李华一直是这店的老客户，跟老板也成了朋友，彼此信任，所以很容易成交。通过两次成功，李华有点摸到门道了。

李华想到了来深圳打拼经商的证券公司的老同学。老同学是李华的同班同学，学习上一直是班里尖子，而且文笔很好，是班主任老师的得意门生，是男生的榜样。在那个年代，老同学也是很少走动的，何况是男女同学。李华只身一人来深圳这事，曾无意间对班主任老师爱人说过，没想到班主任老师听枕头风后知道了，立刻打电话告诉了他的得意门生陈雄。陈雄在李华学习期间打电话联系过李华几次，要请她吃饭，都被李华拒绝了。李华这次就想着是时候请这位老同学吃一餐饭，顺便直接说明自己正式投身保险这个行业，让老同学支持。

李华早知道陈雄也住在帝王大厦不远的证券公司宿舍楼。刚来深圳时，李华考虑到自己还没有决定做什么工作，不想给老同学添麻烦，于是没有告诉陈雄她也住在那里附近。现在不同了，李华认为自己生活上的事自己都解决了，

现在是创业，是谈工作，可以光明正大地请老同学支持了。想到这里，李华会意地笑了起来，拿起手机对陈雄号码打了过去："喂！你好啊！"

那边传来陈雄的声音，李华笑着说："是我，今天约你明天中午吃饭，我请客怎么样？"

陈雄说："哈哈哈，太阳从西边出来了，你怎么会有空请我吃饭呀？我都请你几次了，你都不给面子，还好意思说。来深圳快两个月了，都不见我。要不是班主任告诉我，你肯定不打照面！怎么，有事？"

李华说："请你吃饭，非要有事？你是中午方便，还是晚餐有空？"

陈雄说："好，我上午比较忙，下午开个小会，晚上咱们在帝王大厦附近一个上海饺子馆碰头，再定吃什么好吗？"

李华心想真巧，陈雄也知道那个饺子馆。世界真小，可怎么俩人从来没有撞上？

李华说："好，就依你。咱们六点在上海饺子馆见！"

李华知道这老同学肯定是要打扮整理一下。陈雄的住处离自己上班地方都很近，李华也想多留些时间给陈雄，这样老同学聚在一起可以慢慢聊。两人是老同学关系，李华可以直接让陈雄买一份保险，这一次李华不用转弯谈。

陈雄和李华到店前后不差两分钟，他们都提前了 5 分钟到达。俩人见面都格外开心，陈雄没把李华当外人，也没把她当女同学。李华本来想约陈雄吃好一点，吃湘菜馆的沸腾鱼，结果陈雄说："你也喜欢吃这家饺子吗？"

李华说："喜欢，但是请你吃饺子，是不是太委屈你了？"

"哎呀，这家饺子很好吃，别到处跑了。我们可以多聊聊，这家店离我住的地方很近。"

"好吧，既然你不嫌便宜，别说我不请你吃好的。"

"这家店的饺子比什么都好吃！"

俩人一说一笑走进饺子馆，选择一个靠窗户的桌子坐下来。服务员上前问："还是吃老样的吗？"两个人同时点头："对！老样子！"

俩人又同时笑了，指着对方说："原来你也常来吃呀，怎么没有碰到你？"

笑过后，李华直接说了要完成保险单任务的事，她只需要陈雄买一个小保险单，一年的意外险种。

陈雄说："要买就买人寿终身险种！"

"我现在不建议你买人寿终身保险，因为你也是刚来深圳，事业还没稳定，经济上也不富裕。等你发达了，买房了，再考虑买一个大保单，行吧？现在就一个小保险就好了！"

陈雄说："好吧，就听你的，买那种一年 10 万保额的吗？"

"嗯，给你自己填好表，再给我。"

在等饺子上桌的工夫，俩人很默契地达成了共识。表刚填好，饺子就端上来了。李华趁机说去洗手间，顺便把单买了，另外又加了两份凉拌菜。回头慢慢吃着饺子聊着天，李华心想这老同学真够意思，根本没有做什么思想工作就投保了。

李华知道这是一张友情保险单！

四张小保险单都完成了，如果按这样速度进展，李华不仅能拿到新人钻石奖，还有可能上本月红人光荣榜！但是李华知道，她还需要完成一张大单，人寿终身保险单！

李华想到了小妹曾经对她说过的话："姐，如果在深圳有困难，需要帮忙的时候，可以去找我的学友，荣总！我对他说过，有个姐姐来深圳发展。他非要请你吃饭，我替你回绝了。"

李华算着日期，快到了月底，不得已打通了荣总电话，简单预约了见面地点就把电话挂了。这个电话李华处理得小心谨慎，因为是妹妹的学友，她不知道以什么方式开口谈到保险。这下真难为李华了，她一直鼓励自己，这是谈工作，厚点脸皮不是丑事，保险行业就是很锻炼人。

这话讲师说得一点不假，一个月的保险展业时间倒计时，让李华很紧张，从而也影响了自信心。李华给自己打气，决定看情况再说，氛围不适合谈合险，她就不说，不能让妹妹的学友感到为难。

星期六晚上终于到了约定时间，吃饭地点是小妹学友荣总订的餐厅。李华刚进餐厅，服务员就引着李华走进了一个包厢，荣总已坐在等着李华到来："大姐好，路上好走吗，堵车吗？"

李华说："还好，顺利，给你添麻烦了。"

荣总说："早就想请你吃饭，一直不好打扰你。听你小妹说，你保险做得还不错，有需要我帮忙的吗？"

听到荣总直奔主题，李华担心是多余了，她真没有想到小妹的学友这么直白问她。她想过很多开场白，就是没有想到直截了当！现在李华不担心了，她顺着话题实话实说，荣总听完笑着说："给我儿子做一个少儿一生有保障的保险吧！保费每一年5000内的可以投保。打算缴二十年，是人寿终身的险种，以你的专业可以推荐我投保选一种就行，大姐说了算！"

李华激动无语，这又是小妹一个大人情！李华认真地分析荣总儿子的情况，算了一种最适合的人寿保险。结果荣总一看，很高兴地指着险种说："这少儿一生幸福保障好，谢谢大姐想得周到！"

这晚餐吃得越来越温暖，这也是李华来深圳吃到的最丰富的一次大餐。李华从来没有像今天这样欣慰，她欣赏地看着荣总这代人，真不愧是年轻有作为的一代人。李华真为小妹自豪，也为荣总的善解人意而敬佩。这年头，年轻这一代人真了不起。

月底的表彰大会上，李华站在舞台中央举起本月钻石奖杯，在欢呼声中和所有公司高层领导合影留念。照片记录了这光荣的瞬间，李华的保险展业开了一个好兆头！

第十四章　拜访朋友

　　刚来深圳的这些日子里，除了工作和学习以外，李华经常通过报纸看到新楼盘信息。她喜欢通过看房子打发时间，以此度过一个人的周末。李华坚持从前就喜欢看房的好习惯，从不交异性朋友，她不管有钱没钱，都会去看房地产的新楼盘，也会在售楼部小姐推荐下看样板房，算一算首付款多少钱，付多少成可以成交的计划，看上去就像真的是想买房的女主人。那服务生可献殷勤了，李华很喜欢这种感觉，她暗地里给自己加油：一定要做一个有钱女人！

　　刚到深圳的一个周末，李华去拜访女友万咪。当时她们在福田区就看了三个新楼盘，其中有一区楼盘的面积很小，16.67平方一卫一室的公寓房型。李华开玩笑对万咪说："这个房子我买得起，如果只先交首付，我想把它买到。我不想总是租房子，万咪你看呢？"

　　万咪回答："算了吧，才来几天啊，多看一下嘛。别一下子冲动就买房子，好房子还有的是，慢慢来。要买房子也要等工作稳定了，你确定想待在深圳，我再来陪你到其他地方去看看。真的不要太冲动了。"

　　好友万咪是单身，因为丈夫出轨跟保姆好上并生了孩子。万咪一气之下向银行单位辞职下海来到深圳打拼，现在投靠深圳哥哥，已经打出一片天了。万咪拥有自己的房子，她把自己的房子作为投资，出租赚取租金，自己就在哥哥家居住。

　　万咪早年离婚后就再也不想结婚了。每年万咪回老家的时候，李华和闺蜜珍珍一起接待她，打保龄球，唱歌，吃饭，上美容院，足疗馆洗脚……总之几个女人在一起有很多快乐的时光，这也是同病相怜的友谊。

　　李华说："好，我听你的，不会随便乱买房子。但是我真的很喜欢看样板房的感觉，很享受被人服务当成是有钱人的感觉，真过瘾！"

　　"是啊，我也喜欢买卖房子，因为好像只有房子能给女人安全感。我已经发现了，你和我还有珍珍，咱们三个女人都喜欢房子，这说明我们还是缺乏安全感，缺好男人。哎呀，还是靠自己吧，挣钱以后想买什么房子就买什么房子，靠自己才靠谱，是吧！"

李华说："你说得太对了，靠男人不可靠。现在我的事情你也知道了，男人一个也不靠谱！现在我换个新环境就是想重新开始，所以一定要开始学会多挣钱，过自己想要的日子！等我站稳了脚跟，有实力了我再来跟那个男人说声拜拜。现在我还没想好怎么应对目前的状况。我一点都不甘心，那个女人那么丑，怎么就敢上我的家偷情，那个男人眼瞎呀！想到这些我就会不服气，可是事实就是如此。这个男人我肯定是不会要了，但是不知道用什么办法休了他，我好难呀！"

万咪说："反正你现在是分居状况，安心做你的事情，找到适合自己工作多挣钱，以后走一步看一步。"李华点头赞同。

到了中午时间，两个人不约而同地说："咱们吃鱼吧，补脑子！哈哈哈，都想到一块了！"

这叫默契，这一餐饭吃得真香。饭后继续看房子，就当是散步帮助消化。就这样通过看房子，李华了解深圳很多房产实际需求信息。这个周末就这样过去了，过得充实愉悦。

接下来的周末，李华安排去拜访了妹妹的学生。妹妹的学生也在深圳，名叫黄文，是一位麻城农村男孩，他正在做汽车配件及汽车改装的生意，他还开了一家洗车店。

妹妹介绍说过，黄文一个人先去深圳打工，结果不到两年把农村的一家人都弄到深圳创业打工了。现在的几个店，全部是家人给他们自己打工，真不简单。这么厉害的能人，李华早就想见见他了。

这一天终于等到了。李华打通黄文电话："黄文你好，我是李老师的姐姐！"

电话那头马上听到回应："是李姐啊，你把定位发给我，我开车接你。"

李华不客气地听话照办，发了定位后，就在帝王大厦附近停车场等候。不到半小时，黄文开车来到。李华看到丰田小车里下来一位个头不高，胖墩墩，笑眯眯的一个小伙子。小伙长得很壮实，短袖肩膀结实，人到了李华跟前声音也到了李华耳边："李姐你好，快上车，咱们上车聊！"

"好，谢谢你来接我，给你添麻烦了！"

"不客气，只要你不嫌弃，可以住在我们店的职工宿舍。这次先带你去看看我的三个店，随后中午我的家人，也是我的工人，加上我的老婆还有儿子一起见面，为你接风洗尘。我来接你之前就订好酒店了！"

李华说："不要太麻烦了，我想向你取经，你是怎样在两年不到的时间，把一家人接到深圳创业，而且还买了三套房。听我妹妹说，你太能干聪明了！"

黄文一点架子也没有，看起来很纯朴，憨头憨脑的样子，黄文笑着说："那是李老师高看了我。我做上汽车配件洗车店这行，纯属偶然！"

原来黄文来深圳的第一份工作也是做保险销售，当年人生地不熟，每天从扫店做起。黄文认为要想卖出保险，必须选择有钱的人群，有保险意识的人群。于是他就从汽车装饰店，洗车店及汽车配件店，开始一家一家地搜索，一家家拜访接触，留下名片。当然，在展业中也吃了很多闭门羹和冷脸，遇到不理解的还被拒之门外。

有天正好是中午，一连几天没有一张单成功，正在进退为难之时，黄文肚子又饿又渴，身上的钱也不多了。他舍不得搭车回到租住地方，于是就沿着公路往回走。遇到一家汽车零部件小店，实在走不动了，就停了下来，劝自己再拜访一家客户吧，试试运气。

黄文慢慢走进去，跟柜台前低头算账的中年男人打一个招呼。中年男人没有抬头，继续写着什么。于是黄文自己介绍保险的好处，哪知面前的男人又抬头回话说："把保险产品都给我再讲一遍。"

这时从隔壁洗车店里走出一位妇女，手拿着拖把、抹布，提着水桶从后门走进店里，对着柜台男人说："哎呀，老板，那个车已经洗好了，但是客人好像外出办事去了。要请你把车移动靠边停着，我们才能继续洗后面的车。"

这女人与男人的对话，让黄文高兴地喊了起来："哎呀，我们是老乡！在这里遇见老乡真是两眼泪汪汪。今天算是遇到熟人了，我们是正宗老乡。我是麻城人，你们一定是麻城人吧。"

柜台男人早听出黄文像是老家的人，所以才让黄文再说一遍保险的内容，实际上就是想确认一下是麻城哪里人。男人笑着对黄文说："要不是老乡，有谁听你说保险啊。我叫罗胖，这三个店都是我开的，全家人帮我一起打工，其实也是为了养活他们自己。我们也只来三年，生意还不错。这几年忙生意，没顾上买保险，我听你说后，还是打算买个保险，求个心安和保障。你来深圳

几年了，做保险多久？今天劳烦你给我们家庭每个成员配一个医疗保险，可以吗？”

黄文惊喜得张大嘴巴，激动地说："罗老板，谢谢你关照老乡小弟！我一定把最适合的保险产品给你推荐，做一个家庭保险计划！而且一定让你满意！"

就这样，黄文的保险生涯从这一天才真正开始。有了罗老板一个大家庭成员的保险单，十人的单！罗老板一家三口，加上他姐姐和妹妹两家人，共计十人，全投了人寿保险及医疗保险。

从那以后，黄文只要有空就到罗老板店里来，像自家亲戚一样走动。有时候店里活忙客户多，连罗老板都要亲自拆车修车。黄文很勤快，帮里帮外地见事做事，拖地做卫生，搬卸货物，没把自己当外人。罗老板的家人员工都喜欢这位勤劳的小老乡黄文。

第十五章　调研深圳房产市场

又是一个周末晴天，深圳夏天热起来了，不干活都出汗。黄文一进罗老板的门店，就看到罗老板仰躺在车底下，满脸灰尘的样子，手上不停地拧着配件。罗老板叫黄文把第一格货物架上，黄文机灵迅速地找到了，并一一递给罗老板。也不知道过了多久，汽车终于安装完毕，顺利调试成功，发动机的声音表现很正常了。

这个时候罗老板满脸脏兮兮的，像一张大花脸。黄文看到忍不住大笑起来："你真像唱戏的花旦，快去洗洗！这里我帮你收拾整理归类放着。"

罗老板不客气地去职工宿舍冲凉洗头，换上一身干净衣服。当他再走进店里的时候，黄文已经把地上和货物架上的零配件摆放得整整齐齐。说句实话，罗老板自己也爱有条不紊地规律摆放，但没有想到黄文做得比他还好。黄文正在认真写着配件型号，规格产地，价格表，根本没有发现罗老板进店。

罗老板站在黄文背后，看着他写得一手漂亮整齐的钢笔字，情不自禁地拍着黄文肩膀说："大学生就是不一样！我看你呀，干脆把保险工作给辞掉，来我这里来，咱们一起做吧。我正准备策划再开一个汽车配件店，地址都选好了，就缺人啊。要不你像我一样，把你老家农村家人都带到深圳，我来培训一下，咱们开一个连锁店，怎么样？给你考虑三天时间，三天后我必须请人了，如果你答应干这行，我们就以合作方式，保证带你入行挣钱。"

黄文没有等三天，他只是想了一个晚上，他经过这些时期帮罗老板义务做事，已看懂了这行业的运作模式，这是他留在深圳最佳机会，于是第二天就答应了罗老板。当天直接走进平安保险公司总部申请辞职，决定与罗老板一起回麻城家乡。罗老板也一同回乡，做黄文家人来深圳创业的动员工作。就这样罗老板顺利按计划把连锁店开了起来，也改变了黄文三家人的生活状况，从农村无业人员成了深圳建设者，创业者。以家庭为单位的共同创业平均分配收益，如今他们也买了三套房和三台汽车！

也就是从那天起，黄文把罗老板改称罗大哥。黄文说："我有今天真的很感谢我的老乡罗大哥！"黄文一边介绍店里的情况，一边向李华讲他自己从保险业转行汽车零部件开店的过程。李华听得既佩服又敬畏。

黄文还说，当年罗老板告诉他把家人都带出来打拼的理由：深圳流动性大，创业机会多，要在深圳生存必须抱团取暖。以家人小团体创业会互相牵制，要有同甘共苦的意念，才能有凝聚力生存下来。如果当年请了散工，教会一个修车技术员工就会走一个员工；但是请家人就不同了。如果当初罗老板只请黄文一个人，连锁店开起来就不会这么顺利。罗老板说的这番话，黄文至今都佩服得五体投地。

吃午饭时，黄文的创业故事也说得差不多了。李华听完还是觉得很震撼，久久回味。黄文突然想到看房子的事，下午就带李华去看罗湖及龙港区四个楼盘的房子。

黄文说："这个周末，我一定全程专车当李姐的司机，去看样板房。今天看不完，明天继续看！"

李华很激动地感谢黄文："这次真的没有白来，听你讲的创业史都可以让我给你写上一部书了，这绝对是人生价值的干货！"

那两天黄文带李华四处看房，黄文对地产的形势和未来发展走势作了分析，李华有了参考依据。李华非常兴奋，同时坚定了今后也要投资房产的信心。黄文说的那句话，李华记得最清楚，"李姐，告诉你哈，这几年，只要你手上有钱，在大城市投资买房，房价绝对会涨。买了房就是挣到钱了，李姐买房是时机了！"年轻的城市深圳让李华看到了很多希望和商机。

在接下来的周末，李华又主动约了那位文笔很好的老同学陈雄。李华讲明自己的想法，让陈雄一起去看看小梅沙附近的海景房，相约作伴，顺便观看海边楼盘，就当是度过一次不一样的周末。

陈雄接到电话就答应了："好呀，我来深圳这几年，周末经常加班，研究证券公司的市场调研报告，从来没有犒劳自己。正好这个礼拜跟你一起看房，好好享受海边生活。请带上游泳装，在海边去游泳。那就定在星期六，还是饺子馆见。"

李华说："好的，但是明天不吃饺子了，我们见面后换一个地方，去吃牛肉米粉！我知道哪家好吃！"陈雄说："好的，明天见！"

就这样，第二天早上六点多钟，李华就和陈雄前后不差三分钟到了饺子馆。见面以后李华直接带着陈雄去了那条小吃街，很熟练地走进了牛肉粉店。老板娘非常热情地冲李华打招呼："今天来两份吗？"

李华友好地对老板娘说："对，再加两根油条。"

"好的，马上到，你们先坐下喝茶。"老板娘是重庆人，为人爽快热情。店里的食物味道正宗。

李华对陈雄介绍说："这米粉越辣越好吃，最后剩下的汤汁也不要浪费，你用油条沾上汤汁，浸泡两秒再吃，那味道你绝对喜欢！"

陈雄说："在这方面我得向你学习劳逸结合，边工作边享受。你还考虑投资了，你打算买房子自住，还是想在深圳这里拼搏试试？"

李华说："第一，我确实喜欢看房子，那种感觉让我太舒服了。第二，到合适的机会，如果有适合的投资机会，我当然也不会放过。正好在深圳，也没有其他知根知底的人，咱们是老同学一起出来聊得来，彼此信任。连我们中学班主任袁老师都支持我们要多联系多走动！你的电话号码还是袁老师告诉我的，袁老师真的好喜欢你这位得意门生。"

陈雄说："那是，袁老师最喜欢我，我心里有数。袁老师也喜欢你们这些女生，不然袁老师不会特意交代让我照顾你，带着你一点。我看这是老师多心了，其实都是你在带我玩，感觉你比我更熟悉深圳！"

陈雄的感觉是对的，李华没有一天闲着。她就是利用周末的休息时间，将周边及中心郊区所有的房地产信息，考察了一遍。说起房产分析，李华比陈雄了解的还透彻明了！陈雄佩服地说："我要是没有老婆，我可一定会追求你哟！"

李华笑着差点呛住了："打住，别拿我开玩笑。谁不知道你呀，你在学校的时候就追校花，会跳舞的那个。有一个文笔很好的亚君也暗恋你，你对人家也很好，可你又追校花！当年你是怎么想的？真是一个多情才子，我可不敢想。今天没有别人，你老实招，谈谈你的情史怎么样？哈哈哈！"

陈雄说："那都是过去的事，都还不懂事，别笑我了。说说你，怎么把那体面的机关工作放弃了，你还真勇敢，赶时髦下海呀？"

李华一下子安静了下来，声音低沉自嘲道："不得已啊，被逼无奈……好啦，别谈我了，还是说你吧！"

　　李华不想让老家熟人知道她第二任丈夫于平出轨的丑事，同学同事更不会说。李华忍得住，知道的人越多越有后患。老同学在一起，的确有说不完的话。相处起来轻松亲切，但是没有男女之间的邪念，反而无话不谈。只要不说自己的婚姻状态，说什么都可以聊。

　　吃完早餐，俩人赶紧上了去小梅沙海边的巴士。沿途俩人天南地北聊着，有伴陪着就是好，大约过了一小时就到了。那个时候陈雄还没有买小车，大巴车也很舒服，有空调。这一下车，就看到有举着看房广告牌子的售楼部美女，对下车的人介绍说："跟我们车去看海景房吧，有免费茶水甜点水果，还提供自助餐。"

　　"你信息灵通，佩服！我们就跟这美女走，去看样板房！"陈雄见美女就开心搭上话来。

　　李华和陈雄上了二十多人坐的看房车，沿途的海景尽收眼底。小姐在车上就开始用广播话筒介绍房源、周边环境、交通等条件，各种让人心动的好处，价格每平方只要 4300 元。当时罗湖 6000 元每平方，福田区价格是 6600 元每平方，龙岗房价是 4000 左右，各区的相差价格一目了然。

　　这趟一来，李华把深圳 2003 年的房地产行情统计了一下，心里有数了。按照李华的规划，如果有钱，如果找到适合自己工作，她会在全国大城市范围挑选自己喜欢的城市生活打拼。黄文的那些话她听进去了，她此刻很相信自己看到的房产势头，只要有钱，就要想办法买房。

第十六章 "咳嗽"积劳成疾

　　李华来深圳有一段时间了。深圳秋天的晚上，李华一个人躺在小床上，瞪眼看着房顶，想着如何进一步开展保险工作。此时李华感觉到很孤单，每天晚上就是这样一个人待在窄小的公寓。房间里只有几件简单的生活用品，凑合着生活，这不是她想要的环境。

　　她睡觉前会想起自己期待的家。对她来说，家就是人在哪里房子就在哪里。她不喜欢租房的感觉。这次来深圳就是想从零开始。李华选择了一座新城市，新环境。趁深圳是一座特区城市，发展前景机会更多。但在深圳生存并不容易，在深圳买房也不容易。但是李华有信心，她就这样勤奋，热心于关注房地产的信息，这种意念执着坚持下去，总有一天会有李华一处安身之居，她有感觉她会在即里发展，就一定有自己安身居住的一个小天地。

　　一连几个月的强化培训学习，以及奔波展业的辛苦，加上自己又吃一些辣的食物，最近李华的嗓子有些疼痛。也是因为推荐保险，要比以往说很多话，而且还要注意说的话题，不能直接说保险，得说好像与保险没有关系的内容。通过拉家常，引出保险的话题。这样下来，嗓子很劳累。

　　这时李华的嗓子疼得受不了，不能再拖了，得赶紧吃药打针抑制。印象中这公寓楼附近有一个私人小诊所。白天去帝王大厦的路上，李华有见到门前挂着白红色十字布帘的小诊所。李华虽然很难受，还是得自己从床上爬起来去看病。她随便穿上一件宽松的外套，拿起无论走到哪里都要提着的那个包，那是李华最值钱的东西，装着身份证及银行卡。

　　夜晚九点，小诊所还有一些坐着打针的病人。李华看到里头还有两张空床。

　　李华对医生说："医生麻烦你看看，我有些咳嗽，能打几瓶消炎针吗？我嗓子特别干疼！"

医生拿出小木签叫李华张大口，用小木签压下舌头检查："对，你嗓子出血，已经红肿了，得先打三天吊针消炎，打吗？"

李华说："打，现在就打，能躺在那床上打针吗？我想睡着打会好受点？"

医生说："可以的，要收床费10元。"

李华此刻只想赶紧就医打针，早点好，少受罪。她猛地向医生点点头，从包里拿出银行卡刷了三天的打针费用，另外还开了一些吃的消炎药和止咳糖浆。

小诊所共有两个人值班，一个医生一个女护士，服务态度挺好。十分钟不到护士就配好了药，走到里间床边，对李华喊名字。核对确定是李华，就开始做皮试了。15分钟过后，护士看过皮试对李华说："还好，你不过敏，可以打吊瓶了！"

针水打进李华静脉，李华几乎没有感觉，这护士手法轻巧，打针没有痛苦。看着药水一滴一滴地进入身体，李华精神上好像舒服了一些，也许是思想作用。

这个时候李华衣兜里手机响了起来。李华让护士拿出手机，接通电话递给她。电话里传出她熟悉的声音："华华，你好吗，在干吗？"

真是怕什么就来什么，这个声音搅得她心神不宁。她躲得这么远，还是被于平找到了。从于平出轨后，李华感觉他不配众人习惯的称呼"于先生"，所以在内心里已经直呼全名。

"于平，请你别再叫我小名华华，现在请称呼我全名李华！你是怎么知道我在深圳？"

于平电话声音传进李华的耳边："这不重要，要找到你很容易。重要的是，我要告诉你，我所在广州服装厂离深圳很近，乘火车只需要40分钟左右。我可以来看你呀！听你说话，好像嗓子沙哑，你生病了吗？明天是周末，告诉我详细地址，我来看你好吗？"

电话这头的李华静静听着，心想肯定不能让于平知道她现在住的地方。这里环境太差，如果让于平看到了，那不是让他看笑话吗？

"你不用来看我，我正在打针，吃药就会好的，没有事，我挂了！"

不一会电话又响起，护士没有走远，很机灵地又将电话接通放在李华手上，示意李华还是接电话吧，不然铃声会吵着其他打针的病人。没有办法，李华只得压低嗓子说："你说吧，还有什么事？"

于平温和磁性的声音再次响起："那等你病好了，来我广州服装厂吧。我会去火车站接你，我现在住在厂里单间套房宿舍，吃在职工小食堂。等你嗓子好了，下周来我这里吧。我厂里有一批女装和儿童装出口多余订单回库的衣服，用处理价格就能买到正品质量的衣服。你来玩玩，顺便可以多选择一些你喜欢的款式，还可以帮家人带点适合的衣服！我已经给你挑一些准备送给你，想想你自己来最好，可以多买点。"

于平太了解李华了，听于平说话的语气是诚恳的，因为以前于平也喜欢给李华买一些很时尚的衣服。

怎么办？李华不想让于平来深圳看到她暂住的地方，不想让于平看到她落魄病恹恹的样子，只得敷衍答应："等病好了，我再去广州看看。现在我想睡一会儿，挂了！"

手机终于安静了下来了。其实于平是性情中人，他对谁都好，耳根子软，如果不是图他性格好，当初李华也不会冒险二婚嫁给他。但是于平触碰了婚姻中最忌讳的底线，专一忠诚都没有做到。所以就算于平再好，他已经在李华心目中一落千丈。只是曾经有过的爱和缠绵，常常折磨着李华。

李华暗地里还会把于平跟一些向她示好的男人比较，这证明李华还是没有彻底放下。在李华心里她还是很爱很在乎于平，至今都没有释怀，没有真正地放下。

闭上眼睛躺在病床上打针的时间里，李华的脑袋像在做梦一样，一场一场过往在脑子里快速闪现。她都没有察觉针水什么时候打完，还是护士的声音打断了她的思绪。护士拔掉针头，让李华按住手背针眼的创伤贴。

李华走出诊所已是晚上 11 点了。诊所是 24 小时营业，这私人医生也不容易，这么晚了还得守着诊所的病人！李华走向自己租的公寓，回家倒床就睡了，这一觉睡到天亮。

及时就医，连续三天打针，李华体质还是很好，很快恢复过来了。

一晃又快到周末了，她在考虑要不要去广州看看于平的服装厂，顺便了解他的近况。这也是一个机会，无论怎样她必须面对于平，是分是合都得处理，不能总是这样躲避和拖着。看看于平的具体情况，再做打算。而且还可以去看看广州的房地产，这才是李华去广州的真正原因。

　　说来也怪，每次李华想到什么，就会出现什么。这时手机又显示有人来电，一看手机号码就知道是于平打来的。

　　"喂，好些了吧。这个周末星期六你来广州吧，今天去买好火车票好吗？我等你信息，告诉我火车票班次，我来接你！"

　　李华心里其实已经说服了自己，可不知怎么回事，对于平的邀请，她还是很纠结很矛盾。换句话说就是又爱又恨。

　　李华想了一分钟说："好吧，我来，现在就去火车站买星期六的票。另外你能星期天陪我去广州白云山吗？我想去看一个新开销售的楼盘。"

　　于平秒回："可以啊，你星期六来，把衣服选好，晚上带你去吃广州地道菜。你多喝点广州煲汤，补充营养。星期天就专程陪你看房，晚饭后送你去火车站，返回的火车票我们到了站台再买票。返回不赶时间，几点到几点就走，很方便的。"

　　于平小心说着，李华听到于平的口吻几乎在哄着她。她心里想，早知今日何必当初啊！

　　火车班次多，车票很好买，特快也不到 100 元。李华将火车票拍照片，发短信给了于平。一切准备就绪，到了星期六李华简单地带上小包和一部手机就出门，就像串门的样子，穿着上很有知性女人的味道。病后痊愈的李华还是有些柔弱，反而看起来更显温柔妩媚，更有女人韵味。

　　李华特意挑选了一件很柔软的连衣裙，上身白色背心，下身浅黄色小花裙子。那是 1999 年，李华和于平还有女儿小琳在上海游玩时买了这套衣服，现在穿起来还是那么合身。李华身材很好，标准体重，看起来很苗条。李华戴着一副墨眼镜和一顶白色的大太阳帽，肩上挂一个很小的挂包，里面只能装一个钱包、一部手机。李华喜欢这裙子的质量面料，太适合南方城市穿了，轻装上阵的样子比深圳人还像城市人，到广州这行头也像广州女子。李华想着，虽然瘦了一圈，可人还变漂亮了，这要感谢于平啊！不用减肥都保存着当年的风韵！

　　李华刚上火车就睡着了，就像是眯了一会儿火车就到了广州。近年铁路高速发展，距离很远的人当天就可以相见，这科技发展得太快了。祖国日新月异的变化，城市道路都在扩建之中，马上又有了城际高铁投入各大城市，这座特区深圳发展更为有利，深圳是加速发展城市中的领头羊。

第十七章　就此永远别见了

出火车站的那一瞬间，于平一眼就看见李华站在亮眼的地方，上前就牵着李华的手说："我一眼就认出这条熟悉的裙子。你真苗条，变漂亮了，一路还顺利吧。你看多方便，以后有空休息，可以常常过来聚聚。"

李华没有答话，只是看着于平，心想：让我瘦下来的不是你吗？看来我还因祸得福咧！

李华出站跟在于平身后，直接上了停车场一辆宝蓝色小轿车。这是服装厂销售部的车，到了厂里，于平直接带李华去仓库房，挑选出口转内销的衣服。从儿童到女装和老人服饰，李华都给家人挑选了适合他们的衣服。她忘我地挑选，甚至忘了身体才恢复不久，依然有点虚弱。

李华终于选了三十多件，从来没有这样爽过，就该让这个男人破费了！以前李华省钱舍不得给自己买多少衣服，每次出差总给于平买纪念品，领带、衣服、钱包也没有少买。现在如果还帮于平省钱，谁知道他会把钱贴给哪个贱女人用去了呢？李华这样一想，一下子就心安理得。不管怎样，现在李华还是于平合法的妻子。

李华想到这里，心里骂道："这男人真是贱，对他好的时候不珍惜；没有把他当一家人了，却像哈巴狗一样黏着！"

于平助理对李华说："李姐你放心，于厂长已把你要买的衣服全部付款了。我给你包好，放在于厂长办公室桌上。"

女人都喜欢买衣服，有事情做时间过得就是快，一晃到了下午下班的时间。于平把衣服结账，将服装拎到宿舍楼公寓放好。他在冲凉房洗了个澡，换上一套新的衣服，看上去精神了许多，比他在厂里接单谈事看起来要更精神许多。人靠衣服马配鞍，这话一点不假。

于平跟李华到一个中式餐厅吃晚餐，那里有乐队演奏，气氛浪漫。那汤清淡鲜美，喝完汤后李华没有吃多少东西。瘦了之后，似乎胃也变小了，李华的饭量像吃猫食。

第二天于平带李华到广州白云山楼盘看房，那里的房子看上去很高档，最贵的房价跟北京东三环的价格差不多，6700 元一平方。样板房设计得合理适用，正正方方，一点都没有浪费空间。李华喜欢这房子，但是不太喜欢广州，只是过把看房子的瘾，顺便了解房子在不同城市的行情，对以后最终决定在那个城市发展，就在那里选择房子做一个比较，可以很快速地拿出决定，因为机会总是留给有准备好的人，边攒钱边寻找出路，边努力是李华最有效的办法，就是行动，认真做好每一个阶段该做能做的事情，时间对每个人都很公平，李华不会浪费一点时间，就是短暂的周末休息，也要带着梦想的意念去靠近目标去努力。

这段时间以来，李华最大的收获就是把深圳和广州的房价作了比较，哪里适合生活，李华心中有数。她也意识到跟于平不可能再续前缘了，虽然他们还没离婚，但已分居快两年了。这次来广州游玩，在厂里工人面前，他俩是一家人；但在吃晚餐的那个晚上，于平就像是做了错事的贼——偷女人的贼。

李华也看过于平居住的宿舍，不能更简单普通的生活环境。于平在厂里工人面前才表现出自信和优越感。李华发现于平已经不是那个她曾经深爱的男人，现在的于平配不上自己。李华住厂里宿舍那晚，于平为李华铺床，在隐约的月光下，李华默默望着于平的背影，她看到于平头发稀少，有的地方已经秃顶。她突然又想到于平跟汪芹兰在一起的情景，顿时倒胃口，想吐。她跑进卫生间，干吐几口水，洗口洗头洗脸刷牙，磨磨蹭蹭搞腾了半天才从洗手间出来。那时候躺在床上的于平已经睡着了。

李华盖上床单，慢慢地躺在外沿，不知道什么时候睡着的。醒来的时候，于平早就起来了。李华知道她跟于平一样，心结没有解，两人的生活永远只是赎罪和小心客气。两人都承受着触景生情的精神负担。

这趟广州之行，是开始也是结束，是李华跟于平最后一次的团聚。李华已经预见了他们的将来，如果两人在一起生活，两人的内心没有爱情，只有可悲和无情的罪恶感。这样的婚姻有必要维持吗？

通过这一次广州之行，李华摸清了广州的房地产行情，也知道今后该如何面对于平。她会回老家城市，悄悄地办理该办的法律程序，解除两人的婚姻关系。李华觉得是时候离开这个男人了，对他的感觉没有爱也没有恨，只有可怜。她也理解于平只喜欢待在厂里的原因，在那个环境中他才有男人的自信，能人模狗样地装腔作势。现在的他早不是从前的于平。李华连分手都不想跟于平说，还是怕伤到他，想给于平留下男人的尊严。还是不要说穿吧，悄悄地放下，放过于平，也放过自己。

离开广州火车站已是夜晚七点钟，于平帮李华拎着装衣服的大包，送她到车厢座位上。叮嘱了李华几句就马上出去，在站台上站着，一直等待火车发动才离开。李华看着他远远的影子变小变得模糊不清。火车在夜幕中向着前方冲刺，火车在轨道上奔驰得越来越快，像是在对李华说：一切不顺其自然，终会到头，你终会冲破束缚去往新的目标前进！

回到深圳已经是夜晚，秋风落叶吹过街道两旁，依稀三三两两的人影，有很多情侣在散步，依偎在一起。这是回宿舍的必经之路，夜宵大排档还有很多人吃着聊着，那桌底下摆放着一箱箱空酒瓶子，看来生意很不错。

瞬间李华想起从前跟于平在老家一起吃夜宵的情景，当时两人的恩爱并不亚于现在这些年轻人。当时两人的热恋也让人羡慕，于平高大帅气，说一口纯正的普通话，总能让女人们喜欢。就连长辈们也喜欢于平那身派头，文质彬彬的气质让人不知不觉地对他产生好感。

现在李华能真正摆脱心里的结，她跟于平的恩恩怨怨仿佛在今天晚上做出了结。李华告诉自己，这一次一定得彻底走出来，毕竟对于平的那份恨和爱，已经用可怜的感觉代替了。没有必要再跟于平纠缠不清，事实上已证明彼此之间，无论如何努力宽容和做努力，都会触景生情，带来刚刚淡忘的又重新点燃心中那隐藏在内心的刺痛，真还不如不见，让岁月淡忘自然消失那曾经已逝去的爱情，走吧，走得越远心里会越干净！

想到就做到，李华在下一个周末就果断搬进妞妞的小区房。李华每个月按说好的 500 元租金支付给妞妞，比起以前少 100 元。在创业初期能省 100 是 100。创业真不容易，幸好环境还好，而且两人可以做伴。

自从李华搬进妞妞的房子后，房间经常传出俩人的笑声。这间往日冷清的房子也有了人气，她们同进同出，厨房里也常看到两人忙碌的身影。妞妞会做一道东北乱炖，李华会将湖北的特色菜肴每顿换一个花样。妞妞做东北乱炖一会工夫就好了，两个人就这样喝点啤酒，边吃边聊，穷开心的日子也很简单。

　　这种互补取暖的小日子过得很遐逸。妞妞对李华说："女人离开了男人一样可以过得潇洒，不是吗？"

　　其实李华搬到妞妞的住处，也是为了杜绝自己心软。她怕以后万一于平找理由来看她，她就用与女伴同租一屋不方便为由，可以礼貌地拒绝。因为这是实情，说出口容易。李华不善于说假话，也讨厌谎话连篇的人，哪怕是对一个背叛过自己的男人，她还是坚持着以真性情对待。

第十八章　互诉秘密

妞妞和李华白天一起去人才市场做接待登记工作。因为是朋友推荐的就业登记，公司准时每月将保底金打到卡上。人民币真好，已收到两个月的保底工资了，吃盒饭的钱也有了保障。其他费用，计划买房必攒钱，将在做成保险单后，还会有业绩工资奖励。那些日子除了正常必需的生活费保证，以外的花销全减，李华都将零钱全部归集攒着，攒着到可以用来交首套房子的首付，终有一天，会找到适合自己又有能力购买房的机会，李华不是做梦，她是开始朝着计划目标迈进前行，从没有退缩过，甚至越走越见到了曙光！

对新人来说，前三个月是展业的观察期。适合不适合投身保险行业，在最初的冲刺阶段就能看出来，能在冲刺阶段坚持下来的新人，一般做保险行业是没有问题的。

有一天晚上，妞妞跟李华聊天时突然说到自己的家庭。妞妞拿着一本很旧的影集，在客厅的沙发上坐下来，打开影集拿出一张五岁小女孩的照片："看看我哥的孩子好不好看，我在老家时候经常去看我哥的孩子，我现在非常想她。"

妞妞聊着她家里的事情，谈到侄女就情不自禁地低头抚摸照片上的女孩，接着整理一下情绪又谈到她香港男朋友的事情。她说："我可能会在下半个月离开这个地方，因为男朋友已经有一个多月没来了，这很不正常。在以前每个周末他都会来聚两天，你见过我的男朋友，长得像老板港仔，很帅是吧。你觉得他像没有结婚的吗？他原来只付了半年租金，这里快要到期了，要再续租金才能居住，而且是需要半年一次性交清，如果那港仔不来，证明这爱情必假无疑，我还有必要守着这套空房吗？"

李华说："我感觉他有家庭。如果他最近不来，房子到期，你也没有必要再续租了。一个月3000元的房租不便宜，而且你也没有必要住这么大的房子。我建议你下个月之前几天离开这里，你说呢？"

妞妞说："香港男人在深圳包二奶的事例有很多，我不敢朝这方面去想。但是搞不好，我无意中成了他的二奶，我也不想这样过日子。这保险学到了，但我还没有做成几单。男朋友照顾了我一单，还有其他人买了两单，我都没有完成业绩。看来我不适合待在深圳，如果这港仔不做我的男朋友，不帮我，我也只得回去，看看我哥的孩子。"

说着说着，李华似乎听出妞妞对她的侄女有很深的感情，既思念又悲切，就像在想念自己的孩子。李华猜想那就是妞妞的孩子，两人长相很像。

妞妞无意中说漏了嘴，问李华："孩子长得真像我，你觉得是不是？"

李华慢慢抬头看着妞妞说："对比你的脸型和厚厚嘴唇，小女孩都像你。而且感觉你谈起这孩子特别伤心，好像有什么话要说。如果你有什么心事可以跟我聊聊，第一，我不认识你的身边的人，你跟我谈心事没有任何坏处。第二，你说出来心里会好受一些。第三，这里没有外人，不怕泄密。我最近咳嗽厉害，兴许比你更早回老家治病。"

那时是 2003 年，深圳和广州已经是非典型肺炎的重灾区。李华又说："在非典疫情下，我的咳嗽很耽误保险工作事情。只要有咳嗽，人家都躲得远远的，还真不适合谈保险了。如果你决定换小公寓，我可以在走之前帮你搬家。"

妞妞说："以后你治病还有单位可以报销，我只能回老家，还不知道要做什么工作。东北那地方气候太冷了，回去就不想工作。我估计回去先看看我的女儿。我不瞒你说，我还是要来深圳找工作。你猜对了，那女孩真是我的孩子，她已经五岁了。我离婚了，没办法一个人带孩子，我也舍不得离开她。我的前夫东北爷们好斗，又不负责任，老爱打人。你知道家暴吗？非常可怕，我跟他在一起，他经常打我，扯我头发。所以我把女儿送到我哥身边，我出来打工挣钱寄给我哥，给孩子每个月抚养费。我放心跟你说，也请你别怪我以前骗你。"

妞妞掀开衣服，让李华看她身上的伤疤。除了脸上是好的，全身都是伤痕，特别是乳房周边还有牙齿印。李华心痛难受地对妞妞说："没关系，你不是骗我，这是保护自己的好办法。"李华理解妞妞，善解人意地安抚她："别太难过，回家看一看孩子，想好以后再来发展也不迟。这个月也快要到期了，最近提前与房东中介办好离开手续，我可以走之前争取帮你搬走，把房退掉，这样你不拖欠房子租金了。那港仔不出现，你也不用再交下面的钱。不租房子，那你们俩人的关系就这样断了。顺便告诉他一声吧，QQ留言还是打手机号告诉他吧，不指望也别伤害彼此，毕竟曾经好过一阵子，也许那男人不能给你名分，只有悄悄以离开你这种方式，忏悔吧？"

　　妞妞说："很少打电话给他，我也不想打了。我知道这不是一种正常的恋爱关系。算了，男人都靠不住……那你回老家后，准备干些什么呀？"

　　李华说："我准备回老家，首先住院把病治好，然后趁这段时间把老家自己的房子卖掉。也把父母亲的老房卖掉，然后买一个大一点的房子，名字写老爸老妈的，让俩老人放心。这样我可以安心把他们安排好，再出来创业。也许跟你一样回深圳，也许不再回来了。我感觉来深圳只能顾到自己，父母和女儿我都顾不上。我想去女儿以后读大学的城市，到那里去创业，看是否能做点小生意，开个小服装店或者小茶楼。我很喜欢那种小资小调的生活状态，不需要挣很多钱，但要很干净，很温馨，很体面文艺的工作。我喜欢写作，但是一直想等工作稳定了，思想性情成熟了，再开始做这件事。梦想一定要有，我可要先养活自己为基础。我也可以攒点钱开一家很小店，看书学习那种'书吧'，我很喜欢那种小茶楼，可以疗愈我自己的内心。我很喜欢挑战自己，喜欢尝试各种喜欢的工作。反正不试一试，就是不甘心！"

　　"哇！谈着未来的想法，你说出来想做的事，好像离你生活很近呀，真爽！好佩服你，雄心勃勃！"妞妞笑着回复李华。

　　俩人聊着傻笑之后，李华说："我们都在做白日美梦啊。可若是不做美梦，我连活下去的勇气都没有了。"

　　李华看到妞妞对她讲了自己的隐私，也情不自禁地跟妞妞简单带过几句话，说了自己老公外遇的事情，李华不知道怎么去处理。劝妞妞有一套道理，但自己还是有点茫然，也在探索怎样在没有婚姻的情况下过好自己的小日子。李华对爱情和婚姻已经没有信心了，她也不想依赖男人。她想先回老家，把父母照顾好，把女儿照顾好，一边陪读一边创业。省城离老家不远，李华计划下个阶段就在家乡最近的省城发展。

　　从室内向窗外望去，可以看到繁华的深圳夜景，这是李华和妞妞曾经打拼过的城市。那高耸的大厦和低矮的公寓楼，还有杂乱的小房子，都曾是她们创业的见证者。

　　两个人在阳台看着灯光闪闪发光的风景，深圳的夜景让多少人向往，李华也一样，眺望着天空的繁星说："你看，我们就像这么多星星一样，一闪一闪而过。像我们这样的人，走到哪里都要像星星一样，自带光芒。一定要活得比以前更好，才对得起自己。"李华执着坚毅的眼神影响了妞妞，也给了她希望：离婚的单身女人，也能靠自己创造一切美好的归属。妞妞心里似乎也有了方向和奔头。

第十九章　离开深圳

前些日子李华在人才市场上又认识了一个同乡，是湖北新洲的一个美女，名叫静雯。李华见到老乡格外感到亲切，于是把静雯推荐给东北的妞妞。以后三人经常在一起吃饭，虽然是叫盒饭，每个人点一个菜，凑合起来大家换着吃，这样就可以吃到三种味道了。她们都懂得在外面要节省着过日子。

静雯就像她的名字一样，是个非常文静的姑娘，身形小巧，说话声音很特别。静雯长得很秀气，一眼看去，立体的大眼睛和高鼻子，几乎占了一半脸。妞妞觉得静雯特别斯文，很羡慕她年轻漂亮。

静雯之前的打扮看起来有点妖艳，一头染黄的头发。李华还为此提醒过静雯："能不能把头发染回来？你本来是个很好的女孩，要是不了解你，还以为你是坏女孩，现在人都比较以貌取人。再说我们做这行工作，给陌生人的第一印象最好是着装大方。我的年纪可以当你姐姐，所以我就直说了，你不介意我陪你去把头发染成自然黑吧？"

静雯说："我也知道你是为了我好，染回黑发当然没问题。以前在厂里工作要求统一工作服，所有女生看上去都不突出，有些女生就用染发的方式吸引别人的注意，我也是其中一个，你别笑我哟！"

现在静雯才意识到自己已经换了工作环境，她已经坐在办公室中工作，在这个环境中应该要表现得大方成熟。

静雯说："我听你的，谢谢你没把我当外人。我很感谢你直接提醒我，改掉做事往后拖的坏习惯，今天晚上下班我就去染回来。"

静雯来深圳有两年了，她原在龙华那边一家台资企业厂里工作，最近才在深圳人才市场附近租了一室一卫的公寓房。静雯跟李华说："之前我厂里的台湾老板想追我，才认识两个月，但感觉老板好像是有家室。不想跟老板有不清不白的关系，所以才从龙华那边搬到这边来。我想在这边找到工作，可以不在以前的厂里干，拒绝那位台企老板的追求。这里正好立足深圳市中心生活，我知道必须依靠自己才靠谱，这才是我来深圳的目标。"

静雯在厂里的工作太封闭了，全厂的打工妹都是外地姐妹。一天工作12个小时，很多机械性手工操作工作，还是感觉城市的活轻松些。静雯来到这边也是天意，这里录用门槛低，虽然只是做些没有技术含量的小事：照着已招聘录用的员工名单，经老板同意由静雯带人去到单位报到就好。李华和妞妞也是做相同的工作，把录用的员工与单位对接。将员工送到单位，就算是帮助应聘新人完成了工作交接的程序。

静雯搬家那天李华也来帮忙，静雯说："我这边搞好了，你也可以跟我一起住。我一个人在这边住，有时候弟弟周末过来，吃一顿饭后就走。"静雯是真心留李华住进她的小公寓，这里也方便李华上下班。

静雯很庆幸在这里认识老乡李华，虽然年龄比她大一整圈，但是看得到李华心地很友善，真心喜欢李华。李华也很放心与纯朴静雯做朋友，所以自然地帮助静雯做些实事搬家。李华没有想过任何沾光的想法，纯粹是对老乡给予举手之劳。

李华对静雯说："暂时不搬你这边来，因为我才搬到妞妞那边，住得还好。等过一段时间再说好吗？我得跟妞妞商量，免得误会有你没有她了。而且我感觉深圳气候的不适合我，我在深圳几个月里老在咳嗽。我又爱吃辣的，才打完吊针嗓子刚好，结果因为吃辣老毛病又犯了。现在我的嗓子已经成了慢性支气管炎，常常想咳嗽。你知道吗？我在做保险的时候跟人正在交谈，话才说了几句，突然嗓子痒，又要咳，又要忍。中途赶快跑到洗手间去，或者没有来得及躲避，当着客人面就咳了出来，真尴尬！最近非典太严重了，大家都很谨慎，小心躲避。我知道自己不是非典病，但别人不知道啊，特别是咳嗽的时候，别人下意识就想远离，根本没有心情跟我聊。这样下去，哪能有精力谈成保险，所以最近很费劲。这一个月我根本没有跟进的保险客户，一直在纠结着回老家治疗咳嗽，再来深圳工作。"静雯理解李华，就没有再坚持要李华搬进她的公寓。

那段时间，李华因为咳嗽的问题痛苦不堪。有些时候李华只能睡半天时间，真是连小便都咳出来了。她都不敢穿裙子，随身包里带上一条内裤，备带卫生巾。一旦咳嗽厉害，能立即应急解决。

这深圳的秋天，本来气候都很热，穿的衣服也不多。有一次真难看，不小心尿到裤子外面湿了一片。李华赶快在商场去买套休闲衣服，在洗手间换上，这样才解决了一时的难堪，才能坚持到下午去展业拜访见客户。

李华打针好像已经失效了，家人一直担心李华。坐火车回老家还需要检查要量体温，如果查出发烧，一定要被关在隔离区，还不能及时到医治咳嗽。那时非典传染发烧的人很多，非典的症状也是咳嗽。李华心里清楚自己不是非典病毒，但别人不知道。旁人不知道她是什么原因咳嗽，远离她是对的，这一点不能怪别人。

李华权衡了很多，还是准备回老家医治，其中一方面是有医疗保险在老家。只有把病治好，才能安心工作。这一次可能真的要离开深圳了。李华主意拿定后，选择了月底的前几天与妞妞和静雯商量这件事。

李华说："这段日子里幸好有你们，我们之间有了难舍难分的情谊。我先回去医治咳嗽，不知道会不会回深圳。如果不回深圳，我想我也不会选择在老家发展，我会选择在老家附近的省城，这只是我初步计划。其实我非常喜欢深圳，这里是一座年轻的城市，就业创业机会多啊，可我真的适应不了这里的环境。来了几个月，几乎隔一个月就咳嗽犯一次，实在受不了。身体健康很重要，你看我来深圳已经瘦了，现在还在继续瘦，像这样下去不正常。吃不好，睡不踏实。"

李华搬家退房的那天，深圳的天气很好。李华把自己所有生活用品都留给静雯使用，妞妞准备要退房子，也一同整理自己的行李，所有可用不可带的东西，都交给了静雯。来深圳前后半年多，妞妞走了，李华也走了，留下静雯，还有适合在那里坚持拼搏的人们。在那片土地上依然还有人继续在迷茫寻找中奋斗。

李华在心里说："深圳，我很喜欢你，可又不得不离开你。但是，我不后悔我曾经来过，奋斗过，并找到了适合我人生的转折！"

妞妞对李华说："我真谢谢你，让我下决心找到了人生目标。你转变了我的观点，以前我总指望找到一个爱我的男人就能好好生活，可事实让我清醒了，离婚后的女人要想幸福还是只能靠自己。"

静雯说："你们都走了，我真有些难过，但也很庆幸，很高兴和你们成为好姐妹。若你们再来深圳，无论是今后创业还是来旅游，都到我这里来。不要嫌弃我这个小家，欢迎你们来住，这就是你们的家。"

月底的最后一天，李华来到深圳的火车站。背向火车站，仰望天空，看着远处的车水马龙，人来人往。她意识到自己马上就要离开这里，李华对深圳已经有很深的眷恋。

第二十章　回到家乡

火车的鸣笛声把李华的思绪带回了即将奔赴的湖北，她的老家。

下车的那一天车站果然严查得很厉害，每个人必须量体温。庆幸的是李华在上车之前包里就准备了一包糖浆药片，药片放在嘴里，一旦想咳嗽的时候，就喝点水润喉。李华手中始终拿着一杯水，就这样保证一路没有咳嗽症状发生。

下了火车，李华没有惊动家人朋友去接她，而是自己直接来到熟悉的公交车站坐车。这里正好有一班车驶向李华家的小区，小区门前就有站台。

"家乡我回来了！"

李华真实感觉到在家千日好，出门一时难这句话的道理。李华回到家里，父母亲高兴得不得了，就是觉得李华消瘦了很多。

母亲心疼地问："在外面吃了不少苦吧？"

李华微笑着说："回家看到你们都好，就感觉不苦了。放心吧，一切都过去了。现在我就想直接到医院去把咳嗽治好，省得老妈老爸担心。"

李华父亲发声了："还知道回呀，那么好的工作说不干了就辞工内退，也不想想这把年纪。也不小了，都四十多岁的人了，女儿在读书，这个家没你不就散了吗？不说你了，回来就好。赶快去把病看好，这个咳嗽把人瘦成这个样子，还真不爱惜自己。"

李华父亲是个急性子，但是最疼大女儿李华，从小都是把她当男孩子养。在李华的童年时代，每次父亲周末钓鱼都把李华带在身边。李华跟着父亲一起钓鱼，捉鳝鱼，来改善生活。那个 80 年代，父亲勤奋持家顾家，家里的生活由母亲打点安排，两人配合着把孩子们尽量改善基本生活。

李华放下行李箱，简单收拾了一下，母亲非要李华喝一碗排骨藕汤再出去。李华看到满满一碗最喜欢喝的汤，也毫不推辞一口气喝完，满嘴都是油。这一路下来她也真饿了。

母亲说："别急，慢慢来，别烫着。还有汤，还可以再给你一碗。"

"妈做的排骨煲莲藕汤真好喝，吃饱了，从来没有吃这么饱。老妈老爸我去医院彻底检查，别担心哈！"

李华准备看女儿的事就安排在出院以后，李华不想影响女儿小琳的学习。二妹把女儿照顾得很好，替李华当妈做了很多生活上的事情。李华放心将小琳交给妹妹们照顾，她很信任这个大家庭，亲人对女儿的照顾比自己还周到。

出了小区大院，来到巴士车站，直接两站路程就到了妇幼医院。医生检查完李华的喉咙，对她说："你得的是慢性咽炎和支气管炎，你的喉咙炎症很重，都咳出血丝了。拖这么久才来，有几个月了吧？"

李华回答："是的，三个月前就开始咳嗽。打了十几天针就好起来了，接着不小心吃辣的，又咳起来。气候干燥的时候，反反复复一直咳，一直没有治好，隔一段时间就打两三天针。"

医生摇摇头，直接说："你需要住院，赶快办理住院手续吧。单位就在这附近，对面这么近，怎不来看病？"

医生说的没有错，李华的工作单位就在医院的斜对面。医生不知道李华已不在单位上班了，而是远去深圳打拼。李华也不好解释，只是微微笑着说："是的，现在咳得受不了，才来看病，想彻底治好！"

医生说："你今后一定不要再吃辣的了。辛辣食物一律戒掉，千万不能再吃了。不然会反复，会得慢性支气管炎病，那就更麻烦了，以后治疗都难，一定要爱惜自己啊！"

李华笑着连连说："好的，我戒，我真不敢再吃辣椒了！"

拿出诊断病历，退出医生门诊去大厅办理入院手续，医疗费单位可以报80%，李华只缴了入院费用。

李华此时体会到作为一名单位职工有多好，这些福利是国家给的。她从心里感激能出生在中国，还有一份这么好的福利享受，在生病的时候给她安慰，不用担心看不起病，而是很安心地治疗。

在住院治疗的期间，单位工会主席还代表单位领导特意来医院看望李华，带来了亲切的问候。安慰李华："一定要好好治疗，内退和退休人员都是我们的员工，我们一致同仁。你们也是响应当年组织政策的号召，所以一致同仁。"

这使李华放下了精神压力，从心里感激有国才有家，有家才有个人发展的良好社会主义大环境，这种感觉是走出后才体会到有领导组织关心真好！

李华想起她的好友谢华也是单身女人，当年在市领导迎春晚会上认识。领导还开玩笑说："你们两个名字带华，幸好不在一个单位，以后别弄错了，要经常互相往来哟！"

谢华的老公因为得了癌症去世，年龄只比李华大两岁。谢华长得一双大眼睛，一根长辫子，在当时算是很出众的一位女性。李华和谢华住得近，两人认识后经常在市政府的花园草坪周边见面，沿着湖畔散步聊天。有时相约清晨一起打羽毛球，有时候约在周末下午在李华单位一起打乒乓球，有些时候相伴买菜，再各自回家。

李华想到这里，立马拿起手机给谢华发了信息。通了电话获知李华生病住院了，谢华直截了当问李华在医院几号房："等我半小时，我带些吃的给你，不要吃医院的饭了，我做一些带过来，等我！总算可以见面了，可没想到在医院见你。真是的，怪不得不陪我打球啊，跑了那么远，来了再来说你。"

谢华跟李华的友情还真的没话说。谢华是一个非常爽快的人，而且现在女儿也长大了，去读大学，家里就她一个人，整天在露台里摆弄着一些花，她喜欢养花。李华曾经去过谢华的家，有时候也在谢华家吃饭。谢华的厨艺很好，现在肯定有了更大的进步。谢华说过没事就经常琢磨着怎么做好吃菜肴，现在自己一个人也不想谈恋爱了，反正得把自己的身体照顾好。

谢华走进病房，冲着李华笑了笑："你终于老实了，你只有生病的时候才乖。什么时候跑深圳去了，也不告诉我一声。要是我知道你在深圳，我就该答应我的同学，那个一直对我好的男同学，他一直劝我去深圳发展，让我去他公司工作。我刚办退休了，这个年龄去深圳合适吗？没想到你从深圳回来，你在深圳觉得好吗？"

谢华就是那种大嗓子讲话的女人，人没到屋，声音先到屋。一连串的问话，把李华逗笑了："我知道你来会说我的。听实话，深圳气候真好，如果有熟人在那里，你直接去工作能上班吧，真的值得重新开始你的新生活。再说你那男同学也是单身，对你那么好，人家肯定是认真对你，你应该考虑一下了。你已经单身几年了，自从丈夫去世以后，你就没有一个男朋友照顾你。如果有人真心对你好，我建议你还是去吧！"

谢华说："我现在还拿不定主意，还一直想我那房子怎么办？还有我的单位后面的一些事情，怎么处理？"

李华说："这好说，你跟深圳那边联系好，决定去了，你就把这边的房子卖掉。现在房改已经成为自己的 100% 的产权。"

李华劝说道，也把自己的想法对谢华全盘托出。李华把随身带的本子从包里拿出来，叫谢华记住电话号码，是房地产中介的联系人。李华也想做这件事，她要把自己的房子卖掉，还要把父母的老房子也卖掉。当时李华听进三妹的建议，已经选好了一个绿化非常好的小区房子，准备买一所大房子。把这些想法说完，李华恨不得马上就操作，执行力超强真像李华父亲，同样 A 血型的人性格，具有组织领导能力，还有两种性格，适应能力也强，还特沉得住气，同时又喜欢浪漫的情怀。

李华当面指教谢华，在谢华的面前打通了房产中介的电话："喂！我的美女小秦，你现在方便吗？"

小秦回答："方便，美女姐姐请说，有什么事情要我做？是要卖哪套房子啊？"

李华说："哈哈，你怎么知道我要卖房子？你是孙悟空钻到我的肚子来了？"

中介小秦说："我知道，只要看到你的电话，我就知道你有好事，一定是又要发财了。卖房子又买房子是吧？你把你要卖掉房子的小区、楼层、面积、想卖的价格告诉我。我帮你挂在网上，积极推荐！"

李华说："好的，我马上用手机发短信，把全部信息内容发给你。另外我还有一个朋友也要卖掉房子，我把你的手机号告诉她，这美女姐姐名叫谢华，让你们直接联系。你一定也要帮她卖个好价，她是我很好的朋友。"

挂下电话的李华，马上调皮地冲着谢华笑着说："把电话给抄上，就找这小秦，她人非常好，我几套房子都是她帮着联系买家给我房子卖掉，不用你操心。你把电话先留着，有事直接跟她打电话约，去她办公室好好把你的房子详细情况说出来，她会帮你的。"

谢华开心地笑着说："你就这样三下两下的就可以把房子卖掉了，真服了你。我这次没白来看你，看来你在医院要住几天，我就得天天来陪你一下。没想到你能把我的心病治好了，这么多年我都下不了决心，你让我下定决心了。

这回就听你的，把这房子卖掉。你知道吗？我每次回到那个家，就总想起我女儿她爸。所以还真的要换个环境，换个山头，重新开始。"

李华说："别跟我客气，不要谢我，其实女人都很难，首先要爱自己。轻装上阵才能走远，这卖房子估计要花一个月左右时间。该办的早点办，不要拖泥带水，我们的时间就是金钱！"

第二十一章　写上父母亲名字的第一套房产

　　住院七天一晃就过了，在这七天的时间里，谢华真的做到天天来陪李华，两个人有聊不尽的话题。谢华的房子只挂了五天就有客户相中了，这也不奇怪，房子的路段确实好：谢华从她家走到医院只要五分钟时间，如果加下楼两分钟，七分钟就到了。谢华把房子有买家的好消息告诉了李华，真心感谢李华帮自己解决了大问题。

　　李华的房子在网上也有人打听，而李华母亲那处八十多多平方的小房子，有人看中了。李华按当年行情挂价 4 万 5 千，结果对方买家还价。买房的是一个年轻男孩子，准备结婚当新房用。买方很有诚意，就是想买过来后，第二年装修结婚用。这是一个农村男孩，大学毕业后分到这座三线城市工作。在大学里谈了一个女朋友，准备过些日子和女友领证。如果没有婚房，女方父母不放心女孩嫁给他。他不想让农村的父母亲操心，于是小两口急着买房，做好成家立业的大事。

　　中介小秦跟李华说出实际谈判情况："李姐，我也想给你卖个好价，但是这个小伙子还真的是诚心买房。他已经来我们这边两次了，我都不好意思跟你说。本来你的价格也不高，但他还要砍价，我都不知道怎么谈了。现在把实际情况跟你讲，我想听听你的想法。"

　　李华的妹妹给李华介绍了一套新房，付定金两万就能定下来，后期就可以操作签购房合同了。因为特殊关系，可以先交钥匙装修。想到这里，李华马上回电话说："小秦你跟他谈，如果我降价 5000，那么四万块钱成交，但是他要付定金两万，而且必须确保我在搬家之后延期五个月退房。合同一定要备注退房时间，退房当天补齐尾款 2 万元。如果他同意就签约，这是我最后底线，不能再让了。"

　　小秦欣喜地说："好的，我就按李姐的意思去谈，应该没问题。我也跟他说了，这套房的主人很好。这小伙子是遇上贵人了，你这么帮他，我尽量照你的意见来。谢谢你理解，李姐你不发财都难！"

李华放下电话后，紧张地操作买大房子的事情，那可是将来父母亲的家。人们常说有父母在的家就是最好的风水宝地，李华必须好好操作，让父母亲住得舒服！

李华出院后就办这件事情，选择了一个吉日，按母亲的意思带上一个苹果，图个平平安安。李华在办正事大事时，还是有些紧张，因为家中无男主替她做决定，她必须谨慎行事，全凭自己判断拿主意，签了合同就没有回头的机会，如果犹豫不决也会错失良机。

三妹带着李华来到售楼部，房子已经看好了，李华直接带定金2万签合同。合同写上要在5个月全部付清总款，然后拿钥匙开门验现房。

李华考虑到那个时间点，她自己的现住房肯定已经卖掉了，这样房款就有着落了，今天付款2万定金是父母住房卖出的定金。这事衔接得很漂亮，也不需要把父母的房子卖掉后，还要急着找住的地方。李华想好了，拿到钥匙就可以请装修队伍进场。她跟装修包工头谈好了，两个月时间装修完，放三个月透气除味，正好是五个月时间，应该没多大问题。

想到后来的安排，李华觉得又有正事要干，心里很充实。这才是干实事，为父母亲做了一件最大的好事，也是当女儿最应该要付出的孝心。李华知道这件事必须办成功，给辛苦了一辈子的父母晚年一个好的归宿。父母亲一辈子都在替孩子们着想，从来没有想到过享受生活，总是省吃俭用地补贴着李华的生活。如果孩子们没有回家，父母每餐就吃两个素菜；可孩子们一回来，总有好鱼好肉好菜招待，让孩子们吃好吃饱。饭菜安排上两老简单凑合着他俩自己，李华发现过几次，心里很难受。这辈子亏待谁，都不能让父母受苦了！必须改善父母亲的生活状态。提高他们的生活水平，就从居宅改善做起。

从售楼部出来后，李华长长地松了一口气。房子已经卖了一套，父母亲可以继续住在老房子里，直到5个月后搬迁新家。这是李华此行回老家要办的第一件大事。

李华准备再叮嘱一下中介小秦，把自己的那套房子抓紧时间找到客户尽早卖掉，因为没有太多时间，她不能拖延了。李华希望新房写上父母的名字，如果要这样做就不能贷款。因此一定要赶在交房之前把房子卖掉，付清全部房款。

李华这样做是为了让父母亲住得踏实。身为家中长女，李华带一个好头，为妹妹们做一个孝敬父母的好榜样。做这些事，李华没有跟妹妹们商量，只是跟父母亲长谈了置换房子的设想，然后就大胆稳妥地操作程序。

李华对父母说："这件事你们放心，我一定把它办好。卖出去的房子已经收了定金，我用这些定金购置新房。合同已签，房产证写上你们的名字。你们可以住在原来的老房子，新房子装修好以后敞开透气三个月，再由老妈选择一个吉日搬家就可以了。"

李华母亲关心地问："我和你爸这所房子真的已经卖掉了？人家买了房，会等我们住那么长时间？不会中途要赶我们吧？"

父亲一听这话就急着又问："这么快卖掉了，别人还让我们住几个月？哪有这好的买主呀！"

李华说："人家也不是傻子，他同意我们住几个月，是因为他在房价总款里减了我们5000元。相当于我们反过来让利给他。这相当于租金，从我签合同当日算起，这后期的五个月就算是租了他的房子。这样买主少花5000元钱，对他有利他当然同意，只是让我们租住五个月！不这样操作，我们还要出去临时找房子租住，临时又搬一次家多麻烦，家具都搬散了架！"

老妈又问："新房子首付款还没付清，只给定金2万，他们就可以把新房钥匙给你？"

李华急着解释说："这是三妹夫的面子啊，他跟老板打了招呼，告诉他我购房的思路和可行计划。老板知道我有能力付清全款，他在开发商那里为我担保了。按照合同中备注执行，若是买方失信违约，我会双倍赔款。当然肯定不会发生那种事，我会积极地配合中介把房子卖掉。你们就别担心了，我知道怎么操作，我会抓紧时间办理这件事。"

两位老人真的没有什么可说的了，李华父亲只是叹息道："在这住了三十多年，你们姐妹都是从这里嫁出去的。从小到大就这二室半一厅一卫一厨一阳台的房子，我们一家六口人都住得蛮好的，也不觉得房子小。现在剩下我们两个老家伙了，反而还能住进新房子，大房子。我从未想过会有这么一天，老伴你说说看？"

　　李华母亲回答道："这还不是我们养的女儿孝心！老伴，你别再认为没有生儿子就低人一等，断了这些封建想法吧。那些有儿子的家庭，有几个能帮父母亲买房子住？你看看我们单位有几个儿子女儿给父母买房的？以后再别对女儿说什么'嫁出去的女儿，泼出去的水，女儿就是赔钱货'，真的不能这样说了！我们的孩子们都不错，都很孝敬我们这俩老，没有话说！"

　　李华父亲说："女儿们都是好孩子，我知足，知足常乐啊！那以后搬到大房子去了，那些老同事，老朋友，肯定会高兴羡慕我们。这事我只打算准备跟老董和老吕讲。"

　　李华母亲说："是啊，你这两个好同事好朋友，都认识 40 年了，是值得深交的好人。到时候搬了新家，请他们来家里坐坐，好好喝几杯酒。我亲自下厨，好好招待他们。老董和老吕这两个朋友真的不错，也是你的入党介绍人。当年入党都是他们同意，才有了你后来担任服务公司工会主席的提拔。这两个朋友可都是你的贵人啊，我们应该记得人家的好，好好感恩。"

第二十二章　报答父母恩

　　李华看到父母亲一问一答的聊天，心里涌出许多感慨。小时候的日子虽然过得清贫，但是很快乐温暖，父母亲没有因为贫困，而忽略孩子们的教育。在李华的印象中，父母亲在对待每一个女儿的基础教育方面，都很开明，积极鼓励女儿们好好学习。只要女儿们想读书，父母一定送她们去最好的学校念书。

　　李华上中学那个时候，学校经常搞学工学农活动，一个学期中几乎有一半时间在务工务农。学校会跟农场和工厂挂钩，定期安排学生去学习工人阶级的勤工俭学，学习农民伯伯种田割谷子。半学期的课程学习中，只简单学习部分语文、数学、物理、化学、政治、地理、体育这七门课，当年没有开设英语课程。

　　在李华父母眼中总感觉孩子没有学到真正的文化知识，所以在李华上初二时，李华父亲已经托人把她从农场里接回来，第二天就送进当年最好的县一中学读高中。李华转学后没有多久，这所重点中学又陆续转来几个初中同校的同学，他们跟李华一起读过小学初中。他们的成绩都很好，只是没有分到同一个班。这里的高中分文科班、理科班、重点班、普通班。李华先在普通班学习，后来因为作文写得好，被分配到文科班，担任劳动委员。

　　李华父亲把她从工人厂办子弟学校转到县城最好的高中，这件事遭到很多人的不理解。那个年代批判走资派，知识分子被批为臭老九。李华父亲对孩子们的学习没有掉以轻心，在他眼中这是一件人生大事。父母都非常重视女儿们的学习，一直把女儿送往好学校去念书学习，让孩子们培养起良好的求知欲。李华想到这里，不由得佩服父母亲的高明之处。

　　后来李华母亲鼓励二女儿："老二呀，你那年高考，已考取了湖北艺术学校，绘画专业，因没有学费，家里经济不宽裕，没有让你上大学，为了改善经济，你像大姐一样太懂事了，因为这个家呀，你才当了临时工，现在厂里子女又有两个报考名额，只要考得上中专技工学校读书，我和你老爸就支持你去读书。别当这个临时工了，看你的一双手冻得像肉包子一样，又红又肿，还裂开口子了。孩子啊，乖，听话，考出去学习两年，去当个老师，比现在这份工作更适合你!"

二妹听进了父母亲的话，认真复习，从实习工中考取了技工中专学校。二妹聪明好学，考试被录取了，直到学业完成毕业，并荣幸地留校当了一名大专老师，后期工作每年被评为高级讲师。

时隔一年，李华母亲也鼓励三女儿去当幼师。三女儿能歌善舞，特别适合当幼师。那个年代的人认为没有文凭就没有实力，当幼师必须要有上岗证。三女儿默默利用业余时间复习幼师专业文化课考试内容，终于在参加工作的第二年考到幼师资格证书，成为一名幼师班主任。

后来李华父母把小女儿培养得同样优秀，小女儿在高中时获得全国数学竞赛第二名，直接保送到中国科技大学读书，国家负担一切学习费用。小女儿毕业后分配到北方省城银行工作，一干就是八年。小女儿边工作边学习，最后通过自学，又考取了英国剑桥大学，留学英国两年，获得精算师学位。

李华心想，她们姐妹几个如今在工作和生活上都过得很不错，这跟父母亲的关爱和细心栽培分不开的。李华深深地认识到，是父母亲将无私的爱都给予了孩子们。现在女儿们都长大了，每个人都成家立业，过上了自己的好日子。每个小家庭都有自己的房产和家!

虽然李华遭遇了两次婚姻不顺的打击，家人也从来没有歧视她，而是在精神上给予安慰和帮助。尽自己所能帮助李华，让李华可以专心工作。李华对双亲感到愧疚，他们永远在为自己操心，她永远无法报尽这种无私的养育之恩。

李华按程序奔忙，处理卖房，又处理买房，还处理房子的装修。终于在第三个月将两套房子的尾款、全款处理到位，随时可以办理退房迁移新房程序。此刻全部付清时间还不到五个月，提前兑现了承诺。

这是一个值得纪念的好日子，李华母亲按照易经学，结合夫妻双方的生辰八字选了一个大吉日，定了 16 号搬家。那天真是风调雨顺，乔迁之喜，大吉大利! 终于落户了，李华终于做到让父母亲拥有一套写上他们名字的大房子。

这确实是一套大房子，上下复式楼，每层 160 平方面积——因为是顶楼，享有买一送一的福利，实际面积的 320 平方。共 6 室 3 卫，三厅一厨一阳台。这房子足够住下整个大家庭，四女儿全回到父母家团聚的时候，每个小家都可以暂住下来。父母亲真实享受了四代同堂的温暖幸福生活，在那些时候，李华会感觉到她一点都不孤单，这才是她的幸福大家庭！

这套房子虽然是李华个人出钱买给父母亲，但是妹妹们每人都以家庭成员的身份赞助了两万装修款，同时也都给父母添置了新家具。除了父母亲舍不得扔的老古董五梯柜，穿衣镜，加上那个老祖宗留下的摆件挂钟外，其余的家具和电器，都是妹妹们赞助父母亲的：二妹提供冰箱，三妹购买电视机，小妹买了洗衣机和大理石圆形自动餐桌。室内的小摆设和实用生活品，都是几个女儿买的。遇到逢年过节以及父母亲的生日，在庆贺的同时也找理由给父母亲买些实用衣物及添置家当。

在李华的影响下，当年二妹在昆山也买了一套小户型的现房，给二妹夫用作商住二用公寓房投资。因为二妹夫在外企高管工作，这样操作将单位补贴房租费，加上只投资一点资金就可还银行贷款。房产权还属于二妹夫妻俩，这样等于支持二妹夫安心工作，创造了一个投资自住的环境。昆山的房产当年买的时候，投入只需要首付四万元，其他银行按揭贷款，自住了五年，后期因二妹夫工作调动深圳总部，此房作为出租 4 年，以租还贷款，第十年将贷款全部还清后，卖掉昆山房子后获利 29 万元。

三妹也在第二年鼓励李华下一起又买下了两个小门面，一门面签了十年的租赁合同美发店，一方面为了稳定，一方面也为了利益于朋友租用实惠介绍。对方为了报答朋友，李华承诺每年都不增加租金。此门面房也是以租还贷，两套门面房，都是以租养贷，轻松挣钱。

小妹在第二年就在北京买了一栋别墅，邀请全家老小陪伴父母亲到北京一聚。姐姐和姐夫们都邀请到北京的新家，在这里大家度过了一个有意义的阳春三月天。在那之后，一家人常常在天气暖和的三月份去北京跟小妹团聚，全部费用都是小妹出资承担。

小妹这样说："自从老妈老爸搬进了大姐买的房子后，那里肯定是风水宝地。老妈老爸开心多了，我的事业也很顺利，所以沾光借福，我没有想到在北京第二年我的工作提升很大。这次请家人都来分享我的这栋四层楼的别墅，就想要家人都来陪伴父母亲享福。让亲人们给我添加人气，我听这里一位佛教大师说，房子就是要热热闹闹，多种些绿色植物，特别是要多养些水竹。"

小妹指着一盆有一人高的竹子对家人说："这就是大姐送的竹子，长了一年了，这么高，很旺盛！我好喜欢，大姐帮装修一个月，真是帮了大忙呀！。"

俗话说得好，百善孝为先，只有孝敬父母的家庭，家人才会事业如鱼得水，万事如意！李华和妹妹们都感觉到了，自从父母亲搬迁移居后，李华的整个大家庭都显现出好运连连，大家的事业更顺畅。

女儿们也体会到父母亲在她们成长中付出了多少心血。她们看到父母亲脸上布满皱纹和满头白发的样子，依然能感觉到慈祥和蔼。父母的双手长满了老年斑，皱皱的皮肤显示出岁月的痕迹。

此时的父母亲看到一家人和和美美，打心底里欣慰，欣慰孩子们都长大了，欣慰女儿们都成才了，都过上了美好生活。现在孩子们的生活比他们俩佬的过去，不知道要强多少倍。

母亲是脆弱的一面，小女儿第一个发现母亲用手去擦掉脸上的泪水。小女儿说："老妈别哭了，您和老爸应该高兴啊，只要你们健康长寿，好日子还在后头呢！"

李华接过话："老妈是高兴得哭了，肯定又想到从前为我们受苦的伤心事了！"

父亲开口了："你妈是高兴啊，总算可以不用对你们操心了！"

二女儿笑眯眯地劝着母亲："你们看看，我们老妈这个新发型像不像大教授呀？"

三女儿跟着起哄："我老爸说了，我老妈长得像中央那位女领导吴仪！"

这个时候的母亲被老伴和女儿们逗笑了，激动的泪水也止不住往外涌。母亲说话哽咽了起来："孩子们好，工作顺利，是我这个当妈的最幸福的事情。孩子们呀，有你们这么孝心，看到你们姐妹团结互助，这是我最愿意看到的亲情，一家人就是要这样亲上加亲。"

父亲补充道："你妈一直说，我们家的女儿个个都顶得上几个儿子，甚至比儿子还强！上个月我们的老同事，你们的董伯伯和吕伯伯都说，你们的女儿比他们的儿子强百倍，说他们的儿子在啃老，你们的女儿们却给你们养老，你们多幸福哟！"父亲的一席话彻底把母亲从难过情绪中拉了回来，父亲很会劝母亲，女儿们过得好，也是他们二老的福分，应该高兴。

别说为父母亲买一所房子，就是把所有都给父母亲，李华都心甘情愿，认为理所应当。李华做这些事不图名不图利，就是想让父母亲过上比以前更好的生活，要让父母亲享受生活，这才是她当女儿应该尽的义务。

有时候李华几乎用命令的口吻跟父母说："你们就该享福，不要操心了，现如今我们每个子女的小家都是住新房子，而你们还是住着 80 年代的老房子，叫我们做小辈的于心何忍？肯定是想改善你们老两口的居住环境。如果我们只顾自己住得好，不管你们二老，那不是给别人骂我们吗？"

李华就是想给父母一所足够大的房子，让大家逢年过节好时暂住一起，还宽敞舒服，让父母尽享家人团聚的幸福喜悦有一个自家的氛围，有父母在的家就是幸福的家，女儿们不想留下遗憾，还是想趁早对父母尽孝心。这家风是父母亲教子有方，把女儿们都培育成才，让李华父母同辈朋友们羡慕不已！李华父母深感欣慰！

第二十三章　为女儿买了学区房

　　李华为了报答父母亲，终于将自己的住房卖掉，给父母亲在家乡买了一套复式楼，写上了父母亲的名字，完成了作为长女孝顺父母亲的心愿。

　　房子装修进入尾声环节，安装门窗工程的吴老板与李华结算门窗安装改造款。吴老板为了说明他公司业务做得大，已经做到省城大开发商的工程，无意中聊到第二天要去省城与开发商的工程款也要结账。那是家乡最大的开发商，在省城投资的商业房产项目正在预售，有小户型现房。

　　李华听到这个消息非常兴奋，她恨不得马上就跟吴老板去一趟省城，于是开口问他："吴老板你明天去省城，能方便带我去看看省城开发的房子吗？"

　　吴老板想都没有想就说："当然方便，我一个人开车也是去，多带一个人而已，早上七点开车出发，争取在九点售楼部开门时间到达。我去财务部结账，你在售楼部看房选房，最好让工作人员带你去看看样板现房！"

　　吴老板表现爽快，一是想证明自己与大开发商合作的实力，二是告诉李华他的公司门窗铝材质量好，才能与省城开发商合作，也想让李华介绍一些家装公司客户给他。去结账时顺便带上李华看房，看李华人脉广，对父母又孝顺，心眼好，也愿意攀上业务关系。吴老板很高兴地说着几年来与开发商在省城投资合作的几个大项目，地址分别在不同区域，但是都是好地方，交通方便！吴老板随意与李华一路聊着公司目前主要接工程项目，又聊一些大开发商正在省城其他几个区域正在，明后年都要售楼的信息，李华默默听着，没有打断吴老板的讲话劲头，心里却有了很多进入省城发展的念头！

　　李华这一天有很多想法突然冒了出来，她最近刚好把手上所有零散资金的银行卡都带在身上，好像有预感就是为此事去。她必须抓住时机，购买适合的房型。这件事势在必行，为了照顾好父母，又好照顾女儿，李华选择了在家乡很近的省城创业。李华看来，要想创业，就必须先安居才能乐业。她信仰这种有家为主题的奋斗目标，买房是在省城创业的敲门砖。

在这个时候，李华又考虑到女儿的学业，女儿一定会在未来的两年考进省城念大学，那么就必须为女儿提供省城的学区房。这样自己也好展开创业，既可以照顾父母亲，又可以为女儿读大学期间提供方便和照顾，还可以方便女儿毕业后找工作，提供省城户口，这样在就业分配上有了好的基础。

第二天清晨早早醒来。已是八月，夏季的尾巴秋天的初时，秋高气爽，早上的空气非常爽朗。家乡的小城飘过耳边的微风，让李华感觉到非常舒服。要不是于平婚内出轨，李华很热爱自己的家乡，怎么也没有想过会以这种理由，背井离乡，去省城发展。也许是目标已定，她感觉很轻松，就当今天是短途实际考察房子的第一站行程。

李华要在省城买房安家，让女儿和家人放心。既然以提前内退再创业，这种心境里出来闯荡，没有退路必须积极干出一番事业。为了给家人更好的生活，李华急需一处省城落脚的住处，也为了改善生活条件，也许甚至李华得作好思想准备，寻找第二职业、第三职业。她考虑到只要在投资不超出她的能力范围之外，都会想到以小博大。执行力强，行动快，这是李华成功的特质，而且考虑成熟，一定要会短时间作出行动。前期在深圳、广州、北京、上海、苏州几个城市的考察中，李华已经掌握了房产价格在全国实际情况。此行到省城买房，李华已经做好充分考察的数据准备。

吴老板在小区的门口准时等着李华出现，他说过，如果时间观念不强，到时没看见李华，他会一个人开车离开。李华记住了这句话，比吴老板更早来到。

吴老板的黑色丰田小车，慢慢驶进小区门卫停了下来，按下电动车窗对着李华说："请上来吧，你还挺准时的，是个做生意的女强人。一看你就是很有主见的女人，做事情靠谱，什么都爽快。你看来没有办不成的事情，将来发达了别忘了也照顾我啊！"

李华说："吴老板夸的这话我爱听，起码我也是想认认真真做成这事。也谢谢老板今天顺便带上我，让我少走弯路，直接到考察的售楼部去看一看，也许今天会定一套最小户型。"

吴老板说："我跟你说，这个项目真的很好，是我们这个小城市最大的开发商开发的。我跟他们合作有几年了。还有其他的两个开发项目，今天如果有空都可以带你去看一看，你可以比较一下。我个人觉得这个项目比较适合你，有你想要的小户型，而且投资不大，总价十万多一点就可以拿下一套房子，平均每一平方面积 2030 元。省城有一套房子，对孩子未来读书上大学都有好处，将来在省城创业也有更多选择。"

李华说："是啊，目前省城这所房子的单价确实比北京、上海、广州低，与苏州、云南价格相持平。比较一下，有刚需和投资的空间，值得投资。我想将来价格还会涨，这两年房价一定是往上涨。"

李华和吴老板边聊边向省城开进，一路上聊着很愉快，双方交换了有关房地产各方面的信息，聊到了房产未来走势。李华对这次之行，心里更有谱了，心想这一次一定要把握机会，向省城进军，这是走对走稳第一步。李华总感觉冥冥之中，这都是因为她善心孝顺为父母所做好事遇见了省城机会，如果不是为父母亲买房装修房改造阳台门窗，怎么又会遇上吴老板夸夸其谈的这些及时正需要了解的信息呢？真是说者无心，听者有意，李华把这些及时信息资源都归功于上天照顾她，帮她指明方向！

一个多小时就到目的地了，售楼部的中心门口还没开门。吴老板说："我们就在附近吃早餐吧，这省城的早餐非常丰富，价廉物美，品种繁多。你看喜欢吃什么，今天我请你！"

吴老板把车停好，两人走进对面的一条巷子。真是不看不知道，看了吓一跳。看着不起眼的地方，却有这么多摊位和路边小吃店。省城称吃早餐为"过早"，花样真多，李华都看不过来。有她喜欢吃的味道，如牛肉粉、汤包、油条、面窝、米酒汤圆、葱花卷，小米粥、红枣粥、排骨藕汤……真是看花了眼，不知道吃哪一个才好。到最后，李华还是来了一碗牛肉米粉加一根油条。这是她最喜欢吃的重口味，辣的牛肉粉。

这时候李华更坚定要在这里买房，她觉得这里的生活太便利了，住在这附近感觉很舒服。李华庆幸这次能搭上顺风车，于是很感激地悄悄先把早餐的单买了。她感觉自己买单才能多吃一点花样，不然不好意思再点其他的。李华又点了一盘小糯米饺，点了一个面窝还有韭菜合子，每样都尝一点，吃不完的就打包。李华觉得自己嘴馋，情不自禁笑起来。

吴老板吃完准备买单，没有想到李华将单已买了。吴老板说："刚刚说好了我请客，怎么你已经付了？那好吧，谢谢你。好吃吧，这地方来对了吧？"

李华说："太好吃了，真没想到这里这么方便。正好这时间应该开门了，我们该去售楼部了。"

吴老板说："是啊，只走几分钟就到了。你一定是第一个客人，开发商售楼部的工作人员我都认识，他们会耐心介绍适合的房型给你，我让他们给你优惠打折扣。"

李华说："谢谢你给我优惠，谢谢，谢谢！"李华此时最需要的是能省一点投资成本，哪怕少一个点，都是最实惠的帮助。

吴老板感觉李华很知恩图报，在最近的接触中，给吴老板印象心目中，李华是一位守诚信讲话算数的女人，值得帮忙和交往。吴老板想到这里很热情地走进到售楼大厅，对着工作人员小秦说："我给你带来新客人了，是我们老家的人，请你把最大的优惠价给到她吧。她是我的客户也是朋友，她一定会买一套你们开发的房子。她喜欢这个地段，请你们照顾她。"吴老板对售楼部负责人说着好话，又转身对李华打了个招呼，就直奔财务部。

李华在小秦耐心热情的推荐下，去现场看了现房！当即回到售楼部签下了购买合同，这一下笔这房子就定了下来，首付两成三万元，余下做商业性贷款，等银行贷款批准了，就可以交房装修使用了！李华又有事要干了，这每一个环节衔接得紧凑，没有拖泥带水，甚至可以说是速战速决。

吴老板从财务部走出来时候，看到李华这边已签了合同，在工作人员面前竖起大拇指赞赏道："佩服，太佩服了，第一次来看房，不到三小时就决定签了合同。以你的做事风格，你今后一定能干起来，今天可以庆贺了，这是进省城创业的第一步，以后若还有选房看房需要，保持联系。"

李华也情不自禁地感慨：终于有了自己的一个小窝了，这就是人生新的转折点。也许将来就会在这座城市有自己的发展领域，把自己生活经营好，也把父母亲接来省城和自己居住，让父母亲享受这种天伦之乐的生活。

李华想到这是自己的责任，一种担子。她一定要向前走，先求生存，再寻找梦想，一个接一个小目标实现它。无形的动力和精神意念推动着李华艰难前进，遇到再大的困难，她也从不叫苦，不对亲人诉说。对亲人只报喜不报忧，将乐观的人生态度，感染着周围的单身女友们。那段时间，李华接触的朋友几乎都是单身离异的事业型女强人。李华鼓励自己以她们为榜样，与智者为伍，与勤奋者相随，与成功者为师！相信自己总有一天经过努力，也会在成功路上，成为榜样的一员，被人羡慕以引为自豪的成功女人！

第二十四章　为女儿置换落户婚前房产

李华买的是小户型的学区房，周边环境很好。当年房产的开盘价格比起同年的深圳、广州、北京的房产价格要低得多。当时李华手上的资金仅有三万块钱，首付投资款的房子，只能选择一套 38 平方米的学区房小户型。一是还买得起供得起，将来女儿读大学，每周回家会很方便。李华买了这套房子没有任何压力。这里交通非常方便，从大学校区到小区居住地只需要坐五六站公交车就到了。

为了省钱李华只请了一个装修工，只花了 7000 元简单装修配置。这是李华为女儿在省城投资的第一套房子，在省城武汉市的武昌区。

装修完的那天，李华满心欢喜地把亲人都带到她自己设计的房子参观。那是一间很温馨的住所，进门的正大厅就设有开放式厨房，左手边是一个小卫生间及洗澡的小区域，右边是一间主卧室，阳台放洗衣机，阳光露台放空调外机，阳台和大厅中间隔着一道推拉沙门和玻璃门。卧室里充分利用边角空间，置顶做满了衣柜，整个储存柜都考虑到了。卧室里放一张大床，足够李华和女儿一起睡下，作为休息的一席之地。

从那以后，那几年李华感觉浑身是劲，为家人她必须拼出去，好好工作努力挣钱，让家人过好幸福的日子。李华只想挣口气，离婚不可怕，丈夫背叛不可怕，她不需要婚姻也可以过好自己想要的美好生活。

李华是一个闲不住的女人，在装修父母亲房子的期间，只要有关省城房子的信息，她都很关注。能顺利买中这套省城的房子，这也是前期积累下来的成果。之前李华到了各大城市都要去考察当地的房产市场。刚办内退没有目标的日子里，李华去北京帮小妹装修房子，获取了北京的房价信息。在昆山帮二妹装修房子时，就了解了苏州和昆山房价。在深圳做保险的几个月中，李华了解了深圳和广州的房价信息。因为亲眼所见，充分掌握了真实的信息，李华可以快速比较和判断，做决定能做到快准狠。

　　那几年房价上涨速度很快，几乎只要是投资了市中心的房子，没有不涨价，只要售出都能挣钱。可以说是买房子就可以翻倍挣钱的年代。当然，对于李华刚来省城创业的小白来说，真是一个机会。一方面是生活刚需，另一方面，在买房三年后，也可以根据自己和女儿的实际情况安置规划，进行调整改善住房的需要。后来李华看到购房有落户政策，而且是政府对广大知识分子制定的优惠福利政策。

　　日子过得真快，李华女儿也在省城度过了三年。在大学的第四个年头里，马上要找一个单位实习，需要半学期完成科目学业。为了让女儿得到实习工作的好机会，也为了能使女儿成为省城户口，李华想以女儿的名字购买大一点面积的房子。是非做不可的时机，只有这样，才能享受购房转为省城户口的条件：房款达到 50 万元以上，面积为 100 平方，才有资格落户藉条件。

　　这事必须在 2006 年定下来，女儿就要大学毕业，实习的单位就是省城电讯行业公司。李华不想错过这次购买房子的机会。李华认为最稳妥投资财富项目就是房子，她给父母送了房子；如果要给女儿最实惠急需的爱，李华还是认为房子是最好的礼物。给女儿买房是为了给女儿安全感，一处温暖的港湾。那是给女儿一个高平台起点，养育孩子，引导孩子健康成长，不想因单亲家庭，给女儿带来自卑，要在女儿心目中树立好言传身教做经济独立的好榜样，这才是李华想给女儿最实际最大的母爱。

　　李华看中了武昌的学区房，周边交通发达，可算是武汉文化中心，几分钟就能通过武汉大桥直到汉阳，直达汉口商业街。小区门前的公交车站有十几路班车，可直达中南商业大厦，东湖汉街，乘船可直达的汉正街，这些都是武汉市的商业文化中心。又有配套的医院学校、幼儿园、菜市场，还有首义广场就在黄鹤楼脚下。能在这里生活，女儿的将来该有多方便。如果女儿将来在这边落户成为省城居民中一员，就业就没有问题了。

　　想到这些，李华干劲十足，一点不知疲倦，一鼓作气任劳任怨做着各种烦琐又必须解决的事情。李华的全部心思都是为女儿考虑，没有想过自己。

　　为了买新房，李华要筹集购房首付款。第一念头，就是把这套自己名下已住了三年的房子卖掉。这是最好的解决资金来源的办法，这房子已经涨了两倍价格。看着即将要卖的房子，这曾住了三年的房子，周围的一切都见证了李华三年前的果断英明。在这方面没有谁教李华，父母亲也没有想到，大女儿李华在短短的三年时间里，默默地做着这些投资房子的事情，全由自己领悟到了房产投资中带来的意外惊喜和财富。

这些年的经历培养了李华投资房产的直觉，只要看到好地段的房子，李华要做的就是积极凑足购房的首付款资金，然后马上去售楼部签订购买合同。接下来的就是根据自己良好的银行信誉积分，办理商业贷款。因还贷款及时，信用好，李华又是离异单身，自己的事情自己作主，办什么事情起来很顺畅，这是李华最愿意做的事，就是在购房合同上签名字时刻最过瘾，心情爽极了。

李华还有一个优点就是低调。做购房这样的大事情只是跟家里支持她的人商量，向他们吐露出自己的想法和可以实施的每一步骤。没有办成之前，李华很低调。家人、朋友、同事、同学只知道李华特别忙碌。有时候电话微信上找到人的时候，李华不是在建材市场，就是在哪个城市旅行中看房，有时候又在搬家，有时候又在装修中。其实这些事情落实下来，真的需要做很多实事。那些年搬家对李华来说是常态了，这次又开始面临从前搬家做过的日常事务。李华有时候就是女汉子形象，一身迷彩裤、旅游鞋、T恤上衣，把自己打造成一个包工头的形象，怎么看都不会想到她就是房东。房子没有搞好，李华不会让家人看到她的这一身打扮。

虽然李华很喜欢那种悠闲小资情调的生活，她又是一个具备浪漫味道的女子。但在某些时候，她却像一个不知疲倦工作狂人，一位无私奉献的妈妈，又是通情达理的大姐，在长辈们眼中，更是一个大孝心的长女，从小养成了好强有主见的个性，没有矫情，没有多余的废话，果断踏实做事。李华始终给人沉稳的感觉，充满着活力，好像永不知疲倦，朝着她认准的目标前进，坚忍执着，从不受其他人言语的影响。

李华边在网络上联系房屋中介，将自己名下的这套小户型学区房委托中介公司迅速地卖掉。小户型当年买的时候，房款总价是10万8000元，住了三年，还涨到18万元。李华心里确实舍不得，但这是以小博大操作的第一步，为了顺利出售，最后让利2万元，以16万元总价出售了，为给女儿小琳户名买房，有了省城落户购房的首付款，这是成功运作迈出去的第一步。

李华在一所小学附近，找到了老家来省城开发的新楼盘，选中了一套能享受转户口政策条件面积房子，总价超过了50万，面积是102平方。李华以女儿的名字购买，签约购房合同，两个月后就可以交房装修使用。计划是一环套一环，交易成交时间很重要。

第二十五章　李华的创业史

　　时间就是金钱，此时真的不假，李华知道只有将小户型房子出售的资金到手，后面购房的手续才能顺理成章。不然错过了商机和资金补充，新房那边目前只是下了定金，还没有付首付款。虽然找到了熟人将首付款的时间协调到一个月后再交，但是一旦超时交付，定金不退，房号也不会保留。这是一步险棋，但是李华没有别的办法，她从来不想向朋友们借钱投资，也不想给亲人找麻烦。她宁愿在出售小户型的总价让步，也要尽快成交。目标清晰后，李华显得很淡定。

　　卖房信息挂到网上不久，中介小陈通知李华要带客户来看房。李华积极准备，希望顺利促成这笔房屋买卖。这座城市是火炉之城，夏天的热风让人感到闷热心躁。李华希望买住对房子留下美好的第一印象，她特意选择了一束鲜花，布置在客厅最显眼的地方。李华平日里舍不得开空调，但是这天她将空调调到适宜的温度。房间做了一次彻底的大扫除，整个房间给人温馨浪漫的小文艺氛围。屋子里播放着轻缓的音乐，宁静舒适。似乎让人产生错觉，在这里不是夏天，而是春色满园！

　　一切准备就绪，门外刚好响起敲门声，"李姐，我们来了。"小陈亲切地在门外叫着李华。李华慢慢打开房门，侧身站在一旁，把宽敞明亮客厅显示出来，也将客人的一次性鞋套一一递上。李华服务周到，就好像迎接看样板房的客户。

　　中介小陈愉快说："李姐的房子真漂亮，像新房。如果买下后，根本不用再投资装修了。"

　　李华说："房子虽然小，但配套齐全。"

　　买主是一对年轻人，刚进来就满心欢喜。电器、家具、摆饰，无不显示主人的文化品位，买主看得眼睛发亮。女买主问："这都是李姐布置的吗？"

李华说："是的，我喜欢设计房子装修，每一件用品都是我精心挑选的。即使卖掉了，我也很爱护它们。也许这房子更适合你们小两口居住。"

李华把家里的环境布置得非常好，对买主有问必答，聊天过程而且很愉悦。看着看着，这对年轻的小两口很着急地说："那我们今天去中介签约吧，我们也没有时间再看其他的房子了。跟李姐有缘，咱们就按挂在网上的信息成交吧。我们是商贷，银行批下来很快的。李姐，我们一次性拿不出这么多，但是可以先付你十万元整，另外六万贷款。"

小陈说："好说好说，咱们到中介坐下来谈。你们能买到不用装修的房子，就是买对了。拎箱入住！全房家电全送！"

李华按捺不住自己的喜悦，稳定自己的心情，很礼貌地说"这是缘分，我也希望买到房子的朋友也和我一样喜欢它，这个快乐浪漫幸福的小屋！"

一对年轻人不约而同地说："很喜欢这里，我们想待下来不走了。这音乐光碟也给我们留下哈！"

李华舒了一口气，爱惜地抚摸着光碟说："我也很喜欢这音乐，这是在音乐之家小店淘到的。好吧，就送给你们了！"

小陈带着看房的俩人有说有笑地走向中介所，当天就成交了。这是李华有生以来最快出售的又一套房子。

第二天李华拿着出售小房的 10 万元定金，加上先付款购买新房的定金 2 万元，刚刚是首付款的总数 12 万元整。女儿新房的总房款是 40 万 6 千元，这是李华最满意的一次房屋买卖交易，也最成功的衔接！虽然扣除了中介费奖励小陈的兑现，李华这边获利少了，但是及时补充了投资房的资金款，这一点更为重要。李华抓住了时机，解决了女儿户口落实的事情，也为女儿在省城工作打好了基础。李华给了女儿一个家，一处名副其实的婚前第一套房产，一个安全的港湾。这件事也打开了李华女儿投资理财的智慧大门，等于拿到了开启百宝财富箱的金钥匙，让她从小知道经济独立所给予自己的安全感，要比任何人给予得靠谱。

从那以后，李华女儿的学业、事业、结婚生子都从这所房子受益。这所房子不仅给李华和女儿带来了事业和投资理财的一桶金，而且带来了很多合作商机创业的好机会。买了这所房子之后，李华开始创业，几年来身兼数职，全年无休拼命赚钱。李华做一行专一行，很快在短短三年的投资中见到了成效，突破了百万元的起点，还清了女儿这套房子的所有贷款。还将售后的利润加本金，全部又投入第二套，第三套市中心房产。做到了从一套小房置换成大房，从一套变三套投资房。李华以身作则潜移默化的良好影响下，李华女儿在同龄人中也显现出投资智慧。

这些年来，在夜深人静之际，李华常常会想起自己第一次创业的情景。买了小户型学区房后，于是她想着要做些事情赚钱，解决房贷的压力。李华最初的想法是开一家茶舍，一家 100 平方左右带点小资艺术风格的小茶舍。每年三月都要陪父母亲去北京与妹妹团聚，李华顺便去考察北京茶楼、茶舍、茶馆、书吧、咖啡馆的市场模式。

三月的北京洋溢着春天景色，路边树叶茂盛，沿途大厦繁荣昌盛的景象，能感觉到祖国的日新月异变化和发展的强大。李华陪同父母亲在妹妹的安排下观光旅游，北京的几大景点和一些主要的城市地标建筑都有游览。一到傍晚李华就出门逛街考察，了解北京的一些小型音乐轻吧、小书吧、咖啡馆之类的文化小资格调的茶舍，也考察了一些古朴风格的茶艺文化小茶馆。那段时间李华在北京来考察了几十家小茶楼。

后来李华也将考察的动机告诉了家人，让他们给点建议。大家谈到资金投入、预算、实际装修费、员工聘用，以及开店后的管理运作模式实施方案。家人将问题摆在李华的面前：资金及精力的投入太大，还有后期的守店方案不成熟。这些问题逼着李华不得不打消了开茶馆的计划。

小妹对李华说："大姐你想想，你是为了创业挣钱还房贷。如果你的创业达不到这个目的，不仅失去意义，耽误你的时间，还给你增添更大的经济负担！"

李华听着沉默了一会儿问道："那你有什么好的建议，你觉得我适合做什么事情？"

二妹应声道："姐，你不是很喜欢我们老家黄冈莎街的那家女人品牌折扣店服装吗？每次买一大堆，看你的女友和同学也都喜欢。每次你们买十几件，你又和那家店老板熟悉，还不如也开家服装品牌折扣店。我觉得肯定行，你熟悉这行业，服装价格也便宜，投资成本低，你可以试试这个项目。"

李华心中一亮，以前在老家的时候，她经常光顾的那家女装品牌折扣店。听说服装店女老板的朋友在北京专门发货，她已经开了三家品牌折扣店，店铺虽然都在地县市区，但是生意都很火，几乎进店的女人没有空手出来的。李华和女友们都爱去购买，每次都买七八件。

三妹也说："对呀，大姐最爱买，周边朋友们也都喜欢。每次去逛逛，总是满载而归，没有空手回来过，肯定有你的消费市场。你要是加盟开了这家服装店，不愁货卖不出去。这个事情比开茶楼和咖啡馆简单！"

小妹听后又说话了："是啊，做自己熟悉也能投入的事情。最主要是先谈生存之道，再求梦想。"

李华经妹妹们点拨，脑袋里浮现出服装店老板小洪在店里忙碌样子，每次去店里都看到很多顾客，顾客看每一件衣服都像看着宝贝一样，那些衣服只要零售价的两折，顾客们买起来一点也不心疼手软。李华自己也体验过购买这些衣服的兴奋冲动，说明这个开服装店的建议是目前最好的投资项目，照着做就应该没有问题了。

想到这里，李华马上说："我有办法了，我先打电话给这个品牌折扣店老板娘小洪。我听说过，她驻住在北京发货，可以跟她谈加盟店，需要什么条件，我打电话咨询一下，要是她现在北京就好了！"

第二十六章　先谋生存，再求梦想

　　李华是急性子，做事果断，想法确定后马上去落实。李华信心满满地拨打了老板娘小洪的联系电话，了解到小洪正好在北京。

　　小洪正好在公司准备进货，一听说李华来到北京，立马要见一面，当面来谈。小洪直接说："我来接你，你在公司亲自考察几天，跟我一起住公司这边。我有一间公寓用来发货，现在基本在这里定居。这次你来得真是时候，我正在北京，还正好刚刚买了一辆红色跑车。你现在在北京几环路上？我来接你。"

　　这小洪老板也是个能干事的人，听到李华说在北京的东二环逛王府井的水秀街，让李华在秀水街的星巴克咖啡店等她。

　　电话里小洪老板还这样说："明天我要去公司挑货，你陪我一起就知道怎样进货了。我把公司的流程顺便给你介绍一下，如果你加盟我的公司，我也不收你加盟费，但是我在你服装批发费用上加两个点行吗？好处是你不需要长住北京进货，我把现货帮你选好。你只要把好卖的款式，客户需求的款式、样式说给我听，我按照市场情况综合给你发货。每件衣服我就按成本价上提两个点，其他的多卖都是你的利润。我不需要你加盟费，你回老家找一个适合开店的地址，就可以简单装修开张，这样合作行吗？"

　　小洪接着说："我不会让你吃亏的。我们认识了好多年，你给我们店铺带来了很多顾客，这样的好客人我会以朋友相待。我们的加盟店真的很赚钱，相信你在湖北省城能做起来。为了保证你的利益，我先不收你的加盟费。省出来几万元就用作运营装修费用，也用作进货资金。你来了我们再好好商量一下。"

　　这个喜讯来得太突然了，李华被小洪的话打动，一下子勾住了李华的思绪。她失去了婚姻，她一定不能失去事业，李华很想去尝试一下服装行业带来的收益。小妹的话提醒了她，必须先挣钱多挣钱，先求生存再求梦想，这才是王道。

　　有小洪的具体指导帮助，李华少走很多弯路，这也真是机会。经过亲身考察以及家人的分析，李华也认为开茶舍的资金成本太大，一时不可能实现得了。特别是在创业初期，李华只能投资小成本的项目才能达到快速还房贷的目标。

加盟服装店的想法比较成熟，投资小，几万块钱就可以立马开店挣收益。李华想着还是先试着做挣钱的项目，再来实现自己做小茶舍的梦想。李华懂得先要有米，才能下锅做饭；有了经济基础，才能做到你想要成为的样子。听过服装店老板小洪的一番话，性格爽快的李华二话没说就答应了小洪："好，今天就在这北京二环星巴克咖啡馆等你。你快到了就给我打个电话，我准备好出来。"

大概过了一个小时，小洪就打来电话："可以出来了，我就在星巴克的十字路口。路边打闪灯的那个红色小轿车就是我的。你注意安全看路，快过来，我在车里等你，这里不能久停。"

李华叮嘱妹妹们先回北京小妹家，自己去考察服装公司待两天。李华很快找到小洪的车，上车后小洪与李华俩人分外兴奋，她们都说起家乡话，聊起来很畅快。真没想到家乡的客户和老板能在北京这大都市相逢，并且还在谈生意，成为盟友。

李华这次看来是来真的了，有备而来。小洪边开车边笑着说："行动是实力，说干就干，真佩服你的闯劲，看来茶楼没开成，要开服装店了。"

李华也开心地说："那是肯定的，我觉得跟着你开服装店，肯定能做起来。因为我了解你，我也太喜欢你们家的服装款式了。价格我能接受，我也有这些消费群体，朋友的客人带客户，到时候朋友捧场，价格适中，一个便宜个个爱，这个服装折扣店就能做起来。何况我和你一样好性格，为人随和，一定能做起来。我就不去折腾开什么茶楼了，没有固定的客人，没有稳定的消费人流市场。安心向你学习，还得先挣钱，等挣了大钱，再去开茶楼。"

小洪应声说："到时候我也去你那休息休息，蹭杯茶喝。下午我就带你去公司看，我带你选货，看看要达到多少量。若是加盟服装公司，公司要拿中间管理提成，那样对你压力太大，因为你还不知道适应市场的销售环节的技巧。所以建议你就当我的分销商开个小店，加盟费就不用了。你直接销售多少，我在中间给你提两点就行。这样你的资金压力不大，我来给你发货，你就安心卖货。如果以这种方式操作，就像我家乡的黄冈三家分店一样。那三家店都是这样经营，不用他们进货，我发货就行，他们只管销货。你也看到了，生意挺

好，进去的人没有低于三四件的，往往是七八件。你也体验过，买起来感觉很畅快。"

李华被小洪这一番话打动了，立马高兴地说："今天看了说不定就想飞回去，早点干起来。如果是你说的那样子，我在省城多开一家这样的服装店也有生意。"

俩人聊了一路，李华兴奋地看着车窗外的北京，车水马龙，人来人往。车子路过高楼大厦，逐渐向北京的五环中路驶去。小洪开车很快，没过多久就到了公司附近。原来服装公司在北京的五环九峰，李华这才知道北京的九峰批发服装市场原来在这里。

李华问："服装批发市场怎么选在这么偏的地方？"

小洪回答说："这还偏吗？北京六环的房子都卖得很贵了！你要是想来这里发展也不是不可以，但是在这里可不比湖北舒服。小城市滋润多了，没有压力也能挣到钱。在北京太拼了，处处都需要用钱。"

李华说："所以都需要创业挣钱谋生活。我只有把写作、书吧、茶舍、咖啡馆的美梦放一放，多做几年实际事情。以后挣到钱了，再努力去实现梦想。你觉得我会挣到这第一桶创业基金吗？"

小洪立刻回复："你一定行，冲着你这果断英明的精神。我有信心你一定能成功，所以才甘愿帮助你。你到了公司，就能看到服装款式进货的场景，当你看到价格和质量，你一定会决定回省城开这家品牌折扣店。"

第二十七章　开一家特色的服装品牌折扣店

李华随小洪选择服装发货，果然被公司的大气和服装的价格所震撼了。李华动心了，而且是铁了心要开这家服装店。想到未来和女儿的生活，想到以后要给女儿买房，李华必须创业赚钱，要不然一辈子也别想买房。一想到这些，开服装店是当务之急要做的事情。

李华看着满地堆积琳琅满目的服装，都是分类打包堆放，由进货商自己挑选。有人蹲着，有人站着，有人像看花眼一样，不知从哪里下手。大部分人不停地埋头选择自己喜欢的以及客户需要的服装。

李华兴奋地对小洪老板说："谢谢你把我带到总公司来，我信任你，从现在开始，我也不犹豫了。今天就跟着你一起进货，我决定跟你学着做，直接加盟在你的店里，给你两个点的销售提成。"

小洪老板高兴地说："好的，我们就从今天开始帮你选货。我知道你会果断同意做这一行，要挣钱才能做你想做的事情。只要我带过来老家的人，没有一个不动心开店。希望你在湖北省城好好打开局面，我全力配合你选货发货，你回老家只管选店址，简单装修，开店销售。"

李华兴致勃勃地笑着不停点头，眼里看见的全是满地服装，和进货商们忙碌的样子。也好像未来她的服装店，客户满堂进进出出的情景。

李华风尘仆仆地按计提前回到家乡湖北省城，为女儿定购房子同时，也看好了品牌服装折扣店的地址。选址就在新小区的侧面街上，这里人流量非常大。这条街直通必经菜市场，清早及下班期间，总会有人群路过。右边是一排早点摊位、理发店、小餐馆。走到丁字路口就是有名的重点实验小学，和有名的艺术学校。再向前方就是一座省城有名的人民医院。这里公交车有很多站点。

总而言之，选择这个地址做服装店，真是太适合不过了，闹中取静，有稳定的小区居民人流量，也有艺术学院的老师和学生，还有探望病人顺路逛街的人们。最主要是这条侧街面店铺全部开了不同品牌风格的服装店、首饰品店、

鞋店、儿童时装店，周边还有三家美容院、美甲店、足疗店。这是一个配套设施齐全，成熟的优质生活小区。在这里开一个中青年都适合穿的品牌服装折扣店，肯定有适宜的女性购买人群。

李华认为这店开在这个地段，生意一定能做起来，最主要是服装价格款式适合不同的女人群体。想到这里，李华干劲十足，找到两家刚要转让的老板谈。有一家空店没有装修，但房东一定要预交半年的房租，租金以每个月 3000 计算，半年 18000，没有半点迟疑，因为这里地理位置太好。隔壁那家转让的首饰店，因装修豪华转让费过高，超过了李华的预算投资成本。没有办法，李华只有放弃接现成装修好的店面。

李华说干就干，很快跟空店的房东签合同，并向房东争取赠送半个月装修时间，其它条款都按照房东的规定来办。房东刘老板看到李华有诚意租店，而且个性豪爽说一不二，他喜欢跟这样的租户打交道。他想着空置时间里不也收不到房租，还不如做一个顺水人情。于是刘老板答应租给李华，并赠送半个月时间给李华装修。

这店地点好离李华的新家又近，既然决定了开店，就要早点动起来，事不宜迟。李华看了这个门面，打心眼里满意，果断签了房租合同，立刻紧张有序着手房子的设计布置。为了节省投资成本，只请了一个木工师父将废弃的木头桩子锯成片，将自己手写的三个大字"莲湖缘"朝门面上方中间钉上去。不仅节约了广告费 5000 元，而且效果特别，在整条女人街上的门面店名看上去，就是别具一格。

李华在北京考察茶楼时拍照了一些门牌装饰风格，服装店的门面设计就参考了这样的风格：醒目、艺术、自然、怀旧、古朴、时尚。一下子吸引了路过女性人群的眼球，装修特色正好又符合艺术学院老师和大学生们的喜好，也适合平日出来买菜闲逛的家庭主妇们。

这是一次成功的选址，装修设计又得益于在北京考察所做的功课。世上真没有白走的路，人的思想和努力的行动，总能带来意想不到的收获！

装修服装店正在紧张而有秩序地进行着，同时李华也抓紧与北京发货的小洪老板沟通，全权让洪老板尽快在半个月时间组织好服装店开张的货源保证。在门店装修上面，李华还在色彩、音乐、灯光、镜子做设计布局，让整个只有上下 60 个平方面积的铺面，看起来不仅有特色，还非常实用，有足够多的隐藏空间放置东西。

李华将整个楼下设置成服装店，半面整墙有镜子，上方设计一面紫色纱布遮住客人试穿的空间。左角落一个小吧台作收银台，配备电脑播放音乐。右边是一面从下做到顶的服装展示柜，背景也是紫色，配上"莲湖缘"三个字，与店外的招牌呼应。在过道最里边的角落设置了一个小而实用的卫生间，上方也配备了一台电热水器。

店铺装修细节李华都想到了，到底是搞过装修的人，也幸好李华喜欢自己装修，设计。当李华做着这些男人的活，并没有觉得自己有多累，做喜欢的事情，盖过了一切的委屈和困难。

"莲湖缘"服装店如期开张了，李华既是老板又是服务员，一抹带十杂，什么事都干。她慢慢学习当服装店老板，也在观察摸索客人看货的喜好。起初两个月的守店，慢慢地累积了一些居民客户。逐渐又有了艺术学院的老师和大学生客户。因为价格合理实惠，很容易就让顾客动心购买。李华的服装生意就这样进入正轨了，生意一天天好起来，回头客户多了起来。

李华后来发现，那一排侧街上的店老板全部是单身女人，真是这么巧，李华怎么也没有想到，自己一下子成了服装店老板了，为改善自住条件环境，为家人过得更好，自己必须先要富起来，有米才能下锅做饭，有实力才能去帮到家人！这是实际生活！

有一天，晚上快要关门的时间，李华店里走进一个中年妇女，看着不像是要买衣服，神情看着很疲惫的样子。她手上已经拎了很多东西，这里瞧瞧那里望望。李华还是热心地叫妇人放下东西，慢慢看看有没有喜欢的衣服。这句话妇人听进去了，她把东西放在角落地面上，对李华说："我可以上洗手间吗？"

妇人的神情有点焦急，李华连忙指向洗手间的位置："可以，向里走左边就是！"妇人感激地点头，直接向里面快步走去。李华帮着客人看管着地面放的东西，扫了一眼，感觉是刚买的鞋子和服装一类的东西。有可能是妇人逛街逛了一天了，现在只是路过李华的服装店，随意地走了进来；也可能是尿急没有办法，走进来试试能否解决上厕所的问题。总之肯定不会是为买衣服走进来。

妇人轻松地从卫生间走出来，站在与李华的对面指着衣架上服装说："能取下来摸摸布料手感吗？"

　　李华边取边说：“可以，你慢慢看看有没有你喜欢的，我都给你取下来。我这里白天人多，因为是品牌折扣店价钱，跟刚上季的新款比，这老款便宜多了，来年又时新起来。晚上客人少，你可以慢慢选！”

　　妇人眼睛一下子亮了起来，慢慢看慢慢摸摸，转了一圈，又转过头对着李华说：“老板你有水喝吗？”

　　李华迅速地将一次性杯子装满水递到妇人手上说：“请坐在这沙发上慢点喝，喝完了还有。坐下来歇歇，没有事就坐着慢慢看。”

　　妇人真的坐下来，跟李华边喝边聊。沙发前的茶几上，李华将平时放瓜子和糖果的水果盘移到妇人面前，“你还没吃晚饭吧，先垫垫肚子。这苹果橘子果很甜的，吃点吧！”

　　妇人拿起水果笑着说：“我都没有买衣服，你还给水喝又给水果吃。你这老板脾气真好，这么有亲和力，我感觉怎么你一点不像老板呢？你真是老板吗？”

　　李华大声笑了起来：“美女姐姐呀，我一个人闷得慌，有你陪我说话，还照顾我的生意，这是我求不来的客人。人家说了客户是上帝，一看你就是一个有范的主！买不买都没有关系，咱们有缘，以后随时来坐坐！”

　　妇人满足地说：“我是看见你店铺的招牌有特色，好奇走进来看看。没有想到你人好有耐心，服装实惠，最主要是我喜欢的风格。但是我今天已买了这么多东西了，可还是想在你店再买几件衣服，真怕是冲动啊！”

　　李华说：“没有关系，今晚你看中的服装我给你留着，一个礼拜之内都可以随时退换的！”

　　妇人果然出手了，毫不犹豫地买了七件，连配饰品都挑选了三样，那件挂着的冬季才穿的大衣，也被这妇人买走了！妇人真的很开心地离店。

　　李华关店的时间晚了，平日九点关门，今天却是十点。李华看看墙上电子钟的时间，高兴地一边摇头一边默默笑着，脸上浮起了辛苦值得的神情。原来做生意也要善待每一个客人，说不准谁是一个大买家，一个喜欢你的好客人。李华的生意兴隆是有道理，她在那条街上，最后成了女老板们的聚餐点，聊天拉家常的小茶舍，因为那条女人街的女老板们，几乎隔壁像串门似的，来光顾李华的店坐坐，喝茶聊些天南地北的趣事，常常把客户也逗笑了，甚至有小区邻居客户，也成了李华店铺里的常客和朋友！

第二十八章　待客之道

人们常说同行是竞争对手，可是李华却打破了这个说法，李华跟同行做起了朋友。

"莲湖缘"服装店隔壁是一家首饰品店，老板名叫小林，她开的是真品玉石店，有发晶、水晶、紫晶石等等。相比之下，小林店生意清淡，几乎没有人光顾。后来小林与李华熟悉了，就经常到李华店坐着聊天。

有一天俩人正边吃瓜子边正谈着，旁边运动休闲服装店的女老板欣儿也笑眯眯走了进来："你生意真好，总看到你家客人多，我想来看看取经验。"

李华边起身边说："快来坐坐，吃点瓜子。主要是我的服装便宜，一个便宜十个爱嘛。我看你家店也有很多学生进去买！"

欣儿说："我是为了好玩，做着打发时间。我的店员小君对我说，你去莲湖缘看看，那家店生意肯定好，总是看到进进出出的客人，所以我就来看看。反正我们不是做一个风格的牌子，没有冲突哈！"

小林也插话说："我也想跟莲湖缘买些服装，所以也过来坐坐。"

一条街上的三个女老板就这样亲密地聊起来了，店里的生意照做。

有客人进来指着墙上挂的花连衣裙说："这件连衣裙是你电脑显示的款式吗？"

李华说："对，就只进这一件！"

小林老板接话说："要是我穿的码子，我就买走了！"

欣儿老板说："你店衣服怎么这么实惠，是哪进货的呀？"

李华知道是两位老板帮客人做买的决定，有意帮助李华一搭一搭地促使生意成交。

年轻的客人穿着很时尚，看样子是艺术学院学生，她问三人："你们哪个是这店里老板呀？"

李华走出来说："我是。"小林和欣儿同时指着李华异口同声说："她是！"哈哈哈笑声同时响起，客人和三个老板都笑了起来。

李华抓起茶几上的一把瓜子递给年轻的女客人说："边吃边看。说心里话你真有眼光，这件连衣裙是我店最喜欢的样板。这红色大花大朵的，有范的美女才能穿出那个韵味。你大气时尚，穿上一定迷死人。不信的话，我取下来，你试穿给我们看看！"

一席话让年轻客人做了试穿，站在镜子之前的客人跟之前判若两人了。"像明星，妖艳又性感！"欣儿称赞道。小林也附和着说："真看不出来，穿在身上效果真好。再配上一串项链，在鸡心领胸前吊着，更是勾人啊！这连衣裙还可以帮我进一件吗？"

李华说："总部没有货了，这是断码处理才有这个价格。"

年轻客人边拉上帘子边对李华说："老板，这件我要了！我脱下来，给我包好！"

小林和欣儿佩服地向李华笑笑，友好地说："老板实在，难怪生意好！"

这期间又走进三个年轻女孩子，小林和欣儿同时起身帮着李华招呼接待着客人，李华放心地收着钱，那笔刚谈成的交易。李华已经习惯了由同行的老板小林和欣儿去照应着店里的客人，李华也没有想到，同行一条街上的老板们成了朋友！

一晃神晚饭时间到了，李华打了订餐的电话，叫送餐到"莲湖缘"服装店。餐厅老板马上说："知道了，一个辣椒水煮鱼片，一个青炒红菜薹，一个酸辣土豆丝，三碗米饭！"20分钟后送到了李华店里，李华指着茶几上的订餐说："小林，欣儿一起吃，这家餐馆做的是湘菜味道，尝尝好吃！"

欣儿和小林同时说："哇！还管我们晚饭，以后没事就来你店蹭饭吃！"

李华说："快趁热吃，现在客人正好少。今天谢谢你们俩了，帮我做成了几笔生意！"

小林说："举手之劳！"

欣儿说："都别客气了，生意就是要人捧场，再说你店服装确实划算，客人买得起！"

李华笑着说："我们以水代酒，开喝开吃了，改天我们一起再去 K 歌！"

此时虽然是夏天，三个女老板照样吃着湘菜，不停地说："辣，辣得真过瘾，太地道了。"

小林看着李华的脸已泛红了起来，看着欣儿脑门上冒汗，笑着呛到了，还不忘抢着说："看来以后，我们这条街的生意都会带活起来，为生意兴隆干杯！"

李华的"莲湖缘"服装折扣店在那条单身女人街上生意出奇的好，整体店面装修风格搭配与其它店设计不同，所以很容易找到。就连送餐外卖人员也知道"莲湖缘"服装店，隔壁首饰品店开了多年，送外卖的就是不清楚。小林情急下说："我店就在莲湖缘隔壁！"送外卖的小哥立即回复："哦，我知道，那你就在莲湖缘取快餐好吗？正好莲湖缘老板也点餐了！"

小林哭笑不得地对李华说："唉！我点的午餐，餐馆服务员只知道送到你的店铺。我今后就到你这里才能吃到饭哟！"

李华说："你不怕麻烦，我们俩一起吃哟！我也点了一个烤鱼，应该你喜欢吃！"

果然午饭一起都送到了"莲湖缘"，小林和李华像这样的一起吃午饭已经是常态了。后来这条街上的休闲装店老板欣儿点餐也送到莲湖缘。莲湖缘的客人也增多了起来，在附近的美容院小美女们也会光顾着李华的生意。李华是美容院的优质客户，知道是美容院老板发话让小美女们来照顾李华的生意。生意伙伴之间互帮互助在这个时候体现出来了，李华也很感动，建立的友情是在逐渐加深，彼此之间已很信任了。

2008 年 5 月份的一天，李华像以往一样 7 点多醒来，开始起床整理好店里二楼放的冬季服装库存。这是北京发货的小洪老板所建议的一批分销老款红色的大衣。小洪说只有大批量进货才能享受最低折扣。李华听了小洪建议，先进了 40 件，这也是帮小洪分销一批任务。零售价可以根据自己市场需求来决定。

李华折中了一些客户信息需求，她不想把冬季的衣服积压几个季节再卖出去，于是给 QQ 好友发了信息，也给一些爱打扮的女同学打了电话。直接告诉那些喜欢穿漂亮衣服的旧同事，新老朋友们快来店看看，选择一些适合自己的服装。看中就按进价加点运费，不挣钱只保本销售，尽早吐货减少积压成本资金，顺便帮北京小洪多分销点库存。李华只拿出少量的冬季服饰挂在店里当宣传促销。

消息一发出，第一个回复电话的是旧同事丽丽，她现在工商银行工作。在原来小城市里面，丽丽就住在李华父母家隔壁小区，现在也办理了内退手续，正闲着没事干，听说李华在省城开了一家服装店，好奇心也想来看看李华。

丽丽跟李华在 18 岁时就在一个厂里工作。那个时候丽丽的爸爸是黄冈区的干部，丽丽还有一个哥哥，一个妹妹。丽丽是最得宠长得最漂亮的女儿。

那时候李华是厂里的运动健将，丽丽常常在球场边看李华打羽毛球。最初只是看着李华运动的身影，后来忍不住下场练习，一来二去两人就熟悉了。李华很自律，下班休息几乎都能看到李华在球场打球训练的身影。人们常说，有恒心定力的人都会成大器。

丽丽就是被李华这股干劲吸引，两人成为无话不谈的好朋友，再后来丽丽还为李华介绍男朋友。李华常常笑称，当年丽丽介绍给自己的男生是有名无实的初恋对象。

李华从接到丽丽电话后，有意无意地想到这些青年时代的趣事。时光过得真快，都这些年了，李华盼着丽丽早点来到店里。

想到这里，李华直接对着电话说："丽丽你来吧，住在我店里，我好好陪你两天，让你听听我这几年越来越好的经历，你保证开心！"

电话那头的丽丽笑得像花一样甜美："连住的都替我安排好了！毕竟是上省城了，看把你乐的，我一定会去！对了，我前天同学们聚会，我把你的手机号码给了你初恋情人郭奇志了。我等会把他的手机号码也发给你，你一定要保持联系哟。忘记告诉你，他现在也是单身，还是我们这个城市某税务局副局长呢，人家也在进步。到时候当面说给你听！哈哈，你们俩应该可以续前缘了吧？"

李华笑着说："你真是喜欢当媒婆，还提这些笑话我的事，等你来再谈这些故事！我现在只想心思怎么挣钱养家，哪有你命好，就是做官太太的命，你来了就知道我有多忙！"

第二十九章　好友来捧场

女友丽丽是一位随性洒脱的女人，真的第二天就来到了"莲湖缘"店里。进店的时候正是李华生意的高峰时段，李华刚接待完一个客人，正在收银台收钱。李华抬头看到笑眯眯的丽丽，手上也拿出一件正在促销活动的大衣："这件衣服我要了，这么便宜你不会是亏本清仓吧？"

李华赶紧走出吧台："是你穿的码子吗？穿着让我看看！"

丽丽说："我试穿了，很合身，给你捧场支持。店开张时也不告诉我，不然会给你红包！"

李华凑近丽丽耳朵小声说："给你包好，送给你，你别跟我扯了，让客户看到不好！"

丽丽欲言又止，只能示意让李华替自己包上衣服，随后又来到沙发前坐下来，慢慢环顾店里四周，像欣赏宝物一样看着李华做生意。丽丽怎么也没有想过李华会成为商人，真是时代造化人呀，李华从事业单位退出走入商海职场，从保险行业又转型投资自己开店当个体户，这几年肯定吃了不少苦，也一定见过很多世面。丽丽的眼神里充满羡慕和佩服。

李华接待完最后一个客人，就拿起一张湘菜馆的宣传单说："看看你想吃什么东西，就点什么菜，我们今天就在这里吃晚餐。等关门了，我带你在首义广场走走。在夜市吃点夜宵，这里的小吃街很不错！"

丽丽说："祝你生意兴隆！给你，郭奇志手机号码，装好！先把正事办了，你不忙的时候联系他！"

李华说："再说吧，你都看到了，我哪儿有空？还是挣钱重要！我明天叫女儿顶我一天看店，我陪你去看一个新楼盘。今晚你就跟我一起睡在店里楼上，委屈你一晚上，这里比不上你家豪宅，哈哈！"

说完，丽丽随李华上楼参观。楼上左边摆着一张 1.2 米的床，右边是一张木板大床，楼梯口正上方是服装设计展示柜，楼上还有一间储物空间，放满了进货服装。房间不大，但是干净整洁有序，楼上还有窗户，店铺正面的窗户都做了防盗铁网，后窗是对着小区院里，没有做防盗网。床头上系着一根绳子捆在床脚，丽丽问："这是什么意思呀？"

李华笑得合不拢嘴："我平常一个人睡觉的时候就害怕呀！害怕强盗和火灾，万一有什么灾难发生，前面不好逃，我可以捆住绳子向后窗逃出去。但愿是我多想了，有了预防措施就不慌不怕。"

丽丽听到李华这样说，顿觉得李华真的不容易，便关心地问："你为什么不再谈恋爱结婚呢？有一个爱你的人关心照顾你多好，你的退休金应该够你基本生活消费吧，非要把自己搞得这么忙？"

李华说："你明天跟我一起去看看新楼开盘，就知道了我为什么要做生意了。我看中了一套房子，必须开店挣钱获得流动周转资金。我想买到那套房子，今后一定会涨价。你也买一套吧，涨价了再卖掉，还可以挣钱！如果你想自住，那个地方位置很好，居住和投资都适合！"

丽丽说："你都看好了房子吗？我们明天一起去看看吧！我也喜欢房子，女人就怕没有窝！"李华得到丽丽赞同，高兴点头说："这我就放心了，还担心你明天去哪里玩，还不如做好考察房地产业行情走势，我们好好抓住投资机会获得利益，比开店还挣钱！如果有资金需要，我买房的钱不够的话，哪怕将服装店转让出去，也要买到那套房子，你懂我的意思吗？"

丽丽不停点头同意李华的思路，认为这个决定应该比守店经营更适合李华性格——守店浪费了李华的才能！

第二天是星期六，李华全程陪伴丽丽去看了武汉的三个楼盘，聊起了很多往事，也计划着未来投资房产的想法。李华恨不得把心掏给丽丽，让她相信这是难得的发财机遇。李华讲到这几年去过的几大城市，在房地产方面真的很有发展前景，买到了就是赚到。

李华讲到此话题非常兴奋激动，但是丽丽却说："我看武昌也是很好，我姑妈以前就在这边有几栋房子，后来经历了打倒资本主义那次运动后，被没收了所有的房子。我现在对购买房一点兴趣也没有，我家已有180平方的大房子，就是你去我家见过的那套房。有这样的房子我已经知足了，我可没有你这么拼，房子多了难打理！"

李华没有再说什么了，两个人说到这个话题不在一个频道。李华开玩笑说："那好吧，咱俩今天吃好喝好就行。"

丽丽与李华看完房子后，李华请了丽丽吃了晚饭，丽丽很满足地看看手表说："还得赶最后一班巴士，这里离汽车站很近，今晚我就回市里去。我俩散步走到汽车站，你就回店忙吧！"

李华说："你不多呆两天吗？还有大衣拿了吗？"

丽丽说："一直背包里，谢谢你，我就不客气了。你记得打电话给郭奇志，人家打电话给你，记得接听，聊聊总可以多一个朋友吧！"

李华点头笑着说："你也看到我多忙，身兼数职，又当服装店老板，又帮台湾卞姐销红酒，还有门窗工程要做，恨不得变成会分身术的孙猴子。哪有时间去谈恋爱？不过，如果他打电话给我，我会接的，因为我也过得很充实。还是挣钱有胆呀！"

丽丽一边跟李华说着，一边向汽车站方向走去。俩人在车站就此别过，丽丽坐在车上向李华挥挥手说："快回店去吧，有什么情况给我电话！"

李华说："那是肯定的，不然你会让人睡不成觉！我会告诉你买房进展的情况！拜拜！"

平日里，李华守店生意比其他店好，基本上总有人进店看看。有的客人从路人变成了李华的朋友，甚至其中有些就有李华小区的令居。今天幸好李华女儿帮忙看店，要不然李华还真脱不了身陪同丽丽。

李华女儿很懂事，知道妈妈只是开了一个小店，为了节约员工成本，没有请员工看店。李华女儿平日周一到周五全天工作，只有在周末星期六才能帮忙顶替妈妈守店，常常带着同学同事来照顾妈妈的生意。

李华的女儿这次又带来八个美女顾客，每人都买了三件以上的服装，她们都买了一件红色的大衣，都说太便宜了。这些美女说要一起穿起红色大衣，显得有范儿。

李华知道每次女儿星期六守店都会创收，店里生意都是女儿的朋友们捧场。李华想，这种靠照顾性质的生意是有回数的，也是靠着女儿和李华人缘好，熟人热心帮衬，不可能总是让人家破费包销。

女儿每次星期六到店，都会先穿上店里积压最多的服装。这件红色大衣穿

在女儿身上怎么看都好看，路过的客人看了一眼，脚就停住了。一位小区嫂子问："美女，你身上穿的大衣，有我穿的码子吗？"

李华女儿热情地答应："有，你看你侧面那一排架子上，大中小码齐全。这是公司打折扣最实惠的价格，物有所值，超划算！你看原价399元，现在折扣价只需109元。如果买两件，单件价只需89元。你放心挑选试穿，夏天买冬季款，是最省钱的。有年轻的老师买了两件，说送给儿媳妇当过年礼物，红红火火的寓意多好！"

客人甲说："真的，标签上价格还是399元，这送朋友也拿得出手！"

客人乙说："美女老板有包装的袋子吗？我想买两件，一件M号，一件S号。我自己一件，送闺蜜一件，今年过年红色的衣服搞定了。给我单独包起来，优惠价可以吗？"

李华女儿说："没有问题，给你活动价格，包你满意！"

女儿做生意不比李华差，还且很有创意。客人心服口服，这价钱真实在，寓意又好，中国人本身喜欢过年过节穿红色的衣服，显得喜气。

晚上李华回到店里，跟女儿结算当天的收入，比平时要多1060面额，那天再创最高营业额3080元。

第三十章　闺蜜情谊

丽丽来访一周后，李华在店盘点着销售的大衣，只剩下最后几件了，她心里松了一口气。这时店门口外听到有几个女人的声音，"是这里，你们看莲湖缘三个字。李华电话里说过，是用木头树皮钉上门牌。肯定是这里，总算找到了！"

另外一个女声音说："还真好找，是这家，李华也说过隔壁有家玉石首饰品店。"接着又听到一句话："你们俩真是的，进店看看不就清楚了吗？"

李华在玻璃门里面隐隐约约听出了是谁的声音，赶紧打开门，"哈哈，是你们三个！好找吧，快进来！老同学这么给面子来捧场，我好开心啊！没想到你们三个约在一起！"

同学三人不客气，进店就坐在沙发上。李华把准备好的水果盘和茶叶都拿出来，泡好热茶，招待同学们。她们可是跟李华一起长大的同学，从幼儿园到初中都是篮球队、艺术队的成员。其中有一个会经商的同学叫敏俐，这个莲湖缘的店名，就是沿用了敏俐曾经开过的茶楼起的名字。李华听敏俐说过，初中袁老师帮她的茶楼起了"莲湖缘"的名字。没有想到李华也用来当服装折扣店的店名，一名多用——当然不在同一个地方，茶楼开在三级市里，而且还是几年前的事。现在李华开的是服装店，相同名字用在不同的行业不会引起冲突，庆幸好名字可以重复使用。

敏俐笑着说："我们的袁老师肯定要收版权费，我们俩都要给！"

同学惠珠说："快参观一下服装店，我们先到楼上看看。李华说今晚让我们一起就睡在店里。好想看看我们睡觉的地方！"

同学闺蜜珊妮说："急什么？今天又不走，让你看个够。"闺蜜珊妮说到这里，还是跟着惠珠上了楼，边上边又问："这店里面真宽敞，我们就睡在这木板床上，还是睡在那张小床上？"珊妮指着楼上的两处睡觉地方向楼下李华喊了起来。李华回答道："你们自己选择，想睡在那里都可以。在我这里自由，听你们的！"

敏俐说："我不睡在这里了，你知道的，我武汉光谷金地那边也买了房子。我不凑热闹给你添麻烦，你只管她们俩！"

李华说："没有关系，睡得下，你赶过去多累呀？"

敏俐说："很方便，就在店出门走几分钟是彭刘杨路站台。从你这里到我那边真方便，不累。我经常坐公交车到武广、中南、汉阳钟家村逛街。别担心我，我很熟悉。你忘了我们俩还有娜娜一起在武汉到处看房子？"

李华说："没有忘，告诉你，我最近又去看了新楼盘，真想买，比我们前二年买涨价了 2000 多。我们那个时候闭着眼睛买房都挣钱啊，只需要 4000 左右。现在涨 6000 多，还有涨价的空间，因为大城市人多啊！"

从楼上下来的惠珠和珊妮说："你们两个人又聊房子了，敏俐衣服看中了吗？"

敏俐说："我已选了一件红色大衣，最爱漂亮的两位美女，你们俩快挑！"

珊妮也说："我也拿一件红色大衣，过年正好穿，红色喜气。这么便宜，质量还好。这跟我们以前经常去的黄冈店是一样的服装风格，可以多挑一些！"

惠珠说："我看也觉得像那家店的服装类型！"

李华说："你俩眼光真准，没有错，我就是加盟了小洪老板的服装店。她在北京直接给我发货，我不操心进货了！"

珊妮说："原来是这样，我们以前总去小洪她家总店买衣服，一买七八件，每次李华买得最多！现在自己开店了，你的衣服穿不完了！"

李华大笑说："你们都爱买衣服，哪个少买了？"

大家你一句我一句顶着说，像过去年轻时候一样。有时拌嘴，有时还闹心不欢而散，但过几天又像没事一样，又好了起来。同学就是同学，有事不放在心里，说完了就完了，没心没肺的时光也曾快乐地度过。

李华看着珊妮，突然想起了前几天丽丽提起过的"初恋情人"郭奇志。在那段还没有开始就已经结束的关系中，珊妮也是其中一个当事人。李华本想跟珊妮聊聊这件事，但惠珠和敏俐在场，李华不方便说起这些涉及个人隐私的旧日往事。

只是想起了那段往事，李华又觉得好笑，情不自禁地把笑意挂在脸上，话风一改："快挑，快选，今天中午在店里吃饭。下午关店，晚上在首义小吃街去吃沸腾鱼和烧烤。晚上去舞厅跳舞，我们没有在一起跳舞有很多年了吧？你们不来，我都没有顾得上玩，就是住这么近，我都没有去玩！"

惠珠和珊妮说："这里还有舞厅？"

李华说："有，知道你们俩喜欢。敏俐今晚别回去，一起看看呗！"

三位同学都在李华店里选了自己喜欢的衣服，待客人都结账散去后，都异口同声地说："老板结账买单！"

说完将准备好的钱直接放在收银台上。"不找了，收下！别扯了！"三个同学都这样对李华说。

李华说："你们不用这样，一是一，二是二。你们来捧场，我已经很开心了。真的，我还图你们经常来玩，该怎么样就怎么样好吗？"

李华把该找的零钱，都放到每个人的手上，心里才妥了。珊妮说："好吧，真不怕麻烦，这么认真！"

这天午饭就在店里叫外卖，麻婆豆腐、鱼香茄子、糍粑鱼，这些菜都是很下饭的菜。她们一起边吃边聊着午餐，大家都说好吃。快吃完的时候，客人就来了。李华看着已卖出去了很多衣服，便早早地关店，去吃晚饭的地方附近转转逛逛街！

晚餐选择了吃沸腾鱼的名店。鱼丸、鱼片下锅，那种辣味进入嘴巴里，每人都说："过瘾！味道太正宗了！"

大家都说吃饱了，要出来走走，走出来的时候已经是舞厅马上要开放的时间，晚上八点钟开场，十点钟散场。有乐队伴奏，很有跳舞的氛围。灯光照着人群里，忽明忽暗，气氛暧昧的暖灯光在舞动的人群扫过穿梭。李华看着同学们很放松地跳着舞，自己也疯狂舞动。跳快三华尔兹，还是习惯选择和珊妮跳，珊妮当男伴，李华跳女伴的步伐，还是原来熟悉的舞曲。虽然体力不如当年，但是两人默契地想起了年轻时候跳舞调皮场景，同时不约而同地一下子都笑了起来。

李华说："这么久没跳舞了，还是很爽啊！"

珊妮说："是啊，你比以前重了，我快带不动你了，哈哈！"

李华说："哈哈，是你长胖发福了，你应该继续多运动哟！"

珊妮说："是啊，以后我回市里后约好友阿香一起跳广场舞。"

　　敏俐被大家一起拽进舞厅。惠珠被一位帅哥请跑了，舞厅中飞转。慢曲子的时候，敏俐也被一位男士请去跳了一曲慢四舞步。那晚大家都玩得尽兴开心，全部出汗了。李华说："这才是美容养颜最好的运动，出汗就是全身排毒！"

　　一直跳到舞场十点散场，个个意犹未尽，散步回到店里。四个人洗完澡，直接都挤在地板的木床上，穿着睡衣聊天，不时地发出调侃互相取闹的笑声。一直聊到下半夜，才慢慢地睡去。四个人横躺着那张地板木板上，房内那张 1.2 米的床空着。同学们真愿永不长大，没心没肺地在纯真同学时代停住，这情谊假不了，一聚就这么开心。

　　这就是发小闺蜜之间的亲密关系，不知道今后还有没有这种铁关系，什么都可以说，什么也可以不计较，可以不用装饰掩饰自己的情绪，这样的情谊真可贵，就像那个年代一位台湾歌手唱的那首歌一样，情义无价！

第三十一章　好友的建议

　　第二天早上，三位老同学早早醒来，跟李华一起吃过早餐后，便按照商量好的计划，珊妮和惠珠直接步行去江边乘轮渡，去对面在武汉有名的批发市场汉正街转转；敏俐在附近公交站上车回自家。李华和同学们挥手告别后，才独自散步回店开门营业。李华正想看看日历上写的备忘录内容提示，突然电话响起来："喂！李华呀，明天我上午会来武汉开卫生组织防疫会议，下午可能会和司机一起来你店看看，帮我选一些适合我穿的衣服哦！明天下午争取见，晚上我请你一起吃饭！"

　　卫悦悦高兴地在电话那头说着，李华很开心地说："没事，随你的时间来吧，我都在店里等你。等会我把店铺地址短信发给你手机上，你的司机就知道怎么来了！"

　　李华想，今天真是好日子，刚刚送走一波老同学，又接到了高中时代的女同学卫悦悦来店的电话。平日里卫悦悦话不多说，是李华的朋友中最朴实的一位，但她一直给李华温暖的支持。卫悦悦的爱人祥和也是李华的同班同学，而且还是在高中最后一学期当毕业班的干部，担任团支书。没想到这同学祥和进入社会后成了卫悦悦的爱人。一个从事医务工作，一个经商。更没想到是，因卫悦悦的善良好性格，让李华和这对同学夫妻还成为最好的朋友。后来李华从卫悦悦口里知道，祥和同学有段时间因病住院，这期间认识了卫悦悦而展开追求。

　　李华跟卫悦悦的同学友情一直很稳定，从李华结婚，生孩子，过生日，李华再婚请的证婚同学，也只请了卫悦悦和祥和二人。后来李华还和卫悦悦当了一回媒人，给另外一个单身女同学促成了一段姻缘！

　　李华想到明天下午就可以见到卫悦悦，心里一阵欢喜。李华很喜欢卫悦悦低调稳重大方随和的性格。李华有很多知心话都会告诉卫悦悦倾诉，她知道卫悦悦从不传话也不笑话她，总是在需要帮助的时候出现在李华的身边，默默地

听着李华倒出来的苦恼！这种友情让李华放心踏实，盼着第二天下午卫悦悦的到来，她想好好聊聊！

果然在第二天下午，"莲湖缘"迎接到卫悦悦到来。司机进店就说："卫主任，你和同学先聊着，我去停好车再来！"

卫悦悦说："小李，你先把车上的水果拿到店里，然后你去停好车，再过来坐坐！"

卫悦悦平和地对待同事司机小李的态度非常谦和，没有架子。卫悦悦就是靠专业技术硬水平，一天天成长在专业干部中脱颖而出，最后成为当之无愧的主任医师！

卫悦悦接过李华递过来几件衣服，就进帘子后面试试，不仅合身，而且时尚大方得体！走出帘子卫悦悦说："你挑得真好，再帮我多选几件衣服，看有没有祥和穿的衣服？还有司机小李穿的衣服，你帮他也选择几件！"

李华知道这是卫悦悦照顾她店里生意，来一次不容易。李华也知道医务工作很忙，开会后都想到特意看看她，这份情谊很难得。

李华说："卫悦悦你若是真的全部需要，就拿走；别买些不需要的，不用特意照顾我店里生意，明白吗？"

卫悦悦的司机小李赶紧上前对李华说："你不知道，卫主任在路上就跟我说了，今天到同学店多挑选好衣服，绝对实惠。一进来看了一下，还真的实在，又是品牌折扣，肯定我们都需要才买！"

卫悦悦说："我怎么会跟你客气呢？真的需要！也确实便宜嘛。按男士穿XL码子拿两件，再给我儿子也拿两件上衣。要不然他们会说我只顾自己，不公平。来一趟不能空手回去，一起算钱，分两个包装袋就行了。搞完后我们就一起去吃晚饭，今天就照顾你早点关店休息！"

李华没有多说话，她心里在想，这就是卫悦悦有意照顾她的生意。虚假的话李华也说不出口，她对卫悦悦这任高中同学真是平淡中见真情。平日各自忙碌，一旦哪家工作生活出了点什么事，两个人都会互相替对方着想，尽力提供帮助。

在晚上的酒店饭桌上，司机小李点的菜全部是李华爱吃的湘菜，真是细心照顾到李华的重口味。这都是卫悦悦叮嘱司机小李点菜别忘记的主菜谱，还记得李华爱吃什么，甚至还多点了一些主食，让服务员打包，让李华带店里明天吃。

卫悦悦说："我妹妹以前开过汽车配件店，长期守店，吃饭就是不方便，我经常送饭去。所以我理解你一个人守店不容易啊。吃饭时你用微波炉转一下就可以吃上口，在店做饭不方便，也不容易做出好味道，你说呢？"

卫悦悦总会在生活细节上替李华着想，这一举动让李华特别感动。李华离婚后这么多年单身生活，只有李华把自己当汉子去拼命挣钱照顾家人和女儿，从没有人在生活小事上能陪伴照顾到自己。卫悦悦这些自然有意的关心体贴，让李华在心中很温暖，李华有些感激卫悦悦真诚朴实平易近人的善良。李华很欣赏卫悦悦不温不火的文静性格，稳妥的好印象也是友情走到一起的主要缘故。

李华说："我过段时间要买房，我想好了，接下来就得卖掉房子，才能有资金投资房产。我感觉还是投资房子才靠谱，又没有这么辛苦。一天干12小时，就我一个人全部顶着，又是营业员，又是老板，一抹带十杂，已经练出来了，什么都干。创业就是要做操心的准备！"

那天李华话多了一些，但是讲的都是大实话。那晚上吃得多也聊得多，通过交流，卫悦悦也说出了好的建议："你适合做好任何事情，事实上我们都看到房地产赚钱机会大于目前开服装店。"

李华接话说："是啊，做这家服装店就是为了投资少，资金回笼快。但是守店时间把我限制了，我无法脱身去干其他事情。所以这次考察了几个大楼盘再求突破。这几个楼盘真的很好，像武昌积玉桥金地，还有那地标绿地楼盘，还有汉街楼盘项目。这几个大楼盘，如果有钱买到就挣到了。不知道你有没有计划将来给孩子们在省城买房？"

卫悦悦说："我就一个儿子，我们就让孩子跟着我们身边，等我退休了也好照应儿子，帮帮他。不过你不同，既然已经在省城了，肯定要趁早买房，安居才能安心乐业嘛。如果你投资房子能解放你守店时间，又能多挣钱。那就抓住机会，时间就是金钱！"

李华的心思被卫悦悦看懂了，而且很支持李华。李华心里有数了："我可能会在近期做出决定，让服装店在经营挣钱的时期转出去。收回的投资成本和利润，全部投资两套住房项目的首付款。这样才有买房贷款。如果果断盘出服装店，就可以衔接抓住这次好楼盘的项目投资。我不再纠结了，就这样办！"

卫悦悦对李华温和笑着说："其实你心里早有主见了，只是非要得到别人的肯定。以后可以不用考虑别人的建议，还是跟着你自己的感觉走。我是学医的，但我也认为有些时候女人的第六感很准，相信你自己！"

那次晚餐不仅仅是吃了一顿饭，对李华来说更重要的意义在于获得肯定，坚定执行自己的计划。李华考虑了一整套的转让计划，开出了三种很诱人的条件。果然在一周时间内，迅速转了出去，将押在房东手上半年的租金退回来了。按照合同，将半个月的租金直接奖励给转让接店的老板。这样看上去是李华亏了半个月的房租，但是为了顺利转让，安抚房东不作乱阻止，在各种条件不影响房东利益情况下，房东只有妥协了，并配合李华顺利转让。

由于及时的资金整合，李华把所有收回的成本和利润，全部投资到已经看好的两个楼盘：一个是武昌金地花园，一个是汉口万科楼盘。一切如李华所愿，李华的投资房产操作又成功了，为女儿又一次投资婚前名下的房产，也为自己在省城投资了一套市中心地域的小户型住宅。

就在服装店转出的最后一天，一位意想不到的来客却出现在李华店门外，他是谁呢？

第三十二章　遇见初恋对象

　　李华的服装店转让后，第一时间把房子的事情定好，处理所有最急的事情。在合同章程细则里，李华存放的东西要在一周时间内全部清理。就在快要到退店前两天，李华还有一台电热水器需要拖走。这几天已经把李华忙得够呛了，一刻也没有闲着，女儿也利用休息的时间来帮忙。这个时候，李华的电话铃声响起："喂！是李华吗？"

　　李华听着来电，惊讶地反问道："你是谁，你不会打错吧？有什么事尽管说吧，我现很忙！"

　　对方没有挂机的意思："是我呀！丽丽没有对你说吗？我是郭奇志，现在在服装店门外，怎么看起来是空店啊？"

　　李华说："你在那站着别走动，我在楼上清东西，马上下楼！"

　　虽然郭奇志与李华有十几年没有见面了，但是彼此之间的声音还是听得出来。见面的那一瞬间，大家好像很熟悉一样，一点都不陌生。郭奇志大大方方地跟李华打了招呼："没有想到吧，我来看你了。可惜来得不是时候，怎么店转出去了？如果不是今天来，还找不到你！这是上天帮我呀，来得及时！有需要我帮忙的吗？今天我可以听你指挥，我没有别的事情！"

　　李华正急着要找人帮忙，郭奇志不请自来，这位李华的"初恋对象"出现得太及时了。若是在以前，也许李华还会假意矫情委婉拒绝，把女人的矜持好好表现出来。现在的李华坦然多了，郭奇志也算自己的熟人，大大方方地接受对方的帮助。看着多年不见的郭志奇，李华不自觉又想起那一段过往。

　　那时还是八十年代，李华跟丽丽因为打球结识，两人成为好朋友。有一次丽丽生病住院，李华去医院探望丽丽。刚进病房，李华就看到丽丽坐在在床上翻着杂志书刊，好像准备要出去走走的样子。

　　丽丽问李华："唉！你怎么来了？"

　　李华说："你生病怎么不告诉我呀？"

丽丽说："没有生什么病！我来好事全身发软，上不了深夜班，来医院检查完，说我身体虚弱，需要调养身体。白天住在这里，晚上我要回家啦！幸好你来得早，不然的话我就回去了！"

李华说："没有大病就好，吓得我赶紧来看看你！那我们坐一下，一起回去吧！"

丽丽说："我正好要跟你说两件事，那个财务科长的大儿子文斌你认识吧？就是每天我们一起打羽毛球的时候，向球场这边弹吉他的那个人，你应该有印象吧？"

李华点点头，想起确实有这么一个人。丽丽说："看来人家喜欢你，问你谈了男朋友没有。我说没有，人家就要我帮忙问问你，愿意不愿意当他的女朋友。"

李华大惊："搞没搞错！你可千万别说跟我说了，我不会在厂里谈恋爱的，我不想找厂里的人当男朋友！"

丽丽说："也是，我也不想跟厂里上班的人谈朋友。你跟我的想法一样，要不我帮你介绍一个男朋友吧。我的同学刚从部队转业回来，他父亲是行署办公室主任，他妈妈以前也在我们这个厂里工作的，后来找关系调走了。哪天我帮你联系一下，让你们认识一下，可以先做朋友了解一下。他当然肯定比财务科长的儿子帅气年轻。他明天要来医院看望我，你明天也在这个时间来医院看我吧，就像是偶然遇上的。这是一个机会，我爸的战友给我介绍的男朋友也住在行署大院里，我男朋友的爸爸是行署专员，他们两人的家庭我都了解，都是干部家庭出身，你放心吧。我有男友这事你对谁都别说！"

一下子听到这么多秘密，李华有些心跳紧张了起来。她没有想过要谈男朋友这个问题，她感觉自己生活过得丰富多彩：该工作时上班，下班打球，或者练习跳舞唱歌，周末还去露天的游泳池学习游泳。这样的日子也过得很开心。没想到很快就要面对谈恋爱的问题了，也许是缘分来到了吧。

李华是家中长女，俗话说得好，"一家养女百家求"。为了打消厂里财务科长儿子的想法，李华也想快点公开有男朋友的消息，这样可以让财务科长儿子知难而退，李华也不至于主动拒绝而得罪他，李华也怕得罪他的父亲，财务科长——毕竟李华暂时还在这里面工作生活，李华不希望自己"没吃着羊肉却惹上一身臊"。这方面一定要处理好分寸，为此李华答应了丽丽的安排，就当偶遇跟丽丽的同学见上一面。

第二天李华应约而至。这次李华脚步有意放轻，她不想惊动别人，她想先看看丽丽介绍的退役军人长得怎样，也想听听他们谈论些什么话题。李华轻手轻脚地在门口站了一会儿，听见丽丽说："我介绍给你的女朋友，她可是从来没有谈过恋爱。有几个领导的儿子看中她，可她就是看不上人家。她性格真的很好，人又能干。见面后你留下自己的联系方式，多约人家女孩子，你不会让我教你去谈恋爱吧？"

那退役军人正是郭奇志。郭奇志说："谢谢丽丽介绍，我也是认真的。我妈说过，只要成了我们家的一员，将来会帮忙把李华调出厂，去一个更好的工作单位。看缘分吧，我家庭关系简单，一家四口人，父母亲加一个妹妹。"

李华看着背影对着丽丽说话的郭奇志，听着他刚刚说的一番话，感觉这郭奇志实在沉稳！

这个时候丽丽已经看到李华站在门口，看了李华一眼，又继续问郭奇志："那你准备什么时候带李华见到你父母亲呢？"

郭奇志说："要看李华的意思，我可以选择任何一个周末去我家吃饭。我都准备好见面礼了，一个黄色女军用挂包，一块女式手表，还有女兵军装一套。这些都是我在当兵的时候向退役女兵换来的，既时尚又有纪念意义，现在女孩子们都很流行穿上军装是吧。我的礼物可是拿钱都买不到的。"

郭奇志说了实话，在那八十年代初期，能穿上部队女装裤子，背上黄色挂包，再穿上一双半高跟鞋，就像是高干子弟文艺兵的打扮。穿上这套服装，女孩子显得有身份，而且气质不凡。

李华也是凡人，听到这里心里和丽丽一样有点高兴和得意，情不自禁地笑出声来。郭奇志转身向门口方向看去，站在眼前的女子正是李华。他看到李华身材娇小曲线苗条，刚好配上他的个子高度，一张圆圆的娃娃脸，看着单纯甜美，正是他喜欢的女友类型。

郭奇志说："你就是李华吧，我们正聊着你！"

李华瞧着有些偏黑肤色的郭奇志：大大的眼睛很深很亮，穿着一件白色衬衣，配着部队军裤子，一双黑色的皮鞋，看上去很文雅稳重，以军人习惯的直板站姿正站在病房里，很有一番军人的风范。李华顿生好感，但毕竟是第一次遇到这样的场合，李华还是不好意思多看郭奇志一眼，直接向丽丽笑着走去。

丽丽上前拉着李华的手对着郭奇志说："我的任务完成了，你们以后就自己说好约会时间，我可以不用管了。记得，你是男人应该主动哈！"

郭奇志笑着说："谢谢老同学帮忙，我会的！"

李华大脑飞快地想起了这些，突然感觉时间过得真快，一晃而过就是中年了。以前的小伙子如今变成郭大叔，郭奇志身材微微发福，现在李华自己暗自想笑，她还能心平气和地像对待朋友一样，与郭奇志相聊甚欢，没有一点别的意思了。像是对待一个老熟人老朋友的情感，大方随意却有分寸的距离，恰到好处掩饰住了起初萌发的一点"假设再续前缘"的念头。

经岁月洗礼，爱情和友情同时见光，就很快分清了。已成为郭大叔的男人，就知道自己没戏了！因为站在他身边的李华，无论在脸上在身材在事业方面，一点也没有留下岁月痕迹，倒是感觉在逆生长，反而多了一份成熟女人的韵味，依旧有惜日年轻时代的风采，真不亚于当年初见如故的模样。

第三十三章　青春往事

八十年代的年轻人刚谈恋爱时都害羞。每次李华和郭奇志约会都会把珊妮叫在一起，三个人并排一字行，沿着马路边上散步，李华在中间，右边是珊妮，左边是初恋郭奇志。

第一次约会时，李华不敢随便盯着郭奇志看，就叫闺蜜珊妮多暗中观察看看。就这样每周一次的约会都成了三个人的约会，每次会从李华的单位开始散步，送珊妮到单位宿舍，俩人又再返回李华单位宿舍楼。途中会经过一所中专学校的大体育场，两个人会沿着大操场走两圈，天南地北地聊天。

那个年代恋爱中的情侣连牵手都会心跳加速，有次他们遇到一条水沟，李华跟着郭奇志跳过去，被郭奇志双手紧拉着那一瞬间，俩人都不好意思，难为情地赶紧松开。那是夏天的傍晚，只有零零散散的人在散步，没有谁在意他们。那夜晚的微风从旁边树叶上吹过，树林中知了发出吱呀吱呀的声响，带动起一片水沟的青蛙欢唱——连小动物都在笑这俩人。那时正是李华情窦初开的时节，李华这种羞羞答答的样子，让郭奇志看得入迷。他想早点让俩人关系更进一步。郭奇志迫不及待地说："我们全家想见见你，这周末可以来我家吗？"

李华微笑而不语，这话就当风一样吹过耳边，听着很入耳，心里感觉暖暖的。少女情开，刚刚开始萌发可能是这样的感觉？到此时俩人已边走边聊，回到了李华的单位宿舍大门前。相处的时间真短，情路浅浅，刚刚才开始就走完了。这一次约会李华害羞，并没有及时回复郭奇志的邀请。

又一个周末，李华正在球场上和丽丽一起练习打羽毛球。珊妮已经应约在球场旁边站着，过了一段时间郭奇志也来了。

郭奇志看着李华在球场上挥动着羽毛球拍的身影，李华每一次青春跳跃的矫健活力都把他的目光紧紧吸引住。等李华下场时，郭奇志给李华递水，并对李华说："真看不出你羽毛球打得这么好。"

丽丽接话说："老同学你不知道吧，李华已经是我们这里连续两年女子比赛亚军了，你今天来约会呀？"丽丽扮一个鬼脸又笑着说："我不当灯泡了，我回家去，你们去转转！"

珊妮笑着说："我从头到尾都看你打球，越打越好了！我们等会去哪里？我今天上深夜班，只要不影响晚上十点车间接班，可以陪你们两个小时。"

那时是夏天，虽然已是晚上七点多，但天还很亮，没有黑下来。李华看着郭奇志问："你今天准备带我们去哪里？"

郭奇志深情款款地看着眼前的李华，想说什么又没有说出来，边摇头边看着脚下低声细语地说："我妈叫我这周六把你请到家里去吃饭，和家人见见，今天我是来跟你说这个事情。上次你还没有回答我，我们家里人还等我的消息呢。我们就在附近走走吧，你看呢？"

李华想了一下就说："那我们一起顺道送珊妮回她单位赶上夜班，我们再慢慢走回来，路上都可以聊聊，好吗？"

李华与郭奇志约会总是有闺蜜珊妮的陪伴，在那个年代也很正常，好像如果没有一个证人，就会不自在。李华就是这样的心理，有了闺蜜在旁自己的胆子也大点，敢开一些玩笑，活跃气氛，露出该有的调皮本性。

从李华单位穿过一所中专学校大体育场，就走到一条大街上，再向前走 10 分钟，就可以看到珊妮的床单厂大门。李华和郭奇志每次都会把珊妮送到马路对面的床单厂大门口，看到珊妮走进去，俩人才转身原路返回李华的单位。

回来的路上，郭奇志好奇地问："你和珊妮关系一直这么好吗？"

李华说："是啊，我们从小就在一起上学，打球。我到她家学会了包饺子，她喜欢吃我们家妈妈做的咸鱼咸菜。从小我们就好得不分你我，我有什么好吃的都想着给她一份。她性格好，每天上学总是到我家等我一起上课。我在家是老大，有很多家务活我得干，她就帮我丢垃圾袋。后来又一起参加了工作，只是没有分到同一个厂。"

郭奇志听李华说一些与珊妮孩儿时的趣事，又忘了问李华关于下周六见家人的答复。没多久又回到了李华单位大门口。郭奇志只得说："晚安，可能星期五下午我要抽空来厂里找你，看看你工作的车间好吗？这次就咱俩见面说这个事行吧？"

李华反应迅速："这不好吧，车间是工作地方，有什么好看的？哪有在工作地方约会的？"

郭奇志欲言又止，最终还是没有问出口。看着李华转身走进宿舍大楼后，才赶紧调头快步离开，那步伐就像军人的样子，果断，坚毅，就好像是给自己作一个决定，"星期五下午我一定要李华答应！"

很快就到了星期五，李华正在车间上班，机器嗡嗡作响。车间前面进来了一位陌生人，拾管工闫师傅问话，对走进车间的年轻小伙子："小伙子你找谁？这是车间工作重地！"

来人不是别人，正是郭奇志，他还真行，真的找到了李华的工作车间里。这样会造成不好的影响，李华被闫师傅叫了出来，急着问郭奇志："怎么你到这里来了，这样影响多不好呀！有什么急事，快点说呀？"

郭奇志看着四周，似乎一点不急，只是慢慢地说："我妈、我爸和妹妹，全家人定了这个星期天，一定要我带着你来我家吃饭，你答应我！我马上离开。"

"哎呀！就为这个事儿？你也不应急着在车间工作的时间找我呀？"

李华担心被车间领导看见了挨批可不好，哪有学徒谈恋爱被追到工作地方？李华又催促道："你赶快走，我妈说了，女孩子谈恋爱一定要男方父母亲先上女方家提亲，女方才能再去男方家，这是社会风俗。你们家是干部家庭，难道不懂得尊重这些风俗习惯吗？"

郭奇志纳闷了，接着说："这算什么问题，现在已经是新社会了，还那么封建迷信？只是吃个饭，大家相互了解，这有什么不对？你一定要去，我们家都给你备了见面礼，一块手表、一套绿色军装和黄色军挂包，这是现在最流行的。这次先来我家，下次抽空准备去你家，好吗？"

李华脑子飞快运转，像那一排纺织缫丝飞速运转机器。几秒钟后李华似乎下了决心，压低声音但很严肃地对郭奇志说："你先走吧，我想好了，我不能去你家。我妈要是知道了一个女孩子家先上男方家的门，一定会很伤心的，甚至会指责我不懂事。我妈说过了，女孩子一定要矜持一点，才能得到男方家人真正的尊重！要去，也应该你先上我家去，我家人同意了，再去你家才可以呀！"

郭奇志没有说话了，他有些生气地向车间外走去，最后又慢慢回头对李华说："那我们散了吧，如果你坚持不去，我只有这样跟家人交代！"

李华也生气地顶了回去："这很重要吗？不去就散了？散了就散了！这是

你说的！好，我同意结束了，你爱怎么跟你家人说就怎么说。不送了，我得回去工作！"

两人就这样不欢而散。这场初恋就这样结束了吗？连李华都感觉蒙了，还没开始就结束了？想想都觉得好冤枉！做个好女孩子就得放弃恋爱机会？李华有点烦躁了，听妈妈的话应该没有错，管他的呢？连这点事都不尊重女孩子建议，那以后谁听谁的就更难了？

李华没多说什么，就埋头干自己的活去了。这是她第三次拒绝了谈恋爱的机会，为了听妈妈的话，做个好女儿，做个懂事的女儿。李华觉得自己没有做错，但是人家郭奇志似乎也没有做错，那么是哪里出错了？那个年代造成思想观念，选择标准就选择按传统规则来，不会有错。

反正这个事情黄了，没戏了，值得庆幸的是李华是热爱生活的人，爱好广泛，打篮球，排球，羽毛球，游泳，骑自行车，跳舞，唱歌，织毛衣手工活，都占用了李华的所有休息时间。这样的生活也很充实，李华只不过是又回到了快乐的单身生活。丽丽知道后也没有说李华什么，只是说："你找男朋友挺挑剔的，若是嫁给郭奇志，肯定能给你调出这个厂，安排更舒适的工作。"李华也接话回说："是啊，郭奇志说过他妈妈就是从我这个单位，我这个车间调到行政事业单位工作了。就算他真有本事有关系，但没有耐心。"

一晃三个月平静地过去了。有一天周五下午，李华正准备上班，结果被突然来访的郭奇志拦在路边。

郭奇志说："有件事想求你帮忙，我想跟你的闺蜜珊妮谈朋友，你不介意吧？"

李华一时没有反应过来，她真没想到郭奇志来找自己是因为这样的目的。当时李华感觉到自己可笑，差点自作多情地以为郭奇志后悔了，来追回自己。真没有想到人生的第一次恋爱，竟是这般戏剧性地变化着。

李华故作轻松不屑一顾地说："好呀，我祝福你们。我没有意见，我不会介意，真的！"

李华说完直接走向上班的人群中，谁知道郭奇志又追上去说一声："你能今天陪我去当面说一声吗？珊妮要你说亲口说不介意！"

第三十四章　大气成全

李华停了下来，看着眼前的郭奇志，心里想着：反正都这样了，何不做个好人，成全他们。心里虽然有些不爽，竟和这样的男人谈过恋爱当朋友，李华感觉自己好笑，但很庆幸，和郭奇志什么也没有发生。

这两个人中，一个是好朋友，一个是刚刚开始初恋还没有发生激情的男友。李华对郭奇志并没有爱到深处的感觉，还没有体验到那种死去活来的爱情。他们好像只是牵过手，连拥抱亲吻都没有做过。两人之间的约会就是看了一场电影。这也没有什么不好放下的情感，最起码李华还没有痛苦过，失落过；也没有让郭奇志瞧不起，没有原则上的大错，没结过仇恨，也没说出彼此伤害的言语。

想到这里，李华在人群中喊了一个工友的名字："陈香，麻烦你上班替我跟对班素芬说一声，我有点急事，让她顶我一个班！明天我顶她上连班！"

转头再向郭奇志说："走吧，这个忙帮你，以后就别找我了。"

李华的果断让郭奇志感到惊讶，马上说道："好吧，那我们现在就走！她应该下中班了！"

李华感觉自己好大气，要是别的女人听了这话，一定气死。但李华却异常冷静，两个人一前一后地走着。此时的路，正是他们俩走过无数次的路，地方没有变，变的却是人的心。

真出乎意料，李华都佩服自己能这么冷静，对待郭奇志和珊妮这件事情就像劝解朋友间的矛盾一样。李华也明白，跟郭奇志认识开始，几乎每次约会都跟珊妮三个人在一起，这一段关系里参与者是三个人。若是他们之间产生了感情，也是很正常的，毕竟恋爱是两个人的事情，你情我愿才能走在一起。

唯一的俩人约会，是李华跟郭奇志看了一场电影。那部电影是《少林寺》，李华还学会了电影的主题曲《牧羊曲》。一直以来，只要去了 K 歌厅，李华都会有意无意唱这首《牧羊曲》。这是那个年代留下的精神烙印，李华也用它纪念那段昙花一现的感情。李华自认为的初恋，其实用现代的人情世故来说，那不叫爱情，更不是初恋，那只是人生中上车后，路过的一站必经之路，没有到目的地，在中途的站点就下车了。

十几分钟的路程不长，可李华千头万绪想了一路，想来想去还是觉得跟郭奇志缘分浅薄。

很快就走到珊妮的宿舍门口了，李华常来，对这里很熟悉。李华与郭奇志并排站着敲门，宿舍里珊妮在里面答应道："谁呀？进来！"

李华推门的那一瞬间，珊妮看到李华身边的郭奇志，什么都明白了。没等李华说出口就急着说："别听他瞎说，我还没有答应呢！"

李华很冷静平和地对珊妮说："我是特意请假过来跟你说，真的不用考虑我的原因，你们谈朋友，我真的没有意见，因为我和他什么也没有发生。只要你不介意我们谈过朋友这层关系，我祝福你们，我该走了！"

李华说完话转身走开。郭奇志也被珊妮赶了出来："你走吧，我马上要上晚班了！以后别来找我！搞成这样！"

做了这件事，李华释怀了，好像完成了一个任务，就彻底放下了。谁说女人失恋了就痛苦。李华没有觉得痛，只是理性上觉得惋惜。有时李华会觉得这种惋惜可能是一种心理上的伪装，为错失一次恋爱而装作轻松。李华当时何等镇静泰然自若，只是溜过一丝丝心头的不快，这事很快过去了。看来那不是初恋，只不过是让李华体验情窦初开的感觉。

从那以后，才再次见到郭奇志，是在李华单位大楼。这一晃十几年过去了，李华也没有想过还有跟郭奇志见面的缘分，真像电影。那时李华已是离异的单身女人，一门心思搞工作，正在市局办公室里任中心主任，主要负责单位行政事务，管理食堂工作，包括食材进货、厨师和服务员的管理，还有负责接待省里市里的业务客人，还要抓职工干部食堂的饮食工作。

有一天办公室三楼走进一位高个子的男人，敲门进来就说："请问，李华主任在吗？"

李华正好在办公室里审核进货账单发票，抬头看去那中年男人，长得很帅气，但不认识，便问："请问你找她有什么事吗？"

男人一口黄州人的乡音说："不是我找，是我们的郭局长找她。"

李华听出口音并疑惑地问："哪个郭局长？你是黄冈市来的？"

男人马上回答："是的，是郭奇志局长。他就在楼下大厅等着见李华主任！"

李华心道：是他？他怎么找到这里来了？这多年没有见过面了！李华沉思了一会，上前对男人说："她今天没空，要开会，你们回去吧！"

男人不甘心地问："那什么时候有空，让我下去好回话！"

李华想了想说："那就在 1 月 16 号吧，如果你们郭局长领导还记得这个日子。"

男人似乎明白了，眼前的女人应该就是李华主任，她的打扮也有点奇怪，在办公室里还戴太阳墨镜。男人退出了办公室，低头丧气地慢慢向电梯口走去。李华这个时候才放心了，幸好办公室里她来得早，其他科室里的人也没有串科室碰见。

李华心跳加速，心想：又是什么风把他给吹来了，我可不再怕你，你以为当局长了就不得了？嘿嘿，我也不差，这有什么好怕的！

李华边想边拿出抽屉的镜子，对着自己照了起来。取下太阳镜，慢慢看着两周前才隆过的鼻子，正在慢慢消肿。"要见也得我说了算，十几年没有见过面了，一定要让他见到最好的一面。即使没有什么目的，也得保持良好的形象，何况是这么一个初恋情人，连谈恋爱都变来变去，幸好当年没有谈成，刚才做得真好，拒绝的感觉真爽！"

李华想到这些，就安心地期待着那天到来。她也不明白为何要这么做，是为了证明自己的魅力？

鬼知道李华当时怎么想的，那不重要了。李华说的日子是自己的生日。李华给对方一个见面的机会，就当是跟老朋友相聚一回吧。

生日那天李华像往常一样上班工作，只是穿着上在职业装的基础上多配带了一条亮丽的丝巾。11 点钟郭奇志的电话准时打给了李华："我就在办公大楼前，车子停在前面路边，还是停在单位后院？"

李华说："你就停在大楼前路边车位上吧，你直接上后副楼二楼，我在这里等你！中午我请你吃饭！"

郭奇志说："这样吧，我带了红酒，在外面去吃吧！"

李华说："没有关系，到我这里看我，我请你吃一顿便饭而已，不要跟我客气！"

电话那头停了一会："那好吧，恭敬不如从命！"

郭奇志有些别扭地说着，李华站在二楼走道上，看着这位十几年未见过的初恋，心里突然觉得好笑。她自己都不知道为何要对这个男人这么盛情款待，按理说应该有点恨意吧，毕竟他曾经追过李华最要好的女友闺蜜，这事对一个女人来说怎么都算是一种伤害。郭奇志怎么能把这件事忘了呢？他为什么还有勇气来找自己？真是个奇怪的男人！

俩人见面相互看了又看，"你一点没有变！""你变漂亮了，保养得真好！"

俩人不约而同地夸奖起对方，坐下待客的小包厢里，郭奇志打量四周干净明亮的餐厅，将自己带上的红酒拿在桌上，"今天喝这瓶，好酒！"

李华想，微整形还是有必要的，她不是为别人漂亮，而是为取悦自己开心！年轻就是好，要让脸上看不出岁月的痕迹，她庆幸投资自己做到了。

那个年代，微整形可是一种最奢侈的投资，没有多少人舍得。李华舍得为学习、运动而花钱，也买漂亮衣服，做美容；就是不赌博，不抽烟，没有坏习惯，有自控力，也经得起诱惑！

这是郭奇志这次见面对李华的第一感觉，成熟知性的美，比少女时的李华更有内涵了。他知道眼前的李华经历过生活的磨炼，已不是当年的单纯少女，但依然能感受到她骨子里善良和谦和。李华依然风韵犹存，从职业装都能看出身材丰满而俏皮，那双高跟鞋在走廊上敲着的声响极有韵味。

现在李华的影子在郭奇志的脑海里翻腾，一幕幕地浮现在眼前。来之前想好的话，又不好意思说出来了。他以为自己单身了，又当了税务局的局长，应该还有资格追李华。可不知道怎么的，见到李华后，他害怕失去接触的机会，不敢提情感问题，只有像看望老朋友一样淡定地叙叙旧。

俩人谈到以前一起看的那场电影，谈到郭奇志自己小时候的时光，才知道他也缺乏安全感。郭奇志父亲曾经被运动时期下放劳动，那个时候他还小，还要照顾妹妹吃饭，妈妈也经常加班，很少能照顾到他和妹妹。

李华招待的工作餐已上桌，另外多点了两道菜，李华记得那是郭奇志最爱吃的红烧鲫鱼、五香粉蒸肉。郭奇志很感动，他也不知道为何丽丽要告诉他李华的近况和手机号。他只知道李华是单身，他也是单身了。也许丽丽想促成俩人再续前缘吧。他们俩纯粹是历史性的缘分，让他们之间少了一些陌生，多了一些包容相处的信任！

丽丽老觉得他们俩散了好可惜，又没犯什么大错，甚至想那时候都年轻，错过了一段本可应该有的良缘——不然上天为何又让两个人都又是单身呢？丽丽是他们美好时代的见证人，她太希望李华有个伴了，她总想再次促成李华与郭奇志缘分，但丽丽忘了，人都是在变的，更何况是有思想有主见的李华。

第三十五章　特别的生日

两人吃完饭后，郭奇志问李华："今天你可以请假半天，我们开车出去转转吗？"

李华平日以工作为重，很少休息，就答应了郭奇志，请假半天。还好今天公司不忙，又没有领导客人来访，李华生日提出休息半天，领导立刻同意，只要李华把工作安排好就行。

郭奇志高兴地问："你想去哪里？"

李华不假思索地回答："想去东方山，拜佛庙，抽个签！可以吗？"

郭奇志满口答应，说走就走！两人一起下楼，走向郭奇志那辆白色车子旁。郭奇志为李华打开车门，很亲切体贴地让李华先坐上副驾驶，自己再坐在驾驶座位上，系好安全带。李华照做顺便问道："这是你的私家车还是你单位专坐车？"

郭奇志说："我叫司机休息了，自己开私家车方便。"

李华不作声了，这是第一次坐初恋的车。以前年轻的时候还没有这样条件，约会都是散步，走来送去的都是步行，也挺乐的。没有一点攀比，谁也没有嫌弃过穷。可是现在谈恋爱都要讲房讲车，现在的人也变得很物质了，可偏偏李华对车没有概念，也不知道什么车子好，什么车子是豪车。李华从不虚荣，她只喜欢房子，那是经历过离婚后，她感觉有自己的房子，一处屋子就是家的感觉，才有安全感。

郭奇志问："你会开车吗？有私家车？"

李华说："我会开车，也有驾照，但说实话我不喜欢开车，喜欢坐车。我在空场地开车很厉害，但是一上正道就怕开车，心里打鼓，手脚不灵了。唉！从那以后就不想开车了。"

郭奇志又问："你这几年还有什么计划吗？比方说个人问题，不想再成家吗？"

李华抬头向郭奇志这边看了看："你还是安心开车吧，我们到东方山庙抽一个签，就知道了我的命运了。听天由命吧，就算我心里有计划，还要看天意呀！"李华说的是真心话，她正担忧纠结下一步该如何走。

她喜欢工作，但是不喜欢目前的这项工作。李华很想转行或调动工作，去一个是非少的单位圈子工作。李华不喜欢钩心斗角的工作环境，她没有那么多花花肠子心眼，就靠实干。但是有些领导还是喜欢拉帮结派互相吹捧，玩阴招，搞小动作，经营虚假的人际关系，提干升级！李华受到排挤，有点不舒服，但是不知道跟谁说，只有祈求佛缘观音菩萨给出指引，以求得安慰！

李华这些偶尔悲观无奈的情绪化反应，也是可以理解的。在现实生活中，一个单身离异的女人，需要做到不被少数小人排挤欺负，必须付出比常人的努力要多，还要有韧性钢铁般的性情，勇敢，正气！有实力才能做到众人服气！

车上一搭一问地聊天，时间过得很快，40分钟车子就开到了东方山停车场。因为不是什么节日，上山的人不是很多，庙会的亭子前后香台炉子，一缕缕香火青烟随风飘向天空。李华很虔诚地一个一个菩萨跪拜。郭奇志也站着旁边，双手合十拜佛。程序走完后，李华上正堂大厅找到抽签的和尚，摇出一个签。

和尚应声道："啊！是上上签，大吉！"签的内容是：君若游途出关走，半生银两不用愁，任你东南西北去，四海依旧为你荣。

真是好签，上上签，但是李华不敢相信，这怎么可能呢？李华心里想：我想离开这个工作环境，不工作还能有钱？我又不能没有工作，离了婚的女人必须有更好的工作，若是调到省里的工作有着落了，那也是工作才有"银两"呀？

李华很欣喜求到这个上上签，但不确定签文所说的内容真是自己的指引，内心还有点疑惑，把签文反反复复看了几遍。

这个时候郭奇志从钱包里拿出200元交给和尚，和尚谦和礼貌地敲了三下响钟，示意将钱放在功得箱里，并签一下捐赠者的名字。只见郭奇志提笔，在捐赠名册上写下了李华的名字。那一刻，李华想推辞都不能了，这是做善事积德！李华欣喜地默认接受了。

看来郭奇志对李华是真的上心了，他了解李华所想，如果此时送物质上的东西，李华肯定会拒绝，毕竟无功不受禄！

这一行，这个生日过得真有意义，真的没有想过李华39岁的生日，会与曾经的初恋度过佛系有意义的一天。李华有一个习惯，当遇到大的事情，无主见的时候，她会看一些佛教书和名人的哲理故事名言，慢慢淡化心中焦虑。久而久之就会独自一人上山，叩拜佛庙，听听敲响钟声，都会使心安静下来！

那一天过后，李华跟郭奇志并没太密切的联系。李华认识了于平，并成了于平的妻子。郭奇志也知道这件事，他跟李华的姻缘也没能发展起来。这一晃又是多年过去，再次见面时就是李华的服装店退店的这天，郭奇志及时出现帮忙搬店。

李华猛然想到郭奇志跟她缘分不浅，这次与上次东方山一别，时隔了七年，两人又在武汉相见了。没缘分做情侣，可彼此之间成了熟悉的朋友。

郭奇志很自然地帮李华清理店里的重物，将店里的热水器放到车子后备箱。按照李华说的地址，运到黄冈市温州商城，那里有一处李华多年前投资的三层店铺。

这回该郭奇志吃惊了，李华还在他的城市买了一套门面房！一个小时的车程，终于到了李华投资的那套门面房，郭奇志熟悉这商城的情况，麻利地将热水器搬到三楼。他打量着已装修好的店铺，这里看起来空置多年，一直没出租，只是小幅度涨几万元钱。

李华自嘲道："这是我投资房产没有经验的一次。钱虽然不多，但是快十年了也没有看涨。我被温州炒房团坑了，一位爱炒房的女友巧嘴说服了我，扮演好人让利将这门面摔给我接盘。吃一堑长一智，就是这一次吃亏让我吸取了教训。从那以后，我投资房子每一次都准确，几乎投到哪里就涨到哪里！只要出售都有获取双倍以上的利润。"

李华像讲别人的事情一样，自然大方地跟郭奇志聊开了。郭奇志以开玩笑的口吻说："既然到黄冈市来投资了，你打算买什么房子呀？我那还有一套新房是空着的，你有没有兴趣？要是我到武汉发展，我也不买房子了，就住在你那里，怎么样？"

说完大笑起来，看到李华似乎没被吓住，郭奇志又接着说："我知道我们这小城市房子不值钱，还是你眼光好，投资省城房产，买到就是挣钱了。我建议这套商铺趁早卖掉！"

李华也是这样考虑，来之前就预约了一个房屋中介来看房，准备挂网上转让出去。李华做事雷厉风行，说干就干。中介李经理来了，把房子评估的市场价格报给李华。李华心里有数，这处房产卖掉只要挣回本金和利息就行了。余下的利润，给一万元直接奖励给李经理，唯一条件是尽快出售。如果在一周内找到一次性付全款的买家，李华奖励中介 1.5 万。李经理立马签了出售合同，当即表态一周内听电话通知，保持联系。

李华也补充道："房子你也看到了，就是不做生意当住房也划算。装修都搞好了，连热水器今天也安装了。全房的家具东西都不搬走，全部赠送。唯一条件是全款一次性付清！"

郭奇志佩服地笑着对李华说："事情已经办完，该去吃饭了。我请你去吃特色菜，烧土鸡、暴腌糍粑鱼、红烧鲫鱼，都是你爱吃的，对了，还有锅巴粥。这辈子没有娶到你当妻子，我有眼不识泰山啊，我还有机会吗？"

李华笑得很灿烂，她嫁不嫁不重要，但目前俩人的关系让她感到很舒服。人生没有永远的敌人，也没有永远的朋友，更何况选爱人呢？李华从不后悔她的这些经历，起码她在郭奇志的心目中得到了升华和敬重。这么多年没有白白浪费，应了那句话：善良待人接物，智取打拼才会赢！看来条条大路通罗马！

那餐晚饭吃得很香，酒也喝到位了。李华还执意邀请了房屋中介李经理共进晚餐，笑声从民宅小餐馆里飘出屋外，夜色撩人。三人在愉快的气氛中举杯预祝房产顺利出售。

吃饭过后，郭奇志还答应帮李华处理她父亲住院费报销的问题。但是几天过后，郭奇志发现自己的前妻在相关的部门工作。郭奇志担心前妻若是知道李华跟郭奇志的微妙初恋关系，而且前妻的性格泼辣，要是知道郭奇志是帮李华办理这事，肯定会误会更深，以前妻的脾气，弄出一些乱子怎么办？郭奇志想到这些，又有点害怕了，他不想再去招惹前妻了，免去引火烧身。

为了避免给李华和自己带来不必要的麻烦，郭奇志无奈地打电话向李华告知内情。李华善解人意让郭奇志不必放在心上，本来就不是大问题，她自己去办理就可以。

郭奇志那头无奈被挂机了，想想他自己也只有这点胆，明明可以借这个机会，讨好李华这位还是单身的初恋。二十多年前错过了她，七年前又错过一次，这次可能又是有缘无分了。只感觉李华比年轻的时候更强大，好像什么事情在李华眼里都不是事，总会找到解决问题的办法。应了一句话，办法总比困难问题多，只要遇事冷静，没有攻破不了的问题。

郭奇志恨自己无能追求自己喜欢的人，他感到很懊悔，这么好的机会又一次溜走了。丽丽曾以开玩笑的口吻调侃过他："你这一辈子就是为了官帽子。该做的和不该做的，你都没有做好。你不知道怕什么？你的母亲被前妻欺负，你没有孝敬到位也有责任；老婆也离了，还成了仇人。好不容易李华对你包容，不计前嫌，你也没有抓住机会。你年轻时赌气追了李华闺蜜谈了一场恋爱，这事肯定伤到李华，可李华都没有恨过你，还能去哪里找这么好的女人呢？而且你也浪费了机会，如果李华不是对你有好感，哪个女人还愿意倒请你闲着吃饭呀？"

丽丽也是旁观者清，郭奇志认为丽丽分析得太到位了。可是没有办法，他郭奇志就是这样的性格，一切以事业为重，为了坐稳税务局副局长的位置，也只能委屈自己的心病了！趁着还没有向李华明确表白，就此知难而退，给自己留点男人尊严。一辈子为面子活着！做个小心谨慎的人，也不为过。

谁也体会不到郭奇志此时此刻的无奈，他也怪自己放不下。他明白李华会很快把他晾在一边，李华年轻的时就是这样对待他，他知道李华不是为爱情婚姻放下事业的女人。

李华也确实会这样做，她在第二次婚姻当中吸取了教训。被于平伤害过后，李华再也不敢尝试恋爱了。李华的这份淡定是岁月逼出来的坚毅，李华挺过这些年也真不容易。一个人离开熟悉的城市去异地打拼，从报复的心念阴影中解脱出来。

时间真是良方，这么多年过去，她已经渐渐地学会沉默，释怀了过去的事。对那些伤害她的当事人，也没有恨了，对曾经执着爱过的于平也早已淡忘了。

自从广州那次和于平见面过后，李华就放下了于平。回到老家不久，李华悄悄单方起诉离婚程序了，她需要为自己再做主一次。在那之后，李华不急着恋爱结婚了，她从此对婚姻有点恐惧。但没有想到的是，当李华身兼数职事业有成时，向她示爱的人多的是，郭奇志也只是其中之一。

因此李华对郭奇志的讨好处理得云淡风轻，就好像是遇到了十几年前的一个老朋友，礼尚往来过而已。没有对错，也没有应该不应该，缘分过去就过去了，相聚见了就见了，甚至淡定到没有跟好闺蜜珊妮提过这件事。说了反而不好，李华是这么认为，有的话永远埋在土里，比风传话要靠谱。她还是很珍惜和闺蜜珊妮之间孩时的纯粹友情，也留给郭奇志对她的那份纯粹的好感。善良让一切变得简单。李华的生活已步入了她想成为的样子，财富自由，精神自由。人生中二者兼得的境界状况，是生活平衡的难得。

第三十六章　那条街上的单身女老板们

从小县城处理完门面的事情后，李华又回到省城去处理退店后的收拾。服装店隔壁左右店铺的女老板们邀请李华到自家店聊天，她们想知道李华的店铺说转让就立马转了出去的经验。

她们也想把店转出去，不做这行了。经营守店太难了，熬的时间长，业务需求又没有达到请员工的活，所以基本上都是老板们自己守店经营。经营一个小店，什么活老板都要亲力亲为。这样也有好处，一是进货价格老板们自己清楚，在遇到爱讨价还价客户，可以有个最低限价利润，做起来灵活，挣少挣多自己说了算。

李华一来到这些熟悉的朋友圈里，顿时热闹了起来。李华先到隔壁的首饰店小林那坐了一会，帮忙出点主意，也帮忙处理一些货物盘点。首饰店老板小林说："真佩服你，说转店就果断转出去了，你是怎么做到的？"

李华不急不慢地耐心地说："你也看到了，我把所有货物服装都以进货价格加点运费，全部先促销出去。还有一部分服装半卖半送给好友、同学、同事，让她们来店里以优惠价拿走。还有一些路过捡便宜的客户，一定要满足他们是占便宜的心理，跟他们说只有这一次活动，过了这村就没有这个店了，于是大家都舍得花钱买实惠的东西。"

"当然你这里卖的是奢侈品，不能这样低价促销。你一定要对不同需求的顾客人群挖掘出他们的购买理由。你可以建议顾客买到就是挣到，当作搞好关系的礼物，留着送朋友，送兄弟姐妹，送父母等等。也可以建议年轻人买来送给情侣对象，作为纪念性的饰品。这样你的销售的客户人群就多一些了。还可以搞买一赠一的活动，将饰品全部尽量清空。这样转让店铺成本就低了，新租客只接手空门面的店铺，只负担租金，就很容易找到租户。你就不用这样被动，等待的时间里你也做两手准备。一旦到期了，你也没有积压的货物，这样也容易处理。像空调这些贵重大件，尽量早处理折价卖掉。"

小林说："经你这样一说，我明白该怎么出手了。我豁出去了，折价优惠，买一赠一，这个办法行！"

两人正说着，休闲服装老板欣儿也走进小林首饰店，"李华，你转店后，我的店也盘出去了。今天来是退房的，我有一组长柜没有地方放，你要是有地方放，就送给你了。我舍不得给新来的租户，她接店砍价太狠，不想便宜她！"

李华看了看小林问："你需要吗？今后还开店就留着！"

小林推让说："哎呀，人家欣儿给你留着，你有车库就先放着吧。到时候谁需要谁拿去用！"

欣儿也说："对，先放在李华车库里，你怎么使用都随你便。反正我送给你！走，快跟我去看看！"

小林说："你快去吧，中午咱们一起吃饭！"

李华跟着欣儿到店里一看，好家伙！那么漂亮一组展示柜台，方方正正的黑色油漆木柜，加厚双层玻璃窗，看着就沉重结实，好柜子！丢了确实挺可惜的。放着可真是占地方面。

李华拨通前天帮她搬家的公司电话，讲了店里地址也谈好价格，搬家公司立刻派三个大力士来到，花了两个小时将店里的柜子全部迁移到李华的车库安放好了。看到这一切，欣儿高兴地说："你真行！这组柜子让我愁死了，一个晚上都没有睡好觉！今天晚上我请你唱歌，咱们几个好好乐乐！"

处理完欣儿的事情后，出门正好遇到田园布衣老板娘胡青。胡青跟李华同年出生，开服装店很多年了，她是这条街上唯一坚持下来的女老板，也和李华成了无话不谈的同行朋友。李华有时想想也觉得奇怪，不是说同行是冤家吗？李华却和这条街上的单身女老板们都成了朋友！

胡青看到李华回来了，赶紧把店里关门了，过来跟李华打招呼："你做服装这行比我经营得还好，干吗转了？再说你卖的服装风格跟我店里的风格可以互补，你不经商太可惜了。这以后怎么找你玩呀？欢迎你经常回来找我玩，反正我会一直在这里开下去，没事过来坐坐啊！"

李华搭着胡青的肩说："放心吧，我会来你店挑我喜欢的服装，因为我一直喜欢你这边的服装风格，有民族味道，又有女人韵味！"

胡青笑着说："你们晚上的活动算我一个，我正好有几箱啤酒，我们今晚全部喝完，一醉方休！"

欣儿开心地说：“我是准备叫你一起去唱歌！今天你早点关门吧，7点首义路歌厅见！”

那天晚上，服装街上的女老板们几乎全到齐了。欣儿带上一直帮她看店的单身女友陈君，小林带上追求她的男朋友苏总，胡青带上了她的单身女同学，李华带上了两个客户女友——从客户变成为了李华的私人朋友了，还有同街美容院的老板娘和店长两美女。最让人想不到的是，那天有位不请自来的男嘉宾——这条街上的物业管理公司陈总经理，一口普通话流利好听又会唱情歌的帅哥！这可是太助兴了。

那天晚上大家真的是玩疯了，喝大了，个个都尽情挥歌几曲。从没有这么尽兴过！李华真的有些舍不得这条街上的好姐妹。

李华看着抢着唱歌的同行女友们，暖暖的灯光散发出暧昧神秘的气氛，音乐声中夹带着谈天说地的话语，个个都看起来都那么妩媚性感而富有情调。李华那天也穿出了自己的衣着风格，真不愧是做服装行业的老板们，个个看上去都不失女人的韵味，各有千秋。苏总和陈总看见她们都竖起大拇指夸奖，陈总说：“真没发现这条街上还藏着这么多美女老板，我们这些单身狗在花丛中却找不到属于自己的鲜花，这是我们男人的悲哀呀！”

陈总上台献歌了，“给美女们送上一首老歌《我不想说》，希望美女们喜欢。”

欣儿说：“陈总的普通话好听，没有想到歌声更深情好听！”

小林窃笑说：“可惜呀，他个子太矮了，我喜欢高个子的！”

胡青低声说：“苏总一口东北口音，但是个子像墩子，哈哈！”

欣儿和陈君同时笑呛，水都喷出来了，还不忘急着说：“小心点，我们也不是来选王子找对象的，大家一起聚聚乐乐！”

李华指着台上唱歌的陈总说：“你们听歌选歌，快去跟陈总唱几首情歌对唱。来点高潮怎么样？每个美女都要上哟！一个不能少，不能漏了！”

小林说：“对，唱过瘾！”

李华接过欣儿递来的话筒，“我带头，美女们跟着来。”李华上台与陈总并列站着，开始唱了起来。也许是两个人都很投入歌中角色，两人深情款款的眼神，让歌厅气氛达到了高潮，两人唱歌时候表情像是真的一样，表演是绝配呀！

小林等李华坐下来后，附在她耳朵边说："我看出陈总喜欢你。你们唱歌的时候，真像一对情侣！你不是喜欢他说普通话声音好听吗？我看有戏！"

李华赶紧低头压着小声说："可别这样说，我不可能找一个比我小 17 岁的毛头小伙子。就当是小朋友哟！千万别瞎说，那是不可能的事！"

小林在旁说："我早就看出来了，以前他总是说'带上几个工作人员在你店里坐坐'。我起初以为是工作需要关系，后来发现只要你提出建议，他公司的员工就会及时照办。"

胡青说："今天晚上算是看明白了，要不然这陈总怎么会不请自来参加我们的聚会呢？肯定也想跟李华聚聚。包厢唱歌是苏总买单了，陈总喊着说等会出去请大家吃夜宵。到时继续喝啤酒，我车上还有！"

欣儿说："本来我是想还李华一个人情。以前总是李华请我吃饭，搞得今晚又轮不到我，那下次唱歌再聚吧！"

李华说："别客气了，你送我那么多东西，那能还要你请客呀！"

这一晚上，众人从歌厅散去，又赶到夜市大排档。那晚上实在尽兴，人多热闹。这武汉的夜市灯火通明一片繁华景象，这群单身女老板们连夜生活都这么丰富多彩，哪里还有时间去为过去的事情伤心呢？李华想：我们这些智慧的单身女人不比谁差。看看每一个都是漂亮能干，情商智商都不亚于男人的高手！单身没有什么不好，过得很洒脱！

这条街的单身女老板们，虽然将店转让了，但从此都过得很有品质，个个是财富自由的行家。据说小林去了新加坡做保健品生意发财了，将女儿送到新加坡读大学。欣儿成了艺术学院的音乐钢琴老师，陪伴着母亲一起生活，有些业余时间还带学生补习班做演出前培训，有稳定收入。她还是那甜美的样子，岁月一点也没有使她变老。胡青还在那条街上做着稳定的服装店生意，每天穿着漂亮时尚的衣装，越来越像一个富婆。陈君也找到一个比她小八岁的好男人结婚了，日子过得很甜蜜。

李华在那个时候起，在投资的房地产，几乎是每买一套都能挣到钱。经过那么多年的积累，又遇到好的投资年代，只要勤劳智慧，有商业眼光，在这盛世不发财都难。除了没有婚姻，李华什么都有了。

李华和这条街的女人们一样，大多数都还保持着快乐的单身状态。一是她们的眼光更高了，一般男人驾驭不了。最主要的原因是，女人有了钱后就有了安全感，若是遇到爱自己的男人，又担心对方只是爱她们的钱，所以越来越不好选择伴侣了。

几位好友一直保持联系，商量如果老了还没遇到心仪的对象，那就选择一个好地方，抱团买房住在一起养老！李华一直抱着一颗真心两种准备的想法，向往着有真情实意的婚姻爱情生活，但不刻意去寻找。她知道爱情不是一厢情愿，而是两个人心灵的碰撞，可遇不可求。所以她自己的原则，随遇而安。该干吗就干吗，不会坐等天上掉馅饼那桩好事。她从不幻想不切实际的事，做事还是喜欢脚踏实地。

李华干着干着现已拥有了海景房，大都市里有学区房。在市郊区被闺蜜珍珍的积极推荐下，两个单身女人又一起做了邻居，投资一栋养老小别墅，3 层楼的房子够住了。两个人平日里各忙各的事业，遇到节假日都在别墅小区约定好碰面时间。放松时看看同小区邻居的装修，以备需要入住之前的装修准备。前一段时间，两个女人都按照各自的喜好，进行了基础水电布局的简单装修，框架图效果已经出来了，俩人的创意各有千秋！李华已不需要以婚姻和好男人作为安全感了，她早已依靠自己找到了安全感。

第三十七章　市中心投资两套精装房

服装店转让出去后，李华抓紧时间办两处地产投资房，终于赶在涨价之前签订了购房合同。

那是 2009 年三月上旬，比起 2008 年底看房时的价格，每平方微涨了 100 元。李华看中了武昌江景房精装修一套小户型；还有一套万科精装修小户型房子，位于武汉三镇最繁华的汉口火车站附近。

当时考虑这两套房子的户型，一是解决李华女儿就近上班的问题，以女儿名字投资的婚前房产。服装店转出后，武昌投资小区房已涨价翻了两倍，专门靠转让店盘出的资金，不够投资两套房子的成本。为此李华要卖掉一套房子，这套房子因为地域交通方便，距离学校和医院都不远。一挂在网上，就被附近医院的年轻医生定购。

出售的这套住房，当初为了节约投资服装店租金成本，李华将此房出租给一位条件不错的艺术学校的女学生。想到学生已毕业到期，那时是收回卖掉的最佳时候，李华果断联系房屋中介顺利卖掉了那套旺宅。

想想还是有些舍不得，但是李华一想到只要卖掉一套投资房，可以解决两套投资住房，还是很成功的运作。这也是李华第一次以倍增的方式，做出了很成功的投资转型。既方便了女儿在省城工作，也方便单身的自己在省城生活。

在对的时间办对了事情，李华心里很有成就感，于是积极推荐家人，朋友们来看投资的房子。在李华默默做成功几件事之后，家人自然对李华刮目相看并非常信任。2008 年底全球性房价疯狂下跌，李华一直动员家人劝说父母早点迁移到省城来，大家互相可以照应，一起照顾年迈的父母亲。这样李华才放心！

李华小妹听了建议，2009 年初春节一过，小妹为父母亲投资了这一套省城的住宅，就是因为李华积极推荐。当时李华态度坚定地说："如果你们还不及时出手买，以后涨价了，肯定会后悔呀！"

看中的这套房子，总价 100 万之内，136 平方面积，地段好，老街小巷菜市场都在附近。还有三大银行，小区正面是大道和公交车站，房屋对面就是长江，可以说很有未来发展前景。真的是买到了就是挣到了财富。李华建议小妹给父母亲买房的小区，后期城建扩建地铁站线路就在此小区门口，瞬间房产又因交通方便的有利因素而增值。

一是投资的初衷基于孝心，二是判断信息准，三是时间恰到好处，这次李华推荐小妹成功购房很成就感。李华看到家人获利，减少了购房成本，比自己得益还高兴。

收房登记拿号那天，李华正低头帮父母亲签字拿房钥匙，旁边响起一个女人的声音吸引了李华的注意："这套大户型的房子还有吗？"

物业工作人员回答："早销售完了。"

李华抬头看到旁边背对着她的女人，惊喜地拍拍女人的肩膀："真是你呀，李琳！这么巧，你也买到这个小区的房子了！是自己住，还是投资？"

李琳高兴地说："是你呀李华！好多年没有见过了，怎么会在这里碰到呀？真是有缘啊！"李琳高兴地忙把身边站着的一位男士拉到李华跟前说："这就是我的老公，老李！这是我以前单位的同事！那个时候我们还不到 20 岁呢！"

李华说："是啊，一晃几十年过去，都要做邻居了。你真有眼光，买到这里。"

李琳说："我已经买了，我想让我弟弟也买一套，在一个小区互相好照应！唉，刚问过，一套房没有了，只等二期房推出来，到时候再看看吧。你呢，还好吧，买了几套房？"

李华与李琳谈起投资房子这个共同爱好的话题，俩人聊得没完没了。

李琳说："后面装修你找到了吗？"

李华说："我今天正好约了以前帮我装修过的装修公司赵总谈这事。我们把图纸带上，你先看我家。如果你认为赵总的装修方案实在，你就让他去你家看房，也做一个装修方案的报价，你们直接聊！多比较也是好的。"

李琳和老李点头："可以，可以先看看你妹为父母亲买的毛坯房吧，带我们一起谈！再到你自己住进来的小户型精装房参观一下好吗？"

李华本来就是热心肠的性格，遇见年轻时的同事，高兴地将装修公司老板赵总推荐给李琳，并交代赵总给李琳最优惠最省钱最实在的价格。李琳感到李华一点没有变，还是年轻时那样阳光友好！李琳也是爽快果断的女人，当天就与赵总签了装修合同，现场拍板就让赵总装修。

老李说："我当监督顾问，可以吗？"

赵总说："没有问题，我们就喜欢业主跟我们保持密切联系！我们可以提前商量施工细节方面工作！"

李华补充道："没有问题，到我的小户型坐坐喝杯茶，边休息边聊。先谈好装修方案，这样装修会避免做好了拆，浪费成本！"

这次李琳了解到，李华家在这小区已投资了一大一小两套住房，出发点也是为了方便照顾父母亲，又不影响各自的生活习惯。李琳也高兴地告诉李华，她弟弟在马路对面江景楼盘也投资了一套房子。遇到兴趣和三观相同的知己，是多么庆幸的事情！两个人从见面到分开，一直没有停下聊天。那亲热的友谊，让旁边人都羡慕，更别说家人了。

那天大家都很开心，负责装修的赵总也高兴地说："两位姐姐请放心，我一定把你们的房子当做小区户型样板间房装修！而且价廉物美，包两位姐姐满意，一定对得起姐姐们的信任！"

就这样两位多年前的同事，又开始做起了邻居，而且是一栋同单元。李琳住在 2003 号，李华住在 2907 号。

从此两人经常一起看房和考察投资房。后来李华以女儿的名字投资了汉口万科精装修房，在开发商交房业主验收房子的那天，李琳也在一旁陪同。真没有想到在快要步入退休的年纪，俩人遇到了知音！这也是求之不得的缘分！

那年李华如愿以偿地办成了这两件投资房的大事，对李华来说意义重大。在省城为自己安家乐业打下了基础，方便女儿上班来回节省时间，也能更方便照顾父母。在自己投资的同时，也影响带动了家人一天天地好了起来。

这就是李华为什么有拼命奔跑的动力，为了家人过得更好，她作为长女必须努力。李华心里有责任有担当，她的心愿是亲人能过上更好的生活！自己必须做在前面，当领路人是很操心啊！

第三十八章　英国旅行

　　房子在李华的眼中是大事，别笑话她，在离婚之后她真的最在意房子。在第一次婚姻期间，为分计划性房子变成商业住房，李华需要跟前夫拿钱买下，管钱的丈夫一毛不拔，只丢给李华三个字"没有呀！"就真的不管了。

　　从此李华悟出了钱的重要性，没有话语权的她能感觉到，如果她有一天连房子都没有，那她就真的没有家了。

　　从那个时候起李华想尽办法请朋友帮忙，通过银行贷款总算弄到了钱，顺利把计划房变成了商业住房产权，当真正属于她和前夫共同所有。后来与丈夫的争吵冷战，李华从骨子里不再依赖丈夫了。由此婚姻也走向了离异结果，李华宁愿付给丈夫房产一半的钱，也要求法院判决离婚请求。

　　离婚之前，李华一点也不物质，每月的工资如数交给丈夫管，李华的丈夫管生活。油米茶盐都需要钱，家庭日常开支都是丈夫在管。李华经常工作出差，所以不当家，也是怕麻烦。可是当需要给家里添置大件东西时，想从丈夫那拿出钱来，永远是没有。矛盾就此激化，三观不同，过日子就会闹心。三天一小吵，丈夫第二天又哄李华。

　　李华从来没有主动认过输，她性格的好强是被丈夫逼出来的。每次先是让李华生气，后面又哄李华继续交钱，但始终没有解决实质性问题。所以李华烦了，她不想要这样的生活，于是有了离婚的念头，什么都可以重新再来。离婚后的两年里，俩人各自成家，但后来都又离婚了。

　　李华跟于平的婚姻是基于爱情结合，这一次李华也没有要于平购买婚房。他们的婚姻因于平的背叛而终结。这场风花雪月的爱情，来得快去得也快，几乎伤到了李华骨子里。李华心很痛，迷茫了很久，无精打采，常常白天闷闷不乐地上班，下班就去盲人按摩院按摩。

　　心里的失望和苦，李华不知道能跟谁说，她觉得自己丢不起这个脸。当初被于平追求时，李华对自身的魅力自信十足，得意扬扬。也以为两人结婚后，于平一定会将她宠得像公主。二婚的生活，她过得很是心动，浪漫了一段时间。李华一直忙于工作，她认为工作胜于爱情婚姻，也庆幸自己没有因为婚姻而放弃工作，但却因工作忽略了婚姻经营。她过于自信过于放心，导致自己的二婚又一次失败。

李华心里痛苦，初期她麻醉自己的解脱方式，就是上班少说话，下班静静地享受按摩！因为按摩师是盲人，看不清李华的那张脸，李华很享受那种不被打扰不被窥探的感觉。盲人技师似乎很聪明，每次李华进来说上一句"一个小时"，他就知道是谁。他也从不多说话，好像知道李华的失意的痛苦。甚至有两次盲人技师不收李华的钱，原来是有经常去按摩的同学，还有认识李华的大老板帮李华买单了。原来这里不只是李华有心事，这里客人可能都有一些难以言说的苦闷。按摩的好处在于，身心疲惫，万念俱灰的时候，还是可以让身体放松一下，让盲人的手抚平李华心里的伤痛，获得一点内心的平静。

多年后李华反而在心底感谢曾经的那些乱事，要不是那些过往的痛苦，哪有今天这么有能耐的李华。李华心里真的感谢伤害过她的人，岁月把她打磨成更坚强成熟的一名勇士，此时的李华很有成就感。如果不是那些负心汉和贱小三，她李华也不会有今天，为家人为自己做到了这些看似很平凡的事情，也不曾想过，拿起笔在房产合同签上自己名字，购房大事自己说了算这种豪气。

那些痛苦的经历在李华心里已经不算是事了，眼下才开始醒悟过来，还有什么放不下的呢？男人和婚姻没有了，反而让李华事业财富蒸蒸日上，而且每次投资都是顺利获得成功，如愿以偿。

当两套精装房验收完成，短期内的计划已经实现，李华稍稍放松了下来，她决定彻底地放飞一次，奖励自己出趟远门，好好地享受美好生活，说不准又会遇到什么好运呢。这回听从女友的建议，李华决定去英国旅行。

2009 年 4 月中旬，李华申请的英国签证批准了。一起同去面签递交申请的朋友因没有房产作经济担保没有批，而李华半个月就顺利拿到了去英国旅行签证。

工作人员笑着说："恭喜你，英国签证通过！"

李华不紧不慢地问："批签证需要什么特殊条件吗？"

工作人员说："你肯定通过，你有两套购房合同，还有一套门面产权证复印件，经济上真有实力。你不会留在英国去当非法移民。"

李华说："那是肯定的，中国这么好。我只是去见识见识，去散心旅行。请问我最长能待多久？"

工作人员说："1个月到半年的签证！"

李华看看签证心想：这么长时间？我不需要！我只是去旅行放松一下。

李华迅速听了女友徐姐的话，买好了飞往英国伦敦的机票。这次可真的要一个人飞出世界了。这次长途旅行，徐姐让李华帮女儿带了一套护肤品。徐姐女儿脸上长了痘痘，这是对应治疗的面霜。徐姐是给李华女儿介绍工作的恩人。徐姐大李华5岁，做某事业单位财务总监，人好热情，助人为乐。她帮李华女儿安排工作，没有送礼就办了。李华心里很过意不去，这次李华去英国顺便给徐姐女儿带点东西自然是心甘情愿。李华与徐姐的友谊都已有十几年礼尚往来的交情了，两个人都很懂得感恩。

从中国武汉飞北京飞英国伦敦，只用了11小时。飞机降落在英国伦敦机场时候，已是黄昏，太阳西落。徐姐给英国的英俊帅气的朋友，一名刚退休二线皇世警察艾伦讲明了李华度假的事，艾伦主动来机场接李华。

出机场的时候，等待多时的艾伦一眼就认出了李华，手中举的牌子写着中文李华两个字。李华笑了起来，就像电影院里播放的场面。英国朋友以这种老套管用的方式接到了李华。李华当着艾伦的面，用手机拍了一张合影发给了徐姐，告诉对方已经安全到达。

旅游伦敦一个月后，李华出发前往另外一个城市，去看徐姐女儿。伦敦到徐姐女儿读书的城市，开车就要六个多小时。李华自嘲道："这趟旅程要是没有艾伦帮助，我那点英语水平肯定够呛。"真的感谢艾伦这位英国朋友，及时细心地开车将李华送到徐姐女儿读研的大学，英国剑桥大学。

在校园中找到了在那里等候多时的汪微——徐姐姐的女儿。李华将带来的东西一一交给汪微手上。完成了这个任务，李华这才舒了一口气，还将艾伦送的一大罐糖果，全部交给汪微，艾伦把读书汪微当孩子。后来才知道艾伦与妻子结婚后一直没有孩子，恰巧艾伦妻子出轨，两人离婚，艾伦从此身边再没有女人了。艾伦居住在退役警察聚集在一起的小区，那小镇很安逸宁静。李华应艾伦邀请前去做客，那是一套独门独户的两层楼小别墅，实际只有160平方面积。

汪微真懂事，正赶上是吃饭的点，她带大家到餐馆吃饭。艾伦把汪微当小朋友了，但是人家汪微可机灵，趁点完菜单后，汪微就把账结了。李华吃完饭后去买单的时候，营业员笑着说："单已买过了，你桌子上三个人都来买单，真逗！"原来艾伦也来买过单！同类朋友相处起来真舒服。不用玩心眼！

　　李华替徐姐心意带到后，心里轻松了很多，但是反过来让汪微把单买了！这小女孩也太像徐姐做事风格了，连抢着买单都学。当晚李华将信息告诉了徐姐，少不了夸汪微懂事，让李华做阿姨都失色了，难怪徐姐为何那么放心，将女儿汪微送出国深造。按徐姐的话说"女孩子就是要走出去多见世面，今后人生中，不会因为什么都不懂而被骗，也不会因为无知而失去自信。"

第三十九章　旅行中的创业准备

　　这天晚饭后，李华和艾伦没有及时返回艾伦居住的城市，在就近的酒店入住休息了一晚上，当然是入住在不同单间房。

　　在第二天吃早餐时，艾伦对李华说："我们回程的路上还可以去英格南小镇，在那里你可以看到穿上格子裙子的女人。那个地方山清水秀，还有一些名胜古迹可以参观，你想去吗？"

　　李华马上说："要是你不累，我们就去吧。只要不多走弯路，能顺便就多去一些地方转转，这当然是好事。"李华用翻译器跟艾伦交流着，很快进入自然沟通状态。李华没有客气，直接同意赞同！

　　李华已经习惯说走就走的旅行，也能做到很洒脱。在这一点上，李华跟艾伦还是有点不一样。现在李华跟艾伦已经是很好的朋友关系，彼此熟悉，相处起来很自然舒服，没有任何压力。艾伦很有素质，热情恰到好处的分寸，让李华放松释放出调皮活泼的开朗性格，有时候开心笑起来，反让艾伦腼腆不好意思。

　　想起第一次见到艾伦的时候，李华还感觉这位 1.86 米的高个子男人有点压迫感，直板的腰身，一看就能感受到对方是个训练有素的男人。只是艾伦笑起来的时候，李华发现他的两颗门牙齿有点暴突，不好意思说出来。

　　李华转念一想，自己又不是相亲的，对方只是接机的朋友，为什么要挑剔对方的长相缺点呢？李华当时就觉得自己有点过分，又犯了以貌取人的缺点。女友曾经给李华取了一个雅号叫"外貌协会"！就因为李华对外表相貌，喜欢帅气英俊潇洒的男人！

　　离婚后，李华并没有因为自己离异而降低择偶标准！有了经济实力后，李华更不会委屈让自己下嫁。如果缘分到来，遇到很好的优质男士，李华就可以考虑成家；如果缘分不来，那就永远做一个快乐自由的单身女人，多自由自在，想买房一个人签字算数，想出来旅游，买张机票就如愿了。

　　李华想到第一天到伦敦机场的印象，这里没有想象中那么繁华，老旧的公共设施，让李华放下了来之前的崇拜和兴奋。只是东看看西瞧瞧，和艾伦边聊边走出机场。转了两个弯，经过一个机场外的巴士站，那只能站八个人左右。艾伦推着大箱子走在前面，李华跟艾伦身后问："我们去哪里？"艾伦说："现在去拿车，我的车子停在机场附近酒店的停车场。"

　　艾伦是徐姐介绍的英国朋友，李华信任徐姐，也信任她介绍的朋友，很放心地跟着他走，有一搭没一搭地用简单英语对话。来之前，李华特意去新华书店买了三本英语小册子，随身携带恶补英语短句对话，很实用地运用上了。朋友们也因此称赞李华："真佩服你，拿几本英语书小册子就敢去英国，胆子真大！"

　　李华确实有胆量，这次出国旅游，她可是下了很大的决心。第一是奖励自己把服装店成功转让出去，第二是把多年前投资的商铺也出售了，第三是预定的两套省城住房已经验收。这些大事情在短期内一一办妥，李华也有成就感。李华有个好习惯，从不对自己小气，因此必须给自己放假享受人生。

　　离婚后李华想通了，人生要活得通透点，除了工作挣钱，还是把投资房产的老本行当作自己最爱的投资方式。她认为这种投资能实现时间自由和经济自由。有钱可多投两套，钱少就凑钱，申请银行贷款也得投一套。只要是好的地标房，或是城市中心一首房，没有钱也要考虑！多年来的房产投资给李华带来了经济效益，她才舍得自掏腰包，自费出国旅行实力，兑现奖励自己。在事业单位要混到副局长职位，才能享受公费考察旅游的名额。李华觉得自己能随心出国比依赖单位福利强多了。

　　李华的第一次出国旅游选择了英国伦敦。第一站就去了伦敦的唐人街，吃了一份韭菜肉饺子。这里的饺子很贵，30个一盘，30英镑，当时的兑换汇率是1比11，一盘饺子价格要330元人民币，在国内两三个人都能吃一顿大餐了。一换算成人民币价格，李华就觉得有点心疼，但已经点了，总不能退掉。

　　之后李华每次买东西，吃东西都要换算人民币，心里计算一下，花得划不划算。后来的日子也就不算了，尽量省着用。

　　在英国待了两个月，李华已经很习惯在英国淘宝，还会到二手旧货币市场选购自己喜欢的服装。最初她不知道那是二手店，偶尔经过一家店铺看到很多人在买东西，她也进去看热闹。她看见一件玫瑰红的裙款，看着又像旗袍，腰带特别漂亮，一下子就把李华吸引住了，看着很有古典女人韵味。

李华用翻译工具问了老板衣服大概的情况，再把标签一看，差点没有叫出来：我的妈哟，这么便宜，想不到只需6英镑！换算人民币只需66元，太值了，立刻就买。

结果那天买了很多衣服、包、鞋子，最后才发现那是二手杂货店，售卖各种各样的商品。李华没有想到的是，在英国二手店买东西的人，多数是英国人。亚洲人的面孔有来自日本、韩国、中国、越南。

李华常常把日本女人看成是中国女人，有几次上前用中文问话，结果别人谦和地笑着解释："我是日本人！"认错几次之后，李华再也不好意思随便去问了。路过的亚洲人都是来自全球五湖四海的旅客、留学生、签证过来的工作者。世界真大，英国之行让李华开阔了眼界！

在艾伦的帮助下，李华报了当地旅行团，周游英国各大景点和皇家城堡。李华随身携带多国语言翻译器，每个游客胸前都挂着卡牌，拿着导游小册子，沿途跟从举着小彩旗的导游，住酒店也都是随团队安排，很方便。据说李华报的旅行团是当地做得最好的旅行社，服务信誉第一，费用比其他旅行社高一点，但是安全，到哪里都有巴士接送！

这次长假旅行，让李华又燃点起李华的创业热情。她看到英国人的家里门窗，还是中国人早已过时的白色塑料铝板材料制成，窗型设计还是很老套。出国之前就有一位东北朋友想跟李华合作，开一个门窗工程有限公司。准备由李华接活，签项目合同；东北朋友负责技术制作，铝材的购进，工程施工队伍合作等工作。这个创业计划只谈了开头，李华正在考虑要不要投身到不懂的行业。东北朋友很看好李华，跟她聊了几次。李华行事谨慎，等有周全的计划再答复东北朋友。

这次出国虽然是旅行，可李华总会情不自禁关注各种房子的门窗造型，也将各种家具配搭一并拍照保存在手机中。她虽然给自己放了一个长假，但始终没有忘记回去后要大干一场。这次旅行也变成了创业前的市场考察，游玩过程中不时搜集素材，拍的照片除了李华本人和名城风景外，大部分是一些有关各式各样风格房子、门窗为背景的照片。还将照片在英国当地全洗了出来，李华怕手机储存不够，这样保存放心！

　　李华想好了，回国后要跟东北朋友好好谈谈投资门窗公司的事。她已经有主意了，自己主要负责销售洽谈业务工程。技术、公关、工程施工方面，都交给懂技术的东北朋友，未来的合作伙伴。

　　一旦有了创业的思想准备，李华的英国之行就闲不下来了。后期的一个月旅行，李华几乎走到哪里都会记录那个地方的房屋建筑情况，拍下地标房和各种各样的门窗造型。连旅游景点的卫生间，酒店大厅卫生间的门，只要造型特别，她都会选择一个角度拍下来，而且在照相馆把这些相片全部洗出来。

　　这些举动让英国朋友艾伦好奇，他问李华："你这是要做门窗相关的生意吗？"

　　李华笑着回复："我想把这些漂亮的图片保存，带回去作为造型参考，适合的就用作东西方文化搭配。我们有的私家房也建成别墅区的风格，对那些要求西方韵味的房屋，我们就能提供这些有西方特色的门窗产品，肯定会有市场需求！"

　　人家的旅行就是观光吃喝玩乐，而李华那一行的长假期却在脑海里已打下了创业伏笔。李华认识到不管在哪里生活，都需要经济基础，要食人间烟火。她明白了，想要证明自己离异后的生活过得好，必须从经济方面创造利润。而创业可以比较快达成目标，只要能抓准时代的市场需求。

　　现在已是市场经济，那些年与房产有关联的行业，都会被社会建设行业市场带动起来，例如，房地产，装修行业，门窗工程，房屋中介出租出售房屋，这些行业都能挣到钱。有了投资的大方向，李华就有了主见，她关注新闻，关注房地产任何城市价格比较信息。机会就是留给到有准备的人，英国的这次旅行打开了李华的思维，开阔了眼界。

　　艾伦很欣赏地偷看李华专注看图片的神情，开口询问："你能留在英国吗？我可以帮你留下来！"李华抬头看看艾伦，他是一脸认真的表情。李华有些意外但又很不好意思地说："我英语不好，在中国有我的事业和家人，我的饮食习惯也不适应英国，我更喜欢中国的生活。我只是来度假放松，并不打算长住。谢谢你的邀请。如果有机会你去中国旅行观光，我当你的中国导游！"

　　李华把心里的话一口气全部说了出来，一点都不掩饰自己的真实想法。这或许是艾伦欣赏她的原因，纯粹坦诚相待。当没有心机的李华出现在艾伦的视野中，已经留下了中国东方女人的魅力。艾伦也不知道从什么时候开始，已经悄悄地从喜欢到爱上李华的那么一种情感，在艾伦的心里，默默掩饰了很久了，今天艾伦也不知道为什么自己敢表达出来。

察觉到艾伦微妙的情感变化，李华只得提前结束了英国之行。她有很多事情要做，现在根本不可能有时间有心思谈情说爱。她对爱情怕了，尽管都是男人先喜欢她，但是最后的婚姻都以离异收场。爱情虽然不分国界，不分年龄，可她真的爱不起了，她不想受到情感的伤害。她目前感觉个做一个快乐的单身女人真好，什么都是自己说了算，自由自在。现在李华已经感觉自己的生活如鱼得水，收放自如。目前最重要的不是恋爱和婚姻，而是工作，要有独立的经济基础，有自己的一番事业！

离开伦敦机场的那天，阴天下着小雨。艾伦很绅士地帮李华搬大行李箱，又买了一些路上吃的水果，还悄悄地放进200英镑在李华的包里。进安检后李华才发现，抬头看到艾伦依依不舍的眼神，李华只有低头逃避躲过艾伦有所期待的眼神，她明白自己不能给予爱情，这场爱来得不是时候。她只能装傻，装作轻松的样子，向艾伦的方向挥挥手，立刻转身离去。李华不敢多看依然站在那里的艾伦。心想就此别过就好，她在心里祝艾伦会遇到他的一定会幸福："再见了，艾伦！你是好男人，可我给不了你爱情了！"

第四十章　创办门窗公司

　　李华风尘仆仆归来，与合伙人东北朋友肖总一拍即合，马上开始紧急筹划预备开张门窗工程公司，火速地准备了两个月，选址开张了。

　　李华给公司的第一单见面礼，是她帮忙洽谈的一个三级市里的一栋办公大楼工程。客户介绍给肖总后，技术方案都交给肖总去跟进交流。预审批后，将由肖总安排施工队伍进场。安装工期都写在合同上，共四个月，工程款按进度结算，进场首付30%，中期随材料进场安装为准，尾款以工程完毕全付工程款，预留5%的维修保证金！合同简单明了，因为是跟政府打交道，一切从简，以效率质量获得信任，以确保第一单工程顺利完工。

　　肖总非常高兴，他没有想李华从英国旅行归来就马上投入工作，这说干就干的魄力，真不是所有女人能做到的。李华已经忘记了自己还是女人，除了与甲方跟进施工收回工程款，还每天跟肖总一起去工地现场。有时跟工人一起吃盒饭工作餐，那一身迷彩裤配白色上衣，也很英姿飒爽！就像闺蜜形容的那样，站在什么山头唱什么歌，李华的扮相太适合工作场所了，丝毫不输给男人。干练，稳重，果断，有组织能力和超强的亲和力。

　　工人都服她，肖总也佩服地说："咱们爷们都怎么会听娘们管呢？"一口东北腔调的肖总话说完，工人都笑了。有的扮鬼脸，有的嘟嘟嘴，有的就直接喊："只要李总来了，就会给我们加伙食，加菜，肖总就知道吼我们干活！"

　　肖总继续说："你们把这项活干好了，我请大家吃酸白菜炖排骨，还有饺子，整两瓶二锅头！怎么样？"

　　工人齐声说："好啰，到时候好好喝一杯，现在咱们干活去！"

　　说实话，这帮施工队伍，还真没话说，个个都是以前跟肖总干过活的熟练技术工。其中有一个工头经理是肖总的小舅子，也就是肖总爱人的弟弟。肖总在一次幼儿园门窗工程中认识做幼儿园老师的小许，一来二去俩人认识了。谈恋爱两年就奉子成婚了，第二年又添了一个小子。自从肖总与小许结婚后，从来不拖欠工人工资。甲方有时候没有如期结账，资金周转不灵的时候，什么材料款可以押一个周转期暂放放，可工人工资一个也不少发。

这也是这支队伍愿意跟着李华和肖总干的重要原因。关键是与工人一条心，把工程质量干好，如期完成安装门窗任务。这是一支能战放心的施工队伍，公司分工明确，责任到岗，协调合作好。人手不够的时候，肖总会与工人同吃同住。周末或遇到重大节日，肖总会把工人邀请到公司来吃饺子，一锅东北美食酸白菜炖排骨。

李华肯定是被邀请的人之一，李华本来是单身，平时全身心的时间都以工作为主，很少做饭，这是肖总有意照顾李华的原因。本不吃香菜的李华，已学会了香菜蘸酱、小葱蘸酱、大葱蘸酱，按照肖总的东北话说"李总已习惯吃我们东北伙食了，这才像带好这支农民工队伍的领导啊！"

的确如此，李华没有架子，随和的工作作风，生活上关心农民工，让工人感觉亲切。他们知道公司的业务工程活都是李华接的，她还负责所有甲方合同与人脉关系的跟进。李华真不容易，一碗水端平的微妙平衡，一般人是做不到的，更何况是李华一个女人。李华在公关方面充分发挥肖总东北人的豪爽性格优势，用东北口音讲笑话段子，像当时电视里的小品演员小沈阳一样，把甲方领导哄得开心，说到笑死你。公关费花得少，还把合同给续签了。打那以后，李华把所有的甲方人脉圈子都带上让肖总认识，交给这位军人出身，比李华小16岁的肖总全部跟进，两个人合作愉快默契。

在某个工程完成时，李华鼓动肖总说："你将来会向千万资产进军，我只要达到一半就行了！"

肖总突然想起来一件事，"听甲方大领导说，黄冈有一处地方，有个大胡子的大师算命很准。我们今天去结算工程款之前，去探路问问算算。你觉得怎么样？"

李华接腔斜着眼瞪着肖总说："今天还是早去工程部找到盛处长，把申请结工程款报告递上去。顺便问问盛处长有什么要求和困难，还有那主管我们质量的李处长，一定要跟她谦虚问问结账情况。具体先找谁，找哪个领导谈，你要机灵点随机应变。我去会计那边了解一些具体工程结账计划分配情况。据说有七个施工队伍都需要甲方结算工程款了，时间紧。如果这批计划没有报上去，没有获得八个领导处长签字，我们还是拿不到工程款，这是燃眉之急。把这个事办成了，我一定带你去算命，询问前程。"

肖总说："好的，这是大事。下个月过节还要发工人的过节费，还有进铝材料款。厂里也要跟我公司结算了，结一批才能进下批的铝材给我们！"

李华深深呼吸了一下，"我怎么当初就听了你的话，办起了我不懂的行业，还真开了公司。想到这么多人际关系要处理，我真累了。我干这行才接近一年，却老了5岁。你是爷们，又懂行，你多操点心，我只配合你的工作。需要我出面的事和人，我帮你约，你做公关就好，没有你搞不定的事！"

肖总又调侃道："又拿我开涮，跟你开公司，我是你的专职司机，又是执行总经理，又是跑腿的，还是公关部经理。你真会用人啊，可把我累死了。就这么干吧，谁要俺是爷们呢！如果不挣钱，你肯定不带我出去混了！"

肖总说归说，做任何事真不让李华操心，遇到事商量着办，细节上比女人还细心周到。甲方李处长就很欣赏肖总，喜欢这位属马的东北小伙子。那一期的工程款如期结算划拨批准了，真是解决了大问题！

李华兑现了承诺，特意选择一个阳光明媚的周末，让肖总开着公司创业期间买的二手黑色奥迪车，向黄冈县城的西山方向驶去！

途中景色秀丽，树叶繁茂，一股树枝的清香弥漫在小道两旁。车子开到山下停车场，接着步行上山。山路像是盘山弯道循环转圈，慢慢地向山顶走上去。上山一条道，下山一条道，走到半山腰，想退都难。

李华走在前面，回头看着掉下几十米远地方肖总说："你这都爬不动了？还得趁着有点体力向上走，不能停。到了山上有东坡饼吃，限量排队才买得到。那可是这山中特产，吃后沾点仙气，算命更灵。抽一个上上签，你就乐意来这趟了。我们今天就吃斋饭，保你吃饱。"

肖总调皮笑着说："你今天就这样打发我，请我吃素食。明知道我喜欢吃肉，无肉不欢，这整人整得我吃不好，就没有力气开车回公司！"

李华歪着头向天上看看，"快走，搞不好要下雨了，跑呀！"

肖总连忙小跑跟上。看着天，太阳躲进云中去了，树林就感觉到凉意。山里就是多变气候，空气出格地好，花香树香人也精神爽。小跑步登山，走走停停，边说边笑，不到1小时，就到了西山亭区门口。李华购买了两张门票，直接带着肖总去和尚念经的地方。

静静跟着等待排队的人群，那些少男少女们怎么求签拜佛，肖总就怎么做。李华也虔诚地照做，跪下在佛祖的面前，默念着心里的三个心愿，愿佛祖保佑一切顺利，愿生意兴隆，财源广进，愿一切如愿以偿！

肖总默念跪拜后，连叩拜三个头，随后悄悄告诉李华："我抽了一个上上签，要我去功德箱捐赠钱，你看应该给多少？"

李华看着佛相拜叩，小声说："你自己随心，有诚意就好！"

肖总把手放进兜里，拿出事先准备的 600 元放进功德箱，"图一个顺意！六六顺吧，让我们的公司多挣钱，让我今年也能买套房，当一个千万富翁！"说完，肖总自己都笑个不停。他也知道这是掏钱买一个精神寄托，一个心愿，来了就有诚意呗，肖总贴在心口比画着"求佛祖保佑我顺顺利利。"

肖总拿着签去和尚大师那边解签去了。签上说"明知风和险，但诚心已定，乘风破浪行，定能胜乾坤！"

"好签，好签！"和尚笑着望着这位圆圆泛红色大脸的肖总，敲了三下钟，肖总赶紧下跪叩拜了三个响头。这可是 180 度弯腰叩头。李华同样一脸诚意，将上上签拿在手上，连忙藏在包中。她看懂了签文的意思，心中非常高兴，这趟没有白走。签上说"明君心中有，业绩四海有，无论天涯海角，有君一席地，崇山峻岭求，定是非等之闲辈！"

就是这好签给了李华信念，无论到哪里，李华都把抽的上上签藏在她的一片天地里！

第四十一章　三年艰辛

求到上上签后，李华的心态更积极了，她什么都不考虑，埋头苦干，和合作伙伴肖总一起干过几个有模有样的好工程。在省三镇几个重要的地标性建筑都有她公司的门窗项目！陆续有几个大开发商跟李华公司联手合作。由于质量好，工期按时交付，口碑在同行业中已经有名气了，资质更没有话说。

肖总在辽宁东北找到了一家大型民营企业作为铝材基地依靠，由于信誉好，结货款及时，反而被厂方给予李华公司更大的合作优惠条件，达到了三方共赢的局面。这正是李华愿意看到的发展理念，大家共同致富，共同发展，共同谋取最大的合作利益。合作三年来，肖总与李华的合作一直很愉快，从来没有在利润分红分配上闹分歧矛盾。肖总可是知足了，他想公司有更大更好的发展。

很快到了公司成立三周年纪念日，在庆功酒会上，肖总带着一口东北乡音，激情澎湃地说："我其实不会说正经话，大家平时对我说'你在哪里干，我们就跟随你'，我听了真的很感动。大家对我这么铁，我心里真的很感谢。我没有什么好说的，我就是一个军人出身的粗人，在过去的三年中，大家给了我很大的支持帮助，让我在最困难的时候，顶了过来。"

"这一路走来顺畅，还得感谢我们公司李华李董事长的提携和大力帮助。在公司起步最难的那年，我一点谱都没有，是李董给我们拿到第一项工程合同；后期在我们公司面临资金掉链子的危急时刻，是李董以诚相待求助甲方及时预拨了我们公司的工程回款。那真是及时雨啊，回来的钱都用在工人的工资发放、原材料的结算、运费、厂房租金、水电及所有费用。记得那个时候，我肖总和李董剩下的资金，刚刚好能支付那年团圆饭的钱。"

"可这些，李董从不让我叫苦埋怨。李董说'困难是暂时的，开年初八大伙就上班，干好已签合同项目工程，就会拿到进场首付款。我们干好质量，让领导们放心，钱的事你就不用操心了。'大伙知道吗？我肖总就从那刻起，下决心跟着李董干。在今天把这话说出来，也是借此庆功酒，敬李董一杯，谢谢了！我就说到这里！现在由请李董给我们大伙讲话，大家欢迎！"

当年公司和施工队伍三十多人，人数不算多。会场就设在江景边上的威斯汀酒店小会场，曾经只有和甲方签合同才去这个高级酒店，今天却把同心协力一起打拼的工人师傅们请到这里。这是很有意义的举措，肖总说了就是要让工人们知道这叫有福同享，鼓励大家跟公司同甘共苦。公司好了，工人们就有盼头，现在的公司不是李华和肖总两个人的公司了。

会场中响起热烈的掌声，李华作为公司法人，有准备在这个场合说上几句话——作官场上的总结是一定要有的会议议程。但是没有想到的是，肖总真能说话，把情况都讲到实处了，这下让李华感动，一时忘了准备好的发言稿，脑子一片空白。在欢呼声中走向会场讲台上的李华一个劲地想，我说哪一句话当开头呢？

李华边想着边慢慢地拿起调整竖立式麦克风话筒，抬头扫了一眼台下的人群。在那一刻，她看不清谁是谁，只知道人们在等她发言讲话。"天啊，怎么会这样紧张！"李华转念一想，就当是平时和工人聊天唠嗑说上一段吧。"对，就从这开头！"李华缓缓地放松了心情，话筒扩出一段感人的真情流露。

"大家好，本想给大家做一个总结，结果肖总的话说得太感人，我也因为感动乱了思路，忘记了原来打算讲的内容。现在我想到哪里就说到哪里，说错了大家别往心里去。"

"首先我得感谢肖总，说服了我加入公司合伙一起干，硬是把我这位门外汉，培养成这支专业门窗队友的一员。在大家努力下，这三年工程合作中，我们看到了希望和发展前景。同时最让我感谢的是大家善良、勤劳、坚毅的工作干劲，大家有一股不服输精神。看到工人师傅们在施工现场没有怨言，默默地付出完成工期所有的安装任务，我才有充足的底气和信心去跟甲方商谈，递上工程回款报告申请单。是大伙让我有脸有勇气去和甲方争取，及时拿到公司工程回款，及时挽救公司资金脱节的问题。"

"我能当好大家的后勤工作，配合肖总技术施工各项任务，都是微不足道的事情。比起工人师傅们的辛苦劳累，要轻松很多。在此感谢大家对我的抬爱和理解支持。因为有了大家的同心同德，才使我们公司今天的发展形势一片大好。一句话两句话表达不出我要说的感谢之情，只有借此酒向在座的全体同仁表示最好的祝福。祝大家健康快乐幸福，心想事成，万事如意！干杯！"

之前李华和肖总商量过，决定在公司成立三周年之际，以奢侈的规格在五星酒店做一次高调的总结，以此鼓舞大家的士气。而这一次庆功酒会确实达到了预期的效果。李华看到公司已慢慢走入正轨，工程项目每年递增，还扩大到接外省的门窗项目。这三年来李华的责任越来越大，没有一天休息时间，遇到逢年过节，工人们可以放假，可李华却放松不下来，还得要考虑公司更远的发展。

那一年春节的大年三十，李华坐在电视机前看春节联欢晚会。好像是成立公司后第一次这么惬意，放纵地在客厅的沙发上懒洋洋地躺着，一双秀气小巧的双脚翘着放在茶几上。难得这么放松，毫无顾忌地在自家享受那种暖暖的感觉。

买到这套房时，当时做门窗工程的肖总坚持说服李华，安装上了地暖设施。李华为了省天然气，一直舍不得开地热暖气。真没有想到那一年春节，湖北武汉这座火炉城市却来了一场大雪，天气出奇地寒冷。李华不得已开了地热暖气，感觉真舒服。

老人常说，再怎么想串门探亲也不要选择大年三十夜这天外出。当地风俗是必须守着自己家过年，守财神爷。自从经商后，对于这些风俗，李华全听全信，为了图一个吉利和顺意。再加上天气寒冷，李华更安心待在家里，随心所欲，看看春晚节目，放松自己的心情，真是难得的一次！

这一天只有李华一个人在家，女儿到她亲爸那里过年去了。这是女儿参加工作后，第一次受到她爸的邀请。在去看爷爷奶奶之前，女儿对李华说过："爸爸打电话告诉我，说爷爷奶奶想我去他们家吃年饭，妈你说去不去呀？我听你的！"

李华想了几秒钟反问女儿："你是怎么想的？这么多年没有来往了，你想去看看？你把真心话告诉我。"

女儿小心翼翼地看着李华说："听爸爸的语气挺好的，就是说做了很多我小时候爱吃的过年的菜，想让我和你去吃团年饭。还说爷爷奶奶老提你多好，爸爸说奶奶指着墙上挂着你抱着我的那张相片说，看看这孙女长大了，还不来看看我们。说你是很好的媳妇，她儿子没有福气。所以，我想去看看爷爷奶奶！他们家人只认你是媳妇。"

李华想了想女儿说的话也在情理之中，她与女儿爸爸离婚后，与前夫家人关系处理得很好，没有破面子。李华对女儿说："你去看看吧，把我单位分的油和家里的两瓶好酒带给爷爷奶奶。另外准备送业务关系户的两件羊绒衫，你拿给你爸爸穿，但是千万别说这些都是我给的，明白吗？别提我名字就好。"

女儿高兴地说："好，你同意了，那我三十年夜饭去爷爷奶奶家吃。那你一个人在家过年吗？不如我们一起去，怎么样？"

李华接着说："你去就行了，我去算什么事儿？你去就说你已经大学毕业，找到好工作有了稳定工资，可以孝敬爷爷奶奶了。这些都是你买的，懂吗？其它的废话少说。"

女儿知道李华很顽固，一家人不会再回到从前了。以前她爸也是对李华做得太绝情，如今李华放下个人恩怨，让女儿带上这么多礼物，重建亲情，这是李华的善良大气。李华跟孩子爸爸一家毕竟十几年没有来往，感情淡了；但女儿的血缘关系永远断不了。李华自己可以不走动，不能影响左右女儿的思想吧！李华是明理的妈妈，这方面由着女儿。女儿多些亲情，多些大家庭的爱，她也欣慰了。毕竟曾经是一家人，而且当初也是李华死活要坚持离婚，多少对女儿有一些内疚。

大年三十下午，女儿早早就出门了，李华独自待在家里。电视机一直在播放，李华却不知道什么时候睡着了。那一觉睡得很香，没有人打扰。李华心想，也许只有她自己会在过年时节还操心工作，举国上下的人们都在欢度新年，这个时候还会有谁因为工作的事情来打扰自己呢？于是李华把手机调成静音，也好好享受节日的祥和宁静。

年初一睡到自然醒的李华，被拍打的敲门声吵着懒意全无："谁呀？"

李华打开门一看，原来是肖总带着爱人和项目经理的小舅子一家人来给李华拜年了。肖总可没有忘记大年初一给合伙人李华拜年。在私下，肖总会直接喊这位大他16岁的李华叫李姐，在有些多人场合叫大姐。"李姐，是我们一家人给你拜年，恭喜发财，新年快乐，万事如意，顺风顺水！"

肖总人还没有进门，那东北嗓音已传进了李华耳朵里。李华听起来还是感觉特别亲切，心里暖暖的。这个时候的朋友、合作伙伴、同事的友谊，胜似亲人的关心，是真的难得。李华整理了一下衣服，喝了一口水，迅速地将沙发上的毛毯整理放进卧室，再直奔大门口小跑步走去。

开门的一瞬间，看到肖总一家人，全部是穿着红色外衣，围着红色围巾，小孩带着红色帽子，一番喜气洋洋的过节打扮。

李华连忙招呼他们进屋："一家人红红火火地过节！快进来，外面冷，里屋暖和。"

肖总爱人说："李姐，新年快乐。这是我家土特产，黏米圆子，还有苹果，平平安安，你收下吧，就当是过年开个荤，吃点素，尝点新鲜。"

小舅子边往屋里客厅走，边说："李姐，这地暖效果挺好的，今年冷，真用着了吧。那年我们劝你安装没有错吧？"

肖总接话说："你大姐舍不得享受，这是今年下大雪，第一次打开吧？"

肖总一家人正坐在客厅边吃边喝茶聊天，突然李华女儿也回了，进家门就喊："呀！这么热闹，我还以为我是第一个赶回家，给我妈拜年的人呢。肖总好，大家好！谢谢你们看我妈妈！"

接着又对李华说："妈妈，这是爸爸给你做的辣菜，知道你喜欢这味道。奶奶用瓶子装好，让我带给你吃。还有这是爷爷给你的暖炉，这是姑姑给你的手套，说有时间一起聚聚！"

女儿一口气说了一堆话，都是婆家亲人的关心和祝福。李华心里感动，眼睛也湿润，她没有明显表露出来，对女儿说："你玩得开心吧，快去洗完手，一起吃团圆饺子。这是肖总亲手包的全素饺子，你放心吃吧！"李华一家人吃素，肖总和朋友们都知道。

李华这个年过得真难忘也很快乐，女儿把亲情又系了起来，把以前怨恨心结打开了。那年正是公司创建的第三个年头，一切向好的方向发展，包括亲情和友情。李华忽然感觉，这十几年的委屈已经释怀了。她认为做个好人还是有好报。李华无论多难，都坚持了做好人的底线，做一个有价值的人，才会得到真正的尊重，从内到外的自信，散发出强烈的人格魅力。李华已经炼出一副处事不惊的姿态了，遇事不急不躁，成熟稳重。

第四十二章　转让公司

这几年李华做工程过得很充实，还认识了不同行业的高端人士，学到了不少在学校里学不到的知识。在这龙蛇混杂的社会中，一步步成长，识人长教训，吃过了无数次小亏。遇到过没有素质的企业领导干部；也遇到滴酒不沾，也不贪财的好领导干部。真是什么样的人都有，就看怎么去应付。

当李华遇到男性领导多的应酬，基本上都依赖肖总陪同。她知道肖总有讲笑话段子的公关能力，他能掌控得住应付自如。李华看到肖总的能力已经超越了自己，李华开始打算自己该退出幕后了，该由肖总挑大梁主持工作了。她想把这次工程合同由肖总签订，作为公司的新年贺礼。也想趁这次交接之前，找肖总好好谈一次，将公司法人的 50%，全部转给肖总一个法定人。李华打算彻底放权，自己就专门跟进扩大业务工程洽谈，以销售铝材为主导，配合肖总整个公司运作。

这三年的超负荷的劳累操心，李华已经身心疲惫。夜深人静之时，李华泡完澡后，有时候为了改善睡眠，临睡之前会喝上一杯台湾老板卞姐送的红酒。看着穿上睡袍镜中的自己，似乎近三年来已经老了 5 岁。看着镜中消瘦的脸，李华突然想到，当这次工程结束完成，获得分红利润后一定要对自己好点。当转让公司让肖总正式接手后，李华退出二线，安心地安排微整形医院，对自己全方位进行美容微整设计。

这决定似乎比继续辛苦搞公司重要，毕竟李华是最爱臭美的。她不能将岁月的不堪写在脸上，她要活出自己喜欢的模样。目前的生活不是她想要的状态，钱挣了人却过早老去。她更需要阳光自信的自己，而且现在她也可以做到这点，她有这样的经济实力。那个年代，最时尚的炫富就是你自己美丽的容颜。容颜能不攻自破，容颜姣美胜过千言万语的表白。这个思维的转变，让李华对自己大方了很多，舍得用钱投资自己才华和美貌。

想到这里，李华下了决心，不能为挣钱不要面容和身体健康了。这三年没有好好休息过，少不了熬夜，度过了许多不眠之夜。女人老了真不敢多看自己几眼。想到万一哪天，那些曾经伤害过自己的前任，或者想看她笑话的小人看到自己的老相，那多没面子啊！有这些虚荣也是情理之中，李华非仙人女子，也是普通女人都有的爱美之心。

人活着就是争口气，如果别人只在李华脸上看到满脸沧桑，一副伤痕累累的苦瓜相，有再多的钱和房子难不成总是挂在嘴巴上说吗？如果你看到一个人精神差，一脸老相，谁会相信你过得很好呢？要是李华真遇到那些伤害过自己的人，她要去跟他们去辩解，去炫耀？这些小孩子做的事，李华肯宁干不了。那唯一可以改变的是自己的生活状态，给自己身心放个假，彻底地释放自己。

解救自己不难，就是要学会放下。李华想着这几年已从一穷二白，一步一步地实现了有房有事业。目前女儿学业有成，也能兼顾孝敬父母，经济水平逐年递增，能满足自己的基本开支。一切已经足够美好，没有什么想不开的，也没有什么放不下了。

春节初八，李华公司就与甲方同步正常进入施工现场。安排好工人，又将任务又交给肖总的小舅子后，公司立刻兵分两路，将甲方的有关管理人员领导，小到出纳会计，大到处长干部，都邀请到一处当地有名的足疗城，娱乐放松一下。一是统一感谢他们去年的支持和配合，二是为肖总做好来年业务上的衔接，将甲方关键领导推荐给他认识。李华想毫无保留地将公司的所有业务关系，带给肖总认个脸熟。

邀请的领导都到了，当时公司只有一台二手奥迪车，接送都是肖总一个人。李华联系了一辆长期合作的商务出租车，对司机说："你负责送你接来的这些领导，记得每个人都要送上预先准备好的礼物包，要送到他们手上。现在等这些领导尽兴地玩麻将，你陪着服务好。"

李华交代完司机，又去叮嘱肖总："你去陪爱唱歌的领导们唱歌吧，我就陪李处长还有出纳夫妻俩去足疗。咱们就这样分工，如果有领导提前走，一定发短信告诉我，互相照应一下，千万别掉下那位领导。一定别谈工作！切记，就是放松！"

初八的这天，大雪纷飞，是往年从没有过的冷。这次活动连出纳员普通的家属都一起请了，不只是邀请有权的领导，因此领导处长们才放心参加这个聚会。因为是集体活动，每个参加的人都感受到真诚和尊重。大家都很开心，很放松。这些项目比在外只是吃喝要实在得多，而且针对爱好不一样的人，都基本满足了各自的娱乐消遣。

再说初八是团拜的日子，并不是真正的工作状态，其实是假期收心的缓冲期。放长假后还没有把心思真正放回工作上，这是事业单位办公室的常态。李华太了解事业单位的工作做派了，所以不急不躁地对肖总说："今天只陪好领导，你统一结账，放开嗓子尽情带头唱好第一首歌。唱歌前讲一段感谢的话。"

那天晚上下着满天白色鹅毛大雪，雾霾加雪花挂在路边树枝上。雪花压弯了树枝上，叶子都看成是白色的一朵花，屋顶上的雪已是厚厚的一层白色棉花被。马路上却还是有公交车驶过，很慢很慢地行驶。这座城市真是不简单，这么大的雪还是有陆续的鞭炮声，东边和西边不远处的天空升起五颜六色的烟花。

李华选择坐在李处长旁边的躺椅坐下泡脚，热水的温度刚刚好。李处长也满上了一大木桶热水，李处长对李华说："李总你实在太客气了，这次工作上有什么想法，需要我帮忙的地方你尽管先说出来，我会支持你们的工作。"

李华说："有李处长这句话，我很感激。今天就是让大家好好放松，也是感谢大家对我们工作的支持。以后我公司这边，肖总会请教李处长，请多多关照！"

室内的暖气真足，个个满脸红通通的，享受着足疗带来的睡意。李华先退出足疗室，提前结束自己的足疗按摩。她悄悄对技师说："别打扰他们，如果做完了，请让领导们躺下休息，别吵醒他们。中途端上小吃放在茶几上就退出来。"

叮嘱完服务员后，李华和肖总还有出租车司机都在候客厅大门口必经之路候着。领导们一一出来，按事先安排的那样，肖总把他送来的领导请进自己车上。出租车司机把他送来的领导请进商务车上。李华跟每个领导打了招呼，握手告别，送上车。

直到车子启动远远地离开，李华这才进足疗城环视一番，坐在大厅单人沙发上看看时间表。还有 15 分钟就到晚上 9：30 分，还有最后一趟公交车可以直达李华居住小区那里。估计要 40 分钟时间到达李华家最近的公交车站。

想到这里，她立刻打通肖总电话："肖总，是我，你不用吱声，我说你听。

今天太晚了，而且路滑，你注意安全。你把领导送到家，你不用赶回来接我了，我可以自己乘公交车回家。你辛苦完事后，直接回家。"

电话挂机后，李华迅速地向门外走去，一深一浅地踩着地上的脚印，向对面马路的公交站走去，一不小心摔一大跤。赶紧爬起来，瞧瞧还好没有路人看见她的滑稽狼狈样子，风有些刺骨，刮在脸上，雪下在头顶上的羽绒帽子帘上。没几分钟，李华看着自己就像木偶雪人，很可爱。到了站台还好，车还没来，赶上了在这外面等车。

这一天总算忙完了，不管有没有结果，但是公司的诚意和心意，这些领导应该感觉到了。他们感觉到李华和肖总就是实实在在做事的人，出门上车的领导在跟李华握手的时候，看得出都对李华真诚道谢。

公交车晚到了 10 分钟，9：40 分到站。当李华走上公交车，已成了雪人。之前在站台上不停地踩脚脚踢腿驱寒，上车后直接坐在靠窗的最后一排，选择一个角落靠着。随着车子的颠簸，摇摇晃晃地睡着了。不知是紧张还是根本不敢睡沉，李华老是半醒半睡的状态，生怕坐过了站，那可是不方便回头的路。李华就这样靠近窗户，用手擦掉窗上的雾气向外望去，外面成了一片白茫茫的雪城！

不知道过了多久，公交车自动报站名："彭刘杨路站到了，要下车的旅客，请依顺序从后门下车。"李华惊醒了过来，下车后望着路边最高楼，"终于到了，今晚又是一个不眠之夜！今天太累了，明天一进公司，一定跟肖总谈谈交接的事情了。"

李华一辈子记得那一场雪，坐公交车回家孤单和疲倦场景，可能这辈子也再遇见的那么大的风雪。

到了第二天雪照样下个不停，基本上公司的员工还是沉浸在节日气氛中。李华早早地坐在自己的办公室等着肖总谈话。肖总知道李华的性格，她决定的事情肯定是考虑得很成熟了，才会对他说出来。双方都开诚布公地交了心，肖总很舍不得地说："我理解你退出公司的打算，这样可以一切重新开始。但是能不能永远当我的顾问，有好的人脉继续帮忙引荐。接到的工程项目，我们还是按公司规定奖励到个人，以与甲方签订合同为准，你看怎么样？"

李华笑着说："我就知道你怕我卸掉担子不管你了。不会的，我会一如既往地帮你洽谈好的工程项目，向甲方引荐你，你们直接联系。具体事项和工作安排由你来决定，我再不插手公司的任何业务，不介入你的后期所有人事工作安排，我只配合你签订业务合同成功，这样你才能迅速成长。至于个人奖金就按我们以前定下的规矩为准。其实你已经独当一面了，不用害怕，你想想当初咱们在西山庙会上抽的签。旨意明确，你是未来的千万富翁，我只达到你野心的一半，几百万足以。当你真的成为千万富翁的时候，说好了我们一起去还愿！"

这一年李华彻底悟空了人生哲理，当财富达到自己预期的水平时，还有比拼命挣钱更有意义的事情。这个阶段的李华，只想开始放慢脚步，冷静思考一些问题。她可不是为挣钱而挣钱的女人，而是要把生活过得更有意义。人生不能缺钱，但钱不是快乐的根源。财富可以让人自由，有更多时间积累沉淀，通过投资自己实现人生的梦想，这是良性的循环，是一种完美的境界。精神财富和物质财富相结合的人生，才能享受真正的快乐和幸福，这两种财富不能缺一。有了双重快乐，才算真正的人生赢家。

后来的一周里，这座城市终于出太阳了，阳光洒照着大地，雪花逐渐变成水滴，从树叶、树干，石头缝中流进土地。这么好的春光季节，趁着大好天气，李华跟肖总顺利地办了移交手续，公司法人那栏表格上填写了肖总的名字。肖总满脸羞涩地笑着接受正式移交文本，李华轻松高兴地说："无官一身轻啊，真的可以好好去报名学点兴趣爱好了。"

李华的脑海里已经有了下一个学习目标，她这一生都没有放下的文学梦想。李华将已写好的邮件投进了附近的邮局信箱，那是一份报名学习的书面信函，李华要参加北京人文写作函授班。这将是又一个新的台阶。李华没有间断自我提升的学习要求，在每一个成长阶段，都会给到自己一个目标，也会在那个领域获得惊喜。成就一个想做文人的写作梦想，正潜移默化地从李华内心萌发一种动力。该是打基础学知识实践写作的时候了，现在开始应该也不算晚。

第四十三章　开拓红酒销售市场

九十年代市里主抓招商引资政策，闺蜜珍单位正好负责接待洽谈跟进外企落实项目。珍很有责任心和组织能力，为了尽快让外企在内地的业务开展起来，平时除了正常工作时间接待这些外企老总和相关负责人，周末或节假日也跟他们组织一些联谊活动。珍常说这份工作没有分工作日和休息日。

台企卞总夫妻是闺蜜珍主要服务对象之一。珍为他们做了很多力所能及的事情，娱乐活时中也常常陪伴在他们身边。在周末的娱乐活动中，珍经常带着李华一同参加那些高级别小范围聚会，出席聚会的有事业单位科级、局级干部，有时候还把主管抓这项招商引资工作的市长也请来。

活动中说是不谈工作，但是有大领导在场的时候，卞总有时不经意就会问一些政策性的优惠条件。这些领导人把外企的工作做到了基层，落到实处，有时候就成了现场办公。卞总是一位很有智慧的女老板，她跟丈夫的私营企业来到内地投资，相关的重要事项也是她说了算。卞总是一个很有魄力的女强人。

那年卞总六十差点，珍和李华那时只有三十多岁，正是干事业的黄金年龄。她们是卞总喜欢的同类女性。卞总曾经在市长面前说过："感谢领导这样照顾我们台企，又安排这么得力的美女们配合我们的工作，我很放心把企业引进本市，进入下一步红酒市场的投资。"

李华就是那个时候以朋友身份认识卞总。后来李华的服装折扣店在省城开张期间，卞总打听到了，还亲自去"莲湖缘"服装店请李华出山，再次邀请李华在省内外多个城市打开红酒销售市场，拓展业务，向全国省市销售。

当时李华已身兼数职，没有答应卞总的请求，只是说："我会在需要用到红酒的场合，都会帮卞总推荐，无偿服务。等我忙过这段时间，定在节日之前帮卞总促成几单，卞总您看行吗？"

卞总看到李华确实分身乏术，话都说到这份上了，也没有勉强。她知道李华人脉广，经商思维灵活。李华已经答应帮忙推荐，卞总也算是有收获，她很感激李华的帮助。在那之后卞总不时约李华小聚，维系感情，李华当然也是处处为卞总的红酒业务留意，所以每次与卞总小聚时，总会很随意地约上不同职业身份的好友，介绍给卞总认识。后期红酒市场的几个主要大客户女友，都是李华常去美容院的老板琴琴，还有类似其他行业圈子的女友。

当李华将门窗工程公司转让给合伙人肖总之后，李华心中其实也安排了未来的事业方向。她没有忘记卞总夫妻俩诚意的邀请，她也没有忘记自己做过保险，做过批发站主任，那些商业模式与客户打交道的技巧都是李华的强项。闺蜜珍常说："会做人，就不愁没有事业。"

闺蜜珍在卞总面前就说过："我把李华介绍给您认识，保证以后您会当她是个宝。李华是个人才，真的是销售冠军，脑子反应很快。最主要是她总为对方着想，跟她合作在利润上一定不会吃亏。大家都喜欢跟实在人做生意。她能举一反三成交生意，无论是个体还是单位，又或者是私人喜宴，她全都能搞定！卞总，您现在已把家和公司安在武汉，李华也在武汉，这真是天时地利人和啊，缘分啊！你们一起联手，一定能把红酒推向更多城市，销量只会比往年的更大！"

卞总激动地连连说："谢谢你帮我引荐认识了李华好妹妹，在武汉我只信任李华。不管李华来不来公司报到就职，我都将李华作为我公司的长期合作伙伴，她在家在外电话办公都行，对李华特殊，我不要求李华早八晚五的工作时间模式。"

卞总领教过一次李华成功的随机销售，就是电话聊天，将领导夫人约到美容院，请她做了面部和身体保养，那笔红酒生意就成了！卞总知道李华不是刻意去推荐红酒销售，她的那些营销模式是在先考虑让朋友舒服，这就是先做人！朋友们认可了李华人品，想想后面聊到什么共赢的项目，还会不动心吗？

李华的父母搬到省城生活之后，李华找时间回了趟老家，把给父母亲买的那套空闲的房子卖掉。为了卞总的红酒推广，李华可以把红酒先当人情送人免费品尝，或者当礼物送给合作伙伴。

这次她临时想到一位朋友，银行支行高行长，他知道有些客户有买房的需求，也有买房的经济实力。打通高行长的电话后，高行长关心地问几句客套话："李总这次回家乡有什么好项目呀？别忘了告诉我一声哟！"

李华认真地说："还真有一件事，你可以帮到我的。"

高行长也认真说："什么事，只要我能办到的，一定帮。"

李华接着说："好的，下班后请高行长在凤凰路那家茶楼聚聚，好好谈谈。如果你身边有信得过，有经济实力，又需要买房子的朋友，也可以一起带到茶楼来，边喝茶边聊。当然，今天你能带有诚意买房的朋友来更好！"

高行长想了想，立刻回复："还真有一位做生意的朋友想买房，因为他想让孩子在城里上学。我可以请他直接到茶楼跟你谈。我不传话，你俩当面谈。他有钱在我行存着，房钱应该没有问题。那等会我联系好，下班直接茶楼见！"

高行长是李华的老乡，人很朴实热情，干到今天这个职位上，全靠做人好，有良好的服务态度，而且业务精，在行里储蓄任务完成总是第一名。他的工作范围已经超出了储蓄任务要求，他把客户当朋友，帮忙他们解决困难。因此客户也愿意帮助支持他的工作。李华就是在办业务接触中，了解高行长的为人，知道他乐意助人，值得信赖，所以这次第一个想到了让高行长引荐需要买房又有钱的大客户。

李华回到家乡，喜欢去离茶楼很近的一家美容院做两个小时的放松项目，面部保湿和颈部护理，然后在那里美美地睡一觉。因为办了年卡，平时回来办事中途，又不想麻烦朋友招待，她就到美容院消遣时间。这是李华与闺蜜约定见面的好地方。

三个小时很快过去了，做过美容的李华精神很好，小美容师的一双小手在脸部肌肤上抚摸的指法真舒服。李华在疲惫的时候，总喜欢在这里听着轻缓的催眠音乐，享受那种轻缓到位的按摩。单身多年李华已经养成了好好爱自己的好习惯。为了在办事精神一些，李华常常用这种方式快速恢复自己的体能，消除旅途疲劳。所以朋友们眼中的李华总是精神焕发的样子，感觉李华在逆生长，越来越有女人的那种成熟知性美韵味。

闺蜜珍也来了美容院，做了一个小时的项目，随后李华把此行来的目的说了一遍。闺蜜珍二话没说，把李华请到自己买的一台七座新车。珍高兴地说："这台车以后是接你的专车，只要你回老家，我来接你。另外买这车主要是帮卞总做点红酒推销，方便自己送点货。我自己还在职工作，不能像你一样全职做红酒生意。"

李华说："这倒是个很好的主意，我还想着你个子这么苗条，怎么买这么大的车。现在明白了，你不经商下海真的是浪费了人才。"

　　珍说："我们单位又没有你单位好政策，我必须干到 55 岁才能退休啊！我只是给做餐馆的朋友带一点下总家的红酒，不像你，一拖就是一车红酒 40 箱。今天准备卖房子，打算再卖多少箱酒?"

　　珍的这句玩笑话还真提醒了李华，她灵光一闪想到了一个好主意！

第四十四章　多赢方案

　　傍晚六点钟，李华和珍坐在指定茶楼靠近窗户的座位上。刚刚点了一壶水果茶和零食水果拼盘，高行长就来到了，随同一起来了一位满面笑容的中年男人。高行长在坐下之前，向李华介绍："这是我的朋友刘老板，今天带来跟你谈谈买房子的事，一起喝茶聊聊！"

　　李华向高行长及刘老板介绍了闺蜜珍，这像是正儿八经谈生意，李华忍不住暗自笑了起来。刘老板说："能把房产证给我看看吗？"

　　李华从包里取出来，直接递给刘老板说："我喜欢刘老板这种办事风格，直截了当！"

　　高行长也补充说："刘总就是这个性格，要是今天谈妥，明天就可以照程序走了。等会可以看看现房吗？"

　　李华拿出钥匙说："行，都在这里，今天先看看吧！"

　　"刘总在哪里高就，办了什么公司？"珍从侧面问问刘总的情况，想知道他是什么公司的老总。

　　刘总边看房产证，边答："我就做点钢材，建材生意！"接着又对李华说："这房子是顶楼？面积可以，但是夏天会不会很热呀？听高行长介绍了你的小区情况，我感觉还不错，我确实也需要买一套房子。如果看完现房没问题，我就买了这套房子吧。至于价格上，我给出 52 万，你看怎么样？"

　　李华之前报出的价钱是 54 万，听到刘总一下砍了 2 万元，李华沉默了一会向高行长笑着说："高行长，你没有告诉刘总总价吗？"

　　高行长这样说："我已经把你的报价告诉了刘总。至于成交价格你们俩直接谈，我不介入。"

　　刘总接话说："我这边想法很简单，你李总照顾一下，我们省了中介费，李总这边不亏。如果你同意，我也是爽快人，马上给你看房定金 2 万，怎么样？

我知道李总你也忙，能尽快成交对李总也有好处。最主要是我是真忙，要不是高行长邀约，所以省去了你我共同转弯抹角环节，李总你定！"

话都说到这份上了，闺蜜珍看了李华一眼，接着喊服务员："点餐！"

服务员热情地问："领导们想吃那哪种煲仔饭呀？这是我们茶楼最新推荐的菜式图片。"

高行长拿出一张优惠卡递给服务员，"用这个卡结账！你们想吃啥尽管点吧！"

刘总笑着点了宫保鸡丁煲仔饭，高行长说："我要一份牛排加一份水果沙拉。"珍要了一份鱼香茄子煲，李华叫一份红烧鱼块煲仔饭。

真是众口难调，像这样四人四样饭，还是来茶楼比较合适。李华想到闺蜜珍给她腾出了几分钟的考虑时间。珍的眼神告诉李华，先收下定金，这样的价钱是合理的，目前本地二手房价就是这个行情，可以成交。

李华领悟了，这些中介费差价等于直接让利给买方刘总，而且这次是高行长出面，资金上有保障，不担心卖房后收不到房款。因为没有房屋中介作保，只能相信高行长了，他是行长应该没有问题。

心里评估了几分钟后，李华开玩笑调侃道："哎呀，刘总真会砍价，把中介费都直接减没了。您是高行长的朋友，第一次见面，谈生意也爽快。就听刘总的意思，吃亏上当就只有这套好房子了。现在大家都是朋友了，以后还得多多照顾我的红酒生意哟！就这么定了，卖给你了！这房子可是风水宝地呀！你瞧我们一家都升迁省城了。"

刘总灵光，立刻拿起一杯啤酒对李华就说："为成交干杯！"又拿出二信封银行纸袋钞票递给李华，"这二万元定金先拿着！"高行长也拿起杯子，还有闺蜜珍也抬起头，一起昂头喝完杯中的酒！

高行长放下杯子说："这是我处理过的最轻松的生意牵线，两位老总真是爽快！今天我可以多说两句话了。李总虽然是女士，可谈事做派不比男人差呀，我佩服，来喝一杯！至于红酒推荐的事情，还真可以请刘总帮忙推销！这个忙，你刘总应该帮，人家李总一下子让你 2 万元，大气之人，不挣钱都难！"

高行长使出了激将法，刘总只得表态说："我愿意试试，正好春节之前可以弄一批，搞几箱送关系户先喝，看看效果怎样。"

李华想了想说："高行长是这样的，我之前说过，谁帮我卖掉房子，中介费 2 万元就给到谁。没有想到中介费被让利刘总了——也好，肥水不流外人田，现在咱们都是朋友了。现在高行长牵线促成了双方买卖房子的生意，一点好处也没有得到，我于心不忍；现在还帮我牵线搭桥让刘总帮推销红酒，这情分太重了。我想这样处理，等房子办完过户手续后，房款到位，房子马上当日移交。我会在春节之前，先送 40 箱红酒给高行长和刘总送关系户。品尝的红酒算我送的，如果有销售成交的单，就算我奖励高行长做了好事，帮了我。这四十箱红酒算我全送了！怎么样，没有压力帮我吧！"

李华送红酒开拓市场的大胆做法，让闺蜜珍长了见识。难怪常听李华说，舍不得羊，就套不住狼的饥饿促销法，李华今天给她用实例上了一课。

后面的事情也很顺利，李华的房子不仅赶在春节之前成交，年前收到了 50% 的房款。李华用红酒答谢高行长雪中送炭的及时帮助。李华心想，这比送两万元红包更有好处。第一，两万元红酒批发价与零售价的市场利润部分，给到了高行长礼物心意；第二，给了高行长继续帮推荐红酒市场，先可给供应商铺货铺垫理由，让高行长无压力收下红酒；第三，利用春节之际，许多人情往来需要送红酒最佳时机，顺便帮卞总拓展多层次的销售平台。

当闺蜜珍跟卞总说了李华自垫红酒 40 箱送朋友，卞总对李华更加赏识。卞总对珍说："李华上次还自己垫付 1 万元钱的红酒款，携带好友的儿子学做红酒生意。那一批红酒赚得的利润，都给了那位好友的儿子。后来小伙子继续进货几批红酒，真的挣到了人生第一桶金。李华的好友——那小伙子的妈妈，后来成了李华女儿的干妈。我真佩服李华的为人，她有大智慧，她把一些有销售潜质的好朋友都发展成推荐红酒的赢家，不仅都挣钱了，还赢得了友情。"

那年元旦，卞总夫妻把李华发展起来的做红酒业务的朋友全部召集起来，不光组织大家聚餐唱歌，还赠送高档规格的新红酒产品。卞总公司向李华还了一个大人情，也把红酒推向了多种销售渠道的良性循环。

李华那一年硬是把私人需求的零散生意做活了，例如美容院老板搞活动，李华建议给办会员的顾客送红酒；对于举办私人婚宴的场所，也以批发价出售给举办方，让其获得红酒利润差。李华做这些经销手段只是单纯替对方着想，把利润摆在桌面上说，把利益给到推荐方。有些时候是自己先垫钱，成交挣钱了之后，在收到利润分成的同时，将本钱收回。

卞总有天接到美容阮老板琴琴的电话："卞姐姐，李华让我直接找你，我今年春节要预定 30 箱胜百利红酒做活动，可以按李华一样的价格给我们吗？"

卞总回答道："李华说了算，就按这个价钱给你。只不过要算李华的销量，才能享受这个三级批发价！"

琴琴高兴地说："谢谢卞姐姐，难怪李华这么帮你又帮我。你们俩真好！到时候来我们美容院，送你做项目！我们下个月马上又在中南二路开一家美容院店，规格档次更高。我现在先口头邀请您卞总，到时候一定来享受会员高级服务待遇。一定让您满意！"

李华早就成了琴琴美容院五所店里的终身高级会员。李华在外打拼累了，或者从外省送红酒回来晚了，都会在琴琴的美容院做几套项目。洁面、护颈、卵巢保养、提臀、丰胸等美容物理手法，做着做着李华会不知不觉就睡着。有时候是中午到店，到晚上七点才出来，睡了几个小时的李华，恢复元气精力充沛。这也是李华的一种协调放松的办法，李华也是女人，而且是一位对自己舍得的爱美女人。女儿干妈对李华说过："我就是欣赏李华这点，对朋友都大方，对自己也舍得。不像有的女人，当守财奴，对自己都不投资的女人，那会舍得对别人好！"

同学惠平和珊妮曾经亲自看到李华的一张美容院会员卡值 17 万元，差点没惊掉两个人的下巴，这可是亲眼所见哟，看到李华在事业上拼对自己狠，在生活美容保养方面的开销大，也有力度真狠真舍得啊！羡慕李华有实力也想得开。应了李华说的话："要做金钱的主人！"

李华做红酒销售那些年，红酒销到美容院，餐馆，三级批发站，还给卞总的公司红酒市场拓展到了省外，遍地开花。李华还带出了不少做红酒销售的女性朋友，这些不同行业出身的精英娘子军，都获得"靓女富姐姐"的外号！李华被她们称呼为"靓女师姐"了。

第四十五章　长期聘用

卞总在湖北省这几年的红酒销售中，看中了李华的义气，做事踏实的作风。每笔业务自然成交，从没有去强迫销售。而是从细微处，替对方节约成本着想，这样自然办成事情。李华直接言传身教地做红酒推广，把自己需要还人情的所有机会，都变成送红酒作为感谢礼物。就此举一反三，促成了多次自然销售成功。她还帮助几个没有工作的年轻人学会走进社会，学会了推销自己。在赚得的第一桶金后，获得了经商的自信，学会寻找适合自己的创业天地。他们也懂得了工作挣钱不容易，也看到了父母亲的辛苦。

李华关心后辈们的成长，她对他们的关爱不是给出红包，而是手把手教会他们做生意。让他们熟悉进货、送货、押货、结账的各个流程，学会利润分配。也教会他们挖掘新的需求人群，进行循环进货再销售。将第一笔支助本金，变成了本金加利润，然后再进货再赚钱，像书中所说的成功经商模式那样，滚雪球一样的使利润增大。

只要跟李华合作做过红酒业务的朋友们，都看到了销售挣钱的希望。李华不仅仅是挣了钱，而是学会了替合作伙伴着想，认识到他人的利益越多，结果自己受益更大。人性如此，你真心对别人好，大家共赢，谁都想跟你合作，挣钱的时候都会想着你。谁都信任一位能带动自己挣到钱的人。李华就是这么一个人。

卞总看到李华销售的每一单红酒，都有一个感人的故事。在李华的朴实帮助下，卞总的红酒开拓市场慢慢受益于在广大的消费者。还教会后辈在课堂上学不到的社会知识，智慧、耐心、善良、真诚、韧性、灵活，各方面言传身教！

卞总不想失去李华这么好的朋友，她既是销售高手，又是公司最得力的合作伙伴。卞总与丈夫商量，决定长期聘用李华作为公司的销售人员，兼职或专职由李华自己时间去决定。

李华也知道自己有几斤几两，她明白自己最需要什么，她目前的生活状态适合什么的工作。这些年来李华也体验过多个行业，在每个行业中她都不恋战，能迅速华丽地转身。服装店生意正旺时，她能果断将店铺转让；在门窗公司生意兴隆时，她也舍得将公司转让。她知道不能一味地去追求金钱财富，而忽略了自己的精神需求。

她需要生活来滋润她的梦想，她就需要时间去放慢生活的脚步。她需要更多的时间做一些更有意义的事情。一边兼职做红酒销售，一边做自己喜欢的房产投资，这是目前最适合她的工作。通过业余红酒营销的一年中，她还悟出了做生意的道理。

那次卖房还人情送出 40 箱红酒的举措，卞总知道后很感动李华这样实实在在帮她拓展红酒市场，打开力所能及的销路。那年春节初八日，高行长一上班就跟李华打电话说：“新年好，今天我已约刘总来银行，提醒他给你付房子的尾款，今天全部给你到位。另外，年前送出去品尝的红酒，有的是作为礼品赠送了，其中推荐两个二级红酒批发商感兴趣，想跟你谈谈生意。你看怎么运作，我来当介绍人帮你推荐！”

李华很高兴地说：“谢谢高行长操心了，送出去的红酒都算我应感谢你的礼物。剩下的请你直接与那两个二级批发商谈，直接将零售发票及进货批发价收据给到经销商，这笔销售款及中间差利润，你可以直接与经销商分享利润！这是对你的感谢，这样做当然也是鼓励你以后多帮我推荐红酒，我也可以得到总公司的销量奖励金。”

高行长说：“给这么多？怎么好意思！”

李华说：“没有关系，你以后帮我多推荐多销售，我们一起挣钱。薄利多销，扩大市场！饼子是大家一起吃才能细水长流，感谢你是我应尽的本分！”

卞总知道李华的房款顺利到位，心里才踏实了。大年十五这天，天气特别好，卞总约李华来江景茶城聚餐。李华正好有发展新客户预定红酒的打算，也得当面跟卞总夫妻俩说说计划，作好备货送货准备。

茶城是李华喜欢的谈生意场所，卞总很尊重李华的喜好。卞总很守时，提前就来到茶城选择好一个比较适合说话的雅座包间，李华按卞总说的地址房号也准时到达。她们不约而同将带来的礼物赠送给对方。卞总拿出一条很漂亮的杭州丝巾说：“今年太冷了，送给你保暖，配衣服也好看，戴上漂亮！”

李华笑着说："我们俩又想到一起了，不过我只考虑到保暖，两条大红色洋绒围巾！给卞总和孟董的一点心意。"

孟董说："过去的一年你帮我们创新了销售量，公司准备给你配备专职送货司机。价格在以往基础上，达到 100 箱奖励 10% 的利润！只对你有这样的优待！"

李华感激地说："谢谢，这是我应该做的。通过帮公司推荐拓展红酒市场，我也受益很多。谢谢卞总和孟董给我多方位支持配合，让我有施展的平台！真心话，我接受给公司永远当兼职推荐的销售员！"

卞总说："这正是我们两个老家伙想说的话，正式邀请你永远担任我公司的编外销售总监！这个位置永远给你留着！"

孟董说："今天我们喝公司最好的红酒，还给你备了二瓶好的新产品，带回家给亲人喝。"

卞总说："今天没有别的事，吃完饭后，我们一起唱歌，孟董想与你合唱一首台湾歌曲《爱拼才会赢》！"

就像这首歌的歌词一样，爱拼才会赢，卞总和孟董都已到了古稀之年还在外打拼。有他们作为榜样，李华自然备受鼓舞，继续努力打拼。人们常说"物以类聚，人以群分"，大家都喜欢跟同类人在一起。正能量的人吸引着李华，李华身边就有一群这样的强人能人。正是卞总能力出众办事果断的特质吸引了李华，两人成了忘年之交，事业和生活上的知己。李华想像卞总那样成功，不是说一定要做多大的事业，而是不让自己不闲下来，像卞总一样地干实事，做一位对社会有用的人。

卞总曾经语重心长地对李华说："我和孟董这个年龄还这样干，不仅仅是为了钱。我们的孩子不做我们这一行，不接我们的班，我们俩闲着还生病。自从做熟了这个行业后，感觉很轻松，就当是交朋友做事业。也当为自己谋一份差事，尽心尽力做，把利益分摊出去，没有想到事业越做越好，特别是将这个红酒从西班牙引进国内后。中国这个大市场，人口多，国家对外资企业政策好，再遇到你们这样的好朋友帮助支持，我们越来越轻松，就当是娱乐交友。我们俩一向主张有钱大家挣，愉快合作，共同富裕的理念，做健康生意，交开心的好朋友！"

孟董也知足地说："来湖北通过红酒会友，经你的介绍，我们都认识了你身边的能人好朋友，他们都成了我们的合作伙伴，我们真的很开心。像美容院的老板琴琴、周总、珍珍、珊妮、你女儿的干妈，还有你女友的儿子，你妹妹的女儿，还有电信的那个徐姐，还有联通的严总……他们个个是销售行家了。你带动开辟了另一个大红酒市场，这是我们俩做不到的事情，也是我们俩没有想到的。看来你是不想让我们这两个前辈退休啊！"

卞总也不停点头拉着李华手说："你知道吗？珍等退休了，来和我们一起做全职销售红酒，问你还有什么高招？"

李华笑着说："别这样夸我了，我哪有什么高招呀？卞姐姐，我销给每一个客户，每一个团单，您都知道是怎么促成。我就是有您公司做后盾支持配合，加之以诚相待。对合作伙伴，将利润全部摆在桌面上谈，分配合理，五五分成，做到互帮互助共赢。这样每一笔业务利润及时结算，利润及时到位，从不拖泥带水掖着藏着。利润透明，讲诚信，吃亏留给自己，好处多替对方想。这样办事待人，合作共事，还怕合作伙伴不找讲信用的人合作吗？我没有什么经验，就是办事实在。"

卞总不停点头说："对呀，对呀，这叫老实人有福气。谁都喜欢和你这样的人做生意，谈项目，继续合作。我不管，你是我和孟董永远的合伙人，永远的朋友！"

李华很激动地笑了笑说："我们光顾说话了，我就此机会，为两位老总唱一首老歌《情义无价》，送给我的事业伙伴卞姐孟董。祝你们健康幸福，财源滚滚！祝我们合作愉快，顺风顺水！"

闪光灯照着包厢中舞台上的李华，神情专注的演唱，以真情柔润的嗓音，唱出了情意绵绵，也唱出了歌曲的主题：情义无价。

第四十六章　投资地标房

　　李华有一个好习惯，凡是促成红酒生意后，就会请合作伙伴做美容美甲，以表感谢。另外再将对红酒感兴趣的女友拉上一起喝茶，让已做成订单受益的合作伙伴，与新朋友随便自然分享那种成功喜悦。李华只负责请客买单，引荐新朋友相聚。这样的自然推荐方式是一种良性循环，使李华少说很多客套虚伪的话，李华真心待人，延深影响更多的朋友，自愿地感兴趣与李华合作。

　　李华的销售成功，就是靠这一点，绝不"王婆卖瓜，自卖自夸"，而是借助朋友成功后的喜悦分享，用事实说话，让新朋友对红酒销售产生兴趣。随后言传身教，现场由朋友代教每一步简单的程序。朋友示范出成功的例子，新人看到成交的希望就想亲自尝试，有经验的朋友也乐意教导。这也是李华的销售人脉越来越广的原因之一。李华还有一个优点，喜欢把感谢尽早兑现，哪怕是平日的口头承诺，也会放在心里，在合适的时候给朋友一一兑现友情，兑现利益，兑现感恩。

　　李华与卞总的合作，李华腾出了更多自由支配的时间，空闲时李华就会搜索房地产有价值的投资信息。这一天李华又发现了一个好的投资项目，就在请朋友到附近的茶楼坐坐，便无意地聊到了商机。

　　六月份的武汉，天气渐渐热了起来。合作伙伴美容院琴琴刚刚促成了一单红酒业务，李华把她请到最高规格的江景茶楼喝茶。李华有一位同住江景房的女友琦琦，她同样是一个爱美容、又爱漂亮、又有实力的女强人，这一次李华把琦琦约上了。

　　李华认为，是时候让琴琴跟琦琦互相认识了。虽然两人年龄相差八岁，但两人的情况很接近，都是有实力的单性女性，事业成功经济独立，都舍得给自己花钱养生，大家可以在同一个朋友圈子交往。当大家相聚在一起，可以畅所欲言，交流激发出各种有智慧的点子，思维改变人的命运。

琴琴的喊声打断了李华的思绪："李华你来得真早，我提前五分钟到。你的好朋友来了没有？"

李华忙起身招呼："在这边坐，等会她就到了。琦琦家就住在这附近的高档小区，她有点小资韵味及事业做得好，搞建筑房屋工程设计，很有品位的一个娇柔的小女人！"

琴琴很自信地说："我明白，你身边的朋友个个都是强人，当然也包括我在内。"

琴琴调皮地夸了李华的朋友，也夸了自己，小嘴甜甜的像抹了蜜。李华在琴琴身上看到了机灵内秀，也很会说话，真要向比自己小八岁的琴琴学习。

琦琦从玻璃门向茶楼室内走来，穿着那一身碎花连衣裙，外层全是纱，随微风吹拂，分外妖娆，优雅得像仙女一样。"你们都来这么早，我好像没有迟到吧？"

人和声音同时进入琴琴和李华的视线，琴琴惊掉了下巴："李华，你说你的朋友琦琦跟你同年，你们俩都是美女！真是冻龄啊？太让我妒忌了！真高兴认识后两位仙女姐姐。有空一定要到我的美容院去做身体护理，我送你俩项目保养卡，让你们好好享受！"

琴琴这话一说完，既介绍了自己，又夸得两位姐姐笑得合不拢嘴。李华直接对琦琦说："这位就是我跟你说到过的，年纪轻轻能干大方的美容院老板琴琴，她可是有 5 个美容院实力的时尚达人！"

琦琦将白白嫩嫩的小手伸出来，主动牵住琴琴的纤细小手。琴琴赞叹道："哇，这么会保养，手都这么漂亮，一看就是懂得投资自己，会保养的美女！说真的，真没有丑女人，只有懒女人！喝完茶，去我那里做身体轻松开背！免费赠送！"

李华看着琴琴活跃地推荐自己美容院，恰到好处地自然介绍，很欣赏她的业务能力。李华笑着从包里拿出一个信封递给琴琴："这是昨天结的红酒款项。你推荐的俞总夫人真豪爽，下总司机将货送到后，她直接一在发票签字付款了。这是你的那 50% 利润，收着！"

琴琴应着说："这么快？这么简单就挣钱了？"

李华看着茶单点饮品，回复琴琴："是你能干，关系铁，俞总全货照收，还说谢谢你呢。她端午节就分红酒给员工，她那是私营企业，她说了算！"

琴琴和李华一来一搭的对话，琦琦听明白了，对李华说："你们俩的红酒做成这么轻松，怎么不带我呀？"

李华拍了琦琦的手说："你也知道我一直做红酒，而且我也带你认识了卞总。你的心思，专搞你的工程设计去了，没有瞧上这小生意。我们就是做着好玩，自己也喜欢每天喝点，好睡觉！你如果感兴趣，叫琴琴现在教教你怎么入门。"

琴琴说："我认为琦琦比我能做得更好，因为她人脉关系更关，需求红酒范围人群更多。我们只动动嘴巴就能成单，其他的送货，收款，都由李华配合你服务，真的很简单！"

琴琴边说边查看信封上的钱，"这样，今天晚上我想唱歌，正好我请两位美女姐姐，给我面子啊！"

李华给琦琦和琴琴都倒上带来的新上市最好的一瓶红酒，笑着说："好，今天先去你那里享受美容。如果觉得适合有效果，我办张养颜减龄护肤年卡。"

琴琴说："先去美容院体验享受一下，如果适合，再需要办冻龄护肤提升紧致的张年卡，最主要是今晚可以漂漂亮亮去唱歌。"

琦琦已经笑得差点呛到了，缓缓说："听美女们安排，李华说好办卡，我也需要办一张年卡。反正美容项目一定要做，去别的地方做还不如照顾琴琴，今天还能得到赠送项目。难怪你美容院开了5个店，真不简单。那可是说好了，你要教会我怎么具体做红酒生意，挣到的钱全部投资办美容卡，把自己变得美美的。"

三个女人一台戏，聊着聊着就把美容和红酒的事聊得开心。无意中李华看着窗外的房地产广告，问琦琦："听说那是地标性建筑，琦琦你搞工程设计的，能确定这事是真是假吗？那里什么时候开盘对外销售，还有房价会不会很高，这些信息也帮忙打听一下。抽空我们一起去看看有没有样板房对外开放参观。"

琦琦也跟李华一样喜欢房子，这一问真是问对人了。琦琦连忙说："我知道，这是绿地集团盖的江景房。要建世界第三高，武汉第一高的地标性建筑。打造房地产高档小区、写字楼、商业圈为一体化的策划好项目。第一期预售每平方面积要12000以上，样板房好像在下个月7月1日对外开放。你真是问对我了，前几天我妹才向我打听武昌有没有江景房，所以我全部了解一遍周边的情况。

还有一点补充，听说这里还要开通地铁 5 号线，就在小区售楼部门口。这个楼盘太值了，我准备看看再计划要不要入手。你不会又要去买房吧？这可是目前武汉房价比较高的楼盘。"

李华低头看着手中的杯子，静静思索着，假如到时候看房子情况跟琦琦说的一样，她要怎样盘下一套。她很想投资一套地标性建筑的房子，哪怕改善自住条件也行。其实目前李华居住的小区环境很不错，各方面的配套设施都很齐备，她只是不想放过这个投资好项目。

琦琦奶声奶气对李华说："美女啊，你又想到什么了？"

李华微笑说："你真是我肚子里的一条蛔虫，我想什么你都看出来了！"

三个女人同时大笑起来，琴琴扮一个鬼脸，吐了吐舌头，"别人瞧我们这桌子了，还以为捡到大元宝了！"

琦琦用手轻轻拍着李华的手臂说："我猜你肯定又想买那绿地中心的房子了，对不对？"

李华笑而不语地点点头，可是又发愁地问琦琦和琴琴："你们俩帮我拿主意，如果将我现在的小户型房子卖掉，用那笔钱去预定绿地中心房子，这样运作怎么样？"

琦琦说："从小区投资发展来看，你那边的小区房价已经翻了一倍。如果能迅速卖掉，抓住绿地中心地标性建筑投资，应该还可以有增值空间。"

琴琴也补充道："如果你在绿地中心投资了，我也想去那边找一个小区门面，把美容院开到那里去。你们看房的时候也叫上我，我也去看看。你们买到哪，我的美容院开到哪！哈哈！"

李华笑着用食指放在嘴边："嘘，好，就这么定了！"

李华拿出手机给经常保持联系的房屋中介打电话："小黄，现在我们地铁站银行这边小区的房价能卖多少一个平方？我那套小户型能尽快找到有诚意买家吗？请帮忙了解摸清情况，尽量早点告诉我实情，等会我把房子详细信息发给你。中介费还是按照你的店规，如果在 1 个月之内成交，我愿多付中介费给你作为额外奖励。"

中介小黄电话那头高兴地说："没有问题，马上帮你推到网站上，有消息第一时间回复你！"

　　李华的表情果断而认真，看来这事真定下来了。琦琦盯着李华说出自己的疑问："还是你胆大心细，就这么定了，开始操作了吗?"

　　李华说："如果要投资，必须做好资金准备。我现在没有其他资金来源，又不想找亲朋好友开口借钱。能自己解决的，就决不向家人吐槽资金困难。再说，我已经习惯了买呀卖呀，这是解决资金问题的最好方式。所以我跟房屋中介一直保持良好的业务信誉！放心吧，顺利就是我的财运，不成也影响不了我现有的生活！只要尽力了，就有希望。机不可失，时不再来!"

第四十七章　女儿的理财老师

功夫不负有心人，李华抓紧时间操作投资地标房的计划，一方面跟房屋中介积极联系，一方面抓紧零散资金的整合。在中介积极的推动下很快有两个买家，一个是从上海回武汉发展的白领年轻人，一个是本小区的业主，他想替自己家人买在同一个小区，互相有一个照应。中介小黄问李华："李姐，你想卖给哪一家？"

李华了解客户情况后说："尽量优先一次性付款的买家，在同样价格的情况下，选择能一次性付款的客户。如果都是按揭贷款的方式，就选择买方是单身的买家，当事人能直接办理过户手续。"

小黄说："那还是选择从上海回武汉创业的白领年轻人吧！他正好可以全款，而且买房也很有诚意。只是在总价上，买方要求减少2000元，你看怎么样？如果同意减掉这部分，我可以通知买方明天上午带定金六万过来办手续。也麻烦你把房产证和所有购房合同发票都带过来，在中介门店签订委托买卖合同，明天见！"

小黄办事一向有魄力，这是李华看好小黄店长的原因。当然李华每次给小黄的中介费都比别人多。李华想早点把房子出售，抢到下一个投资机遇，衔接好资金来源，这样比去银行贷款利息要划算。好地段的房子比较难逢到，而且这座绿地中心项目楼盘，离现在居住地方只隔三站公交车路程，交通便利，还有名牌幼儿园，银行，菜市场。主要那里是地标性建筑，比现在居住的房子更有增值空间。

虽然处理起来有些折腾，卖掉旧房子后又要退房，又要搬家具。但是一想到住上三年后，还净挣房款价钱一倍的利润，也值得折腾。只是这个过程确实有点辛苦，清理，拖运，搞卫生，打包行李等各项琐事。为了投资挣钱，李华目前还没有享受生活的实力，她还需要奋斗，还需要去迁移住所，只要有挣钱的利润空间，李华都会果断卖掉。以后再寻找适合自己养老的好地方。

李华当即答应了小黄店长，说好了签合同的时间。接着马上给女儿打电话："乖乖，今天下班早点回来，我们一起在楼下对面鸡汤馆喝鸡汤，有事要对你说！"

女儿说："你现在说呀，我7点才能到家！"

李华卖关子说："还是等你到鸡汤馆当面说吧，就这样！"

女儿真听话，下班后直接在鸡汤馆与李华碰面。"有什么事情，还神秘兮兮的要见面说？"

李华已经点好了两份鸡汤罐，两份凉菜，一个烤鸡爪子，这是李华和女儿都爱吃的简单晚餐。女儿已经习惯了妈妈的做事风格，进店边问边坐下来，笑着向李华打招呼。李华这当妈妈的也笑着说："今天晚上你做好准备，把你最喜欢的生活用品和衣服整理好；把不需要的，可要可不要的东西整理在一起。估计我们要把东西暂时搬到三姨家的空房子放一段时间。我们可以在姥姥家的客房暂住。我准备把现在住的房子，明天办手续卖掉，然后拿到卖房子的钱，去买我带你看过的那套绿地中心的房子。下个月开盘，我还想说服你二姨也买一套。"

女儿脸上笑开了花似的说："我猜到了，但没有想到你会这么快卖掉房子。你跟哪个中介谈好了？别上当受骗。"

李华得意地跟女儿说："就是你认识的那个房屋中介小黄店长！"

女儿说："原来又是她，黄店长真行，一个礼拜就帮你找到买家了？不过我们家这小户型也好卖，有很多人买得起。听说这房子还有涨价空间，不过我已经习惯了，反正这是你的房子，只要能挣钱，你想卖就卖吧，我没有意见。反正我上次搬家过来的一大袋鞋子，我都没有打开穿过，还有一些衣服也没有开包！嘿嘿，我就知道新家住不长。"

女儿调皮又很理解李华的心思，李华反而有点不好意思，"妈妈暂时倒腾几次房子挣钱，以后一定会给你一处大房子，好房子。你相信妈妈能做到！目前苦一点，是为了以后能住更好的房子，相信我。"

女儿很自豪地开玩笑地说："你知道吗？我同学同事都说我妈像我姐姐，还说我妈一定很有钱。来我家玩过的同学说，这里那里都有我的房子。我说住个几年那些房都卖了，她们还不信，硬说我妈看着就像一位有钱的姐姐，说我是富二代！嘿嘿，我徒有虚名呀！"

李华很酷地对女儿说："那你认为呢？我们每一次都是住好房子，经过努力也越来越好呀，不是吗？等再奋斗几年挣钱了，我们会过上想要的生活，会住上更适合我们俩的好房子，现在暂时选择一个适合投资项目，让钱生钱。最适合我的挣钱方式就是投资房子。股票那种方式我不懂，投资实体店又太麻烦，还要守店经营。开公司也心累，太多事情要处理。所以，还是投资房子最舒服。"

女儿不停地笑着点头："我当然懂你，我的同学同事还说，以后他们家人买房，请你去看，带他们发点财。她们真的羡慕我，把你夸得天上去了，就好像我生来只是享妈妈的福！她们可没有想到我经常搬家的辛苦！"

李华静静听完女儿的话，接着说："你的同学同事没有说错，你真是幸亏有我这个妈。你已经少走很多弯路，你的起点比别人高，婚前就拥有过两套住房投资的经历，对你以后投资的眼界成长绝对有帮助。还有，你从小跟了我，我没有让你住过租的房子吧？回头想想看，我们俩到处搬家，是不是从小城市搬到大城市，从小公寓换成大房子，从学区房换成市中心房子？我们可是越换越好，这叫越努力越幸福。"

李华和女儿就像朋友一样有商有量调侃着，难怪女儿的同学同事们羡慕这对母女关系。女儿也受李华潜移默化的影响，对理财和投资房屋也很有自己的独到见解。

李华这边已经准备好，第二天直奔主题，去中介门店签订买卖合同后，当天收到了定金6万。一星期之内办理过户手续，交易当日收到房子全款！

一切如李华所愿，这笔房款来得及时，刚好赶上绿地中心售房第一期开盘剩下不多几套房子。李华还说服了二妹，也通过卖房买了一套绿地中心的房产，还解决了入武汉市户口问题，一举两得。从那以后，二妹买房都听李华建议，投资一处增值一处，获得了钱生钱快乐。二妹的本职工作是普通老师，但也通过这种投资方式达到了小康生活水平，不用亲人操心。李华就喜欢做这些能带动家人和朋友们一起致富，又提高生活品质的事情。

没有听李华建议买房的丽丽常常后悔，错过了买房挣钱的好时机。这些后悔的朋友还不止一个，还有后来进修湖北师范学院同学招娣；犹豫购买海景房的琦琦。当初承诺跟李华一起买房开店的琴琴，没有错失机会，不仅真的在地标建筑那里开了美容院，还为自己投资了几套市中心住房。琴琴也是李华众多

单身女友之一，一样爱房子，也享受房子带来的安全感。从那以后琴琴似乎更愿意跟随李华的眼光，说到哪里就会看到哪里投资到哪里！琴琴在房地产投资，已经轻车熟路的地步，出师了！

李华耳边常想起平时闲聊时妈妈说过的话，"其实我最喜欢的是那种带一个小院子的家，有自己的一片天一块地，没有别人住在我们家头上，有独立空间，感觉很自在。"

说者无心，听者有意，李华在心里又默默地开始新的人生规划。心中有孝，到哪都想着娘，有娘才是真正的家。李华心中又涌动出一个新的理财目标，有动力就有去探索和尝试的执行力。李华想着一定要让自己的母亲实现这个愿望。李华暗暗地笑了，心想继续这样努力下去，应该不是问题！

第四十八章　将父母接到省城

　　人们常说安居才能乐业，李华在省城已经实现了这个目标，拥有环境很好的居住单元，生意也做得顺风顺水。李华的小妹帮父母亲在省城买到新房子，而且听了李华的建议，买了同一个小区，方便李华照料老人。这房子的户型很不错，面积有 137 平方，在李华监督下完成了装修，并通风透气几个月。

　　将要离开已生活了几十年的家乡小城市，老人家心里还是有些依依不舍，毕竟那是四个女儿出生成长的地方。他们在那里度过了大半辈子岁月，他们的工作、青春、老同事、老邻居都在那里。

　　李华母亲经常鼓励女儿们"好儿志在四方，人往高处走，水往低处流"。所以李华母亲也说服自己的老伴尝试体验新的生活环境，生活也会有更多乐趣。这是女儿们的一番心意，安然接受就好。而且跟女儿住得近一些，孩子们才能放心打拼。

　　李华家中凡有大小事情需要择日，大家都听从李华母亲的意见，让老人家选定好日子。这次李华母亲经过推算，选择了 2009 年 9 月 16 日从老家小城搬迁到省城市中心的房子，让女儿们完成了孝敬父母的心愿。

　　迁往省城的那一天果然真是风调雨顺。搬家那天，当家具全部装上车后，天空就下起了毛毛雨。去往省城的路上，李华坐在大厢式货车副驾驶座位上，还担心着下雨，会把家具淋湿，心里着急。老妈选日子向来很准，怎么这次自己搬家却下雨呢？

　　父母坐在三妹私家车上，三妹问母亲："刚刚还阳光灿烂，怎么这一会儿就下起雨了？老妈您算的搬家日子不是没有雨吗？这雨要是一直下，怎么搬东西啊？"

　　李华母亲不慌不忙地说："三闺女，你别担心，到了省城雨一定会停，这叫风调雨顺！安心开车吧！"

　　李华母亲真说准了，快到省城一半的路程雨停了，太阳当空照，天气晴朗，根本没有下过雨的痕迹。

　　三妹高兴地说："我老妈真会算日子！这边省城真的没有下雨了，这真是个好日子，太神了！"

　　李华母亲不言语，在小车后座位上闭目养神，听着女儿们一搭一问拉家常。从李华母亲的神情看，这一切就是预料之中的事情，没有什么大惊小怪。

　　到了省城小区大门口，李华的货车先出发先到达。李华提前办好了物业小区通行证纸条，在门卫工作人员的指挥下倒车入位停下，然后开始向自家单元楼层搬家。看着一切按部就办进行着，李华刚刚在大货车上还担心下雨，这会儿已放心下来。

　　过了不久，李华的三妹也跟父母到达小区。打开房门后，李华听母亲的话先进屋，她提着火炉，手上还托着一盘苹果和柑橘。接着三妹进屋，她要提半桶水，还有米和扫帚。这都是按搬家的风俗习惯来办，先入户的物品是有讲究的。总而言之一切听从李华母亲的指示来做。这次搬家得让父母亲舒服和喜欢，毕竟今后这是父母亲的新家。父母亲心里踏实，这次他们和大女儿李华住在同一个小区，能互相有个照应。

　　有正规搬家公司负责，这次搬家很顺利。所有东西安装摆放到位后，李华事先将父母亲喜欢老古董旧家具量好尺寸保留，搬进新家。摆放在哪个房间，全由李华安排。虽是新旧混搭，却有着一派中式风格。李华母亲的书房，做了一整面墙的书柜，从下到上全部摆满了书。搬家师傅说："这一箱子一箱子的书真重，怎么这么多书？"李华母亲看着书柜对师傅说："师傅们辛苦了，这书可是黄金屋啊！小心摆放，谢谢师傅们了！"

　　父母看着新家很满意，李华也很高兴，直接走近父母身边手指里屋，"这是老妈的主卧房，这隔壁是老爸的次卧室。老爸出门斜对面就是洗手间，也是为了老爸方便，特意做的装修设计。现在带你们去社区附近转转，这里腾地方让师傅们搬东西。"

　　李华领着父母亲和家人乘电梯下楼，从小区外面绿化带环境中走过，那里有水池喷泉，五颜绿色的花朵。走在绿荫小道旁，见到椅子就让父母亲坐一会，闻一下树叶的清香。李华兴奋地介绍说："早晨出来这里走走，运动一下，享受清新空气。向东门走，有理发店、足疗店、干洗店；向后门走就是菜市场和中百超市和学校；向正门出去，就是银行、地铁、公交车站、早摊点、中餐馆、美容院。过了马路就是江边，晚上的江景可漂亮壮观。江堤坝上有跳舞的、散步的、遛狗的、谈情说爱的，很热闹。这就是现实生活中看到的江城，也是有名的江城武汉。"

李华边走边介绍，选择了附近最大的一家青灰瓦砖四合院农家乐餐馆吃饭。家人都坐下来之后，李华老爸发话了："这里真方便，什么都有。老伴啊，你满意了吧！"

李华母亲回复说："肯定满意，我也说过'好儿志在四方，人往上走，水朝下流'！孩子们都辛苦了，我们俩老知足了！"

三妹补充说："现在快点菜，大家都饿了。这里有很多老妈老爸爱吃的土菜！很地道好吃，保证大家还要再来！"

这是乔迁之喜的第一次团圆宴，家人欢聚一堂。李华二妹一直忙着看东西，小妹已从北京乘飞机赶回来。父母最高兴的时光，就是同孩子们团聚，人都到齐了的那份天伦之乐氛围。此时此刻母亲对大家说："孩子们快坐下，多吃点，从早忙到晚，总算图一个顺顺利利。放心吧，这里人丁很旺，我们为四代同堂欢聚一堂，碰一杯酒，老伴今天高兴吧！"

搬家的第二天，小妹带了好酒好烟和水果特产孝敬俩老。父母亲能迁移到省城新家定居下来，全靠小妹在经济上支持买下房子。这次乔迁之喜她也从百忙之中抽出两天时间赶回来，跟家人团聚。看完新居后，李华带上一家人到小区附近的足疗馆做足疗。小妹对父亲说："老爸老妈可以每周来一次足疗店，刷卡就行了，我刚给你们办了年卡。做足部按摩对身体好，促进血液循环！"

小妹为人细心体贴，在家也是父母亲的骄傲。姐姐们都以小妹为自豪，读书好，人品好，乖巧，善良，有主见，有自控力。小妹从小学习名列前茅，先是保送科大，后来到英国留学，学业完成回国定居北京。小妹一直从事金融行业，每年为父母亲在经济上资助最多。三个姐姐都很佩服小妹，外表看似柔弱娇小，却很有内涵，是成熟稳重的知性管理类型。小妹处事风格平和，从没见她说一句狠话，也没有大声讲大道理，但是如果跟别人聊天，每一句话都会说到对方心坎上去。父母亲最喜欢和小妹聊天，也最疼爱小妹。

父母做完后足疗，心疼小女儿花了太多钱，对小女儿说："你就别操心了，这里有你几个姐姐照顾，什么都有，挺好的。你大姐还帮你爸办一张刮胡须洗

头的会员卡，那美发店就在这附近。你二姐也带我找到了打五谷杂粮粉的摊店。我们生活中需要的都被满足了，你放心，你今晚就飞回北京安心工作吧。再别给我们俩老花钱了，钱够用了！"

三妹答话补充说："已经给老妈请了钟点工，每星期都做全房卫生打扫。该做的我们都安排好了，放心吧。"

李华对小妹点点头说："要是再不放心，你有空经常飞回来也行，我们大家可以多沾光聚聚。"

李华说完全家人都笑了，气氛真好，一家人和和美美的。李华的女儿小琳羡慕这老一辈亲情，让她感受到大家庭的温暖，全是实打实的相互支持！这温情浓浓的情景，给了李华女儿后辈竖立了尊老爱幼的好榜样。

李华的父母在这新居的房子里，一住就是几年，像其他老百姓一样，日复一日地过着平凡而又简单的生活。李华有时候回自己的小房子居住，有时候在父母亲的客房暂住——那客房就是给来照顾看望父母的亲人备用。谁来看望父母，谁就可以在此房间休息！

在同一个小区买房真是好主意，既能互相照顾，又不干扰彼此。在大家庭中，也不会有什么代沟问题。一到节假日，李华父母家里经常是四代同堂，一起团聚。餐厅里一桌人聚餐；茶几旁几个小辈聚餐；客厅、阳台、书房都可以坐下来与亲人谈笑风生，这样的情景让人羡慕。李华父母老一辈的同事和老友，经常从小城市来省城探望他们。有客人来临时，李华父母亲比过节还开心，热情地招待老同事和老家的亲戚朋友。那是父母的精神支柱，李华父亲最爱对老友说的一句话："有空常来坐坐！"

第四十九章　那一年发现父亲晚期肺癌

李华将父母亲接到省城在一起居住生活，老人家过得舒心如意，这样的日子过了好几年。

在 2016 年上半年体检中，李华父亲确诊为肺癌。经住院医治后，出院直接回到了老家疗养。为了父亲动过手术后生活方便，三女儿特意又给父亲买了一层楼的四房二卫二厅大房子，并请了护工 24 小时照顾陪护。李华母亲一直陪伴左右，望着一天天老去的父母，李华在跟时间赛跑，她希望把手头上的工作做好，多挣点钱，好给父亲多一些营养费用，也好支付长期的护工费用。可父亲还是在 2016 年 12 月 8 号那天晚上去世了。

父亲离开的那天，李华在省城和老家回来跑了两趟。李华多想父亲好好活着，她就可以安安心心地去工作，她不怕辛苦不怕累，就怕失去亲人阴阳相隔。现实没有因为李华的恐惧和不愿而改变，所有一切都按自然规律发展，李华的父亲还是被病痛夺走生命，离开人世。

父亲离世那天，李华还想着明天干完最后一件事，一定好好陪父晒太阳，散步，放松说说话……可是这一切都是李华的一厢情愿，父亲还是没有留给李华这点时间，父亲这突然一走，给李华留下了终生的心痛！

李华父亲生前将一些喜爱的物品集中放在一个抽屉里，这些东西都成了老人家的遗物。抽屉里装满了女儿们在各个时期送给他的礼物，有金戒指、手表、佛珠链、衣服、帽子、领带、手套、围巾等等。这些东西整齐地摆放在抽屉里，有的都还没有用过，父亲舍不得穿上它们。

看见这些父亲留下的件件物品，似乎在告诉女儿们，这些都是身外之物，哪样都无法带走。父亲走了，可是生前最爱不释手的东西，却留给女儿们——物归原主。这是父亲生前已经交代过李华的事，将每个女儿送的礼物退回给送礼者本人。

父亲很帅，年轻的时候经厂里最大的领导介绍认识了母亲，母亲也看中了又红又专的父亲。父亲出生在一个贫困的农村家庭，整个村里就培养了一个初中文化水平的农村小伙子。父亲是当年从村里第一个考进厂里的工人。父亲勤奋好学，在工厂生产线上对项目进行技术改造，也对机器改革创新做出了很多贡献。他逐渐成为厂里的骨干力量，被选派到北京大礼堂，参加过五一劳动节表彰大会，被厂里授予极高的荣誉：五好标兵、优秀共产党员、先进工作者等。光荣榜上经常有父亲戴着大红花的照片。

那时李华的母亲很年轻，是革命后代。书记夫人亲自做媒为俩人牵线，成为一生伴侣。结婚那年，李华母亲才刚满 19 岁，父亲 23 岁。李华母亲曾笑着对女儿们说起过，"那时你们父亲很穷，为了结婚时体面一点，将黑色的雨鞋当作皮鞋穿着与我结婚。那时的生活条件很朴素简洁，住在厂里分的一间平房，里面就一张桌子，一张木板床，一个煤油炉子，这就是我和你们爸爸所有的家具。"老人家年轻时的婚姻，没有任何物质作基础，却也在风风雨雨几十年岁月中恩爱如初，一直度过了金婚岁月！

李华看着墙上父亲 23 岁时的照片，那时父亲真的好帅，文静俊俏，嘴唇抿着微笑上扬的弧度，一双小小的单眼皮眼睛目光深邃，像是在看着李华。旁边挂着一张父亲自己亲自去照相馆拍的黑白照片，照片上显示着那年还是六十六岁。墙上还挂着两位老人跟李华四姐妹一起拍的全家福照片，那是父亲去世之前的最后一次全家合影，那年父亲 75 岁。2013 年 3 月小妹在北京为父母举办了金婚纪念，父亲与母亲的俩人合影，这张珍贵的照片挂在全家福旁边。

记得父亲曾经对女儿们说："这辈子我和你妈搬了七次家。前两次搬家你们都很小，那时候叫厂里职工宿舍平房。第三次搬到连排三层楼上面的第一间套房，老大在那里高中毕业，几个小女儿们都在那里中小学毕业。第四次搬到独门 5 楼左边 501 房，那是 87 平方面积，二房半室一厅一卫一厨的房子，你们三个大的女儿都工作了，就是小女儿在科大读书。后面搬的三次家是，是老大在市区以我和你妈名字买的大房子，上下复式楼 320 平方面积。没有想到后来小女儿又在省城买了我们老两口住的房子。六年后三女儿又在老家为我们老两口买了 200 平方面积的一楼大房子。生活上一直有老二来改善我们的伙食，变着花样地做一堆好吃的，包好素菜馅饺子放在冰箱里备用，有你们几个好女儿孝敬我们，这一生值啊！"

父亲说这些话的时候，已经是大手术后出院回到家乡。当他看到宽敞明亮的新房子，有感而发说了这些肺腑之言。

父亲晚年的卧室总是住在次卧，父亲为了让母亲休息好，总是把最好的主卧室留给母亲。像许多中国老一辈的婚姻一样，父亲一生一世就守护着的唯一的结发妻子，女儿们的母亲，两人磕磕碰碰地走过了一辈子。父亲从来没有在嘴上对母亲说过一句"我爱你"的话，从来也没有听过父亲的任何绯闻。虽然他们经常顶着几句嘴，为生计牢骚满腹——父亲的脾气不太好，可当遇上大事情都会互相忍让。就这样几十年平平淡淡地走过了金婚岁月，父亲度过了他的一生。

李华拿起她在父亲 70 岁那年送的生日礼物，那枚黄金戒指，回想起当年的一些细节。当时为了凑大黄金的重量克数，李华悄悄地告诉母亲说，"我想把我的所有黄金首饰，项链，耳环耳坠耳钉戒指都拿到黄金加工店铺，换成一个大戒指，送给爸爸的 70 岁生日礼物。经常听爸爸说他的戒指小，和老同事们打麻将总是显得小气。爸总说那个当官的何伯伯手上戴的是儿子送的大戒指。我知道爸爸就是爱面子，反正我也不爱戴这些老款式饰品，就给老爸换个大戒指吧，省得我爸总觉得养了女儿抵不过养儿子！"

母亲说："你爸就是这个心结，养了几个女儿，总想有个儿子多好。你是老大长女，给我们家挣个气，给你爸挣回面子。不过你把这些首饰都换了，你不需要？"

李华说："没有关系，旧的不去新的不来。既然你同意了，那我就拿去黄金首饰店换了，商场正好做活动。这个事不要对爸说，你知道就好，这回我要让老爸戴着大戒指去和他的老友们打麻将，显摆显摆！"

那时候李华还在创业初期，手上也没有多少现金流，有点资金就会零存整取用在投资房地产上面。在没有取得效益的时候，李华害怕家人为自己担心，总是瞒着父亲，默默地早起晚归做自己看准的事情，从来没有提过困难和资金欠缺的问题。

有一次投资市中心地标房时，李华看准了商机，可手上就差几万元定金。母亲知道后，悄悄把攒了多年的积蓄拿给李华："老大，这 10 万元拿去急用吧，别担心还！"

母亲的举动让李华鼻子一酸，眼泪都快要出来了。她半天说不出一句话，硬是把眼睛憋得红红的。李华赶紧走进卫生间，冲刷掉了脸上的泪水和鼻涕。李华半天不敢出门，因为看着镜子里的自己眼睛还是红红的，肿着像灯笼一样的眼泡。

李华暗自发誓，一定要让父母亲过上体面的好生活，一定要让父亲为她而骄傲！养女儿怎么啦？养女儿一定要比别人家养的儿子强！

想到这里，李华才平静下来，坚定不移地对自己说：我一定会让父亲戴上最显眼的戒指，一定让父亲住上市中心的大房子，一定不会让父亲失望后悔，一定要让父亲以我们几个好女儿为荣！

李华和妹妹们都做到了，都很争气，2008 年小妹在省城为父母亲买了一套地铁口的新房，从家乡迁移省城居住了六个年头，日子过得越来越好。父亲带上李华送的黄金戒指后，每次打牌回家，也会跟母亲聊一些外面的事情："老伴，你知道那些牌友们怎么说吗？哈哈，夸我们俩老有福气，比那个当官姓何的强。这几天姓何的都没有来打麻将了，牌友说他儿子犯了经济问题双规了。你看看，当官若不正直，就会出事。这有什么好？还是做百姓安稳！"

母亲平日里喜欢看书写日记，从年轻时候就养成了爱学习的好习惯。在家庭地位上，大事全部由母亲说了算。母亲声音不大但很有威严，母亲语气凝重地说道："老头子呀，你打你的小牌，别再笑话别人了。养儿防老，养女无福的歪理，那都是封建迷信社会的产物。现在不同了，时代进步了，该改变你的死脑筋了！少打牌少抽烟，没有事情去运动运动吧！学打太极多好呀！"

父亲说："是啊，现在三缺一，也打不成了！明天开始就去小区学打太极去。"

父亲听进了母亲的话，真的开始戒烟。从每天的两包到一包烟，后来又从一包烟减掉几根烟。慢慢全部戒掉烟的时候，是父亲住进了医院，医生严肃地说："必须一根烟也不能抽。"父亲这才彻底戒掉了三十几年的烟瘾。

说起吸烟这事，李华深感内疚。从事工作后，李华坚持送烟孝敬父亲，每月 4 条从没有间断过，逢年过节更是多送好烟给父亲以备待客之需。父亲抽了多少年的烟，李华就送了多少年的烟。后来李华感觉是她害了父亲得了肺癌。李华想，父亲是烟吸多了吗？

第五十章　父母的欣慰

　　李华父亲是在 2016 年上半年体检中发现了肺癌晚期。出院之后，就没有回过省城的住宅。考虑到父亲疗养期间要经常出行透气晒太阳，经常上下楼会很不方便。母亲和三妹考虑周到，说服了父亲回老家住新房。父亲出院的时候，李华已将父母的家具全部搬迁到了老家的新房子中。

　　父亲回来的路上感觉到精神格外兴奋，李华和家人一直瞒着父亲的真正病因，没有告诉父亲是肺癌。她们知道父亲一旦知道真相肯定会接受不了。李华也常常听到很多人说，癌症并不可怕，可怕的是人失去了精神支柱，心里的恐惧情绪对身体伤害极大。所以有些善意的谎言既是美德又是无奈，李华和家人都希望父亲在不知情的情况下，能保持平和开朗的心态，这样没有坏情绪压力，配合康复治疗，也许父亲会活得更长一些时间。

　　在医生办公室里，李华第一个知道父亲的病情，她清楚地听见医生说："你父亲就算做了手术，也许只有三个月的时间。之后他想吃什么，想去哪里旅行，都尽量满足他。如果调养得好，也许他会活得长久一些，可能撑到半年。"

　　李华问医生："不能控制吗？"

　　医生说："发现太晚了，肺癌细胞已经扩散到周围了。这次切肺部时候发现了更多的转移……"

　　二妹和三妹都在医院走廊上陪伴着母亲，等着李华出来。李华大脑一片空白，出来看到母亲和妹妹们，只有如实回答医生说的每一句话。她们在走廊里简单开了一个家庭会议，大家决定先瞒着父亲。不然以父亲的性格，如果知道实情，精神必然会垮掉。大家说好了不提此事病情，还要装着若无其事的样子。像往常一样，该怎么聊天就怎样聊天，别让父亲看出来，更别让父亲起疑心。

　　母亲在妹妹们的搀扶下走进病房，看着刚刚从手术后醒来的父亲。病床上父亲躺着，想吃力翻动着身体，但是动不了，可能是麻醉药的作用，父亲有些

无力。医生对父亲说："手术很成功，想要吃什么东西就跟女儿们说。您看您女儿们多好呀，都来看您了！"

隔壁病床上的老汉开始哭泣了起来，哭诉抱怨自己命苦，哭得很伤心。父亲后来才从护士那里听说，这老汉只比父亲大两岁，有三个儿子一个女儿，却没有一个儿子来看他，送他来住院的也是女儿。但是女儿很困难，是一个环卫工人，在经济上帮不了他，只能下班后，做点吃的送过来就得赶回家，因为家里还有两个孩子需要她照顾。

父亲在这间病房里，突然发现了自己的优越感。父亲知足地劝慰病友说，"老伙计别想太多，来多吃一点营养鱼汤，女儿给我做了很多。我们早点好起来，就是给儿女们减少负担！"

父亲安慰别人说起来轻松，到了自己头上还是有顾虑。没过几天，听说父亲的病友在做手术之后两天，就转到重症监护室抢救无效而去世。护士长让李华别对父亲说这个消息，因为病房里又添加了一个新病人。在病房里不能谈论病人的事情，这对病人会产生心理阴影。自从换了病人之后，父亲的语言少了，经常吵闹着要出院回家休养。

医生同意了，等伤口愈合拆了线再观察一周，如果没有问题就出院。那时父亲的面容憔悴得不成人形，脸色苍白，瘦成皮包骨，看着有点吓人。李华看到父亲这个样子，心里很难受，一股悲伤的情绪从心里涌出来。李华强忍着不让眼泪掉下来，赶紧换一个角度站着，不被父亲看到。她背对着父亲拿起床头上的碗到洗手间清洗，直到平静下来才敢再进病房。李华让父亲放心睡觉，她会看着药水瓶吊针打完，及时叫护士换药。

只有在睡着的时候，父亲才会舒服一些。杀死癌细胞的药物和止痛药都不能太打多，而且也不能让父亲在清醒的时候过多地胡思乱想。当伤口愈合拆线过后，医生让父亲出院，在家里好好疗养。医生知道没有什么药物能够救得了父亲，只是说延长生命只能靠自身的体质。

父亲在不知情的情况下，以为是身体恢复过来了，所以才安排出院。出院后父亲的精神状况也好了起来，自我感觉不错，但是李华和家人心里却特别难受。想着如果能用一种药物延长父亲的寿命，该多好啊。女儿们个个都争气，在各自的岗位上干得有模有样，能让父亲感到欣慰，而父亲却要在很短时间内离开他们。李华越想越难受，那些时间装得很辛苦，心里清楚知道父亲的生命已进入倒计时，却不能表现在脸上让他看出来。

出院那天，天气晴朗，上车的那一会儿，父亲仰起头向天空长长地望了一眼，感受到阳光下微风吹在脸上的舒适。父亲深深地呼吸了一下新鲜空气说："在医院里很长时间没有见到太阳了，今天真的很舒服，还是回家好！"

李华说："是的，老爸！医生就是说让您回家以后要多晒太阳。我们在家里也给你买了一台自动控制的轮椅车，家里请了那个你喜欢的护工，经常推您出去外面晒太阳。多喝汤多补钙吃健康的食物，这样能很快恢复体质。"

三妹也赶紧扶着父亲上车说："家里都安排好了，陈志（三妹夫）在家等您，做您喜欢吃的墨鱼汤。还有房子都搞好了，他跟他家的亲弟说了，每天可以捉活鱼给您吃。新农村承包了鱼塘，土鸡炖汤，您会很喜欢的。我们这次买房陈志特意选择了一楼，也不用上下楼了，就是为您出行方便。您不用操心了，只管吃。陈志的同事听说他把房子送给岳母岳父住，都夸他孝敬老人，品德好，说做陈志的父母太幸福了，对岳父岳母孝心故事，一传十，十传百。陈志很高兴公司所有人夸奖他孝敬老人的举动，越夸他做得越带劲！"

李华说："说句实在话，陈志这次做了一件大好事。能把岳母岳父当自己的亲生父母一样对待，真的没话说。这个女婿就是一个儿子，老爸本来很喜欢他，有什么事都跟陈志直接说。"

父亲听着大女儿和三女儿的对话，心里明白了，这是直接回到三女婿准备好的新家去。父亲看着旁边坐着的老伴，笑着说："老伴还是你说的对，养女儿好呀！我们这几个女儿都是好孩子，我们比养儿子的老董老吕强。住院期间老大天天陪着跑上跑下去照顾，几个女儿把工作安排好也轮流看护我，小女儿住得远，但是治疗的费用她出的最多。我这次真的想通了，还是生女儿好！"

老妈回应道："是啊，有儿子的老董夫妇一起攒钱给儿子买房子娶媳妇。你的好友老吕夫妇攒了一辈子的钱，给两个儿子买房子，还因为大小面积不一样闹矛盾。现在他们俩还分居帮两个儿子带孙子，没有自己的晚年生活。"

父亲满足地点点头："他们到老了还在给儿子们当牛做马打工，哪像我们早早享福了，我抽了几十年老大送的好烟，女儿们也经常送好酒好水果孝敬，好衣服都穿不完，我知足了！"

老妈赶紧接着说："老伴啊，这次回家你就好好养好身体，别再耽误影响孩子们的工作了。让老大抓紧时间把省城市中心的房子卖掉，现在行情好，卖了把钱可以还给小女儿，她现在两个孩子在国外读书，也需要用钱。"

李华马上接话说道："你们俩老别再操心了，我已经挂在房屋中介公司了。放心吧，老爸好好养身体，老妈陪着吃好点，让我们都省心。所有的事情办好后，我也会告诉你们。你们安心生活，俗话说得好，家里有老是我们的宝！"

三妹说："就听大姐的，你们就别操心了。吃好喝好，少让我们担心比什么都好。只有你们老两口健康快乐，我们的事业才会越来越顺利，也能多挣钱！"

李华和妹妹们把父亲从医院接回老家新家后，安排好一切，请了一个 24 小时全程陪伴的男护工。这是李华从医院中介联系上的男护工，每月包吃包住付 4000 元护工费。这笔钱都由四姐妹分担，放在老妈保管的共同账户上，及时按月付出。

父亲出院一连几个月里，李华和妹妹们又赶紧抓紧时间，都各自忙着自己的小家庭生活和工作，日子还是要继续。父亲生了这场病住院后，李华意识到钱的重要性。如果当时手上没有储存的周转资金，也不能及时第一时间帮父亲交上住院费用 10 万元，后来小妹也拿出 10 万元。虽然父亲已经出院，但后期的营养费和护工费，同样需要花钱。

李华想到医生说过的话，"您父亲只有几个月日子了！"她也意识到这句话有另一重意思：要做好后事的准备。

这个念头让李华充满了恐惧，李华惊慌得想逃避父亲这个现实状况，而唯一逃避现实的理由是不停地工作，创造更多挣钱的机会。李华将父亲曾经住过的房子全部打扫清理干净，将父亲所用过的东西，全部安排车子运回新家的储藏室，包括照片也全部包装起来，运送到老家。

李华没有请人做这些卫生工作，她自己一个人抽空就来整理。当房子腾空打扫干净后，立刻被中介推荐的买主看中，只看了三波人，就敲定预售退房的时间。李华全权代理签了买卖合同！也收了定金和首付款。这是在李华买卖房子出售得最舍不得最有感情的一套房子，这里记录着李华和父母相聚愉快的时光。

第五十一章　突发状况

小妹在北京居住，这套房子全权委托了李华办理所有过户手续。时间就定在 2016 年 12 月的 9 号，马上就要到预约过户的时间了。

12 月 8 日下午，李华和装修公司经理赵总在建材市场已忙到下午 3 点多钟。两人随便吃了一碗热干面，就直奔汉西大建材市场，准备购买一些基础装修材料。

在半路上，李华包里的手机不停响起。开车的赵总向坐在副驾驶的李华看了一眼，示意李华有电话打进来。李华有些累了，正迷迷糊糊地打盹，被吵醒后拿出了手机按了接听键。电话里传来二妹和三妹焦急的声音："大姐，你今天赶快回来吧。老爸从昨天开始就没吃什么东西了，只喝点粥。老妈让我们打电话跟你说，如果不忙就赶紧回家看看老爸。叔父从老家赶来了，你也今天回来吧！"

李华两眼立刻睁大："什么情况，叫我现在回去吗？我正忙着呢，不能过几天吗？"

李华有点焦虑急躁，对着手机嘀咕道："我还没忙完呢，正准备把这手头上的急事安排好。明天就要过户房子了，手续必需要我本人办理。我准备把这大事办完了，再回去好好陪老爸一段时间，就等一天不行吗？"

李华说完就挂断了手机，整个人闷闷不乐。开车的赵总听到电话里说话内容，忙关心地问，"李姐，家里有事，你还是回家看看吧。这边装修的事情你放心，我会按照你交代意思去选装修标配的好材料。"

听到赵总的话，李华稍微在愁思中解脱一点，就在这个时候，手机又响了。李华赶紧接听，原来是小妹打来的电话："大姐呀，今天你别忙其他的事情了。一定得赶回去看看老爸，过户的时间不是明天吗？你今天赶紧坐高铁回去一趟，爸有什么情况也及时告诉我！"

这边的消息都通知远在北京的小妹了，小妹也催着李华赶紧回去。接到这样催命一样的电话，李华很无奈，恨不得要分身出来同时应对这两件重要的事。

看望父亲很重要，第二天的房产买卖过户也很重要。买方早在两个月前就签了购买合同，李华已经收了定金。中介已在一个月前排队，才预约了 12 月 9 日的过户的时间。明天三方约好在市政大厅办理过户，如果违反合同，李华这边要双倍赔偿定金和首付款 100 万。

这两件事都很重要，都到了重要的关头，不管哪件出了什么差错，对李华都会造成沉痛的打击，因此李华才这么无奈焦虑。表面上李华看起来很不耐烦，也很生气，但又不知道生谁的气。她还是赶紧拿起手机搜索购买回老家的高铁车票，查看了几趟车都显示今天已没有票了。

李华有些崩溃了，心中一阵绞痛，无助到极点。赵总看着焦急的李华说："李姐，我开车送你回去吧。装修选材料的事，今天可以放一放。我马上送你回去，你看看会放心些。如果你父亲没有什么情况，我们就及时开车回来。这样你心里踏实一些。"

李华感激地对赵总说："真的谢谢你，那你辛苦了，来去费用我给！"

赵总跟李华合作有十几年了，李华亲朋好友所有房子的装修都是交给赵总来办。赵总人品好，报价格理，两人合作一直很愉快，他们已经合作装修了 13 套房子。赵总做事让人踏实放心，赵总的为人值得信任，也因此李华愿意将所有工作交给他去办。多年合作下来，李华已经把赵总当兄弟一样真诚对待，从不掩饰自己喜怒哀乐，赵总也知道李华一些家庭情况。

赵总开始调头，打开车上 GPS 上导航，边操作边说："别分得那么清，李姐照顾我公司这么多年，我去看看你父亲也是应该的。你父亲生病住院及搬到老家后，我一次也没有见过了。正好今天我遇上了这个事，别跟我客气！"

一路上赵总默默开车，偶尔向李华确定一下方向对不对。李华思绪万千，想了很多很多见到父亲的场面，一幕幕地瞎想瞎琢磨，有种不好的预感……

赵总以最快的速度把李华送到老家，全程 100 多公里，1 小时 20 分钟就回到了三妹为父母准备的新家。李华刚进屋就被母亲二妹三妹团团围住，打了一下招呼就一起走进父亲卧室。李华进门就看见父亲侧身面向墙壁躺着，床前有叔父和护工两个人守着。

见到李华进来，叔父马上对着李华父亲喊："哥，老大华子回来看你了！"叔父叫着李华小名，把父亲唤醒。李华示意叔父别这么大声叫醒父亲，就让他睡觉，等他自然醒就好。

　　叔父说："你爸没有睡着，他在等你们回来看他，他心里明白得很！"

　　果然，父亲慢慢地动起手脚，似乎要从床上撑起来看看李华。好一会也没有翻过身，费了好大劲才伸出一只干枯苍老皮包骨的手，想握住大女儿的手。李华看到几个月没有见到的父亲，已经瘦得不成人形了。以前那么高大的身躯，现在成了皮包骨，身躯躬着，瘦成了虚弱的一团。好像被子盖上去都看不出下面有人躺着的感觉。

　　李华想去抚摸父亲的双手，但又害怕地收了回来——那完全不是记忆中父亲的手。李华眼睛里已经涌出满满的泪水，喉咙堵住了，嗓子发不出声音，鼻子酸酸的。李华只喊出老爸两个字，剩下的话又被哽住了。李华用手轻轻拍拍父亲的肩膀，停顿1分钟，稳定一下情绪后，贴在父亲耳边忍住抽泣轻声说："老爸我回来了，你安心睡吧。"

　　此时李华已掩饰不住自己的难过，不想让父亲和叔父看到她脆弱伤心样子，赶紧低头跑出父亲的房间，到卫生间关上门默默流着眼泪。泪水擦了又擦，就是止不住。李华沉重地走近镜子前，打开水龙头，赶紧用冷水不停地向脸上浇着。让那冰凉的水洗掉脸上不听使唤的泪水。

　　李华想让自己尽快镇静下来，好面对外面等候她说话的家人。李华是老大，是家里长女和顶梁柱，从小父母就把她当男孩子养。在父母亲眼里，她就是最要强的孩子，也是最敢担当，是妹妹们主心骨。李华从卫生间走出，看见母亲和两个妹妹坐在大厅中，叔父和赵总也在一旁坐着。

　　李华艰难地说："看老爸这样子，只要让他吃进东西，应该可以好转吧？要不我们把他送去医院吧？"

　　叔父摇摇头说："送医院也没有用，医生早就说过了，只有三个月。你们照顾得很好，已经延长到了半年，多活了三个月。没有多少时间了，如果吃进粥，还可以维持一周；如果吃不进东西，那就这几天的时间，我们得做好后事准备。"叔父说的是实话，接下来也交代了一些重要的准备事项。对李华及妹妹们交代了一些要做事情，一件一件落实到了每一个人。

　　除了远在北京的小妹还没有回来，基本上父亲最亲的人都见上一面了，相信他也不会有遗憾了。李华看着坐在一旁的赵总，忽然想起另一件重要的事情，连忙对家人说："老妈，叔父，还有二妹、三妹，你们大家都在，今天我等会就跟小赵总车子返回省城。我明天真的要办理房子过户手续，约定时间是上午

10 点，签字过户才能收到房子尾款 230 万。如果违约，我要倒赔定金和首付款双倍。如果更改通知其他人，会很麻烦的。我办完这件事，就迅速赶回来。"

家人理解李华的难处，母亲只得说："你去吧，办完事赶紧回。你爸理解孩子们，我带你去跟你老爸打个招呼吧。"

李华又随母亲来到父亲床前，喊了一声："老爸你要吃东西，我明天办完事就回来陪你一段时间。"

母亲接着说："老伴你安心休息吧，我们都在。老大这么忙也回来看你了，她现在要回去忙明天的事，忙完了就回来陪你。别拖孩子们的后腿呀，孩子们也难！"

父亲似乎听懂了母亲的话，轻轻挥了一下手，又侧脸睡了过去。李华将父亲的被子被角向上扯了扯，给父亲盖严实了一点。沉默看了一会儿，什么话也说不出来。这种情况说什么话都显得多余，此时此刻还什么比父亲重要呢？可是今天又必须走，明天的事也很重要。

李华在心里跟父亲说："老爸，请你给我明天一天时间。我忙完了一定会回来好好陪你，跟你一起出去晒太阳，到你老友们叙旧，有女儿孝顺。也可以听你啰唆唠嗑，我保证不跟你争论了，全听你说年轻时候事情……"

李华为了赶时间，跟家人打了招呼就回去了。赵总也和李华家人告别打过招呼说："放心吧，我会把李姐安全送到家！"

李华头也没有回，赶紧向门口车上走去。三妹赶上车子旁，递上一袋橘子和两个苹果，几瓶水，叮嘱道："赵总和大姐在路上吃，开车慢点，安全第一！"

二妹说："有事我们会给你打电话，你就安心办你明天的事情吧，这里有我们在！"

赵总替李华与家人点头告别，此时的李华不敢多看家人一眼，低着头小声对赵总说："开车走吧！"

车子启动了，李华的泪水又不争气地像涌泉一样宣泄出来，完全止不住。李华不知道为什么哭，为什么这么伤心，为什么做人这么难！她是父母的好女儿，女儿的好妈妈，妹妹们的好大姐，同事和朋友们佩服的女强人，可这一切做到了又能怎么样？能留住父亲多活几天都是一种奢望。李华的成功足以让父亲骄傲自豪，但是父亲却没有因为李华的努力和成功而长命百岁。

第五十二章　最后的陪伴

赵总把李华送到小区楼下马路边，车子停了下来："李姐，已经到家了！"

李华从迷糊中睁开眼睛："不知道什么时候睡着了，赵总到我家吃饭再走吧，这个点吃晚饭都过了！"

赵总说："李姐不客气，你早点回家休息吧。明天你还有那件大事要办呢！"

李华想了想对赵总说："好吧，今天太谢谢你了，改天忙完了，我好好请你做足疗保健！小别墅装修的事情，就由你选择一个好日子开工吧。"

赵总回答说："放心吧，你安心办你的事，有什么事都会给你办好！我走了！"

望着赵总开车离去的方向，直到看不见车子了，李华才快步地向女儿家走去。明天有很多东西要准备好，过户用的房产资料，委托书，自己的身份证，有关买卖合同全部要整理放在一起，今晚也很忙。想到这里，电梯已经到了27楼，按了门铃，女儿小琳开门说："还没有吃晚饭吧？锅里有鸡汤，喝点吧！今天外公怎么样？"

李华说："好像时间不多了，应该撑不过几天。我真的很担心你外公，但愿他能够多活一些日子！我明天就要帮你小姨的房子办理过户手续，我今晚上整理好资料。"

小琳端着一碗鸡汤放在桌子上："妈，先喝碗鸡汤再去整理吧，快趁热喝！"

人是铁饭是钢，李华一天没有吃过正餐饭菜了。看到女儿懂事体贴的样子，李华心里暖暖的，埋头吃了起来。喝完汤后，就直接进书房整理资料。

快到九点的时候，李华手机突然响起来。李华愣了半天，不敢接电话。女儿忙拿起床头柜上正在充电的手机，递给李华。电话是李华母亲打来的，"老大，你爸半小时之前刚刚走了，告诉你一声，回来吧！"

李华父亲真的走了，一天也没有撑住。李华就害怕这个电话，结果还是躲不过。李华自言自语道："这个老爸真是的，非要跟我抢时间，非要在这个时候走，跟我争跟我抢！"小琳打断李华："妈，你别这样说，赶紧回去吧。我打电话让熊阿姨来带小宝，我开车送你回老家去！"

李华此时有点情绪化，像小孩子跟父亲生前争论一样，继续说着："这老爸就是不讲理，生前倔强老爱跟我争，走了还要跟我抢时间。我真的很生气，这太折磨人了！好好的日子不过，非要赶着上天堂！"

小琳默默安排好一切，等着熊阿姨来后就出发。李华像木头人一样，呆呆地看着墙上的时钟，秒针一摆一摆地继续向前走着。时间不等任何人，对谁都一样，它不会因你想在人世间多待一会，而停止转动。李华无法也不愿接受这个事实，父亲已经离开了人世，不相信也得面对现实。

李华说："我明天的事情怎么办？如果今晚回去，明天我也要一早赶回来办事！"

女儿小琳说："如果你今晚不回去，你一晚上也睡不好。还不如我开车送你一起回去听听安排，先处理好家里的事，明早再赶紧回来办事。"李华轻轻叹了一口气，也认可了女儿的方案。

熊阿姨是小琳一直请在家里做清洁的阿姨，跟女儿已经相处了 5 年，俩人已经超过了雇佣关系，成了亲人。家里发生了这么大的事情，熊阿姨二话没有说，赶上九点之前的公交车立刻到了小琳家里。一进门就说："你们快点去吧，我这几天就在这里照顾小宝，你们安心去吧！"

小琳说："谢谢熊阿姨，我们可能要在老家那边待上三天。"

李华说："我可能明天早上坐高铁回省城，办完事再乘坐高铁接着赶回老家，料理我老爸的丧事。家里我们小宝拜托你了！谢谢熊姐！"

小琳开着车，不时通过后望镜看着后排座椅上的李华。小琳安慰说："妈，外公走了算是解脱了。癌症痛起来很折磨人，我同学的妈妈也是肺癌，痛起来时都受不了，不能吃，不能喝。其实外公走了也是福气，没有受那么多痛苦，不然多煎熬啊。"

李华没有接话，一直在后坐上流着眼泪。她好像第一次这样为父亲感到愧疚，明明知道父亲的日子不多了，却没有陪伴在身边；还在父亲离开的时候，责备父亲跟自己有意过不去。无论如何，在心里就是接受不了父亲在这个时间去了天堂。几个小时之前父亲还在，可是为了办事还是狠心丢下了父亲往回赶。

没有想到会这么快，父亲连一天时间也不留给李华。这就是李华的父亲，走了还让李华难受！不让李华省心。

小琳将车子停在老家的后门口，前门车子都停满了。进入大门的那一刻，李华看见父亲已经躺在客厅的中央的一块木板上，遗照和灵堂就设在客厅里。进门的时候，叔父就叫了一声："哥，华子又回来看你了，请你闭上眼睛吧，孩子们都在回来送你的路上！"说完带着李华和小琳向灵堂磕三个头。

说来也怪，李华看到父亲就像睡着了一样，脸上也是抿着嘴唇微笑的样子，像极了遗照的神情，安详熟睡着的感觉。李华情绪低落地问母亲："我走后，老爸是不是很生气，一定怪我了！"

母亲马上走过来说："没有怪你，你爸不是不讲理的人。老大，你是长女，今天晚上你就在这里守候着你爸的灵堂，负责写追悼会的悼念词。"

李华问："由我来写合适吗?"

三妹夫走过来说："你写最合适不过了。这是笔和纸，今晚写好。出葬那天，由你念出来，最后烧掉，就完成了对老爸的悼念仪式。"

李华没有说什么，安静而小心翼翼地坐在灵堂边桌前，看着父亲的遗像，想起了小时候和父亲一起生活的点点滴滴。从七岁记事开始写起，写出了父亲的四大人生转折点。父亲为了这个家庭的付出，全部历历在目，就像放电影一样，一幕幕浮现在李华的脑海里。李华低头默默地迅速开始写了出来，一张张纸稿按顺序排列，不知不觉写出了十一张信纸，三个小时一气呵成！

写文过程中，李华一直埋着头，有时泪水瞬间模糊了双眼，擦掉后又继续写。李华写的是内心深处对父亲思念，感受着最柔软细腻的温暖。她写出了生活中父亲对女儿们成长的关心。在贫穷的六十年代初，每年过年姐妹们都跟父母亲一起准备大年三十年货。那时候是父亲洗、切、腌制、油炸翻身面果，给女儿们当零食。不管多困难，父母亲也会为女儿们买来新衣服摆放在床头。李华想起父亲工作出差，忘不了为李华买了一件橘红色的毛线针织衫，那件衣服温暖了她整个冬季，也让少女时期的李华，度过了几个青春漂亮的秋冬——那是李华穿过的最美的衣裳。

那个年代已经远去，却无法淡化女儿对父母亲爱的记忆。父母对女儿们朴实无私奉献的付出，女儿们都在长大成人的过程中吸取父母亲善良的品格。在父母年迈的岁月中，大爱无疆已显现出，并回报在父母亲的身上。但是李华却感觉到还不够，她总是感觉当父母老去需要她的照顾陪伴，她却还是各种原因，没能守候在父母的身边，这让李华深深感到愧对父亲！

李华的父母亲从来不担心没有新衣穿，女儿们为父母提供最好的居住环境，让他们吃到最可口的美食。细心耐劳的二女儿在每年的团年饭中都担任大厨，为父母和家人亲手做出丰盛的饭菜。这些美味的菜式曾出自父母之手，成了女儿们最爱的纯粹朴实的味道。这些美味由女儿们传承下来，这也是亲情和大爱的回报。这种尊老爱幼的家风美德，潜移默化地影响着女儿们的成长，向善，向前，向着美好的未来，一天天呈现恩情回馈，延续温馨亲情。

李华也回想起父亲在教育上的付出，为了帮女儿们获得更好的学习机会，父亲多次亲力亲为求人帮忙，将孩子们转入重点学校学习。在工作上，父亲也支持女儿的决定和选择。李华记得有一次工作上受到了很大的委屈，也为某个决定犹豫不决，父亲在紧要关头给了李华最坚强的支持。父亲对李华说了一席话："我相信你，没有过不去的坎，大胆地向着你认为正确的方向去走。无论前方遇到什么情况，我都会坚决支持你。"这些朴实无华的话语足以让李华解压释怀。想想几十年来，女儿们成长走过的每一步都有父亲陪伴，父爱如山，每个孩子们成长过程中都留有父亲的鼓励和默默付出的痕迹。

李华起身走到父亲灵堂前深深地鞠躬，将写完的追悼词交给母亲。没有想到李华母亲看完后直接泪崩，不停地点头，看着写好的初稿悼念词对着父亲遗体说："老伴啊，你在九泉之下会感到欣慰，老大写得好啊。大女儿把你一生中对家庭的责任担当，对她们的爱护，都记在心里去了。你瞧瞧孩子们多懂事，都记得你的养育之恩，你放心去吧！"

李华在旁边扶着母亲说："这样写行吗？我没有按那悼念词格式写，我是按着心里想起小时候点点滴滴，老爸对我们的很多爱护情景去写的，想到哪就写到哪，这样行吗？"

母亲将信纸放在父亲灵堂桌前，对着李华说："老大这样写就很好，有真情实感，一个字都不用改。"

母亲转身又走近父亲灵堂前说："老伴，你没有白养我们的好女儿。小女儿今天也在赶回来看你的路上，你放心吧。"

追悼词写了父亲与女儿之间的真挚情感，这篇文章被母亲认可，李华也松了一口气。她也没有想到，突然之间想起父亲那么多闪光点。这篇悼词内容写得很流畅，李华将父亲身上平凡的故事写得生动感人，也写出了父亲对女儿们守护了一生的情感，将内心对父亲的爱淋漓尽致地表达出来。李华后悔没有在父亲生前告诉他，女儿们有多爱他，李华后悔她没有亲口对父亲说出一句"爸爸，我爱你！"

希望天堂的父亲能够听见李华的心声："老爸你安息吧，我们爱你！"

第五十三章　人生的意义

考虑到早上还要处理房屋过户的问题，清晨时分李华必须出门回省城了，她要赶上最早的那趟高铁班次。李华小声跟着母亲交代后，又跟二妹说："我必须早点回省城去，这里白天家里的客人安排，有你和三妹商量着办。房屋过户的事情也很重要，我该去办这件事了，我想老爸会理解我。"

二妹点头，向李华挥挥手："大姐你快去吧，我明白，老爸也懂你。你是在为小妹办事，你是为家人过得更好才操这个心，知道你有责任！"

得到亲人的理解，李华不想麻烦家人，招了网约司机后立刻向高铁站奔驰。

坐在高铁里的李华，这时才长长地舒了一口气，看着车窗外一晃而过的风景，不知不觉沉沉地睡着了。李华太疲惫了，从昨天到今天就像跟时间打仗，一直没有休息过，她真想像孙悟空那样有分身术。李华认识到在这个时刻她不能倒，必须办好这件事。这不光是挣钱的问题，还是信誉的问题。做生意讲诚信的品格，多年来已经成为李华的做人基本准则，也因为这样的人格魅力，才使李华做什么行业都有很大的收获。几十年来李华尝试过各个行业，在每个领域中从小白到有所成就，都来源于李华做人办事认真，替他人着想。在商业运作中，不光要衡量利益，还要看人品，有鼓舞人心的正能量才能凝聚力量，才能做大做强。

李华提前到了省市政大厅等候，三方按协议程序顺利地办完了所有法律手续。当李华看到手机显示交易完成，收到全房尾款230万时，心里的那块石头终于落地了。她深深地呼吸着空气，拿起手机小给北京的小妹发送微信，"房屋交易顺利完成，尾款马上转给你指定的银行账户上，请及时查收回复信息。我现在准备带买方和中介在房子里交接钥匙和物业费水电费。今天全部将此房移交完成后，立马乘高铁赶回家。小妹放心，保持信息畅通。"

小妹此时已从北京乘飞机赶到湖北老家，正在母亲身边看到了李华发的信息，向李华回复道："大姐，我已收到房款，也赶到家了，你放心吧。慢慢来注意安全，在外记得吃点东西再办事。今天晚饭之前回来就好，我们都在家等你！"

一切事情都办妥了，李华真的好佩服自己，原来自己这么能干，两件看似需要分身术才能办成的事情，李华先后顺利处理完毕。李华走出住宅大楼，看着这个曾经让她陪伴父母亲住过的小区，既感到亲切又有些依依不舍。她看着小区里遍地青枝绿叶，又看向着蓝色的天空，那天阳光正在头顶温柔照耀着她。一股柔柔的微风加带着一丝丝的细雨，开始绵绵地洒落在李华的身上。李华感觉到这是父亲给她的及时雨，一种温暖的拥抱，她明白一定是父亲在天上看着她，李华就这样想的，不然怎么解释天空的雨又突然间停了呢？

李华终于放松了下来，她感谢亲人的理解，也感觉到有一种暖暖的感觉，一定是父亲欣慰地对她说："快回去吧，你办事我放心，我的好女儿就是能干！"

李华想，父亲如果还活着，一定又会在老友们面前夸奖她，显摆炫耀一番吧。想到这里，李华赶紧急匆匆地乘地铁赶去高铁站，直奔老家，跟家人汇集再讲办事经过。她知道家人肯定关心这件事的过程和相关细节，她会给家人满意的答复。

第三天是父亲出馆仪式荣归故里追悼会，在父亲的老家稻谷场地举行。那天父亲真的接天缘，晴空万里。微风中传来李华为父亲，亲口念出自己所写的悼念词，稻谷场上空飘着缅怀不舍的情感，这悼念词如此温情感人，让所有在场悼念哀悼的亲朋好友都落泪了。李华对父亲真挚的情感一定也触动了父亲的灵魂，相信他能感受到亲人悲伤不舍，也会为女儿们的表现而感到自豪。

那天是父亲最荣耀显摆的一天。李华一直以为父亲最爱面子，有时候总认为父亲活得太累了，为虚荣心而活。父亲生前总是将女儿们孝敬他的礼物视为至宝，父亲已在天堂，可昔日女儿们孝敬他的礼物却静静地摆放在抽屉中。

李华突然号哭，她瞬间悔恨自己明白得太迟，父亲生前喜欢在人前炫耀，不是因为父亲虚荣心强，那是父亲在炫耀他女儿们的孝心，显摆作为父亲享受的幸福。他认可女儿的孝心，也希望别人认可女儿们的美好品质，这同样是对女儿一种爱的宣示。李华回想起那一幕幕父亲得意扬扬而谈笑风生的情景，领悟到父亲的用心良苦。父爱大于山，李华有点自责，原来一直以来都误会父亲了。

那天在场来参加追悼的亲朋好友们，被李华诚挚啼泣宣读的悼词而感染。大家回想起父亲生前为工作、家庭及女儿们所做的每一件事，每一次付出。他对女儿们深沉的爱意将永远留在亲人的心里。他们也明白，父亲的炫耀才是女儿们最想看到的幸福。那是因为女儿们的成长一路都有父亲的爱在陪伴。

父亲的离世让李华对人生有了新的认识，特别是在物质财富与精神财富方面有了很大的心灵冲击。李华看到在生死关头，物质财富显得那么苍白无力。父亲生前那么多贴身随带的宝贝黄金饰品，当人离开世界的那一刻，这些东西都不能带走，留下的也只是在世的亲人珍藏的回忆。随着时间的流逝，恐怕连记忆都会随着岁月淡去。

人生中挣再多钱却舍不得花钱，那样攒钱有意义吗？李华开始怀疑自己是否还需要那么辛苦去打拼。人生不仅仅是工作挣钱，还有很多事情可以去做，还有很多生活的方式会更有意义，这些事情与金钱无关。

李华开始重新调节自己的工作、生活、学习、娱乐、休息时间，她开始将节奏放慢。记得有位哲学家说过"生活必须平衡，不然会乱了方寸，会使你焦头烂额，生活一团糟。"

父亲的去世让李华悟出了一个道理，人活着还要有价值感，应该要创造出精神财富。因为精神财富是人本身可以分享，感悟，与心灵交融在一起的体会。那种感受，无人可替代。给一个穷人一笔钱，在短期内可以改善他的生活；如果在他心里植入积极的人生信念，也许能改变他一生的命运。这些年来李华一直以积极的心态影响着身边的人，这些就是她自己创造出来的精神财富。只不过，一个人接触的人有限，影响力也有限，能不能有更好的方式将自己的精神财富分享给更多人呢？很快，李华找到了答案：通过写作来实现这个目标。那就是余生要做的事情，那种从内心深处对文学创作的冲动欲望又回来了，现在不为，何时才能为之？李华想这是父亲告诉她，现在做还为时不晚，活好当下。

第五十四章　奖励投资提升自己

李华每次在投资房产受益后，都会奖励投资自己。这种良性循环的好习惯一直保持着，能激励李华再接再厉地去努力工作，寻找新的投资商机项目。

以前李华对自己的奖励主要集中在物质方面，或者是身体保养方面的投资。自从经历了三年艰辛的门窗公司创业，又经历了父亲的离世，李华对物质财富已不像过去那么看重。在她这个阶段，她可以放缓对物质财富的追求，而用更多精力转向精神财富的追求。

李华年少时热爱写作，后来忙于生活，忙于生计，忙于创业，只能把写作梦记在内心里。如今李华不需要再为金钱辛苦工作，实现了基本的财务自由和时间自由。近年来李华对自己的投资主要是提升自己的思想和精神面貌。

2017年春节刚过，李华就报名参加了本市老年大学，报了两个班，一个是歌咏班，一个是T台模特儿班。她还加大了写作上的投入，报名参加了有书写作训练营班，报名简书写作。后来还陆续报了齐老师散文人物传记写作班，宁老师长篇小说学习班，王老师纪实文写作班。并参加了2019年知音故事大赛，获得优胜奖。在学习写作中得到认可，更激起了李华对写作和学习的浓厚兴趣。

接下来的几年，李华不断深入故事和小说领域的写作学习。先是参加了陈老师的短篇小说写作班学习，后来又参加一鸣老师的长篇小说写作课程。在学习提升自己的同时，李华已经创作完成了两部长篇小说，这两部作品的初稿已经在报纸上发表出来。李华将这些报纸整理好，排列铺满在地面，拍照发到母亲的微信。母亲一直支持李华写作，也乐意分享女儿在写作上获得的成绩。

在写作的这些年来，李华笔耕不辍，并获得了一系列的成绩：李华加入了武汉市作协；获得2019年《知音》故事参加比赛获优胜奖，含税奖金1000元；作品发表在淮南作家文化媒体、有书、简书、美篇、17k小说网络媒体、每天读点故事媒体、小小说、婚姻故事、城市故事等刊物和网络平台，其中包括长篇小说两部，精品短篇几十篇。也在省级报纸刊物发表了一系列文章。

李华想象着母亲认真出神看着自己作品的样子，觉得很幸福。果然不出所料，母亲谈起李华的写作感到非常自豪，不停地说："这多有意义呀，给孩子们留下房子都比不上留下一本书更重要。钱花光了，就什么也没有了，人走了房子也带不走。而留下了作品，子孙后代都能阅读，精神财富可以永远传承，写作多有意义啊！"

有时母亲看完了李华的作品也会发表一些阅读感想，"老大，我正在看你写的那篇《我以父母亲名字买的第一套房产》，这故事情节让我哭了，孩子啊！写得真好……"

李华母亲说的这些话，是用微信语音一段一段发到李华的微信上。听到语音中母亲的哽咽，李华感受到母亲欣慰和骄傲。父母都有望子成龙的心愿，母亲在情感上生活上精神上都很依赖李华。李华出生在 60 年代，那时还残留着重男轻女的现象，养女不如男的封建思想还比较严重。母亲总希望李华争气，要比男孩子强。她从小培养李华一定要好好学习，好好做人，对李华的要求严格得多。而这些年来，李华一直没有让母亲失望。

妹妹发微信告诉李华："老妈可喜欢你的文章了，有时她会在一些段落下面用钢笔划上一条条波浪线，标记出这些精彩的部分反复看。"

有时妹妹也假装吃醋对李华说："你一直是老妈的骄傲，我们对她再好，可老妈还是最喜欢你！"

母亲常常对妹妹谈起李华小时候的事，李华七岁就会生火炉子做饭，冬天还用小手做煤炭球，周末洗油污的工作服，还要照顾妹妹们。说到动情时，母亲还流了很多眼泪："那个年代你们的大姐吃了很多苦。小学班主任陈老师常夸你大姐懂事，学习又认真，放学就赶回家帮大人做家务事。你大姐总是把好吃的都让你们。第一次领到 22 元工资的时候，交给家庭 10 元，留下的生活费 6 元，吃了一个月的食堂素菜。后来她每周回家都给你们带回油炸麻花条之类的零食，甜的咸的各一半，十条十条买。她还带回腌制好的小鳊鱼，每次都不会空手回家。这些东西都给了你们吃，你大姐自己舍不得吃，八十年代还是很困难的时期啊！"

母亲的爱从来没有说出口，她总是鼓励影响着李华一定要多学习知识，要上进，一定要自己优秀，这样才不被欺负。后来李华姐妹个个都不输给周围同龄的孩子们，这离不开母亲的教导和影响。

母亲的眼神让李华至今都忘不了，她的精神一直影响着李华。李华突然明白，为什么这些年能一直坚持写作，就是为了母亲期望的眼神。李华很享受母亲流露出欣慰的目光，这正是当初的期望已经被满足。

成为作家是李华的梦想，也是母亲的期望，母亲希望家里能出一位知性的女作家，而这个心愿被李华实现了。得益于写作前辈的介绍，李华已经加入武汉市作协。如果李华能将长篇小说出版纸书，李华有望加入湖北省作协。这既是李华自己的目标，也是社会对李华写作成绩的认可。李华此刻心中又多了一个更大的文学目标，让自己写出更多更好的优质作品，努力成为中国作协一员！

之后李华有了更强的写作动力，每周至少保持 8 千字的写作发表量。每当看到自己的作品在报纸杂志发表出来，李华内心激动又快乐。为了将长篇小说出版成书，李华活学活用精益求精，大幅度修改整部长篇小说，从故事大纲、故事结构、情节场景、人物对话、人物塑造、文笔语句全方位修改，将作品提升了一个档次。让读者的阅读体验更好，也更容易感受到作品表达的主题。李华的作品获得编辑的赏识，已经签下了纸书出版的合同，再过不久就能上书架销售。

在长期的写作过程中，李华一边学习一边思考，李华的三观也在写作中得到升华。李华不是为写作而写作，也不是为出书而凑字数，而是用灵魂表达内心的感悟，力求让读者有所收获，并得到与读者情感的共鸣。李华的目标是写出好作品，为后代留下一笔精神财富，而不仅仅是房子、车子、票子。她更希望自己留下的精神财富可以供几代人享用，她坚信不管时代怎样发展，做事的方法，正确的信念，善良的品质是每个人都需要具备的。

这些年不管赚多少钱，又或者成功购买了几套房子，李华觉得其中的乐趣都不如自己的作品以书的形式发表出来。那是一种发自内心的快乐和自豪。李华暗暗决定，为了母亲能继续分享自己的快乐，也让母亲为自己感到骄傲，李华在家人和文友一老师面前，都表态了，一定要写到老！余生为写作而活！

第五十五章　已拥有海景写作复式公寓

　　李华在投资提升自己的同时，还继续关注投资房地产。无论哪个城市有好的房源信息，李华都会赶去实地看房。李华曾带上 5 名同班女同学去广东阳江看海景房；带女友去广东珠海和中山看房；带家乡的闺蜜去市郊区域看别墅；带亲人去市中心看学区房……

　　李华积极搜索投资房地产信息并踏实地落实，为了节约成本，在房子的装修上一直亲力亲为。也将装修的过程发展成个人喜好。谁都知道装修是累活，但是到了李华这里，却看不到辛苦。她是把房子当成艺术品去塑造打磨。能把毛坯房变成自己想要的样子，是成就梦想的过程。李华从头到尾都在享受这种创意被自己支配的满足感。装修过程很累，但是却让李华感到无比充实。

　　李华的生活节奏时紧时缓。有一天李华接到女友杨阳的电话，邀请李华聚一聚。李华正在装修施工现场，想都没想就婉言拒绝了："美女，我最近太忙了没时间聚会，等会我发现场视频给你看看。"

　　李华说完就挂掉手机电话，立刻将手机交给项目经理，拍了 1 分钟内的短视频，发到杨阳的微信。杨阳看到视频中李华穿着白色 T 恤上衣，戴着白色太阳帽子，下身穿着一件绿色的迷彩服裤子和一双黑色的高帮皮鞋，整个人看起来精神干练。从鞋子上的灰尘泥土看，就知道李华还在做土建施工现场。现场还堆积了很多水泥、沙子、地砖。视频中还看到干活的工人，传来各种干活的嘈杂声响。

　　杨阳说："知道了，看来你确实来不了。你在装修哪里的房子？"

　　李华谦虚小声说："在市郊乡下的一个小镇。等我忙完了这阵子，再请你出来坐坐。"

　　李华只能客气地解释，并附上现拍摄视频发给杨阳。之前杨阳已经几次邀请李华，每次都碰上不合适的时机，杨阳几次打电话给李华，她都在干活，不是在建材市场买装修材料，就是跟设计师调整设计方案，或者像今天一样在现场做一些应急的事情：衔接电工、泥工、油漆工及木工之间的交代事项。因为是半包工程，所以什么事情都得自己亲力亲为，把控好进场和出场的工人交接。

项目经理跟做装修的赵总正在现场进行员工安排，决定相关的装修工序。赵总体谅李华，让李华放心离开去参加聚会，这里有他主持大局。李华挥挥手说："现在哪有心思去唱歌？赵总你一天不把整体布局图和现场施工图搞出来，我都不能放心。"

赵总说："你就给我一年时间，包给你装好。你又不急着住进来，反正市中心还有那么好的房子。"

李华说："这是两码事，装修头期一定要布置合理，不能想到哪里就做到哪里！这样会浪费时间又会浪费成本。一定要计划好布置好，才能一鼓作气地把事情做好。千万不要做了拆，拆了又重做，那样不仅丢了钱还耽误时间。"

赵总明白李华的意思，就不再劝了。他很了解李华的个性，毕竟赵总跟李华一起合作装修了 13 套房子，每次都配合得很默契，还省钱省事。李华每次都把装修房子的细节考虑周到，并提醒赵总。

拒绝朋友们的娱乐应酬多了，李华也担心被朋友们误解。所以直接拍视频澄清，让她知道自己确实正忙着，不能一下子赶回市中心。一方面节省解释的时间，另一方面也省得绕弯子引起误会。当朋友问起这是谁的房子，李华不能直说都是自己的房子，就说跟装修公司老板一起监督管理，学习看看他们的工人是怎么处理一些现场施工的问题。

李华习惯低调，不喜欢炫富显摆。有些人猜测李华有多少套房子，挣了多少钱，想要打听李华的实力情况，拐着弯来探寻李华的实力。对这些试探李华一笑带过，闭口不说此事，口风紧得很。李华不买车，不穿大牌子，跟着女友们逛街也是购买品牌换季打折时的衣服、包、鞋子。只是女友们都知道李华喜欢进美容院做保养及微整。李华有时尚的理念，她在乎内心的强大，也很在意外表。有哪个女人不爱美呢，除非虚伪。李华一直认为最好的炫富是女人的一张脸，以及不留岁月痕迹的健康身材。

这些年回归单身生活，李华不仅没有显老，反而看上去越来越年轻。精神压力少了，气质也好了，按照李华自己的话说，就是要精神和物质两手抓，两不误。不仅仅是质的变化，也要让那些曾经伤害过她的人看到她只会越来越好，让那些人看到她风生水起，看到她越来越有底气，看到她越来越高贵。李华一直在心里佩服自己，鼓励自己，劝慰自己，要做到争气而不是生气。这几年不经意间就这么走过来了，而且一路上走得很顺利。

李华有时抽空到广东珠海与中山这些城市，实地考察房产信息真实性。亲自去体会道路运输、城市交通、生活节奏、生活配套各方面的情况。这一次李华要去中山办理一些已投资的房产项目，两套房子手续，一套等增值出售，一套自留备用。

从武汉坐城际高铁到广州，再转珠海和中山。李华已习惯一个人的旅途奔波，出门在外列车上几小时的孤独，常常让李华可以冷静思考一些问题，也学会很多独立技能。从广州开往中山北站过程中，李华有一种奇妙的预感：今后会经常去珠海和中山。很可能在这次看现房过程中，她就会交购房定金。

在中山北站出来，李华已经看到接她的陈司机。陈司机是当地小镇人，很熟悉跟购房相关的单位路线，这也是售楼部小芸推荐陈司机的原因之一。从中山北站到售楼部有 20 多分钟的车程，小芸已经在大厅等着李华了。陈司机对李华说："你看房就由售楼部美女陪同，有电瓶看房车。你看完房后，打电话给我，我来送你去酒店入住。晚上还可以去海鲜街吃虾、鱼、螃蟹。"

李华回复陈司机："好的，谢谢你。我忙完后联系你。这里风景真好，气温也像春天。就是公交车太少了，的司都没有？要不是陈司机接送就太不方便了。"

售楼部小芸立马说："以后发展起来会很方便，会有小区到公交车站的电瓶车，接小区的人到车站。这里还有温泉酒店，购房客人入住会打折，标准间168 元。"

李华点点头，笑着对已经在微信上保持密切联系的小芸说："走吧，带我先去看房子再说。"

李华对房子情有独钟，只要是看房选房，一切烦恼都没有了。这天晴空万里，天气作美，售楼部大厅装饰得大气奢华，已经让李华喜欢了。整个下午李华跟着小芸看了六套现房，另外还看了海景房公寓样板间三种类型的房间。李华看中了两套房子。她不是一时冲动，而是有备而来。她选择了一套 138 平方面积，四房三卫二厅四四方方的房子；还预选了一套海边的复式公寓。

当看到实景现房，李华心情变得更好。站在现房阳台上向海边望去，能看到远远的山，海水浪花一波一波拍向岸边，不停地随风吹动着水面。再打开朝向小区的阳台，小区里的小桥流水，绿色植物沿着院里的小路长着小花小朵的五颜六色，还有池塘里的荷花，院里小花，李华只觉得好看，可是叫不出来花名，李华看着想着入了迷。

此时李华有实力冲着浪漫而来，脑子里闪过诗人海子的名句，李华悄悄地对自己说："我已拥有面朝大海春暖花开的海景房了。"

这一天李华就可以实现它，拥有它。跟大海之间的距离就这么近，看着蔚蓝的天空，闻着清新的空气，耳边传来海浪拍打的声响，由远而近的宽阔，看不到边际，这环境已经让李华胸怀澎湃。李华毫不犹豫地在心里下了决心：买！一定要拥有它！

小芸对李华说："李华姐姐，这里美吧？"

李华说："是啊，真美！最主要是这个户型方正，像我现在湖北住的家，一样的布局，一眼看见就感觉是熟悉的样子。走吧，去签合同吧，就买这两套。你们的宣传广告那句话好听，温泉海岸！"

小芸乐得脸上笑开了花，很开心地对李华说："你是我这周见到的最爽快的好客户！上个月有一位从澳门来的老板也是上午看过房，下午就签了两套房子。她说这房子离澳门近，周末回来居住或者投资都很适合。她还说房子买得太值了，以后肯定会涨。"

听着小芸说的话，一个信息给李华提了醒，自己也可以带喜欢买房的女友来投资海景公寓房，让她们也一起受益。像琦琦和珍珍，肯定也会喜欢这里的房子。李华经常做这些事情，把好的信息分享给一帮喜欢投资房产的女友们。

小芸高兴地对李华说："走，咱俩去签订购合同。今天只缴定金，七天后交齐全款就行，我还免费送你一个月的物业费。"

另外小芸告诉李华，接她的陈司机其实就是装修公司的老板。陈总也兼顾帮助业主办产权证，因为办理地址他什么都熟悉，加上陈总微信很多方便。

这天李华心情特别好，在落笔签名时突然发现付出的辛苦是值得的。说不定哪天故地重游，李华从这次投资中的获益会远远超过今天的付出。她坚信自己每一分付出都会有回报，她坚信随时做好准备的人更容易获得成功。

真没有想到时间过得这么快，一晃又是几年过去了。李华又做回自己，能随心所欲自由自在。李华享受这种成长带来的快乐，享受这种愉悦的生活状态。李华在生活中兜了一圈，发现还是自己说了算的生活才叫有意义的人生。

李华深情地将眼神转向大海的方向，这里太美了。在这里她可以一个人待下去，在这里遐想，在这里从事最喜爱的写作。在这里创作故事小说，将文字出版成书，在这里实现那缠绕着李华多年的文学作家梦想！

小芸微笑望着李华，眼神里能看到明显的情绪：佩服、羡慕、崇拜。小芸说："李姐，你太牛了！这辈子我能做到你现在这个样子，我睡着了都会笑醒。"

李华说："你这么努力，你也一定可以！女人只要经济独立，安全感就来了。记住，靠谁都不如靠自己，特别是我们单身女人！"

第五十六章　淡化在岁月中

　　李华的生活在繁忙和充实中度过，她自己都没有察觉到，单身的生活一晃都十几年过去了。

　　从前的婚姻生活就像她手上戴的玉镯，如果碰破了，断裂了，无法还原，只能扔掉，再选择适合自己的新镯子。李华明白"旧的不去，新的不来"的道理。这就是现实生活，人要是没有爱情和婚姻，原来也可以活得潇洒自信美好。

　　李华早已把怨恨远远抛在脑后，时钟不停止地旋转，随着岁月运转前行，怨恨都已经在岁月中淡淡逝去。李华的生活越来越好，生活品质不断提高，原有的失落感一去不回！想起从前的一些人和事，李华已经释怀，她学会了理解人性，善待自己也放过他人的错误。失去婚姻之后，亲情和友情一直带给李华支持和温暖。

　　距第一次离婚已有二十多年，有一次李华刚从苏州笔友新书发布会回到女儿家中，一进门李华习惯性向女儿小琳打声招呼："我回来了，人呢？"

　　小琳从主卧跑向客厅，笑眯眯地说："回来正好，这几天太忙，我叫老爸帮我做几餐饭。他的老伴阿姨也在厨房帮忙做卫生，等会一起吃晚餐！"

　　李华没有反应过来，迟疑地问女儿："怎么回事？那我趁他们俩在厨房还没见到我，我赶紧走，你们吃吧，这多尴尬！我要知道他们在这里，我也不会回来。你怎么不打声招呼告诉我？我真白养你了！"

　　李华边说着边将行李箱子递交给小琳，用眼神示意快把箱子拿进次卧室放着，那是女儿特意给李华保留的卧室。

　　李华随后压低嗓子说："我去美容院做护理，正好休息几个小时，你们吃吧。他们走了发微信告诉我，我走了，别说我来了！"

　　正开门出去的时候，前夫从厨房端出做好的菜，放在桌子上，一眼看见站在门口的前妻李华和女儿。前夫愣了一下，马上像没有事一样，走上前打招呼："哟，回来了，正好有你喜欢吃的红烧鱼，还有榨菜丝炒辣椒，来吃点！"

前夫老了许多，从外表上看，已经和李华不像是一个年代的人了。前夫还是那个大嗓门，说话带着地道汉腔，性格一点没有变；而李华从外表打扮上，却显得年轻、朝气、大方、时尚、知性美。真是时代造化人啊，李华突然见到前夫这般模样，想起他们俩在一起的那段婚姻。以前丈夫一直认为自己出身大城市而得意自傲，看不起来自小城市的李华。可现在倒觉得两个人的身份调换了一样。

这些回忆在李华脑子里闪现了几秒钟，记忆犹新，恍然间还有点走错家门的错觉。李华很客气地推辞说："我真的有事，你们吃。"

这时候前夫的老伴也从厨房出来了，李华脑子里迅速闪过女儿小琳说的话："老爸现任妻子大老爸三岁，阿姨条件也很好。是阿姨追老爸，老爸还是蛮有女人缘，对我也很好……"

前夫的现任妻子，看上去朴素娴熟地帮着女儿做家务活，真没把自己当外人，也客气礼貌地对李华说："已做好了，一起坐下来吃饭吧！"

这个时候倒显得李华不像自家人，站也不是，坐也不是，忙后退在大门外，挥挥手说："你们快趁热吃吧，我真有事！"李华其实心里高兴，这些年来她也放下了。女儿多些亲人的关爱，这不是李华想要的吗？

李华说完脸红了，头也不敢回地向电梯口跑去，按下电梯键才感到轻松一些。女儿追了出来："妈你吃饭再去嘛？真是的，他们都很随和。你也看到了，你多年轻洋气，他们没法跟你比！人家都不计较放在心里，你还躲？"

李华直接拒绝说："去你的，让他们来又不对我说说，搞得我真难堪！"

小琳忍不住笑着补充道："妈你又可以有新的素材写故事了，哈哈哈！"

李华瞪着眼看了小琳一眼，"唉，瞎操心！你快去吃饭吧，我去小区美容院做护理，饿不着我。你这个白眼狼，我把你带大，还抵不过你老爸做餐饭功夫？心被狗吃了！唉，算是明白了，亲爹还是亲爹啊！"

小琳赶紧顶嘴："哎呀，都过去了。你们各自都有自己的生活，大家都是亲人。你看到了，老爸还记得你喜欢吃的菜，对你很好。爸家里还挂着你抱着我的照片呢！人家一点都不恨你，当初可是你不要老爸的！"

电梯门开了，李华冲进去，按下关门键，向站在走道女儿扮了一个鬼脸，"你快进屋吃饭，他们等你呢！"

电梯从最高层直达一楼，李华舒了一口气，缓过神来，向着小区绿荫树旁边小道走向小区后门，美容院就在那附近。做美容保养是李华最喜欢的一种休闲消费。李华想，如果做完了美容护理，前夫他们还没有走，她还有一个地方可以去。李华在小区附近办了足疗会馆的会员卡，那就再做一次足疗护理。如果他们还没有走，李华再去美发店做一套头部护理，反正也办了卡。生活上李华很会合理安排和享受，也很注重健康保养。这些年来，也幸亏李华懂得调理自己的生活。每当工作累了，心里孤独想一个人静静的时候，都会通过以上几种方式休息，缓解身心疲惫。

岁月就在弹指之间流逝，那些过去的人和事，现在就是放在李华眼中，也激不起怨恨了。时间真是最好的良医苦药。李华都怀疑自己怎么欣然放下了一切，有时李华想到这些事会忍不住偷笑，情不自禁地摇头。李华心想，这些事没什么大不了，一切都过去了，现在只有李华自己，不也过得挺好的吗？别人也没有她以前想的那么坏。也没有多少人去在意谁与谁的过去。再说，谁没有过去呢？

李华想着想着，在舒适的美容床上睡着了。美容师们的一双小手，按摩手法到位，让李华感到很舒服；店里轻柔的催眠音乐，也让李华无比放松。

这年春节前几天，女儿对李华说："老妈，姑姑兰兰和老爸说，叫我们去奶奶家过年，三十夜年饭，你看怎么样？"

李华顺着女儿意思试探道："你去就可以，我就算了，要不然你爸的现任怎么想？"

小琳说："奶奶说了，那天没有请老爸的现任老婆，就是为了让你回去吃年饭。老爸说阿姨很善解人意，特意说自己娘家也要吃年饭，故意不在场！"

李华沉默片刻说："那阿姨对你老爸那么好，我就更不用去了。你要你爸爸好好对人家，好好过日子。你这次去就把我单位分的物质带过去，那些水果给爷爷奶奶，那件羊绒衫是给你老爸的，那手套送给你的后妈，那丝巾送给你姑姑。这些东西别说是我给的，就说是你工作有钱了孝敬他们的。只希望他们都对你好，别恨我就行了。你代表我去看他们一样，你对他们说，老妈要守新房子过年三十。就这么说，其他的都别谈！"

李华其实真的只想自己安安静静地在自己的新居过一个踏实的年。那感觉好像自己就是女王，随意躺着，跷起腿放在茶几上，这样舒服地看看年欢晚会比去哪里都自在。还可以悄悄地看看女儿小琳给她复印出来的一封信，那是小琳藏了很多年的一封电子邮件。

李华一直没有联系的那个人，也几乎忘了的那个背叛过她伤害过她的男人于平。那封信就是于平写的，这个时候小琳把它拿出来给李华看，一定是有特别的用意。

多年都过去了，小琳察觉到老妈一直不再恋爱不再结婚，心里一直对于平又爱又恨，并没有放下他。小琳不想让妈妈活在痛苦仇恨中，她想让妈妈彻底释怀走出阴影，于是这封信该是时候拿出来给妈妈看了。

这封信是当年李华通过法院起诉与于平离婚生效之后，于平给女儿的电子邮箱转发信的内容。那年头，李华还不会电脑操作，女儿设置了一个共同使用的邮箱账号。要不是看到这封信，李华早就忘了这个电子邮箱的存在。小琳经常用电脑，有什么信息她会最先看到，这封信就是在李华不知情的情况下，被女儿小琳看见后收藏。

李华本不想打开看，但又想起小琳走之前说的那句话："妈，你要是感觉无聊，可以看看这封信。不过看完后你可以烧掉，处理掉，别留着！"

此时的李华，好奇心萌发，里面写了什么内容，看了要烧掉？

第五十七章　于平的忏悔

李华迅速拿起信封，靠在沙发最舒服的位置，跷起腿垫在茶几上，漫不经心地看着信。看着看着，表情凝固，眉头深锁，不知不觉眼睛溢满了泪水。李华无声地擦掉模糊住眼睛里的泪水，继续看那封信。

信是这样写的：

亲爱的华华，我其实早收到你的起诉状了。幸好是我收到看见了，妈妈没有看到信。妈妈在死之前都还不知道你与我离婚的信息。当然我也没有机会对妈妈说这些了。

她八十三岁那年得了阿尔茨海默病住进了医院，当年就去世了。一直陪伴她的程伯伯送她去了殡仪馆。程伯伯那么痴情专一地爱着妈妈，守护了后半辈子，两个老人却还没有在一起，现已天堂人间两分离。我突然感觉到，我真不是人啊！这辈子我最对不起的人是你，我的华华。

我写这封信的时候，是我一个人在医院度过了 60 岁生日。我早已经看到了法院传票通知，我知道那是我的错，导致你对婚姻失望，才以这种不伤体面的方式提出离婚。我知道一旦你做了决定，说什么都没有用了，都晚了。

另外我很感谢你在诉讼卷上没有提我婚内出轨那段丑事，给一个男人留下了颜面，保全了我的自尊。我顿时醒悟过来，你是对我真好的那个人。但我也没有脸面求你回到我身边。虽然我已经跟那个女人断了联系，但也知道你不可能与我重归于好。我知道你的性格倔强，永远不会原谅我。这一点我自知之明，我不怪你，只怪我自己，也请你别再恨我了，我只有忏悔的心。我这辈子没有心思再去爱上别的女人了，我把我们的爱情婚姻搞砸了，丢失了，我好心疼啊！现在身边没有一个女人，但满脑子里都是你的影子，我天天想着我们曾经在一起的快乐时光。

写这封信给你的时候，我正一个人在上海的某医院里治疗，我已经偏瘫在病床上两个月了。医生说我可能遗传了父亲的病，脑血栓。不知道在哪一天会突发心梗病，然后突然离开人世。离婚开庭现场，我要是没有出庭，你可以直接拿到法院判决书，离婚生效，恢复单身。我现在是快要死的人，只能为你做到这些了。

也许当你看到这封信的时候，我已经不在人世间了。我知道你不常守在电脑旁查看电子邮箱。

最后说几句真心话，我对不起你，请原谅我所做错的蠢事吧！也请你别再为我去惩罚你自己了，华华对你自己好点，我活着或者走了，都想以这种方式道别，因我无脸再见到你。这辈子我最后悔的事，是我没有好好珍惜和你在一起的日子。我的糊涂刺伤了你的善良，让我彻底地成了孤魂野鬼！

原谅我吧，不然我死不安心。

一直还爱着你的人：于平！

2012 年 11 月 5 日（你还记得吗？今天是我的生日。）

于平就是李华的一个心病，一生都还不了的一笔情债。于平临死都可能不知道，李华要在多年之后才看到这封信。于平知道，善良心软的李华会原谅他过错；可于平不知道李华被曾经爱过他的那份痴情，伤得极深，以至于从那以后，李华不再相信爱情。

于平信里的文字像多情种子，惨兮兮的文字情景让李华悲哀伤心。她不知道是为自己伤感，还是为于平感到惋惜。此时的李华懂得了小琳的心思，明白了女儿良苦用心，希望李华振作起来。过去的都已经过去，爱过恨过的人都走了。不要再为不值得的人和事惩罚自己的生活，该好好正视自己，从心底阴影中走出来。人生除了生死，还有什么坎坷过不去呢？放下所有的恩怨，好好活着就是对过往伤害最有力的诀别。事实证明李华也是这么走过来了，没有了爱情和婚姻，不也过得很好吗？

像往日一样，珍珍在电话跟李华约定在大年十五这天见面，还是在老地点碰头——约在她们俩一起买的别墅小区里。正月十五那天，珍珍和李华前后差5 分钟都分别到了别墅区物业公司碰面。

小区里绿化带让人心旷神怡，省城市郊空气清新，沿小区大门两旁挂着喜庆的大红灯笼，给节日带来了喜气洋洋的传统文化氛围。能住在这个小区里的人都不简单，有一双慧眼，特别是第一期购买这里的人。选择在这里买房，不管是投资还是自住都很值得，是明智之举。

这些小区房价廉物美，发展几年后的小区环境越来越美了。李华和珍珍都很喜欢这里，这是她俩投资房产项目的杰作，看来想去还是决定留下来，作为自己将来养老的好地方！这里绿草如茵，去省城的交通很方便，是一处闹中取静的休闲好地方。珍珍爱摄影，李华爱写作，平日里有自己工作和爱好学习要忙碌，俩人互不打扰；但相聚时又能彻夜长谈，心心相印。人生中有这样的知己，一生足矣！

李华和珍珍沿着小区小道边走边聊，珍珍对李华说："我有一封于平的公证书快递交给你，这是由于平的律师转交给我代办。不知道放了多久？我是在初十上班时，发现我办公桌上有一堆信件，其中有这个大的邮件快递纸盒。我打开纸盒后，就看见了交代转交给你的一份公证书，还有于平要交给你的一套房钥匙和一封私信。我马上带着全部交给你，我的任务完成了！你打开慢慢看看吧。"

李华看了一眼珍珍，当面打开那封信，信上一行行字，那笔迹李华太熟悉不过了。信的内容如下：

华华，你收到这封信的时候，也许我已经不在人世了，所以请华华耐心看完，好吗？

我在世的时候做了一些对不起你的事，现在我要在即将离开人世的时候，做两件正确的事情，弥补我对你的愧疚。第一，在我死后我将全身有用的器官全部捐赠，帮助有需要的病人。第二，把我唯一对你保留的那套上海房产办理赠予给你做了公证。做了这两件事，我没有牵挂了。

做完这件事后，我心里好受些。我明白你压根就没有想过，我会私下买下了上海那套房产。现在这套房产价值已达到千万元。这是我们俩婚后购买的房产，房产信息也是你当年极力推荐的，只是后来我没有机会告诉你，当年我及时买下了这套房子。那时是妈妈的钱买下的缘故，我不知道怎么跟你开口说起这事。我还幻想着有一天你能原谅我，我们会在这所你喜欢的房子继续生活下去……这些意外增值的财富，让我想起你的投资智慧。是因为你的眼光让我受益，而这些本该是属于你和我共同的财富。

这么多年我身边也经历过很多女人，大多是贪图我的钱财而逢场作戏，当发现我生病偏瘫后，身边的女人都销声匿迹了。在我住院期间，是我最孤独最明悟的日子，我静静地望着病房上的天花板，四面冰凉的墙壁，突然感觉到我这一生中的悲凉。

我想起了关于你的一切，我们在一起的时候，你的好，你的善良，你的粗心大意。你一直傻傻地相信我编织的谎言，直到婚外情被你发现为止。我看到了你的痛苦和失望无助。你咬了我手臂上的那一口牙印，还在我的手腕上，那是我一辈子的污点。我没有对你还手，我忍着也想着让你解恨。出事过后的冷战期间，我知道你保留了那张我第二天写下的悔过书。我记得那两句话内容，那是我一辈子都很难说出口的悔恨。

李华当然永远记得于平留在纸条上的内容："我对不起你，我离开去另外城市发展了，我走了……"

看到这里，李华眼睛红红的，鼻子开始不通气了："真难受！"

李华装着很轻松的样子，背过珍珍直视关心的目光。珍珍很理解李华此刻的心境，眼睛只看前方的路，继续边走边说："看淡点，向好的方面去看。于平能以这种方式去忏悔，说明他还是真的后悔做了那些伤害过你的事情。人无完人，我们得念他曾经对你的好。想想他余生最后的日子，心里全是你的好，他一直记得你的善良。于平用心在行动上，为你偿还这笔情债。这多年过去了，你不也一个人走过来了？其实你已经释怀了，只是我们俩从不提过去那段日子，从不提于平这个人，有意回避这件事、这个人。可是我知道，你心里一直有他，所以你一直没有接受其他人的情感。我作为知己想对你说，你现在可以平静地接受这些事实了。时间是最好的疗伤药，我永远理解你！"

李华一脸蒙地继续小心打开快递袋子，里面展现公证书和钥匙，正是那年李华和于平去上海看房的那个小区——上海文闵区，离麦当劳店只相隔十分钟的路程。正是当年看到最后尾盘的其中一套房 2001 房。没有想到的是，于平竟然在隔天去定下来了。而且没有对李华提过这购房的事情。

事隔这么多年，如今这套房子的实价已涨到了一千多万元。这也证明了，当时李华的看房眼光有多厉害。那年李华和女儿随于平来上海旅游，李华无意中看见报纸上的房屋宣传信息，坚持要去看这套现房尾盘。看完后，李华坚持说，如果有钱买了这套房子，闭着眼睛都会涨价。那时于平心动赞同买，可过后又说了一些理由没有购买，实际上隔二天就去定购了那套房子，想着将来总会给李华一个惊喜。结果过了不久就发生了那件不愉快的事情，于平一直没告诉李华这件事。

看见公证书内容，此房产权归属赠予李华名下，以法律文书方式传给到李华手上。李华思绪万千，她在想，现如今人都走了，还留下房子有什么用呢？

李华用很镇定的眼神对着珍珍说："我决定了，我把于平这套上海的房产变卖，卖出去的钱全部捐给穷远山村的儿童。最好能给偏远山村的孩子们建一所希望工程学校，让孩子们都能上学！珍珍，你现在当副市长了，关系渠道比我广，这事还是由你这个朋友帮我运作，找到律师进入拍卖，我到场办手续就好！"

珍珍一点也不惊讶李华会这么做，她知道李华现有的财富早已超出了于平赠予的这套房子的价值。

珍珍知道李华爱房子，多年来一个人打拼，房子已经不再是李华安全感上的依赖。精神上自信的李华，早已实现了财富自由，成长为经济独立的女人。没有婚姻，没有爱情，她照样可以靠自己挣钱买到理想中的房子，再不是昔日的李华！

第五十八章　已做到喜欢自己的模样

处理完于平赠予房子这件事后，李华一身轻松。珍珍打心里佩服李华这样淡定从容，毫不犹豫淡然处之的态度。想到如果老了还有这么一位知己做伴，俩人还住同一个小区，还用担心孤单寂寞吗？

珍珍也感谢李华信任她，当初珍珍只是提议一下要在一起买房，俩人相约看了一次房子，李华在第二个月就签了购房合同。有经济实力真好，一次性全房款付清，这就女神的范儿！在珍珍眼里，每次投资项目，李华只要实地考察过，都会将一切细节想好，把最好最坏的利益分析透彻，并果断出击。

李华执行力非常强，只要有合理的方案，不管怎样先试着干下去，做着做着就上路了，遇到困难再一个接一个应对解决。如果把所有困难都想一遍再实施完美方案，以求避开一切风险，很可能什么事情都办不成，做之前就已经吓住自己了。

李华在周末经常跟珍珍约在别墅区碰面，有时会顺便探讨一些事情。因目前两个人还是居住在不同的城市。

李华环顾小区四周葱郁的环境对珍珍说："这一次你把于平这套赠予房子公证书转给我，简直是一个烫手山芋。庆幸我从未指望这天上掉馅饼的事，能这样平淡处理这件事，也是替于平做了最后一件善事。过去的都过去了，我也放下了。希望他在天有灵能看到善果，偏远地区的孩子能健康成长，好好读书。为国家培育栋梁之材做件好事，这样比房子放在我的名下要有意义。"

李华跟于平分开后就再也没有考虑过自己的婚姻问题，在往后余生的岁月里也不打算去追寻完美的爱情。李华除了工作就是投资财富投资提升自我，把自己的时间填满，让自己像机器一样运转，不感到孤单。

人们常说，越是渴求的东西越难得到，反而不求不想的好事会突然来到身边，让人惊喜。李华最近就是遇见了让她犯难的好事。

李华跟于平分开后，这些年来其实有不少男士向李华示好，如服装街的物业管理公司陈总经理，还有李华的"初恋对象"郭奇志。那时李华四十多岁，忙于事业打拼，没有心思回应。一晃又是多年过去，李华没有想到六十岁的她怎可能有什么爱情呢？但是，现在真的遇到了，并被两位优秀的男士惦记着。难道这世上还有真情所在？

李华开始警觉地提醒自己，他们是爱她这个人吗？李华心想自己确实会保养比同龄人显年轻十岁，但即便自己再有姿色和魅力，也抵不过岁月留下的痕迹，毕竟已是年过半百。李华又担心他们只是冲着自己好的条件财富。才好奇关注获得一些好感罢了。

想来想去，李华有时觉得自己想多了，那两人的"惦记"也许只是自己的错觉。因为两位男仕途都很好。李华不怎么相信自己能遇见一段黄昏恋。再好再优秀的男士，也进不了李华的视线和内心。几十年都孤单已习惯了，她也不朝爱情和婚姻这个方向去想。能继续自由自在地过后半辈子，已经不知道有多少人羡慕自己，李华知足了。

这些年来，李华也遇见不少会说甜言蜜语的男人，对男人的讨好也有点麻木了。她能从容应对男人的试探，会给没有真情实意的男人自觉退出的台阶，也会应付那些只为保持事业合作关系的假意示好。李华有很好的识人能力，能把握好距离和分寸。

李华并不抗拒真情，但不刻意去追求。如果这时真的有合适的人选出现，李华不会像年轻时那样喜形于色。她会先默默观察一段时间，如果对方有真情必然会有恒心。如果两人确实有缘，对方不会因为一段"观察期"而退缩——如果当年郭奇志能坚持追求李华一两年时间，他未必没有成功机会。

过了不久，李华的长篇小说出版上市了。出版方特意为李华召开了一次小型的新书发布会。在发布会的现场，有一位男士始终关注着李华的一举一动，流露出无限欣赏的眼神。这是一位体型微胖结实宽肩的中年男子。李华认得他，在一次开发商举办的楼盘项目首发销售会上，经三妹夫介绍，李华认识了这位房地产公司的尹董事长。

尹董是一位地道的北方男人，为人稳重大方，做事有耐心细腻，平时默默做事从不多语。尹董身高一米八，眼睛很小，一笑就眯成一条缝，加上微胖的体型，看起来反而觉得有憨厚的气质。李华对他有好印象，总感觉这种人朴实有安全感。据说尹董夫人在几年前去世，之后尹董一心扑在事业上，一直单身。

不知道什么原因，李华虽然没有与尹董深交，但是彼此之间都留下了好印象。李华爱关注开发商房源新楼盘信息，自然也就经常关注尹董公司的项目走向，更是在这些项目中投资过三套住房。一来二去，李华几次见到这位房地产公司的尹董事长。

有一天三妹夫在酒会上对李华说："大姐，我们尹董人真的很好，单身几年了。身边好多单身女性朋友喜欢套近乎，可尹董都没有放在心上。上次听我谈到你准备新书发布会的事，尹董问我哪天举办，还问我拿入场券。我感觉有点突然，是不是我们尹董看上你了？你能把新书发布会的邀请函给我几张吗？"

李华笑着说："当然欢迎你们来捧场，但是一定要带有诚意购买新书的朋友来。对你带来的朋友，不限购买书的数量。"

第二天李华就将邀请函给了三妹，让她转交给三妹夫。至于三妹夫交给谁，李华也没上心去猜测，她只知道来的人越多越好。众人拾火士气高，捧场的人越多，发布会的气氛就越热闹。李华期待多年的文学梦想，终于美梦成真了。她希望签售新书圆满成功！

很快就到了新书发布会的这一天。站在台上讲话的李华，首先向台下扫了一眼来宾，她看到了亲人，看到了朋友，看到闺蜜，看见了老同学，还看见前排右边走道坐着的尹董事长，一双眼睛已笑成一条缝的男人。说起来也怪，李华见他就想笑，那虎头虎脑的憨厚样子，甚至让人感觉有几分滑稽而可爱。这就是李华印象中的尹董。在脑海里已是一位随和的老朋友了，好像很熟悉，有很多好感。

对于尹董的前来，李华并不感觉惊讶，反而有几分窃喜。三妹夫之前提起尹董对自己有意，李华是听进去了，只是没有过多表露出来。几十年单身日子形影孤独，李华只是深藏着，只能对事业上心，对异性朋友淡漠变得有些麻木了。在事业职场上，李华把自己当男人使，跟异性相处只谈合作，不谈风花雪月的浪漫。以前也有一些异性朋友对李华关怀备至，但都被李华巧妙地回避过去了。而这次怎么就有点不一样的感觉呢？真出了鬼？李华心里想着的那个"鬼"。

尹董没有当面向李华刻意示好，但他们却能像熟人朋友那样大方相处，也有好几次不期而遇——李华觉得这也是两人有缘的迹象。有时两人会自然地在意彼此的动态，微信朋友圈也互相点赞。有时候李华感觉尹董真像一位好大哥，在有意无意地暗中帮着她，例如，提供最好的新房售房开盘信息。只要李华看中要买，尹董都会给售楼部打招呼，以公司最优惠内部员工价格售给李华及其家人！当然，三妹也帮了很多忙。有时直接鼓励提醒李华去投资尹董公司的房地产项目，间接给尹董公司造势捧场。而这些都是好项目，李华每次投资他们的房产都能获得很好的收益。因此形成了良好的循环，李华跟尹董间接上也有好几次合作。

今天尹董前来捧场，果然出手不凡，一口气就签售了 500 本新书。当主持人念到购书单位，姓名，数量之时，这才让李华感到吃惊。尹董把新书当饭吃吗？买这么多是要包销？

李华当然不怀疑尹董的经济实力，但是书是用来阅读，买了这么多如果只是为了捧场，让这些书放在阴暗的角落里吸灰，李华又觉得太无意义了。尹董似乎看到李华的心里去了，那眼神似乎对李华说："放心吧！我会帮这些书找到适合它们的读者人群！"

一瞬间的眼神对视，李华不好意思地赶紧把目光收了回来。按照之前的活动安排，接下来轮到李华讲话。当李华准备发言时，才突然发现刚刚的眼神对视打乱了自己的思绪，她一下子忘词了！幸好李华见过场面有经验，沉默了几秒就马上调整回来，慢慢发出温文尔雅，不缓不急的声音："首先感谢前来参加签售新书活动的领导，亲朋好友们。谢谢大家的鼓励和支持帮助！我身为作者，向大家表示最真诚的感谢。感谢大家一路陪伴我走在写作路上；感谢有大家的鞭策使我写出了好作品；感谢大家的抬爱和喜欢。最后也因为有大家的鼓励，才使我有动力坚持写作。我会在今后的创作路上，写出更好的文学小说作品。最后预祝新书发布会圆满成功！谢谢大家！"

在几百人的会场讲话，对李华来说已不是头一回了。尹董本来很紧张的情绪，被李华讲完话后的掌声冲淡了。尹董悄悄起身离开座位，跟礼仪小姐说了几句话。接着只见礼仪小姐像变戏法似的，从托盘下方端出三束粉红色的鲜花。穿着合身大红色旗袍的礼仪小姐领着三个美女，在音乐声中缓缓走向舞台中央，向刚刚发表讲话的李华献上了三束鲜花。

　　李华看见那是她喜欢的粉红色百合，不由得心花怒放。她明白是尹董送她这些有涵义的百合鲜花。她情不自禁也毫不掩饰地，在众人欢呼声中收下鲜花，也收下尹董的深情厚谊。此时无声胜有声，尹董还是没敢说出什么甜言蜜语，但李华已感受到了满怀心喜的甜蜜。

　　尹董总是以行动代替说话表白，李华就是看中尹董这优秀朴实的一面。这种有实力、有责任心、又有担当的、好男人品质。在李华这个年龄阶段，能跟尹董有这样深的缘分，确实是可遇不可求。此时李华冻结多年的芳心再度怦然涌动，久违的少女情怀盈满李华内心。难道在夕阳落日的黄昏，遇到真爱了？李华真没想过在这个年龄还能感受到这样心动的情感。

　　新书发布会后，闺蜜珍珍兴奋地说："李华你现在可以将一部分创业挣来的钱，用于改善写作环境。拾起以前曾经梦想，开办一间书吧或者茶舍、咖啡馆——喝杯咖啡还能提神醒脑，适合你写作。你现在可以去策划实现你的美梦了。"

　　李华被说动心了，认真思考这件事，现在确实是实施运作的最佳时机。好友嘉嘉在旁提醒李华："哎呀，你可以就把你一至三层楼的小别墅改造，一楼全部按照茶室会所去装修办起来。现成的房子，小区环境又好。你可以每天在那里好好享受生活和写作；周末邀请一些志同道合的文友，绘画朋友，爱好摄影朋友，还有能歌善舞的朋友相约在一起，多自在！"

　　李华应声道："我也是这样想，珍珍，嘉嘉你俩听听我这样设计安排妥不妥。把一楼大厅设置一面墙为展示柜，从下至上满墙都可以摆上我出版的书，还有所有文学书刊，还有家人作的画画作品。我将它们裱一下镜框，挂在需要的位置展示。客厅柱子角落装饰制作一棵大树，客厅顶部全部布置成榕树，一眼看去绿叶茂盛，像春天一样。我们感觉是在大树下品茶聊天，谈天说地，尽情享受美好时光。这个装修设计我很早就有图纸方案了！告诉你们，那棵树里面打开全是柜子，关闭时看上去就是一棵仿真树。我特意在红军的故乡红安县城，找到了一位民间很有名的手艺人阮老师制作的仿真树。等装修工程全部完成。你俩可以是常客。哈哈，有你俩忙的！"三个人大笑起来。

　　这时候尹董笑眯眯地走过来，看着李华放桌子上的手机保存着的设计图纸，指着一楼餐厅中央设计厨房大操作台说："如果需要请厨师，我很乐意为美女们下厨，露露厨艺。我做李华喜欢吃的沸腾火锅鱼宴，包你们都喜欢吃！不知道能不能录用我入职？”

尹董认真地对李华说，也是在婉转地示好，也想让李华的朋友们知道，他已经把李华当成将来共度余生的人选。尹董知道李华才是他要选择的伴侣。凭实力李华什么都有了，在尹董心目中，李华已是财富自由了，不图他的钱财，因为尹董已身价过亿了。

尹董更乐意从实事小事上帮助李华，他理解李华最想要的人生价值，他心甘情愿地为之付出行动。细微之处见真情，一次就签售李华出版新书 500 本；在装修之中，暗中提供最好最实惠的施工材料，为李华减轻装修成本。尹董为人实在，已经让李华动了芳心暗许，只是她从不表露出来——毕竟是即将步入晚年的女人，李华不敢去奢望爱情。可眼前的女友们都为李华高兴，在晚年能遇上这样一位贤德的知己，可以托付余生的伴侣。她们都异口同声地喊了出来："李华快答应，我们赞同！"

好友们都希望李华聘用尹董成为她一辈子的高级厨师！李华和尹董腼腆笑了，李华像情窦初开的少女，脸颊飞快地红晕起来，一颗心怦怦直跳。这种初恋的感觉藏在李华心里，她默默地享受着这种久违的幸福感。

如今的李华都被好友们夸奖，羡慕她已经活到自己想要的生活境界：衣食住行无忧无虑，清晨写作六小时，半天时间养养花，做点自己喜欢的事，看书学习，坚持做健身运动。周末和朋友们一起品茶练舞，畅谈未来，有时候还约在一起去远方旅行，好不乐乎！

李华做到了她曾经梦想的样子，如今万事齐备，只需再乘风破浪，顺势而行，活好当下。

第五十九章　岁月如此妖娆

像很多人一样，李华也珍惜活着的每一天，享受岁月芳华。作为一名文学爱好者，她需要不断地学习和寻思着创作源泉。如今李华已经经济独立，她想多走走祖国的大好山河。为了写出作品中的真实感，李华通过旅行的方式，走出国门，先后去过英国、澳大利亚、美国，亲身感受当地的生活方式，文化风俗，并采访了大量人物，其中有部分成了小说中的角色原型。

通过这样的走访和考察，两年多来李华已创作出两部长篇小说，共计六十多万字。这些作品在报纸媒体上连载发表，后来都顺利出版成纸书。在创作长篇小说的同时，李华也写出了大量女性情感、婚姻、观点，情感等领域的精短小说及散文，发表在各种省级刊物和网络平台上。

在刚开始写作的时候，有很多人并不理解李华，放着舒服的日子不过，还半夜三更写作折腾，真是有福不会享啊。还有的人认为，李华只是一时心血来潮，坚持不了几天。还有的人说，要是文章能在刊物上发表，甚至出版成书，那才叫作家——这些李华都以实力行动做到了，而且做得很好。

初期听到这些风凉话，李华像是早就预料到一样，并不生气，依然我行我素，该干吗就干吗。从没有因为别人的冷嘲热讽去争辩，照常报名学习写作班。经过前后两年不间断地学习写作知识，结合老师给的写作任务，持续写作投稿，退稿再修改，修改后再投稿。就这样李华每隔一段时间，都有散文，短篇小说，长篇小说陆续发表在各大媒体平台。

李华取得这些写作成绩，不是天上掉馅饼，那是常人做不到的付出。李华对写作有高度负责的态度，认真对待写作字句，尽可能客观反映作品中善与恶，美与丑，正与邪的较量，引导人们崇尚正义，崇尚善良，并告诫女性一定要做到经济独立，思想独立，行动独立。

在全篇小说快要完成结尾期间，李华感到兴奋又感到焦虑，一方面是想尽早完成这耗费两年时间的作品，另一方面又担心结尾太仓促。夜里李华常常处于半睡半醒之中，虽然眼睛闭上了，但脑子里一直在构思作品的故事线该如何布局。

一直以来，李华都没有成为作家的梦想。当处于人生的低谷，李华就当自己在储备精神财富，将生活中的素材甚至苦难，加工成激励人们崇善自强的良方。她珍惜生命中给予她帮助的每一个人，每一位恩师，每一位志同道合的文友。她庆幸有这么好的亲人理解、鼓励、支持，让她成为从事文学创作的一员，一名不问前程，只想默默写出好作品的作者。

李华想对亲人们说，往后余生，我会在面朝大海的海景房，或者在春天的市郊小别墅里，写出更多好看感人的小说故事。这些年来，李华旅行到哪里，哪里就能给她文思泉涌的创作灵感。李华一直有敏感的洞察力，正如当年在英国旅游时获得很多关于门窗产品的灵感。

李华把写作出书，当成生活中不可缺少的一部分。她想将人生中所有美好的感受和获得的智慧感悟，以文字方式传承下去。她认为人生的意义在于向世人奉献出自己的价值，物质或者精神皆可分享。而她更想让后代子孙获得自己的精神财富，那是一种积极向上，努力拼搏的精神，不气馁，不低头，像朝阳下的向日葵，永远面向光明！

"无论何时何地，必须要做善良的人。"这是李华母亲常常在她耳边叮嘱的话。

以前李华在工作中遇到委屈而气愤的时候，母亲常这样对李华说："孩子，你要学会看淡，给小人让路，你转过弯就过去了，小人横冲直撞总会遇到绊倒他的路障，用不着你出手。另外，放过伤害你的人，也是放过自己。这世界还是喜欢善良的人多些，有些事情会因为你的善良而成就你。这世界遵循因果法则，善有善报，恶有恶报，不是不报时候未到。因为你善良，很多事情冥冥之中都会不解而破；也因为你的善良，美好会回到你未来的生活中。你要知道古人没有说错，记住要做一个善良的人。"

李华用几十年的人生经历，反复验证出母亲的话是对的，这个世界就是这样的规律。

李华从小受父母亲的影响，在成长过程中学会了忍让、谦和、换位思考。当然也加设了识人的一条底线：可以让对手三招，给三次改过的机会。那是李华做人自加的一条保护自己的法则，事不过三！

　　李华的人生就像"开挂"了一样，对正能量的事物，以积极心态去追寻；对负能量的人和乱事做减法。严以律己，宽以待人，不以物喜，不以己悲！

　　李华有时会想起跟女儿父亲离婚的事，庆幸自己当年的善良包容了前夫的自私过错，在前夫生病的时候，李华暗中伸出援手，变卖首饰凑钱，让信得过的亲戚转交给他。那时李华没有去医院看望，因为亲人都理解李华的难处。那时前夫已经二婚，正被当时的妻子冷落。这个男人悔恨自己的草率冲动，赌气闪婚。经历那一场大病过后，前夫也放弃了第二段婚姻，又过回单身生活。

　　经过女儿小琳协调带动，前夫已经与李华家人像亲戚一样走动了。

　　李华在异地闭关写作期间，有一天小琳在家人群里发出了一段视频。视频中出现了一位李华熟悉得不能再熟悉的人——曾经一起生活过十年的前夫。李华睁大眼睛仔细看着视频中的男人，如今也是六十岁的人了，脖子上戴着很粗的一根黄金项链，手上框着一个大黄金戒指，头发还烫着微卷。他正手舞足蹈大声讲着自己照顾母亲的故事。为了讨李华母亲欢喜，前夫可没有把自己当外人。

　　视频中的前夫没一点拘谨，讲着他如何做好吃的给年迈的父母，如何护理照顾已患上了阿尔茨海默病的母亲，说得很生动形象。那段困难时期，他因为对父母细致的照顾，在邻里街坊中获得了孝子的美名。接着被现任妻子看上，并追求成婚。如今前夫也有了幸福的家庭，找到了爱他并适合他的幸福婚姻，李华在心里默默送给祝福。

　　前夫将这些年的经历，用着地道汉腔说给李华的家人姐妹们听，逗得大家一个劲地点头，不时大笑。李华从这一幕中感受到大家庭的祥和氛围，她没有想到会这么和谐。这一刻李华感到很欣慰，她明白了女儿的苦心，明白了女儿让前夫走近大家庭的原因：为了完成她爸的心愿，成不了李华的丈夫，还可以当亲人！

　　李华的母亲已经八十岁了，常年喜欢一个人安静生活。生活过于简单，也不太爱做饭，导致营养不足。李华前夫从女儿那边得知这些信息，很想为李华母亲做些力所能及的事情，于是就出现了视频中的那一幕。前夫通过讲自己照顾老人家的经历，也劝解李华母亲注重身体，注意饮食。之后他会不时上门给李华母亲做些好吃的，也好让李华母亲接纳他的一片善意。

　　前夫现场直播的真情实意，让家人重新接纳了他，信任他心意真诚，但是李华母亲还是委婉拒绝了。李华母亲说："你的心意我领了，能来看我，我就很高兴。不过，我还是喜欢安静，就周末两天，我自己动手做点饭菜吧。我没有那么矫情，别麻烦你两头跑。现在看到你们都很好，我就很高兴了。"

看到这里，李华很庆幸听了母亲的话，做个善良的人。当年李华的前夫做得很绝情，可李华后来还是原谅他了。跟前夫离婚时，他将所有家具电器搬空，只留下一所空空的房子给李华和女儿。甚至在准备二婚之前，受二婚女人的指使，到李华单位办公室逼着李华写下承诺，放弃法院判决书上前夫应给女儿的抚养费，这样他才不再纠缠李华今后的生活。

想起这些往事，李华也真佩服自己当年的大气包容，这些善意现在都以不同方式回馈到李华身边。此时李华心中早已没有了恨，只有无限的幸福感。没有想到她婚姻虽没有了，但家人还是享受着因善良带来的亲情，而且这是前夫心甘情愿地报恩付出。

李华佩服母亲的智慧，母亲曾经多次教导："出现艰难困惑的事情，先别急于发泄情绪，要善解人意，替对方着想，慢半拍冷静处理，放放就过去了。做一个善良的人，要有宽广的胸怀格局。只有这种人才具备遇事不惊的人格魅力，什么事都可以跨过去！"

以前听到母亲这些话，李华会觉得厌烦啰唆。现在她理解了母亲善良和智慧，李华家几代人的身上都流传着这种善良的品质。母亲身边的老一辈同事朋友都羡慕她，夸母亲培养的孩子个个孝顺，也羡慕她越老越有子孙福，逢年过节都是亲人团聚，四世同堂。

视频中的场景温馨真实，李华看着甚至有一种错觉，里面的男人还是她的丈夫，他们之间什么事情也没有发生，一晃就过了几十年，他一直是这个大家庭的一分子。李华看着前夫戴着围巾在厨房忙着，为李华家人做上一桌可口的饭菜，有时又会到客厅里说上几句话。那样子就像在自家厨房一样，忙进忙出，真实自然。李华心生感慨，因为自己善良待人，曾经割断的亲情在几十年后又续上了。虽然李华与前夫没有直接的接触，但这份亲情还是回归到这个大家庭中。

当李华看到这段视频时，她正在珠海和中山之间的海景房长住写作，享受着面朝大海，春暖花开的闲暇生活。李华在几年前就买下了这一处海景房，特意为了以后可以实现在海风和涛声中写作的美好愿望。李华装修完成后一直忙

于事业，也奔波于家庭事务，没有时间享受这种闲暇的度假生活，更没有在这里居住过。

当李华的长篇小说出版之后，她开始找到写作和生活的平衡点，也找到适合自己的创作方式。在安静的环境中独处一段时间，李华的灵感和写作状态更好。她意识到当年的海景房真是买对了，这里正是长期写作的绝佳环境。在这四季如春的海边，她可以真正享受面朝大海的开阔愉悦感。阳光照射下海浪拍打着银色柔软的沙滩，迎面而来海风吹拂着海的气息，空气中弥漫着绿色植物的芳香，眺望着落地窗海景，一边写作一边沐浴着洒落的阳光。只要身在这样的优美环境中，李华心中就会涌出写作的冲动。

李华相信，遇到就是缘分，只要善良努力，岁月一定会以美好回报。瞧，岁月如此妖娆！还有比这更美好的蓝图吗？

李华沉浸在时光悄悄走过之中，欣慰地享受大自然无限风光，释放着内心深处的那片芬芳岁月，时光如棱，艰辛的、美好的、那些曾经的伤痛都已经随风而去，她自信未来的生活，一定会越来越好，人生的磨炼使她逐渐变得温文尔雅。

李华依在自家的窗台前，放眼眺望东方升起的太阳，阳光下的余辉照着海面，泛起一波一波的海浪，蓝色大海与慰蓝天空相互呼应，白云在浩瀚的天空中，自由舞蹈游移中飞翔，真美。

这一切仿佛就在昨天，岁月的长河就如同时光悄悄走过……

后记

　　《时光你悄悄走过》，历时二年多，终于付梓。窗外，秋日阳光播撒，苍穹格外明朗，蓝天游云，令我欢欣。

　　《时光你悄悄走过》一书的谋篇、初创、写作过程中、初稿完成及修改，得到了家人、朋友、老师、主编、出版社等各方在精神、心里、写作各个方面的大力支持、热心帮助。使我深深感到人间有大爱、世间有大善。所有这些，让我深深感动，并在此一并表示感谢。因此，我也将以写作为生活的一部分，认真投入写作之中，写出好的作品，写出更多作品，报答有恩于我的所有人。写作无止境，我将继续文学创作，续写新篇，活好当下！

赵舒娴

2024 年 2 月 28 日